death is not enough

By Karen Rose

Have You Seen Her?

Don't Tell
I'm Watching You
Nothing to Fear
You Can't Hide
Count to Ten

Die For Me
Scream For Me
Kill For Me

I Can See You
Silent Scream

You Belong to Me
No One Left to Tell
Did You Miss Me?
Watch Your Back
Monster in the Closet
Death is Not Enough

Closer Than You Think
Alone in the Dark
Every Dark Corner
Edge of Darkness

Novellas available in ebook only
Broken Silence
Dirty Secrets

Karen ROSE

death is not enough

HEADLINE

First published in 2018 by
HEADLINE PUBLISHING GROUP

1

Cataloguing in Publication Data is available from the British Library

Hardback ISBN 978 1 4722 4406 2
Trade Paperback ISBN 978 1 4722 4407 9

Typeset in Palatino by Avon DataSet Ltd, Bidford-on-Avon, Warwickshire

Printed and bound in Great Britain by Clays Ltd, St Ives plc

HEADLINE PUBLISHING GROUP
An Hachette UK Company
Carmelite House
50 Victoria Embankment
London EC4Y 0DZ

www.headline.co.uk
www.hachette.co.uk

To Robin Rue, who believes in me when I doubt myself.

And, as always, to Martin. I love you.

Acknowledgements

Terri, Kay, Sonie, Mandy, and Amy for all your love and support.

Chris, Cheryl, Brian, Kathy, Susan, and Sheila for the plotting.

Julie Gerhart-Rothholz for making sure I described my Julie just right.

Sarah Hafer for editing all the pages (even the ones that make you blush).

Beth Miller and Sarah Hafer for the proofing.

Claire Zion and Alex Clarke for guiding me in making this an even better book.

All mistakes are my own.

Prologue

Nineteen years earlier . . .
Chevy Chase, Maryland,
Sunday 10 January 10.30 P.M.

'Sherri, give me the damn key.'

Rolling her eyes at her boyfriend's growl, Sherri Douglas closed the driver's-side door, locked up, and tossed the key to her old Ford Escort over its peeling roof. 'There you go.'

Thomas's scowl was interrupted by the grimace of pain that twisted his bruised face as he reflexively caught the key in midair. He froze for a second, then hissed as he lowered his arm. 'Shit,' he muttered.

Sherri sucked in a breath, instantly regretting her thoughtlessness. 'Oh, Tommy, I'm sorry. That was stupid of me.'

He schooled his battered features and swallowed hard, pursing his lips then quickly opening his mouth because his lip was split too.

She wanted to cry. His beautiful face was . . . still so beautiful. But hurt. Her chest ached as she catalogued every wound. She wanted to hit something. Someone. Four someones, actually. She narrowed her eyes, thinking about the boys who'd done all that damage. Hating them. Her fists clenched and she shoved them in her coat pockets. Hitting them wasn't going to help Thomas.

And her father would kill her if she got in trouble too. Her dad wasn't terribly keen on her dating a white boy to begin with. Ha. A white boy. It would have been funny had it not been so frustratingly sad. Thomas's dark skin wasn't white enough for him to fit in here

1

at school, but he wasn't black enough for her father. At least he hadn't forbidden them from seeing each other. Because Sherri would have disobeyed her father if he'd tried. But if she got expelled along with Thomas? Her father would make sure they never saw each other again.

Expelled. They'd *expelled* him. She still couldn't believe it. It was so *unfair.*

'Don't you *ever* call yourself stupid,' Thomas said quietly.

She blinked in confusion, then realized he was referring to what she'd just said. But it *had* been stupid to make him move so quickly. 'I should have thought.' Because it wasn't only his face that was battered. They'd kicked his arms and legs too. She clenched her teeth, willing the tears back.

They'd hurt him. *Those bastards.* They'd *hurt* him.

Thomas shook his head. 'It's all right. I'll live.' He walked around to where she stood and held out the car key, his expression one of weary defeat. 'Sherri, please. Give me the *right* key. I'm too tired for games. I just want to get my bass and get out of here. Get back in the car and keep it running. You should stay warm.'

Her eyes filled with tears she couldn't hold back. 'I'm going with you,' she whispered fiercely.

His dark brows lifted, his split lip bending down. 'No. You're not.'

'I'm . . .' Her voice broke and she looked up at him helplessly. He was so big and strong and . . . *good.* Better than any of those bastards. One on one, it would have been no contest. At six-three, he was the tallest, strongest boy in their class. But there'd been four of them. *Four.* They'd beaten him and yet *he'd* been blamed. *He'd* been punished. *He'd* been expelled.

Because Richard Linden – even in her mind, Sherri hissed the entitled bastard's name – thought he had the right to touch any of the scholarship girls. *Just because we're poor. And he's not.* And because Thomas couldn't ignore poor Angie's terrified face as Richard held her against the wall and groped her. And because when Thomas pulled Richard off Angie, Richard and his posse of thugs attacked him and beat the crap out of him.

2

The principal had blamed Thomas. *What a shock*. Dr Green did whatever the Linden family said because they were rich. And white. *And Thomas and Angie and I are not*. And to make it all even worse, somehow Richard or one of his crew had gotten to Angie, because she was denying Richard had even touched her.

So they'd expelled Thomas. He'd worked so damn hard to look good to the colleges. He'd needed a scholarship or he wasn't going. Now? He'd have to go to his local high school, the expulsion on his permanent record. Would the colleges even want him after this?

Richard Linden and those bully friends of his had stolen Thomas's future. She was going to make damned sure they didn't touch anything else of his. A blink sent the tears down her cheeks. 'I'm going with you,' she repeated. 'It's just the band room. It's not dangerous.'

'If you get caught, you'll be expelled right along with me.' He cupped her jaw in his huge hand, gently swiping at her tears with his thumb. 'I won't let that happen to you.'

'It shouldn't have happened to *you*. It's so unfair, Tommy.' She bit her lip hard, trying not to cry anymore. She knew her tears ripped him up.

He drew a deep breath. 'Yeah.'

'We need to fight this. *You* need to fight this. You did the right thing. You protected Angie. You were the hero.'

'Fighting it won't do any good.'

She held his gaze, desperately hoping to make him see reason. 'We can sue.'

He laughed, a huff of disbelief. 'What? No!'

She took his free hand in hers, twined their fingers together. Her skin dark, his a few shades lighter. 'We can get a lawyer.'

'With what?' he scoffed. 'Willy counts every bite of food I put in my mouth, for God's sake. You think he's gonna pay for a lawyer?'

Thomas's stepfather was a nasty, abusive man. Sherri didn't like being around him. He made the hairs stand up on the back of her neck. He didn't make any secret of the fact that he thought Thomas was inferior. Thomas, who was better than all the other men.

Thomas, who Sherri loved with all her heart.

'We can call the ACLU,' she said.

Thomas blinked down at her. 'No way. I'm not suing anyone. Nothing ever gets solved in court.'

'That's not true.' Her voice was trembling again and she closed her eyes to fight back tears. 'Tommy, this is your life.'

Wearily, he leaned down until their foreheads and noses touched, a gesture he'd learned from his real father, with his Maori roots. His real father, long dead, whose memory Thomas quietly worshipped.

Sherri, only five feet nothing, leaned up on her toes so that he didn't have to bend down so far. She barely caught his whispered reply.

'I can't fight the Lindens, Sher. You know it as well as I do. Nobody is going to stand up for me. Nobody but you.'

'But some of the teachers might. Coach Marion or Mr Woods . . .' The soccer coach loved Thomas, and their history teacher did too.

He closed his eyes, shook his head, pivoting against her forehead. 'They won't stand up for me either.'

'How do you know?'

He drew in an anguished breath. 'Because they *didn't*,' he snapped, then sighed. 'They had a chance on Thursday.'

'They pulled the boys off you,' she murmured. 'Then walked with you to the main office.'

Except that Thomas hadn't been walking, not really. He'd been too badly hurt, dizzy from the kicks to his head and limping because one of the boys had repeatedly stomped on his knee with a heavy boot. Coach Marion and Mr Woods had actually been holding him upright.

'They had the chance to tell Dr Green what happened, but they didn't.' Thomas shrugged. 'Woods started to, but Green called him out into the hall and said something about contract renewal.'

Sherri's eyes widened. 'He threatened Mr Woods's job?'

'Yes. I assume he said the same to Coach, because *he* didn't speak up for me either. And they were the best allies I had.' Another defeated shake of his head. 'Hell, Miss Franklin could have let you take my bass with you on Friday, but here we are, breaking into the school to get it. I bet Dr Green threatened her too.'

4

It would have sounded paranoid, except that it was true.

Miss Franklin had said as much when she pressed three keys into Sherri's palm late Friday afternoon. One was to the school's outer door closest to the band room, one to the band room itself, and the third unlocked the instrument cabinet.

I can't give him the bass myself. But if someone breaks in and takes it? Miss Franklin had shrugged. *That would be a real shame. Especially if it happened on Sunday night. Nobody's here to stop any would-be thieves on Sunday night.*

Miss Franklin wanted to help, but she wasn't willing to defend Thomas either, and the realization was devastating.

'Tommy . . .'

He pressed his finger to Sherri's lips. 'Nobody's gonna stand up for me, Sher, and that's just the way it is. I'll go to the high school near my house. I'll be okay. I'm more worried about you, staying here without me.'

She wanted to say she'd go with him, that she'd leave this fancy school with its rich white brats and follow him wherever he went. But her father wouldn't allow it. Her parents wanted her to have a future, and Ridgewell Academy was her ticket to an easier life. There had to be an answer for Thomas, but she wasn't going to figure it out standing here in the school parking lot.

She straightened her shoulders and lifted her chin. 'Come on. Let's get your bass.' It had been his father's – his real father, not that piece of shit who was his stepfather. His real dad had died when Thomas was five, and the bass was all he had left of him.

The instrument wasn't worth a lot of money, but it was everything to Thomas. He never left it at school overnight, but the principal hadn't let him get it Thursday after the incident. Dr Green hadn't allowed Sherri to get it for him either, the ass.

She set off at a half jog toward the rear of the building, well aware that one of Thomas's strides required two of hers. At least on a normal day. He was still limping and she reached the door before he did, scowling as she unlocked it and slipped through, holding it for him.

'Dammit, Sherri, go back to the car. I'll meet you there.'

'Nope.' Because she wasn't sure what they'd find in the instrument closet. Yes, she had the keys, but it had been forty-eight hours since she'd seen the bass. She wanted to be there to support Thomas if someone – like Richard Linden and his friends – had gotten there first. If the bass was gone . . . or, even worse, broken?

Thomas was going to lose it.

The heavy outer door closed behind them, automatically locking with a click that echoed in the quiet. 'Let's do this,' Sherri said, and started jogging toward the band room. She could hear Thomas's heavy steps behind her. Normally he moved like a panther, swiftly and silently, but Richard's friends had done a number on his knee.

Abruptly, his footsteps halted. 'Sherri,' he hissed. *'Wait.'*

She slowed and turned. 'I'm not going back to the . . .'

Thomas was limping down one of the side corridors, and Sherri followed, catching up as he reached the stairwell at its end. 'Sherri!' he shouted, panic in his voice.

'I'm here,' she said, a little out of breath. 'What's wrong?' A second later, her eyes adjusted to the dim light . . . and she saw. Horrified, she stumbled backward. 'Oh my God. Who is it?'

Because the boy on the floor wasn't recognizable. Someone had beaten him until his features were one big bloody mess.

Thomas crawled under the stairwell and pressed his fingers to the boy's neck. 'He's . . . still alive, but God, Sher. I don't see how. Looks like he was stabbed.'

'What do we do?'

'I'll try to stop the bleeding. You call 911.'

'I don't have any quarters.'

'You don't need them for 911. Go!' He shrugged out of his coat, wincing in pain because his arm still hurt. She turned to run, but from the corner of her eye she saw him freeze.

'Shit,' he whispered, then looked up to meet her eyes. 'It's Richard.'

'Oh no,' Sherri breathed. 'Oh no.'

Thomas's jaw tightened. 'Go. Call 911. He's lost a lot of blood. Go!'

She turned at the snapped command, then stopped short when he called her name again. He'd taken off his coat and was now ripping off the sweater she'd given him for Christmas. 'What?' she asked as he flung the sweater away and began taking off a long-sleeved T-shirt.

He balled the T-shirt up and pressed it to Richard's stomach. 'Once you've called 911, get out of here. I don't want you involved.'

'But—'

'Don't argue!' he shouted. 'Just . . .' His voice broke, and he blinked, sending a tear down his battered cheek. 'Just go,' he whispered hoarsely.

And then she understood. When help came, Thomas would be caught in the school. With a dying Richard Linden.

'They'll blame you.' She choked on the words. Dropping to her knees, she grabbed his arm, but he shook her off. 'Thomas, come with me. We'll call 911 and then leave. Together.'

Thomas shook his head and resumed putting pressure on Richard's stomach. 'Somebody has to stop the bleeding. He'll die otherwise. He's not even conscious. I can't leave him to die.'

She stared at him helplessly. 'Tommy . . .'

He met her eyes, his misery unmistakable. 'For God's sake, go! Do *not* come back. *Please.*'

She pushed to her feet and backed away, then ran for the payphone. She'd make the damn call, then she'd go back and sit with him. There was no way she was leaving him to face the blame for something else he had not done.

The payphone was next to the front office. With trembling hands she dialed 911.

'What is your emergency?' the operator asked.

'We . . .' Sherri drew a deep breath through her nose, tried to slow her rapid pulse. 'We need help. There's a guy—'

The doors flew open and men poured through them. Men in uniforms.

Cops.

Cops? How did cops—

A burly man grabbed her arm and squeezed hard. 'Drop the phone!'

'But . . .'

7

The man clamped his other hand around her wrist, drawing a cry of shocked pain from her throat. 'I said drop it.'

Her fingers were forced open, releasing the phone, which hung on the tangled cord. She stared up at the cop, stunned. Roughly he spun her around and shoved her against the wall. The next thing she knew, he was snapping cuffs on her wrists.

Behind her, she could hear Thomas screaming her name. 'Sherri, run!'

She grimaced, her temple pressed against the wall so hard that it hurt. It was too late for that now.

Montgomery County Detention Center, Rockville, Maryland,
Wednesday 13 January, 11.15 A.M.

Laying his head on the cold metal of the interview room table, Thomas closed his eyes, too tired to wonder who was behind the mirror and too exhausted to be worried about what this meeting was about. He hadn't slept in three days, not since they'd brought him to this place.

To jail.

I'm in jail. Words he'd thought he'd never say. *Goddamn Richard.* The fucker had died. *I ruined my life and he died anyway.* Bled out from stab wounds to his gut. Thomas's first aid had been too little, too late.

Murder. They'd charged him with murder.

He was almost too tired to be terrified. Almost.

He hadn't seen Sherri since he'd been here. He hadn't seen anyone. Not even his mother. His mom had written a letter, though. He laughed bitterly. Yep, she'd written him a letter, saying she was disappointed in him and how could he kill that nice Richard Linden? *And oh, by the way, we will not be paying your bail or for a lawyer.*

Thomas was on his own.

The door opened, but he was too exhausted to lift his head. 'Thank you,' a man said. 'I can take it from here.'

'Fine.' That voice Thomas knew. It was the guard who'd locked him inside this room. Leaving his hands cuffed behind him. 'If you need anything, just ask.'

'Wait,' the new man said. 'Uncuff him.'

Thomas lifted his head enough to see the man's dark suit and tie. And his wheelchair. Thomas jerked upright, staring.

The man wasn't old. He was young, actually. Maybe thirty. It was hard to say. His hair was cut short, his suit expensive-looking. He was studying Thomas clinically.

'Thomas White?' he asked.

Not for much longer. He'd be ditching his stepfather's last name as soon as possible. He was sure the bastard was the reason his mother had turned her back. Part of him wondered what his stepfather had needed to do to force her to write that letter. Part of him worried about his mom. Part of him was too tired to care.

'Who are you?' he demanded.

'I'm your lawyer,' the man said blandly. He turned to the guard. 'Uncuff him. Please.'

The way he said *please* wasn't polite. It was . . . imperious. Commanding.

'If you're sure,' the guard said with a shrug.

'I'm sure,' the lawyer said.

Thomas gritted his teeth when the guard jerked his arms under the guise of unlocking the cuffs. 'One move from you, kid,' the man growled in warning.

Rubbing his sore wrists, Thomas glared and said nothing.

'That'll be all,' the lawyer said, waiting until he and Thomas were alone to roll his eyes. 'All right, then, Mr White. Let's start—'

'Thomas,' Thomas interrupted. 'Not White. Just Thomas.'

'I can do that. For now, anyway.' The lawyer rolled his wheelchair to the table, appraising Thomas with too keen an eye. 'Have you been eating?'

'No.'

'I didn't think so. I don't have to ask if you've been sleeping. You've got bags under your eyes.'

Like you care. This guy, with his expensive suit and lord-of-the-manor attitude. 'Who are you?' Thomas asked again, more rudely this time.

The man pulled a silver business card case from his breast

9

pocket and gave one of the cards to Thomas. 'My name is James Maslow.'

The card was sturdy and not cheap at all. *Maslow and Woods, Attorneys at Law.*

No way I can afford this guy. 'I have a lawyer already.'

'I know. The public defender. If you choose to stay with him, I'll honor your wishes. But first let me explain to you why I am here. Your history teacher and my law partner are brothers. Your teacher asked me to speak with you, as a favor. He thinks you're innocent. I reviewed your case and thought he might be right.'

Mr Woods talked to this lawyer? For me? Why? His lungs expelled air in a rush. 'You believe me?' he asked, his voice small and trembling, because no one else had.

Maslow nodded once. 'Yes.'

'Why?' Thomas's voice broke on the single word.

Maslow's smile was gentle. 'For starters, because your teacher told me what really happened the day you defended that young girl from Richard Linden's advances.'

'Mr Woods will lose his job,' Thomas whispered, remembering the principal's barely veiled threat. Had that been only six days ago? Really?

'He decided to risk it,' Maslow said, and there was a spark of pride in his eyes. 'Mr Woods has written a letter to the school board on your behalf.'

'Wow.' Thomas cleared his throat. 'That's ... really nice of him.'

'Well, he's a really nice guy. I think you probably are too.'

Thomas lifted his chin, stared Maslow in the eye. 'I didn't kill Richard Linden.'

'I believe you, but the prosecutor thinks he has a case. He wants me to tell you that he's offering voluntary manslaughter. Eight to ten years.'

Thomas came to his feet, shoving the chair backward. '*What? Eight to ten years?*'

Maslow patted the table. 'Sit down, Thomas, before the guard comes back.'

Thomas sat, his body shaking. Tears burned his eyes. 'But I didn't do it.'

'I know,' Maslow said soothingly. 'But I'm required to tell you whatever they offer. Let's discuss your case and then you can decide what you want to do about representation.'

Thomas rubbed his eyes roughly, clearing the moisture away. 'I can't pay you. I can't even make bail.'

'Don't worry about my fees. If you agree, I'll be taking your case pro bono. That means for free.'

Thomas frowned. 'I know what it means,' he snapped. 'I got seven-eighty on my verbal.' Not that his SAT scores mattered anymore. No college would take him now. Nor was it this guy's fault. He drew a breath. 'I'm sorry, sir. I'm . . . tired.'

'You look it,' Maslow said sympathetically. 'You've also made bail.'

Thomas's mouth fell open. 'What? Where did my mother get the money?'

'It wasn't your mother. I'm sorry about that.'

His stomach pitched. *Not my mom.* 'She really has cut me off, then.'

Maslow's brows crunched in a disapproving frown. 'I'm afraid so.'

'That's why I don't want to be White. Her husband changed my name when he married her. I want to change it back. Take back my real father's name.'

'What name was that?'

'Thorne. I want to be Thomas Thorne.'

One

Present day
Baltimore, Maryland,
Friday 27 May, 5.30 p.m.

He sat back in his chair, waiting patiently as one of his most trusted aides walked into his office with a bright yellow folder. He truly hoped Ramirez would deliver, but he didn't really believe he would. Which was unfortunate indeed.

'Here's the information you asked for,' Ramirez said, placing the folder on his desk, looking as relaxed as he usually did.

That Ramirez had been betraying him for so long . . .

If he hadn't seen the evidence with his own eyes, he never would have believed it. Ramirez was like a son. A trusted son.

'Have a seat,' he said, using his normal tone, unwilling to give away what he knew just yet. He opened the folder, flipped through the contents. And sighed. 'This is incomplete.'

Ramirez frowned. 'It is not. I compiled the data myself. That is everything that anyone knows about Thomas Thorne.'

'It is not,' he said, intentionally repeating his clerk's words. 'I know this because I also had Patton do the same search. The file he compiled is twice as thick. What you've given me is less than I could have gotten from searching Google myself.' He deliberately closed the file and folded his hands. 'What do you think I should do about this?'

Ramirez licked his lower lip, his first sign of nerves. 'Do? About what?'

'About you, my friend.' From his drawer, he pulled out the

13

photos Patton had taken of Ramirez. And Thomas Thorne. Conspiring together. 'Care to explain?'

Ramirez drew a breath. 'You had me followed?'

'I did. Thorne seems to know a great deal about my operations. I wondered how he'd gotten all that information. I had all of my inner circle followed – by the person who'd get their job should they be shown to be the betrayer.' He smiled. 'Patton was extremely thorough. He'll make a very good head clerk.'

Ramirez swallowed hard. 'I never betrayed you.'

'I don't believe you.'

'Patton photoshopped those pictures.'

He turned on his cell phone and swiped through the photos he had stored there. 'Ah, here it is. You with Thorne.' He held his phone out so that Ramirez could see the image. 'I took this one myself.'

Ramirez paled. Then he squared his shoulders and lifted his chin, acceptance of his fate in his eyes. 'My wife had nothing to do with this.'

He shrugged. 'Then it's a pity she has to die too.'

'*No.*' Ramirez leaped from his chair, reaching out as if he'd strangle him with his bare hands. But at the sight of the gun aimed at his head he stopped abruptly and froze, breathing hard.

'Why?' he asked the clerk simply, holding his gaze. 'Why did you give Thorne information?'

'I didn't,' Ramirez insisted.

'You're going to die either way, old friend. I can make it quick or make it last. I can also do the same for your lovely wife. Quick or slow torture? Tell me why.'

Ramirez closed his eyes. 'You killed my nephew.'

He lifted his brows. 'I did?'

'Your people did. He was sixteen, just a kid. Got caught in the crossfire when your guys did a drive-by two years ago. Except they picked the wrong fucking house and it was my sister's son who was filled with your bullets.' Ramirez's eyes filled with fury and grief. 'You weren't even sorry. I've worked for you for twenty years and you *weren't even sorry.*'

'I'm still not sorry,' he said, then lowered his aim to Ramirez's gut and pulled the trigger three times in rapid succession, creating a tight grouping of bullets. Ramirez slumped to the floor with a groan.

He stood, peering over his desk at the man writhing on his hardwood floor. Ramirez looked up, the fury and grief in his eyes now joined by shocked realization, intense pain and all-consuming hate. 'You said it would be quick,' he gasped. 'You lied.'

'So did you.'

'No, no.' Ramirez groaned. 'I told you the truth. I told you why I gave Thorne that information.'

'Too little, too late, my old *friend*.' He spat the final word. 'You lied to me every single day that you came in to work for me, took salary from me, all while you betrayed me.'

Ramirez's pain-glazed eyes narrowed to a sneer. 'And it's all about *you*, isn't it? My old *friend*?'

He blinked at that. 'Of course. It's always about me.' He stared down at Ramirez for another full minute. How had he missed that grief? That fury? That absolute hate?

He settled back in his chair, knowing full well the answer to that question. He'd missed it in Ramirez's eyes because he'd seen it in his own. In the mirror. Every damn day since the prison had delivered his son to the morgue in a body bag, minus his guts. Those had been spilled onto the dirt in the exercise yard when his son had been eviscerated, quickly and skillfully. But he'd suffered before he died.

He closed his eyes, a wave of fresh pain rolling through him, clenching his chest so hard that he had to fight not to gasp. His son had suffered before drawing his last breath. God, how he'd suffered.

Ramirez was getting off easily, he thought coldly.

He pressed the intercom button. 'Jeanne, can you send Patton in? Tell him to bring in Mrs Ramirez and two body bags. Mr Ramirez isn't quite dead yet, but he should be soon. Also give me a few minutes to dispatch Mrs Ramirez, then send someone in with a wet-vac. My floor seems to be covered in blood.'

'Certainly, sir,' Jeanne said with an equanimity that he'd long admired. His office manager was pushing sixty and he dreaded the day she'd retire. At least she was training her replacement, and he had to admit the girl had all of her mother's organizational skills.

Jeanne's younger daughter, Margo, was as close to a daughter of his own as he'd ever had.

And Jeanne's older daughter, Kathryn, was as close to a soulmate as he'd ever have again. Kathryn warmed his heart and his bed, but they both knew that he would always grieve his Madeline. That Madeline had hand-picked Kathryn to be her replacement had made the transition smoother, but Kathryn would never be his wife. Luckily she didn't expect to be. She was happy to be the mistress of a powerful man.

'Can I get you anything else?' Jeanne asked.

'Yes. Tell Margo that I need to meet with her in about thirty minutes.' The mother of his grandson, Margo, and little Benny were all he had left of his son, Colin. Anguish speared his heart, but he welcomed the pain. Avenging his son's death was what gave him the strength to wake up each morning. 'I have a job for her.'

'You bastard,' Ramirez gasped when his wife was brought in, bound and crying.

He smiled. 'What is the expression? Pot, meet kettle? You have much nerve, Mr Ramirez. Your betrayal will hurt so many more people than only yourself. You can excuse us, Mr Patton, but don't go far. We'll need those body bags soon.'

Standing, he removed his clothes, folding them neatly and storing them out of the way in the wardrobe. He liked this suit and didn't want it bloodied. Carefully he lifted the leather thong over his head. From the end of it dangled a small vial containing Madeline's ashes. Soon he'd mix Colin's ashes with them.

Feeling the burn of pure rage, he put the vial on top of his clothes and shut the wardrobe door. 'Now, Mrs Ramirez. I will apologize in advance for the pain I'm about to cause you. When you are screaming curses, aim them at your husband. You're here because of his betrayal.'

'I won't,' Ramirez's wife stated forcefully. 'I will never curse my husband.'

But she did. They always cursed the one whose missteps had put them under his knife. In this case, his auger. Mrs Ramirez suffered terribly before he finally took pity and put a bullet in her head.

Then he ended his former aide with a final bullet to his heart and showered off the mess. Once he was dressed again, he called for Patton to remove the bodies and sat down to read through his new head clerk's much fuller folder.

Patton had indeed been thorough, finding nearly everything he himself had found. There was nothing new here. His plan to bring Thomas Thorne to his knees had been in progress for months.

Thorne would beg for mercy, just as Ramirez's wife had. But just like with Mrs Ramirez, there would be none.

Baltimore, Maryland,
Saturday 11 June, 11.45 P.M.

'I'm out,' JD said, tossing his cards to the table with an annoyed huff. 'Fuck, Thorne. Do you have to win every damn hand?'

Thomas Thorne gave the five men sitting around his poker table a smug grin as he began to stack his chips. 'Yes.'

The others grumbled good-naturedly as they fished out their wallets.

'Your luck's too good tonight,' Sam muttered, throwing a ten on the table. No one ever lost more than ten in an evening. They played for fun. And to win, of course. None of them liked losing.

Across the table, Grayson rolled his eyes. 'I'm thinking his luck is *way* too good tonight. Maybe we should investigate. Sam? JD?'

'Lots of ways a man could cheat,' JD agreed.

Grayson Smith, the city's lead prosecutor, decorated homicide detective JD Fitzpatrick, and former Baltimore PD officer Sam Hudson would certainly know about many of those ways, but Thorne knew none of the men were really upset. Nor did they believe he'd actually cheat.

He'd earned their trust, just as they'd earned his.

'Knock yourselves out, boys,' he said loftily, then made a point of looking at his watch. 'Except you'll need to make it fast, on account of your curfew. You poor married boys have to go home.'

JD snorted. 'Asshole,' he said, but it was with affection. JD was married to Lucy, an ME who'd come back from maternity leave to work part-time in the Baltimore morgue. But she and Thorne had been friends for years before JD came into the picture. For the past eight years, Lucy had been Thorne's partner in Sheidalin, the nightclub they owned with Gwyn Weaver.

Who Thorne had studiously *not* been thinking about all evening. *Liar.*

Fine. Yes, he *had* been thinking about Gwyn all night, wondering if she'd actually gone on the date she'd been so excited about. If her date had any brains at all, the answer would be no. Either way, Thorne would have to wait until tomorrow to hear about it.

'Nah, he's not an asshole. Not a total one, anyway.' Sam had left Baltimore PD the year before, taking a job as a PI for Thorne at the law firm he fondly called his 'day job', even though the firm was his major focus. Sheidalin was primarily Gwyn's to manage. Thorne and Lucy were there mainly for the music, performing occasionally.

Although Thorne hadn't done so in some time. Four and a half years, to be exact. He missed it, playing his bass onstage in front of a live audience. But he'd had other things that needed his focus. There'd been his godson, Lucy's little boy. Jeremiah. He loved that kid.

And he'd had to take care of Gwyn, as much as she'd let him. Which wasn't that much.

Mostly, though, he'd focused on his firm. He'd built it up from a solo operation to one that employed two other attorneys, a paralegal, who managed the office, and a death investigator. And Sam, who'd proven himself a skilled PI. Thorne felt lucky to have him.

Sam was chuckling. 'Thorne's just jealous because he's got to clean up this mess all by himself.'

Yes, Thorne admitted, but only to himself. He was jealous of the married guys who had partners to go home to. Once they all left, his house would be far too quiet. But he'd never admit that to any of them, because they'd all conspire to fix him up. They were worse than old women in that respect.

Instead, he raised one brow. 'Ruby cleans for you?' He pulled out his cell phone. 'Should I ask her?' Sam's wife Ruby, formerly Lucy's

ME tech, was now Thorne's death investigator. He highly doubted she would actually clean up after Sam.

Sam laughed. 'Please, no. I value my life.'

'We single guys have to go too,' Jamie said with a sigh. He backed his wheelchair away from the table with an ease that came from a lifetime of practice. Born with spina bifida, he'd used a chair from the time he was a child. 'I'm getting too old for these late nights.'

Jamie's movements were only a little slower than they'd been when he and Thorne had first met, nineteen years before. Jamie Maslow had started out as his attorney, but had quickly become his friend and mentor. And the closest thing he'd had to a father since his own dad had died when Thorne was just a boy. Now Jamie was his employee. Newly retired from his own firm, he did pro bono work for Thorne's.

'You wouldn't be single if you'd just marry Phil and make an honest man of him,' Thorne said blandly. It had taken him months to stop calling Phil 'Mr Woods' when the two men had taken him in as a scared and abandoned teen.

His old history teacher had left the fancy prep school Thorne had attended years ago, dedicating his career to teaching kids in the inner city. Thorne admired them both, so damn much. They'd been the role models he'd so desperately needed as a miserable kid. They'd given him a home when he had nowhere else to go.

'I keep asking him,' Jamie said, a twinkle in his eye. 'He says that when he retires, we're going to elope to Vegas and get married by Elvis.'

Frederick snorted. 'I think if you elope, you'll have a revolt on your hands.' The newest member of their group, Frederick Dawson had recently come to Baltimore from California. Once a high-profile defense attorney in Oakland, he had recently become licensed in Maryland and worked with Jamie and Thorne on a pro bono basis. He gestured to the empty chip bags and beer bottles. 'Seriously, you need help cleaning up before we haul our asses out of here?'

'Nah. It won't take me long.' Thorne knew he was lucky. He had good friends, loyal and respectable. There had been a time when he didn't know if anyone respectable would ever give him the time of day. But even the best friends in the world had to go home sometime.

And I'll be alone. Still. Always.

Someone rapped briskly on his front door, opening it before Thorne had a chance to push away from the table. Lucy peeked into the room. 'Can I come in?'

JD's face lit up with a smile of surprised delight as he hurried to greet his wife. 'I thought you had to work the office.'

Thorne, Lucy and Gwyn had managers who worked the front of Sheidalin, but the three of them liked to have one of the owners in the office on Friday and Saturday nights, the two busiest – and most lucrative – nights of the week. Gwyn normally took those shifts, but Lucy had pinch-hit tonight so that Gwyn could go on her date.

Since Lucy was here, Thorne assumed that Gwyn's date had not occurred. He felt relief ripple through him.

'Gwyn took over,' Lucy said, then laughed when JD dipped her low and kissed her soundly. 'She told me to go home, but not to have any fun.'

JD's brows shot up. 'Why?'

Lucy sighed sadly. 'She's in a mood.'

'Are we going to listen to her and not have any fun?' JD asked.

Lucy shook her head. 'Hell, no.' She waggled strawberry-blond brows. 'The kids are staying with Clay and Stevie tonight. We're going to take full advantage of an empty house, then lie through our teeth and just tell Gwyn we had a terrible time.'

'I'll get my gun out of Thorne's safe and we can head home.' JD took off, a distinct spring in his step.

'Show-offs.' Thorne gave Lucy a hug. 'I've got one of your casserole dishes in the kitchen. Come with me and I'll find it for you.' He led her away from the prying ears of his poker buddies, who were awful gossips. 'Why did Gwyn come in?' he asked carefully, hoping to confirm his assumption. 'I thought she had a date.'

Lucy made a face. 'She got stood up. Again.'

Yes. Her date had been smart after all. 'That's awful,' Thorne said soberly, and with anyone else he could have pulled it off. But he and Lucy had been friends for nearly a decade and she knew him far too well.

20

'It is,' she said, frowning at him thoughtfully. 'This is the third guy who's canceled on her. She's only been on one date since she started going out again, and he never called her back.'

Because that guy was smart too, Thorne thought balefully. 'Maybe it's the dating service she's using.'

Lucy narrowed her eyes. 'She's not using a dating service. She's been fixed up by friends. Which you knew. Tonight's date was someone I personally vetted. He's a nice guy. Wouldn't harm a flea. Much less be so rude as to stand her up. You wouldn't have had anything to do with this, would you, Thorne?'

Abso-fucking-lutely. Thorne gave her a look of disbelief. 'What? Why would you even ask me that?'

'Because you should be as pissed off as I am on Gwyn's behalf. But you're not. What's the deal? She's been alone so long. She's *finally* dipping her toe into the dating pool and you're . . . what? What *are* you doing?'

Suggesting that they ought not touch her. In a roundabout way, of course. But at six-six and two hundred fifty pounds, even his indirect suggestions were crystal clear. 'Nothing.'

Lucy blinked at him. 'Thomas Thorne, you're lying to me.'

He winced. 'Not . . . exactly.' He'd simply needed more time to tell Gwyn how he felt himself. *Because she's mine.*

Lucy stared at him for a long moment, then her eyes widened. 'Oh my God. You . . .' She struggled for a word. 'You *want* Gwyn? For yourself?'

Thorne could feel his cheeks heating. He could fool a whole courtroom, but not Lucy. Who was, it seemed, a lot more aware than Gwyn herself. He'd been hinting – openly flirting even – for weeks, but Gwyn was oblivious.

He said nothing, reaching into a cupboard to get Lucy's glass dish. 'I washed it,' he said, shoving it into her hands.

'Oh no,' she said, shaking her head. 'You don't get to shoo me away. What the fuck, Thorne? Do you want her or not?'

Only with every breath I draw. He had for years, but they'd never been single at the same time. And then . . . Gwyn had been broken by a vicious killer, her confidence shattered along with a few bones.

21

That had been four long years ago. She'd crawled into her shell afterward, nursing her wounds, physical and emotional. He'd waited. Patiently. She was finally emerging. He was finally seeing glimpses of the woman she'd been before a killer had destroyed so many lives.

The woman who loved life, loved music, loved to laugh. She was still there, but stronger now. More beautiful. A survivor.

If she was going to dip her toe in anyone's pool, it was going to be his.

And you realize how that sounds, don't you? The small voice was not so small on this topic. It was actually a scream. *You're a fucking stalker!*

If I ask her to go out with me and she says no, I'll walk away, he promised the scream in his most rational tone. He just needed to ask her. Sometime this century. It was just . . . He'd be shattered if she said no, and that was a vulnerability he didn't know if he could deal with.

'Not your business, Luce,' he said quietly.

'Bullshit,' Lucy said, just as quietly. 'Whatever you're doing, for whatever reason, is hurting her, Thorne. You don't want that.'

'No,' he admitted. 'I don't. I just need some time.'

She skewered him with a glare. 'Tomorrow. You have until tomorrow.'

'And if I don't fess up?' he asked acidly.

'Let's not find out,' Lucy replied, then swallowed hard. 'She was crying tonight, Thorne, and you know how rare that is. Wondering why all these men have rejected her before they've even met her. I had to hold her while she cried. You better make this right.'

Thorne bowed his head, Lucy's words sharp knives to his heart. She was right. One hundred percent right. 'I will. I promise.'

'By tomorrow?'

'Yes.'

Lucy sighed. 'Okay.' She grabbed his collar, pulling him down so that she could kiss his cheek. 'I love you both,' she whispered in his ear. 'But I'll castrate you if you continue to hurt her. Swear to God.'

Thorne winced. 'I believe you. Go home. Make JD happy.'

'I will.' She released his collar and smoothed his shirt. 'I want you to be happy too. Like I said, I love you both.'

Thorne walked her out, finding his friends gathered by the door, car keys in their hands. He said his goodnights, then closed the door and sighed at the mess they'd left behind. Normally he'd get right in there and clean, but he was tired tonight.

No, he wasn't tired. He was heartsore. He had been for a long time. He could fix it. Maybe. If he ever got up the courage to tell Gwyn how he'd felt for too long.

Tell her, you fucking coward. You know where she is. In the office at Sheidalin. She'll be there till two. Don't wait until tomorrow. She's hurting now.

He needed to man up. Grabbing his car keys, he shoved his feet into shoes, locked all the doors to his house, and set off in his Audi SUV.

He was minutes away from Sheidalin when his cell rang. Caller ID said it was his answering service. 'Thorne,' he said.

'Hi, Mr Thorne, this is Brooke from the answering service. I have a caller on the line who says she must speak with you. Her name is Bernice Brown.'

'I know her.' Mrs Brown was one of his newer clients, a forty-five-year-old woman accused of attempting to murder her husband. Thorne was unsure of her guilt or innocence, but was leaning toward the latter. They were still pulling together the details of her case. The woman didn't strike him as the type to call for a frivolous reason. 'You can put her through.'

'Mr Thorne?' Mrs Brown's voice was unsteady. Barely audible as she whispered, 'Can you meet me? Tonight? I wouldn't call if it weren't important.'

'What's happened?'

'I was almost run off the road earlier.'

Thorne frowned. 'Are you all right?'

'Yes. I . . . I got away. I'm scared.' Her voice broke. 'Really scared.'

Thorne glanced at the clock on his dash. 'Where are you?'

'At a bar. It was the first place I came to that looked open. It's called Barney's.'

'I know it. I'll be there as soon as I can. Stay at the bar and don't drink anything that anyone gives you.'

'I had a whiskey.'

'All right. Don't drink anything else. I need you sober. Ask the bartender for a pen and write down everything you can remember about the car that tried to hit you. I'm on my way.'

Baltimore, Maryland,
Sunday 12 June, 6.15 A.M.

'I'm going to *kill* him. I'm going to fucking kill him.' Gwyn Weaver gripped the steering wheel so hard that her hands hurt, the discomfort circumventing the devastating need to cry. 'I'm going to . . .' She swallowed hard. 'How could he do it, Lucy?' she whispered. *'Why* would he do it?'

Why would Thorne *deliberately* ruin her date? It was . . . beyond cruel.

Her best friend sighed into her phone. 'You'll have to ask him that question,' she said quietly, almost crooning the words. Lucy was awake, nursing Bronwynne, her one-year-old daughter, Gwyn's goddaughter. They'd had many crooned conversations over the months, usually at six a.m.

Lucy had always been an early riser and Gwyn didn't sleep that much. Not anymore. Not in four years. Although it had been getting better. Until this.

Thorne . . . Why? She bit the inside of her cheek to stop the burn of tears. She would not cry. Would not allow the man to see how much it hurt her. Because it did hurt, so goddamn much.

'I thought we were . . .' The word *friends* evaporated from her lips as Lucy's words sank in. 'Wait. You knew?'

Lucy sighed again. 'I suspected, but only last night. I told him he'd better fix this by the end of the day or . . .' Her voice changed abruptly. 'Thank you, Taylor,' she said warmly.

Gwyn frowned. 'Where are you?'

'At Stevie and Clay's. Taylor was babysitting the kids last night. I woke up and . . .' Her chuckle was self-conscious, 'I missed my

24

little girl and my boobs were about to burst, so I drove over here to nurse Wynnie. Taylor made me a cup of tea.'

Well, that made sense at least. Taylor was the twenty-something daughter of their mutual friend, Clay Maynard, and had been a babysitting godsend, caring for Wynnie and Jeremiah, Lucy's two-year-old son, when Lucy had returned to the ME's office from maternity leave. Gwyn had been their sitter until Taylor dropped into their lives the summer before, and although she was grateful for the free time, Gwyn missed the children, who were as close to her own as she was ever likely to get now.

She'd been given the chance to be a mother once and she'd blown it. *No*, she thought. *You didn't blow it. You gave your son a chance at a normal life*. With two parents who loved and cared for him. She knew this was true. In her head, anyway. Her heart still hurt whenever she held Lucy's babies. But it had gotten easier, and . . .

Aaaand, I'm not going there. Not thinking about it. Not now. This wasn't the time to worry over her past mistakes. This was the time to nurse her anger with Thorne and let it sweep away the hurt he'd inflicted. Because what Thorne had done *had* hurt. *Goddammit*.

'So?' Gwyn prompted. 'You were saying? You found out last night?'

'I picked JD up from the poker game and Thorne asked about your date.'

'That he *sabotaged*?'

'I . . . think so.' She was back to crooning. Usually it soothed Gwyn as much as it soothed Bronwynne, but not today. 'How did *you* find out?'

'I got pissed off when Jase called to cancel. I kept wondering why guys kept breaking our dates before I even met them. I'm getting a goddamn complex.'

'I know,' Lucy said quietly. 'So what did you do?'

'I paced for hours, then went to the jogging track near the high school where you run. I figured Jase would show up eventually.' Because Jase was Lucy's running friend. And a doctor, for God's sake.

At least my mother wouldn't have been able to complain about that.

Not that her mother would have had any trouble finding a million other things to criticize. If they'd been on speaking terms, which they hadn't been since Gwyn was sixteen years old.

'You went to the track alone?' Lucy asked with a hint of alarm.

'No.' And that admission hurt too. It had been four and a half years, for God's sake. Yet she still rarely left the house alone, and never at night. 'I had Tweety with me.' *Because nobody fucks with a hundred-and-fifty-pound Great Dane.*

'That was smart. I take it that Jase was running this morning?'

'Yes. I lucked out,' Gwyn said bitterly. 'I didn't have to wait long, because he wanted to run before the sun came up and it got too hot. He said Thorne had paid him a visit. In person. Threatened him.'

Lucy gasped. 'No. No way. He actually said Thorne *threatened* him?'

'Well, no,' Gwyn admitted. 'Thorne "suggested" he find another date. Jase said that Thorne made himself perfectly clear. And as nice as I seemed to be, he didn't have room in his life for any drama right now.'

Lucy made a strangled sound. 'Thorne,' she murmured, as if the man were in the room with her. 'What was he thinking?'

'I'm sure I don't know.' Which was what made this so hard. She'd been shocked within an inch of her life. 'What did he say to you?'

'That it wasn't any of my business.'

'The fucking hell it's not! Wait, you're not on speaker, are you?'

Lucy chuckled. 'Never when I'm talking to you, sugar-lips. Look . . .' She hesitated. 'Ask him. But . . .'

Gwyn was almost at Thorne's house. 'But *what*?'

'God.' Lucy drew in an audible breath. 'Gwyn, have you ever thought about Thorne . . . you know. Like that?'

Gwyn blinked. 'Like what?' And then she understood. 'Like *that*? Like . . . *romantically*?'

'Or just physically, even.' Lucy's voice held a wince.

No, Gwyn started to say, but stopped herself. Because it would be a lie. A vicious, hateful lie.

'Oh,' Lucy whispered into the quiet. 'Good to know.'

26

'Only once or twice.' *Liar.* 'A long time ago.' *Dirty liar.* 'We're co-workers.' *That* at least was true. 'It . . . it never would have worked out.' But her protest sounded weak, even to her own ears.

'Okay.' Lucy drew the word out, then cleared her throat. 'Well, you might not have been alone in . . . you know, whatever it was that you did or didn't feel, once or twice, a long time ago.'

The thought rocked Gwyn soundly. 'Really?'

'Maybe. Just . . . stay calm. Hear him out. Then if you still want to kill him, call me and I'll come get you. You can work it out on JD's punching bag in the basement.'

Gwyn shuddered out a breath. 'Deal.' She ended the call as she pulled into Thorne's driveway. Cutting the engine, she fished his house keys from her purse. She'd had keys to Thorne's house for as long as she could remember. They watered each other's plants when they traveled, picked up each other's mail, and fed the other's pets.

She looked in her rear-view mirror at Tweety, who was strapped in his harness in the backseat. 'You know where you gotta go, dude.' Thorne had a special area set aside for Tweety in his yard, because his cat tended to hide whenever they came over.

She'd named the yellow Dane Tweety because Thorne's cat was a tiny tuxedo named Sylvester and it had seemed cute at the time. Ironically enough, Tweety loved Sylvester, but because the feeling was not mutual, they had to keep the animals separated.

Yet another reason it would never have worked.

Except . . . Gwyn closed her eyes, thinking of Thomas Thorne, all six feet six lickable inches of him. Dark hair, square jaw, just the right amount of stubble all the time. Muscles. Acres of muscles. He was like a god. Seriously. The man could have been a Hollywood star. Women swooned after him wherever he went. But he generally didn't date.

Not recently, anyway.

Not in four and a half years. Gwyn swallowed hard as the realization hit. Not since . . . Evan. The killer she'd taken into her bed. The man who'd had an obsession with Lucy. Who'd killed so many people, who'd . . . *used me. He used me to lure Lucy. So that he could kill her. After he killed me.*

27

Which would have been bad enough. Except he'd done more than lure Gwyn. He'd . . .

Her eyes flew open and she blinked rapidly, trying to banish the pictures in her mind. Images that still had the power to freeze the blood in her veins.

He'd done a lot more. Things she'd never shared with a living soul – not even Lucy. And especially not Thorne. In the aftermath, there hadn't seemed to be any point.

Evan was dead. He'd lied for months, tricking her into believing he could be 'the one'. *Telling me that he loved me.* Just so that he could get close to Lucy. Everyone who had an Internet connection knew that she'd been humiliated.

But that she was a victim of rape? No, she didn't want anyone looking at her with even more pity. So she'd kept that ordeal to herself. Until sixteen months ago, when she'd finally found a therapist who'd helped her begin her recovery.

She could hear her therapist's voice in her mind. *It's not happening now. Repeat after me, Gwyn.* Gwyn had obeyed, saying that phrase over and over. *It's not happening now.* And after months of repetition, she'd finally started to believe it was true.

Hands shaking, she unlocked her phone and swiped through her photos, replacing the nightmare in her mind with real faces, just as her therapist had taught her to do. Real people. Real people who loved her.

Lucy, JD. Their babies, Jeremiah and Bronwynne. *Named after me.* Little Wynnie had Gwyn's middle name. A different kind of hurt squeezed at her heart, just as it did every time she looked at Lucy's children. She loved them like they were her own, but they weren't her own. Yet she'd had her own child. Once.

She studied Jeremiah's photo, feeling the old yearning descend, suffocating her. Allowing her son to be adopted was still the hardest choice she'd ever made in her life. It had been the right choice for him, though. She knew that. She'd been alone and too young to care for a child then. She'd finally stopped second-guessing herself after a decade, but it had re-emerged the first time she'd held Lucy's son in her arms.

She'd never told Lucy. Never told Thorne. It was too personal. And although she knew she'd done the right thing, the fact that she'd given her child away . . . It shamed her.

Anxiety began to build and her heart began to race and . . . *I'm not going there. Not today.* Redoubling her focus on her phone's screen, she looked at picture after picture. Her friends, her dog, the publicity shots she'd taken of the dancing crowd at the club . . . She studied each one for a second or two, until she came to Thorne's photo.

Everything inside her relaxed. He was real. And he did love her. Even if it was only in friendship.

Except . . . what if it wasn't only in friendship? She'd taken this photo last week, wanting to capture the look on his face when he saw the gift she'd left in his desk at Sheidalin. The coloring book. The Kama Sutra coloring book, actually.

Which she'd given him after he'd left a Kama Sutra playing card on her desk, his way of teasing her about her ability to twist her body into positions no other performer could achieve. She'd thought it a little risqué at the time, even for Thorne, but she'd laughed it off.

He'd followed that first card with fifty-one more, because it had been a set. One or two a week. She'd started looking forward to them. And when she'd stumbled on the coloring book, it had seemed the perfect gift.

Except she hadn't really stumbled on it so much as typed the phrase 'Kama Sutra products' into her browser. She'd been flirting back, she admitted, ever since she'd started performing again a year ago, beginning with the aerial silks on Sheidalin's stage.

It had been out of expediency at first. Lucy had been out on this latest maternity leave, creating holes in their schedule that Gwyn had been unable to fill with reliable bands. But after some initial nerves, hitting the stage again had felt right. It had been time. And Thorne had been delighted to see her come back to them.

It had been years since Gwyn had last performed. Not since *him*.

And she was *not* going there. Not right now. Not ever, she wanted to promise, but she knew that was a promise she couldn't keep. Her therapist had assured her that would be the case, and the woman had been correct.

29

I wonder what she'd say about Thorne. About him threatening my date. Maybe all of my dates.

What if Lucy was right? What if Thorne had feelings? *For me?* She looked at the photo on her phone once again. His face had gone slack with shock when he'd found her gift, but then he'd turned a look on her. A smolder.

She hadn't wanted to admit it at the time, but now . . . Yeah. It was there.

And it scared her senseless.

Thorne and Lucy were her very best friends in all the world. If she and Thorne did start something and it failed? She'd be risking everybody's happiness.

Her phone buzzed in her hand, making her jump. A text from Lucy.

Well?

Gwyn sighed. *Still sitting in my car*, she typed back. She'd been sitting there for a long time, she realized. Thinking. Wishing.

GET IN THERE, Lucy replied.

'Fine, fine,' Gwyn grumbled aloud, then typed *I will* and hit SEND.

After putting Tweety in the backyard and making sure he had water, she gathered her courage and as much dignity as she could muster and opened Thorne's front door. 'Thorne?' she called. 'You here?'

She stepped into the living room, then frowned. Thorne's dining room was a mess. Chip bags and half-eaten bowls of dip covered the table, along with empty beer bottles and Coke cans. The dip had hardened, the melted cheese on the nachos congealed.

In all the years she'd known him, she'd never seen him leave a mess. Never.

Maybe he's sick. Frowning now with worry, she went to his bedroom and knocked lightly. 'Thorne? It's me. You okay?'

Silence. Quietly she opened the door, complete darkness meeting her eyes despite the rising sun. Thorne had blackout shades because he sometimes slept late after a long night at the club. Occasionally he got migraines and the light pained him.

30

'Thorne?' She stepped into the room and stumbled. Over a shoe. A woman's shoe.

She bent down to scoop it up, checking it in the dim light from the hallway. An expensive shoe. Louboutin, about seven hundred retail. *And not mine.*

Fury began to bubble inside her once again. 'Sonofabitch,' she muttered. Having a woman here? *After sabotaging my dates?*

She shone the light from her phone on the floor, noting the discarded little black cocktail dress, the black thong and matching frothy bra. Probably a push-up, she thought scornfully. She herself had never needed one of those.

Picking it up gingerly, she smelled a woman's perfume. Again, expensive. Again, *not mine.* She tossed the bra back to the floor.

Because there in the bed was the master of the house himself. Thorne lay on his stomach, one huge arm hanging off the side of the bed, his knuckles dragging on the floor.

Gwyn snarled. 'Son-of-a-fucking-bitch.' She crossed the room, making sure to grind her shoe into the woman's pricey lingerie as she walked. 'Wake up, Thorne.' She poked his hard biceps with her forefinger, her fury boiling over at the lump under the sheet beside him. *Fucking bitch.* 'Wake the fuck *up.*'

Neither he nor the woman stirred. Gwyn balled up her fist and slugged him hard. *'Wake up.'*

But . . . nothing. Except now that she was closer, she caught the iron tang of blood in the air.

Dread filling her, she switched on the light. And screamed.

Thorne lay utterly still, his face slack.

The woman beside him . . . had no face at all. Not anymore. And the sheet was covered in blood.

Gwyn glanced down at the floor, because there was something hard under her shoe. A knife. A butcher knife. Covered in blood.

'Oh God. Oh God.' She was panting, hyperventilating. Frozen. 'Thorne? Oh God. Don't be dead. Please don't be dead.' She chanted the words aloud, the sound of her own voice jarring her into action. She pressed her fingers to his throat, relieved when she felt a pulse. But it was weak. Damned weak.

She closed her eyes, drew a breath. Lifted her phone to her ear. 'Call Lucy, mobile,' she whispered.

Lucy picked up on the first ring. 'Well?' she demanded, the sound of the road in the background.

Gwyn tried to breathe. 'Lucy, come. Please. It's Thorne.'

A beat of silence, followed by a horrified whisper. 'Gwyn, what did you do?'

'Not me. I found him. He's still alive. But unconscious, I think.'
'How?'

'I don't know, but there's blood, and a knife.' Her voice rose, hysteria gripping her throat in a vise. 'Please come,' she whispered. 'Please hurry.'

'I'm almost there.' Lucy's voice had taken on the calm that she drew on like a cape during times of stress. 'I want you out of his house. Walk backward the way you came.'

'No. I'm not leaving him.'

'Gwyn, listen to me. Whoever hurt him might still be in the house. Get out. *Now.*'

Gwyn hadn't thought of that. 'I have Mace. I'm staying here.'

'Did you call 911?'

'Not yet.'

'I'll call them.'

'Lucy, wait. There's someone else here. In his bed. I think she's dead.'

'Holy shit.' Lucy swore on an exhale. 'All right. I'm pulling into his driveway.'

'How? How are you here?'

'I thought I might be needed to referee, so I left Clay and Stevie's house as soon as we hung up,' Lucy said grimly. 'I'm going to call 911 now.'

Gwyn heard brakes squealing outside, then the slam of a car door, followed by the sound of the front door opening.

'Gwyn?' Lucy was in the house. It would be okay. Lucy would know what to do. Lucy always knew what to do.

'I'm . . . I'm back here. In his bedroom.'

Lucy ran to her, phone in hand. 'Oh my God. Thorne.' She

handed Gwyn the phone, putting in her earpiece. 'Yes, I'm still here,' she said to whoever was on the line. She looked over her shoulder at Gwyn. 'I called JD. He's on his way.'

She pressed her fingers to Thorne's neck. 'His pulse is thready, irregular. God. Maybe fifty?' She frowned. 'Yes, I *am* a doctor,' she snapped. 'I told you. My name is Dr Lucy Fitzpatrick. I'm with the medical examiner's office.' She rolled her eyes. 'Yes, I can still work on live people. Have you sent the ambulances?' She drew a breath, nodding. 'Good. We have one live and one dead.'

Again she looked over her shoulder. 'Do you know who the woman is?'

Gwyn shook her head. 'No.' Then she sprang into motion, snapping photos of the room with her phone. 'The EMTs will take him to the hospital and destroy the scene. I'm going to get as many pictures as I can.'

'Good thinking,' said Lucy, the praise in her voice helping to calm Gwyn further.

'My best friends are a defense attorney and an ME who's married to a homicide cop,' Gwyn said grimly. 'I've picked up a few tricks along the way.'

TWO

Annapolis, Maryland,
Sunday 12 June, 2.20 P.M.

'He's not dead.'

He breathed a silent sigh of relief at Margo's words. The men he'd sent had given Thorne enough GHB to take down an elephant. *Idiots.* 'Is he awake?'

'Not yet,' she answered, the sound of a car starting in the background, 'but he's stabilized. I had to wait to call you until I was alone.'

'Thank you, my dear. I appreciate the update.' He also appreciated the risk she was taking. *For me. For Colin.*

'Any time, Papa,' she said warmly, and the constriction in his chest relaxed just a little. His daughter-in-law was one of the few bright spots in his life. Her baby was the other.

'Are you bringing Benny to dinner with you tonight?'

'I've hired a sitter because I thought we were talking business, but I can bring him if you want to see him.'

He could respect Margo not wanting her son to hear any of what they were going to discuss. He'd kept Colin from the darker aspects of his business until his son had been sixteen. But Colin had always known.

'I'd really like to see him,' he murmured. 'I'm missing Colin today.'

A sigh. 'Me too, Papa. I'll bring Benny. Once he's had his evening bottle, I'll put him in his crib in the nursery, and then we can talk.'

The nursery. The room on the upper floor of his home that had

34

been painstakingly decorated by Margo. *And Madeline*. The thought of his late wife had his chest constricting again, and he had to concentrate to take a simple breath. *I miss you*, mi alma. *My soul*. 'Thank you. I'll leave the gate open for you.'

'Thank you, Papa. *Te amo.*'

'*Te amo*, Margo.'

He hung up the phone and walked to the office he used for disciplinary procedures. Closing the door behind him, he looked at the two men chained to chairs in the middle of the room. *Idiots*. Soon they'd be dead idiots. 'He's not dead.'

Both visibly relaxed.

The one on the left swallowed hard. 'So . . . you're letting us go, right? I mean, he's gonna be fine.'

He rolled his eyes. *God. I should have done it myself.* And he would have, if Thomas Thorne weren't a damn behemoth. He could never have gotten the man into his house.

'I wouldn't say that.'

The one on the right's nostrils flared. He looked a little green. Some of that might be the slight rolling of the vessel, which, anchored far out in the bay, was as private and soundproof as a vault. But most of the man's distress appeared to be fear. 'You wouldn't say what?'

He let his mouth quirk up. The one on the right wasn't quite as stupid as the one on the left. 'Either. Both.' He began removing his clothing, hanging each piece carefully in the antique wardrobe adorning the far wall. Suit coat, trousers, silk shirt, tie. His shoes and socks went on the wardrobe shelf. He shucked off his boxers, folded them neatly and placed them on top of his shoes.

Hesitating, he gripped the small vial, then lifted it over his head and carefully tucked it into the pocket of his trousers.

He closed the wardrobe and turned to face the two bound men, who stared at him in horror. Good. They should be afraid. They could have spoiled everything before it had even begun.

The one on the left's eyes dropped to his groin, widening comically. 'What the fuck are you going to do?' he whispered hoarsely.

He rolled his eyes again. 'For heaven's sake, get your mind out of the gutter. I'm not going to sexually molest you. I'm just going to kill you.' He indicated the wardrobe with a nod of his head. 'That's a two-thousand-dollar suit, and blood is a bitch to explain to the dry-cleaner.'

'But Thorne's not going to die!' the one on the right sputtered. 'You can't do this.'

'Oh, but I can. And I will.'

The one on the right tried rocking his chair back, but it was bolted to the floor. *Not my first rodeo.* He'd learned a thing or two over the years. How to properly restrain his prey was one of them.

He stood studying them for a long moment.

'What?' demanded the one on the left, appropriately scared out of his mind.

'I'm just trying to decide which of my skills I want to hone. See, I told you the exact amount of the drug you were supposed to use on Mr Thorne. For whatever reason, you disregarded my instructions. I can't let that stand.'

The one on the left gulped. 'But . . . But he was huge, man! One *heavy* motherfucker. We just . . . we wanted to be sure he didn't wake up while we were dragging him into his house.'

'Well, he very nearly didn't wake up *at all*. Had you given him the amount I specified, he would simply have slept several more hours. As it was, you nearly killed him. If I let your incompetence go unpunished, what kind of a message would I be sending to the rest of my employees?'

He didn't wait for an answer, instead opening his weapons case and drawing out a simple bludgeon. He'd decided on a physical approach. He needed to work off some excess stress.

Baltimore, Maryland,
Sunday 12 June, 3.35 P.M.

Thorne swallowed hard, confused when his throat felt raw. His head hurt too. *Dammit.* And there was beeping. Something was beeping.

Close to him, someone was murmuring. He drew a breath and

relaxed. Lavender. *Gwyn is here.* She always smelled like lavender because she soaked in scented Epsom salts every night. It kept her muscles from hurting after performing at the club.

He turned his head toward the scent and breathed once again. 'You're here,' he whispered, then jerked awake, because she wasn't supposed to be here. He was asleep and she was . . . here. In his bedroom.

His eyes flew open at the same time he tried to sit up. Pain sliced at his wrist and he yanked his arm to get away from it, only to have it hurt even more. Two sets of hands pressed against his chest, both female. Both familiar.

All he could hear was his own roar and the clang of metal until Gwyn's voice broke through his confusion. 'Thorne. Stop. Please. Stop before you hurt yourself.'

Wide-eyed, he stared into Gwyn's dark blue eyes, then at Lucy's pale face. Both were urging him back down. Suddenly exhausted, he dropped his head to the pillow. Then turned to stare at the handcuff that cut into his wrist.

He was handcuffed. To a bed. He scanned the room. White walls. Monitors that beeped incessantly. He was handcuffed to a *hospital bed*.

Swallowing again, he drew a breath that he hoped would calm his racing heart. But it didn't. 'What happened?' The words came out as a hoarse croak.

Lucy abruptly turned her back to him, shifting her body so that she blocked Thorne's view of the door.

Gwyn's gaze flicked over Lucy's shoulder to the doorway, then back to his face. 'You were drugged,' she whispered fiercely. 'You're in the hospital. The police will ask you questions. Don't answer them. Wait for Jamie to get here.'

'Gwyn. Lucy.' The voice and the sigh were familiar. JD Fitzpatrick was here. This couldn't be good at all. 'Step away from the bed, both of you.'

Gwyn's chin lifted. 'He's not talking to you without Jamie in the room.'

'I figured as much,' JD said, sounding a little bit . . . hurt? 'But I need to be here in case he does say something. You two can stop acting like I'm the enemy, you know.'

Lucy stepped aside and Thorne realized she hadn't been blocking his view of the door, but JD's view of him. 'I didn't expect it to be you coming through the door,' she told her husband, sounding relieved. 'I thought Lieutenant Hyatt had taken over.'

Hyatt? Thorne wanted to groan, but his throat hurt too much. If the arrogant, abrasive, grandstanding homicide lieutenant was on point, things really had gone to shit. *Wait*. Homicide detective? *What the hell happened to me?*

'He has,' JD said. 'He had to take a phone call. He'll be in here as soon as he's done. Now, can the two of you step away from the bed, please?'

Neither Gwyn nor Lucy did what they were told. Both took a step backward so that they stood on either side of Thorne's head. His sentries.

Thorne might have smiled had his head not been splitting in two. 'Can I get some water? Maybe some aspirin or something too? My head feels like I got kicked.'

As did the rest of his body. Now that he was awake, he hurt all over. He had been in enough fights to know that whatever had happened, he'd soon be covered in bruises, if he wasn't already.

What time is it? He was in a single room cubicle. With no windows. In the hospital. *What the fuck happened?*

JD studied his face, the cop's expression one of genuine concern. 'That's the doctor's call. She's on her way.'

Gwyn's small hand stroked the hair off Thorne's forehead. 'Where else does it hurt?'

'Everywhere.' He closed his eyes, tried not to panic. 'What happened to me?'

JD came to stand at the foot of his bed. 'You don't remember?' he asked carefully.

No. I don't. And it was terrifying, because he was *handcuffed* to a *hospital bed* and a *homicide detective* was in his room in case he said anything. *What happened? What the fuck did I do?*

His lips started to move, but Gwyn's hand over his mouth kept him from saying another word. 'Wait for Jamie,' she said.

She was right. It was what he should have told himself, but he cut himself a little slack because the other words she'd spoken had finally kicked in. *You were drugged.* He opened his eyes to meet hers, a deep dark blue that he'd dreamed of waking up to so many times. *Just not like this.*

Drugged. It explained a lot, actually. Except . . . *How? And by whom?*

'Can you unlock the cuff?' Lucy asked JD. 'He's not going to flee.'

JD frowned, his gaze dropping to the handcuff fixed to the bed rail. 'Who cuffed him?'

Lucy's mouth tightened. 'The detective who brought him in. Brickman.'

'And against his doctor's orders,' a woman said as she strode into the room wearing a frown. And scrubs.

She glanced at the monitors, then flicked a light in Thorne's eyes, nodding at whatever she saw. 'If you have to restrain him, we can use softer restraints.'

JD simply unlocked the cuff and removed it from Thorne's wrist. 'I don't have to restrain him at all.'

Thorne flexed his fingers, then gently removed Gwyn's hand from his mouth, hesitating before placing it on his cheek. Needing her to touch him right now, he was relieved when she didn't move her hand, curving it instead to cup his jaw. 'I'll wait for Jamie,' he murmured, then looked at the nurse. 'Water?'

'Let me take your vitals and I'll get you a cup and a swab. You can't drink until the doctor's been in and changed her orders, but you can at least wet the inside of your mouth.' She glanced at Lucy. 'Can you move, please?'

Lucy complied, standing next to JD at the foot of the bed, watching every move the nurse made. Thorne closed his eyes again, secure in the knowledge that Lucy wouldn't let the medical personnel hurt him and that Gwyn wouldn't let him say anything stupid before Jamie got there.

'Am I under arrest?' he asked quietly.

'No,' JD said quickly, then sighed. 'Not yet. But it doesn't look good, Thorne.'

What doesn't look good? he wanted to shout, but held it back because he was so tired.

The nurse returned with a cup and a small sponge on a stick. 'There is an angry-looking bald man on his way to this room. If he causes a problem, I'll call security.'

Lieutenant Hyatt was coming. The man was mostly trustworthy. Mostly. But he tended to make decisions first and ask questions later. And it was no secret that he had no love for defense attorneys. And if things didn't *look good*? Thorne didn't like the odds that Hyatt would be on his side of things.

'Thank you,' Gwyn said, then took the cup and sponge from the nurse. 'I'll take care of him.' When the nurse had backed away, Gwyn leaned in close to wet Thorne's lips with the sponge. She was *very* close, he realized seconds before he heard her whisper, 'I found you in your bed at a little after six this morning, unconscious. You were lying next to a woman. She was dead, beaten and stabbed.'

His eyes widened in shock, but after flicking a glance at the door, Gwyn leaned in even closer, blocking his face. She made a show of re-wetting the sponge and swabbing the inside of his mouth. 'There was a knife on the floor, placed as if you'd dropped it before passing out.' She rested her forehead against his, her swallow audible. 'You nearly died. If I hadn't found you when—'

'Miss Weaver.' She was interrupted by a deep, booming voice that Thorne also recognized, unfortunately. Lieutenant Peter Hyatt had arrived. Thorne and Hyatt had butted heads far too many times over the years. But Hyatt did seem to know the meaning of loyalty, and Thorne had done the homicide department a few favors in between the head-butting.

Maybe it wouldn't be so bad.

'Say nothing,' Gwyn whispered as she pulled away. 'I was just swabbing his mouth,' she told Hyatt with a sweet smile that anyone who knew her would realize was a charade. Gwyn was many things – most of them good – but sweet wasn't normally one of them.

Which had only made Thorne want her more.

Then, once again, his brain seemed to catch up. *A dead woman in my bed? Stabbed? Beaten? What the fuck is happening?*

He clenched his jaw, determined not to say another word.

'Mr Thorne,' Hyatt said grimly, then frowned at JD. 'Who removed the handcuffs?'

'I did,' JD said flatly. 'He's not a flight risk. He can barely lift his head, much less run, and the cuff was causing injury.'

'Mr Thorne is a suspect in a homicide,' Hyatt growled. 'He will be *treated* like a suspect in a homicide. I need to chat with him. You all need to leave.'

'He's not saying a word without his attorney present,' Gwyn said, all pretense of sweetness gone.

'His attorney is here.' Jamie Maslow wheeled his chair into the doorway. 'I'm going to need everyone to clear out so I can talk to my client.'

Thorne saw a flicker of something in Hyatt's eyes. Relief? It certainly looked that way. JD's relief, on the other hand, was unmistakable.

And mine? Off the fucking chart. He was finally going to find out what was going on.

Gwyn started to move from his bedside, but he caught her arm. 'Stay,' he murmured, then glanced over at Jamie. 'I need her to stay. Please.'

She found me. In my bed. With a dead woman. That part hadn't entirely sunk in yet, because the words felt . . . surreal. Why had Gwyn even been in his bedroom? Why the fuck was another woman there? A *dead* woman? *Jesus.*

'You're entitled to talk to your attorney,' Hyatt said tightly. 'No one else.'

Thorne's temper stirred and suddenly he needed not to be flat on his back. He jabbed at one of the arrows on the side of the bed and raised himself a few degrees. His head spun, but he gritted his teeth and locked his gaze on Hyatt's face. 'Am I under arrest, Lieutenant?'

Hyatt pursed his lips. 'Not yet.'

'Then I can speak with whomever I choose,' he said coldly.

'However, if it makes you feel better, Miss Weaver is a paralegal with my office.'

Hyatt's eyes narrowed. 'She manages your nightclub.'

'I'm a multitasker,' Gwyn told him. 'I'm also a licensed paralegal.'

'She assists me part-time,' Jamie chimed in. 'She helped me write a brief just last week.'

Because the case had been a sensitive one that Thorne hadn't trusted to just anyone. He trusted Jamie and Gwyn with his life.

Hyatt's nod was curt. 'Very well. I'll be waiting to take your statement, Mr Thorne.'

Jamie backed his chair away from the doorway, allowing Hyatt to exit.

Shaking her head, Lucy pressed a kiss to Thorne's cheek. 'We'll wait outside too. Don't worry. We've got your back.'

He met her eyes, unable to hide his dread any longer. 'What did I do, Luce?' he whispered.

'Nothing bad,' Lucy whispered back. 'I know you, Thorne. You did not kill that woman. We'll get to the bottom of it. I promise.' She forced a smile. 'Now I've got to find a quiet room and pump. My boobs have to weigh fifteen pounds each.'

His lips twitched, as she'd meant them to. 'TMI, Luce. Way too much.'

She gave him a wink. 'See you soon.' Then she took JD's hand and led him from the room, leaving Thorne alone with Jamie and Gwyn.

When the door was firmly closed, Thorne turned to Gwyn and repeated his question. 'What did I do?'

And then his throat closed, because her expression grew shuttered. But not before he'd seen the accusation flickering in the dark blue eyes he knew so well.

He shrank back against the bed, suddenly too damn weary to hold his head high. She believed it was true. Gwyn believed he was guilty.

Not again. This couldn't be happening again.

death is not enough

He glanced up when Patton came in, looking disgusted and the tiniest bit scared. He already knew why, but he wasn't nearly as upset about it as Patton seemed to be.

On the other hand, Patton had disposed of the bodies of both Ramirez and his wife after his former clerk had died such a painful death. He knew the price of failure, so a few nerves were understandable.

'Yes?' he asked softly. 'You look upset, Mr Patton.'

The man called himself George Patton, but he'd really been born Arthur Ernest, his parents farmers in Kentucky, as traditional as they came. A former soldier, Patton had been dishonorably discharged, narrowly missing serving time for the death of another soldier killed in a bar fight. Not that any of that really mattered, except that Patton believed he'd gotten past his extensive background checks. Foolish man. But he was also a power-hungry man whose loyalty could be bought.

I'll use his greed as long as it suits me. And when it no longer did, there were thousands of Pattons out there just waiting for a chance to shine.

Patton squared his shoulders. 'Thorne was discovered hours too early. I had the person who should have found him set up and ready to go, but his business partner found him instead. The scene was set as you directed, but because he was discovered early, the GHB was still in his system.'

He met Patton's eyes directly, reluctantly impressed when the man didn't look away. 'That's unfortunate, but no surprise. I have eyes and ears in the hospital,' he explained when Patton's eyes widened. 'I am, however, disappointed that you waited so long to tell me.'

Patton scowled. 'I waited until he woke up, to see what he remembered.'

He blinked. 'You went to the hospital?' There were only a million surveillance cameras there. *Good God, man.*

43

Patton's scowl deepened. 'No. Of course not. I have eyes and ears too.'

Well, at least there's that. 'What does he remember?'

'Nothing so far. The problem is that the presence of GHB in his system will make the cops doubt his guilt. He doesn't have an alibi, but he was drugged and bruised. Your goons were not careful.'

Because he'd told them not to be. He'd wanted Thorne in pain. A few broken bones would have been lovely, but his *goons* hadn't been that resourceful. 'It doesn't really matter. The police would have doubted his guilt regardless. He's done too many favors for them in recent years.'

Patton frowned. 'Wait. What? You mean you never intended for him to be arrested for murder?'

'I did intend for that to happen, yes.' *But that isn't the end goal.* 'He will be arrested when all is said and done, so don't worry, Mr Patton.'

Patton gave him a long, assessing look. 'What is this really about? I mean, I could have put a bullet in his head twenty different times already. Now he'll be on his guard.'

'I don't want a bullet in his head,' he snapped, then drew a breath. He hadn't meant to show his temper. Immediately he calmed himself. 'There are worse things than death, Mr Patton.' *Like living alone for the rest of your life. Like watching your family die and knowing the person who killed them still lives.*

He didn't actually want Thomas Thorne to die. He wanted Thorne to know his pain. To *live* his pain. Preferably behind bars, where he'd be hunted like the animal he was.

'I agree,' Patton said evenly. 'So what would you like me to do next?'

'These two.' He passed a photograph across the desk. 'Bring them here.'

Patton's eyes were flat as he studied the photo. 'Where can I find them, and what did they do?' he asked.

'What they did is not important.' Because it really wasn't. The two men in the photo were tools. Nothing more. 'They'll be at Sheidalin tonight.'

Patton folded the photograph. 'I'll let you know when it's done.'

'Thank you. In the meantime, please dispose of the two currently tied to chairs next door.'

Patton's jaw grew taut. 'I see. Are you going to kill me too?'

'No. First, you did tell me about the error. Second, it really wasn't your fault that they were colossal idiots. Do be careful when you go into the office. The floor is slippery.' Because the two who'd botched Thorne's drugging had both bled out. From multiple wounds and orifices.

It had been . . . cathartic.

'Where do you want them dumped?'

'Over the side is fine. They're fairly tenderized, but you should cut them up a bit more. Don't want any identifiable parts washing up on shore.'

'Of course not. May I go now?' Patton asked.

'Please. Have a good afternoon, Mr Patton.'

Baltimore, Maryland,
Sunday 12 June, 3.50 P.M.

Frederick Dawson rubbed his forehead with a sigh. He'd hoped that the files he needed to read would take his mind off the fact that he was sitting in a hospital, but no such luck. He really hated hospitals, but he was pretty sure nobody gathered here in the waiting room liked them either. Yet more than a dozen people waited for news on Thomas Thorne, the atmosphere tense and disbelieving.

It didn't look good. Thorne had been unresponsive when he'd been brought into the hospital that morning. That would be bad enough, but the circumstances under which he'd been found . . .

None of the people waiting for news believed Thorne had killed the woman discovered in his bed. Frederick had heard the shocked words 'He wouldn't do that' so many times.

But these were Thorne's friends. His employees and co-workers. Of course they'd say that. Most of them even believed it.

Frederick wanted so badly to believe along with them. He didn't want to think Thorne could commit such a heinous crime, but he no

45

longer trusted his own judgment in such matters. He'd believed the liar he'd called his wife for years, after all. Not once had she set off his bullshit detector.

Still, he desperately wanted to believe in Thorne's innocence, because he truly liked the man. He'd only known him for ten months, but he'd been impressed with Thorne's ethics and his dedication to getting justice, especially for clients nobody else would touch. Not because they were guilty – many of them were guilty as sin – but because they couldn't afford private counsel. Given representation by the public defender, they'd probably do far more time than was fair. Or, in the rare case of a truly innocent client, they'd get railroaded because they had no advocate.

Many of them had found an advocate in Thomas Thorne, and Frederick respected that. Thorne was the kind of attorney Frederick himself had once been, before he'd been forced to leave his practice and go into hiding to protect his adopted daughter, Taylor, from the biological father they'd believed would harm her. That belief had been rooted in the lies that Frederick's wife, Taylor's mother, had told him for years. Lies that hadn't been revealed until after her death.

Frederick had given up his practice, his home and ten years of his life based on an unforgivable lie. Worse, he'd forced his family into hiding, stolen years of freedom from his daughters. The cost of his choices had been . . . immeasurably high. To his daughters and to the man he'd hidden Taylor from. A good man, who'd been innocent of any wrongdoing. All those years.

I judged him, found him guilty, hid his daughter away from him. And I was wrong. A year later, this remained a hard truth to swallow.

That same biological father was now lowering himself into the chair next to Frederick with a weary sigh and two cups of coffee from the Starbucks in the lobby.

Clay Maynard was not the monster Frederick had been led to believe. Now, unbelievably, he counted Taylor's biological father as a friend. *Unbelievably* because Clay had forgiven him. Now, if Frederick could only forgive himself . . .

'Hey,' Clay murmured quietly, offering him one of the coffees.

Closing the file he'd been reading, Frederick took the coffee gratefully because it wasn't the sludge he'd been drinking from the pot in the waiting room. 'Thanks. Any news?'

'Nope. I checked at the nurses' desk on my way back in, but his status is unchanged. I really just needed to take a walk. The quiet here was getting to me.' Clay grimaced. 'But the zoo outside changed my mind.'

'How many news vans?'

'I saw at least six before I hightailed it back in here. Vultures,' he snarled.

Frederick lifted his eyes to the TV mounted on the wall, its screen set to a cartoon channel even though there were no kids in the room. 'We had to change the channel. The media have already declared him guilty.'

'Vultures,' Clay snarled again, then drew a breath to calm himself. He cast a look at the file. 'I don't mean to bother you. Keep reading if you need to.'

'Nah. I wasn't absorbing any of it. Just trying to stay busy. I met Anne in the office and we pulled the files as soon as I heard what had happened.' Anne Poulin, Thorne's receptionist and paralegal, was one of the most steadfast voices in his defense. 'Whatever happens to Thorne, we have to protect the privacy of our clients.'

'We're going to clear him,' Clay said, his jaw tight.

'I know.' Frederick wasn't so sure about his own judgment anymore, but he'd bow to Clay's any day of the week. 'But in the meantime, his clients will still have trial dates. Jamie and I will figure out how to split Thorne's caseload. It'll be fine.'

Clay studied him, narrow-eyed. 'You're not sure, are you? If he's innocent?'

'I'm sure that *you're* sure, and that's good enough for me.'

Clay sighed. 'Frederick. Dammit, man. How many times do I have to say this? Donna lied to us both. You're gonna have to let all that shit go. I have, and so has Taylor. What does your gut tell you about Thorne?'

'That he would never do anything so heinous.'

'Then there you go. He's being framed. That's clear to me and . . .'

47

He sat up straighter, brightening at the sight of the daughter they shared coming through the waiting room door holding a red-headed toddler on her hip. 'Taylor.'

Frederick smiled, because the joy on Clay's face was infectious, just as it was every time Taylor walked into a room. Clay appeared to have truly put the pain of his and Taylor's twenty-plus-year separation behind him. Every time Frederick saw the man's face light up, he told himself that someday he might forgive himself.

'Hey, baby,' Frederick said, leaning his face up for a kiss. Taylor complied, kissing his cheek, then Clay's.

'Any word?' she asked, sighing when both he and Clay shook their heads. 'Well, Miss Wynnie here was missing her mama.' She dropped a kiss on top of the baby's head. 'I texted JD and he said to bring her in, that Lucy could find a quiet room to nurse her. And before you ask, Pops, I left Ford on babysitting detail. Mason is in good hands.'

Ford Elkhart was Taylor's fiancé and Frederick liked him very much. Mason was Clay and Stevie's new son, already six weeks old. That Clay was getting to experience fatherhood from the beginning for the first time made Frederick very happy.

'I never figured you'd leave him alone,' Clay said mildly. 'And don't call me Pops.'

Taylor just grinned at him. 'You know you love it.' She sat down next to Frederick, settling the baby on her lap. 'Oh, Dad, I heard from Daisy. She's coming for Mason's christening.'

Frederick raised his brows at this news. His middle daughter had been enjoying the new-found freedom that had come with Taylor and Clay's reunion. No longer needing to stay in hiding, she'd been backpacking in Europe for the past four months. She wasn't supposed to be back for another two months. 'Is she okay?'

Taylor moved her shoulders in an uncertain shrug. 'I don't know. She said she was. But I worry about her.'

So did Frederick. Daisy's sobriety had been only one of the casualties of their years of forced hiding. His twenty-five-year-old was now a recovering alcoholic because of the choices he'd made.

'Dad, stop it,' Taylor chided. 'I can see you going into guilt mode.'

'I keep telling him,' Clay muttered.

The two of them huffed such similarly aggrieved sighs that Frederick found himself smiling. 'Fine, fine. Is she planning on telling me, or am I supposed to act surprised?'

'She said she was going to text you. I only know she's coming because I went online about five a.m. and saw she'd posted new pics on Facebook. You don't want to see them,' she added quickly when Frederick started to look on his phone. 'She met this guy. With a motorcycle. So . . . save your blood pressure and let those photos just pass right on by.'

Frederick only nodded. He'd look at the pictures later. And then he'd check out the guy to make sure he was legit. Nobody messed with his daughters.

'Anyway,' Taylor said, 'I saw she was online, so I called her. Had a nice chat while I shoveled out horse stalls. Then I did a few therapy sessions at the farm.'

Taylor was an intern at Healing Hearts with Horses, an equine therapy center that provided services to child victims of traumatic violence. It was what she'd been born to do, and Frederick's heart nearly burst with pride every time he thought about it.

'Jazzie was one of my sessions,' Taylor went on. 'She's doing really well. She's gotten over her fear of riding and she smiles much more often. See?' She took out her phone and showed them a photo of a smiling young girl astride one of the farm's horses. 'I thought if Thorne was awake, I could show him. She doesn't know what he did for her, but . . . Well, he still asks about her.'

Jazzie had been one of Taylor's first clients. A little girl who'd discovered her mother's brutally beaten body, she'd lived in terror that the murderer would find out that she'd seen him leave the scene. When he had indeed come after her, Thorne had provided key evidence that enabled the police to bring the killer to justice, ensuring the little girl's safety.

The memory of Thorne's actions in that case dispelled the remaining doubt in Frederick's mind. *See? He's a good guy.* 'Send me the photo,' he told his daughter. 'When he wakes up, I'll make sure he sees it.'

Taylor smiled up at him. 'Thank you.' Then she twisted in her seat, because everyone around her had come to their feet.

Lucy and JD had entered the room, their expressions relieved. An audible sigh of relief rose from Thorne's group of friends.

Lucy made a beeline for her daughter. 'Thorne's awake,' she announced. 'Ask JD for details. I've got a baby to feed.' She took Wynnie from Taylor. 'Thank you,' she said fervently. 'You're a lifesaver. I was about to go pump or explode. This is so much nicer than either.'

Without another word, she hurried from the room with the baby, and Taylor sat back down with a slight grimace. 'You know, I'll sometimes start thinking about how sweet babies are. Then she reminds me about exploding . . . well, you know. I hate to break it to you dads, but it'll be a while before you get any grandchildren out of me.'

'Fine by me,' Clay said. 'You're too young.'

'Older than you were when I was born,' she retorted.

'Which was too young,' Frederick echoed. 'Live a little, baby. Go to Paris like Daisy. Have fun.'

Clay pushed to his feet. 'What he said. Now excuse me while I go listen to what JD has to say.'

Taylor laid her head on Frederick's shoulder once they were alone in their corner of the waiting room. 'I'm not the Paris type. And I *am* having fun. My life is good, Dad. I promise. So no feeling guilty, okay?'

He pressed a kiss to the top of her head. 'Okay. Then I'll go talk to JD too. You planning to stick around?'

'Until Lucy's done with the feeding, then I'll take Wynnie back to the house.' She tugged on his sleeve when he stood up. 'Dad, let me know what I can do to help Thorne. Please? He's a good guy. There's no way he did this.'

'I will,' Frederick promised. 'And I agree.' He was happy to realize that he really did. His new boss was a good guy and he wasn't going to allow his own ridiculous insecurities to convince him otherwise.

50

Three

Baltimore, Maryland,
Sunday 12 June, 3.50 P.M.

Gwyn closed her eyes against the heavy silence that descended on the room. 'Who was she?' she asked, her voice far less steady than she'd hoped it would be.

'I don't know.' Thorne's whisper was barely audible. 'But I didn't . . .' His voice broke. 'I didn't kill her.'

Gwyn's eyes flew open, stunned to see him looking defeated. 'I know you didn't, you asshole,' she snapped.

He frowned. 'Then what?'

'Then *what*?' she parroted, scowling at him. 'There was a woman in your bed, Thorne.' And after the initial shock had subsided, seeing her there had hurt.

From the corner of her eye she saw Jamie glance from her to Thorne. His grey brows rose. 'Oh,' he said in a way that told her he'd already jumped to the wrong conclusion.

Gwyn narrowed her eyes at the older man, her temper closer to boiling than it had been in years. 'No. There is no "oh". There is no anything. There is only a dead woman in his bed.'

Thorne was blinking at her, confusion clouding his handsome face. Why did he have to have such a handsome face? She wanted to smack it. She wanted to smack Lucy for getting her hopes up, for insinuating that Thorne had cancelled her dates because he might have *feelings* for her. She sneered as the word bounced around in her mind. *Fucking feelings.*

He'd had another woman in his bed. Naked in his bed. Tears

51

stung her eyes, making her even angrier. Sucking in a breath, she concentrated on cutting the waterworks. She would *not* cry.

'Gwyn?' Thorne's voice rumbled in the quiet of the room.

She looked away. 'What?'

'Look at me. Please.'

Gritting her teeth, she dragged her gaze to his. 'What?' she repeated as coldly as she could muster. But it wasn't nearly as cold as she wanted, because understanding filled his eyes. Understanding and something else that she was not going to allow herself to even consider.

'I got a phone call last night,' he murmured. 'From Bernice Brown.'

Jamie rolled his chair closer to Thorne's bed. 'What time?'

'Close to midnight.' Thorne spoke to Jamie, but his stare remained fixed on Gwyn's face. 'It came through the answering service to my cell phone. There will be a record.'

Gwyn tried to draw a breath, then realized she had her arms clamped tight across her chest. She forced herself to relax her grip, closing her eyes to visualize her arms dropping to her sides, relieved when she felt it happen. It had been a useful takeaway from therapy, visualizing her body relaxing. If she could see it happen, she could make it happen.

'Gwyn?'

His voice was deep and quiet and . . . calming. He'd always been able to do that. *To calm me. You trust him*, she told herself. *You've always trusted him. He didn't kill that woman.* He'd been set up, that was already a fact in her mind. So maybe the woman was a setup too.

Opening her eyes, she watched his shoulders sag in relief as he correctly read her expression. Another thing he'd always been able to do. 'Who is Bernice Brown?' she asked.

'A client. She's been in hiding from her husband, who she's in the process of divorcing.'

It was Gwyn's turn to be confused. 'You're not a divorce attorney.'

'No. She has one of those too.' Blinking hard, Thorne rubbed his eyes. 'What the fuck was I drugged with?'

'They don't know yet.' The memory of him in his bed, so damn still . . . She shuddered. 'Lucy asked your doctor to run all sorts of extra tests to try to figure that out. But whatever it was, they gave you a shitload of it.' Because he was so big. So big that they'd had to extend the hospital bed to its full length and his feet still bumped against the footboard.

Gwyn had always thought Thorne was invincible. Indomitable. But this morning they'd nearly lost him.

'Hey,' he murmured, once again reading her mood. 'I'm here.'

Yes, he was. Here. *Alive.* She lowered herself to the chair beside his bed. 'So why are you this woman's attorney, and why did she call you?'

'She's accused of trying to kill her husband. She stabbed him. She says it was self-defense. I believe her. She was released on bail, but has been hiding because her husband was stalking her. He denies it. She called because someone had tried to run her off the road.' He sucked in a sudden breath. 'Describe the dead woman,' he demanded.

'Brunette, maybe five-nine.' Gwyn grimaced, remembering. 'Her features were unrecognizable. Whoever killed her didn't want her visually identified.'

Thorne exhaled harshly. 'Not Bernice Brown, then. She's only five-two.' He glanced at Jamie. 'Check on her. I never made our meet. I hope she's safe.'

'Which bar?' Jamie asked calmly.

'Oh.' Thorne rubbed his eyes again. 'Dammit. My brain is all foggy. She called me from Barney's. I told her to sit at the bar where lots of people could see her, and wait for me there. I got there about twelve fifteen, parked in the lot, and . . .' He closed his eyes. 'I can't remember going into the bar, but I might have.'

'We'll check,' Jamie promised. 'And then?'

'I woke up here.'

Jamie sighed. 'Well, this is what we know. You were found by Gwyn in your bed at six thirty-five. You were unconscious, your blood pressure dangerously low. There was a knife that matches the set in your butcher's block on the floor by your bed, where it would appear you'd dropped it.'

'If I was guilty,' Thorne said from behind clenched teeth.

Jamie nodded once. 'The blood on the knife matches the victim's type. Your fingerprints are on the handle.'

'Of course they are,' Thorne bit out. 'It's my fucking knife.'

'Both under and on top of the blood,' Jamie added, still calmly. 'There was blood on your hands.'

'Of course there was.' Thorne stared up at the ceiling. 'Hyatt's going to arrest me, isn't he?'

'Probably not today,' Jamie said. 'He's going to want all his ducks in a row before he does that.'

Because the state would have only seventy-two hours to arraign Thorne if charges were brought.

'Plus,' Jamie continued, 'I don't think he believes you did it.'

Thorne lifted his head at that. 'He doesn't?'

Gwyn agreed with Jamie's assessment. She'd seen the flash of relief in the lieutenant's eyes when the lawyer had shown up and interrupted the interview. She didn't like Hyatt because he was an overly dramatic, condescendingly arrogant asshole who reminded her far too much of her father. Both of them could make her feel like a worthless piece of shit with barely an effort.

Hyatt had insinuated that she'd gotten what she'd signed up for when she'd cozied up to a strange man like Evan so quickly. Even though it hadn't been quickly. She'd waited months before letting her guard down. Evan had been determined. He'd been so slick that he'd fooled everyone.

So they'd all told her. Except for Lieutenant Hyatt. When he'd interviewed her in the hospital, he'd treated her as if Evan's killing spree had been her fault, or worse, that she'd somehow suspected. Even though he'd *fooled everyone*.

At least Hyatt never hit with his fists, so in that way he was better than her father. Still, the very sight of him made her furious. She couldn't even think about the time he'd set Lucy up to be human bait to lure their would-be killer. He didn't care who he used or who he hurt.

And now Thorne's future was in his hands. She'd just have to be extra vigilant, to make sure the lieutenant kept everything above board. At least at this point she didn't think Hyatt believed Thorne was guilty. If that changed, though . . .

'The whole setup was too pat,' she said. 'And your alcohol level was under point zero two when the medics arrived. Barely registered. Plus, you've got bruises all over your body. Some are finger-shaped. Like you were grabbed. Some are big and nasty-looking, like you were kicked. Whatever happened, you put up a fight.'

Jamie nodded. 'And Hyatt knows all this. But . . .' he shrugged, 'he's got the prosecutors watching him, making sure he doesn't play favorites because so many of his people like you. He's going to be playing this by the book, every step of the way. For your protection as much as anyone's. You've done favors for Hyatt's detectives in the past. He knows where key leads have come from. The man's a damn bull in a china shop, but he's fair. And, to a certain extent, loyal. We just have to figure out how to play this ourselves.'

Thorne's expression had gone neutral. Which meant he'd shut his emotions down and was thinking. Good. 'The scene was contaminated by the medics, so CSU didn't get photos of the original setup.' It wasn't phrased as a question. 'That could be good or bad for me, depending on how well those responsible set the scene.'

Jamie handed Thorne his phone. 'Gwyn took photos of your bedroom, living room, kitchen and bathroom before the medics got there.'

Thorne's glance shot to Gwyn. 'You did that?'

Gwyn nodded once. 'Yes.' *Because I was falling apart and had to keep busy. Because you were dying. And because there was a woman in your bed.*

Planted there. The woman had been planted there. Those were the facts.

Unless – or until – they were proven false. *Because everyone lies about something.* Except Thorne. He'd never lied to her. Ever. Not in twelve years.

She shut down the doubts that continued to nag. This was her anxiety talking. And her anxiety was a lying, deceitful bitch.

Thorne's lips curved. 'Thank you. I don't think I'd have had the presence of mind to do the same if I'd found you the same way.'

The praise warmed her, shining light in the darkness of her mind, driving away those nagging doubts. But before she could respond, he'd dropped his gaze back to Jamie's phone. 'How did you send Jamie these photos, Gwyn?'

'I uploaded them to the Cloud, then deleted them from my phone. I called Jamie from a burner phone later and told him how to get the pics.'

Thorne was nodding. 'Good. There'll be a trail, but only if they can get a warrant for your Cloud account.'

'Which is not in my name,' Gwyn said, miffed that he hadn't assumed as much.

His grin was quick and sharp. 'Excellent.' In seconds, though, the grin was gone and he was frowning at the photos. 'What was supposed to have happened?'

'You mean if Gwyn hadn't shown up?' Jamie asked.

'Yes.' Thorne shot a look at her. 'Why were you there?'

Gwyn opened her mouth, then closed it, shaking her head. 'We can talk about it later. In the grand scheme of everything, it's not important.' Except that it might be. Especially if Lucy was right and Thorne really did have feelings.

But do I?

Well, yeah. Because to begin with, I'm pissed to holy hell that there was a woman in his bed. Which is irrational under the circumstances. Obviously I have feelings. And those feelings might be important. But later.

Thorne continued to stare at her for another few seconds. 'Okay,' he said finally. 'So if you hadn't come at six thirty-five and found me nearly dead with a dead woman beside me, what might have happened? Would I have died? Was I supposed to die?'

Gwyn bit at her lip. 'It doesn't make sense that they'd go to all that trouble only to kill you. They could have just killed you after they drugged you, and left you behind Barney's Bar. Instead, they dragged you home and staged that.' She gestured to the phone. 'I think finding out what drug you were given might help answer that question, but it seems like there were a few possible scenarios.'

Thorne handed Jamie his phone, then lay back in the bed, his eyes closed, his jaw tight as if he were in pain. 'Like?'

Standing, Gwyn leaned over the bedrail and pressed her fingertips to his temples, rubbing in little circles. He immediately hummed in relief. 'Your headache's worse?' she murmured.

'Hurts like a bitch,' he admitted.

'They probably won't give you any painkillers. Not until they're sure all the shit is out of your system.'

'I figured as much. But that pressure feels a little better. Tell me the scenarios, because Hyatt's not going to give us much more time.'

'Well, for one, you might have died and one of us would have found you and the dead woman tomorrow when you didn't show up for work.' *Which probably would have been me.* She sent a little thank-you heavenward. *I'm so glad it wasn't this scenario.*

Thorne grimaced. 'We need to find out if whatever I was given would have worked its way out of my system over a certain amount of time, making it look like I died – and murdered that woman – while stone-cold sober. What else?'

Gwyn saw Jamie punching notes into his phone. The older man looked up and gave her an encouraging nod. 'Keep going, Gwyn.'

'Well, you might have woken up on your own and discovered a dead woman in your bed. What do you think you would have done?'

'Probably the same thing you did. I'd have called Lucy.' His smile was grim. 'I mean, why have a friend who's an ME if you can't call them when you have a dead body in your bed?'

'She would have called JD,' Gwyn said. 'Just like she did this morning.'

'I know. I still would have called. I would have called 911 too.'

She watched the two men share a long, long look. 'What?' she asked. 'What was that look for?'

'This isn't the first time Thorne's been set up for a murder,' Jamie said quietly. 'The thing that saved him from a conviction the last time was that he made his friend call 911.'

She opened her mouth to ask more questions, because how could she leave a statement like that alone? She'd known he'd been tried for murder and found not guilty, but she had never heard the details.

She could have looked them up, but she'd always figured that if he'd wanted her to know, he would have told her.

Thorne shook his head. 'Keep giving me scenarios. We're running out of time.'

'Okay,' she said unsteadily. 'If you were supposed to wake up at some point, perhaps someone else might have been supposed to find you. Or maybe whoever did this took their own photos.'

'Blackmail,' Thorne said flatly. 'Or extortion.'

'Which would only have worked if you'd woken on your own and not called 911,' Jamie said.

'What might they have blackmailed you about, Thorne?' Gwyn asked.

'Money. Influence on a case.' Thorne frowned. 'Or it could have been targeted at the club. I get threats all the time there. Little mobster wannabes trying to distribute through Sheidalin. I threw a sleazebag out just last weekend. He threatened me and my little dog too. I didn't tell him that I only have a cat.'

'You didn't tell me about that!' Gwyn exclaimed.

'I don't tell you about those things.' He closed his eyes again. 'You've got enough on your mind with running the place.'

'And you don't think I can handle a few thugs?'

He sighed. 'I don't want you to have to handle them. I was just trying to help you.' He winced. 'Don't yell at me. I have a headache.'

She drew a breath, let it out. 'Well, when you no longer have a headache, Mr Thorne, we shall have quite a lively conversation.'

'Then I think I'll have a headache forever,' he said glumly. 'I'm serious,' he added when Jamie chuckled. 'Wait.' His frown deepened. 'Where *is* my cat? Is he okay?'

'Clay came to get him,' Gwyn told him. 'He's got Tweety too.' Which also gave her peace of mind. Taylor was at Clay's, watching Lucy and JD's children, who loved her dog.

'Good.' Thorne glanced at Jamie. 'What should I do next?'

'For now, nothing. You say nothing to Hyatt. We will investigate this. We have resources. The doctors will tell us what you were drugged with and we'll start looking into all of these scenarios.

I will personally contact Bernice Brown and make sure she is okay. I'll also ask her who else knew you were coming to that club to help her.'

'I have cameras at my house,' Thorne told him. 'The footage gets uploaded to an offsite server in addition to being DVRed in my house.'

'We'll find out if the DVR is still there. If it is, we'll compare it to the recordings on the server.' Jamie glanced at his phone. 'Text from Phil. Hyatt's coming.'

'Phil's here too?' The hopeful, almost boyish note in Thorne's voice was hard to miss. The two men were like fathers to him, Gwyn knew. She didn't know how that had come about, but they'd been part of his life since she'd known him.

Jamie's smile was gentle. 'Couldn't keep him away. He's been pacing outside in the hall. Don't worry, Thorne. We'll take care of this. We'll take care of you.'

Thorne stared at him, then abruptly closed his eyes and cleared his throat. 'I could use some more of that water, Gwyn.'

Gwyn swabbed his mouth. 'Here you go, Mr Tough Guy.'

'I am a tough guy,' Thorne muttered, but his voice broke a little.

'I know.' Gwyn stroked his cheek. Feelings or no feelings, this man was one of her two best friends. 'Jamie's right. We'll take care of you. Let us.'

He nodded, rubbing his palm over his eyes, then wiping it on the sheet. 'I hate getting framed for murder.'

She placed a kiss on his forehead. 'We'll figure it all out. I promise.'

There was a knock on the door, and a few seconds later, Hyatt entered. 'I have news,' the lieutenant said. 'We've identified the victim.'

A few beats of silence passed. 'And?' Jamie prodded.

Hyatt's brows crunched. 'Her name is Patricia Segal. Her husband is a judge.'

Gwyn and Jamie looked at Thorne, who was staring up at the ceiling in silence. 'He's not going to talk to you, Lieutenant,' Gwyn said. 'On the advice of his attorney.'

Hyatt moved further into the room and stood at the foot of the bed, his gaze intent on Thorne's face. 'Her maiden name was Linden.'

Thorne's body went stiff. As did Jamie's. But Thorne's gaze remained locked on the ceiling. Gwyn desperately wanted to scream, *Who is she?* But she held her tongue. Kept her expression neutral.

Hyatt swore quietly. 'Goddammit, Thorne. I can't help you if you don't help me.'

Thorne lowered his gaze at last. 'With all due respect, Lieutenant, I've heard that before. I'll be invoking my right to remain silent.'

Hyatt blew out a breath. 'Fucking defense attorneys. But I figured you'd say that.'

'Are you going to arrest my client?' Jamie asked.

Hyatt shook his head. 'Not at this time. Please don't leave town, Mr Thorne.' He took a step back, then hesitated. 'I'm going to put surveillance outside your house and anywhere you go.'

Thorne frowned suspiciously. 'Why are you telling me?'

Hyatt's jaw muscles twitched as he visibly ground his molars. 'Because the woman's husband is a judge. I have to do this textbook. But also for your protection.'

Thorne scoffed. 'Really?'

'Yeah. Really.' He lowered his voice to a bare whisper. 'Because Judge Segal claims the two of you were having an affair. Says he can prove it. And because somebody ripped that woman open stem to stern. All while you lay unconscious in the bed beside her. Whoever did that is capable of ruthless violence, and they seem to have a hard-on for you, Mr Thorne. You've done me a solid or two in the past. Consider this a debt paid.'

Hyatt left the room, and for a long moment there was only silence.

Then Thorne's lips drew back into a snarl. 'Fuck this. *Not again.* I'm not *doing* this again, Jamie. Not with them. Not with the Lindens.'

Jamie dragged trembling palms down his face, but once he'd done so, he firmed his expression. 'Yeah, you will. So will I. And we'll beat this to hell, just like we did before.' He lifted his brows.

'Look on the bright side. I'm an even better lawyer now than I was then.'

Thorne stared at him, then, unbelievably, he chuckled. 'Yes, you are. I learned from the best.'

'That's the spirit.'

Gwyn's patience was at its end. 'Will one of you tell me what the fuck just happened here?'

Thorne sighed. 'Yes. But get Lucy in here too. I only want to tell this once.'

'And Frederick,' Jamie added. 'He's in the waiting room. As are Sam and Ruby and Clay and Stevie and Paige. They all want to help you.'

Because Thorne had touched all their lives for the better. *Just like he's touched mine.*

Sam and Ruby had been a cop and an ME tech respectively. Now they were private investigators for Thorne's practice. Sam sometimes provided personal security when clients needed it. Ruby was Thorne's death investigator. Gwyn knew that the pair trusted Thorne with their lives, because Thorne had dropped everything to help them when they'd needed it most.

It was the same for Clay, Stevie and Paige, who ran their own PI agency. Clay and Stevie were former cops and knew that the law didn't protect everyone as it should. Stevie would be especially helpful as she'd worked for Lieutenant Hyatt for years. She'd be able to predict his actions and behaviors. Paige managed personal security for Clay's firm, kind of like Sam did for Thorne. Between Sam and Paige, Thorne would be protected.

Gwyn was suddenly, overwhelmingly, relieved. Thorne wasn't alone in this. He had a . . . family. Maybe none of them related by blood, but they all cared about this man.

Not as much as I do. Well, maybe Jamie and Phil, who considered Thorne their adopted son. But it wasn't the same. Gwyn wasn't sure what she felt, but . . .

It was way too big to go back in the box where it had been hiding for so long. The realization came with an abruptness that stole her breath.

Thorne opened his mouth, then closed it on a snap. He nodded once. Then rubbed his hand over his eyes, drying it on the sheet once more.

Gwyn took that hand in her own and squeezed it gently. 'I think we're going to need a bigger room.'

Four

'Dammit, Gwyn, your house is made for Smurfs or something.' Thorne's grumble was not a new one. He said the same thing every time he came to Gwyn's condo. But this time his voice was softer, his groan a little more authentic as he dropped his big body onto her low sofa. Built especially for short people. Because that was what she was.

'It's not forever,' Gwyn snapped back, mostly because she was just so damn glad to see him out of that hospital bed. She pulled his feet from the floor to the sofa, putting a pillow behind his back. 'Just until your house is released by the cops and we're sure it's clean.'

Because he was afraid it had been bugged or wired for cameras by someone other than himself, and it was not a paranoid fear.

Her front door opened and Lucy barged in, pocketing her key, and was followed by a . . . horde. A welcome horde, to be sure, but more people than Gwyn had ever had in her place all at the same time. The doctor had come into Thorne's hospital room right after Hyatt's departure and Thorne had signed himself out, against her orders. The doctor had wanted to admit him for observation, because even though the drugs had sufficiently worked their way out of his system, he'd had a very close call.

But Thorne had wanted out of there and Gwyn couldn't blame him. She always hated hospitals too. More importantly, he wanted to be in a private place when he told them what Gwyn was anticipating to be a very painful story.

Lucy had a small duffel bag in one hand and Thorne's bass in the other. She dropped the bag on the floor and put the bass in the corner. Of all Thorne's things, the bass was the one possession he treasured, because it had belonged to his father. He kept it locked up in a special safe. Gwyn had only heard him play it once.

'I packed you some clothes,' Lucy told Thorne. 'JD and that horrible little Detective Brickman were with me in your house the whole time, so don't say any of those things you're getting ready to say, because I was safe.'

Thorne scowled. 'Thank you,' he grunted. 'And thank you for getting my bass.' He lifted his cheek when Lucy bent to kiss it. 'Do I have a swarm of media around my house?'

'Yep,' she said. 'Part and parcel, Thorne. You knew to expect it.'

'I know. But I don't have to like it. At least getting in here was easier than getting away from the hospital.'

Because Gwyn's new condo had excellent security. She paid for it through the nose, but along with a kick-ass security system and several handguns in her safe, it enabled her to sleep at night. Sometimes.

Lucy checked Thorne's eyes and nodded at whatever she saw there. 'You're looking better. Did they tell you what they found in your system?'

'Yeah. I'll cover that.' He looked to the door with a sigh. 'When everyone gets here.'

Within five minutes, Gwyn's small living room was packed to near bursting. Jamie had positioned his chair at the foot of the sofa. Phil was sitting at his feet. Sam and Ruby were on the floor along with Paige. Clay and Stevie took the only chairs because they'd accumulated enough injuries over the years to make walking painful, so sitting on the floor was not going to happen. Stevie still walked with a cane after being shot nearly three years before, and probably always would. Clay was noticeably slower after his last brush with a bullet – taken while guarding his adult daughter, Taylor.

Clay had brought Tweety back, and the dog followed Gwyn around, looking puzzled at all the people.

Taylor's stepfather, Frederick, filled out the group. He pulled two of the milk crates she used to store her vinyl albums from a corner, carefully stacked the albums on the floor, then made the crates into a makeshift chair. 'I worked a ranch for years,' he said when Clay tried to make him take his own chair. 'I've sat on a whole lot worse, trust me.'

The two men had bonded over their love for Taylor, who was absent. 'Is Taylor babysitting?' Gwyn asked.

'She is,' Lucy confirmed.

'And loving it,' Frederick added, then gave Thorne his attention. 'What the hell happened, Thorne? Who is Patricia Segal, and why was she in your bed?'

'And why is she dead?' Clay added, and heads nodded throughout the room.

Thorne sighed. 'Okay. Look, this is hard. I haven't talked about this in nineteen years. So . . .'

'So . . . ?' Clay prompted.

'Take all the time you need, Thorne,' Paige said quietly. 'We'll be patient. Won't we, Clay?'

'No,' Clay answered. 'Because this is really bad.'

Heads bobbed in nods again, murmurs rippling through the room.

Her dog curled up at her feet, Gwyn perched on the arm of the sofa, leaning against Thorne's rigid back. Here she could give him support, but the mirror on the opposite wall allowed her to see his face. There were mirrors all over her condo. Nobody would ever sneak up on her in her own home, ever again. 'At least he's honest,' she murmured in Thorne's ear. 'You want me to tell them what we know so far?'

Thorne nodded gratefully. 'Please.'

Gwyn proceeded to tell them everything she, Thorne and Jamie had discussed in the hospital room, including the possible scenarios. 'Hyatt says the woman is Patricia Linden Segal. This means something to Thorne and Jamie. All I know is that Patricia Linden is the sister of the boy Thorne was accused of killing nineteen years ago.'

65

Thorne twisted abruptly so that he could look up at her over his shoulder. 'Did I tell you that?'

'No, but I *can* Google,' she told him, keeping her tone sarcastic. Sarcasm was both her weapon and her best shield, and she wielded it as bravely – and as often – as she could. 'It wasn't easy to find, but I was determined. You were being seen to by the doctor and I needed something to do.' She'd always respected his right to privacy, but the game had changed the moment she'd found a dead woman in his bed.

It would have been nearly impossible to find the article about the murder of which Thorne had been accused if she hadn't known his legal last name had once been White. He'd changed it to Thorne when he was eighteen and she'd never asked him why. But now she thought she knew. The name change had been filed in the court only a few days after the jury had returned with their not-guilty verdict.

She wondered why he'd chosen Thorne as his new name and not Jamie's last name – Maslow. When they were alone, she planned to ask. *Among many other things.* Her list of private questions was steadily growing.

'So the murder of Patricia Segal is a deliberate link to your past,' Clay said.

'Deliberate and painful,' Phil murmured, and Gwyn remembered that the man had known Thorne back then. He'd been Thorne's teacher in high school, and he and Jamie had taken Thorne in. But that was all she knew. Neither Thorne, Jamie nor Phil ever talked about that part of their lives.

'Yeah,' Thorne murmured, then bumped her lightly with his shoulder, indicating that she should continue.

'The only other thing I know,' Gwyn went on, 'is that the doctor said that Thorne had been given GHB – and a lot of it. It is possible to OD on the stuff, and he'd come very close to full cardiac failure.'

Angry murmurs filled the room and Jamie's jaw clenched. 'The doctor also said that had Gwyn not found him when she did,' he said, 'there wouldn't have been enough of the drug left in his system

66

to find. It has a short half-life. Levels had already dropped considerably. The doctor wasn't exactly sure when he'd been dosed, but she guessed at the minimum he could have been given based on his body weight, considering he'd been knocked out. She believes he'd been dosed at least four hours before Gwyn arrived, maybe a little more.'

'How long had the victim been dead?' Stevie asked.

Lucy shrugged. 'Her wounds were fresh. I've recused myself from the autopsy due to my friendship and business relationship with Thorne. Neil Quartermaine will do it, but I trust him to do a good job. We'll have to wait for the report, but I can tell you that rigor had only started to set in. I noticed that her jaw was affected when I tried to find her pulse, but her extremities were still fluid. I'd guess that she'd been dead no more than two to four hours.'

'Does Hyatt know this?' Stevie asked.

'Yes,' Lucy said. 'Well, he knows my two-to-four-hour guess because I told him that when they first brought Thorne in. Unless Thorne gives his permission for the ER doc to share his medical information with Baltimore PD, she hasn't told Hyatt yet about the time frame in which he was drugged.'

'I didn't give my permission,' Thorne said. 'I'm not sure if I will or not. It depends on what else we find.'

'We'll come up with a plan of action, but we can't do that until we hear the whole story.' Clay grimaced as Paige elbowed him. 'Dammit, Paige, that hurt.'

'You're supposed to be being patient,' she hissed.

'You're supposed to not hurt me,' Clay shot back.

Stevie rolled her eyes. 'Guys, enough. See what I put up with every damn day? They call themselves professional business partners, but they squabble like siblings.'

Clay had brought Paige into his PI firm three years before, but their work styles – and their personalities – had meshed together as if they'd known each other forever. The two grinned at one another before turning back to Thorne expectantly.

Thorne shook his head. 'I'm so sorry for you, Stevie. I'd have knocked their heads together a long time ago.'

67

'Like to see you try that,' Paige muttered, but it was said with humor. Paige was a black belt and an international sparring champion. Thorne had her by about eight inches in height and a hundred pounds of solid muscle, and Paige had recently given birth to a beautiful daughter, but it would still be a fairer fight than most.

Gwyn chuckled. 'I'd buy tickets.' She had a lot of respect for Paige. The woman had helped her immeasurably over the last few years. The self-defense classes she taught had enabled Gwyn to feel confident enough to leave her house again. Now Gwyn had her own brown belt. Her personal goal was to be a black belt by the time she was forty. That gave her two years, and Paige believed it was possible. Paige was her hero and one of her greatest allies.

Now she gave Gwyn an encouraging wink that managed to convey as much sympathy as sass, and it struck Gwyn that her *sensei* was there for her as much as for Thorne. That at some point the woman had become one of her friends as well. It shouldn't have surprised her so much. But it did. Maybe they'd been friends for a while. *Maybe I just never noticed.*

It made her wonder what else she hadn't noticed from within the walls she'd hidden behind for the last four years. *Maybe it's time to come out now. Thorne needs us. All of us. All of me.*

'You're supposed to be on my side,' Thorne murmured.

Gwyn leaned in close. 'You know I am,' she whispered, so that only he could hear.

He drew a deep breath, then let it out. 'I know,' he murmured. 'Let's do this.'

She lifted her eyes to the mirror to find he was looking at her reflection as well. There was something there. Something grim but also . . . hopeful.

'Yes. Let's,' she murmured back, and felt a tiny spear of terror because she was promising him . . . something. She wasn't entirely sure what, and that scared the bejesus out of her. One step at a time. It was how she'd lived her life for the past four years. She'd get through the next few days. And then they'd see.

Baltimore, Maryland,
Sunday 12 June, 7.30 P.M.

This story . . . Thorne didn't want to think about it. He never wanted to think about it. But he always did. Every time he walked into Sheidalin he thought of it. And he thought of Sherri.

'I wasn't born in this country,' he started. 'I came from New Zealand as a child.'

Every eye blinked at that. 'I never would have thought that,' Stevie said. 'You have no trace of an accent.'

'Because I left when I was young. And I was . . . persuaded to lose it when I moved to the US.'

Lucy's eyes narrowed. 'Persuaded by whom?'

'My stepfather, but I'll get to him in a minute. My father's name was Thomas Thorne Junior. I'm actually a third.' He swallowed hard, remembering his dad. How much the man had loved him. *How much I loved him back.* 'My dad died when I was five, and my mother remarried. She told everyone it was because she'd fallen in love with Willy White, but that wasn't true. She told my grandmother – my father's mother – that it was because she could no longer afford to support me on her own, but that wasn't true either. My grandmother paid the bills and made sure I saw every one of them, in case I ever had to do it myself someday. The life-insurance money my father had left my mother was more than enough.'

'Why would your grandmother think you might need to pay the bills when you were only five years old, Thorne?' Lucy asked, and he realized he'd gone silent.

'She didn't really expect me to pay bills, but she was old and she worried about what would happen if she died, because after my father's death my mom started drinking. She drank a lot. Anyway, she met up with this man, Willy White, in a bar and brought him home. He was not a nice man. But by then my mother was no longer a nice woman either, so they got along all right. I was another story. He liked to use his fists and he was a big guy. I wasn't this big then.'

'Because you were only a baby,' Ruby murmured, her voice thick. 'He beat you?'

Thorne smiled down at her where she and Sam sat on the floor, twined around each other. He'd always had a soft spot for Ruby, starting back when she worked for Lucy in the ME's office. She was fiercely loyal. 'It's okay, Ruby. I turned out fine.'

Her smile was teary, but that was because she was pregnant and her hormones were all over the place. That would make what he was about to say next hard for her to hear. He gave Sam a glance that he hoped communicated some kind of warning. He was relieved to see Sam's arm tighten around her. *All right then.*

'My mother married him because she got pregnant. He continued to beat the shit out of me. What I didn't know at the time was that he beat her too. In any case, she lost the baby. All I knew was that she'd miscarried and that they yelled at each other a lot afterward. I didn't understand why at the time. It made sense later. Anyway, he was an American working in New Zealand on a visa, and if his abuse became known and he was arrested he could lose his job, because his visa would be revoked. I only know this because it's what they argued about most often. My mother would threaten to tell, and I wished she would. But she never did. His job ended and he was called back to the US. We came too. We became citizens a few years later, right about the time he lost his job. He'd come back from lunches drunk too many times. He blamed my mother and me, right up until the year I turned fifteen.'

'Because then you became bigger than him,' Sam said quietly.

Thorne knew he'd understand. Sam's father had been an addict. Sam knew the drill.

'Yeah. I told him that he'd laid hands on us for the last time. He hated me even more after that. He was barely making ends meet then. We counted every penny. But by some miracle . . .' he grimaced as he said the word, because it still left a bad taste in his mouth, 'I won a scholarship to a very fancy prep school.'

'Ridgewell Academy,' Gwyn supplied. 'It was in the article about Richard Linden's murder.'

He nodded. 'Yeah. I hated it there. I was so hopeful at first. It was my ticket out of my own life, you know? I worked hard.'

'So hard,' Phil murmured. 'You were my very best student.'

Everyone blinked in surprise once again. 'You knew him then?' Clay asked.

'Phil was my history teacher,' Thorne said, then smiled at the older man. 'The only one who spoke up for me when the shit hit the fan.'

'Because the others were fucking cowards,' Phil growled.

Jamie petted his partner's hair. 'Easy,' he soothed. 'He turned out okay, remember? We did good.'

Thorne swallowed a laugh. 'Yes. You both did good.'

Jamie gave him a wink. 'And you were already potty trained. Bonus.'

Thorne cleared his throat, conscious of the stares pointed in their direction. 'They kind of adopted me. But I'll get to that in a minute. There were a few of us scholarship students and I think we were all equally disappointed. The school really didn't want us there, except for a couple of teachers like Phil. Maybe Coach Marion, but that was only because I was lead scorer on his soccer team. We made the state finals every year I was on the team. But even he didn't stand up for me when the chips were down. He started to, but the principal threatened his job. Threatened Phil's too, but Phil did the right thing.'

'Your coach had a wife and five kids,' Jamie said softly. 'Phil had only me, and I had a trust fund.'

Phil gave Jamie a questioning look, and Jamie nodded. Phil turned to Thorne. 'Your coach contributed to your bail. He made us promise not to tell. He . . . he never really got over not standing up to the principal for you. But he cared. You should know that.'

Thorne stared at the two men who'd been his fathers all these years. 'Really? I . . . I'll need to think on that later. I need to get through this.' Because he was coming to the worst part. Sherri. He shuddered out a breath. 'I had a girlfriend. Her name was Sherri.'

Behind him, Gwyn inhaled sharply. 'Your letters,' she whispered.

He'd known she'd figure it out. 'Yes.' He closed his eyes, remembering Sherri's face. Her laugh. The way she'd looked at him that very last day.

'When we started the club,' Lucy explained quietly, 'we each

71

contributed three letters of the name of someone we'd loved and lost. The L-I-N at the end was for my brother Linus, who died when I was fourteen. I'm guessing S-H-E was Thorne's Sherri.'

Everyone looked over Thorne's shoulder at Gwyn, whose body had grown tense against his back.

'I-D-A was from my aunt,' she said stiffly, and he had the distinct impression she was lying. He wondered why.

A glance in the mirror revealed that her expression had grown shuttered. 'None of us told the others who the letters were for,' he said, trying to take the group's focus off Gwyn. She was probably at her nerves' end just having so many people invading her private space. She'd had lots of parties before Evan's betrayal four and a half years ago. She'd moved immediately afterward, and this condo hadn't had more than a few people in it at one time. 'We just put the letters together to make Sheidalin and moved forward.'

His attempt to divert attention hadn't worked. Everyone was still staring at Gwyn, and she shifted behind him uncomfortably.

Until Paige spoke. 'Wait. *Lucy and Linus?* Lucy, your parents were the worst.'

Lucy rolled her eyes. 'I know, right?'

That Lucy's father had physically abused her as much as White had Thorne would be left unsaid, because chuckles filled the room and behind him, Gwyn relaxed. In the mirror he saw her throw a grateful glance Paige's way. Paige's slow smile was a silent 'you're welcome'.

'Anyway, back to Sherri.' All eyes returned to Thorne and he drew another deep breath. 'We dated all the way through high school. Her father wasn't crazy about me, but I called him sir and treated Sherri like she was precious. Because she was.' His voice cracked a little and he cleared his throat again. 'So he didn't hate me.'

'Who was Richard Linden?' Clay asked. 'The brother of today's victim.'

'The school bully,' Phil said bitterly. 'Goddamn, I hated that kid.' He aimed a look of challenge up at Jamie. 'I can say that now. I'm almost retired.'

Jamie smiled down at him. 'I was fine with you saying it then. He was a piece of shit. So were his parents.'

It was true. 'They were very wealthy and they donated a lot of money to the school. They donated the money for our scholarships, actually. And never let us forget it.' Thorne raised a brow. 'Because we had little originality, we called Richard "Richie Rich". He really was a total piece of shit. Thought he was entitled to everything. And anyone.'

Sam frowned. 'He went after Sherri?'

Thorne found he could honestly chuckle at that. 'Hell, no. Sherri was only five feet tall, but she would have kicked his ass if he'd laid a finger on her. No, there was another girl. Another scholarship student. Her name was Angie. And Richard thought she was his private little toy. I disagreed. We'd had a shouting argument about it earlier in the week that everything went to shit. I told him he was a privileged little . . .' He winced. 'Well, it wasn't very nice.'

Phil laughed. 'He called him a "privileged little limp-dicked Napoleon".'

'You remember that?' Thorne asked, surprised.

'I thought it was fantastic. You managed to blend an honest insult with a historical one. I gave you an A.' Phil sighed. 'But Richard had a posse and Thorne didn't.'

'I was known as a bully, but I'd never laid a finger on him,' Thorne said sadly. 'I was huge by then – six-three and still growing. I was also browner than tan because my father, my birth father, had been part Maori. I did not fit in at Ridgewell Academy. That I had the highest GPA in the school after Sherri made Richard even angrier. He went after Angie when he knew I'd see. He was pawing her in the hallway right near my locker. I pulled him off her. It was the first time I'd ever touched him. Next thing I knew, his friends were on me.'

Phil's smile had evaporated. 'Coach and I had to drag them off him. The boys were vicious. They were all athletes, all big guys. Not as big as Thorne, but there were four of them. And they kicked his head first. Then his ribs. It was . . . shocking. I'd never witnessed a fight like that. I was a good bit more sheltered then. But even later, after I'd gone to the inner-city schools, I rarely saw fights like that. Coach and I got Thorne up and took him to the office to see the nurse. He could barely walk. They'd destroyed his knee.'

'Well, not destroyed,' Thorne grumbled. 'It got better.'

'It took a year, some surgery, and a lot of physical therapy,' Jamie said mildly. 'But because the boys who'd attacked him said Thorne had started it, he was expelled. The girl – Angie – had been threatened into silence by Richard, I'm sure. She denied he'd ever touched her. No cameras back then. It was Thorne's word against Richard's.'

Thorne shrugged. 'When I got expelled, my mother was upset. My stepfather was publicly upset but privately smug. Said he always knew I'd be a thug like my father.'

Stevie's brows lifted. 'Your father was a thug?'

'My father was a professional rugby player. He was a good man.' His voice cracked again. 'A damn good man.'

'I'm sorry,' Gwyn murmured as her hand ran down his arm comfortingly. Then it was gone. But it was enough.

'Thank you,' he managed. 'My father also played the bass guitar, and I'd taken it into school that day because we were practicing for a music assembly. The principal refused to let me take it home and wouldn't allow the teacher to give it to Sherri either.'

All eyes shifted to the bass standing in the corner, then back to Thorne.

'Why not?' Ruby asked, then sighed. 'Because he was afraid of the Linden family. They were the deep pockets.'

'Essentially,' Thorne said. 'That was on Thursday. But on Friday, the music teacher slipped Sherri the keys to her room. That Sunday night, Sherri and I broke into the school to find my guitar, but we found Richard instead. He'd been beaten and stabbed, and he was bleeding badly. I wanted to run.'

'But you didn't,' Lucy said confidently.

'You wouldn't,' Gwyn added, and he met her eyes in the mirror. She looked defiant and pissed off. *Just like her old self.* It almost made him smile. But he was thinking about Sherri and what came next, and the almost-smile faded.

'No, I didn't. I gave him first aid, tried to stop the bleeding. Told Sherri to call 911 and then run. I didn't want her involved because I knew the cops would assume I'd done it. Richard and I hated each other. But I couldn't leave him there to die.' He dragged air into his lungs. 'Sherri had just called 911 when the cops piled in. She'd barely started talking to the operator. Someone else had called first.'

'We never found out who,' Jamie said with a sigh. 'But that Sherri had called at all was one of the things that saved Thorne. That and the fact that they found a bloody knife outside in the bushes. The prints didn't match Thorne's.'

Lucy straightened. 'Someone left a bloody knife with your prints on it at the crime scene this morning.'

'Yeah,' Thorne said grimly. He'd noticed the knife immediately while looking at the photos that Gwyn had so cleverly taken. 'Back then I was arrested because I'd fought with Richard a few days before. It didn't matter that he'd started it. It didn't matter that his friends beat me up. It only mattered that I was seen putting my hands on him.'

'But Sherri was a witness that you hadn't murdered Richard Linden,' Clay said, studying Thorne carefully as he made the observation.

'Yes. She was arrested too. For trespassing, as it turned out. Her father came to bail her out, but I hadn't been arraigned yet so I was stuck in jail.' He closed his eyes. 'She and her father were struck broadside by a pickup truck on their way home from the jail. Neither survived.'

A heavy silence filled the room. Then Gwyn's hand gripped his biceps and squeezed. He covered her hand with his and held it there. She laid her head against his back, cuddling him. Comforting him.

'I was . . . devastated,' Thorne confessed, his eyes still closed because they'd filled with unexpected tears.

'The police ruled that the crash was deliberate,' Jamie said into the silence. 'The truck had been waiting for Sherri's father's vehicle. Witnesses said that it accelerated, knocked them off the road, then sped away. Its license plate was covered in mud. No one got the number. The truck was never found. That was the other thing that saved Thorne. His only witness was murdered.'

'Jamie and my brother had their own firm back then,' Phil said. 'My brother's specialty wasn't criminal law, but Jamie's was, so I asked him to review the case.'

Jamie nodded. 'I would have done it because he asked, but I was compelled to fight for Thorne after talking to his mother and stepfather. He was this awesome kid, and they just threw him away,' he said sadly, and Thorne's throat closed at the memory.

Jamie cleared his throat. 'His stepfather painted Thorne as a violent boy, said he feared him. Told the police that too. He told the jury that Thorne had beaten his mother, that when he tried to stop him, Thorne would hit him too. He made a credible witness on the stand. The fact that Thorne was so much bigger than he was by that point didn't help. The jury believed Willy White. I could tell.'

'But that night after he testified,' Thorne said bitterly, 'Willy went home, argued with my mother, and she ended up dead.'

'Oh, Thorne,' Lucy murmured. 'I'm sorry.'

He shrugged. He'd never stopped missing her, despite her betrayal. 'My stepfather was tried for her murder. Went to prison. Died there.'

'Good,' Ruby stated furiously, and Thorne found himself smiling at her again.

'You're very bloodthirsty, Ruby,' he said.

She firmed her trembling lips. 'Damn straight.' Then leaned into Sam, who kissed the top of her head tenderly.

'Jamie was able to get the judge to issue special instructions to the jury to disregard my stepfather's testimony. The prosecutor didn't fight him because he'd witnessed my mother and stepfather arguing over it. My mother apparently had some conscience. She wanted to tell the truth the next day, that I had never laid a finger on her, that my stepfather lied. But she never got to. That's what they'd argued about the night she died.'

Gwyn rubbed her cheek into his back and he could feel his shirt growing wet. She was crying. *For me.* It gave him . . . hope. 'So, the jury found me not guilty because there were 911 records of an earlier call. And they did have Sherri's statement from her trespassing arrest. That was allowed into evidence. And right after that, I changed my name to Thorne and moved in with Phil and Jamie. Tried to put all the ugliness behind me.'

'Until today,' Frederick said. He'd been so quiet that Thorne had almost forgotten he was there. Frederick had a way about him. Like he could fade into the woodwork if he wanted to go unseen. But the older man's eyes were sharp and Thorne wondered what he was thinking. Frederick had proven himself a formidable man. He never spoke much about his past, but he wore . . . strength like an invisible mantle. It was something about the way he moved. The way his eyes were always assessing. Clay moved that way. So did JD Fitzpatrick. Thorne attributed it to their military training.

Thorne himself was far too big to disappear. He'd never wanted to. His strength was his physical presence and he'd learned to use it to his best advantage.

Regardless of how Frederick moved in the physical plane, his mind was always working the angles. He'd proven himself invaluable in the short time he'd been handling cases for the firm pro bono. Thorne was interested to hear his proposal for action. That the man already had a plan was not even in question.

'Until today,' Thorne agreed.

Stevie's forehead was bunched in a frown. 'Was no one else ever arrested for the murder?'

'No,' Phil confirmed. 'I don't think the cops even tried.'

'So the real killer walks free,' Stevie said thoughtfully. 'At least one person knows what really happened that day.'

Gwyn came to her feet, her hands on Thorne's shoulders. In the mirror he could see her looking at the assembled group with grim determination.

'Somebody knows about Thorne's past. Somebody who wants to hurt him. All this shit is going to come to light and people will wonder. They'll make assumptions. That the victim this morning is the sister of the victim from nineteen years ago will make everyone ask if Thorne was guilty before as well. Just the hint of scandal could ruin his career. Let's figure out how to keep that from happening.'

Annapolis, Maryland,
Sunday 12 June, 8.00 P.M.

He was smiling as he rejoined Margo, who'd taken her brandy to the library, curling up in one corner of the sofa. She smirked when he sat beside her. 'How many times did Benny get you to read it?'

He had to chuckle. 'Only three. Well, two and a half, technically. He fell asleep halfway through the third time.'

'You spoil him,' she said without any real heat.

'He is my grandson.' His throat grew suddenly thick as grief for Colin hit him hard. 'My only grandson. All I have left of my son. *Lo extraño.' I miss him.* Sometimes so much he thought he'd die from it. That his heart would simply stop beating.

He missed Madeline. She was his heart. His soul. But she'd been sick for a long time before she died, and he'd had time to prepare himself. Colin . . . 'He was too young.'

Margo leaned toward him, brushing her fingertips over his upper arm. Her dark eyes were haunted. 'I miss him too.'

'I know you do,' he murmured. Closing his eyes, he held out his palm and she grasped it, sharing his pain. 'How could you not?'

They'd grown up together, she and Colin. They'd been best friends from the time they could crawl, and from there had become so much more.

'When did you know you loved him?' he asked, his eyes still closed.

'I always loved him,' she whispered hoarsely. 'From my first memories, I loved him. But when did I know that I loved him like I do now?' She cleared her throat. 'We were fifteen and he brought a DVD of my favorite movie when I had a bad cold.' Her chuckle was teary. 'He hated that movie, but he endured it so bravely. That's when I knew.'

He smiled, grateful for the shared confidence. For just a little bit more of his son to tuck away in his heart. 'What was the movie?'

'*Twilight.*'

He grimaced. 'My son has more bravery than I.' And then he

realized . . . '*Had*,' he corrected himself. 'He *had* more bravery than I.'

For long moments they said nothing, the ticking of the grandfather clock the only sound in the otherwise silent room.

'We will make him pay,' Margo whispered.

'Yes.' His tone was flat to his own ears. 'We will.'

She squeezed his hand hard. 'Let's get down to business, Papa.'

Opening his eyes, he drew a breath and sat up straighter. 'You have all the information we need?'

'Of course.' Margo looked insulted. 'I know how to dig for information, Papa.'

He released her hand, then patted it fondly. 'I know you do.' His daughter-in-law had many talents, including fluency in six languages, necessary for the international trading deals he made routinely. He'd long planned for her to take her mother's place as his office manager, but now . . . now he was considering grooming her to take over the organization he'd built over the course of his life. She might even be better at it than Colin would have been. *I mean, I loved him, but I knew his strengths . . . and weaknesses.* 'Indulge me, if you would. They do not suspect you?'

'Not even a little bit.' Her lips curved, giving her a feline look. 'They're distracted at the moment.'

'All part of the plan,' he murmured. 'Tell me everything you've learned.'

Five

Baltimore, Maryland,
Sunday 12 June, 10.00 P.M.

'Thorne, wake up. Wake up, honey. Goddammit, Thorne, wake your ass up!'

Thorne blinked hard, the voice familiar but his surroundings not. Gwyn was punching his shoulder and he winced. 'Fuck, Gwyn. That hurts.'

She pulled back immediately. 'Sorry. I couldn't wake you up. I got scared.'

He rolled onto his back and looked around the room. Gwyn's bedroom, actually. Over the years, he'd had a lot of fantasies about this room. This bed. But nothing like that had ever happened. And it definitely hadn't today, especially since he appeared to be fully clothed, dammit. 'How did I get here?'

She perched on the side of the bed. 'That you can't remember should tell you that you really did need to sleep. You're a stubborn sonofabitch, Thorne.' But her voice was soft, the fingers on his cheek gentle. 'I kept trying to get you to lie down, but you wouldn't. Then you just . . . passed out. Nearly rolled off the sofa.'

At least that sounded right. 'Because it's too small.'

'It's not too small for me, and it's my place. It's just right.'

He made a face. 'How did I get in here?'

'Sam, Clay and Paige.' Gwyn smiled. 'Stevie directed the effort. I videotaped the whole thing so we can laugh about it later.'

'You didn't.'

She rubbed her thumb over his lip. 'No. I didn't. Lucy did.'

Thorne rolled his eyes. 'Ha ha. Just keep your stand-up routine off the stage or they'll throw rotten fruit at you.'

'So noted. But the others are ready to talk to you about next steps. While you've been sleeping, we've been planning.'

Others? Next steps? He frowned, and then it all came back. 'Fuck,' he whispered, now fully awake. 'This is bad, Gwyn. Really bad.'

'I know. But we've been through other bad shit. We'll get through this.'

He lifted his hand to her hair, which fell in dark ringlets around her pretty pixie face. It had gotten long in the last four years, now halfway down her back. But her face was exactly the same as it had been that morning twelve years ago when she'd shown up to interview for lead singer of the band he'd played with back then. 'You don't ever age.'

She leaned into his caress and his heart did a slow roll in his chest. 'Oh, I age all right. I just moisturize.'

He pressed a fingertip to her mouth. 'Just say thank you.'

Her swallow was audible, her cheeks going rosy. Thorne stared. Gwyn Weaver did not blush. 'Thank you,' she whispered against his finger.

It was his turn to swallow. 'Why were you at my house this morning?'

Her eyes narrowed, the soft moment abruptly over. 'Because *you* canceled my date. He said you insinuated that I was unbalanced.'

Shit. Busted. He hadn't thought she'd actually ask her dates why they kept canceling. 'I never said that.'

Her eyes narrowed further. 'Then what exactly did you say?'

'Um . . .' He tried to sit up. 'You said the others were ready to talk to me?'

She shoved him back to the mattress. 'They can wait another few minutes. They have pizza and beer, so they're occupied.'

He blinked up at her, stunned that she'd been able to push him back so easily. 'You are either surprisingly strong or I'm more out of it than I thought.'

'A bit of both. Fess up, Thorne.' She winced, her eyes vulnerable.

81

Not a look she ever let anyone see. 'You . . . you had no right to do whatever it was you did.'

He closed his eyes, not wanting her to know what he was thinking, what he was feeling. Not wanting her to guess that he'd do it again in a heartbeat. 'I didn't say you were unbalanced. I just said they would be very unhappy if they went out with you.'

'Because I'm toxic or something?'

His eyes flew open to stare up at her, horrified to see hurt in her gaze.

Shit. Shit, shit, shit. He should have known that this was where her mind would go. Unwittingly harboring a killer in her bed had decimated her belief in herself. It shouldn't have, because the bastard had been a slippery liar. He'd fooled them all. '*No.* God, no.' But her lip was quivering now, and the truth came barreling out. 'It was because I'd go ballistic on them. I couldn't stand the thought of any of them touching you.'

She looked away, swiping a hand over her eyes. When her gaze returned to his, it was wary. 'Why?' she asked simply.

He felt his own cheeks heat. 'Isn't it clear by now?'

'No. *You're* the genius lawyer. I just manage a nightclub.'

She said it lightly, but he could see that she was serious, and it pissed him off. 'You don't "just" do anything, Gwyn. You work harder than I do and your job is every bit as challenging.'

She shook her head. 'Okay. We're done.' She started to stand up and he grabbed her wrist, making sure his grip was loose enough that he didn't hurt her and that she could pull away if she really wanted to.

'What?' he asked. 'Where are you going?'

'You're blowing bullshit out your ass, Thorne. There is no planet where my job is anywhere near as important as yours. You give me lies like that, and nothing else that comes out of your mouth will be believable.'

He scowled at her. 'Did you always think that? Or is this more bullshit from that asshole Evan?'

The asshole who'd lied to her, made her feel special, touched her body, all while he was using her as a cover for a string of murders

82

that was intended to end both her life and Lucy's. *I want to kill him. Too bad the fucker was already dead.*

She looked away. 'Don't go there, Thorne. I'm not talking about him.'

'Fine. We'll talk about you. How many people does Sheidalin employ, Gwyn?'

'Currently thirty-one,' she answered promptly. 'Twenty are part-time. Why?'

'How many of them have families? Someone they are responsible for supporting?'

'All but ten,' she said. 'What does that have to do with anything?'

'How many of those twenty-one employees have children?'

'Fifteen.'

'How many are dependent on Sheidalin for their rent, food, health insurance?'

She rolled her eyes. 'All of them. That's . . . a ludicrous argument, Thorne, and we both know it. You are protecting people's rights. Sometimes protecting their lives.'

'You're protecting people's lives too, Gwyn. And, I might add, people who are generally more deserving than my clients, because we know for sure that none of our club employees have committed any crimes.'

Her lips twitched. 'That's a fair point. But come on. Really?'

'Really. You manage our club effectively and efficiently, without drama. People who work for us love their jobs. They have security. They know they can provide for their kids. *You* do that, Gwyn. So don't be telling me that I'm any smarter than you or better than you. It's not true.'

'Fine,' she agreed, far too easily. Then her eyes narrowed to slits, her pretty mouth falling open. 'You fucker. You totally changed the subject. I asked you why you didn't want my dates touching me.'

He laughed. 'See? You're smart. I can't get anything by you.'

She socked his arm softly this time, and in the only place he didn't seem to be bruised. 'Tell me.'

His stomach tightened, any hope of avoiding the topic

evaporating like mist. He drew a breath. Closed his eyes. 'Dammit, Gwyn. I don't want to have this conversation today. I'm ... not myself. When we have this conversation, I want to be in control of my thoughts. I want to say it right.'

She leaned into his space, and he could feel her frowning even though his eyes remained tightly closed. The scent of lavender tickled his nose and a strand of her hair brushed against his neck. 'Say what, Thorne? Why would you tell perfectly nice men, vetted by people I trust, to stay away from me?'

Her questions were flatly uttered, like she was daring him to speak. Or not to speak. Either way he was fucked, and most likely not in a good way. He needed to get this out on the table so it was plain and visible and she'd know it had nothing to do with her.

And everything to do with her.

He blew out the breath he'd been holding. 'Because I want you for myself,' he blurted, then groaned. 'I had at least twenty ways to say that better.'

The scent of lavender faded as she slowly straightened. Dead silence filled the room, silence that went on so long, he opened his eyes to see her staring at him.

He rolled his eyes, choosing to be embarrassed by the whole ordeal. Because the alternative was the gut-wrenching disappointment that was already rising in his chest, threatening to stomp his heart. Because he'd hoped. He'd really hoped.

After the way she'd looked at him in the living room, the way she'd held his gaze in that damn mirror of hers ... he'd hoped. He'd been wrong.

'Really, Gwyn? You really didn't know?'

'No,' she murmured. 'I didn't. Lucy suspected, but ... I didn't know.'

He rubbed his forehead. He was getting another headache, the pain a welcome distraction from the pain in his chest. 'Just forget I ever said anything.'

'I can't.'

Great. One of the best friendships of his life and he'd totally fucked it up. 'We're friends. First and foremost.'

'But . . . you want more.'

He swallowed hard at her careful tone. He'd heard it in his own voice often enough when he'd tried to let a woman down gently. 'Can we please talk about this later?'

'No. It's a simple question, Thorne. Do you want more? You can answer yes or no.'

He wanted to glare at her, but her face was pale, the bags under her eyes more pronounced than usual. 'No, it's *not* a simple question,' he snapped. 'Yes, I want more. But if you don't, I have to respect that and I *will* respect that. Because you're my best friend in the world and I don't want to lose you.'

She nodded unsteadily. 'How long?'

'You mean how long have I felt this way? I don't know. For sure, for almost five years, but on some level? At least seven years.'

Her mouth fell open. 'Seven years?'

'That is what I said, yes.'

'But . . . you never said anything.'

'Because we were never free at the same time. And then . . . *he* came along.' Fucking Evan, who'd poisoned everything he touched. 'You seemed so damn happy. Until you weren't.'

'Until I wasn't,' she murmured. 'All right. Where do we go from here?'

'Right now? This minute? We go back into your living room and talk to the people who hopefully have a plan to keep me out of prison.'

She nodded. 'Okay. But we aren't finished with this.'

'I didn't think we were,' he said grimly.

She lifted her brows. 'I didn't say no, Thorne.'

'You didn't say yes either.'

She lifted her chin, the pose classic Gwyn. 'I have to think about it. Consider all the angles.'

Which was what she did best. She was one of the finest strategic thinkers he'd ever known. He closed his eyes again, fighting the urge to press his hand against his heart. Because it hurt like a motherfucker. 'Just . . .' he swallowed hard, 'don't run away. I couldn't bear that. Whatever we have to do to stay friends, that's what we'll do.'

'I can agree to that.' She slid off the bed. 'Come. We have work to do.'

He opened his eyes to find her hands extended. As though she could actually pull him to his feet. 'That's okay. I'll manage on my own.' Like he'd always done.

Regret flickered in her dark blue eyes. She opened the bedroom door. 'Sam!' she called. 'Need some muscle back here.' She backed away. 'We'll talk later,' she murmured, and disappeared through the door.

What did you expect? he asked himself bitterly. *That she'd throw herself at you?* She wouldn't have done that *before* the asshole murderer came into her life.

I should have just stayed out of it. Should have never approached her dates. I've ruined everything. But he'd waited so damn long for her to emerge from her shell. He'd worked so hard to make her feel safe enough to do so. It was just . . . the thought of her spending a moment alone with another man had made him crazy.

So crazy that now he'd scared her away. No, she hadn't said no. But did he want to have to coax her along every step of the way? Would he?

He should have more pride than that. He should. Whether or not he did was the million-dollar question.

'Here, boss.' Sam hurried into the room, hand outstretched, and Thorne waved him away irritably.

'I'm fine.'

Sam's look was knowing. And compassionate. 'If you say so.'

Thorne glared at him, but Sam didn't shrink away. He'd always liked that about the younger man. Thorne knew he intimidated people with his sheer size, but Sam had never been one of those people. Never a yes-man, for damn sure. It was why Thorne trusted him with such a critical part of his business. Investigating clients and their claims could be tricky and sensitive, requiring both a quick mind and the ability to read people. Now he was trusting Sam – and the others – with far more.

Helping him mount his own defense. Because if someone found a way to make the murder setup stick? It wouldn't matter what Gwyn did or didn't want. He'd be spending the rest of his life behind bars.

Thorne sighed, then shoved himself to his feet. 'Are you guys gonna save me from prison?'

Sam gave him a decisive nod. 'Absolutely. Come on, boss. We'll get you some food and then present your options.'

'Give me a second.' Thorne picked up his phone, thumbed through his messages. Ninety-five percent of them were requests for media interviews or statements. Ignoring those, he continued to scroll until he found the one he was looking for.

And frowned. It was the reply he'd been hoping for and dreading all at once.

All quiet. No one planned you ill. Altho now gunning for your club. BOLO snow, blow and TNT.

Wonderful. He'd texted Ramirez as soon as Frederick had gotten him a new phone. No way was Thorne trusting that his own phone hadn't been tampered with by whoever had been in his home that morning.

Ramirez was his contact in Cesar Tavilla's organization. A rising star in local organized crime, Tavilla had been the first person Thorne had thought of when he'd considered who had the motive and means to construct such an elaborate frame. The drug lord had hated him for years, blaming him for the incarceration of his son. He'd made attempts on Thorne's life before, causing Thorne to seek out a Tavilla insider to warn him of the next attack. Tavilla had been quiet for several months, but he certainly had the cash and staff to carry off this scheme. Ramirez had, however, provided Thorne with accurate and verifiable information for several years now, and Thorne had no reason to doubt that had changed.

He'd wanted it to be Tavilla, simply because he'd wanted an actual target. But he'd dreaded it being Tavilla because the man was ruthless and powerful. Thorne had managed to stave off the drug lord's bids to take over his club and his career, but he'd always known it would come to a confrontation.

At least Tavilla only wanted Sheidalin at this point. And at least Thorne knew what to be on the lookout for. *Snow, blow and TNT.* Heroin, cocaine and fentanyl.

Wonderful.

Six

Baltimore, Maryland,
Sunday 12 June, 10.15 P.M.

Gwyn dragged the milk crates Frederick had been sitting on to the side of the room and claimed them as her own. Tweety, sensing her mood as he always seemed to, lumbered over and sat by her side, resting his head on her thigh with a sigh. She scratched behind his ears as she studied Thorne, who was lowering himself to the sofa and looking anywhere but at her.

To be fair, there was a lot around the room for him to look at. The team had stuck large chart pads to the walls, with tape that Clay had assured her wouldn't damage the paint. They were covered in scrawled notes and bulleted next steps. Each of the pads was 'owned' by either an individual or a team because they'd divvied up the leads, each developing a plan. Frederick had supervised and Gwyn had been incredibly impressed with the clinical way his mind worked.

If she ever got in trouble again, she'd totally want him on her side. She was so glad he was on Thorne's. Just looking at all the notes, the completeness of the plans . . . it made the knots in her gut loosen. A little.

Mostly because the knots weren't there because of Thorne's current situation. That was clearly a frame-up. She had no doubt that he'd be cleared, and quickly. Her primary goal was to minimize the fallout to his personal life as they proved his innocence. Even if prison was something Thorne was worried about, it was nowhere near the top of her concerns.

No, the majority of the tension she was feeling was because of Thorne himself. *Seven years.* He'd wanted her for himself for seven fucking years?

And he never told me. Never gave me a single goddamn clue.

Except that he had, now that she thought about it. The notes. The little gifts. The teasing flirtation. The long looks when he thought she wasn't watching. She hadn't taken any of it seriously, though.

Or maybe she'd just been too scared to. She was scared right now. Scared of this thing that simmered between them. She was scared of taking a next step with him. Because what if it didn't work out? He'd said their friendship was the most important thing, and with that she agreed.

But as scared as she was about taking the next step, she was equally scared about *not* taking the next step. What if it *did* work out? What if she had someone . . . forever? Like Lucy had JD? *What if Thorne and I could have something like that?*

What if they fucked it all up? *Argh.* She wanted to yank her hair out.

Lucy came over to sit on the floor beside her, resting her head against Gwyn's other thigh. 'I'm worn out,' she murmured. 'And I have to pump again. When this is all done, can I use your room?'

Gwyn stroked Tweety's head with one hand and her friend's hair with the other. 'Of course you can.'

Lucy sighed happily, as much a glutton for having her head stroked as Tweety was. But her next words were serious. 'Are you okay?'

Gwyn might lie to anyone else, but she couldn't lie to Lucy. 'No.'

'He told you how he felt?' she murmured, so quietly that Gwyn had to lean in to hear her.

'Yes,' Gwyn whispered back.

'And?'

Gwyn glanced around the room to be sure no one was listening to them, relieved to see that the others were having their own conversations about the plans on the walls. She bent her head to Lucy's. 'And . . . I'm considering the angles.'

Lucy rubbed her cheek against Gwyn's thigh comfortingly.

'Don't consider too long, okay? And before you do anything, run it by me, if you don't mind. I have to be forewarned if there'll be pieces to pick up. For both of you.'

That Lucy actually thought she might tell Thorne 'no' was . . . unsettling. And a little liberating, if she was being honest. But mostly it was sobering, because a 'no' would have consequences that impacted them all.

'All right,' Gwyn promised, then turned her focus to the group surrounding Thorne, whose handsome face was intense as he took everything in.

Frederick took point for leading them through the plans. 'We divvied up the work. I'll give you the CliffsNotes version, okay?'

'I think that's about all I can cope with,' Thorne murmured, which wasn't true. His eyes were narrowed and sharp, his concentration absolute. He did that. Dropped into a situation and gave it one hundred percent of his focus.

At the very beginning of their friendship, Gwyn had wondered if he applied that same complete focus to his lovers. But she hadn't had to wonder about it long. The long line of Thorne's women had been happy to brag about his expertise in the bedroom. It had made her grind her teeth. It still did, she realized, and she forced her jaw to relax.

At least everyone but Lucy would believe she was just worried about the situation. Which Frederick seemed to have well in hand.

'So, the leads so far,' he said, 'are Bernice Brown, who called you through the switchboard; the connection to the murder of Richard Linden; your arrival at and abduction from the bar; and the setup of the crime scene in your bedroom.' He pointed to the various chart pads. 'Also of interest is the victim herself, Patricia Linden Segal, her relationship to her husband, the judge, and her movements – and interactions – in the days before her abduction . . . because we assume she didn't willingly show up at your house, strip herself naked, and offer herself up like a sacrifice in your bed.'

'I think that's a fair assumption,' Thorne said grimly. 'I haven't really been able to wrap my mind around Patricia's being there. And the fact that she's dead. I have only a vague recollection of her from high school. She was two years younger than us, so we didn't hang with each other. I didn't know her. And now she's dead. It hasn't sunk in enough for me to even feel bad for her and her family.'

But that would come, Gwyn knew. It was a sadness, a regret that Thorne battled with every case he took, with every client, whether they admitted to guilt or maintained their innocence. He represented each one with equal rigor, because they were entitled to a fair trial or the best plea he could negotiate.

But regardless of guilt or innocence, every one of his clients left victims. Some were victims of the crime of which they were accused, but others were their own family members, who often struggled without them while they did their time.

That someone had drawn Patricia Linden Segal into their plot against Thorne was beyond cruel – to her family and to Thorne himself. He would have to live with knowing the Segals mourned her loss because someone had wanted to hurt him.

'We'll dig until we get to the bottom of why she's dead,' Clay promised. 'Stevie, Paige and I are going to investigate Mrs Segal and her husband. I mean, her husband is a judge. What if this isn't about you at all? What if it's about him? What if someone's trying to get revenge on him or threaten him in some way? You could be the collateral damage rather than the target.'

It was clear from Thorne's expression that he hadn't even considered that. 'Oh,' he murmured. 'Good point.'

Clay's smile was equal parts feral and gentle. 'We thought so. We're going to look into her husband, any vendettas against him, any unpopular cases. We're also going to track Mrs Segal's movements over the past two weeks, talk to her friends, that kind of thing.'

'I've got the bar,' Sam said. 'I'll find out when you got there and who you left with. I know the owner from my days on the force. He's not a bad guy. Hopefully he'll cooperate.'

'I'm going to interview Bernice Brown,' Frederick said. 'I'll find out what happened last night. I've already contacted her. Told her that you were hospitalized unexpectedly and that I'll be taking on her case until you've recuperated. She sends her best.'

Thorne's brows shot up. 'She didn't mention the call?'

Frederick shook his head. 'Nope. I've also requested the transcripts and call records from the switchboard.'

'You think someone else called me pretending to be Bernice?' Thorne asked.

Frederick shrugged. 'Maybe. I'll find out.'

'Ruby and I are going to work the setting-up of the crime scene,' Lucy said. 'We have contacts in CSU who owe us favors. I'm keeping JD away from our activities.' She made a face. 'He'd want to help, but I don't want him to get trouble from Hyatt. He's technically not supposed to be working your case because we're friends. He'll help us anyway, but we figure if the information is coming from a couple different places, it'll be less likely to point to him.'

'Together again,' Ruby said with a quirk of her lips. She'd reported to Lucy for several years when both women worked at the morgue. 'And this time *you* can get the coffee.'

Lucy laughed. 'I brought you coffee when I was the boss.'

'Oh, right.' Grinning, Ruby waved her hand, her long red nails sparkling as they caught the light. 'Then nothing's changed. Same old, same old.'

'Except that it's decaf now,' Sam cautioned.

Ruby blew out a breath. 'I know, I know. Don't rub it in.'

Jamie smiled at Ruby indulgently. He really was a kind man. Gwyn had always thought so. Now, knowing what he and Phil had been to Thorne when he was a scared kid, accused of murder? She better understood Thorne's devotion to the two. 'It's not for much longer,' he told Ruby.

'The hell it's not,' Lucy called. 'If she decides to breastfeed, she can cut out all the good stuff for a good while longer. Speaking of which, hurry this along, because I have to pump.'

Jamie rolled his eyes. 'Go pump. This isn't your part.'

'The hell it's not,' Lucy repeated. 'It's about Thorne, so it's all my part.'

Jamie gave her a sober nod. 'Fair enough. Phil and I are going to go back to Chevy Chase and find out who's been digging into

Thorne's past. It's possible that someone simply obtained the court transcripts, but we can find that out too.'

'I'm going with you,' Thorne stated, his tone brooking no argument.

'We figured you'd want to,' Phil said. 'I've kept tabs on a lot of the old academy staff, so I can ask questions without getting too much undue attention. You, son, are going to draw plenty of undue attention. So we need to use your presence sparingly.'

'That means you'll stay in the car a lot,' Jamie said, shaking his head when Thorne opened his mouth to protest. 'We are protecting you, Thorne. As best we can. We need to make sure someone is with you at all times. Your alibi from here on out needs to be unimpeachable.' He looked over at Gwyn. 'Ready to stay in the car with him?'

'Yes,' Gwyn said without hesitation. 'Try to stop me.'

'All right.' Frederick clapped his hands. 'We have our marching orders. Let's go.'

'Wait.' Thorne pushed to his feet and looked around the room. 'Thank you. I . . . I never expected any of this. I don't know how to repay you.'

'We're repaying *you*,' Stevie said. 'You've helped all of us at one time or another, Thorne. Not that anyone's keeping track. You're . . . family.'

Thorne swallowed hard. 'Thank you. Be careful. And don't take any unnecessary risks. I don't want anyone getting hurt, not physically, and not your careers or reputations. Not because of me. It's not too late to back out.'

There was a moment of silence, then everyone began to move, taking down the chart pads, clearing up remnants of pizza and beer, and returning Gwyn's living room to how it had been.

Lucy excused herself to Gwyn's room to pump, and for a moment Gwyn stayed where she was, studying Thorne. He looked a little lost as he watched everyone busy around him. Mystified. Like he was still unsure of why all these people had mobilized themselves on his behalf.

He'd never been good at accepting the goodwill of others. Not even herself or Lucy, although he did allow them to fuss over him from time to time. She understood his reluctance – she'd never been able to accept kindness either, but Gwyn knew where her own insecurities came from. It troubled her that she hadn't known the source of Thorne's until today.

It troubled her that she'd never thought to ask.

I'm kind of an asshole. Dammit.

Her chest grew tight and she didn't lie to herself about why. Tenderness wasn't something she often felt. But when she did, it was usually directed towards the man sitting on her sofa, and usually at moments like this when he was clearly blind to his own worth.

Carefully, she moved to perch on the arm of the sofa once again. Just as carefully, he kept his gaze everywhere except her face. *I hurt him. I didn't mean to.* But she'd hurt him more if she accepted his declaration before she was ready and had to change her mind later. Instead, she offered what comfort she could.

'No one is going to back out,' she murmured.

'I know. I don't actually understand it, but I'm thankful for it.'

They fell silent, and for the very first time in all the years she'd known him, it was awkward. Finally he cleared his throat. 'I'm going home with Jamie and Phil. I'll stay in their spare room while we sort this mess out.'

A stab of disappointment speared her and she frantically searched her mind for words that would make him stay. Because she was afraid that if he left, it would be over. What 'it' was, she didn't yet know. But her gut told her to keep him close.

If only so that she could take care of him. As his best friend, that was her right. Right? But as his best friend, she'd die before she hurt him any more than she already had. 'If that's what you want to do.'

His laugh was quietly brittle. 'What I want and what I'm likely to get are often two different things.'

'You don't know that. I don't know that. What I do know is that I'd like you to stay. I have a spare room too. This condo has better security than Jamie and Phil's house. I know, because Clay installed it for me.'

Because after Evan, she hadn't been able to sleep, worried that someone would invade her space. Even though she'd let Evan in. Voluntarily. And . . .

Stop. You're not thinking about him right now. Evan was gone. *I am still here.* And Thorne was not Evan. The very notion that the two shared anything in common was beyond ludicrous. Thorne would never hurt her.

'And,' she added when inspiration – and reality – struck, bringing with it a brand-new fear, 'I'll be safer wherever you are. You'll have police protection, even if Hyatt is calling it surveillance.'

Because she might be targeted. Again. Because of who her friends were. Evan had targeted her because she'd been his gateway to Lucy, but Gwyn wouldn't have abandoned Lucy even if she'd known Evan's intent. She wasn't abandoning Thorne now. Still . . . the sudden realization scared the piss out of her.

He looked up at her sharply. 'You're not involved in this.'

She shrugged, trying to be calmly logical. 'If someone has researched your past enough to stage a murder just like the one you were accused of nineteen years ago, they know that your girlfriend was also murdered because she was a witness.'

His mouth twisted, then firmed. 'But you're not my girlfriend.'

That stung. 'No, but we're publicly very good friends. And what better way to hurt you than to hurt those you care about? Everyone in your sphere needs to be on their guard.'

Thorne shuddered out a horrified breath. 'Oh my God. I didn't think of that. Why didn't I think of that?'

'You've been a little busy,' she said, fighting the urge to pat his shoulder the way she might have before he dropped that whole *seven years* bomb. Because now it was awkward between them when it never had been before. She wanted to snarl at him about that.

But . . . what if he was right? What if they *could* have more than mere friendship? What if they could have a life together?

Goddammit. Focus. Everyone in Thorne's sphere could be in danger. Everyone, including the men who were basically his parents. 'You should go to Jamie and Phil's, and I should go with you. Jamie can't stay here because my place isn't wheelchair-adapted.

If I go there, we can all be monitored by Hyatt's surveillance. Plus, the four of us can get an early start down memory lane in your old hometown. Okay?'

Thorne's jaw worked as he ground his teeth. 'Jamie and Phil only have one extra bedroom.'

'Not a problem. I'll sleep on the sofa. I'm small. I fit nearly anywhere.'

Jamie rolled his chair up next to them. 'We overheard, and we all agree.'

Gwyn lifted her brows. 'That I'm small?'

Jamie's grin was quick. 'That too. But mostly that you should both come with us, for all the reasons you said, Gwyn. Everyone else here either lives with a cop or was a cop, so they can protect themselves. But we should band together. And we do have a state-of-the-art security system, by the way. Maybe not as good as one Clay might install, but still top-notch. You'll both be safe with us.'

'We'll all be safer if I stay alone,' Thorne growled. 'I'm not putting anyone else in danger. I'm not going anywhere with any of you.'

Jamie frowned at him. 'Thomas,' he said quietly. Disapprovingly, even.

Thorne instantly went quiet. That was a really good trick, Gwyn thought. 'I don't want anyone to get hurt,' he murmured. 'Not because of me.'

'Well,' Jamie said pragmatically, 'now that you know to watch your own back and you're bouncing back from the GHB, don't you think we're safer *with* you? I mean . . .' he indicated Thorne's size with a wave of his hand, 'if I didn't know you, you'd scare the shit out of me.'

Thorne stared at his hands. 'Gee, thanks.'

'You're welcome,' Jamie said, a little curtly. 'Do we have to have this conversation again?'

Gwyn looked from one man to the other. 'What conversation?'

Thorne's shoulders sagged wearily. 'The one where he reminds me that I'm not a thug, but that if people are stupid enough to be afraid of me, then I should make the most of it.'

'The conversation that you and I have had a hundred times?' she asked. 'I didn't realize anyone else was telling you the same thing.' She lightened her voice to hide the anger that speared at the slump of his shoulders. 'You've been double-dipping in the wisdom well, Thorne.'

He didn't smile. 'It's not just my size.'

'I know,' she said softly.

She'd heard the racial slurs over the years, both as his paralegal in the early days and as the club manager more recently. Thorne was a burnished bronze all over. All. Over.

Not a tan line on the man. Anywhere. Which she only knew because she'd once accidentally walked in on him in the shower at the club. She'd nearly swallowed her tongue. The memory still made her want to fan herself.

All that gorgeous, flawless skin made him even more beautiful, but people were often assholes, and the fact that Thorne loomed over nearly everyone he met didn't seem to deter the most stupid of them. Racists usually spewed their toxic bullshit when they were thrown out of Sheidalin or if Thorne refused to take their case, whatever his reason. If he lost their case, the slurs sometimes morphed into death threats.

Which could be the case here. This whole orchestration could be an angry client or family member looking for revenge. It made her so furious, because Thorne was the best man she'd ever known.

'What's really bothering you?' she asked softly.

He didn't say anything for a few beats, then shrugged. 'All this talk of those days brought back a lot of bad memories, I guess. The prosecutor made me out to be some juvenile delinquent, even suggested I ran with one of the gangs, despite the fact that there was no actual evidence of that at all. Gang activity had begun taking hold in the city then. White neighborhoods were afraid of anyone who . . . didn't look like them. And I didn't. Jamie shut the prosecutor down fast, objecting that there was no basis for the intimation, but it still hurt, hearing someone accuse me of being a thug. I'd tried so hard to stay out of trouble.'

That didn't come as a surprise either. Thorne had a kind of fluid ethnicity. He could pass as a member of several minority groups and had occasionally used that fact to go undercover, doing his own investigation into prospective clients. He was choosy about the cases he took on. He wanted the facts before agreeing to representation.

He enjoyed all the undercover intrigue. Gwyn had enjoyed going with him, but she hadn't participated in any of his UC adventures in . . . She wanted to sigh. Four and a half years. *Dammit.* He'd been doing it all on his own since Evan. How many things had she just let go because of that fucker? Too many.

'Good thing you didn't have the tats then,' she said, tongue in cheek. She knew he hadn't, because she'd gone with him the day he'd had his first session. They'd just met, but there had been a connection from the beginning, fast and fierce. So fierce that he'd trusted her to accompany him to the tattoo artist. His first visit had been on the anniversary of his father's death, taking on the tattoo that had adorned his father's skin. The entire design had taken four visits. She'd held his hand through all of them.

They had history, she and Thorne.

Her comment finally elicited a small grin. 'God help me if I had,' he agreed. 'I figured I'd never get a fair trial as it was.'

'But you did,' Jamie said firmly, bringing both of them back to the present. 'I, for one, am happy you're as big as a freaking house. I'll feel safer tonight.' He gave Gwyn an approving nod. 'Go pack a bag. Bring a sweater. Phil keeps the A/C on sub-arctic.'

'What about my dog?'

'Bring him,' Jamie said. 'We've got a fenced-in yard with a lot of shade. Does he like to swim?'

'Like a fish.'

'Then we'll put him outside tomorrow and he can play in the pool if he gets hot.'

Gwyn slid off the arm of the sofa. 'I'll be quick.'

College Park, Maryland,
Sunday 12 June, 11.30 P.M.

Frederick accepted the cup of coffee with a smile. 'Thank you for seeing me so late, Mrs Brown.'

Bernice Brown frowned as she took the chair at her cousin's kitchen table, sitting opposite Frederick. 'I saw the news about Mr Thorne. I don't understand any of this.'

'None of us do. Yet. But we know he's not guilty. And it seems you've been involved in the situation.'

Her eyes widened. 'Me? How? I never . . .' She trailed off, her words suddenly failing her.

'Bernie?' Her cousin came into the room, his expression concerned. 'What's going on?'

Bernice threw him a panicked glance. 'Wayne, they think I'm involved in that woman's murder! The one on the news!'

'Whoa,' Frederick said soothingly, trying to calm her. 'I don't think that's the case. I said you'd been involved – we believe by someone else.' He gestured to her cousin. 'Would you mind joining us?'

Wayne complied, sitting close to Bernice and wrapping his arm around her shoulder. Wayne Bullock was in his mid fifties, Bernice a decade younger. From what Frederick had gleaned from Thorne's files, Wayne had been a father figure in Bernice's life. Now retired, he lived in a trailer, which had provided a convenient hiding place for his cousin. When her husband had begun stalking her, Wayne had moved his trailer to a park two counties away. Having a portable home had its advantages.

'Start talking, Mr Dawson,' Wayne ordered.

'I will. I'm Mr Thorne's associate. I've been with him for about a year. I'll be taking over your case, Mrs Brown, while he is under investigation. As I said, we have the utmost confidence he'll be cleared.'

'How is Bernie involved?' Wayne asked.

'Mr Thorne was attacked and abducted from a bar called Barney's last night.'

Bernice frowned. 'I've never heard of that place. What does it have to do with me?'

'He was going – he believed – to meet you, Mrs Brown.'

She gasped. 'Me? No!'

Frederick nodded calmly. 'I believe you.' Mainly because he'd traced the call and it had come from an untraceable cell phone. 'The call came through our answering service. The caller identified herself as you, Mrs Brown. She told Thorne that a car had tried to run her off the road and that she was afraid.'

'So he came,' she whispered. 'He would, wouldn't he?'

'He would,' Frederick agreed. 'He did. That's the last thing he remembers. He was beaten and drugged.'

Bernice was shaking her head. 'I didn't call him.'

'I didn't think so. I traced the call to a disposable cell phone.'

'I have one of those,' Bernice said slowly, as if considering each word, 'but I didn't use it.' She looked troubled. 'Mr Thorne gave it to me. Told me it was for my safety.'

'You can continue to use it,' Frederick said. 'Or I'll get you another one. Either way, can I ask where you were last night around midnight?'

'Here,' she said. 'We were watching a movie on Netflix. But I can't prove it.'

Wayne's arm tightened around her. 'Will the police be looking for Bernie? She's in enough trouble already because of that piece-of-shit husband of hers.'

'Thorne didn't mention her to the police.'

Bernice's eyes widened. 'But it's part of his alibi. I could tell them that I didn't call him, that he was lured.'

'He won't give your name, ma'am,' Frederick reiterated. 'He won't disclose his clients. He just won't.'

Bernice seemed to relax at that, even though she bit at her lip. 'What can I do?'

Frederick smiled at her. 'For now? Stay under the radar and stay safe. He was worried about you. It was one of the first things he said when he woke up. He asked us to check on you, to be sure you were safe. So that's how you can best help him.'

Wayne was frowning. 'But if someone pretended to be Bernie on the phone, that means they knew she'd hired him.'

'True,' Frederick allowed. 'But that's a matter of record. Thorne is registered as her counsel.'

'But they knew details,' Wayne pressed. 'They knew that it was even possible that she'd be run off the road.'

Frederick nodded. He'd thought of this already. 'True again. But Mr Brown's stalking is also known because it was covered in the newspaper. Having said that, it doesn't mean we don't have a leak in our own firm.' It was Frederick's fear, one he hadn't expressed to Thorne in Gwyn's living room. Thorne only kept a handful of employees in the firm, and as far as he knew, all were loyal. But it was a possibility, and Frederick would not allow it to go unexamined. 'I'm investigating that.'

Wayne's nod was shaky. 'All right. Should we move again?'

Frederick sighed. 'It might not be a bad idea. Just in case.' He gave them his card. 'If you do, contact me. And keep that disposable cell phone charged and on your person at all times. If you are afraid someone is coming after you, call 911, then call me. All right?'

Bernice took the card in trembling fingers. 'All right. Thank you, Mr Dawson.'

Frederick got to his feet. 'It's my job, ma'am. We'll proceed with your defense.'

Wayne also rose. 'At the same rate? Mr Thorne was giving her a discount.'

'I work pro bono,' Frederick explained. 'I'll bill Mr Thorne for any expenses I incur, but my hours are free.'

Bernice's shoulders sagged. 'Thank you.'

He smiled down at her. 'You're welcome.'

He was opening the front door when she called his name. He turned, brows lifted. 'I . . . Please thank Mr Thorne. For being willing to come and help me, even though I didn't really need him.'

'I'll tell him.' There was something in the woman's eyes, something she was holding back. 'If you think of anything else that can help him, please call me.'

'I will.' She drew a breath, and he waited. 'I have this friend. Sally Brewster. She called me on Friday. Said she'd gotten a weird call from someone claiming to be a cop. They said they were trying to locate me to ask me questions about my husband. She told them that she didn't know where I was, which is technically true. But she also told them that they should be ashamed of themselves, that I was too afraid to leave hiding because my husband wouldn't leave me alone. They called her on her cell phone.' She frowned. 'She's listed on my paperwork with your firm. As my emergency contact, after Wayne. You might call her.'

Frederick smiled at her. 'Thank you. I will. And I'll make sure she knows to be careful too.'

Baltimore, Maryland,
Sunday 12 June, 11.40 P.M.

'Sit, Thorne,' Phil said, reaching up to push at his shoulder.

Thorne turned away from the large kitchen window that looked out into the blackness of Phil and Jamie's backyard. In the daytime it was a tranquil place, their inground pool surrounded by weeping willows. A babbling brook ran through the trees along with a paved path for Jamie's chair. At night, though, it was inky darkness, the surrounding trees blocking out not only the lights from the city, but the starlight too.

He wasn't sure how long he'd been standing there, but it had been long enough to put a worried look on Phil's face, and he hated that, so he sank obediently into the chair at the kitchen table.

'I made hot chocolate,' Jamie added, 'just the way you like it.'

With the milk frother, Thorne noted, thankful for that as well, because the whir of the machine had drowned out the sound of the shower. Which Gwyn had been in at the time. Naked.

She hadn't said no, he reminded himself for the thousandth time. That she hadn't said no outright was . . . He sighed. A piss-poor hope to hold onto.

His old friend slid the cup of chocolate across the table, making Thorne wonder if Jamie had timed his use of the frother that way on purpose. When Thorne caught the sympathy in Jamie's eyes, he had his answer.

Well, that's just perfect, he thought crossly, dropping his gaze to the frothy chocolate that really had been made exactly how he liked it. He pushed Gwyn to the edge of his mind and made himself

103

remember the first time he'd sat here, at this very table. 'You made me hot chocolate that day too.'

Jamie reached across the table to squeeze his forearm. 'A genius move on my part,' he acknowledged.

'Which day?' Gwyn asked from the kitchen doorway where she waited hesitantly. Her face was flushed from the hot water and devoid of makeup, the way Thorne liked her best. Her damp hair was pulled back into a ponytail that made her look so damn young. Her loose sweats and oversized sweatshirt hurt Thorne's heart because that was exactly what she'd worn in the weeks and months after Evan tried to kill her and Lucy. It was like she'd been trying to hide in the baggy clothing. Like somehow she'd . . . enticed the bastard. Like she'd caused him to notice her, which of course hadn't been true at all.

Now she stood there watching him. That she wasn't sure of her welcome – that she was hiding from him too – made Thorne's heart hurt even more. *Damn me to ever-fucking hell. I should never have said anything. I have ruined everything.*

'Come in,' Phil said warmly, gesturing to the chair opposite Thorne's. 'We're just having a snack before bed.'

Thorne schooled his voice to something he hoped sounded polite as he answered her question. 'Jamie made this for me the day he and Phil bailed me out. It's good hot chocolate. You'll like it.'

Phil put a cup in front of her and took the chair at the head of the small table while Jamie parked himself at the other end. 'It's my recipe,' Phil asserted. 'Jamie just likes to run the frother.'

'At my age, my entertainment options are limited,' Jamie said, and Thorne snorted, because Jamie still participated in wheelchair races and still won them.

'I've seen the photos of your limited entertainment,' Gwyn said dryly. 'Thorne's papered his office walls with them. The skydiving one is my favorite. I only hope I'm half as spry when I'm as aged as you.' She pronounced 'aged' with two syllables and a roll of her eyes, because Jamie wasn't quite sixty. She pointed to the folders neatly stacked on the table. 'What's this?'

'I'm compiling a file, just like I would for any client,' Jamie answered.

104

'This stack is what we've uncovered on the major players in the trial nineteen years ago,' Phil added. 'We've started pre-planning tomorrow's visits. We figure someone could have gotten all the information about Thorne's trial from the newspaper, but . . .' He let the thought trail off and glanced at Jamie.

'Somebody dug up all this shit for a reason,' Jamie said. 'It will call Thorne's innocence into question – today and nineteen years ago.'

Gwyn bit at her lip, her habit when she was trying to stay calm. Thorne wasn't sure if she even knew she did it. 'This is so wrong,' she said. 'All of it.'

Jamie hesitated. 'Stevie's point is still ringing in my head. Richard Linden's killer was never caught. He's still out there. And he's the only one who truly knows what happened the day Richard was murdered. Assuming it was a he.'

Thorne jerked his attention back to Jamie. 'You're proposing *we* find the true killer?' he asked, unable to keep the acid from his voice.

Jamie met his gaze, unfazed. 'Yes. Why not?'

Thorne took a deep breath, forcing himself to be polite once again, because he really wasn't sure why the thought made him so furious. Because he wished he'd done it already? Which he knew was illogical. He'd been a kid, not a detective. *But I should have at least tried.* Richard's killer was running free, but so was Sherri's. *I'm sorry, Sherri.* 'Because the police couldn't do it nineteen years ago?'

'We'll take a fresh look,' Jamie said, sipping his hot chocolate calmly.

Gwyn opened the top folder and began sifting through its contents, pausing to look at a grainy photograph copied from an old newspaper article. 'Is this Richard with his family?'

Thorne's stomach roiled just looking at them. 'Yeah. How did you know?'

'Because they look rich,' she murmured. 'Like the tourists that used to hire my father to take them crabbing in the summer.'

Thorne was surprised. Gwyn rarely mentioned her family, and never her father. There was bad history there and she'd never told him what had happened. Whatever it was, she'd run away from home at sixteen.

'Your father was a crabber?' Phil asked curiously.

She nodded once. 'Folks like the Lindens would come from the city to play for the day, dressed in clothes that cost more than my family made in a year, snapping their fingers like we were their servants.' One side of her mouth lifted as she tapped Richard's face. 'He looks like Draco Malfoy.'

Thorne found himself chuckling, because Richard did resemble the bully from the Harry Potter stories. 'We just called him Richie Rich.'

Both sides of Gwyn's mouth had tipped up when he'd chuckled. 'And Richard's father? Was he as bad as Draco's papa in the book?'

'Worse.' Phil was unsmiling, his whole body gone tight. 'He testified against Thorne. Painted his little darling Richard to be such a martyr. Painted Thorne to be a . . .' he swallowed hard, 'a hardened criminal who would kill without remorse. He fabricated threats that he claimed Thorne made to his son in his presence. Linden Senior sat on the stand and lied without blinking an eye, except to dash away a crocodile tear.'

Gwyn bit her lip again. 'He perjured himself? Why? I mean, I get that he wanted justice for his son, but was the prosecution's case so thin that he thought he had to lie to make sure the jury found Thorne guilty? Or was he unbalanced?'

'More the first one,' Jamie said. 'The case should never have gone to trial to begin with. The state's case was weak, but the police commissioner and the prosecutor pushed it through. Nobody wanted to make enemies of the Lindens.'

Gwyn looked up from the photo. 'But they had enemies? Other than Thorne?'

'I'm sure they did,' Jamie said. 'You're wondering who else had a motive to kill Richard? I pressed that back then, but hit a brick wall every time I turned around. Linden wanted Thorne found guilty and he did not want anyone else even considered. Yes, I thought it suspicious back then, but no, I couldn't find anyone who'd talk to me.'

'But,' Phil added, 'maybe someone will be willing to talk now.'

'Who's on your list?' Thorne asked, more out of curiosity than any real hope. The chances of getting to the bottom of a nineteen-year-old murder were slim to none.

The look Phil gave him was mildly reproving, like he knew exactly what Thorne was thinking. 'The detective who worked the case, for starters. Prew is his name.'

Gwyn blinked at them, surprised. 'You suspected the cops were complicit?'

'Not Prew,' Phil said. 'But he's a good place to start because he might be able to shed light on Linden Senior's enemies. Jamie hit a brick wall, but Prew may have found something.'

'Makes sense,' she said, leaning toward Phil to see his list. 'Who else?'

Phil glanced at Thorne and pointed to the next name. 'The young woman you tried to defend the day everything started. Angie Ospina. Also Richard's three friends who beat you up because you forced him to stop groping her.'

Thorne's gut churned. None of these were people he ever wanted to see again. 'I have no idea where they are. Any of them.'

'I do,' Phil said. 'Some of them, anyway. Detective Prew has just retired from Montgomery County PD. He's expecting us tomorrow. He's invited us for coffee.'

'You called him already?' Thorne asked, surprised.

'I called him as soon as I heard Patricia was the victim,' Phil said. 'I had time in the waiting room and not much else to do except worry. Plus, I've known Prew for years. He's not a bad guy. I taught one of his sons. Not at Ridgewell Academy, but later, when I went to the next school. Another of his sons is a history teacher today, so we've kept up too. He has two sons of his own now. Twins, just about a year old. Expect the detective to take a few moments to show us photos of his grandchildren.'

'All right,' Thorne said. 'What about Angie?'

'I don't know where she is,' Phil said. 'I'm hoping Prew will know.'

'And the assholes who beat Thorne up?' Gwyn asked sharply.

Thorne had to smile at her fierce loyalty, despite the hollowness in his chest.

Phil pulled another piece of paper from the stack on the table. 'We found two of them. Darian Hinman is the VP of his father's shipping business.'

'Of course,' Thorne said bitterly, clearly remembering the boy Hinman had been.

Phil shrugged. 'Old money, Thomas. You know it exists and the privilege it allows.'

'Hey,' Jamie said with mock outrage. 'I'm old money.'

Thorne's mouth bent up. 'Most of which you give away.'

Jamie waved that statement aside. 'Let's withhold judgment on young Hinman until we meet him. Maybe he's grown up.' Because Jamie himself had. He'd been an impetuous youth. Some of that was natural rebellion, but a lot had been a need to press his physical limits past the chair he'd used since he'd been old enough to sit up.

Phil looked unconvinced at his optimism. 'We'll see. Friend number two, Chandler Nystrom, is now a cop.'

Thorne's mouth fell open. 'No fucking way. He was a thug, the worst of them.' He gritted his teeth, knowing full well that some cops sought the job for specifically that reason. They wanted to be legal thugs.

'Hopefully he grew up too,' Phil said philosophically, 'otherwise he's a thug with a badge and a gun.'

'And the third?' Gwyn asked.

'Colton Brandenberg,' Thorne said quietly. 'I never knew what to make of him. I remember being surprised that he'd thrown any punches at all. He seemed so gentle when he wasn't with Richard. You don't have a location for him?'

Phil shook his head. 'No, not yet. Again, I'm hoping Detective Prew has some ideas.'

Thorne pulled the other folder closer. 'This is your file, Jamie?'

'So far. Mostly I just have the photos that Gwyn took. I don't expect to see anything from Lieutenant Hyatt regarding the official crime scene photos unless you're formally charged. So, again, good job, Gwyn. If you hadn't been so quick-thinking, we wouldn't have shit right now.'

Thorne opened the folder and spread the enlarged photos across the table, wincing a little at the sight of his own bare ass. 'They just *had* to strip me,' he complained.

'Well, you were supposed to have had a woman in your bed,' Gwyn said.

Thorne glanced up and saw no accusation in her dark eyes. No anger. She believed him and he was grateful for that. 'Yeah, well,' he muttered, 'they could have left me a little modesty, for God's sake.'

She pulled one of the photos closer, grimacing. 'Whoever did this didn't just stab her. They cut her open.'

'You don't need to look at those.' Jamie started to take the photo from her, but she rolled her eyes at him.

'I took the photos, Jamie. I saw her live.' She winced. 'Or dead. Plus, I was Thorne's paralegal, don't forget. I've seen worse than this. Unfortunately.' But then she frowned. 'Thorne, what's this?' Rising from her chair, she pushed the photo toward him, leaning across the table as she followed it. 'It's . . . I don't know what it is. I didn't notice it this morning.'

Thorne looked where she pointed. And his blood ran cold. 'Phil.' He had to clear his throat. 'Do . . . do you still have that magnifying glass you use for coupons?'

Phil got up to rummage in a drawer, retrieving the magnifier and handing it to Thorne without a word.

Hand trembling, Thorne placed the glass over the photo and shuddered out a breath. 'Motherfucking sonofabitch,' he said quietly, then looked at Jamie. 'It's a medal. And a key.'

Jamie's eyes went wide. 'What the fuck?' He lurched from his chair to grab the photo and magnifier before sliding back to sit. 'Holy shit,' he murmured.

Gwyn was looking at the two of them like they'd lost their minds. 'What kind of metal?'

'Not me*tal*,' Thorne said. 'Me*dal*. Like a trophy.' He scrubbed at his face with his palms, suddenly numb. 'There was one stuck in

109

Richard Linden's body, in about the same place. A medal with a key attached.'

'So this is a copycat murder,' Gwyn said.

Thorne shook his head. 'The medal wasn't made public. I mean, I saw it when I was trying to stop his bleeding, but when his body got to the morgue, it was gone.'

Seven

Gwyn was staring at Thorne. 'It was just . . . gone? How could a medal have just disappeared from a dead body?'

Jamie set the magnifier aside, his hands trembling.

Patricia Linden Segal's murderer was no ordinary copycat. It was somebody who knew details that weren't public.

Jamie rubbed his eyes wearily. 'We thought at the time that one of the EMTs or morgue employees took it. We never knew why. We didn't press, because it was better for Thorne that it disappeared.'

Gwyn's frown deepened. 'Why?'

'Because I had one of those medals,' Thorne said. He swallowed hard, forcing back the bile that burned his throat. 'They were given to everyone on the soccer team for making it to the state championships that year. I put mine with all my other trophies in my bedroom, but Richard had a hole bored in his and made it into a key ring. That's what I saw shoved into his gut. It still had a key on it.'

'But it disappeared,' Jamie reiterated. 'And so had Thorne's.'

Phil stood behind Thorne, hands covering his shoulders. 'Thorne's mother and stepfather cleared out his room when he was arrested. By the time we got him out on bail, they'd put all this things on the curb and the garbage truck had come by and taken them.'

Thorne watched Gwyn's expression morph from shock to sympathy to rage.

'Everything?' she asked.

'Everything,' Thorne confirmed. 'Every photo, comic book, piece of clothing. All my CDs. All my trophies. All my notes from classes. My bicycle. Everything.'

Jamie's voice was bitter. 'When he came to us, he didn't even have the shirt on his back, because he'd used it to try to stop Richard's bleeding.'

Gwyn swallowed hard, her expression going carefully neutral. Which meant her temper was boiling. 'So you didn't know where your medals were. Which meant that you couldn't prove it wasn't one of yours in the body.'

'Essentially,' Thorne said quietly.

'So who *did* know about the medal in Richard Linden's body?'

Jamie sighed. 'Thorne knew. And the real killer, obviously, assuming he was the one who'd put it there. The EMT would have seen it. Possibly the morgue tech, if it was still there when the body was cleaned up. Whoever plucked it out of the body knew about it.'

'The cops knew.' Thorne's jaw tightened, remembering. 'Because I told them. I told Detective Prew. I don't think he believed me.'

Jamie looked sick. 'I advised Thorne not to press it. Maybe I shouldn't have done that.' He ran a shaking hand through his hair. 'Shit.' But then he looked up and over Thorne's shoulder, meeting Phil's eyes. 'It'll be all right,' he promised, making a visible effort to be calm.

'I know,' Phil said unsteadily, his hands clenching on Thorne's shoulders protectively. Almost painfully.

'It means that whoever killed Patricia Segal did not get all his info from court transcripts,' Thorne said, trying to calm his racing thoughts.

'But it would have been in the police report.' Gwyn cocked her head. 'Right? If you'd told the police you'd seen it, the detective would have listed that in the report. Patricia's murderer could still have gotten the info that way.'

Thorne shook his head. 'No. It didn't end up in the police report either.'

She blinked. 'Why not?'

'Don't know.' He closed his eyes. 'But I saw the report, and it wasn't there. There were moments when I thought I'd fabricated it in my mind. That I was delusional.'

'I imagine it's normal to second-guess yourself in that situation,' she said quietly. 'You were so young and under so much stress. Grieving Sherri.' A beat of silence. 'Did Sherri see it?'

Surprised at the question, he opened his eyes to see hers narrowed thoughtfully. 'I don't think so,' he said. 'I didn't see it until right at the end. Just before the cops showed up. I'd been using my shirt as a makeshift bandage, so that I could put pressure on the wound. But it was so huge, the wound. It soaked my shirt, so I took off my T-shirt to use, and when I removed the first shirt, that was when I got a glimpse of the medal with the key in the wound. Sherri was on the phone up by the office by then. Seconds later, the place was swarming with cops. So if you're wondering if she was killed for seeing that, no. Unlikely anyway.'

'That was what I was wondering. What was the key to?'

It was Thorne's turn to blink. 'I have no idea. Never even thought to wonder.'

'You're wondering if the key itself was the reason it was removed from Richard's body?' Jamie asked, respect in his tone.

Gwyn shrugged. 'It just seems like a weird thing to steal off a body. It didn't have any real worth. Not like Richard was a celebrity or the medal was from the Olympics or anything. The medal wasn't diamond-encrusted and . . . I mean, ew. They had to stick their hand in a frickin' body to get it. That's just gross.'

Jamie seemed to be considering the notion. 'Not if the EMT took it, or someone in the morgue. EMTs get bloody on a routine basis, and morgue employees can't be too grossed out by bodies or they wouldn't last long. We need to add the names of the EMTs and the morgue personnel to our list of people to interview.'

Thorne suddenly felt a million years old. 'I don't remember their names.'

'Neither do I,' Jamie said. 'But they're listed in the court transcripts because they testified for the prosecution. I've got all those files in a box in the basement.'

'I can fetch it for you,' Thorne offered, but Jamie shook his head.

113

'That's okay. I know exactly where it is.' And he had a small elevator that transported him to the basement and back again.

Thorne knew better than to argue, so he just nodded.

'Well,' Gwyn said on a sigh, 'the ME is going to find the medal in Patricia's body, if he hasn't already. He'll tell Hyatt's detectives and they'll ask you questions about it. What will you tell them?'

'The truth,' Thorne said without hesitation.

Phil's hands clenched again, and Thorne winced but said nothing because he sensed that Phil was holding on by a thread.

'I think that's the wisest thing at this point,' Phil murmured. 'Offer nothing. Answer what you can when asked. Besides, many of us saw Richard with the medal after he'd made it into a key ring. Your coach thought he was a total dickhead for drilling a hole in it, by the way. Any one of the old teaching staff still around can ID it as belonging to Richard.' Giving Thorne's shoulders a final pat, Phil moved away, clearing the mugs from the table to the sink, and Thorne noticed with a start that the older man's face had grown gray. 'Phil? You okay?'

Phil smiled. 'Of course. Just tired.' He pointed to the clock on the wall. 'We're seeing Prew at nine thirty tomorrow morning, so we should get some sleep. Rush hour's a bitch. I'll get you some sheets and blankets, Gwyn.' He moved slowly, and Thorne was distressed to realize that age was creeping up on the two men who'd taken him in when he'd had no one.

On Phil, at least. Jamie still looked ten years younger than his partner. He always had. He'd been nearly forty that day in the jail, but Thorne remembered thinking he looked about thirty. Which had seemed ancient at the time.

He stayed Phil with a touch to his arm. 'I'll take the sofa,' he said. 'Gwyn can sleep in my room.'

Gwyn frowned. 'No, *I'm* taking the sofa. You'll never fit.'

'Doesn't matter. I'm not planning to sleep.'

Three sets of eyes now frowned at him. 'Thorne,' Jamie said with a shake of his head. 'Please. Don't do this to yourself.'

'I have to,' he murmured. 'They could come after any of you. All of you.' *Because of me.* It was too overwhelming.

'And you're our *guardian*?' Gwyn asked, a thread of annoyance in her voice that Thorne hadn't expected, and he jerked around to stare at her.

'Yes,' he snapped back. 'You have a problem with that?'

Her chin went up. 'Yeah, I do. I never asked you to be my guardian. I don't want you to be my guardian. There is a good security system here and a cop sitting out on the curb. What I *want* is for you to be well rested so that when we leave this safe place tomorrow, you can be on your guard in case someone tries to hurt you in the light of day. I want you well rested so that you can listen to what people are telling you and what they are not saying. Because if you think they're just going to fess up like you're some Perry-fucking-Mason, you have another think coming.'

He found himself snarling at her. 'Back off, Gwyn. You're the one who said everyone in my fucking sphere is in fucking danger. You're the one who said you'd be safer with me. That all of you would be safer with me.'

She straightened in her chair. 'No, I didn't.'

From the corner of his eye he saw Jamie blanch, as if realizing that his own words were at fault. But Thorne's attention was riveted once again by Gwyn, who pushed to her feet, leaning across the table until he was breathing in the scent of lavender and vanilla.

'What I said was that I wanted *you* safe, with people who care about you.' She gestured to Jamie and Phil. 'I wanted *these* people who care about you to benefit from the cop on the curb. Yes, I did say that everyone in your sphere was in danger, but I never said you were responsible for guarding anyone other than yourself.'

'That was me,' Jamie said quietly. 'And I was wrong to have said it. I'm sorry, son.'

Helpless fury surged in Thorne's chest and he heard himself utter a frustrated growl. 'Don't apologize. You were right,' he snapped at Jamie, then pointed at Gwyn. 'And you're wrong. This is happening because of me. That it's not my fault doesn't matter. What does matter is keeping you safe. All of you. So I will sit on that fucking sofa and keep watch.'

Her jaw tightened, but she kept her voice calm. 'I am not sleeping in your bed, Thorne.'

That she managed to stay calm when he wasn't . . . it just made him angrier. Which he knew was ridiculous, but damned if he could stop himself.

'Fine.' He stood slowly and watched her eyes narrow, because in her bare feet she was a full foot and a half shorter than him. He leaned across the table, purposely looming over her, and watched her eyes flash with resentment. 'Stay awake all night then, but stay out of my way while you do it.' He grabbed the copy of the crime scene photo she'd taken and slapped it on the table between them. '*This* is what they're capable of doing. Do you think I want that to happen to you? To any of you?'

She craned her head back to lock her gaze with his. 'Of course you don't,' she said, still maddeningly calm. 'Nobody said that. But there is a cop sitting out there on the curb and it's his job to keep the bad guys away from us.'

She might seem collected, but her eye had started to twitch. He'd known her long enough to be aware that that was her tell. She was one tiny push away from losing her temper, and he suddenly needed her to. Needed to know he wasn't the only one scared shitless by this whole situation. 'Like the cops can be depended on to keep people safe?' He hated the sneer in his voice, but he had to make her recognize that the threat was real. That four walls and a cop outside weren't enough to ensure her safety. 'How'd that work for you and Lucy four years ago?' Because cops had been guarding Lucy, and Evan had still managed to get them both.

Gwyn flinched, growing pale, and Thorne instantly knew he'd overstepped.

'Thorne,' Phil murmured in shocked reproach. 'Stop. Now.'

'I'm s—'

She interrupted his apology with a raised hand. 'Don't,' she whispered, but her voice cracked on the single word. She took a step away from the table. Away from him. When she spoke again, it was at a normal volume, but shaky. 'Suit yourself. Stay awake all night. Then tomorrow, when you need decent reflexes and you have none because you are exhausted because you were fucking *drugged* last night and should still be in the goddamn *hospital*, your reflexes will say "Sorry, dude, we're plumb tuckered" and you'll get hurt. And then what? Who'll have to bind you up and call 911 and hope you don't *fucking die*?' Her finger jabbed at the air between them and tears filled her eyes.

Her tears shocked him like none of her words had. 'Gwyn, I'm sor—' he started, but once again she swept her hand between them, silencing him.

'*Me*,' she spat. '*I'm* the one who'll have to watch you bleed. Or lie so still that I didn't know if you were alive or dead. I had to call them this morning.' Blindly she indicated Jamie and Phil, who watched wide-eyed. 'I had to tell them that you were non-responsive. They freaked out because you were *fucking non-responsive*, Thorne. And because they love you like a goddamn son, which makes you lucky, because not all of us get that. So go ahead.' She blinked and the tears streaked down her face. 'Go ahead and stay awake all night worrying because you think that's all we need you for.'

'Gwyn . . .' He wasn't sure what else to say, but it didn't matter because she'd already marched herself out of the kitchen.

'I assume the room with all the posters of Pamela Anderson in a tiny *Baywatch* bathing suit is Thorne's old room?' she called behind her.

Phil coughed. 'Yes,' he called back. 'That's the one.'

Thorne rubbed his chest, because it physically hurt. She'd cried. *Over me*. And he'd hurt her when that was the last thing he'd really wanted to do. But he couldn't put words to any of that now. He forced his eyes to roll. 'Really, guys? I took those posters down years ago.'

Jamie's eyes were still wide. 'We put them up today because we assumed you were coming here to recuperate. We thought it would make you laugh.'

He blew out a sigh. 'Sure,' he drawled. 'This is a laugh riot.'

Phil pursed his lips. 'Gwyn's right, you know. She was terrified for you this morning. I knew it was bad, because she was falling apart. In all the years I've known her, all the times we've talked, I've never seen her as scared as she was today.'

Thorne sank back into the chair, exhausted. 'I know.' He'd considered how she'd felt finding him in bed with another woman, but not how she'd felt at finding him near death. She was always so . . . strong. So *Gwyn*.

Except right after Evan, and even then she'd kept her trauma buried deep. Nobody knew that she'd sat in Thorne's bed and rocked herself for hours after she was safe. Nobody knew but Thorne, because he'd held her every painful minute that she'd been lost in her own mind, reliving the worst experience of her life. He'd held her as she'd rocked, willing her to come back to him.

She'd never let herself fall apart in front of anyone else. Yet today, she had.

'You were a dick to her,' Jamie stated.

Thorne dropped his head in his hands with a groan. 'I know. I'll apologize when she cools down. I just . . . I lost it. Today's been a shitty day.'

Phil was pragmatic as usual. 'You may have to wait until morning to apologize, because she's really upset. And now she's taken the bed, so you're stuck with the sofa. We do have an inflatable mattress. We're told it's quite comfortable. I'll go get it.'

That left Jamie and Thorne alone. Jamie reached over and rubbed Thorne's arm lightly. 'You need to talk about it?'

Thorne recoiled. 'No. God, no.'

Jamie's chuckle was low and familiar. 'Well, for what it's worth, she cares about you. That much is clear.'

'Squarely in the friend zone,' he said, fighting tears of his own. He'd already lost it once. He was not going to cry on top of it all.

'Maybe. Maybe not. She's been walking in a fog for four years, Thorne. Let her wake up a little more. Let her feel like she's in control of her own decisions. Let her *be* in control of her own decisions.'

'And if she decides that I'm not worth the risk?'

Jamie sighed. 'Well, I would question her sanity, but I'm a little biased in your favor. But seriously, if she decides that, then you respect it and find a way to move forward. Easier said than done, I know. But you won't be entirely alone. You still have family, Thorne. And we won't leave you. Ever.'

Thorne's eyes stung. 'Thank you.'

Jamie rolled his chair away from the table. Moments later, Thorne was enfolded in strong arms that had been there for him for more than half his life. The same strong arms that had held him when he'd collapsed after learning of Sherri's death, too shocked to cry. He'd shaken so hard he'd thought his bones would separate, and it had been Jamie who'd held him together.

'Thank you,' he whispered. 'For being all I've ever needed.' He lifted his head and rested his forehead against Jamie's, the gesture one he'd learned from his father and had shared with Jamie all these years.

Jamie's palms held Thorne's cheeks lightly, then he backed away. 'I've got to get some sleep. As Gwyn so wisely pointed out, we need to be alert and on guard tomorrow. And every day thereafter until this is just a bad memory.'

'This too shall pass,' Thorne murmured, and shoved to his feet as wearily as Phil had, which made him worry about his old teacher all over again. 'Jamie, is Phil okay?'

Jamie stiffened. 'Why?'

Thorne rolled his eyes, but new dread seemed to settle around them. 'Oh, like *that* was subtle.' He could hear the panic in his own voice. 'Tell me what you know.'

Jamie scrubbed his palms over his face. 'He's seeing a cardiologist. He'll be okay, but he might need a procedure before it's all fixed up. Probably just a balloon angioplasty. It's not that bad.'

Thorne had trouble sucking in a breath. Fear, even more visceral than before, had taken hold of his throat, and he had to force the words out. 'Which one of us are you trying to convince? How long has this been going on?'

'Not long. A few weeks. He wanted to tell you, but couldn't find the right time. Today was definitely not the right time. But let him tell you himself, Thomas. And when he does, know that he *will* be all right.' Jamie's lips trembled and he firmed them resolutely. 'He's a tough bastard. A lot tougher than he looks.' He raised a brow. 'So get some rest tonight. Don't make him worry about you even more, okay?'

119

Thorne exhaled in a rush, suddenly lightheaded at the thought of losing Phil. It could not happen. But Jamie looked terrified, even though he was trying to hide it, so he dug deep and found some sass. 'Guilting me much?'

Jamie pasted a smile on his face. 'Only because it works. Goodnight, Thomas.'

'Goodnight.' Thorne waited until Jamie had wheeled from the room before sinking back into the kitchen chair and dropping his head into his hands once more.

Baltimore, Maryland,
Monday 13 June, 12.30 A.M.

Gwyn carefully closed the door to Thorne's bedroom and slumped, wanting to bang her head against the wall. *God, I'm such a bitch.* Throwing that tantrum in front of her hosts. *Why can't I ever just keep my damn mouth shut?*

But she *had* kept her mouth shut. For the past four years she'd been holding everything inside.

And Thorne had been silently waiting. All that time.

The knowledge thrilled and terrified her in equal measures.

A quiet knock on her door made her jump. She pulled it open to find a tired-looking Phil. 'I'm so sorry to bother you, Gwyn. I need to look for the air mattress.'

Cheeks heating, she stepped aside to allow him entry. 'You really don't need to. I'll sleep on the sofa.' She glanced at the California king bed that took up nearly all the square footage of the room. 'This is his bed. Besides, I can't take all the *Baywatch*.' She gestured to the posters. 'That's a lot of cleavage.'

Phil winced. 'You can take them down if you want. We put them up as a joke. Ended up not being the right night for that kind of humor. But good luck getting Thorne to change his mind about the sofa, although Jamie and I thought you made an excellent attempt.'

Gwyn sighed. 'I'm not normally so impolite.'

'We took no offense. Just the opposite, actually. You care about

120

him. And you saw him near death today. I'd say you're entitled to a little upset.'

Her legs went rubbery at the reminder and she sat on the edge of the bed. 'I've never seen him so still,' she whispered. 'Thorne is always full of life. But today he wasn't. He scared me.'

'You acted quickly and probably saved him. We're grateful.'

'I . . . He's important to me too.'

Phil patted her shoulder and sank down to sit on the bed beside her. 'You didn't know he had feelings for you?'

'No,' she whispered, then frowned. 'Did he tell you?'

'No. Thorne's never been that open with his feelings. But we could tell by the way he speaks about you, and the way he looks at you. And we could tell something had happened when you went to wake him up earlier. You both looked upset. You looked bewildered. He looked shattered.'

Gwyn closed her eyes, regret a sharp spear in her chest. 'I didn't mean to hurt him. But I didn't know.' Not until Lucy had raised the possibility early this morning. *Or at least I didn't know that I knew.* She looked into the kind eyes of Thorne's foster father and decided to trust him because Thorne did. 'I'm confused. I don't want to hurt him, not ever. I just don't know what to do.'

'You're allowed to be confused. You're allowed to take your time to figure things out. And once you have, you're allowed to say no. Although,' he continued when her mouth fell open, 'I don't know why you would. He's a fine catch.'

'Yes, he is. All the women want him.'

'And yet he's had no one for years.'

'Four years,' she murmured. Again the knowledge that he'd waited all that time. 'I don't know why he'd even bother with me. I'm . . . messed up. And not always very nice.'

'He seems to like you anyway,' Phil noted. 'You don't have to decide tonight or even tomorrow. Just don't keep him hanging too long. I have to say, though, the timing of his revelation is very unfortunate. Blurting it out on a day that was already intense doesn't sound like the careful Thorne we know. Why now?'

She pursed her lips, considering her answer, then shrugged. 'I found him in time this morning because I'd just discovered that he'd been chasing all my dates away. I'd gone to yell at him.'

Phil chuckled. 'All right. *That* sounds like the Thorne we know. It was a shitty thing to do, but I can picture him doing it.'

'This evening I made him tell me why. Lucy warned me that this might be the case, that he had feelings for me, so I wasn't, like, blindsided.'

'But?' Phil prompted.

She shook her head, uncomfortable saying more. Uncomfortable that he'd felt that way for seven fucking years. That was a fifth of his life, *wasted*.

'He needs to be focused right now,' was all she could think to say. 'We all do.'

'I agree,' Phil said. 'And on that note, I'll say goodnight. I'll leave getting Thorne to sleep in your capable hands. You'll find sheets and a blanket in his closet.'

He left the room, but Gwyn didn't move. Sitting on the edge of Thorne's big bed, she stared up at the wall of posters featuring Pamela Anderson and every other big-bosomed actress of the 1990s. It was a side of Thorne that she hadn't anticipated, and it made her . . .

Irritable, she decided. *Because if that's what Thorne wants, he's shit outta luck. That is not me and never will be.*

It wasn't like she was unhappy with her body, because she wasn't. She was thirty-eight but barely looked thirty. At least that was what she was told. And she was vain enough to want to believe it.

Thorne, of course, was built like a god. That was indisputable. And if she said she'd never wondered what it would be like with him, she'd be a dirty liar. She hadn't gone to all his neighborhood league soccer games because she'd been a sports fan, for God's sake. It was because Thorne in a pair of shorts was too much perfection to pass up. But she'd never let it go beyond idle wondering – and maybe some lusting – because they'd been friends.

And because she'd never thought she would have a chance in hell. He'd always dated women who looked like the airbrushed bimbos on the posters. Flight attendants, traveling saleswomen, singers who played Sheidalin on their tours. Nobody who was permanent. She'd never seen him in a real relationship.

Because he was waiting for me.

Bullshit, the small voice in her mind said very loudly. *He can't be serious.*

But he'd seemed to be. And she trusted him. More than anyone except Lucy. *I'll figure it out, but not tonight.* She found a blanket and sheets in his closet, then went looking for him, hoping she could convince him to go to sleep.

Approaching the kitchen, she heard Thorne and Jamie in deep conversation. About Phil's heart. *Oh shit. Not now. Goddammit.*

Her own heart stuttered at the fear and pain on Thorne's face. When Jamie rolled his chair out of the kitchen, he didn't see her because he was heading down the hall in the opposite direction. But she saw him stop a few feet down the hall to wipe his eyes and square his shoulders before heading off to bed.

Poor Phil. Poor Jamie and Thorne. Quietly she dumped the blanket on the sofa and went to the kitchen, where Thorne sat with his head in his hands.

Baltimore, Maryland,
Monday 13 June, 12.50 A.M.

Thorne's chest hurt, burning from the shuddering breaths he was forcing in and out. When he caught the scent of lavender, he didn't move. Didn't look up. A chair dragged across the floor and she was there, sitting close enough that he could smell her vanilla shampoo. The next breath he drew was easier, the next even easier.

'I'm sorry,' she whispered.

'For yelling at me?' he asked.

'No. I'm not sorry for saying you needed to rest or that you were much more than a guardian. I'm not even sorry for the way I said it.'

'Then for what?'

'Taking your bed.'

He snorted a half-laugh. 'Really?'

'Well, no, not really. I would have totally slept there, but I couldn't take all the Pamela posters. That much boobage, Thorne . . . That's just wrong.'

He laughed quietly, then stiffened when her hand touched his knee. Quickly she retracted it. 'And I'm sorry about Phil.'

He sighed. 'You heard what Jamie said?'

'Yes. I was coming back to tell you to sleep in your own bed and I heard.'

He sighed again, his head still in his hands. 'I have to figure out how to fix my face so that Phil doesn't know I know. He's bringing me an air mattress any minute.'

'Not tonight. He came to look for the mattress and I told him I'd just take the sofa.'

Thorne lifted his eyes and met hers. They were filled with compassion and kindness and affection, and the sight made his eyes sting. 'I remember the day I came home from school and found all those posters on the walls.'

'You didn't put them there?'

He scoffed. 'Hell, no. They did, thinking I'd like them because I was seventeen and straight. Women like that aren't my type.' *You are,* he wanted to add. But he didn't. He'd give her space to be in control of her own decisions even if it killed him. 'I took them down eventually. They just put them up today as a joke.'

'Why didn't you tell them you didn't like Pamela? I think those guys would move heaven and earth for you.'

'They would. They did.' The memory was bittersweet. 'I had no home. No one who cared. Sherri was gone, and I thought my life was over. At seventeen. But Jamie and Phil, they cared when they didn't have to.'

Her swallow was audible. 'I love them for that. For being what you needed.'

'They always have been. During the trial, I continued my studies with a tutor – paid for by Jamie – because Phil asked me not to give up. Not to assume I was going to prison. He had faith in Jamie, so I did too.'

'When did you realize they were together?'

124

'The first day.' His lips turned up. 'They told me. Said they didn't want me to feel pressured to stay if I didn't want to. But Phil already knew I was okay with it. He was also coach of the debate team, and Sherri and I were both members. We'd debated the topic of marriage equality and Phil knew where Sherri and I both stood. We'd seen the wrong side of discrimination too many times to be okay with doing it to someone else. But I felt . . . more secure that they told me. Because it meant they trusted me in their home, with their private lives. They weren't afraid I'd kill them or steal from them or betray them.'

'I'm so glad you had someone who loved you,' she whispered fiercely.

He turned to search her face. 'You didn't?' Because they'd never spoken of any of this, not in all the years they'd been friends. He knew precious little about Gwyn's life before she'd joined his law firm. She'd had her secrets and he'd respected that. Now . . . now he wanted to know. Everything.

'Not really. I had my aunt, but I was on the outs with my family long before I ran away from home.'

'And joined the circus,' he supplied. He knew that much because it had been on her résumé. He'd found her fascinating then. He still did.

'Yep.'

It wasn't enough, not nearly, but he could hear Jamie telling him to give her time and space. So he didn't push. Just drew in her scent, letting it calm him as it always did.

'I was lucky, I know,' he said. 'And after the trial, they kept doing nice things for me. It took me a long time before I could just accept it and say thank you.'

'Kind of like today?' she asked, and there was a wistful note to the question. 'When everyone came together to help you?'

'Yes. Exactly like that.'

She nodded once, thoughtfully. 'It's hard, learning to accept that people might want to help you, to do things for you, for no apparent reason.'

'Maybe that they love us is reason enough.'

She was quiet for a moment. 'I think *that's* the very hardest thing to accept,' she said, and he wasn't sure who she was talking to, him or herself. She stood, the movement fluid and graceful. 'Go to bed, Thorne. And please sleep there, under all the Pamela posters. I'll be fine on the sofa. I promise. Tweety will sleep next to me.'

He swallowed hard, clenching his hands into fists because he wanted to touch her so damn badly. 'All right. We'll have to leave by eight.'

'I'll be ready.'

Annapolis, Maryland,
Monday 13 June, 3.15 A.M.

He woke with a jolt as cold feet pressed against the backs of his legs. 'Wha . . .' But then he smelled coconut and Kathryn. She'd showered with the special body wash that he'd bought her to cleanse the stink of her job from her body. 'Mmm,' he hummed when her hands roamed up his chest. One thing about a woman in her twenties, she had voracious appetites and he loved that.

'Did everything go to plan?' he asked her.

'It did,' Kathryn purred in his ear, then nipped his ear lobe. 'Just like clockwork. How was your day?'

'Had to get rid of the idiots I sent to bag Thorne. They nearly killed him.'

'And I missed it? Did you film it?'

He chuckled. Kathryn was as bloodthirsty as Madeline had been. 'No.'

She smacked him lightly on the shoulder. 'What do I keep telling you? Those sessions are training gold. You show videos of them to your new recruits and I guarantee they will never fuck up.'

'Next time you can film it,' he promised.

'Good. Now can we get on to the fun stuff?'

'*Absolutamente.*' He rolled onto his side to look down at her. She was so very pretty. 'That means "absolutely",' he said teasingly.

She chuckled. 'That one I figured out on my own.'

Kathryn didn't have Margo's capacity for numbers or languages.

Margo had inherited her mother's proficiency with languages and was fluent in six of them, while Kathryn often had trouble even with English, her Spanish deplorable. But Kathryn was a strategic thinker with a killer body, and he was happy to have her in his bed for the foreseeable future.

He never would have wanted Margo anyway. From the time she'd been old enough to crawl, she'd been Colin's. The thought made him sigh.

'Aw, don't be sad,' Kathryn murmured.

'It's . . . I miss him.'

'I know.' Kathryn pushed him to his back and straddled him. 'But I can take your mind off all that for a little while.'

That would be welcome. 'Then by all means, please proceed.'

Eight

It was remarkably the same, Thorne thought as Jamie navigated the streets leading through Chevy Chase. The houses had always been grand and well kept. The cars had always been luxury models. The signage in the yards had always warned trespassers to keep away.

Grand houses gave way to smaller homes in more middle-class neighborhoods, until they stopped in front of a bungalow painted a cheerful yellow with a garden full of roses. Jamie put his van in park. They'd brought his vehicle because it was easiest for him to enter and exit with his chair.

It wasn't the most maneuverable of automobiles, but Jamie had mad driving skills, which was good because they'd had to lose no fewer than five news vans and four cars. Some of those cars probably held reporters. At least one had been the cop tasked with their surveillance. Thorne felt safer without the constant police presence, especially since they were hoping Prew would give them real information. He might be loath to meet with them if he thought the cops would find out. The man had a pension to hold onto, after all.

'Detective Prew is expecting us,' Jamie said into the quiet of the car, because no one had said a single word since they'd left that morning.

Thorne had been lured from his room by the smell of coffee, to find Jamie and Phil at the kitchen table with Gwyn, already dressed. They were all elbow-deep in paperwork. Jamie had brought up the

128

box with the file from his trial and they'd located one of the EMTs and the ME who'd done Richard's autopsy.

Thorne could only blink blearily at them. He'd fallen asleep only an hour before. He'd tried to sleep all night, he truly had, but he'd only lain in bed looking at the ceiling and alternating between thoughts of the woman who'd died in his bed and the very live woman asleep on the sofa. Everything within him had wanted to go to Gwyn, to lose himself in her scent, in the soft feel of her skin. But he hadn't.

He'd made his case. The ball was in her court.

But this morning she was clearly as messed up as he was. He only had to look at her to realize she hadn't slept at all either. She had dark circles under her eyes, well hidden by her makeup but still visible to anyone who knew her. And Thorne had watched her face for twelve long years. He knew every curve and line intimately.

She was dressed conservatively and that annoyed him. Gwyn didn't dress conservatively. Gwyn was out there, flashy. *Herself.* But he knew she'd be trying to make a good impression today, so he said nothing. Although it annoyed him even more that she thought she had to be someone else to make that good impression. That she'd thought it the night before as she'd packed her bag with the clothes she only wore to funerals and to court.

There was absolutely nothing wrong with who she was. He'd tried to figure out how to tell her that, but no words had come, so he'd let it go.

Now the four of them were in front of Prew's house, and Thorne found he was nervous. Not a feeling he cared for at all. 'Who's on point with Prew?' he asked when they'd exited the van.

'I am,' Phil said. 'At least at the beginning. I'm thinking Jamie should take over if Prew is comfortable talking to all of us.'

Thorne stopped mid-step. 'What do you mean, "if"? Doesn't he know we're about to descend on him?'

'No,' Phil said, 'he's only expecting me, but he knows it's about you, so I think he'll be okay with the four of us. Come on, Thorne. We don't want to be late.'

Thorne followed with a scowl until he caught Gwyn scowling back at him. 'What?'

'Behave, Thorne,' she hissed. 'Phil is nervous enough.'

'So am I,' he hissed back.

'But *you're* supposed to be the pro at this. How many times have you walked into a detective's office to ask questions?'

'This isn't his office. It's his home. And I've never been asking about myself!'

'Then pretend it's not about you. Pretend it's about me. That I'm being set up for murder. Then you find that fire of yours, because I want this over. I want you to be able to live without either murder hanging over your head for the rest of your life.'

He stared at her, then realized she was right. He shook himself, irritated that he'd allowed a homicide detective to rattle him. It was just . . . 'This whole thing makes me feel seventeen again,' he confessed.

Her smile was patient. 'I know it does. Just remember who you are. Thomas Thorne, who eats prosecutors for breakfast and spits out their bones.'

He swallowed a laugh. 'I think you should keep that visual to yourself. I am being framed for homicide, after all.'

'True,' she allowed.

'Thank you.' He'd needed to laugh. He'd needed her to steady him.

Her expression was sober as she nodded. 'You're welcome.'

They were greeted at the front door by a gray-haired African-American man around Jamie's age, and the years seemed to fall away. Thorne remembered this guy, remembered his eyes, which had been so hard to read. He'd never seen Prew in anything other than a suit and tie, but today he'd dressed casually in a polo shirt and khaki pants. A set of golf clubs leaned against the foyer wall. It appeared that the man was enjoying his retirement. He looked a little surprised to see a group instead of just Phil, but he rolled with it.

'Please sit down,' he said, once he'd led them to the living room.

'Thank you for seeing us on short notice,' Phil said. 'Christopher

Prew, this is Jamie Maslow, Gwyn Weaver and Thomas Thorne.'

Prew nodded at each of them, but when he came to Thorne, he gave him a long look. 'I've watched your career over the years. I've been impressed, even though I think defense attorneys are one step down from IRS agents.'

Thorne found himself smiling. 'Thank you.'

Prew grinned. 'You're welcome. I apologize that I don't have refreshments to offer. My wife is out and . . . well, I didn't realize there would be four of you. You'd have to fight over the two Danishes I bought this morning.'

'Our apologies for not warning you. We weren't sure that Thorne would be up to the trip,' Gwyn said. 'He was in the hospital yesterday.'

Prew frowned at that. 'I heard. You've got yourself some trouble, Mr Thorne. Although I remember you as Mr White.'

'I changed my name back to that of my birth father after the trial. My stepfather was a cruel man, as I'm sure you recall. I didn't want to bear his name.'

'I don't blame you,' Prew agreed. 'White was a piece of work for sure. A bully and a thug. So. What can I do for you all this morning?'

'We're here to talk to you about Thorne's case nineteen years ago,' Jamie said. 'The murder yesterday was set up to appear similar to that of Richard Linden.'

Prew's brows went up. 'Shit.'

Gwyn leaned forward, meeting the detective's eyes. 'Somebody wants to hurt Thorne. We need to know how they got the information about the Linden case.'

'They could have read the court transcripts,' Prew said, but not unkindly.

'There were a few details that the court transcripts didn't contain,' Jamie told him. 'Because Montgomery County PD, for whatever reason, held them back.'

'Patricia Segal's body had a key ring embedded in one of her wounds.' Thorne watched the man's face for his reaction. 'It appeared to be made from a medal. A key was still attached to the ring.'

131

Prew's brows shot up. 'We never released that information.'

'Exactly,' Thorne said quietly. 'Yet someone knew. Someone deliberately chose to murder the sister of the young man I'd been accused of killing in a way that was similar to his murder. I want to know how and why. We're hoping you have some thoughts on it, or at least can help us find a few of the people who were involved in my case back then.'

'Like?' Prew asked, again not unkindly.

'Like the EMTs who took Richard to the hospital,' Jamie said. 'The cops first on the scene. The ER doctors who declared him dead. The ME and any morgue personnel who touched his body. Anyone who was involved in the episode that led to Thorne's expulsion, because they either perjured themselves on the stand or disappeared and refused to testify at all. But before we discuss any of those people, I'd like to know why the police chose to suppress the existence of the key ring.'

Prew scrunched his eyes closed. 'Starting with the softball questions, are we?' He sighed. 'I shouldn't be talking to you at all.'

'Then why are you?' Gwyn asked softly.

Prew met her eyes. 'Who are you exactly? How do you connect? Phil I know, and Jamie I remember. You're new.'

'Well, not so new,' Gwyn said, flashing the retired detective a sweet smile that made Thorne want to chuckle because it was so utterly bullshit. 'I work with Thorne. I was his paralegal for several years. Now we partner in our club.'

'Sheidalin,' Prew said, surprising both of them.

'You know it?' Thorne asked.

'Took my wife there a few years back. She'd heard about this violinist. One of your other partners, as I recall. We enjoyed the performance. Although it was . . . different.'

'That was Lucy,' Gwyn said, and Thorne could tell she knew exactly where the detective was going with this. She was a better bullshitter than Prew was. 'Who is, as I'm sure you know, an ME and is now married to one of BPD's finest, JD Fitzpatrick. So do we pass muster, Detective Prew?'

His lips twitched. 'Yeah. Fitzpatrick is a good cop and I've

132

worked with Lucy Trask in the past. My wife went to the club with me on my request. I couldn't believe the prim-and-proper ME was the performer shown in the paper. But she was.' He gave Gwyn a shrewd look. 'You run the place yourselves?'

'With a few managers, yes. Why?'

'Because after Phil called me yesterday, I was curious. And a little . . . cautious. So I visited your club again. The mood was decidedly different than it was the first time I went. Much more tense, but not in a good way.'

Thorne stiffened and glanced at Gwyn. He hadn't even thought about the club last night. She just lifted a brow and turned back to Prew. 'How so? According to the manager on duty, there were no fights, no disagreements. Everyone liked the band.'

Prew didn't blink. 'Well, your manager on duty left a few things out. There was a major disturbance. Your bouncer grabbed two guys by the collar and carried them out like they were puppy dogs. Tossed them out like garbage.'

'Which,' Gwyn said amiably, 'as it turns out, they were.' She glanced up at Thorne. 'More assholes trying to deal out of the club.'

Thorne shrugged, some of his stiffness receding. 'That's a near-nightly occurrence, Detective. Tell us something we don't know. Our club is clean and we work hard to keep it that way.'

'So said your employees. You were definitely the topic of conversation, Mr Thorne. Your employees are loyal. And they didn't trust me, for sure.'

'They don't know you,' Gwyn said, still amiably. 'They know us. They know we're honest and we don't tolerate anything illegal. They know we pay their salaries and health insurance on time, and that we create a safe space for them to work. We even have a part-time nursery in the back now. Soundproofed, staffed and secure.'

Her tone was mild, but her chin lifted and Thorne caught the pride in her eyes when she looked up at him. 'Right, Thorne?'

'Absolutely. It's not an easy job, but Gwyn runs a tight ship. What does this have to do with the question Jamie asked you?'

'It doesn't. I'm answering the question Miss Weaver asked me.'

'Oh,' she said with a nod. 'Which was why you're talking to us. I still don't get it. I mean, we could have paid our people to say nice things. We *are* performers, you know. If they couldn't play their role, they're not much good to us on stage. Yes?'

Prew chuckled. 'Yes.' Then he sobered. 'I was more interested in what the people who got kicked out said. I followed them for a block or two. I mean, they were drug dealers and it wasn't so long ago that I was a cop. They were pretty rattled, actually. They stopped to call their boss, who'd apparently figured that with you out of the way, Mr Thorne, the way would be clear for them to deal from your club. I couldn't hear what the boss said, but he didn't seem too happy if their expressions were any indication. They were literally shaking in their shoes.' He shrugged. 'I figured that spoke well of you, so I'll tell you what I can.'

Jamie crossed his arms. 'Then start by telling me why the police suppressed the key ring Thorne found in Richard's body.'

Prew looked uncomfortable. 'My boss decided it should be so. At the time he wanted to hold the existence – and disappearance – of the key ring back in case it was discovered during the course of the investigation. Whoever had it couldn't claim they were a copycat because, theoretically, only the killer would have known about it. I didn't get it, but I was pretty new to homicide then. I didn't know him that well, so I pushed back. I wanted it in the record because at the very beginning I wasn't sure if you'd killed Richard or not, Mr Thorne. My boss told me to back off. That I had no idea what I was stirring up. I didn't realize he was so susceptible to community pressure.'

'I assume you mean from Richard's father,' Thorne said. 'But why? That doesn't make any sense.'

'I don't know,' Prew admitted. 'I heard later that Mrs Linden had a nervous breakdown, and the "violation" of her stepson's body was what pushed her over the edge.'

'Stepson?' Gwyn asked.

Prew nodded. 'Richard's mother was the first Mrs Linden. She didn't have a nervous breakdown. I was surprised that the second Mrs Linden would. She seemed too controlled to lose her cool – or to have admitted it, anyway. It also bothered me that the medal had

134

shoved her off the edge. I mean, Richard was gutted like a deer. That someone had shoved something inside his body didn't seem all that much worse. At any rate, I think it makes more sense that it was pressure from Linden rather than any desire to preserve the investigation that kept the key ring out of the records. The existence of a key ring made from a sports medal would have been a major clue, especially since your medal had also gone missing, Mr Thorne.'

'Which was why we didn't push it back then,' Thorne said. 'But I'm pushing it now, because that damn key ring, or at least a replica, has turned up again.'

'I wish I'd pushed harder to have it included in the trial now,' Prew said, his regret evident.

Jamie sighed. 'So do I. Okay, we know now that this key ring is of vital importance. Back to the people who might have come into contact with it.' He handed Prew the list of first responders and morgue personnel who'd handled Richard's body. 'Know any of these?'

Prew scanned the list. 'I would have interviewed them as part of the investigation. I've kept all my notes, so I can check, but I don't remember any of . . . Oh, wait. I know this name. The morgue tech. Kirby Gilson.'

Prew hesitated and Thorne grew impatient. 'What do you know about him?'

Prew looked up. 'Well, mostly that he's dead. He was shot at a scene he was responding to. First responders didn't know there was still an active shooter, so they'd called the morgue techs in. I didn't investigate the homicide, but I remember the funeral. He had a wife, and a kid who had leukemia or something like that. We took up a collection for them.'

'When was this?' Thorne asked, making a note to have Lucy check on the man's work history.

Prew frowned. 'Maybe ten years ago? Fifteen years, at the most. Are you thinking he was shot deliberately?'

'We don't know *what* we're thinking,' Thorne said, frustrated. 'But we have to start somewhere. What about the others on the list?'

Prew handed the paper back to Jamie. 'I know the ER doctor,

because my kids played sports and we ended up in the ER too many times back then. He's passed on too. Stroke, I think. Or maybe a heart attack. He was a good guy. The rest of the names, I don't know. I'm not saying they're good or bad. I just don't know. It's been nineteen years.'

'Well, then, what about Angela Ospina?' Phil said. 'She's the girl who Thorne was trying to protect when this whole debacle began. I couldn't find her.'

'Oh, that's an easy one. She runs a hair salon in Bethesda. Upscale. Very high-class clientele.'

'Good for her,' Thorne murmured. She'd pulled herself up by her bootstraps.

The retired detective made a face. 'Maybe. Maybe not. You know we tried to get her to testify for you in your trial.'

Thorne sat back in his chair, surprised in a warm way. 'No, I didn't know that. Thank you.'

'You're welcome, of course, but I was just doing my job. Angie Ospina was a missing link, a loose thread. After your arrest, she disappeared. Her father said she'd run away, but we didn't believe him. He was far too eager to see us go. Most parents want the cops' help when their teenaged daughters run off.'

'Where do you think she went?' Thorne asked.

'She was with her aunt in . . .' Prew frowned. 'Somewhere west. Kansas or Iowa or Nebraska. Some state with corn.'

Thorne chuckled, surprising himself. 'Okay,' he said. 'But when she came back, what happened? Did the Lindens bother her?'

Prew's frown intensified. 'No. On the contrary. They fronted her business. She came back two years after your trial. She'd finished high school in whichever corn place she went to, then got a job with one of the local beauty shops. Then about ten years ago, she up and starts this new salon. Rumor has it that the Lindens loaned her a lot of money.'

'Rumor?' Jamie asked. 'Or fact?'

'Rumor,' Prew said. 'I kept tabs on her after she came back. I wondered if the Lindens had put pressure on her to leave back then, so that she couldn't testify that Richard had started the whole mess by groping her. If they had, that would have been witness tampering and I really wanted something on Linden Senior. I was also worried that they'd give her trouble, but she claimed they'd been nothing but kind to her.'

Thorne snorted. 'Right.'

'I didn't believe her either,' Prew admitted, 'but I couldn't dig deeper unless she made a complaint.'

'Why were you hoping to get something on Linden Senior?' Phil asked curiously.

'Because he makes my skin crawl. His son made my skin crawl. His daughter . . . I never knew her well enough to form an opinion, but Dick Linden Senior is a shark. I don't trust him, so I keep tabs on his businesses. Just in case something looks amiss.' He shrugged. 'I'm retired. I look back at your case as a blight on my record, Mr Thorne. I didn't believe you did it, but I couldn't prove it. I've always been sorry for that.'

'You're talking to me now,' Thorne said. 'It's far more than I expected. Is Angie's business successful?'

'That I don't know. It seems to be, from the outside. For instance, I saw her at a community fund-raiser recently. She was wearing shoes that had to cost a month's salary. And before you ask, my wife knows shoes. She told me that.'

'Her place is called Heavenly Salon,' Gwyn said, looking at her phone. She glanced up briefly. 'I Googled Angie's name. She's listed as the owner. I'm considering a whole new look,' she said, tossing back her hair, which she'd allowed to dry in ringlets. It was Thorne's favorite of all her hairstyles. Just free and natural. Just begging for him to run his fingers through it.

And that's enough of that, he thought. *Focus.*

'What do you hope to gain?' Prew asked.

'Information. If she's indebted to Linden, I'd like to know. If her business is thriving, good for her. If she's having trouble making ends meet?' Gwyn lifted a shoulder. 'She'd be vulnerable to someone either paying or extorting information.'

'She wouldn't have known about the key ring,' Prew cautioned, but then he nodded. 'But she knows something, otherwise Linden wouldn't have given her a dime. I've assumed it was payment for not testifying, but without her cooperation, it makes for a weak case. Which is why I never pursued it.'

'We'll need to see when she got the loan,' Gwyn said thoughtfully. 'I mean, why then? Why not nineteen years ago, when she ran away to corn-town to keep from having to testify on Thorne's behalf?'

'We don't know that they didn't pay her then,' Thorne said. 'Maybe she went back for more.'

Gwyn shrugged. 'You could be right. Either way, I want to talk to her. Worst that can happen is that I come away with a nice hairdo, but I may be able to get more.'

'You really think you can get answers?' Jamie asked.

Gwyn gave him a coy smile. 'Counselor, I know how to get hairdressers to gossip. It's one of my best skills.'

'It's true,' Thorne said with a smile of pride. 'When we first started out, Gwyn would pose as whoever she needed to be to get information for our clients' cases.' He'd nearly forgotten about that. 'I'm glad she used her powers for good and not evil.'

'Evil probably pays more,' she lamented, then tapped her phone. 'I'll make an appointment as soon as the salon opens at ten.' She pressed the back of her hand to her forehead. 'I'll tell them it's a fashion emergency.'

Jamie smiled at her dramatic delivery. 'I don't even want to know what that entails.' He checked his own phone for the names of the people they'd wanted to interview. 'Next on my list are the three friends of Richard who beat Thorne up the day he got expelled. We know where Chandler Nystrom and Darian Hinman are. But we couldn't find Colton Brandenberg.'

Prew's smile dimmed. 'Be careful there. Darian is a chip off his old man's block, and that's not a compliment. Chandler . . .' He shook his head. 'Some people should not be given a badge. He's had some run-ins, gotten written up by IA. I can't give you details because I don't know them. But I do know he left the force abruptly and got a job in private security.'

'What about Colton?' Thorne asked.

'I don't know,' Prew admitted. 'He left town for a while after

Richard's murder. Came back to testify, but he was messed up.'

'I don't remember him being messed up,' Thorne murmured.

'I do,' Jamie said bluntly. 'I worried that he was on something. He was like . . . a zombie walking. I was prepared to go to the judge and have his testimony stricken if he said anything wacky, but he just confirmed the facts as we already knew them – except for Richard Linden starting the fight with you by groping Angie Ospina. That he claimed he couldn't recall.'

Prew was nodding. 'After the trial, Colton left town and, to my knowledge, hasn't been back. His sister is still local. She's a seam-stress. Makes draperies. Talented, or so my wife says. I'll get her details and send them to you.'

'Thank you,' Thorne said. 'Really, thank you. You didn't have to tell us any of this.'

'Yeah, I kind of did. We all get that one case, you know? I was there at the school that day. I remember talking to Sherri and thinking, goddamn, if they'd just given the poor kid his guitar, none of this would have happened. And then Sherri died. I hated that. She seemed like such a nice girl.'

Thorne swallowed hard. 'She was. She really was.'

Prew sighed. 'And then I talked to you, and you were just . . . lost. Abandoned by your mother and stepfather. Targeted by Linden. So . . . yeah, Mr Thorne, I really had to. Just . . . don't make any more trouble, okay? I mean, I don't think you made any back then, but somebody has a hard-on for you. Don't give them any rope.'

Thorne made his lips curve. 'I'll do my very best,' he said tightly.

Prew winced. 'Ouch. I knew I should've shut my mouth while I was ahead. I didn't mean I thought you were guilty. Not then. And from what I hear at the water cooler, not now.'

Jamie cocked his head. 'What do you hear at the water cooler?'

'Well, Gil Segal – the victim's husband – is a judge, right? Rumor has it that he and the missus were having some hard times. They bought a lot of property and then Patricia's business tanked. So that was bad. But my wife heard that Patricia was having an affair.'

All four of them blinked. 'Where did she hear that?' Phil asked.

Prew grinned. 'Beauty parlor.'

'Told you so,' Gwyn said. 'Any water cooler rumors about who she was doing on the side?'

'Not that my wife told me, but I'll ask her that too.' Prew shrugged. 'She wasn't well liked, Mrs Segal. So take whatever rumors you hear with a grain of salt.'

'What business was she in?' Thorne asked.

Prew frowned. 'I'm not sure. Something she was doing for her father. Again, my wife will know.'

'What salon does your wife use?' Gwyn asked him.

'I have no idea. I'll ask her.' He checked his watch. 'I have to be going soon. I have a tee time at eleven. Keep me up to speed, if you don't mind. If there's any arresting of Linden, I'd really like to be there to witness it. You know, for old times' sake.'

'We will,' Thorne promised.

Baltimore, Maryland,
Monday 13 June, 10.30 A.M.

Frederick turned a three-sixty on the deserted dance floor of Sheidalin. 'Hello?' he called. 'Anybody home?'

'Just a second!' A voice came from an open door behind the bar. Sheldon Mowry appeared, an iPad clutched in one hand. The club's assistant manager frowned when he saw Frederick hurrying over. 'What is it? Is Thorne okay?'

'Yes,' Frederick said. 'I just talked to Phil and Jamie. Thorne's . . . you know. Thorne.'

Mowry rolled his eyes. 'Yeah, I got that.'

Frederick studied the man for a moment. He was in his early thirties, slender, with wild hair that looked like it hadn't seen a comb in a decade. His arms were covered with tattoos. But his eyes were clear and without guile. Almost . . . innocent. Thorne vouched for the guy, but those innocent eyes rang an alarm bell in Frederick's mind. He'd checked Mowry out before coming here this morning, but had found nothing pre-dating his time here at Sheidalin, and that raised too many flags. There was something going on with this guy, and Frederick needed to know what that was.

He'd come to Sheidalin with two goals in mind: first, to check out the employees, especially those who'd known Thorne a long time. Whoever had set this plan in motion knew Thorne well enough to know where to dig for his past. The second goal was to meet with Sally Brewster, the friend of Bernice Brown who'd been harassed by a detective. Frederick wanted to know why a detective had been looking for Thorne's client. Miss Brewster should be arriving in twenty minutes, so he had a little time to dig into the employees before then.

'How long have you known Thorne?' he asked Mowry.

The assistant manager's smile was wry. 'If you've got a question about me, just ask.' His smile slid into a full smirk. 'You won't find what you're looking for any other way.'

Frederick's lips twitched. 'A challenge.'

A shrug. 'Do your worst. Why are you here? I didn't call for legal assistance.'

'I needed to make sure everything was running smoothly. Gwyn and Thorne aren't going to be able to give this place their full attention for a while.'

Mowry's eyes narrowed suspiciously, but he didn't call bullshit. 'Look, I ran this club before Gwyn became the full-time manager. She did the books then, and some event planning, but she was mostly busy doing paralegal shit for Thorne. I was in charge of the day-to-day. She was basically a performer back then, like Lucy and Thorne are now. So I know what to do.'

The man was defensive, Frederick thought. And maybe a little bitter? 'Did you take a pay cut when Gwyn took over?'

Mowry sighed, kind of impatiently. 'Nope. Hold on a minute.' He turned back to the door through which he'd come. 'Laura?' he called, and the bartender stuck her head out. 'Can you finish the inventory yourself?'

'Of course. Give me the iPad.' She met him halfway, taking the tablet before giving Frederick a worried look. 'Why are you here, Frederick? Is Thorne okay?'

'He's fine,' Frederick assured her. Twenty-six years old, Laura had been born in Russia and had been adopted by a family in

Virginia when she was an infant. Most of her Facebook photos were of her and her little boy. From what information he'd been able to gather, the toddler's father was not in the picture. Laura's mother was a big help, though. According to her employment records, which Thorne kept on file at the firm, Laura had missed not one shift in the six months that she'd worked for Sheidalin.

She gave him the same suspicious look that Mowry had. 'Okay. I'll be in the back if you need me,' she added to Mowry before leaving them alone.

Mowry's gaze had become perturbed. 'If you're looking for dirt here, you won't find it. We are all loyal to Thorne.'

'I don't doubt it,' Frederick said, and Mowry snorted.

'Come on.' He led the way to a table near the empty stage. 'Let's sit. I've got a long day ahead of me, so I'll rest my feet now.' He waited until Frederick had taken his seat, then launched them in an unexpected direction. 'You know what happened to Gwyn, right? Four years ago?'

Frederick nodded. 'I've seen the police report.' He'd read how Gwyn's boyfriend had been using her to get to Lucy because the man had a sick obsession for revenge, believing that Lucy had been involved in the death of his sister. She hadn't been, of course, but others had. Those people who Evan wanted to kill had been truly bad, but Lucy had been caught in the crossfire. Gwyn had been an unwitting front for him, providing him with easy access to his prey. 'She was abducted by a killer so that he could lure Lucy. Both Lucy and Gwyn were saved. Gwyn was credited with saving Lucy's mother.'

Mowry gave him a disgusted look. 'That's all?'

'That's all there was in the report. All that concerned Gwyn, anyway.'

'Exactly. See, nobody in the media ever goes back to find out how the victims of the crime are doing years later. Yes, Gwyn was saved, and yes, she saved Lucy's mother. But she had to leave Lucy behind with a killer. Lucy forced her to.'

Frederick exhaled carefully. 'I see.'

Mowry gave him a yeah-right look. 'Do you? Do you really?'

Frederick nodded. 'I was in the army. Special Forces. I had to leave a man behind once so that I could get two others out. I went back for him, but it was too late. He was dead.' He swallowed hard, pushing the memory away when it knocked at the door of his mind. 'He was my friend. One of my best.'

It wasn't something he spoke of. Ever. But at least it had been the right thing to share, because Mowry's expression softened.

'Okay, so maybe you do. I don't know how it affected you, but I do know how it affected Gwyn. She was duped by a man who claimed to love her. She had hearts in her eyes for the first time.' He shook his head. 'I always thought she and Thorne would end up together. I was pretty shocked when she brought this Evan guy in.'

'What did you think of him?'

A sigh. 'I wish I could say I hated him, that I thought he was "off". But I didn't. He fooled me too. I got on with him. We went to ball games together. He was a likable guy.'

'Evil often wears a pretty face.' How well Frederick knew that. Taylor's mother had duped him for years. So he supposed he understood Gwyn better than he'd realized.

Mowry's chuckle was hollow. 'Evan did. And Gwyn believed him. She . . . used to be different. Vibrant. Alive.'

'Not dark and sarcastic?'

'If you only knew. See, you met her on her way out of the worst of it. After Evan, she imploded. She wouldn't perform. For anyone. Lucy wanted her to sing at her and JD's wedding, but she couldn't.' His sigh was ragged. 'I found her at the piano one day. Nobody was here and it was dark. She was crying because she couldn't make herself put her hands on the keys.'

'She did last summer. I saw the tape of a wedding for which she and Lucy provided the processional music. It was beautiful.'

'Yeah, well, like I said, she's been coming out of the dark place. She's been singing. And recently she's been doing the silks.' He pointed at a contraption on the stage, a twenty-foot-tall A-frame with two long pieces of white silk dangling from the highest point. 'It's like Cirque du Soleil. Gwyn is damn graceful. I have to admit,

143

the first time she got back on the stage, I cried like a baby.' One side of his mouth lifted. 'I wasn't alone. Not a dry eye in the house. She's well loved here. So when Thorne asked me to back off my daily duties and allow Gwyn to take over, I did. Not that it was easy, mind you, but I didn't argue.'

'But you didn't want to back off.'

'Not at the time. And sometimes I get a little annoyed, still. But Thorne's a mensch. He knew I hated being idle. He also knew I'd never gotten to go to college, so he's paid for me to go. I take classes part time. One more year and I'll have my degree in hospitality. I can write my ticket.'

'Will you leave Sheidalin?'

He smiled. 'Probably not. I like it here. It's home, and Gwyn, Thorne and Lucy are my family. None of us had much family of our own, so we banded together. So you don't have to come here and look over my shoulder, Freddie. I know my business and I do my job well. I love those guys. We all do, all of the employees. We won't let them down.'

'So you don't think Thorne did it. The murder, I mean.'

Mowry scoffed. 'Please. You really need me to say it? No, he didn't. Full stop.'

'And the other employees? Are they as certain as you are?'

'Ask them. Ming!' he shouted. 'Laura! Come out here, please.'

The two came from two different doors. Ming from the main office in the back, while Laura returned from the storeroom.

Ming was the head of security – aka 'the bouncer' – and every bit as big as Thorne. His real name was Clive, but Frederick didn't think anyone called him that out of sheer fear. He had been with Sheidalin from the very beginning. He and Thorne had played college rugby together. When Thorne had needed muscle, Ming had been the first person he'd turned to. The man was the most upstanding citizen you could think of. Took care of his mother, went to church, and did unpaid work with Meals On Wheels. He even volunteered to hold the abandoned babies of drug addicts in the neonatal wards of the local hospitals, posting photos on social media of the tiny creatures in his enormous hands.

The sight had made Frederick's eyes tear up. But Ming knew Thorne better than almost anyone, excluding Jamie and Phil, so he was on Frederick's suspect list.

The two of them dragged chairs to the table and Ming put his tablet in front of him. It showed the camera feeds, Frederick realized. The security man was vigilant.

'What's up?' Ming asked cautiously.

'He's worried about the day-to-day,' Mowry said, one brow raised. 'Since Thorne and Gwyn are out for a while.'

Frederick nodded, well aware that the other two hadn't bought the excuse either. 'Yes. So . . . is there anything you need in order to function?'

'No,' Laura said. 'I just finished the inventory and placed the order.'

'And I just finished this week's schedule,' Ming added. 'So far so good. Nobody's quit and none of our booked bands have cancelled on us.'

'There's notoriety in playing Sheidalin right now,' Mowry said.

Frederick figured that was true. 'I understand there was some trouble last night.'

'No more than usual,' Ming said. 'We toss drug dealers out three times a week on average. These guys were opportunists. Figured they'd give it a try since Thorne was . . . well, not here.'

Mowry's eyes flashed. 'Sons of bitches,' he grumbled. 'But seriously, we have this covered. Yes, we're getting a lot of media exposure right now, but we'll make it work for us. Thorne and Gwyn don't need to worry.'

'They weren't,' Frederick said. 'I was.'

Ming gave him a dubious look. 'Who made you the boss?'

Frederick smiled at that. 'Old habits die hard. I'm kind of used to taking charge, and I like Thorne. He's a good man. I'd like his businesses to be intact when he comes back. Having said that, I've got some law firm business to take care of. I arranged a meeting with someone here. I hope that's okay.'

'Make yourself at home,' Mowry said. 'If you need privacy, we can make ourselves scarce for a while.'

'Thank you.' Frederick checked his watch. 'She should be arriving soon.'

Ming glanced at his tablet. 'I think she's here.' One of the camera feeds showed a woman approaching the backstage door. 'How did she get to the alley? There are news vans all up and down the street.'

One point for Sally Brewster. She listened and complied with instructions. 'I told her to park at the movie theater and cut through the bookstore next door. They let her out their alley door. Said they owed Thorne a favor, so they were okay with it.'

Frederick stood up, wondering if these three could really be as loyal as they seemed. He hoped so, because Thorne deserved loyalty. 'Thanks for putting my mind at ease. If you end up needing any help, please call me.' He gave them his card. 'My cell's on there. I'm serious about wanting to help Thorne. Now, if you'll excuse me, I've got to let my appointment in before the news vans see her.'

Nine

Annapolis, Maryland,
Monday 13 June, 10.45 A.M.

He stepped out of the shower in his discipline room to see Patton waiting by the door, revulsion clear on his face as he stared at what remained of the drug dealers he'd picked up the night before.

'Is something amiss, Mr Patton?'

Patton turned slowly to face him, swallowing hard. 'No. Sir,' he added belatedly. 'It's . . . fine. It's fine.'

He almost smiled. Big strong men reduced to green-faced little girls at the sight of a bit of blood and gore. Making sure he stepped around the affected areas, he went to his wardrobe and began dressing.

'I have a list of tasks for you to complete this morning.' He pulled on silk boxers and then his trousers, finding the folded paper in his pocket. He held it up, waiting for Patton to come to him to get it. 'Mr Patton?'

With an effort, Patton tore his eyes from the carnage on the floor and walked toward him, gingerly avoiding a puddle of something nasty. The head clerk's gulp was audible.

He was amused. 'One cannot eviscerate a man without a little mess, Mr Patton.'

'I know. I remember.'

'I should hope so. It was less than forty-eight hours ago.'

Patton hadn't seemed as shaken at the sight of Patricia's body, though. Mostly because she hadn't been as thoroughly worked over as the two dealers from the night before. On those two, he'd spent

147

hours cutting and carving. Patricia had been dealt with quickly.

Because I was so angry. Too angry. Seeing Thomas Thorne lying there unconscious had been more difficult than he'd anticipated. He'd wanted to plunge his knife into the man's body so badly . . . but he had not. Because death was too good for him. He wanted him to live. And mourn.

Just like I am. So he'd been quick about it, slicing the woman's throat before carving her open and pushing the weathered key ring into the wound. He'd dropped the knife on the floor at Thorne's side after pressing the man's fingerprints into the blood.

And then he'd left the room, going to the garage to lie on the tarp they'd laid in the backseat of Thorne's very luxurious SUV. It had been the hardest thing, walking away from Thorne's breathing body. But he'd done it, because the payoff would be far more satisfying.

He'd taken the tarp with him when he'd exited to his own vehicle, ensuring that there would be no trace of him in Thorne's Audi. And then he'd left Patton to return the Audi to Thorne's garage and to finish setting the scene. He now wondered if Patton had looked the same way after beating Patricia until she was unrecognizable.

'What the hell?' Patton's voice jerked him out of the memory. He looked up from the paper he'd been reading, his eyes flashing with fury. 'You could have texted this to me. Or called me.'

'Of course I could have.' Calmly he continued to dress, watching Patton from the corner of his eye as he shrugged into his shirt and buttoned it.

'But you made me come all the way down here.'

'I did.' He tucked his shirttail into his trousers and began tying his tie.

Patton's face hardened to stone. 'You just wanted me to see this.' He gestured behind him, to where the bodies lay.

He smiled. 'Just a little reminder of how failure is punished.'

'But these guys didn't fail you.'

'Well, when you consider that they pledged allegiance to my rival, I'd have to disagree.' He snugged his tie and pulled on his coat. There. He always felt more put together when he wore a suit.

He nodded toward the paper in Patton's hand. 'Complete those tasks and call me after each one. Then return here. You'll need to transport these two back to their masters.'

Patton's eyes widened. 'Excuse me?'

'You heard me. I want these bodies dropped at the Circus Freaks' warehouse at seven sharp.'

'Why seven?'

Because that was when Sheidalin opened their doors. He wanted shock and awe and media coverage when the police stormed the place. 'My reasons are not for you to question, Mr Patton. Should I search for another replacement?'

Patton's gulp was, once again, audible. 'No. Sir.'

'Good. Then please get to it. You don't want to be late.'

Baltimore, Maryland,
Monday 13 June, 10.55 A.M.

Frederick hurried to open the backstage door. 'Miss Brewster?'

She'd raised her fist to knock, but lowered it. Her eyes widened, startled, although she didn't physically flinch. 'Yes. Mr Dawson, I take it?'

'Yes, thank you for coming to meet me here. Please come this way.'

She followed him into the main hall, blinking to get accustomed to the darkness. Sally Brewster was the woman who'd warned Bernice Brown that someone claiming to be a detective was poking around. She was fifty-two, widowed with two grown children, and was a nurse in the pediatric ward of a local hospital. She volunteered at the animal shelter and played the cello in her neighborhood orchestra. She rode horses in her 'spare time', and had gone to Ocean City on vacation the month before, where she'd looked very, very nice in her extremely modest bathing suit. And she really, *really* needed to make her Facebook page private.

He pulled out a chair for her. 'Please sit down.'

She looked around the club curiously. 'I've been here before, for a concert. It looks different in the off hours.'

'All smoke and magic, I assume. Mr Thorne, your friend Bernice's attorney, is part owner of this club.'

'I know. That's why I came – to observe Mr Thorne. I wanted to get a look at the man who's helping Bernie. This has been a nightmare for her. If he has to drop her case, I don't know what she'll do.'

'I'll be taking on her case,' Frederick assured her. 'At no charge. I understand you called Mrs Brown last Friday and warned her that someone was asking where she was.'

'Yes. He said his name was Detective Hooper. I don't talk to people I don't know on the phone. You hear of scams every day. He might have been hired by Bernie's husband, who is a complete piece of garbage.'

'So you told him nothing?'

'Not a thing. Not really. I gave him an address where he could find Bernie, but it was just a vacant lot at the trailer park. Plus, he was trying too hard. Gave me the creeps. I called the police department he claimed to be with. They'd never heard of him.'

'You were very smart to be cautious.'

'Some people say I'm paranoid.'

'Some people are careless. You were not.' He'd drilled that kind of caution into his daughters. He approved of Miss Brewster's vigilance in this regard, even though she needed to block her Facebook page. 'Do you have the number he called from?'

'Yes.' She found it in her cell phone call log. 'I think it's fake. I tried calling it back.'

'From this phone?'

She gave him a small smile. 'No. From a payphone outside the grocery store. Like I said, he gave me the creeps.'

'Good.' He wrote the number down. 'Is there anything else you can remember about the call? Any background noises?'

She frowned thoughtfully. 'Birds.'

'Birds? Like . . . outside in a tree?'

'No, more like . . . at the beach. Seagulls.'

Frederick's pulse took a leap. 'That's good to know. What else?'

'He had a little bit of a Southern accent. Not at first. It came out

150

when he started to get annoyed with me. That's when I hung up on him. Sorry, I wish I could tell you more.'

'Do you think you'd recognize his voice if you heard it again?'

She looked uncertain. 'Maybe. I've read that voice recognition is even less reliable than eyewitness testimony.'

And she was well read too. 'That can be true. Sometimes it's enough to give the police a search warrant, though.'

Her brows rose. 'I would have thought you'd be against helping the police to get warrants.'

He wasn't offended. It was a common misconception that defense attorneys lived to thwart the police. 'Not necessarily. If the warrant is executed legally and there really is due cause for its issuance, then that satisfies the law. That is the expectation that every defendant should be allowed to have.'

She nodded slowly. 'I see. Do you think Bernie has a chance in court?'

'Yes, I do. I've read her file, I've spoken with her, and I've consulted with two of the other attorneys in the practice. I'll do my very best for her.'

She nodded again. Then she squared her shoulders. 'I knew who you were before I came here,' she stated baldly. 'I wanted to check you out, both for my own safety and for Bernie's. She's putting her life in your hands.'

Frederick sat back in the chair, wondering where she was going with this. Why she seemed so defensive. 'Checking me out was prudent. You should know that I checked you out too. You really need to change your Facebook privacy settings.'

She sucked in a surprised breath. 'Oh. I had no . . .' Her cheeks bloomed pink. 'I will. Thank you.'

'You're welcome.' He started to rise, but she held up her hand.

'I'm not finished.' She waited until he'd resettled himself. 'I checked on you a little more deeply than you checked on me.' She lifted her brows. 'You don't have a Facebook page.'

And he was the tiniest bit smug about that. 'True.'

'But you do have an Internet presence. Or your daughters do, at least.'

He drew a very deep breath. 'What do you mean?' he asked ominously.

She didn't blink. 'I mean that your daughter Taylor was in the papers last year for helping to take down that man who murdered his wife and threatened his little girl. Jazzie. I tried to call her, by the way. Taylor, I mean. I posed as a reporter. She wouldn't answer any of my questions. However, your other daughter did.'

'That's impossible,' he said flatly. Because Daisy only accepted calls from numbers she knew. Otherwise she'd have blown her travel budget on cellular fees and not easels and paint in Paris. Besides, he monitored her bills. Closely. He'd never tell her, but he watched her credit card receipts for trips to the liquor store or the wine shop. He'd allowed her alcoholism to run unchecked for too long the first time. He was not making the same mistake twice.

Her drinking had been his fault, after all. He'd been trying to give her 'space' then, which was ludicrous considering he'd all but sentenced her to a life of seclusion on the ranch in California for her entire adolescence. And all that after he'd already lost one daughter to addiction. Thinking about Carrie hurt too much, so he focused on the children he could still save.

Yes, he continued to watch over Daisy as best he could, and from the accounts he'd received from those around her, she was clean and sober and happy. Just as she should be. And due to this vigilance, he was quite certain that she'd taken no calls from strange phone numbers. At least not from the US to Europe.

He stared Miss Brewster down coolly. 'You must be mistaken.'

'No, I'm not. Julie was quite frank with me on the phone.'

Frederick drew a shocked breath. '*What?*' Hearing someone say his daughter's name was like taking a high-voltage jolt. Julie was the youngest of his four daughters and . . . special. Born with cerebral palsy, she also had an intellectual disability. At twenty-one, she read at a fourth grade level, although she thought she might be making progress at the new therapy center she attended. Regardless, he kept her safe from the world. From anyone who'd hurt her. Fury began to blaze within him at the very thought that someone, *that this woman,*

152

had breached that protective wall. 'That is impossible,' he said, his voice shaking with anger.

She gave him a sympathetic look. 'You may not have a Facebook page, Mr Dawson, but Julie does.'

'Julie's never touched a computer,' he declared, confident of that fact.

Her brows lifted. 'Because she has CP? Think again, Mr Dawson. Look, I harbor no plans to hurt you or your children. I'm a mother. I'm a nurse. But I also like to continue breathing, and this thing with Bernie is damn terrifying. Her husband stalks her, she fights back and wounds him, so he stalks her *more*. And then she gets *arrested*, for God's sake.' Her voice rose a little more at the end of every sentence. 'And then her *lawyer* gets accused of *murder*? And then her replacement lawyer asks me to meet him *alone*?' Her eyes flashed in a mixture of fear and anger. 'Damn *straight* I was going to check you out before I met you. Damn *straight* I told someone exactly where I am and who I'm with so that they know where to start looking if I fail to check in later.'

She looked away, visibly gathering her composure. When she spoke, her voice was quiet again. 'I wanted to know what kind of man you are. Your daughter Julie adores you, by the way. That's all I really wanted you to know. For her sake. But I think she's picked up more at the new therapy center than you might have realized. You might see her as a child, but just because she might read at a lower level, she is *not* a child. She doesn't speak like a child, she doesn't think like a child, and she has the needs and wants of an adult.'

Frederick could only stare at her. *Oh my God. Julie.* She had a caregiver who attended to her personal needs and who stayed with her when Frederick was working, which wasn't that often. He thought he'd been paying adequate attention. *I guess I thought wrong.* Yet again. A feeling of despair crept into his chest, making it hard for him to breathe. He'd failed another one of his daughters.

'I don't know what to say,' he managed, his voice rough and unsteady.

Sally Brewster's mouth curved sadly. 'Say thank you. And then make sure your daughter is safe. She could attract the wrong kind of attention so very easily. I couldn't have lived with myself if something happened to her and I hadn't told you.' She stood up, her hand outstretched. 'Thank you for supporting Bernie. I know she appreciates it. And please call me should you have any questions about her situation. She's my best friend.'

Frederick rose too, locking his knees to keep them from buckling, and shook her hand. 'Thank you. I'll walk you to your car.'

'That would be nice. Thank you. This isn't a bad neighborhood, especially during the day, but it's prudent to be careful.'

On autopilot, he guided her to the backstage door, but stopped before opening it as a thread of reason wound into his brain. 'Wait. How did you get my home phone number?'

'Julie gave it to me after I messaged her on Facebook.'

His jaw tightened. 'You had no right. She's a *child*. My child.'

Her eyes flashed again, and this close, he noticed they were blue. Like the sky. She opened her mouth to speak, then her anger was abruptly gone, her shoulders sagging as she met his gaze directly. 'You're right. I didn't. I apologize. She's not a child, but still, I didn't have the right. At the same time, aren't you glad it was me, and not someone . . . else? Someone who actually might want to hurt her? Now at least you know about the problem.'

He shook his head, unable to find words of absolution. Because there was nothing about this that was okay. Julie was off limits. 'Let's just go.'

But her hand had reached out to cover his as he clutched the door-knob. 'I was afraid. But you're right. I shouldn't have contacted her.'

He jerked a nod, too damn aware of her hand on his. It was gentle and . . . He swallowed hard, trying to remember how long it had been since he'd had such a simple touch from a woman. *Years*, he realized. Long before his wife had died. She'd been sick for a long time. But it was more than that. When he found out how she had lied to him for years, telling him they had to hide because Clay was a threat to Taylor . . . When he realized how much she'd stolen from all of them . . . He could no longer remember any of her touches with anything but contempt.

So it had been a long time. Maybe not since his first wife – Carrie,

Daisy and Julie's mother – had died. Twenty-one years. Too damn long. *Way* too damn long if such a simple touch had him as tongue-tied as a schoolboy.

He stared at Miss Brewster's small hand with its neat, unpolished nails. Her hands cared for people every day. This was not a woman with an evil agenda. Although he *had* believed every word Taylor's mother had said, so he would never trust his own judgment again, at least not when it came to women.

He swallowed hard, forcing himself to put himself in her place. Yes, she'd been right to be cautious. 'I suppose I understand your being afraid.'

'Well, that's kind of you,' she murmured. He thought she'd remove her hand then, but she didn't. Her gaze had dropped to their hands as well. 'But you are wrong about a few things, I think, Mr Dawson.'

'Such as?'

'Well, for starters, Julie is *not* a child. I've said that several times, but I don't think you're completely hearing me. She's a twenty-one-year-old *woman*. She might read at a lower level, but her interests and desires are most definitely adult. As are her hormones.'

He sucked in another startled breath. 'What do you mean?'

She glanced up at him, a small smile on her lips. 'She has a boyfriend.'

He blinked at her, shocked once again. 'What? Who?'

'His name is Stan and she met him at their therapy center. I'm sure they are adequately chaperoned while there, but you might want to talk to her about it. You know, about birth control.'

Frederick winced. He couldn't help it. 'Oh my God.'

Miss Brewster's smile grew rueful. 'Be gentle when you talk to her. She's afraid you'll "have a cow, man".'

He pounced on the phrase, because the thought of Julie having a boyfriend – and needing birth control, for God's sake – was messing with his brain. 'So she's watching *The Simpsons* too? I must really be falling down on the job.'

Miss Brewster's small smile faded. 'She worries about you, you know.'

155

Once again, he blinked. 'About me? Why?'

Sadness filled her expressive eyes. 'You should talk to her, Mr Dawson.'

Dread felt like a sixteen-ton weight on his chest, and he dragged in a harsh breath. 'You're not helping, Miss Brewster.' He could see her choosing her words carefully. 'You are scaring me. Just spit it out. Please.'

She sighed. 'All right. Julie sees more than you know. She knows you're worried about Daisy.'

'She told you about Daisy?'

A nod. 'She loves her sisters very much. She told me about Taylor, who is apparently a cross between Wonder Woman and Annie Oakley.'

That made him smile a little. 'That's accurate.'

But Miss Brewster did not smile. 'She told me about Carrie. She misses her.'

Frederick felt the blood drain from his face and the hand on his tightened.

'She knows you feel guilty that Daisy drank too much,' she continued, 'and that you sent her to "camp". She knows you had some mini-strokes last year. She's not sure if you're telling her the truth when you say that you're okay.'

He felt like he'd been shot. Multiple times. 'I . . . didn't know that she knew.'

'Like I said, she seems to absorb more than you think. She doesn't want to worry you any more than you already are. But she wants more from her life than she has at the moment. She knows you've made sacrifices for your girls – all of them, including her. She doesn't want you to think she's not grateful, because she is. She's worried you'll think she doesn't love you, but she does.'

He stared, the deluge of information smacking hard against the wall of his brain. 'How long did you talk to her?'

'About an hour. She sounded eager for someone to talk to. Her caregiver has an addiction to *The View* and won't allow Julie to bother her when the show is on.'

He gaped at her. 'The caregiver came recommended.'

Miss Brewster's smile was gentle. 'I'm sure she did. And how you deal with that is your business. I can recommend some other agencies, though. If you'd like.'

He nodded, even though a small corner of his mind remained suspicious. It would be an excellent way for her to get more information. Although it appeared that she'd already harvested plenty. She knew his secrets. Not all of them, for sure, but enough.

'Or not,' she added, as if sensing his suspicion. She gave his hand an encouraging stroke before pulling hers away. 'I won't keep you any longer.'

He shook his head hard, trying to clear it. 'Oh, right. Of course. I was about to walk you to your car.' He opened the backstage door. 'After you.'

Baltimore, Maryland,
Monday 13 June, 10.55 A.M.

Gwyn ended the call with a mix of satisfaction and frustration. 'I got an appointment with Angie's salon.'

Phil turned from the front seat of Jamie's van. 'What time?'

She made a face. 'Not until tomorrow at five thirty. She's penciling me in.'

Phil's eyes twinkled. 'I was impressed. I would have given you an appointment for sure. And maybe even a trousseau.'

Gwyn's cheeks heated. She'd been hesitant to use the elopement ploy with Thorne sitting beside her. It seemed . . . cruel. But they needed to get to the bottom of this tangled mess, so she would do what she needed to do. 'I wasn't sure if she was going to buy my story, but I guess she's a bit of a romantic. Elopement is always good for a fashion emergency. That way I'll have her just style it in an up-do without taking scissors to me.'

Thorne narrowed his eyes at her. 'Don't let her dare touch your hair with scissors. It's perfect the way it is.'

Gwyn's heart did a little dance inside her chest at the compliment, but also at the fierce way he was staring at her. She wondered if that look had always been there and she simply hadn't noticed. It did wonders for her ego, that was for damn sure. 'I won't. It's taken me four years to get it this long again.' Evan had cut it short because he knew she loved her hair. But then she cursed her words when a shadow passed over Thorne's face.

'I'm sorry,' he said quietly. 'I didn't think.'

'It's all right, Thorne,' she assured him. 'We can't keep walking on eggshells about it. Evan did . . .'

Things to me. Terrible things. And I can't go there. Not today. And never with Thorne. She'd told the story in counseling. That would have to be enough. Chopping off her hair was the least of the things he'd done.

She exhaled, then drew in another breath. 'I'm learning to move on, to not let it control my every decision. Honestly, his cutting my hair seems trivial compared to all the things he did to other people.' *And to me.*

'But it was a reminder whenever you looked into a mirror,' Phil said gently.

Gwyn shrugged uncomfortably. Her reflection hadn't really mattered. She hadn't looked in a mirror for months afterward. 'Yeah, well, it grew back.'

Jamie glanced at her in the rear-view mirror. 'Who is Amber Kelly?'

It was the name under which she'd made the salon appointment. 'My alter ego. Amber Kelly was my stage name when I was with the circus. I was a tween when *Saved by the Bell* was in its first run. I was a fan.'

'I thought that might have been the case,' Phil said with a knowing nod.

Jamie frowned. 'I'm not seeing the connection.'

'Because you never taught middle school or high school,' Phil said with an indulgent smile for Gwyn. 'Tiffani Amber Thiessen played Kelly Kapowski. She was the main character on the show. Definitely the good-girl overachiever. Kelly was the most popular girl in the school.'

'I wanted to be her so badly,' Gwyn confessed. 'I copied her hairstyle and everything.'

'Why?' Phil asked.

'She had it all. Looks, good grades, lots of friends. She was the head cheerleader and everyone loved her.' *And don't I sound pathetic?* She shrugged. 'It was pure escapism.'

'And then you actually joined the circus?' Jamie asked. 'I always thought that was just your stage story.'

'Yes, I was the kid who ran away to join the circus,' she said with a self-deprecating laugh. 'Good times. So we need to be in Bethesda at five thirty tomorrow. What's next?'

Thorne shot her a curious look at her topic change, but didn't press her to share more. Neither did the men up front, for which she was grateful. Thorne knew part of her circus story, but not all. And certainly not the painful parts. She'd been far too raw to share them when they'd first met. And now she was far too vulnerable. So those stories would stay locked in the vault until she was ready to bring them out.

'We're almost at the home of Brent Kiley, one of the EMTs who brought Richard into the ER,' Jamie said.

'Where did you get his address?' Thorne asked.

'From Anne.' Jamie glanced at them in the mirror again. 'I gave her the names of anyone we hadn't yet located. She's been working on addresses all morning.'

'Anne's at our office?' Thorne asked sharply. 'All alone? She might not be safe. And there have to be a million reporters swarming the area.'

'More like four million,' Jamie said grimly. 'And no, she's not at the office. Frederick had already told everyone on the payroll to stay home today. Anne can access all the search websites we use from wherever she is. She uses a proxy program, so nothing she does can be traced to her. But she's . . . nervous about her job. Understandably.'

That didn't surprise Gwyn. The firm's receptionist was young and rather timid. Her boss being accused of murder wasn't something she'd process easily.

Thorne tensed. 'Did you tell her that she shouldn't be? That I didn't do it?'

'Of course I did,' Jamie chided gently. 'She doesn't know you as well as we do.'

Thorne snorted. 'She's worked for me for a year.'

'And I've known you for nineteen.' Jamie sighed. 'Locating addresses will keep her busy. Give her less time to worry. It's a win-win.'

'I'm surprised she didn't have them all in her head already,' Gwyn said dryly. The young woman was organized to a fault. She'd overhauled the firm's filing system in her first week and knew where everything was located. She also remembered everyone's birthday, at both the firm and Sheidalin, making sure Thorne sent at least a card to everyone.

'Anne's good, but not quite that good. I heard back from Lucy.' Thorne studied his phone. 'She texted about Kirby Gilson.'

'The ME tech that was killed,' Gwyn murmured. She'd had a terrible feeling about what they'd learn when they dug deeper into the man's background. 'What did she find out?'

'That Eileen Gilson, Kirby's widow, lives in Chevy Chase, in the really ritzy part. Her son, who did not die of leukemia – thank goodness – now goes to a private university. Mrs Gilson doesn't have an income-generating job. She participates in a lot of charities.'

'But she's living well if she's got a place in Chevy Chase,' Phil said quietly. 'So we add her to the list?'

Gwyn nodded. 'Absolutely. I mean, I can understand selling out to pay for your child's health care, but it sounds like she's continued to receive benefits from *someone*. I wonder if we can get into her bank records.'

'JD can – if we give him the information,' Jamie said. He parked the van in front of an apartment complex. 'For now, let's talk to this EMT. Brent Kiley has been a medic for twenty-five years. That's all we know about him at this point. I'm still waiting on the address for the other EMT, his partner back then. If Anne hasn't found it by the time we're done here, we'll move on to Richard's posse. Darian Hinman, VP of his daddy's business, is first on the list.'

'Who's going in?' Thorne asked. 'It looks like the places are small. We don't want to overwhelm the guy with all four of us.'

Phil was eyeing the lobby of the building balefully. 'I see stairs, but no elevator. What floor does this guy live on?'

'Third,' Jamie muttered. 'Shit.'

'If it's a walkup, Thorne and I will take it,' Gwyn said quickly. She didn't want Phil taxing himself on stairs, but she wouldn't say it out loud since they weren't supposed to know about his heart condition. 'You two stay here and figure out where we're going next.'

Thorne shot her a grateful look. *Thank you*, he mouthed.

'You need witnesses, Thorne,' Jamie said through clenched teeth. 'Remember? Unimpeachable alibis?'

'Gwyn can be my witness. I won't cause any trouble, Jamie. I promise.'

He waited until they were in the lobby to bend down and whisper in Gwyn's ear. 'Thank you. I wasn't sure how to keep Phil from overdoing it.'

She patted his arm. 'I know. We'll keep him covered, okay?'

His arm tensed under her palm and his eyes skittered away. 'Okay. Let's go see if Brent Kiley is home. We may have to try him at the firehouse if he's not here.'

Brent Kiley was home. He opened his door looking rumpled and bleary-eyed, as if he'd just tumbled out of bed. His sweatpants had grass stains on the knees and his T-shirt was on inside-out. His graying hair stuck up in all directions. Clearly they'd dragged him out of bed.

'I'm not interested,' he snapped, and started to slam his door.

'We're not selling anything,' Gwyn said, leaning forward enough to put her palm on the wood. 'I promise. We just want to ask you a question.'

Kiley's eyes had dropped to her bosom, and a familiar fear shivered down her spine. Her blouse was conservative. She showed no cleavage whatsoever, but that never seemed to matter. She resisted the urge to step back, to flee. Barely.

But only because Thorne was standing behind her. His very presence made her feel safe.

'Mr Kiley,' she said sharply, channeling her old self.

His gaze lifted to meet hers, his expression growing dark. 'If this is about the Bettuzi case, I can't talk about it.'

Gwyn blinked once, startled for a second. Recovering, she shook her head. 'It's not. This is about a call you responded to nineteen years ago.'

Brent Kiley had been staring at Gwyn, but now he seemed to realize that Thorne was there. His bleary eyes widened and he took a step back. 'What do you want?' he asked, a thread of panic in his voice.

'Not to hurt you,' Thorne replied calmly. 'Do you . . . do you know me?'

Brent shook his head, but his eyes told a different story. 'I saw you on the news, is all. You killed some woman. Why are you even out, walking the streets?'

'Because he's not guilty,' Gwyn snapped. 'Look, we need to ask you a question and we'd appreciate a straight answer. Can we come in? This may not be a topic you want your neighbors to overhear.' With her head she gestured left, where a door had opened a sliver. 'And that one is listening to every word we say.'

Brent scowled, holding up his phone. 'Fine, but I'm dialing 911 if you make a move I don't like.'

That he so readily agreed was a blinking neon sign that he knew something – hopefully something he wanted to tell them. No sane person would allow into his apartment a man Thorne's size who'd also been accused of vicious murder.

The inside of the apartment was typical man-cave, Gwyn thought. Empty pizza boxes were piled high on a dinette table and the trash overflowed with beer cans and paper plates. It gave her new appreciation for the neatnik Thorne was. She'd never seen his place messy, except for the previous morning. It had been her first clue that something was wrong.

Brent went into the kitchen and called, 'You want a beer?'

'No, thanks,' Gwyn replied. 'Too many carbs.'

He emerged with a can and popped the top. 'Huh. I figured you'd tell me that it wasn't even noon.'

Gwyn shrugged. 'I run a nightclub. It's five o'clock somewhere.'

'True. My schedule at the firehouse fucks with my brain. I never know what the hell time it is.' He gestured to a sofa that was quite nice. And clean. 'You want to sit?'

'Sure,' Gwyn said.

'I'll stand,' Thorne rumbled.

'Yeah,' Brent muttered as he flopped into a ratty recliner. 'You do that. So, what's your fuckin' question?'

'Richard Linden,' Gwyn said levelly, aware of Thorne standing right next to the edge of the sofa, within grabbing distance if she needed him. 'You responded to the scene of his murder.'

'Yeah,' he said shortly. 'I remember. Kid was carved up like a deer.' He glanced over at Thorne. 'You were arrested for that.'

'And tried, and cleared,' Thorne said, menace edging into his tone.

'Yeah, I remember that too. What do you want to know?'

'Yesterday's victim was Patricia Linden Segal, Richard's sister.'

Brent froze, the beer can only an inch from his lips. Slowly he lowered it and put it on a side table. 'What?'

'Yeah.' Gwyn tilted her head. 'I'm surprised you hadn't heard.'

'I did a shift yesterday. I caught the murder on the news before I started. When I finished my shift, I came home and fell into bed. You woke me up.'

'Sorry,' Gwyn murmured. 'I work nights too. I hate to be woken up.'

He waved his hand. 'Whatever. What's your question?'

Gwyn focused on his face, watching for any flicker of guilt. 'Did you see any foreign object in Richard Linden's body when you transported him to the ER that day?'

'Yes,' he answered readily, making Gwyn blink again. Beside her, Thorne stiffened.

'What?' he asked. 'Really?'

'Yeah.' Brent shrugged. 'I told the cop what I saw. Not the detective, but the first-responder cop. Nobody ever followed up and nobody ever mentioned it. And if you tell anyone I told you, I'll call you a liar.' He straightened abruptly, frowning again. 'Are you wired?'

163

Gwyn rolled her eyes. 'No.'

'Good. Nobody ever threatened *me*.'

Gwyn's brows shot up, struck by his odd segue and the emphasis on *me*. 'But your partner was threatened?' she guessed.

Brent just toasted her with his beer can. 'He pushed because it wasn't in the police report. The cops gave some song and dance about how they were holding it back so that they'd have details only the killer would know. I figured it was healthier to keep my mouth shut.' He opened his arms and gestured broadly to the room. 'And here I am.'

'Where's your partner?' Thorne asked quietly.

Because neither Jamie nor Anne had been able to find his address.

Brent shrugged. 'Don't know. He up and walked a few months after your trial. Well, limped. Had a car accident. Some asshole came at him broadside, shoved him off the road and into a ravine. He managed to climb out with a broken leg. When he got the cast off, he quit and walked. Never saw him again.'

'So why are you telling us this now?' Thorne asked.

'I'm not,' Brent said with a slight smile. 'I said nothing.'

'Meaning you won't tell anyone else,' Thorne said with a frown. 'Like the cops, even if this is important somehow.'

Brent shook his head. 'You were a nice kid,' he murmured. 'You stayed there at Richard's side and did all you could to save that prick's life. If you hadn't been acquitted, I'd planned to tell what I knew to the papers. That evidence had been manipulated. But you were acquitted. And I liked my legs, attached and unbroken. So I shut up.'

From the corner of her eye, Gwyn saw Thorne nod. 'Did your old partner see the truck that hit him?' he asked.

Brent gave Thorne a mock salute. 'I saw what you did there. I never said it was a truck.'

'Was it?' Thorne asked levelly.

Another shrug. 'Yeah. Just like the one that killed your girlfriend the year before. Scared the shit out of me. So I kept quiet. Call me a coward, but I had kids to feed.' He looked around him morosely.

'Not anymore, though. They're in college, and when they come home, they stay with their mother.'

'You're divorced,' Gwyn said softly. 'When?'

Another salute. 'You're smart,' he said with undisguised admiration. His eyes dropped to her breasts again, then jerked back up to her face when Thorne growled. 'My wife left me right after his trial.' He pointed at Thorne. 'I'd started drinking. Partly because I was so damn scared that truck would come after me or my kids. Partly because I knew I'd stayed silent to save my own skin and I was ashamed. So, now you know it all. I won't share this again. With anyone.'

'Got it,' Gwyn murmured. 'Okay. Thank you for your honesty. You take care of yourself, okay?'

He nodded, but didn't move from the recliner. 'You can show yourselves out.'

Gwyn rose and left, Thorne close behind her. 'That was enlightening,' he murmured when they were back in the hall, headed for the stairs.

'Yeah. I'm thinking we're not going to find his old partner. If he's still alive, he's reinvented himself as someone new.'

'I agree. You were good in there. Thank you.'

She smiled up at him. 'Come on, let's get back to the van so you can stop looking around for ninja assassins.'

Because he was, his eyes constantly circling, checking the corners for anyone lurking. 'Fine,' he grunted. 'And for the record, I really don't like assholes like him checking you out like that.'

Surprised, she could only stare up at him as they made their way down the stairs to the lobby. 'I . . . I wasn't provoking him.'

He shot her a startled glance. 'I know that. Did I say that?'

'No.'

'I never even implied it, and if I did, I'm sorry. I just meant that I don't like it. It's disrespectful.' He hesitated for a moment. 'And I wanted to rip him apart for making you feel afraid.'

'I wasn't afraid.'

He glanced down. 'No?'

She smiled up. 'No. I knew you were there.'

The taut line of his jaw seemed to relax. 'Good,' he said as they exited the apartment building. The sun was bright and Gwyn stopped abruptly, dropping her head to keep the glare from her eyes while she searched her handbag for her sunglasses.

Then it all seemed to blur. Glass shattered and she was suddenly being launched to the grassy area to the left of the sidewalk. She coughed when Thorne landed on top of her, nearly suffocating because her face was buried in the grass. She struggled, her protests coming out as muffled noise.

The weight pressing her into the ground receded as Thorne braced his body on his forearms. 'Stay down,' he barked. 'Somebody just shot at us. At you.'

What the fuck? Her breath was coming faster, warm against her face because the pocket of air was so small. *Thorne.* He was vulnerable, all six and a half feet of him. She wanted to throw him off her, to drag him to safety, but she couldn't move and he wouldn't budge.

Behind them, a vehicle gunned its engine and approached. How? They were at least fifty feet from the parking lot. It came to a screeching stop on the sidewalk, and suddenly Thorne's weight was gone, and Gwyn was scooped up in strong arms and all but thrown through the open side door of Jamie's van. She landed on the floor between the front and middle seats, pain streaking up her back.

'Hurry!' Jamie barked.

Thorne climbed in behind her and the van sped away before he could even close the door. It shut automatically and she could see a white-faced Phil looking around wildly, his cell phone in his hand. He'd called 911 and was on the line with the operator now.

Jamie threw the van into reverse, drove across the grass to the parking lot, and took off with a squeal of tires. 'Stay down. All of you.'

'Where are you going?' Phil demanded.

'I have no fucking clue,' Jamie snarled, then ground his teeth and grabbed his partner's hand, quieting his voice. 'Yeah, I do. To the hospital. I'm getting everyone checked out. No arguments.'

'All right,' Phil said calmly. He spoke into the phone. 'We're going to the closest hospital . . . No, I don't think it's smart for us to stay put.' He glanced back at Thorne. 'You can send your officers to the address I just gave you. We'll be at the hospital if they wish to interview us.' He gave the operator his phone number, then disconnected. 'I'm all right, Jamie,' he said quietly.

Jamie's nod was frantic. 'Let's make sure, okay?'

Gwyn stared at Thorne's pale face. 'What the fuck just happened?'

'You were almost shot in the head,' he whispered. 'If you hadn't stopped to look in your bag . . .'

'For my sunglasses,' she murmured, still feeling numb. 'My bag's back there somewhere. My ID is in it. I'll need it back.'

'We'll have the cops pick it up. We're not going back there.' Thorne was already punching a number into his phone. 'JD? It's Thorne. We have a situation.'

Ten

He hit the button on his intercom when it buzzed. 'Yes, Jeanne?'

'Mr Patton is on line one, sir.'

He pressed the blinking button. 'Yes, Mr Patton? What news do you have for me?'

'I did what you said to do,' Patton said, his confusion still evident from his tone.

'Excellent.' He consulted the notes on his desk. 'Your next mark will soon be leaving a Greek restaurant at the corner of Old Georgetown and Wisconsin. The place is called Kaia's Kouzina.'

'Same instructions?'

'Yes. Call me when it's done. I'll have the next mark and the next location.'

'Yes, sir.'

He hung up the phone, pleased. Patton was following his orders without question. Finally. The man was also acquiring manners. It was about time.

A soft knock on his door had him looking up. And then smiling. His daughter-in-law stood in the doorway, her blond hair shining like gold in the light coming through the porthole window. 'Margo. What can I do for you?'

She didn't smile back. In fact, she looked very worried. 'I got a call from the babysitter. Benny is running a slight temperature, just a degree.'

He straightened. 'He was fine last night!'

'Yes, he was, but sometimes babies get fevers. He could simply be teething. But I'd like to go home, if it's all right. I can take care of your to-do list from home if you grant me remote access to the office network.'

'Of course.' He had to tell himself not to panic, that she was right, that all babies got fevers sometimes. 'Should we take him to the doctor?'

'No, Papa. But if this continues, I promise I'll take him in.'

'Of course you will,' he murmured. It was just that the thought of losing Benny . . . The boy was all he had left of his son. 'Call me and let me know how he's doing.'

'Of course I will.'

He frowned at her, because she looked a lot more worried than was warranted by a teething toddler. 'What are you not telling me?'

She drew a breath. 'You're not going to like it.'

He forced himself to remain calm. 'It's not just a teething fever, is it?'

'Yes! It really is. Benny will be fine. This is something else.'

'That I will not like.'

'Right.' She squared her shoulders. 'You remember Bernice Brown?'

'Yes. That was only two days ago, Margo. I've not become forgetful in my dotage,' he added, his lightly mocking tone carrying a definitive warning. Just because she was his daughter-in-law and the mother of his grandson didn't mean she could treat him with disrespect.

She blushed, embarrassed. 'I'm sorry. I didn't mean that.'

'Good. So. Bernice Brown? The woman who supposedly called Thorne to lure him out of his home on Saturday night.' It would have been far simpler to attack him *in* his home. Except getting into his home had proven difficult. The man had an excellent security system. So they'd decided that luring him out was more effective.

'Yes, her. Well, one of the things we did before using her name was to find her and make sure she couldn't tell anyone that she hadn't made the call.'

'Exactly. Patton located her and eliminated her.'

169

She winced. 'Well, he thought he had.'

He came to his feet, his fury white-hot. 'What? What do you mean?'

'He set fire to the trailer she was living in. Or so he thought. But she'd moved, and the trailer he burned wasn't hers. She and her cousin had relocated to a new park. It wasn't Patton's fault,' she added quickly. 'He contacted her best friend, posing as a cop. She gave him the address, but it turned out it was the wrong one.'

'And how do you know this?' he asked coldly.

'Because we have eyes on Thorne's nightclub, and the friend – Sally Brewster – met with one of Thorne's attorneys this morning. I don't know what they discussed, but I was concerned that they'd connected at all. I checked the victims of Patton's fire. They were not Bernice Brown and her cousin. The occupants were a professor on sabbatical and her husband. They'd just arrived at the park.'

He lowered himself back to his chair. 'I see.'

Her eyes were wide and full of entreaty. 'Please, Papa, if you're going to blame anyone, blame me. Patton thought he was doing the right thing. I should have visited and made sure it was the right address.'

He nodded slowly. 'It was an honest mistake,' he said stiffly. Mistakes happened. He'd even made one or two himself. *Million*, he added bitterly. 'Does Patton know of his mistake?'

'Yes.' She hesitated. 'I just told him. He is understandably concerned about your reaction.'

As he should be. 'All right.' He quickly considered his options. He could eliminate Patton and move to the next person in his organization. He'd reminded Patton of the cost of failure just hours before. It was reasonable to believe that the man would be even more vigilant – and obedient – from here on out.

'What would you do?' he asked Margo, curious to know her thoughts. She might sit behind this desk someday. It was time to begin her training.

She bit her lip. 'I think mercy in this situation would create an even more loyal employee. I like Patton. He's smart and ambitious.

I think he's keen to take on more responsibility. I'd leave him in place. He'll work harder to please you.'

'My thoughts exactly. You mentioned that Mrs Brown's friend met with one of Thorne's attorneys. Which one?'

'Frederick Dawson. He's new to Thorne's firm, recently relocated from California.'

His brows lifted, the name all too familiar. 'Dawson?'

She nodded, immediately understanding his question. 'He's related to the woman who was involved in the Jarvis case. Dawson's daughter, Taylor, was providing equine therapy to Jarvis's daughter, Jazzie.'

Because the child had seen her mother murdered. Jarvis had tried to murder the therapist, but Taylor Dawson had shot back, wounding him. That had been the moment his relationship with Jarvis had ended. Unfortunately, not before he'd been linked to the despicable man. By Thomas Thorne, of course. Thorne had provided photographic proof to the police that Jarvis had dined with him in his favorite Italian restaurant.

He'd been furious at the time. He still was. But his confusion over how Thorne had obtained that photograph had led him to an investigation of all of his employees, which had revealed Ramirez to have been the traitor. Now Ramirez was dead. But it had given the police cause to watch him. He'd had to be careful where and when he appeared in public ever since. He always had a tail he needed to lose.

It was the reason he now did business on his yacht. The police didn't know of its existence, so he was left free to conduct himself as he saw fit.

That anyone connected to the disaster of the Jarvis case was now poking around in his business was extremely annoying.

'Do we know where to find Mr Dawson?' he asked, his tone clipped.

'I'm sure I can find out.'

'Please do. You may do that from home, once you're certain that Benny is all right. Go now. Call me if he worsens.'

She nodded once. 'I will. I'll send you Dawson's address and I'll

171

keep you updated.' She closed the door behind her as she left.

Margo was a good mother. He should trust her. Still, he'd have his personal physician look in on the baby this afternoon. Because she *should* have checked the address before Patton torched a perfectly good trailer. He'd be second-guessing her decisions for the foreseeable future, but she had a good head on her shoulders. She'd make a worthy successor, given the proper training.

She was young. They had lots of time.

Baltimore, Maryland,
Monday 13 June, 12.45 P.M.

This is all my fault. All my damn fucking fault. Thorne paced back and forth in the small ER cubicle. The beds here were separated only by curtains, unlike the hospital where he'd been taken yesterday, where there were rooms with physical walls. And doors.

That could stop bullets. Or at least slow them down. He gave the curtain a smack and a curse. Which was met with an aggravated sigh from the woman sitting on the bed.

'Thorne, stop it,' Gwyn snapped. 'You're driving me nuts. It's going to make my blood pressure go up and they won't let me fucking leave.' She drew in a breath that flared her nostrils. 'Come here. Now.'

Grudgingly he obeyed, sitting on the edge of the bed when she patted it. 'Jamie and Phil are in that cubicle right next to us, and Phil's health might depend on you staying calm. Okay?'

He closed his eyes. 'You're almost as good at guilting me as they are.'

'I watch and learn,' she said wryly. She took his hand and squeezed it hard. 'I'm fine. I have a few bruises. You're fine. Those two over there are shaken up, but they're fine too.' She hooked a finger in his collar to pull him closer, smoothing her palm over his cheek. He leaned into the caress, drinking her in. 'You saved my life. You did good.'

He let her voice soothe him. 'You're not going out with me again.'

'Oh yes I am,' she said in a murmur. 'The faster we figure this

172

out, the faster we can get back to our lives, currently in progress.'

He huffed a low chuckle, then once again remembered the terror of hearing that glass break behind her. It had been the plate-glass window of the building's lobby, shattering into a million tiny fragments. He probably still had glass in his hair. Which didn't matter. Gwyn was safe. That was all that mattered.

She was safe. But she'd been targeted. Shot at. *Dammit. Because of me.*

'Not your fault,' she murmured, as if reading his thoughts. 'But do the others know? They should take precautions.'

The others. All of their closest friends. The people who'd banded together to save his sorry ass. If one of them got hurt, lost a single drop of blood . . . *I'll never forgive myself.*

'They need to go under,' he muttered. 'Into a fucking bunker.'

'That's not going to happen,' Gwyn said pragmatically. 'Look at me.' She tapped his cheek with one finger until he obeyed, meeting her gaze. 'They want to help you. Clay, Stevie, Paige? Sam and Ruby? All of them investigate crime for a living. The others have done so as part of their jobs, risking their lives – and for strangers, Thorne. People that walk in off the damn street. You're family. They are going to help you. I am going to help you. So just accept it and we'll go on.'

Family. His heart squeezing hard, he closed his eyes and savored the feel of her palm on his cheek, her soft words in his ears.

The curtain beside them opened, revealing Phil and Jamie. Awkward to be caught in such an intimate position, Thorne lurched back and Gwyn dropped her hand to her lap. Ignoring the heating of his cheeks and the amused surprise in Jamie and Phil's eyes, Thorne studied his old teacher carefully. Phil looked so much better that he shuddered out a relieved breath.

'You're okay,' he murmured.

'He is,' Jamie confirmed. 'We're lucky.'

Phil ignored them both with an irritated wave of his hand. 'Gwyn speaks good sense. You're going to have to let us help you, Thorne. Are *you* okay, Gwyn?'

Her smile was downright sunny. 'Right as rain. You?'

He looked annoyed. 'Fine. But now you know my secret.'

'We knew last night,' Gwyn said with a shrug. 'Nobody told me, if it makes you feel better. I'm a dirty rotten eavesdropper.'

Phil's lips twitched. 'You're absolved. These two, not so much.'

'Absolved my fucking ass.' The curtain behind them parted, revealing a furious JD Fitzpatrick.

Gwyn winced. 'Go easy on us,' she whined. 'I have a headache.'

'You're right as rain,' JD parroted sarcastically. He whipped the curtain closed. 'What the ever-lovin' fuck, Thorne? You were specifically told not to go investigating this on your own.' He held a finger to his lips, then pointed over his shoulder. 'Hyatt,' he mouthed.

Fan-fucking-tastic, Thorne wanted to growl, but he kept his mouth closed because he understood. JD was playing a part, acting angry in front of Hyatt.

He frowned. But that made no sense, because JD wasn't supposed to be on his case at all. Conflict of interest and all that. Unless Hyatt had instructed him to get information. Thorne wouldn't put it past the lieutenant.

But you trust JD. He's earned it. Which was true. Hell, JD had just warned them that Hyatt was listening. So he tamped down his anger and paranoia. For now.

JD lowered his voice. 'Seriously, guys, what the fuck?'

'You knew what we were doing,' Gwyn whispered, eyes narrowed.

JD rolled his eyes. 'Not exactly,' he whispered back. 'Lucy and I agreed she shouldn't tell me. Plausible deniability and all that.' He gave all four of them the once-over. 'You're okay? Really?'

Gwyn shrugged. 'A few bruises, that's all.'

Because he'd slammed her into the ground, Thorne thought regretfully. Then tossed her into Jamie's van like she was a sack of potatoes.

'Stop,' she snapped again, but less fiercely. Clearly his poker face was nonfunctional at the moment. 'You saved my life, Thorne. A few bruises is a small price to pay.'

'You've given your statement to the locals?' JD asked.

'Kind of,' Thorne said with a shrug. 'We told them we were visiting an old friend and that we got shot at.' He pursed his lips, fighting hard against the guilt threatening to suck him back into the irrational desire to grab Gwyn, Jamie and Phil and hide on an island for the rest of their lives. 'But it wasn't "we". It was Gwyn. Once I'd covered her' – *with my body*, but he wasn't going to think about that now, even though she'd felt so damn good against him – 'there were no more shots.'

Gwyn's eyes widened, as if the reality had just suddenly hit her. 'You believed they'd shoot at you. But you still . . . Goddammit, Thorne. You believed you'd be hit and you made yourself a giant target?'

'What would you have had me do?' he snapped back. 'Let you die?'

She inhaled sharply, her lips quivering, her dark eyes growing abruptly shiny. 'No,' she whispered. 'But . . . dammit, Thorne. I don't want you hurt. I don't take up much space. Your back is a target they could see from space.'

That was true. But that wasn't his point. What *was* his point? He blinked hard, then forced himself to look at JD. 'They stopped shooting when Gwyn was covered. They could have shot me, but they didn't. They could have killed me Saturday night, but they didn't.'

'They nearly killed you Sunday morning,' Gwyn retorted.

'That was probably an accident,' JD murmured to her. 'They gave him too much GHB.' He turned to Thorne, his face growing pale as understanding dawned. 'I think you're right. They don't want to kill you, Thorne. They wanted to kill Gwyn. Because she's important to you.'

As is Lucy went unspoken. As was everyone who'd sat in Gwyn's living room promising to help him stay out of prison.

This . . . sucks. Suddenly exhausted, Thorne let his head fall forward. 'I'd just give myself over if I thought it would make this stop.'

'*Thorne*,' Phil gasped. 'Don't you dare.'

'Shh,' Jamie soothed. 'He won't. He won't even think about it again. Will you, Thorne?'

Thorne didn't have the energy to argue. He went still as Gwyn's hand smoothed over his hair. 'No, he won't,' she said quietly. 'And if he does, we'll hide *him* in a bunker.'

'I don't think it would help anyway,' JD said with grim resignation. 'Whoever's doing this is trying to fuck with your life, Thorne. Killing you is not the priority. So the only way to make it stop is to make *them* stop.'

Thorne didn't look up because Gwyn was still stroking his hair and it felt so damn good. But he was listening, and he knew JD was right. 'Then that's what I'll do,' he said quietly.

Gwyn stopped stroking his hair and gave it a gentle tug. 'Not alone, Thorne. You are not going to face this alone. The rest of us have a stake in it. I, for one, am not going to abandon you because some asshole wants to hurt you. Besides, JD's right. That wouldn't help anyway, because as long as you still care about us, you have a vulnerability. We're in this with you. So suck it up, Buttercup.'

The snort of laughter escaped him before he could contain it. 'Buttercup.' He glanced up to see her smirking at him. 'Really?'

'Yeah, really.' She looked up at JD. 'What did they find at the scene?'

'Your purse,' he said. 'It'll be held for a while as evidence. You should probably cancel your credit cards and get a new driver's license.'

'Fuck,' Gwyn muttered. 'Pain in the ass. What else? Did they find the bullet?'

'Yeah. It was embedded in one of the concrete walls inside the lobby. We got lucky. The concrete stopped it. Had it gone through, its next stop was a living room where kids were playing.'

Thorne's blood ran cold. 'Oh my God.'

'But it did *not* breach the concrete,' Gwyn told him sternly. '*Nobody* got hurt. Right, JD?'

'Right,' JD said decisively. 'Hyatt's taking the case from Montgomery County PD, because it's being linked to the murder of Patricia Linden Segal. I can't tell you much right now except that nobody saw anything. Of course.'

'Does this help clear Thorne?' Phil asked hopefully.

'Right now? No,' JD answered. 'But in the longer term it should. That's only my opinion. Who knew you all would be at that apartment building?'

Thorne's gaze met Jamie's troubled one. 'Detective Prew did,' Jamie said.

'He said he didn't know the EMT,' Phil whispered.

Jamie shook his head. 'He saw our list. He knew we'd be contacting him eventually.'

'Who is Prew?' JD asked sharply.

'The detective who handled the murder of Richard Linden,' Jamie said. 'He's retired now.'

'What did he tell you?'

'Not much,' Jamie replied non-committally, making JD scowl at him. Jamie glanced over JD's shoulder, focusing on the curtain. Where Hyatt was probably listening. He mouthed his next words. 'What we did hear, we've passed on to Lucy.'

JD's jaw tightened, but he nodded. 'So then you went to the apartment to see Brent Kiley. Why?'

Thorne answered this time. 'He was the EMT who responded to the scene of Richard Linden's murder. He was belligerent. Didn't tell us a thing.' Then he mouthed, 'Later.'

He'd tell JD everything, but he didn't trust Lieutenant Hyatt. Not with the lives of his friends, anyway.

JD nodded. 'How long were you there?'

'Only a few minutes,' Gwyn said. 'It's unlikely that was long enough for him to summon a shooter.'

'Probably not,' JD agreed. 'Who else knew?'

The four of them stared at each other for a long moment before Jamie sighed. 'I thought I'd lost all the tails this morning, but it's possible we were followed. A few news vans, a few unmarked cars. One was Hyatt's man, I'm sure of that.'

'Yeah, you lost him,' JD confirmed. 'Hyatt was pissed.'

Jamie looked pleased. '*Yesss*. I've still got it. The ability to lose tails, I mean. I never lost the ability to piss off cops.' He sobered. 'I called everyone who's helping out to warn them, just so you know.'

Thorne stared at him, surprised. 'You did that? Already?'

'He needed something to do,' Phil said indulgently. 'So I gave him the task.'

JD checked his phone. 'Lucy texted me about it. She says for you to be careful.' One side of his mouth lifted fondly. 'And that she loves you guys.'

Thorne rubbed a palm over his chest. That was bittersweet. He loved that Lucy loved him. He could only pray her love didn't get her killed along with Gwyn and all the others.

'We need to get out of here,' he said hoarsely. 'We have things to do.'

The curtain opened, revealing a very irritated-looking Lieutenant Hyatt. 'Yes, you have things to do, Mr Thorne. Like talking to me. Come with me, please. We're going to a secure location.'

Thorne didn't immediately move and the others followed his lead. 'What will we talk about, Lieutenant?'

Hyatt met his eyes directly. 'About all the people who hate you.'

'That'll take a week,' Gwyn snarked.

Thorne glared at her, then at Hyatt. 'Am I under arrest?'

'Not yet,' Hyatt replied, just as he'd done in the hospital the previous day. This time, however, the expression on his face was quite different. Yesterday he'd been frustrated and angry that Thorne wouldn't talk to him. But now . . . There was something sharper in the man's eyes. It looked like fear. 'But we need to discuss your friends.'

Yes, Thorne thought, and once again his blood ran cold, because it *was* fear in the lieutenant's eyes. Somehow he managed to keep his voice level. 'What about them?'

'At least four people in your little vigilante posse are important to me,' Hyatt responded, shocking him. 'And one of those people was just shot at. Not hit, because her husband's reflexes are as quick as yours were today.'

'Oh God,' Gwyn gasped.

'Stevie,' Thorne whispered. She was the only person that made sense. She had worked for Hyatt for years.

'Yes. She's on her way into my office.' The lieutenant drew a careful breath. 'So you *will* talk to me, Mr Thorne.'

Thorne closed his eyes. 'Yes. Let's go.'

Wight's Landing, Maryland,
Monday 13 June, 1.30 P.M.

Frederick double-checked the contents of Julie's suitcase. He thought he'd packed everything. If not, he could come back for it, but he was getting Julie out of this house and somewhere she'd be safe.

Behind him, he heard the whir of her motorized wheelchair as she entered her bedroom. 'Where are we going, Dad?' she asked, her words labored but understandable. She'd made great strides since Frederick had moved them to Maryland. Back in northern California, they'd lived in an area so remote that there hadn't been adequate physical or occupational therapy.

He zipped up the suitcase. 'You're going on a little vacation, to Clay and Stevie's house.' The couple had generously offered one of their spare rooms when Frederick had shared what Sally Brewster had told him. He was doubly grateful for it after he came home and found the caregiver parked in front of the television, just as Julie had told Sally.

He'd fired the woman on the spot. He still wanted to flinch at the raw hatred that had filled her eyes. *So much for recommendations.* He'd been sequestered in California for so long, his people-judging skills had grown rusty. *I used to be so much better at this.* He'd had to be, for his job. He'd have to be again, both for the work he did for Thorne and to protect his family.

Regardless, next time he hired a caregiver, he was installing a nanny-cam.

Julie's blue eyes lit up. 'To see Taylor?'

Julie and Daisy had inherited his first wife's blond hair and blue eyes. Only Carrie had looked like him. The familiar pang of guilt and grief hit him hard and fast, then dissipated because Julie was smiling at him.

'To see Taylor,' he confirmed. 'She's got a new cart for one of the horses at the farm. She's looking forward to taking you for a ride.'

Taylor was actually chomping at the bit herself, wanting to take a swing at the supposed 'caregiver' who'd been neglecting Julie.

179

She'd missed her baby sister, so this visit would be a good thing. He wouldn't have to worry about Julie with Taylor on point.

'Yay!' Julie clapped her hands, the movement perhaps appearing awkward to some, but it filled Frederick with joy. He loved seeing his baby girl so happy.

He sat on the edge of her bed so that they were eye to eye. 'We need to have a little talk, honey.'

Julie's gaze dropped. 'Are you mad at me?'

'Of course not,' he said softly. He tipped up her chin. 'But I was a little scared today. I talked to Miss Brewster.'

Julie smiled. 'She was nice.'

'She seemed so. But she's a stranger, Jules, and you gave her our phone number.'

Julie's eyes flickered with trepidation. 'Am I in trouble?'

'No, baby. But you can't do that again. Miss Brewster was nice, but some people might not be.'

Her eyes clouded with confusion. 'But Taylor's dad turned out to be nice.'

He understood the connection she'd made. And she was right to challenge him on this. He'd assumed terrible things about Clay and his children had suffered because of it.

'Yes, he did. But there are some really awful people in the world, who might try to . . .' He searched for the right words, finally deciding on the simplest. 'Hurt you.'

'All right,' she said, not sounding entirely convinced. 'Will I still be able to go to the center?'

'Yes. Maybe not for a few days, but yes, you'll go back to the center.' He gave her a sly smile. 'You want to tell me about Stan?'

She blushed so prettily. 'Daddy.'

He leaned in to kiss her cheek. 'I'd like to meet him. You know,' he added teasingly, 'to make sure he's good enough for my little girl.'

'He's very good,' Julie assured him. Then she waggled her brows, startling him into a laugh.

Miss Brewster had been right. His baby girl wasn't a baby. *God. Am I ever going to get this right?*

He loaded up the car, then secured Julie's chair in the back. His land in California hadn't sold yet, but he'd had enough investments that he'd been able to outfit her with all the things she'd needed when they moved. He was grateful for that.

He had so much to be grateful for. He had a new life here. Good friends. A job he really enjoyed.

'Daddy?' Julie said, as he got behind the wheel.

'Yes, honey?'

'I got another message. From Miss Brewster.'

He twisted in the driver's seat, frowning. What the hell was the woman doing contacting her again? Julie shrank back, her grip on her tablet faltering – the tablet he hadn't known she owned.

'Where did you get that?'

'From Miss Selma,' she said, eyes wide.

The caregiver. She'd probably given it to Julie to keep her quiet. That had *not* been their agreement. Good riddance to the woman, then. He'd need to make sure the tablet was safe, that any harmful Internet sites were blocked.

'Okay,' he said, forcing his voice to stay calm. 'What does the message say?'

'She wants to call me again. But I'm not at home.'

'I'll call her,' he assured his daughter, immediately dialing Sally Brewster's cell phone. 'Miss Brewster,' he said sternly when she answered.

'Mr Dawson?' she replied cautiously.

He was going to dive right in. 'Why did you message Julie again?'

Julie looked up from her tablet, where she was now watching a video of cats sitting in small boxes.

'But I didn't,' Miss Brewster exclaimed. 'I swear to you.'

'Oh.' He felt curiously embarrassed. But terrified. All at once. Because . . .

'Somebody messaged her?' Her voice became alarmed as well. 'Pretending to be me?'

Smart lady, cutting right to the chase. 'Yeah.'

She was quiet for a moment. 'Like someone called Mr Thorne

pretending to be Bernie? Or like someone called me pretending to be a cop?'

An unpleasant chill ran down his spine. 'Perhaps,' he said, maintaining his calm for Julie's sake. 'I'm going to check into this. Where are you right now?'

'I just walked into work. I'm on second shift.'

'Stay there, please. Around a lot of people. Don't leave, even to take a break.'

'I won't,' she promised, sounding appropriately afraid. 'Call me to let me know that Julie is okay.'

'She's with me now. We're temporarily relocating.'

'Good. Just let me know how you are.'

'Call me as well.'

'I'll do my best.'

They ended the call and Frederick drew a breath. 'Julie, honey, can I see your tablet?'

She frowned at him. 'You'll give it back?'

'Yes,' he promised.

She handed it to him. He opened her messaging app and looked through her communication.

'How are you reading this?' he asked. Julie's reading comprehension was not this advanced.

'VR, Daddy.'

He lifted his gaze to hers. 'What is that?'

'Voice . . .' Her brow wrinkled. 'It talks to me. I tap it.'

He tapped the message and a computerized voice read the message. 'From Sally: Can I call you again?'

Again. Dread was like a live wire, shocking his body from the inside out. If Sally Brewster was telling the truth, someone knew she'd called Julie already. He thought back to when he'd dropped her off at her car. Still shaken by their conversation inside the club, he'd asked her to contact him if Julie called her again and she'd agreed. If someone had been following them, they could have overheard. They would have known Julie would respond to a message from Sally. Or, if Sally was lying, she could have set it up. Either way, he needed to get to the bottom of this.

He typed into the messaging app: *I'm not at home. Why do you want to call?*

A new message popped up. *I have a present for you. I want to know where to send it.*

His hand shaking, Frederick clicked on the information button, to see from what number the message had originated.

He couldn't control his gasp. The message was from the same number that had called Sally Brewster. The number used by a man who'd posed as a cop.

Baltimore, Maryland,
Monday 13 June, 1.45 P.M.

This is a fucking nightmare, Gwyn thought as she, Thorne, Phil and Jamie followed Lieutenant Hyatt through the maze of desks leading from the elevator to Hyatt's conference room at the Baltimore PD headquarters. They were a depressed-looking bunch, all worried expressions and plodding steps. Even Jamie's wheelchair seemed to be moving more slowly than usual.

Thorne was on autopilot, and Gwyn hated seeing him like this. His face was stark, his shoulders slumping wearily. He seemed to have aged twenty years in the moments after Hyatt told them that Stevie had been shot at too.

It was as if all the fight had been drained from him.

'This will not do,' she muttered. Gesturing Jamie and Phil into the conference room ahead of her, she grabbed a handful of Thorne's suit coat and yanked until he stopped walking and stared down at her.

She stared back up at him, wishing for the millionth time in her life that she were taller. 'Come here.' Keeping hold of his jacket, she led him to the nearest desk with an empty chair and pushed him into it. That he made no complaint, uttered not even one question, told her how utterly defeated he was. *This won't do. At all.*

She stepped between his spread knees, now face to face with him. Cupping his jaw in her palms, she tugged until he looked at her numbly.

'Thorne, come on,' she whispered fiercely, acutely aware that

183

several detectives at nearby desks were watching their every movement.

'And do what?' he whispered back, so bleakly it was like a knife to her heart.

'Do you remember the day you brought me out of the hospital? After Evan?'

He nodded slowly. 'That was a shitty day.'

'Why?' she asked, knowing how he'd answer.

'You were alive. But your light was gone. I couldn't find *you*.'

'But you didn't give up. You let me grieve and mourn and heal. And it took me four and a half years.'

His eyes slid closed. 'Longest years of my life.'

'Yeah. Mine too.' She stroked his cheeks with her thumbs, his stubble lightly scratching her skin. But in a welcome way. She loved touching his face. She always had. 'You let me sit in your bed and rock, and you held me until I fell asleep.'

'You remember that?'

'I remember everything,' she said quietly. Everything Evan had done to torture and hurt her. And then everything Thorne had done to help heal her.

His eyes flew open, his distress apparent. 'I hoped you hadn't. I couldn't reach you. I hoped that meant you'd escaped someplace nicer in your mind.'

'No, I was with you every moment. And I appreciate everything you did for me, every kindness.' She sighed. 'Today is another shitty day, but I'm not going to be as patient with you as you were with me. I'm going to tell you to get your head back in the game. *Now*. Because if you don't, we're never going to figure out who the hell hates your guts enough to try to pick us all off.' She gave his cheeks a light squeeze and a pat. 'I can't give you time to feel like shit and get all morose. We need you *now*, Thorne. So stop moping. Stop dragging yourself around like you're a fucking zombie. We need you.' She leaned forward until her forehead rested against his, their noses lightly touching. '*I* need you.'

He let out a shuddering breath, his hands reaching for her hips to hold her close. 'All right.'

It felt so good, so natural to be held by him this way. Like it always had, except . . . not. This moment was far more intimate than mere friends might share. And it wasn't awkward, not at all. It was right. She hesitated for a moment, then went with her gut and pressed a kiss to his forehead.

His gaze was searching, but he said nothing, just let his hands drop from her hips when she took a step back. Again going with her gut, she extended her hand, breathing a sigh of relief when he took it. She gave it a tug and he came to his feet.

Drawing a breath, he squared his shoulders and held her hand tightly. 'Let's go figure out who hates me.' But he didn't move just yet. Hesitating much like she had done, he kept his eyes on her as he brought their joined hands to his mouth and kissed her fingers. 'Thank you.'

Her throat grew thick and a shiver rippled down her back. 'You're welcome.'

When he walked into Hyatt's very crowded conference room, it was with his back straight and his head high. Until he saw Stevie. She held an icepack to one hip and clutched her cane so hard that her knuckles were white. Her face was tight with pain, one cheek scraped and raw.

'Oh, Stevie,' he murmured. 'I'm—'

Stevie glared at him. 'If you say you're sorry, I will kick your ass, Thorne. I swear to God.'

That made his lips twitch. 'You can't kick that high.'

That earned a snort from Clay, who stood behind Stevie, his hands on her shoulders. Both of them were pale but steady. 'You'd be surprised what she can kick when she puts her mind to it,' he said. 'I wouldn't push her, Thorne. Plus, she's right. This isn't your fault and we're going to make it stop.'

'Damn straight.' The declaration came from Hyatt, who sat next to Stevie, arms crossed over his barrel chest, his face set in his trademark scowl.

Gwyn blinked a little to see Special Agent Joseph Carter sitting on Hyatt's other side. His expression was unreadable, but then it always was. The man was a damn enigma. Joseph led a joint task

185

force comprised of BPD detectives and federal agents. JD was often on loan to his organization, so Gwyn supposed it made sense that the Fed had become involved.

JD sat at the far end of the table, looking appropriately grim. Lucy was at his side, giving both Gwyn and Thorne worried looks.

'We're fine,' Gwyn assured her, then frowned. Another detective stood leaning against the wall, glaring at them with contempt and suspicion. Gwyn glared right back, because the man was a fucking asshole. His name was Brickman, and he'd been the one to handcuff Thorne to his hospital bed the day before.

Thorne either wasn't aware of this fact or he was ignoring the sour-faced man, because he drew a breath and gave Gwyn's hand a squeeze. 'Okay. Let's figure this out.' He pulled a chair out for Gwyn, took the one next to it himself, then focused his attention on Stevie. 'What happened?'

Stevie glanced at Hyatt from the corner of her eye. The man appeared carved out of stone. 'Lighten up,' she said to her old boss. 'Nobody's dead.'

'Yet,' Hyatt growled. 'I should have locked you all up last night.'

'And then you'd have nothing,' Stevie countered. 'Thorne, he had tails on all of us today. It was one of the reasons you were allowed to leave the hospital so freely.'

Sonofabitch, Gwyn thought, but bit it back. 'I knew that felt too easy.'

Thorne had stiffened. 'I knew you'd have surveillance on me. But on all my friends too? Why? Because you thought I was guilty?'

Hyatt rolled his eyes. 'No,' he snapped. 'Because I'm pretty sure you're not, and I knew your friends would gather round like . . .'

'Friends?' Stevie supplied helpfully when Hyatt was unable to find the right word.

Clay coughed to disguise a laugh. Lucy covered her mouth and JD pursed his lips, hiding their smiles. Joseph Carter didn't even bother to hide his chuckle. 'It was a fair prediction, Peter,' he said to Hyatt. 'You guys kept us busy today, I have to say.'

Gwyn bit back another curse. 'You were in on this too?'

'It was my idea,' Joseph said mildly. 'And before you go off on a rant, listen. I know Thorne's not guilty of this. I also knew that you weren't simply going to sit still and wait for us to investigate. So we let you do what you were going to do anyway. We just made sure you were protected as you did so.'

Gwyn had to concentrate on not grinding her teeth. 'And that you got a bird's-eye view of the action was a pleasant by-product?'

'Hell, no,' Joseph said. 'A view of the action was the primary goal of the plan. Your protection was a pleasant by-product. Well, not *yours* specifically because *you* shook your tail this morning.'

Gwyn's gaze shot to Jamie, who looked very pleased with himself. The asshole detective's face, though, had grown dark with anger.

Thorne was frowning. 'I thought Stevie was saved by Clay's quick reflexes.'

'She was,' Clay replied, grim again. 'I heard glass shatter from the missed shot and shoved her out of the way.'

'Which is how I got scraped up,' Stevie said. 'Clay threw himself on top of me, but unfortunately we were on asphalt.'

Gwyn looked up at Thorne just as he looked down at her. 'Sound familiar?' she murmured.

Thorne nodded. 'Yeah.' To the group he said, 'That's what happened to us, except for the asphalt. Was it just the one shot fired?' he asked Clay and Stevie.

Stevie nodded. 'Yes. I was terrified that Clay was about to get shot.' She aimed a glare over her shoulder at her husband. 'Again.'

'It was the same with us,' Thorne said quietly. 'I was sure another bullet was coming, but none was ever fired.'

'What *was* different,' Joseph said deliberately, 'was that Clay and Stevie had not shaken their tail, who was one of my best agents. He was able to get the make of the shooter's van and a partial plate, but the shooting occurred in a crowded shopping area and he couldn't return fire. It was a white panel van. Did you see anything that looked like that?'

Jamie shook his head. 'I didn't, but I also didn't stop to look. I just wanted to get us all out of there.'

Phil looked unsure. 'I don't think so. It happened so fast.'

Thorne shot Phil an *it's okay* look before turning back to Clay and Stevie. 'Where were you when the shots were fired?'

'Coming out of a restaurant,' Stevie said. 'Kaia's Kouzina. It's an expensive place in Bethesda. Patricia Segal was supposed to have been there for a meeting today with one of her fund-raising committees. Clay and I went for lunch. I don't recommend the place, by the way. Small plates started at fifty bucks.'

Clay winced. 'Yeah. Man, that hurt. But we got an earful about Patricia. Seems like nobody on the committee liked her, although it took several bottles of wine before they loosened up enough to say so.'

'And when they did, it was loudly,' Stevie added. 'She was having an affair. Maybe more than one.'

Just like Prew's wife told him, Gwyn thought. 'Did anyone say with whom?'

Stevie made a face. 'Some guy half her age. And she was only thirty-four.'

'Wonderful,' Jamie muttered as Phil made a distressed noise.

'No names?' Gwyn pressed, forcing herself not to think about the sexual assault committed against a seventeen-year-old boy.

'No,' Clay said. 'She'd bragged about him to a few of the ladies after too many cocktails. She was afraid her husband would find out, though.'

'The thing is,' Stevie added, with another glance at Hyatt, 'Patricia has a son who's seventeen going on eighteen. The young man she was ... "seeing" might have been the same age. And she might have known him through her son.'

A son who's seventeen going on eighteen.

Gwyn drew a quiet breath, focused on keeping her expression static while pain constricted her throat. Over the years she'd had a significant amount of practice at hiding her reaction whenever someone mentioned a son. Especially one who was the same age as her own. Eighteen years and four months to be exact. About the same age she herself had been when she got pregnant.

A moment later, the pain had passed, just as it always did. 'She was a young mother,' she murmured.

Hyatt's scowl remained unchanged. 'How do you know all this, Stevie? How did you know her committee would be meeting at that restaurant today?'

'She and Clay Maynard probably hacked into the victim's computer,' Detective Brickman said suspiciously. He really was an asshole.

Stevie rolled her eyes. 'You're just mad because a *minivan* driven by a *lawyer* shook you off this morning, Brickman. You don't know jack shit, so just chill with the insults.'

Brickman started to open his mouth, but Hyatt raised a hand. 'So,' he said quietly, 'if you didn't hack, how did you know?'

'Facebook,' Stevie answered testily. 'Patricia's account is not privacy-protected. Anyone can see it. Even cops like you, Brickman.'

Ouch. Stevie apparently didn't like this guy any more than Gwyn did.

'We checked her account,' Brickman said stiffly. 'She hadn't posted anything about the lunch.'

'No,' Stevie said with exaggerated patience. 'She hadn't this month. But if you'd taken the time to go back a month or two, you'd have seen that she met with this group the second Monday of every month at the same restaurant.'

Brickman's glare could have melted rock. Stevie looked away, unimpressed. 'Anyway,' she went on, 'the point is, there might be reasons why she was targeted, other than her connection to Thorne through her brother. There is the issue of the possible affair. These committee ladies were speculating that the husband might have ended her if he'd found out about the young man. They also speculated that she might have been having an affair with Thorne.'

Thorne's jaw went so tight that it cracked. 'I wasn't,' he said coldly.

'I know that,' Stevie said with a dismissive wave. 'But they were what-iffing all over the damn place. And then they found your photo and all but swooned.'

Clay nodded. 'They said they couldn't blame Patricia for risking her husband's fury for you. The media is speculating that this was a setup because you weren't arrested and you were unconscious too.

189

The ladies ran with that, wondering if her husband was responsible. If he was, then the kid could be in danger too.'

Stevie shot another irritated look at Brickman. 'And because we haven't hacked into her personal email or anything of that nature, we haven't identified this kid. Yet.'

Gwyn was aware that Stevie hadn't specified whether the 'yet' referred to her hacking or her identification of the young man. So, apparently, was Hyatt, because the lieutenant looked like he'd sucked on a lemon.

'How were you planning to ID him?' he asked.

'The old-fashioned way,' Stevie said sincerely. 'By getting a list of Patricia's son's classmates and teammates – anyone she might have come in contact with.'

Thorne's mouth had turned down doubtfully. 'I'd love it if I weren't the target here. But you and Gwyn were shot at today.'

'And they missed,' Stevie said pointedly.

Gwyn sensed where Stevie was going with this. 'They missed us both, Thorne. They didn't take the opportunity to hit either you or Clay. We've assumed this is a campaign to hurt you by hurting – or killing – your friends. But is it possible that they're just trying to make it *look* like you're the target? That they shot at us to shine the spotlight on you and away from whoever might have hated Patricia enough to eviscerate her?'

Eleven

*W**as it?* Thorne thought. Was it possible that today's shootings were merely a diversion to take the focus off whoever had killed Patricia Linden Segal?

'Maybe,' he answered slowly. 'I suppose so. Except for the key ring.'

Joseph lifted his brows. 'And how did you know about that?'

'Crime scene photos,' Jamie cut in with a small smile.

Hyatt shook his head. 'Nope. We didn't give you access to those. Thorne hasn't been charged.'

Thorne glanced at Gwyn regretfully, but saw her chin already lifted in defiance and felt a welling of pride. 'I took some photos before the EMTs got there,' she said. 'I knew Thorne was being set up. I also knew the EMTs would make a mess of the crime scene getting him out of there. So I snapped some pictures.'

Eyes flashing, Hyatt drew a deep breath and let it out. 'You might have shared those with us, Miss Weaver.'

'Why?' she shot back, outraged. 'You *followed* us.'

'I *told* you I would,' Hyatt said icily. 'I *told* you I'd have surveillance on Thorne.'

'Yes, but you followed all our friends too. If any of them had found anything that looked bad for Thorne, you would have pounced on it. You say you believe he's innocent, but at the end of the day you're cops, with your own fucking agenda. You'll take any evidence you can to make your case, even if that evidence is completely out of context.'

191

Hyatt's glare was cold. 'You don't have too high an opinion of me, Miss Weaver.'

She frowned. 'No, I really don't. Yes, you do the right thing most of the time, but I've seen the times that you haven't. I was a paralegal for a lot of years. I worked hundreds of cases for people who were brought to trial unjustly. Your officers take liberties with searches and twist testimony to fit their own needs. Not all of them.' She shot a quick glance of apology at JD, then at Stevie, before turning her glare back on Hyatt. 'I know cops who are good, who have integrity, who carry a badge because they truly wish to serve. But some don't. And some of them have worked for you, Lieutenant.' She shrugged. 'But I don't work for you. Anything I choose to share is voluntary unless I'm subpoenaed. Or arrested. Yes, we knew about the key ring. And had you asked the right questions, respectfully, instead of depending on us to do your work for you, you might have predicted we'd be at Brent Kiley's apartment. With or without a goddamn tail.'

Thorne stared down at her, warmth spreading in his chest. It was pride, yes. But it was far more than that. She was back. This was Gwyn before Evan ripped her confidence away. *She's back. And she's fighting. For me.* It was damn heady.

Hyatt ran a frustrated hand over his bald head. 'You defense attorneys . . .' He bit off whatever he'd planned to say. 'Are you going to trust us or not?'

'*Not*,' Gwyn stated firmly, just as Jamie said the same.

Joseph nodded calmly. 'I can see your point, Gwyn. Truthfully, I don't expect you to trust me. However, I *do* expect you to be honest with me so that I can do my job and keep you all safe.'

The heady feeling that had filled Thorne seeped away and he sighed heavily. 'I don't trust either of you' – he gestured between Hyatt and Joseph – 'completely. However, I don't think you'd lie or intentionally trick me.'

'At least Joseph wouldn't,' Gwyn muttered.

One side of Thorne's lip quirked before he could stop it. Focusing, he schooled his features once again. 'I also don't want to live with knowing that somebody I care about got hurt because I didn't share the right information. The key ring is important. One that looks to be similar was shoved into Richard Linden's torso. I saw it when I was trying to stop his bleeding.'

Joseph's eyes went wary. 'I saw the court transcripts. I don't remember reading about a key ring.'

'Yeah, well,' Thorne said, 'that's because it disappeared.'

'Brent Kiley is an EMT,' Hyatt said slowly. 'Was he one of the first responders to the Linden kid's scene?'

Thorne had to give him credit. The man might be an asshole, but he was sharp. 'Yes. But he doesn't remember seeing anything.'

There was no point in saying anything else, because Kiley had promised that he would say exactly that to anyone else who asked.

'Yet you stayed in his apartment for several minutes,' Joseph commented. 'So says his nosy neighbor, anyway.'

'We did,' Thorne confirmed, but said no more.

Joseph rolled his eyes. 'So this is the way we're playing it? Really, Thorne? Both Gwyn and Stevie are shot at and you're going to make me guess the right questions to ask you?'

'I've told you the one important thing that I see as a connection,' Thorne said evenly. 'The key ring. The one I saw on Richard Linden's body belonged to him. Or resembled the one that belonged to him, anyway. The EMT couldn't say where it disappeared to.'

'Have you located Kiley's partner?' Joseph asked. 'Maybe he saw it.'

Thorne considered his words. 'When we asked Kiley if he knew where his partner was, he said he'd quit about a year after my trial. This was after a car accident in which his car was broadsided by a truck that came out of nowhere.' He lifted his brows and Hyatt's scowl deepened.

'Your girlfriend at the time died the same way,' Hyatt said reluctantly. 'She would have been a witness. What happened to Kiley's partner?'

Thorne shrugged. 'He just . . . disappeared. Quit his job and never came back.'

'We'll start a search for him,' Joseph said. 'Who else was involved in handling Richard Linden's body?'

Thorne glanced at Lucy, who'd been sitting silently at JD's side. She was still wearing a lab coat and had probably come straight from the morgue.

Thorne dipped his head almost imperceptibly, giving his assent, and she cleared her throat. 'I read the police report detailing the murder of Richard Linden,' she said. 'Richard was declared DOA in the ER. The doctor who called his death died a few years ago of a heart attack, so that's another dead end.' She winced a little at her unfortunate word choice. 'Anyway, according to the report, there wasn't much done in the ER. Richard may have been dead even before he was put in the ambulance.'

Everyone aimed a look at Thorne. 'Was he?' Joseph asked.

Thorne shrugged. 'He had a pulse when I discovered him. I thought so anyway.'

'He was convinced enough,' Jamie said acidly, 'to stay at Richard's side to try to save his life, even though he knew he'd be blamed.'

Joseph met Thorne's eyes and Thorne was momentarily struck speechless by the kindness and respect he saw there. 'I gathered that from the court transcripts,' Joseph said. 'It was . . . above and beyond decency, Thorne.'

Wow. For a second, Thorne just stared. Then years of training in the art of interrogation kicked in. Joseph Carter was very good at his job. That wasn't to say he was insincere or untruthful. But he definitely knew how to manipulate a witness.

Thorne smiled at him, allowing his amusement to show. 'Thank you.'

Joseph held his gaze for a long moment. 'I meant it.'

'I know. It almost worked too.' He sobered, reclaiming the thread of the conversation. 'Richard had a pulse when I found him. I tried to stop the bleeding, but I was only seventeen. I'd had Red Cross first aid training because I'd been a lifeguard, but I didn't know how to deal with a wound like that. I knew he was close to death, though. I mean, I could see his internal organs.' He swallowed hard, remembering exactly how it had looked. How

194

fucking scared he'd been. 'Then the cops stormed the place and ripped me away from him. They had me cuffed and face down on the floor before I could say a word.' Beside him, Gwyn tensed, and he glanced down at her. 'It really did look bad,' he murmured. 'I was bent over him, covered in his blood. I couldn't blame the cops for that part.'

'I could,' Jamie said flatly.

'And I did,' Phil added.

Smiling ruefully at them, Thorne returned his attention to Joseph. 'I don't know what happened after that with respect to Richard. I only know what I saw in those minutes that I was trying to help him. The key ring was there then. That's what I know to be fact.'

'I interviewed the ER doctor as part of my trial prep,' Jamie said. 'I asked him about the key ring, because Thorne was so adamant that he'd seen it and by then it was gone. The doctor said he didn't do an exam. He called Richard's time of death less than a minute after he was brought in. He deliberately hadn't touched the body any more than necessary because he knew there would be a homicide investigation. And he said there was police presence the entire time. The cops accompanied the body to the morgue. The doctor didn't have any more contact with the body or the Linden family.' He looked to Lucy. 'I also interviewed the ME. He denies having seen the key ring as well.'

'I know the ME who did the exam,' Lucy said. 'He was my boss until he retired, and he was always a man of integrity, personally and professionally. His autopsy report lists no items found inside the body, and according to court transcripts, nothing meeting that description was taken into evidence by the police. That leaves the ME tech who prepared the body for autopsy as the only person left in the chain with access to Richard's body. That tech is dead. He was killed at the scene of a shooting incident fourteen years ago.'

'Lots of dead or missing people,' Joseph commented. 'What was the significance of this key ring?'

'I don't know,' Thorne said truthfully. 'It was made from a medal Richard received for soccer. As I recall, he carried a single key on it. Both key and ring were inside his body. Until they no longer were.

Can you describe the key ring you found in Patricia's wound?'

Brickman, the asshole detective still leaning against the wall, made a disagreeable sound. 'That information is confidential,' he said stiffly. 'It's part of an ongoing investigation. As are you, Mr Thorne.'

Thorne stiffened, and beside him Gwyn drew a deep breath, her cheeks darkening. She opened her mouth to say something sharp and snarky, but he squeezed her hand and gave his head a mild shake.

Joseph was giving Brickman a disapproving look, but he said nothing, probably because Brickman was Hyatt's responsibility.

Hyatt harrumphed. 'Not your call, Detective,' he said, injecting the proper level of sharpness into his tone. 'We are *cooperating* here. And Mr Thorne is here of his own volition. We are grateful for his help.' He turned to Thorne. 'Having said that, we really can't tell you much about the key ring, but that's because it's being analyzed in the lab.'

Thorne nodded slowly, hoping his expression showed his disbelief. 'I see.'

Gwyn tugged at his hand. 'I think we should go now,' she said. 'They'll never *cooperate* with us.'

Hyatt rolled his eyes. 'For God's sake. It really is being analyzed. Knowing that it might be a sports medal is helpful. Currently, there's so much buildup on it, we can't see what was inscribed. The lab will tell us what the item is when they're finished. Jeez.'

Gwyn gave him a narrow-eyed nod. 'Thank you. That is co-operation.'

Another eyeroll from Hyatt. 'Now, what would be even more cooperative is if you tell us who you suspect is behind this.'

Thorne drew a breath and let it out. Frederick had drawn up a list of clients who'd been unhappy with their sentences, but no one had jumped out. Other than Cesar Tavilla, he wasn't aware of anyone who hated him *this* much or had enough muscle to pull off such an elaborate setup. And according to Ramirez, this was not Tavilla's doing. 'I don't know and that's the truth. I tend to make enemies in my line of work.'

Detective Brickman made another offensive noise. 'No kidding.'

Gwyn's hands clenched into fists. 'Motherfu—'

Thorne wrapped one of her fists in his big hand and squeezed. 'That's what he wants,' he murmured. 'Don't give him an inch.'

'Sorry,' she muttered. 'But he's an asshole.'

'Yes, he is,' Thorne agreed, as if they were the only two people in the room. 'But he's trying to make me mad. You need to keep me calm. Okay?'

Gwyn visibly reined in her temper. 'Okay.'

He squeezed her hand again before turning back to Hyatt and Joseph. 'No one has made any explicit threats, and implicit threats happen every damn day.'

Joseph's gaze was . . . unsettling. Like he knew something that Thorne didn't. 'Tell me about the implicit threats, Thorne. Give me something to work with.'

Thorne stilled. 'Why are you even here, Joseph? I thought you and JD had recused yourselves because we have . . . a not-unfriendly relationship.'

Still standing behind Stevie, Clay laughed out loud. 'Not-unfriendly. That's priceless. But I was wondering the same thing. What gives, Joseph?'

Joseph's lips had twitched at Thorne's words, but he sobered quickly. 'I would have thought you'd have asked me that question when you first walked in.'

'He was a little preoccupied at the time,' Phil said, leaping to Thorne's defense with just the right amount of paternal outrage.

'I could see that.' Joseph was very serious. 'And I understand, believe me.'

'Then answer his question,' Gwyn said quietly. 'Please.'

'All right.' Joseph slid a single sheet of paper across the table to Thorne. 'I did some research of my own this morning. Did you know that Cesar Tavilla's son is dead?'

Startled, Thorne grabbed the paper and scanned it quickly. Colin Tavilla had been killed in a fight in the prison exercise yard. Two weeks ago.

That was impossible. *I'd have known. Ramirez would have told me.*

'I didn't know,' he said tightly, wiping his expression clean. But if it was true? This was going to get really, really bad.

Hunt Valley, Maryland,
Monday 13 June, 2.35 P.M.

Frederick didn't draw an easy breath until he and Julie were safely in Clay and Stevie's house. Taylor was waiting for them with a huge smile.

'Julie, look at you!' Delighted, she stroked a hand over her sister's hair. 'Your haircut is super-cute!'

Frederick blinked. Julie's hair *was* shorter. He hadn't even noticed.

Taylor chuckled. 'It's okay, Dad. It's kind of a girl thing, right, Jules?'

Julie beamed. 'The hair cutters came to the center. I like it!'

'Hello, gorgeous.' Taylor's fiancé came up and brushed a gentle kiss on Julie's cheek. 'Long time no see.'

Julie giggled. 'Hi, Ford.'

Frederick frowned, mentally checking the day. 'It's Monday, right? Why aren't you at work?'

Ford straightened, shooting Frederick a cautious look. 'I took some vacation days.' He glanced at Julie. 'You know, to help Clay and Stevie get ready for the christening.'

Which was in less than a week. *Shit.*

Taylor continued smiling at Julie, fussing with her hair. 'We're watching all the kids. Just so everyone can get their jobs done.'

It was then that Frederick saw the telltale gun-shaped bulge at Taylor's side, covered by the loose-fitting jersey she wore. She was carrying. In the house. While watching children. His gaze quickly flew to hers and then to Ford's.

Ford looked positively grim for a brief moment before schooling his features back into a smile for Julie. 'I've got all kinds of fun stuff to do downstairs, and Cordelia's picked out some DVDs she said you're going to love.'

Julie clapped her hands. She loved Stevie's ten-year-old daughter, and the feeling was mutual. *I was right to bring her here.* One thing done right, at least.

Frederick kissed Julie's forehead. 'Have fun, baby girl.' He looked at Ford. 'Can you carry her down the stairs?'

'Daddy,' Julie said, frowning. 'They have an elevator. I can do it myself.' She waved, maneuvering her chair toward the elevator to the basement, Ford at her side.

'She knows the way,' Frederick murmured.

'She does,' Taylor said wisely. 'And Ford knows to let her do it herself. But he'll be there if she needs him.'

Frederick met his daughter's dark eyes, so like Clay's. 'When did they install an elevator?'

Taylor's lips curved, watching her fiancé laughing with Julie. 'A few months ago. Stevie was having trouble getting up and down the stairs to the basement with her cane, and one day she tripped. The next day Clay had the elevator company here.' Her eyes softened. 'Stevie was mad about the expense, but then Clay pointed out that if they got an elevator, Julie could play with Cordy. Stevie was on board after that.'

Frederick's heart squeezed painfully, overcome with gratitude for the man who'd opened his arms and his home to their family, when very few would have been so forgiving.

'Yeah,' Taylor murmured, as if reading his mind. 'He's pretty special.' She cleared her throat. 'We've had a situation.'

Frederick's shoulders sagged. 'More than someone trying to get to Julie?'

Taylor looked as grim as Ford had. 'Yes. Stevie was shot at.'

He gaped. 'What? When?'

'As they were leaving lunch. She's fine, but Gwyn got shot at too.'

'Clay never mentioned it when I called him.'

'He said you sounded freaked out enough. That I should let you get here before I told you.'

That made Frederick feel both grateful and annoyed at the same time. 'I guess that explains the gun you're carrying.'

'Nobody is going to hurt my family,' Taylor said fiercely. 'Come on.'

He followed her to Clay's study, where Sam, Clay's PI, was staring at a large monitor on the desk. Alec Vaughn, his IT whizz-kid, sat on the floor, a computer on his lap and stacks of paper arranged in a semicircle around him.

Both men looked up, expressions also grim. 'You get your daughter settled?' Sam asked.

'Ford's with her,' Frederick said. 'What are you doing?'

'I'm viewing video from the bar where Thorne got attacked,' Sam said, 'and from one of the businesses down the road from the bar.'

'Anything yet?' Alec asked, but Sam shook his head.

'No. But when I find what I'm looking for, I'll send it to you.'

Alec nodded. 'In the meantime, I've been checking into that phone number that called Bernice Brown's friend and tried to contact your daughter. So far, all I know is that it's a throwaway.'

'I'd have been shocked if it weren't,' Frederick muttered.

Taylor leaned up and kissed his cheek. 'Julie's safe with us. I'm going downstairs to help Ford.'

'He took vacation to help out,' Frederick said quietly, again overwhelmed by the way these people pitched in to support each other.

Her lips twitched. 'I keep telling you that he's a nice guy.'

'I believed you the first time. I'm . . . glad.'

She nodded, understanding. 'We were self-reliant for too long, Dad. Hard to get used to having so many people willing to help. Are you going to stay here today?'

'No. Whoever contacted Julie knew that Sally Brewster had contacted her first. Miss Brewster could be in on this. If she's truly honest, then we were overheard. If that's the case, I need to know where it happened.'

Taylor looked like she wanted to protest, but she nodded. 'Keep yourself safe, got it?'

'Yes, ma'am,' he said.

'She told you about Stevie and Gwyn?' Sam asked brusquely.

200

'Just that they were shot at.'

'Only them. Both Thorne and Clay made themselves targets by throwing themselves over them, but they weren't shot at.'

Frederick better understood the tight set of the younger man's jaw. Someone was looking to pick off Thorne's friends, but was, for some reason, being choosy. 'Where is Ruby?'

'She and my mother were going shopping for baby things. I told them to go straight back to my mom's house. I'm going to get Ruby now.' Sam shut down his computer, and when he stood, Frederick saw that he too was wearing a weapon.

God. What had they come to, that they were armed in a secure house? 'Poor Thorne,' he murmured. 'This has got to be wrecking him.'

'We haven't talked to him yet. Clay's going to get him to come here. They're all at the police station now, being grilled by Hyatt *and* Joseph Carter.'

Frederick whistled. 'I'm sure that's doing wonders for Thorne's mood.'

'Which is why we're all going to be here when he arrives,' Sam said. 'We need to show him that we've got his back and that we're going to fix this before it gets any worse.'

Baltimore, Maryland,
Monday 13 June, 2.45 P.M.

Thorne's gut twisted painfully. Colin Tavilla was dead. *How did I not know this? I should have been told. Ramirez should have told me.* If there'd been radio silence from his man inside Tavilla's camp, he'd have been worried. But he'd heard from Ramirez. Yesterday.

Gwyn's small, trembling hand came into view, sliding the report of Colin's death over so that she could read it. 'Shit,' she whispered, then passed it to Jamie and Phil. Both men had paled. All of them knew what this could mean.

Exhaling heavily, Thorne looked up to meet Joseph's concerned gaze. 'How did you know to look for this?'

'I've been keeping my eye on Cesar Tavilla since last summer,'

201

Joseph said. 'Ever since you gave us evidence that helped us bring in Gage Jarvis.'

'What?' Jamie demanded. 'Thorne?'

Fuck. He hadn't told them for a reason – the fear on their faces right now.

Joseph registered surprise. 'You didn't tell them?'

'No,' Jamie bit out. 'He did not. Please correct that oversight right now, Agent Carter.'

Joseph shot Thorne a curious look, then shrugged. 'Last summer, an attorney named Gage Jarvis killed his ex-wife and was looking for his daughter because she'd witnessed him leaving the scene. She was eleven.'

'Was?' Phil asked sharply.

'I'm sorry,' Joseph said immediately. 'She *is* eleven. She's healthy and in therapy. Lots of therapy.'

'Oh, thank God.' Phil shuddered out a breath. 'I thought you meant that she was dead.'

'No.' Joseph's mouth curved up in a small smile. 'But we owe some of that to Thorne. JD turned to him for information because Gage was a defense attorney. JD hoped that Thorne might know who Gage had been friendly with so that they could find his hiding place. Thorne did us one better. He had a photo of Gage having dinner with Tavilla, taken a few days before, so we knew our suspect was in town and for whom he was working. Except Tavilla washed his hands of Gage when we turned up the heat. The long and short of it is that Tavilla isn't stupid. He knew we had inside info. At the time, Thorne told us that he'd had reason to believe Tavilla had targeted him in the past, and that he had a man inside. I worried then about what Tavilla would do if he found out. So I've kept watch. He's gone under, by the way. He's only been sighted a handful of times, usually at the same restaurant where he met with Gage Jarvis. He knows we're watching. He somehow manages to lose his tail every time. We're investigating that too.'

'I see.' Jamie's voice was low and controlled. 'That's certainly enlightening. Both the help Thorne gave you last year and the man he had inside.'

Thorne could feel Jamie's fury, and had to resist the urge to drop his eyes like a scolded child. 'I'm sorry. I didn't want you to worry.'

Jamie swallowed hard. 'Well, too bad. I worried anyway. You should have told me.'

'Jamie,' Phil murmured. 'Not here.'

On the other side of Thorne, Gwyn was uncharacteristically quiet. He didn't know if he had the courage to look at her expression at the moment.

Instead he fixed his attention back on Joseph and Hyatt. 'I would have thought news of Colin Tavilla's death would have made headlines.'

Joseph's brows rose. 'Your informant didn't mention it?'

'No. And I've heard from him recently.' *And I'll be reaching out to him again as soon as I leave this room.* 'How was this kept from the media?'

'Good question,' Hyatt said. 'It seems that Colin was stabbed in a fight in the exercise yard. It was . . . unpleasant. The crowd around him dispersed, leaving him where he fell. The prison had him air-lifted to the hospital. They spread the word among the inmates that Colin had made it through surgery and was recovering. In reality, he died in the exercise yard. We're guessing the prison didn't want any publicity about it because they'd have gang violence erupt inside. They must have figured that anyone who knew differently wasn't going to speak up and incriminate themselves in the murder.'

'Either that or Tavilla wanted it kept quiet,' Thorne muttered.

'Certainly a possibility,' Joseph agreed. 'I have to say I was surprised. I was supposed to be told if he died as well. But his death certificate was filed. When I couldn't find out where he was "recovering", I looked for the certificate. I'm thinking this changes things in your mind, Thorne, in terms of who could be responsible?'

Thorne nodded, his thoughts spiraling everywhere. 'Yeah. I immediately thought Tavilla, but . . .'

'But you'd heard from your man inside,' Joseph supplied. 'If you give us his name, we'll check up on him to make sure he's okay.'

Thorne almost smiled. 'I don't think so, Joseph.'

Joseph shrugged. 'It was worth a try.'

Hyatt wasn't as easily placated. 'We need that name, Thorne. We need to know who we're looking at for this. If it's Tavilla, we want to take him down.'

Thorne simply shook his head. He wasn't going to reveal Ramirez to the cops. They'd bring him in just to get at Tavilla. He owed Ramirez too much to do that to him.

Hyatt gave another frustrated sigh. 'Can you at least explain why Cesar Tavilla hates you so much? Because I don't buy the explanation I was given. That you refused to represent his kid in court is not a valid reason for his orchestrating this vendetta against you, if he's even done so.'

Thorne rubbed his forehead. 'Not entirely, no. I did refuse to take his son's case. Twice. The first time was five years ago. Cesar was displeased, but another attorney was able to get him off. The second time was two years ago.'

'Why did you refuse?' Hyatt asked.

Thorne resisted the urge to roll his eyes. 'Because I don't want to be in the pocket of someone like Cesar Tavilla. Nor did I want to start a feud, but that's what I did. Colin Tavilla went to prison for killing his partner in crime, one of the other young members of Cesar's gang. The two had robbed a jewelry store. Made off with a few million dollars in diamonds. The store owner was distracted because he was receiving a delivery from another young man, Avery, who'd been hired by Colin. Avery is the son of a rival gang leader, which I didn't know when I took the case. Avery didn't know either, but—'

'Wait,' Hyatt interrupted. 'This Avery kid didn't know his father was a gang leader?'

'He didn't know his father even existed,' Thorne said. 'His mother raised him alone. His father knew about Avery and kept watch over him, but he'd never met him in person. Apparently someone else found out, because Colin Tavilla knew. He deliberately set the kid up to take the fall for the theft.'

'To get to the rival gang leader,' Hyatt said with a slow nod. 'Okay, then what?'

'Avery couldn't prove he'd been tricked, and even when I found out who his father was, I stuck with him. He was being railroaded for a crime he didn't commit because of who his father was.'

'Why don't I remember this?' Hyatt asked suspiciously.

'Because Avery's case wasn't a homicide, for one,' Thorne answered. 'But mostly because this happened in DC. It was handled by DCPD and tried in a DC court.'

Hyatt's eyes narrowed. 'Still not seeing why Tavilla hates you so much.'

'Because it became a homicide,' Joseph supplied. 'Colin Tavilla's buddy stole the entire haul instead of simply taking his half. Colin found out and killed him.'

Thorne grimaced. 'And it wasn't pretty. Colin gutted him, very similar to what was done to Patricia. Cesar approached me and asked me to represent his son in court. Not only did I say no, but Avery became a witness in Colin's murder trial. His testimony was credible because I was able to get the grand theft charges against him dismissed. It was crucial to finding Colin guilty. Colin went away for twenty years. Which he apparently did not serve, because he was killed.'

Hyatt was frowning. 'So why does Tavilla hate you and not this Avery kid?'

'Because I sat in court next to Avery. He'd been afraid to testify. He was only sixteen at the time. But he's a good kid. He did the right thing. And when he was interviewed afterward, he credited me with giving him the courage to speak up.'

'Ah.' Hyatt nodded now. 'That makes more sense. What happened to Avery?'

'He's gone off to university. Changed his name. I'm sure Tavilla knows where he is, but if Avery's harmed, his father will blame Tavilla and it'll cause a gang war.'

'Tavilla's not strong enough to survive that,' Joseph added. 'Not right now.'

'He's made attempts on your life before?' Hyatt asked.

Thorne shrugged, conscious that Phil, Jamie and Gwyn were all holding their breath, waiting for an answer. 'A few. None of them

205

successful, obviously. But it was enough for me to seek a contact inside. I've kept my eye on Cesar ever since Colin was incarcerated.' He met Joseph's gaze, then Hyatt's. 'Am I free to go?'

'Of course,' Joseph said. 'You are not under arrest.'

An exasperated sound came from the other side of the room, where Detective Brickman still leaned against the wall. 'You're just letting him go? Again?'

'Yes,' Joseph fired back. 'We are.'

Hyatt gave the younger detective a dangerous look. 'In my office, Brickman, as soon as we're done here.' To Thorne he said, 'Yes, we are letting you go, but it's against my better judgment. Not because I think you're guilty, but because I know you're stupid. Do *not* try to do any further investigating on your own.' He turned to Stevie with a glare. 'That includes you too.'

'I'm going home,' Stevie promised. 'I've got a baby to nurse, a hip to ice, and a christening to plan.'

Thorne chanced a glance at Gwyn. She sat eerily still, her hands folded in her lap. *Shit*, he thought. *She's going to blow her stack when we leave here.*

'We're going home too,' he said. 'Should I assume surveillance will continue?'

'Of course,' Joseph said mildly. 'You've got my cell phone number. If you change your mind and decide to give us your confidential informant's name, I'm happy to help.'

Like that's ever going to happen. Thorne stood and helped Gwyn to her feet, and they all filed out, Jamie still shooting him angry looks. Phil looked wearily resigned.

I should have told them. But he really hadn't wanted to worry them. *And I'm thirty-six years old, for fuck's sake.* Old enough to manage his own life and the consequences that came from his personal choices. But he'd hurt them and he hadn't meant to. He sighed quietly. Just another fuck-up that he needed to fix.

Clay and Stevie followed them, Stevie limping and swatting Clay's hand away when he tried to help steady her. Lucy and JD brought up the rear. Nobody spoke until they reached the elevator.

'Everyone's coming to our house,' Clay murmured in Thorne's

ear. 'We have gates to keep out Hyatt's men. Nobody will be able to listen to us there.'

Thorne nodded once. He considered asking Clay if he was sure, if he was really okay with the shitshow Thorne had already brought down on their heads. But he respected Clay Maynard, so he took the man at his word. 'All right. Thank you.'

Baltimore, Maryland,
Monday 13 June, 3.35 P.M.

Gwyn remained silent as they walked to Jamie's minivan, conscious of the way Thorne loomed over her. Her shield. Again.

She didn't argue with him, largely because she'd decided that whoever was behind this didn't want Thorne dead. They wanted him hurt.

And if it was Cesar Tavilla pulling the strings? She swallowed hard and willed her nerves to settle. But her nerves were not cooperating. Not in the least. She felt ready to leap out of her own skin.

Instead she turned her attention to Phil and Jamie, who'd also gathered around her protectively. Thorne was at her back, while the two older men flanked either side.

'I didn't know either, so don't feel bad,' she murmured as they got to the minivan.

Jamie looked up at her sharply. 'You mean about Tavilla?'

She nodded. She'd known Thorne had given Joseph and JD information about Jarvis, the rogue attorney who'd killed his wife, but she hadn't known that the information had involved Tavilla. She wouldn't have been able to sleep if she had. 'I was at Lucy and JD's house with him the night he helped the cops with Jarvis, but I'd gone upstairs to help Lucy bathe her son. By the time we'd finished, the conversation downstairs was over. I assumed at the time that Thorne would tell me everything I needed to know and that whatever he kept to himself was because of client confidentiality.'

'You didn't need to know about all that,' Thorne insisted,

sounding aggrieved. 'I was trying to keep you from worrying. And I'm right here behind you, so stop talking about me like I'm not here.'

'I know exactly where you are,' she said evenly, because she was so angry. Angry that he'd kept this from them. Angry that he'd taken so many risks with his life. Angry that he'd continue to do so, because she knew he'd try to find his man inside Tavilla's organization, just to make sure the guy was okay.

Because that was Thorne. He was loyal and he didn't leave people behind.

Which is why you . . . care for him. She'd come so close to the L word. The thing was, she did love Thorne. The question was – in what way, exactly? She knew that she wasn't in the proper frame of mind to figure that out at the moment.

They got in the van, Jamie behind the wheel, Phil shotgun, and Thorne and Gwyn in the backseat, just as they'd ridden around all day.

There was absolute silence until Jamie turned the key in the ignition. He set the A/C and sighed. 'You're going after him, aren't you?'

Thorne was stone-faced. 'Who exactly?'

'Your source inside Tavilla's organization,' Jamie answered impatiently. 'And probably Tavilla himself. Don't play games, Thorne. It pisses me off.'

Thorne said nothing, which was answer enough.

'I think we need to regroup,' Phil said, his voice shaky. 'Let's take Clay up on his offer of hospitality for the time being. There's safety in numbers.'

Jamie put the van in gear. 'Fine. I'll need directions. I've never been there.'

'It's in Hunt Valley,' Thorne said. 'Give me your phone. I'll set your GPS.' He did so, before firing off a text – probably to his contact inside Tavilla's organization, Gwyn thought. Then he leaned back in his seat and closed his eyes.

He looked so tired. *And alone.*

Alone was the last thing she wanted him to feel. She reached for his hand and held it, twining their fingers. 'You don't have to bear this yourself, Thorne. We said we have your back, and we do. We're pissed off at you, but we're not going away.'

He shuddered out a breath, but said nothing, so she brought his hand to her lips and kissed his fingers as he'd done hers earlier. She watched his nostrils flare, but that was the only indication he'd been affected at all.

Twelve

Hunt Valley, Maryland,
Monday 13 June, 4.35 P.M.

Clay opened his front door before Thorne could even knock. 'Welcome.' He gestured them in with a wide sweep of his hand. 'We're all here, just waiting for you guys.'

'Sorry we took so long,' Jamie said, wheeling himself up the ramp that led into the house. 'We went by our house first to pick up Gwyn's dog. Now that we're finally here, thank you for the invite. And the ramp. That doesn't happen very often.'

Clay closed the door, locked it, and reset an alarm panel. 'Stevie and I put in ramps. Steps are hard for her.' He pointed to a frosted glass door through which an elevator was barely visible. 'If you need to go upstairs or down for any reason, feel free to use the lift. All the rooms upstairs are accessible, wide doorways and all.'

Jamie smiled his thanks. 'Good to know.'

Clay took a moment to peer up at a monitor on one of the walls. It was the feed from six different security cameras. He pushed a button and the screen flashed, six new feeds appearing. One of them was from the front gate, where an unmarked car sat parked. 'Please tell me that your tail's not that prick Brickman.'

Thorne shook his head. 'It's Agent Ingram. He works for Joseph's joint task force.'

'I know Ingram,' Clay said. 'He's a good man.'

Thorne had heard the same. 'Joseph handpicked him, apparently. I hope Brickman's getting himself a new one torn by Hyatt right now. Guy really is a prick.'

'Brickman's the one who cuffed you to the hospital bed,' Gwyn said, resentment clear. 'Fucking asshole.'

Thorne found himself chuckling. 'He should have been more afraid of you.'

Gwyn craned her head back to glare at him. '*You* should be more afraid of me too.'

Thorne abruptly sobered. 'Oh, I am. Trust me.'

Clay's lips twitched. 'Then you are a wise man, Thorne. Come. We have food. Have you eaten?'

Thorne's stomach had been rumbling for the past hour. 'No. Thank you again.'

Clay aimed an irritated look his way. 'Shut up, Thorne. Stop thanking us. Just get your ass in there, get some food, and find a chair.'

'There' was Clay's living room, filled to capacity. Everyone who'd been in Gwyn's condo the night before, plus a few others – old and young and super-young. The group was having a late lunch, a buffet laid out on a table in the dining room, visible through another wide doorway.

'Uncle Torn!' The squeal was followed by a shock of dark hair and chubby little legs running across the room, a small body flinging itself into Thorne's arms. Lucy's son, Jeremiah. His godson. He lifted the boy off the floor and swung him around, and was rewarded with another squeal, this one so joyful that his heart squeezed. He wrapped Jeremiah in a bear hug before kissing the top of his head.

'What are you doing here, little J?' he asked, tickling the boy's ribs.

But no giggles ensued. Just a sober-faced little boy, who reached out and grabbed Thorne's cheeks. 'To see you.' Dark blue eyes studied him with an uncharacteristic concern. 'Still hurt?'

Lucy sidled up next to them, Wynnie on her hip. 'He knows you were in the hospital yesterday. He was worried. We told him you were okay, but he needed to see for himself.' She kissed her son's soft cheek. 'You've seen him now, Jeremiah, so it's time to go back downstairs with Taylor.'

Frederick's adopted daughter left his side to approach, arms

211

outstretched. She transferred Wynnie to her own hip, then smiled down at Jeremiah. 'Come on, kid. Ford's got Legos downstairs. Let's go play.'

Those were evidently magic words, because Jeremiah wriggled out of Thorne's arms. 'Down.' Then, at his mother's raised brows, he added, 'Please.'

Thorne set him down, wishing he could go downstairs and play too. He wished all of these people had gathered for a party rather than for his sorry ass. But they *had* gathered for him, so he shoved away his longing for Legos and straightened. 'Thank you, Taylor. And thank you for sending me that photo of Jazzie. That was nice of you.'

Clay's biological daughter smiled. She always looked like him, but when she smiled, the resemblance was enough to make a person blink. 'I heard that whatever you did to help her has caused you trouble. I'm sorry for that, but I still appreciate that you did it. So does Jazzie. Every so often we get that magic moment when she smiles and . . . forgets what happened to her. You gave her that chance, so . . . thank you.'

Thorne swallowed hard. Knowing that a little girl was alive and happy made whatever happened to him personally worth it. He only hoped he hadn't doomed his dearest friends in the process. 'Thanks, Taylor.'

With a nod, Taylor held out a hand for Jeremiah. 'Let's go, pumpkin.' To the rest of the room she said, 'I'll take him downstairs to Ford and then come back for the others.'

'The others' were the two infants in the room. Paige and Stevie had given birth within months of each other, so Taylor and Ford would have their hands full. Literally.

Clay pointed the new arrivals toward the food. 'Help yourselves. We're ready to begin whenever you are.'

A few minutes later, the four of them had found chairs in the Maynards' homey living room – where another large flat-screen security monitor hung on one wall. 'How many rooms have monitors?' Thorne asked Clay.

'All of them. I take my family's safety very seriously.'

212

Thorne nodded, wondering if Gwyn, Phil and Jamie might be safer here. *Without me.* But he bit back the question, because Gwyn was giving him a warning look, almost as if she were reading his mind. Instead, he studied the faces of the people in the room. No one looked angry or put out.

Two faces stood out, having not been with them the night before. Clay's IT manager, Alec Vaughn, sat on the floor, a sleek computer on his lap. The young man frowned at the screen, his fingers alternating between being still and flying over the keyboard. He had a reputation as something of a wunderkind in the hacking world. Thorne was happy to see him there.

'I hope you don't mind that I asked Alec to join us,' Clay murmured. 'I have him running some searches for us.'

'It's fine with me,' Thorne told him, because his attention was already focused on the only other person who hadn't been with them the evening before.

JD Fitzpatrick sat next to Lucy on one of the loveseats, his arm protectively around her shoulders.

He caught Thorne's questioning gaze and gave him a sober shrug. 'I'm officially on vacation. Lucy could become a target – which is not your fault. That doesn't change the danger, though. I'm here as a private civilian through the duration.'

Thorne was well aware that wasn't how it worked, but he said nothing. Nothing he could have said would've made a difference anyway. JD was immovable and he was relieved to see it.

He clapped his hands. 'So. Who's leading this clusterfuck?'

Chuckles rippled through the room, and Frederick raised his hand. 'I guess that'd be me. Before we debrief everything we've discovered since last night, I think we need to understand about Tavilla. What is the threat level?'

Thorne took out his phone and checked his messages. Still nothing. 'I don't know. I sent a message to my contact inside Tavilla's organization while we were driving here, but I haven't heard back. I got a message from him last night saying that all was quiet and that no one wished me ill. Now . . . I have to wonder if he's all right.'

'What are you going to do?' Frederick pressed.

Thorne forced his mouth into a small smile. 'What makes you think I'm going to do anything?'

Everyone in the room scoffed in unison.

'Give us a break, Thorne,' Sam said from the sofa where Ruby sat on his lap. 'We're not stupid.'

Thorne sighed. 'I wouldn't have hired you if you had been. I don't hire fools.'

'Fuck,' Paige muttered. 'He's flattering us now. Which means he's going straight to his contact's house when he's done here. Luckily *I* know where that is.'

Frederick's head tilted in interest. 'You do? How?'

Of course Paige had figured it out. Goddammit, the woman was smart. Thorne sighed. *Which was why I sought her out in the first place.*

'I hired her to track him once, after one of our meetings,' Thorne admitted, still unwilling to give up and acknowledge his plans. Not because he didn't trust the others with the information, but because he didn't want to put targets on their backs. Because they would insist on accompanying him, and if this was Tavilla's work . . . he was not a man one wanted to make angry. 'I wanted to know who I was dealing with before I got in too deep.'

'And?' Jamie pressed. 'What did you find, Paige?'

She shrugged. 'His address. That's all I was asked to find. I didn't even know who the guy was at the time.'

'You didn't ask?' Gwyn asked, sounding incredulous.

Paige looked amused. 'No. I was hired by a client to find a specific piece of information. Found it. Job done.'

'When did you know it was his contact you'd followed?' Jamie asked, genuinely curious.

'Just now,' Paige said with a smirk.

'And you'll take us there?' Gwyn pressed, clearly *not* amused.

Paige shook her head. 'No way in hell am I taking *you* there. But I will accompany Thorne, should he require assistance of a personal security nature.'

'I do not need assistance,' Thorne growled. 'And I sure as hell don't need a bodyguard. I'm going to wait to hear from him before I do anything.'

'And if you don't?' JD asked quietly. 'Then what?'

'Then I'll see.'

Everyone shook their heads. 'No way, Thorne,' Sam said. 'We'll follow you if we have to.'

Thorne rubbed his eyes. 'Let's see what happens. I sent him a message and I will wait. For now, let's debrief, because it's still possible this has nothing to do with Tavilla and everything to do with Patricia Segal.'

It was clear that nobody believed him. *Shit.* This was the downside of associating with smart people. They could cut through BS like a hot knife through butter.

Still, he was grateful to have every single one of them on his side. 'Sam? What did you find out about the bar?'

Frederick gave Thorne a side-eye, obviously unhappy that he hadn't answered his question and silently promising that the matter was not dropped. Still, he nodded at Sam. 'Go ahead, Sam.'

Sam shifted Ruby off his lap so that he could reach for his computer bag. 'Basically, Barney, the owner of the bar where Thorne was lured, wasn't there that night. He'd been given four tickets to see the Orioles. Right behind the dugout. The gift was anonymous, the tickets in an envelope thumbtacked to his office door. Just said, "Thanks, boss." Barney figured it was from his employees and went to the game. His employees have since denied giving him the tickets.'

'Which would have been too expensive for them anyway, most likely,' Thorne murmured. 'Four tickets behind the dugout would run you a grand, easily, and that's if you could get your hands on them to begin with.'

'Irresistible lure,' Jamie agreed, because he was also an O's fan and had box seats. 'Did Barney save the envelope?'

'No,' Sam said. 'He felt awful when he heard about what happened to Thorne. He was pissed that his place had been used that way, that he'd been manipulated. Immediately gave me the security tapes from Saturday night, but they were all conveniently blacked out. Not one usable image.'

'Of course,' Thorne muttered. 'Did Barney give this info to the cops?'

Sam shook his head. 'He said some asshole cop named Brickman showed up, swaggering around like he owned the joint. He didn't tell him diddly. But he said he would if a nicer cop showed and if Thorne said it was okay.'

'Tell him it's fine to spill,' Thorne said, almost smiling, because that sounded like Barney.

'I will. Now, after I left Barney's, I went door to door along that road, asking other businesses for their tapes. Most of the folks were receptive, especially because Barney wrote me a note saying "Help this guy."'

Thorne did smile now. 'Did you get anything good?'

Sam inclined his head. 'Yes, as a matter of fact, I did. I've been sitting here going through the files while we waited for you to get here. A liquor store caught your Audi. It drove by as it left the bar, but no other cars followed. You can see the vague outline of two people in the front seats. Neither was as tall as you. I know how much space there is between the roof and your hard head.'

'Thanks,' Thorne muttered.

'Any time, boss. These guys were a good four to six inches shorter. So, still tall. There's no sign of you. I'm betting you were knocked out, on the floor of the backseat or in the cargo hold. The car passed at twelve forty.' He brought the image up on his laptop and turned it so that everyone could see the screen. It was exactly as he'd described.

It gave Thorne an odd feeling in the pit of his gut to know he'd been unconscious at that point. And that Patricia Segal would have still been alive.

'So you were drugged then already,' Lucy said. 'I've heard through the grapevine that the ME confirmed my TOD estimate for Patricia based on the lack of rigor.' Which either meant she'd heard it from the current ME, or that she'd peeked at the autopsy report. 'She hadn't been dead more than four hours before Gwyn found the two of you.'

Alec Vaughn looked up from his laptop. 'Can you give me those files, Sam? I'll see if I can clean up the video at all. Maybe we can get descriptions on the driver and his sidekick.'

Sam dug in his computer bag and tossed Alec a thumb drive. 'They're all there.'

Alec caught it with one hand. 'Thanks.' He bent back down to his laptop, seeming to tune them out again.

'I passed around a photo of Patricia at Barney's,' Sam went on. 'Nobody had seen her there, so I'm thinking she was brought to your house from somewhere else or transferred to your vehicle somewhere along the way, because your security video shows only your Audi being driven into the garage.'

Thorne sat up straighter. 'You got my home security videos?'

'Well, not from the DVR in your house,' Sam said. 'The whole unit was gone. But they hadn't counted on your cameras uploading video to the off-site server. When they arrived, there were at least three people sitting upright in the vehicle.' Again he brought the image up on his laptop and turned it to show the group. All three faces were covered with ski masks. They hadn't been taking any chances.

Sam pointed at the screen. 'There's a shadow here that could be the top of a woman's head. No sign of you, Thorne, so I'm still betting you were in the cargo hold.'

'That's how they got into my house,' Thorne said, that odd feeling in the pit of his gut growing exponentially. How simple it had been for them. *I locked up, but didn't set my alarm*, he thought, wanting to bang his own head into a wall. 'How did they exit?'

'Here,' Sam said. 'It was at one ten on Sunday morning.' He played the video, in which Thorne's Audi could be seen exiting the garage, backing out of the driveway, then driving away. He fast-forwarded. 'It comes back five minutes later and there's just the one guy driving. He stays in the house for two hours.'

Thorne winced. 'He was there that long? No telling what he was doing.'

'Drinking your bourbon, mostly,' Sam said. 'One of your back porch cameras provides a partial view of your kitchen. He comes in periodically to have a swig. Always has the damn mask on, though.'

'Why?' Phil asked. 'If they believed they'd disconnected the security cameras, why cover his face?'

217

'He probably worried that Thorne would wake up,' Gwyn said quietly. She looked as freaked out as he felt. Probably because she knew what it felt like to have a killer walking freely through her home. 'They gave him a lot more GHB than they needed to. They were overcompensating.'

'Because if he woke up, he'd kill whoever was messin' with him,' Ruby concluded, her tone matter-of-fact. She snapped her fingers. 'Like that.'

Thorne wanted to point out once again that he was right there, listening, but he didn't. The thought that this man had moved around so freely – *in my home* – was truly unsettling. 'He changed his clothes at some point,' he pointed out instead. 'His T-shirt is dark there and it was white before.' His stomach roiled, telling him that the sandwich waiting on his plate was no longer welcome. 'He probably did that after he killed Patricia.'

'Probably,' JD concurred, but he looked troubled, and that bothered Thorne more.

Phil frowned. 'But . . . the video still clears Thorne, right? It shows these men going into and out of his home. Shows this man' – he pointed to the screen – 'there for two hours.'

JD shook his head, and now Thorne understood what troubled him. And . . . yeah. It was a problem.

He hoped his voice was steady. He didn't want to frighten Phil any more by showing his own fear. 'I'm not visible in any of these videos. Nothing shows me drugged and unconscious at this point. The police or the prosecutor could still say that I was there, directing the whole thing. That I paid those thugs to bring Patricia to me and that I killed her. And then OD'd on GHB out of remorse or a desire to kill myself or something. The time when I was dosed is really just a guess. These videos don't exonerate me, I'm afraid.'

JD's expression said he'd nailed it. Damn.

Phil paled. 'Goddammit, Thorne.'

'Hold on,' Sam rumbled, giving Phil an encouraging smile. 'I wasn't finished. We do have video of you leaving your house. It was before you got the phone call luring you to Barney's, though.'

Thorne felt his cheeks heat. *Oh, right.* He'd actually forgotten about that. Forgotten that he'd been read the riot act by Lucy and was going to the club to come clean to Gwyn about his role in her canceled dates. 'I was going to the club. Our club. I got the call shortly after I'd left the house.'

Lucy lifted her brows at him. 'Really?'

His cheeks flamed hotter. 'Really,' he mumbled.

Gwyn's eyes flashed with sudden understanding, and damned if her cheeks didn't heat too. 'All right,' she conceded.

Sam was giving them all an appraising look, one side of his mouth lifting in a half-smile. 'All right,' he echoed. 'After I viewed all this video, I went back to the liquor store's tapes and rewound another hour's worth of footage. And got this.' Once more he turned his laptop to show them. Thorne's car was racing past, headed toward Barney's Bar. 'You drove away from your house and to the bar, but you're not shown returning. Yet you were found in your bed, so you can argue that you were unconscious the whole time.'

Phil shuddered visibly, glancing over at Thorne with raw relief in his eyes before turning to Sam. 'Thank you, Sam. We appreciate it.'

Sam's smile was gentle. 'We're going to get through this,' he promised, then pulled up a grainy photo showing the lower two thirds of a man's face. 'This isn't a clear picture of Thorne, but this is how tall he sits in his car. You can see it in the video taken as he leaves his house earlier. So we don't have a perfect alibi for you, Thorne, but it does support your story. That's all I've got for now.'

'That's a lot,' Frederick praised. 'I'll go next.' He told them how he'd found Bernice Brown and how frightened she'd been. And how she'd thanked Thorne for being willing to come to help her even though she'd been used to lure him. 'Then I met with the friend she told me about, the one who'd gotten a call from a Detective Hooper – who, by the way, does not exist. The "detective" was asking her questions about her friend's whereabouts and her attorney. The friend, Sally Brewster, felt uneasy and hung up. She gave me the number, which was providential,' he finished grimly.

Thorne could feel Frederick's fear. It was palpable even from across the room. 'Why? What happened?'

219

Clay gave Frederick a sympathetic look. 'Someone messaged Julie from the same number to try to get her to give them her home address.'

New dread – more new dread – settled on Thorne's shoulders. 'I'm sorry,' he whispered.

Frederick shook his head. 'We are not going there, Thorne. Miss Brewster, Bernice Brown's friend, had messaged her first and Julie gave her our home phone number.'

'What? Why?' Gwyn demanded.

'Because she was scared and she wanted to check me out. I'm grateful, actually. I didn't realize that Julie was so connected into the Internet. I didn't realize a lot of things about Julie,' he added ruefully. 'The point is, we know someone has used that number at least twice, once to try to find Bernice Brown, and once to try to find – presumably – me.'

'I haven't been able to trace the number,' Alec said, sounding annoyed with himself.

'I thought you couldn't track disposable phones,' Phil said.

Alec shrugged. 'There are ways. Not necessarily pretty ways, but ways. The number's 301-555-2495, right? I'd hate to be chasing down the wrong number.'

Frederick checked his notes. 'That's right.'

Thorne sucked in a harsh breath. That was Ramirez's number. *Goddammit.* His chest went tight. This was very, very bad. *Shit. Damn. Fuck.*

But before he could utter a single word, a piercing alarm ripped the air and Clay jumped to his feet and ran to the monitor on the wall. 'Somebody just cut the fence and came through. They're somewhere on the property.'

Hunt Valley, Maryland,
Monday 13 June, 5.35 P.M.

Gwyn fought to stay calm, but the screeching alarm had hold of her brain and she just wanted to *run* as far and fast as she could. Thorne lifted her, setting her on his lap, then wrapped his arms around her.

It was then that she realized she was trembling so hard that her teeth were chattering.

'Shh,' he whispered in her ear. 'Look. They know what to do.'

It was true. Everyone except for Gwyn, Thorne, Phil and Jamie had scattered in an organized way that helped her calm herself a little. Just a little, because the alarm was still blaring.

Clay, Sam, JD and Frederick were standing around an enormous gun safe that had been hidden in a closet behind a normal-looking door. Clay was passing out weapons. Paige and Stevie had already drawn their guns from holsters Gwyn hadn't noticed but was unsurprised to know they had. Paige was scanning the monitors while Stevie and Lucy headed down the stairs to where the children were.

'Oh God,' Gwyn whispered. 'The kids.'

'The kids are safe,' Thorne assured her. 'Do you really think Clay would allow a playroom for children to be breachable?'

'No.' She'd seen Clay's security first-hand. He'd installed the system in her own condo, for God's sake. The man took care of his family. The babies were safe.

'Remarkable,' Jamie murmured. 'They've practiced this, clearly.'

'Like a finely tuned machine,' Phil agreed. 'I feel like a slug, just sitting here.'

The alarm was abruptly silenced and Gwyn's bones seemed to crumble into dust. She'd held herself so tensely before that she was a puddle now. A puddle whose arms were tightly wrapped around Thomas Thorne's neck.

His hand was slowly gliding up her spine and down again. Gentling her. Just as he'd done in those horrible days after Evan. Thorne had been the only one who'd held her afterward. Because Thorne had been the only one she'd trusted.

'Sorry,' she whispered, mortified by her reaction to a stupid alarm. But obviously not mortified enough, because she hadn't let him go. *I don't want to. I don't want to ever let him go.* He was solid strength and he'd been so generous, sharing that strength with her whenever she'd needed it.

'Shh.' Thorne's deep voice rumbled up from his chest. 'It's fine.' She felt his chin lift. 'What can I do, Clay?'

'Depends.' Clay's voice reached them from the other side of the large living room. 'Which of you is the best shot?'

'Gwyn is!' Paige called over her shoulder. 'Give her a Glock. We've drilled at the shooting range.'

'Well, all right then,' Clay said, but he looked doubtful, probably because Gwyn was still clutching Thorne like he was her lifeline. 'Who's the second best shot?'

Gwyn forced herself to release the chokehold she had on Thorne. Sliding off his lap, she held out her hand, proud that she'd controlled the trembling. 'It's fine. *I'm* fine. Give me the fucking gun.'

'Yes, ma'am,' Clay drawled, and obeyed, watching closely as she checked the magazine and racked the slide, making sure it was loaded properly.

She looked up at him, drawing on her defiance for strength. Just as she'd done for the last four and a half years. 'Go. We're good here.'

Clay gave her a single nod, then he was out the door leading to the backyard.

Only Alec stayed behind, his fingers flying over the computer keys, his eyes glued to his screen. He paused only to connect a cable from his cell phone to the device he wore behind his ear.

'Does he have a cochlear implant?' Jamie whispered, fascinated. 'One of my clients has one. He has the same cord for his phone.'

'Yes,' Gwyn whispered back. Clay's IT whizz-kid had pretty clear speech, so she tended to forget his deafness. She watched Alec now, mesmerized by his calm confidence. She envied him that confidence. Her own was mostly bravado.

'I found him on camera two,' Alec said into the phone. 'He got away on a dirt bike. He's headed through the woods.'

There was a pause, and Alec nodded. 'I'll keep watching. You keep your fool head down. Pops,' he added irreverently.

Gwyn calmed a little bit more upon hearing that news.

'Who is "Pops"?' Phil asked.

Gwyn chuckled. 'Taylor calls Frederick "Dad". She needed a

222

name for Clay and tried "Pops". He hated it, so of course *all* the kids have taken to calling him that.'

Phil nodded, also looking a little calmer, although he was clutching Jamie's hand hard. Or maybe Jamie was doing the clutching. It was hard to say, and in the end it didn't matter. 'Who is Alec to Clay?' Phil asked.

Gwyn smiled. 'Kind of like an adopted son. They met when Alec was a kid and had been kidnapped. Clay found him.'

'Saved my fucking life,' Alec said, surprising them all.

Gwyn stared at him. 'Oh. I didn't know if you could hear us and the phone at the same time.'

Alec still didn't look up from his screen, his eyes darting back and forth. He was probably scanning the security feeds. 'I got a second cochlear implant on my other side. I get bilateral input now. So you can stop talking about me like I'm not here.'

'Join the fucking club,' Thorne muttered.

Gwyn let his voice ground her, just as she always did. She sat perched on the arm of the loveseat, leaning into him. 'If you didn't shut us out of the important stuff, we might be able to talk *to* you instead of *around* you.'

Thorne's lips thinned. 'There is nothing to tell.'

She shook her head. 'Whatever, hotshot.'

His phone buzzed loudly, and he flinched, then checked the screen. 'It's my contact,' he said.

A few seconds passed, with Thorne still staring at his phone.

'Well?' Jamie asked impatiently.

'I asked him how he was doing. He just messaged back, "I'm fine. Why do you ask?"'

Jamie sighed. 'That doesn't sound fine.'

Thorne scowled. 'I know. I'm trying to figure out how to respond.'

Gwyn's eyes narrowed at what she saw on the screen. 'Wait just a fucking second, Thorne. *That's* the number your contact uses?'

Thorne abruptly shut off his phone, but it was too late.

'What?' Jamie asked.

Gwyn turned to the others. 'The number for his contact is the same damn number that Frederick just gave for the fake detective who was harassing Bernice Brown's friend, and the one used to message his daughter.'

'*Thorne.*' The single syllable out of Jamie's mouth carried disapproval, disappointment and more than a little fury.

Thorne shook his head stubbornly. '*No.* I'm not telling you anything more. Any of you. You'll insist on "investigating", and get yourselves killed.'

Several beats of enraged silence were broken by Alec's low whistle. 'Whoa. Way to piss off your posse, dude.'

Thorne's face darkened. 'I don't need—'

Alec looked up at that. 'What?' he asked sarcastically. 'You don't need what? Our help? Fuck that. Our support? Fuck that squared. You don't *want* to need it.' He shook his head in disgust, his affected drawl mocking. 'Big strong guys like you don't need nuthin'. At least be honest with yourself.'

Thorne's mouth fell open.

Jamie snorted softly. 'Touché.'

Gwyn gave Alec a hard nod. 'Nicely done, kid. Couldn't have said it better myself.'

'Yeah, well, I work with a whole company *full* of idiots who don't want to need anyone. Gets old after a while.'

Thorne's lip curled in a sneer as his eyes locked onto Gwyn's. 'Right. Like *you* want to need help? Bullshit.'

Gwyn's chin came up. 'We're not talking about me. We're talking about you.'

'Hush, children.' Alec held up a hand, once again talking into his phone. 'I didn't get the bike's plate. It didn't have one. Are you coming back? . . . Fine. I'll stay on the line until you're all safely inside.' He looked up again. 'They lost him. He cut himself a path through the woods just wide enough for a dirt bike.'

'How long a path?' Thorne asked.

'Long enough to get him back to the main road. It had to have taken him a while to clear that much undergrowth. Probably worked at night. There's no light in the back. Trees are too dense for moonlight and our floodlights only reach so far. Clay thinks it took at least three or four nights.'

'How did he know Thorne would be here?' Phil asked.

'I don't think he did, babe,' Jamie replied. 'He was probably planning to strike here again anyway. He already went after Stevie once today. All in broad daylight.'

'Stevie and Clay have kids,' Thorne said tightly. 'Cordelia is JD's goddaughter. If he hit here, he'd hurt a lot of my friends.'

Jamie sighed. 'Normally I'd tell you that not everything is about you, but this time, it is.'

'What are you going to do about your contact?' Gwyn asked sharply. Thorne winced, and she knew he'd hoped she'd be distracted enough to forget about it. 'No, I didn't forget. Spill, Thorne. Now.'

'Or what?' he mocked.

'Don't,' she said quietly. 'Don't shut me out. Don't shut *them* out. The kid is right. You don't want to need our help, but that's too damn bad. Tell me.'

Thorne sighed. 'I'm going to ask him to meet me. And you're not coming.'

Her jaw tightened. She wanted to argue, but she knew there were those in the group who could protect him better than she could. The knowledge irked, but she shoved it away. 'Who is?'

'I don't know,' he hissed, enunciating each word. 'I will figure it out.'

The door from the backyard opened, admitting those who'd gone after the intruder. Everyone who'd been downstairs with the kids joined them and together they reclaimed their seats. Cautiously they looked from Gwyn to Thorne, because they were still glaring daggers at each other.

'What'd we miss?' Clay asked.

Thirteen

Gwyn stared up at Thorne's stony profile. 'Tell them or I will.'

His jaw clenched as he gritted his teeth. 'That call to Bernice Brown's friend and the message to Julie were made from my contact's disposable cell.'

'Well, fuck,' Frederick spat angrily. 'Were you going to tell us, Thorne?'

'Of course I was,' he snapped. 'I wasn't going to tell *them.*' He gestured to Gwyn and the two men who were by all rights his fathers.

Jamie huffed a sigh. Phil looked resigned. Gwyn bit her tongue, because the temper she felt bubbling was going to yield words she'd never be able to take back.

'So your contact harassed Bernice Brown's friend?' JD clarified.

'Or at least someone used the contact's number to do so,' Alec challenged. 'There are spoofing sites that will allow you to mask your call with another number. They didn't have to have his actual phone.'

'I know,' Thorne said. 'That's how I message him. His returned texts are forwarded from my disposable cell to this phone.' He held up his smartphone. 'I got a message from him while you all were gone. He says he's fine and asks why I'm asking.'

'Tell him you want to meet,' Frederick ordered.

Thorne nodded stiffly. 'That's what I was planning to do.'

'But you're not going to the meeting place,' Paige said, watching

226

him. 'Because whoever made that call might be there waiting. You're going to his house.'

'That was my plan, yes.'

Everyone went quiet, considering it.

Finally JD spoke. 'Send your message, Thorne. I'm going with you to the contact's house.'

Thorne surprised Gwyn by nodding again. 'All right,' he said. 'Tell Joseph and Hyatt to have boots on the ground at the meeting place, just in case we luck out and Tavilla shows up. They'll want to be sure they have surveillance and enough cameras to film anyone passing through the meeting area. If it's not Tavilla but one of his goons, we'll want to capture their faces.'

'Good plan,' Clay said. 'What can we do?'

'Just . . .' Thorne's voice went husky. 'Just don't get killed. Please. I can't live with that. Not again.'

Gwyn knew he was thinking of Sherri, his first love, killed because she'd stood with him when nobody else had. And of course he was thinking of the shootings today. Even if the shooter had missed, he'd come so very close to both her and Stevie. 'We'll be careful,' she insisted.

He nodded once, unconvinced. 'Okay.'

She lowered her voice, leaning in to whisper in his ear. 'And we *will* talk about this. Later. In private. You will *not* keep things from us. From me.'

She watched the clench of his jaw, the way his throat worked as he swallowed convulsively. And she sighed. This need to keep them safe was ripping him apart, and that was the last thing she wanted. 'Look,' she whispered. 'You are important, Thorne. To me. I promise not to get myself killed, if you do the same. Can we at least agree on this?'

She felt his small shudder and suddenly wished they were alone so that she could put her arms around him and give him what he needed. Whatever that was. But he'd already pulled away, physically and emotionally, and the knowledge . . . hurt.

Rubbing his hands down his thighs, he stood up. 'I'm going to text him now. I'll be back.'

Fuck, she thought miserably. *He could text from right here. Next to me.* But he was practically race-walking from the room. *Away from me.*

Could she blame him? He'd declared his . . . feelings, whatever label they bore. She'd pushed him away, then told him he was *important* to her. The lamest thing ever. And she still expected him to share with her?

Well . . . yes. I do. Because we're still friends. But the words echoed dully in her head, and her throat thickened. *Aren't we? Can we be?*

She was terrified that she already knew the answer to that question. Remaining where she was, she watched him leave the room and felt a piece of her heart crumble.

She glanced over at Lucy, who looked sad. Their eyes met, Lucy's full of sympathy and helplessness. Gwyn looked away, focusing on the handgun she still held but feeling the weight of every gaze in the room. All on her.

A strong arm slid around her shoulders. Sam. 'Give him a few minutes to get his head on straight, Gwyn,' he murmured kindly. 'You know this kind of shit is hard on him. He feels like he has to be Superman. This has got to be his worst nightmare.'

Carefully she flipped the safety on the handgun. 'I know.' Pointing the barrel down, she slid off the arm of the loveseat and gave the gun back to Clay. 'What will you do about your fence?' she asked him.

'We repaired it already,' he told her, but there was sympathy in his eyes too. 'And now we know where we need to beef up security.'

'The woods gave us a false sense of safety,' Stevie added. 'We'll be installing more cameras. We tried motion detectors once, but that was hard because we have deer back there and they kept setting them off.'

Gwyn felt her stomach lurch. These people – good people – felt the need to take such drastic measures simply to protect themselves and their families. And why? Because they'd stood up against criminals. And now they were threatened again. Because of their friendship with Thorne.

Sam was right. This was Thorne's worst nightmare. *And I'm being selfish, my feelings hurt because he walked away from me.* Because he needed more from her than demands that he be upfront with information.

He needed more than her assurances that he was 'important' to her. Because he was. He was . . . he was everything.

She wanted to say something to him. She *needed* to say something to him. But no words would come.

Then make *the words come, girl. And do it fast. He's hurting, and . . .*

And God only knew what he was planning. The man truly did believe that he was Superman. *Because he usually is.* Bigger than life, he always seemed invincible. *But he's not. He's just a man.* An amazing man. A handsome, strong man who made her feel safe and warm and . . . loved. *He loves me.* And somehow she'd always known that, down deep where it was . . . what? Safe?

Yes. Safe. And loving him back? *Not so safe.*

But you do love him. You know you do. You always have.

Yes, yes, she had. She'd also known that. Also down deep where it was . . .

Safe? the voice in her head mocked her. She had learned that there was no such thing as true safety. There was hiding and there was living. And through all of it, there had been Thorne. *So tell him, for God's sake. Don't be such a fucking coward.*

She felt lightheaded at the notion. *Why is this so hard?*

'Gwyn, honey.' Lucy's voice was soft in her ear, but the smack to Gwyn's back wasn't. Her best friend had thwacked her a good one with the palm of her hand. '*Breathe*, girl. You need to breathe.'

Gwyn sucked in some air, then realized she'd been standing in the middle of the room staring at Clay and Stevie but not hearing a word they'd said. Nobody was saying anything now. The room had grown painfully quiet.

Her cheeks were suddenly on fire. 'I hate this day,' she muttered.

Lucy huffed a chuckle. 'I know. Me too. Come. Let's go somewhere quiet.'

Annapolis, Maryland,
Monday 13 June, 7.00 P.M.

'Hey,' Kathryn shouted.

He held the phone away from his ear with a wince. Kathryn always had to yell over the pounding beat of the music. He hated her job. Hated that she had to be there night after night. 'Are we ready?'

'*Absolutamente,*' she said.

He could hear the grin in her voice and it made him smile. 'Excellent. Patton has completed his task.' His aide had dropped the carved-up bodies at the Circus Freaks' front door, just as he'd asked. 'Let me know when everything is complete.'

'I will. See you tonight if I'm lucky.'

'You will be lucky,' he said firmly. There was no way he was allowing her to spend the night in any jail. Her place at night was with him. Soon her job would be over and she'd be back in his bed every night, just as nature intended.

'Then open a bottle of wine and run me a bubble bath. I'm going to need it.'

Hunt Valley, Maryland,
Monday 13 June, 7.15 P.M.

Lucy led Gwyn into the Maynards' dining room and pulled at the pocket door, sliding it closed as Gwyn sank into a chair and covered her burning face with her hands. 'God. How long was I standing there like an idiot?'

Lucy drew a chair close and stroked her hair. 'Not like an idiot. You suddenly looked so . . . sad. Unbearably sad. You . . .' She let the thought trail and huffed out a sigh. 'You used to do that after . . . well, you know. Evan. Zone out, with that expression on your face. I was afraid you were back . . . *there.*'

There. Back in the huge deserted factory where she and Lucy had been held for hours. Where Evan had intended for them to die. Both of them.

Gwyn wrinkled her nose. 'It smelled like fish.'

Lucy snorted a surprised laugh. 'Yeah, it did. Fish factories usually do.' She gave Gwyn's hair another stroke, her voice softening. 'Are you okay?'

Gwyn considered the question carefully and was relieved to discover that yes, she really was okay. 'I am. About Evan, I mean. About all this? Probably not, but mostly because . . .' Closing her eyes, she leaned into Lucy, taking comfort from her solid frame. 'I'm so worried about him, Luce.'

'I am too. What did you say to him, right before he left the room?'

Gwyn sighed. 'Basically that he needed to keep himself alive. Because he was important to me.'

'Ouch,' Lucy murmured, her hand going still in Gwyn's hair.

'I know,' Gwyn said miserably. 'I need to fix this.'

Lucy resumed her stroking. 'Not unless you mean it. Do you?'

Gwyn didn't pretend to misunderstand, but the word was so damn hard to say out loud. *Yes. Just say yes.*

'It's acceptable to feel however you feel,' Lucy said when Gwyn still hadn't said anything after a minute of silence. 'Thorne will . . . He'll be okay.'

But the unspoken truth hung in the air between them and Gwyn felt her eyes sting. He wouldn't be okay. *Neither will I.* 'Why is this so hard?' she whispered.

'Because you feel how you feel,' Lucy murmured, 'even though you don't want to. You care for him. We both do. But that's not the same as loving him.'

'I *know* that,' Gwyn bit out, feeling Lucy flinch. 'I'm sorry,' she muttered. 'I didn't mean to snap at you.'

'It's okay,' Lucy said with a hint of humor. 'I'm used to it.'

'You shouldn't be. Nobody should. Goddammit, I'm . . . I am not a good person, Lucy. I'm mean and selfish and . . .' She halted abruptly when her voice broke. 'Dammit, I do.'

'Do what?' Lucy asked cautiously.

'Love him,' Gwyn choked out, so glad her face was hidden behind her hair.

'Okay.' Lucy drew the word out, making it more of a question. 'How so?'

Gwyn jerked her chin up, peering at Lucy through narrowed eyes. 'How do you think?'

Lucy shrugged, exasperated. 'I don't know. You haven't actually *told* me anything.'

Which was true. And the admission made her eyes sting again. 'Why can't I just say it? Other people just say it. All the fucking time. Love you, love you, love you,' she sing-songed mockingly. 'What the hell is wrong with me that I can't just say it?'

Lucy drew a breath. 'Okay. Let's step back here. There is nothing *wrong* with you. You're not abnormal. You've had a trauma. Tell me something, honey. Did you ever tell Evan that you loved him?'

Gwyn reared back as if Lucy had slapped her in the face. 'What? No.'

Lucy lifted her hands in a placating gesture. 'Okay. Asked and answered.'

Gwyn looked away. 'But I was about to.'

'Ah.'

She glared at her friend from the corner of her eye. 'What does "ah" mean?'

'It means that the last time you felt this way, it ended really shittily.'

'You can say that again,' Gwyn mumbled. 'So, what do I do?'

'How should I know? I'm far better with dead people.'

Gwyn chuckled, just as Lucy had intended. 'You liar. You love JD. You love your kids. You even love my sorry ass.'

Lucy smiled. 'I do. All of the above. It wasn't easy for me to say the words either, you know. At first. To JD. Now, to my babies? I tell them every day how much I love them. They'll probably get tired of hearing it at some point. I'm not going to be my parents. That abusive cycle stops with me.'

'Why wasn't it easy?' Gwyn asked, suddenly brutally aware that whatever issues Lucy had been having at the beginning of her relationship with JD had been dealt with alone. *Because I was deep, deep in the fog. God, what a shitty friend I am.*

'Stop it,' Lucy warned. 'I can see what you're thinking and it's not true.'

'What am I thinking?' Gwyn challenged.

'You're feeling guilty because you weren't there for me when JD and I first started out. Ha! I knew it,' Lucy crowed when Gwyn rolled her eyes dramatically. 'So you weren't there for me. It turned out okay, I swear. I understood. I was in that smelly fish factory too. Remember?'

'Yes,' Gwyn bit out. 'I remember. And yet you got over it.'

Lucy laughed, then stopped and blinked. 'Wait. You don't really think that, do you?'

'Well, yeah. You're . . .' Gwyn waved a hand from Lucy's head to her toes. 'Well adjusted.'

'I guess it's nice I appear that way, but I'm not, not really. I still have nightmares.'

Gwyn blinked up at her. 'You do?'

'Of course I do. JD does too. He wakes up screaming sometimes,' she added in a whisper. 'But keep that to yourself. He has a reputation to protect.'

'I won't say a word,' Gwyn whispered back seriously. Because this *was* serious.

'Thanks.' Lucy smiled sadly. 'Maybe the difference is that coming out of the fish factory, I got my Prince Charming and you got . . . the memory of Evan.'

'I'm *glad* you got your Prince Charming,' Gwyn whispered fiercely, because she was. 'This isn't me being jealous of you.'

'Oh, I know that.' Lucy sighed. 'I kept hoping that you'd be okay, you know? Because you were asleep for most of it. He'd drugged you and you were still asleep when he got me.'

Gwyn drew in a breath, forced her face to appear calm, even though she was screaming inside. *No. I wasn't asleep.* She exhaled slowly. *Not thinking about that. Not happening anymore. It's over. It's not happening anymore.* It was the mantra her therapist had drilled into her over and over. It stopped the downward spiral into panic. Most of the time.

'Gwyn?' Lucy said very quietly. 'What have you not told me?'

233

Gwyn shook her head, slow wags back and forth. 'Don't ask me. Please. I can't go there. Not right now.'

A long, long silence stretched between them before Lucy cleared her throat. 'Does Thorne know?'

'No.' Gwyn choked out the word.

'Then you need to tell him.' Lucy's voice had grown impossibly gentle. 'At least tell him that there are things he doesn't know. He'll give you time.'

'He's wasted years on me already,' Gwyn said bitterly.

'He doesn't see it that way.' Still so damn gentle. 'You know that.'

'I don't know anything. Except that . . .' She closed her eyes, because they burned. Two tears escaped and she quickly dashed them away.

'Except that?' Lucy prodded.

'I don't want him to hurt.' Gwyn swallowed hard. 'I don't want him to think it's him, when it's really me. I'm broken.'

'No, honey, you're not broken. You're healing. There's a difference.'

Gwyn opened her eyes to stare at Lucy, her vision blurred. *Healing. Not broken.* That too was true. That too she knew deep down in her bones.

Lucy was appraising her thoughtfully. 'Do you love him *that* way? You know?' She waggled strawberry-blond brows and made kissy noises.

Gwyn snorted, grateful for the subject change. 'Are we twelve?'

Lucy smiled. 'Maybe. So? Do you? Do you think of him that way?'

Gwyn huffed a breath. 'Of course. Doesn't everybody?'

Lucy pursed her lips, eyes now sparkling with either amusement or mischief. But at least it wasn't that gentle compassion, because *that* was like a knife in the gut. 'I can honestly say that while I've appreciated Thorne's very fine form, I have never thought of him that way.'

Gwyn frowned. 'You are lying to me.'

'Nope.' She held up three fingers. 'Scout's honor. And yes, I was a Girl Scout, so it's a valid vow.'

'Never? Not even once?'

'Nope. Not even once. He's always been like a brother. And I would never think that about my brother.' She shuddered. 'That's just . . . so wrong.'

Gwyn considered it. 'Not even one time? Not even to wonder how it would be?'

'Gwyn, I have never once thought about Thomas Thorne in any sexual position. Whatsoever. Although I take it you have?' she added slyly.

Gwyn rolled her eyes again. 'Yeah. God. I really can't believe you haven't. He's . . .' She made an amorphous gesture with her hands. 'Like . . . wow.'

Lucy laughed, and it was a beautiful sound after the heaviness of their conversation. 'Yes, dear. Very articulate. Now, JD?' She hummed. 'Like . . . wow.'

Gwyn felt her own laugh all the way to her gut, and it felt so good. Like an icy bottle of water on a really hot day. A relief.

Lucy's brows arched. 'Although I have to wonder how that will . . . you know. Work. You're . . . you.' Her hands made a 'small' gesture, then widened comically. 'And he's . . . him.'

Gwyn's cheeks burned again. 'It will be *fine*. I've been with men nearly his size.' Like Evan.

No. She visualized pushing that shit into a closet and locking the door. *I am* not *going there.*

Lucy had sobered as well. 'Thorne is not Evan.'

'I know. I guess I need to make sure that *he* knows that I know.'

Lucy leaned forward until their brows were touching, the gesture one they'd learned from Thorne. 'Then I'd say you have some work ahead of you. These conversations are not the most fun to have, but the rewards are pretty damn awesome.' She pulled back to kiss Gwyn's forehead. 'Good luck.'

'Yeah. I'm going to need it. Because I have to do something big before he does something stupid.'

She stood up to go, but Lucy gently gripped her wrist, holding her in place. 'No,' she said, very seriously. 'You don't have to do "something big". You just have to let him know that he's yours.'

Gwyn nodded once. That didn't sound so very difficult. Because he was. *Mine. He's always been mine.* 'I can do that.'

'Good.' Lucy released her. 'Go, break a leg.'

Gwyn managed a small grin, then frowned slightly when her phone began to buzz. It was Mowry, who managed the club when she wasn't around. Normally he called her much later. They had a standing time to talk at two a.m., after last call.

She was debating declining the call because she needed to talk to Thorne. But then a text popped up, also from Mowry.

Answer your damn phone!

New dread descended as she answered. 'What's wrong?'

'Thank God,' Mowry said, breathless. 'I tried to call Thorne, but he's not picking up. Is he okay?'

'He's . . . okay, yes,' Gwyn said, not wanting to explain the entire situation to their club manager. 'Why? What's happened?'

'You know how I told you about the two guys who tried to deal from the club last night?'

'Yes.' The same two men Prew had followed. The ones who'd hoped Thorne's troubles were a green light for them to use Sheidalin as their own. 'What about them?'

'They just turned up dead.'

Gwyn's legs turned to jelly and she sat back down blindly. 'Where?'

'At a warehouse near the docks.'

Relief whooshed out of her. 'Oh God. I thought you were going to say they were found at the club.'

Lucy's brows were winging up urgently, but Gwyn shook her head because Mowry was talking. 'It would have been better if they had been. Gwyn, that warehouse is the headquarters for the Circus Freaks.'

It took her a moment to make the connection, but it still made no sense. 'The motorcycle gang?' She blinked for a moment, trying to process. She'd heard about the Circus Freaks on the news. They, along with a few other gangs – including Tavilla's Los Señores de la Tierra – were jockeying for ownership of the city. Because of the harbor and shipping and . . . She was sure there was more, but she

236

couldn't remember it now. 'How do you even know that? How do you know any of this?'

He huffed impatiently. 'I know the warehouse is the Circus Freaks' because I keep up with that shit. I know their colors, their members, their hotspots. So does Ming, and all the other bouncers too. Freaks come into the club sometimes, trying to deal, and I have to know who to boot.'

'All right, that makes sense.' She'd never even thought about that. She wondered if Thorne and Lucy knew. 'Why didn't I know this?'

'It's been within the last few years,' Mowry said more gently. 'So we didn't drag you into it. But this is serious, hon, so you have to catch up, and fast. The bodies were found with their pockets – and their mouths and their wounds – stuffed with Sheidalin match-books.'

'Oh shit,' she breathed. *That* she understood. Another setup, this time implicating the club. 'Mowry, Lucy's with me. Can I put you on speaker?'

'Is JD there?'

'No. Just Lucy.'

'Okay then.' He repeated what he'd told her for Lucy's benefit, then went on. 'Both men were . . . eviscerated. Like the woman found with Thorne yesterday morning.'

'Oh fucking shit,' Lucy muttered. 'How do you know about these bodies? I haven't heard it on the news. And JD would know.'

'Because I pay one of the Freaks for information,' Mowry spat. 'I don't want to give a penny to those drug-dealing sons of bitches, but I do. It helps me keep this place clean. Just like Thorne demands.'

Gwyn closed her eyes. 'Got it. Does that come out of club funds?'

'No. Not exactly,' Mowry admitted grudgingly. 'It's not a traceable thing. Just petty cash.'

Fuck, fuck, fuck. That, in and of itself, was going to ring bells if the cops investigated. Best case, it would look like they were paying extortion money to organized crime. Worst case, it would look like Mowry had been embezzling. *Or that I have, because I do the mother-fucking books.* Or worse still, that someone at the club was buying product from a drug-dealing gang. *How did I miss this?* Because she'd been in a four-year fog, that was how. *Fuck.*

She met Lucy's eyes and saw that her friend had also connected the dots. 'This is bad,' Lucy murmured.

'Y'think?' Mowry snapped.

'All right,' Gwyn said calmly. 'We'll explain it to Frederick and Jamie and then we'll come to the club. Because sooner or later the cops are going to show up.'

'Ah, fuck,' Mowry muttered. 'Too late, sweetie. They're here.'

In the background she could hear loud voices. Demands and shouted protests. Lucy dropped her head into her hands. 'Oh my God.'

'All right,' Gwyn said again. 'We'll be there as soon as we can. Don't say anything to anyone. None of you.'

'I won't,' Mowry promised grimly. 'I haven't worked for a defense attorney for years for nothing.'

A much louder voice yelled, 'I said, off the goddamn phone!' The shout was followed by a sickening thud. The call ended.

Gwyn rose, feeling oddly . . . in control. 'Let me tell Thorne. I'd like him to have a few minutes to process this before he has to be Superman in front of everyone else.'

Lucy nodded wearily. 'Yeah. This is going to gut him. I swear to God, if this is Tavilla, I want to see him roasting on a spit.'

'For hurting Thorne like this? I want him to roast *alive.*' Gwyn stroked Lucy's hair, returning the favor from before. 'Don't worry, Luce. We'll figure this out.'

'I know,' Lucy murmured, but she didn't sound convinced. She pushed herself to her feet. 'I'll bring everyone up to speed. You tell Thorne.'

They slid the pocket door open and every eye in the room cut over to stare. Ignoring her residual embarrassment, Gwyn left Lucy to brief the group.

She needed to get to Thorne.

Fourteen

Thorne stared out into Clay's backyard, lit up like the middle of the day with floodlights as the sun began its descent. This was so fucked up. Clay and Stevie had worked so hard to create a safe space for their little family, for Cordelia and baby Mason.

And because of me, they're on alert once again.

It wasn't right. But he knew what he needed to do about it.

He'd known Tavilla was behind this. He just hadn't wanted to admit it, because, quite frankly, the man scared the everliving *shit* out of him. *I was a coward. And now innocents are paying the price.*

It was time to call Tavilla out. To *take* him out.

It was a dangerous game they'd been playing, and he'd known it. Watching each other, dancing around the fact that Tavilla wanted him dead. Dancing around the fact that it was just a matter of time before the snake struck.

It had also been just a matter of time before Thorne's man inside either gave up, gave in, or gave up the ghost. He feared it was the last one, because Ramirez's texts were not normal.

He stared at the new message on his phone's screen. He and Ramirez had devised a code phrase to indicate trouble. Thorne had used it in his message to Ramirez, asking to meet him. Ramirez had not responded appropriately.

Meet me at 11 p.m.

That was all Ramirez had replied, so something was wrong. Wrong in Ramirez's world meant he was probably dead. That could be because he had been passing information to Thorne, or it could be that he had simply been caught in the kind of situation that normally killed a drug dealer's right-hand man.

Ramirez had been willing to risk himself because he hated Tavilla more than he hated Thorne. Thorne had been willing to risk himself because he wasn't about to cave to monsters like Cesar Tavilla. Once he caved to one, the others would swarm, all demanding he represent their incredibly illegal enterprises. No. *Just . . . no.*

But this was no longer about only him. He'd drawn innocent people into the fray. Innocent people he cared about.

One that he loved.

And, as if he'd conjured her just by thinking of her, the scent of lavender tickled his nose. He stiffened. Everywhere. And cursed himself. *I should never have said a word.* He'd only added unnecessary drama to this rapidly unfolding shitshow that had become his life.

Her small hand pressed into his back and rubbed gently. He had to swallow back a groan. He wanted her affection. Her support. Her friendship. But he wanted so much more. But now . . . even if she succumbed to his 'vast charms', he thought bitterly, anything she gave him would be suspect. He'd always wonder if she'd given in because she felt guilty. Or worse, pitied him.

He couldn't deal with that. He wouldn't.

He deserved more. They both did.

'Thorne,' she said softly. 'I'm sorry.'

He swallowed again. 'For what?' he managed.

'For being selfish and insensitive, mostly. For other things too.' She leaned into him, resting her forehead against his back.

'What other things?'

She laughed quietly. 'You're not going to protest my being selfish and insensitive?'

He found himself – unbelievably – smiling. 'Nope.'

'I . . .' He felt her body shift as she drew a breath, heard her exhale. 'I think we need to talk about what you told me last night. In my bedroom.'

His smile vanished. 'I wish I never had.' Because this was headed toward rejection. He could hear it in her voice.

'No,' she said softly. 'I'm glad you did. I needed to hear it. I needed to wake up.'

He held himself perfectly still. Waiting for the axe to fall. He hoped she'd be quick about it.

'Stop,' she whispered. 'I'm not saying no. Stop waiting for me to say no.'

He kept himself upright through sheer stubborn will, because his knees had gone wobbly as a newborn lamb's. 'Are you saying yes?'

'Maybe.'

He couldn't stop the laugh that rumbled out. The answer was so *Gwyn*. 'Maybe?'

She sighed. 'I . . . want to tell you some things. Good things,' she rushed to add when he tensed again. 'Mostly. I mean, I hope. But, um, most of that's going to have to wait a little while.'

He cleared his throat, clawing for control when he wasn't sure if he wanted to laugh or cry. 'Why are you here, Gwyn?'

'Well . . . I'd started to come to find you for the good reason. And then I got waylaid by a really bad one. You need to hear both.'

He turned, gripping her arms gently when she leaned back so that she could see his face. He always worried she'd topple backward on those damn high heels of hers when she did that. One side of her mouth lifted, acknowledging the move.

'I wish I were taller,' she said with another sigh.

'I like you just the way you are. Short and selfish,' he added, just to see her smile again.

She obliged him, her smile sweet and shy. He hadn't seen that smile before. He would have remembered it. He wanted to think that only he had seen it, that she'd never smiled like that at anyone else. 'You sweet-talker, you,' she said, but not with her usual bite of sarcasm. Her words were soft. And uncertain.

He wanted to close his eyes, to just breathe her in, but he knew that this was . . . important. He also knew that this uncertain Gwyn was not the woman he wanted. *In for a penny, in for a pound.*

'Can I ask a boon?' he asked quietly.

She blinked, the word surprising her out of her uncertainty. 'A boon? Really? Did we fall back into Victorian England?'

'No, we did not. And yes, a boon.' He let go of one of her arms to run his thumb over her bottom lip, caressing.

Her eyes softened, and that was fine. He liked soft Gwyn. Just not uncertain Gwyn. 'What is this boon, Mr Thorne?'

'I'd like to hold you just for a minute before you give me the really bad reason you're here.'

Instantly she reached for him, going up on her toes to cup his face between her palms. 'Yes. We deserve that, I think.'

Not waiting to pick that statement apart, he ran his hands down her back, lifting her effortlessly, hiking her skirt up so that he could urge her legs around his waist. She sucked in a breath, then seemed to surrender, just as she did after a long argument that she knew she'd already lost but wasn't quite ready to concede. Her shoes dropped to the floor, first one, then the other, as she tightened her legs around him.

Shuddering, he buried his face in her neck. And breathed her in.

She rested her cheek on the top of his head, her fingers threading through his hair, petting him. 'I always wondered,' she murmured.

He had to search for the simplest of words. 'What did you wonder?'

'How it would feel if you held me like this.'

'I've held you before.'

'Not like this. It was different before.'

'How?'

She brushed her lips over his temple and he shivered, head to toe. 'I was broken before. I'm not broken anymore.'

His chest contracted with a strength that had him fighting not to gasp. He wasn't going to breathe hard. He wasn't going to tremble. He wasn't going to do anything to disturb this moment. Because it was important.

She pulled back far enough to see his face, her expression wary. 'You don't believe me.'

He gave in and let go of the air in his lungs. 'No. I mean, yes, I do. I mean . . .' He gave up trying to find the right words, because there was something off. She wasn't telling him the truth. Not the whole truth, anyway. He'd known her long enough to know her tells. His heart felt suddenly brittle, his mind shouting at him to put her down and walk away. He gently pushed at her legs until she released her hold. She slid down the front of his body until her bare feet hit the floor and she stood looking up at him, her eyes filling with something that looked like panic.

'You don't believe me.'

The panic in her eyes had his own dread rising. 'I want to.' He swallowed hard. 'I want to so damn much. But . . .'

'But?' she whispered.

'I don't want you saying this because you feel sorry for me.' His voice went raspy as his throat grew too tight. 'I couldn't survive that. It would kill me.'

Her breathing became shallow. 'Don't go.'

'I won't,' he said, trying to keep his tone gentle. 'I promise. I said we would stay friends, no matter what you chose. I meant it, so you don't have to—'

'Stop,' she hissed. 'I'm *not* feeling sorry for you. I'm trying to tell you that this . . . that I . . .' Her hand shot out, grabbing hold of his shirt, and her eyes closed briefly as she muttered, 'I don't have time for this right now.'

He frowned, feeling a mix of hurt and irritation. But before he could say a word, she opened her eyes, tilted her head back and met his gaze directly. The panic was gone, replaced by the grim determination he saw in the eyes of clients who'd decided to fight in court to prove their innocence.

'I . . . I need to tell you some things,' she said firmly. 'Important things.'

He braced himself, certain he wasn't going to like any of those things. 'The bad reason you came.'

'No. Just . . . Well, that too, but this first.' Gracefully she lowered herself to kneel on the floor and patted the carpet beside her. 'Sit with me, please.' Uneasily he did so, remaining silent because he had no idea of what to say. Still kneeling, her hands gripped his face and she visibly braced herself, just as he had done. 'I wasn't drugged the whole time.'

He blinked at her. 'What?'

'Evan. I wasn't drugged the whole time. Before he abducted Lucy. Things . . . happened.'

For a moment he could only stare as the full import of her words registered. Then he was struck by a wave of horror, of rage. Of the need for disbelief. 'No,' he whispered. But it was true. He could see it in her eyes. This was what she'd been holding back.

No. No, no, no, no. He could hear the chant in his head. Had to bite his tongue to keep it from coming out of his mouth. Because she was watching him, waiting for his reaction.

This was important. He knew that. His reaction could break her into small pieces. Break her again. And that was something he would not do.

Except he didn't know what to say. He wanted to howl. He wanted to scream. He wanted to dig Evan up and kill the motherfucker all over again.

But none of those things was going to help Gwyn. Not right this instant anyway. Not when she was looking at him with hope in her eyes.

Hope that he could accept it? Hope that it wouldn't matter?

But it did matter. It mattered. Tears burned his eyes and he forced them back. He reached for her and she came into his arms willingly, trembling as he settled her on his thigh. He held her carefully. So damn carefully. Because if he held her as hard as he needed to, he'd break her into pieces.

He tipped up her chin so that he could see her face. 'Like what?' he asked, and it sounded harsh, even menacing, to his own ears.

But it must have been the right thing, because relief flashed in her eyes. 'Things I can't talk about here and now. But things that make it hard for me to tell you how I really feel.' She dropped her gaze. 'Because I am afraid.'

He blanched. 'Of me?'

'*No.*' Her eyes flew to his, her hands tightening their grip on his face. 'Not of you. And that's one of the things I need you to understand. *Never* of you. You're my safe place. You're . . . mine, Thorne. Mine. And I didn't want you to . . .' Her expression twisted painfully.

'I guess I didn't want you to worry about me. Or think I was irreparable.'

'I wouldn't,' he said hoarsely. 'I couldn't.'

'I know that. I *do* know that. But I also can't let you go on thinking that it's you that I'm afraid of. Because I'm not.'

'Then what is it?'

'I don't even have words for it.' She faltered. 'Maybe I'm afraid that once I tell you, everything will shatter. That this is just . . . borrowed. And I know it doesn't make any sense.'

But it did. It really did. 'You might be surprised,' he murmured.

She considered him, pain in her beautiful eyes. 'Maybe I would be. And we will discuss it, I promise. Just know . . . know that I *feel*. I do. I have trouble putting words to it, but Thorne, you are mine. I promise. If you still want me.'

His mouth went dry. Bone-fucking-dry. 'How could I ever not want you? You are here. With me. Whatever that bastard did to you, you survived it. And nothing will change that. Nothing will change how I feel.'

Relief flooded her eyes. 'I have to confess one more thing.'

He drew another breath, trying to ready himself. 'Go ahead.'

She leaned close, brushing her lips over his cheek. 'I dream about you. Really good dreams, Thorne.'

He released the breath he held in a hot rush. 'You tell me this here? And now? Is this some new kind of torture?'

He felt her smile against his cheek. 'No. I just wanted you to know. Because, you know, I thought everyone felt this way about you. But as it turns out, not everyone does.'

He frowned a little. 'I have no idea what to think about that.'

She hummed, and the vibration rippled over his skin, straight to his cock. 'It means I used to think that what I felt for you was normal. You know, like maybe ninety-nine percent of the women out there want you too?'

'I don't care about ninety-nine percent of the women. I want you. I've always wanted you.'

He felt her smile again. 'Good to know. But for me, finding out that other women *don't* feel that way let me know that this is . . .

special. And I wanted you to know. Because I'm not saying no. I'm not even saying maybe.'

'Then what are you saying?' he asked, his voice hoarse.

She slid her lips over his cheek to his lips and kissed him. Chastely. More like a teenager's shy kiss. But it was so much more. He froze, a growl deep in his chest.

'God, Gwyn,' he whispered when she lifted her head.

'I know.' Her smile was as sweet and dreamy as her kiss had been. 'I was asleep for so long, Thorne. Why didn't you wake me up?'

There was no recrimination in her voice. He swallowed hard. 'I didn't know how. I was afraid I'd . . . hurt you. Permanently.'

She was still touching him and he wanted to close his eyes and purr like a cat, but he held back, keeping his gaze focused and watchful.

'You've been patient.'

'You're worth it,' he whispered.

She swallowed hard. 'Thank you.' Then she drew a breath and he knew the moment was over. 'I needed to be able to tell you this much. I wanted to be able to tell you a lot more, but . . . This is going to have to last us for a little while.'

He shook his head hard to clear it, fighting the urge not to dig his fingers into her soft skin and take what he craved. But something stopped him. Her words stopped him.

Patience, asshole. Remember what she told you. That *things* had happened. Things that still frightened her four years later. *Fucking Evan.* For the millionth time, Thorne wished the man weren't dead so that he could kill him himself. With his bare hands.

'Shh,' she whispered, and he realized his teeth were grinding and he wore a scowl. 'It will be okay. You're mine. That means I'm yours too. It *will* be okay, Thorne.'

'You promise?' he said, feeling ridiculous. Like a damn child.

'I promise,' she whispered, brushing another chaste kiss over his lips. 'I need you with me, though, because we have another situation. Tell me when you're ready to listen.'

He dropped his brow to her shoulder and held on until the rage had passed, until the desire had passed, until the sheer euphoria of hearing her say that he was *hers* had passed. 'All right. Tell me.'

He listened as she told him about the club, about the two dead bodies, about the implication that the owners of Sheidalin had retaliated against the Circus Freaks.

'Oh my God,' he breathed when she was done.

'I know. And this is not your fault.'

'No, but I know whose it is.'

'Cesar Tavilla.'

'Yeah. He tried to get his rival's son charged with grand theft, but that didn't work, so now he's trying to get the Freaks to attack us. He wants to get his hooks in a rival gang and incite them to hurt the club.' He leaned his head against the wall. 'So what is everyone doing now?'

'Don't know. Lucy was filling them in. I wanted you to have time to come to grips with this before you had to put on your Mr Teflon face.'

His lips twitched, despite the gravity of the situation. 'Mr Teflon?'

'Yes. The one that says nothing fazes you. Everything just slides off.'

'That face fools most people,' he said lightly.

'Most people don't know you like I do. Most people don't . . .' her cheeks pinked up so damn beautifully, *'feel* for you. Not like I do.'

Emotion overwhelmed him, foreign and intense. Yes, she'd told him that Evan had hurt her worse than he'd known. But she'd also told him that he was hers. And she was his. He knew this woman. He'd loved her for years. She needed him to focus on the strong woman she was today, not the broken woman she'd been before.

He tipped her chin up, staring at her mouth, hoping his intent was crystal clear. 'Please?'

She swallowed hard. 'Please,' she whispered.

He bent down, taking her mouth with his, feeling her melt into him. Her hand gripped his cheek and held on. Her lips parted when his tongue stroked. And it was good. So good. He kept it as gentle as he was able, pulling back to stare down at her face. Her eyes were still closed, lashes fanned out on her perfect skin.

Her lips curved in a satisfied smile. 'And?'

'I'm already wondering when you'll let me do that again.'

She opened her eyes and he swallowed, his mouth gone dry once more. Because there was want there. Lust and want and everything he'd always hoped to see. She'd dreamed about him. He wished to heaven and hell that they had more time, because he desperately wanted to know what those dreams entailed.

A carefully cleared throat had them jerking apart, turning to the doorway as one. Lucy stood there, arms crossed over her chest, an uncomfortable expression on her face. 'I gave you as much time as I could,' she said apologetically. 'But they've closed down the club and arrested Mowry, Ming and Laura.'

'Mowry said he'd been paying the Freaks out of petty cash,' Gwyn explained. 'Ming was the one who threw the two men out last night.' She looked at Lucy. 'Why did they arrest Laura?' Their bartender was one of the most upstanding citizens they employed. Single mother, putting herself through business school.

Lucy bit at her lip. 'They said she was dealing from behind the bar. They found drugs back there. Coke and some fentanyl. All packaged up to sell.'

Thorne came to his feet, stunned. 'What the fuck?'

Lucy sighed. 'I know. Jamie and Frederick are on their way to the police station. JD is taking me to the club so we can close it up properly. We'll have to figure out what to do once we get all the information.'

Thorne gritted his teeth. 'You can't go, Luce. He's already shot at Gwyn and Stevie today. I don't want you anywhere near the club.'

'That's what I told her,' JD said, coming in to stand next to his wife, scowling.

'Sheidalin is our business,' Lucy protested. 'We can't just hide from it forever.'

'You can't go in there anyway,' JD said. 'They've declared it a crime scene, because of the drugs.'

248

'Oh, for God's sake,' Gwyn said angrily. 'We employ at least thirty people. We can't just let them close us down.'

'This is Tavilla's doing,' Thorne said, then extended his hand to Gwyn, tugging her to her feet. She immediately slipped into her shoes, making herself four inches taller and bringing the top of her head level with his shoulder. He found himself hunching a little and realized he'd done so thousands of times over the years. But unlike those thousands of times, she sidled closer, sliding her hand to the middle of his back.

'Did you text your contact about meeting you?' Lucy asked, eyeing them with what looked like relief. JD wore the same expression. Somehow it made the situation a little easier to bear.

'Yes,' Thorne replied. 'But after this latest clusterfuck, I don't know that the cops are going to want to cooperate in a sting.'

'What did your contact say?' Gwyn pressed.

'He said he'd meet me at eleven p.m.'

Gwyn huffed. 'That's original.'

Thorne shrugged. 'It's our normal meeting time. I could slip out of the club and back without being noticed.'

'Don't think I didn't see you guys changing the subject,' JD said, irritated. 'Lucy and Gwyn need to stay away from the club.' He closed his eyes. 'Please, Lucy,' he added in a whisper. 'You can't take chances. You just can't.'

'He's right, Luce,' Gwyn said. 'You're a mommy now.'

'Hey,' Lucy snapped. 'If I'm not going, you're not going either.'

Gwyn crossed her arms and made an unimpressed face. 'I know.'

She looked like a five-year-old who was being sent to bed early. Thorne might have smiled had the situation not been so serious. 'I'll go,' he said. 'He doesn't want to kill me. Just . . . ruin me, apparently. I need to borrow a car.'

'I'll take you,' JD said. 'You two' – he gestured to Gwyn and Lucy – 'stay here. We'll come back for you.'

'Did Phil go with Jamie and Frederick?' Thorne asked. 'Or is he still here?'

'Neither,' JD said. 'Sam took Phil home.'

Lucy held up her hand when Thorne started to protest. 'Relax,

Thorne. He had some medication to take or something. Sam's going to stay there with him until you get home. And you'll still have your tail. Agent Ingram is covering Phil because JD's got you. I trust Ingram to keep Phil safe.'

'Meet me at the front door,' JD said. 'I need to get my gun from Clay's safe.'

Lucy waited until her husband was gone before lifting one corner of her mouth in a tiny smile. 'You have a minute to finish what you were doing when I interrupted you.'

Gwyn wasted no time, grabbing Thorne's shirt collar and hauling herself higher on her toes. 'You take no chances,' she growled. 'Got it?'

'Got it,' he murmured, then bent down and kissed her just as he'd always wanted to. She responded just as he'd always dreamed she would. Hard and hot and so damn perfect.

Too quickly she ripped her mouth away, panting. 'Come back to me, Thomas Thorne,' she whispered. 'Promise me.'

He understood, both what she was asking and what he might be giving up to make the vow. He'd have to take backup with him to Ramirez's house. He'd have to take *JD* to Ramirez's house. And if by some miracle the man wasn't dead, Thorne would be breaking his promise to him, because JD would be compelled to arrest him. Ramirez was too high up in Tavilla's organization to have committed no crimes.

Still, he couldn't make himself refuse the desperation in her eyes. 'I promise.'

Fifteen

Baltimore, Maryland,
Monday 13 June, 10.45 P.M.

'This is a nightmare,' Thorne murmured.

JD gave a grunt of assent as he exited off the parkway and slowed to stop at the light at the end of the ramp. 'Right now? Yeah, I'd concur with that assessment.'

Going to Sheidalin had been a huge mistake. The cops had not only shut down the club, the media had been there to cover it. Now Thorne, Lucy and Gwyn were the focus of headlines and soundbites. Especially Thorne.

The cops hadn't let him anywhere close to the club. Someone had applied liberal amounts of crime scene tape to the doors, which made the reporters very happy because the bright yellow 'popped' against the club's dark exterior.

Thorne's arrival had caused quite a stir, with the vipers descending upon him with microphones and vicious accusations they didn't even bother to veil. He'd managed to hold his temper, but barely. Eventually JD got them out of there, taking them to the police station, but Thorne hadn't gone inside because Jamie had warned him against it.

There was no warrant out for Thorne's arrest, but showing up at the police station might push them to that extreme. Plus, Jamie and Frederick had everything under control. They'd gotten Ming, Mowry and Laura out on bond and were disgruntled to have to owe that favor to Lieutenant Hyatt, who'd greased the skids to make it happen faster.

251

Thorne and JD had transported Ming and Mowry back to their respective homes while Jamie and Frederick waited for Laura to be released.

And now Thorne and JD were on their way to Ramirez's house.

Thorne sighed. 'What are we going to do, JD?'

'You're going to keep doing what you're doing,' JD said resolutely. 'You're going to prove who's behind all this shit and then you and Gwyn and Lucy will give an exclusive to whichever reporter has the biggest audience.'

The reporters had been there front and center, looking oh-so-disappointed to have to report that the owners of Sheidalin were 'allegedly' involved in a territorial drug war. *Allegedly, my ass,* Thorne thought bitterly.

'Once they say we're guilty out loud, no amount of "allegedly" or after-the-fact retractions will change public opinion.' He opened his phone, scrolling through the coverage. 'They could at least get my ethnicity right, for sweet fuck's sake. One reporter says I'm Samoan, so at least he got the right hemisphere. The rest of them have me as everything from Hispanic to Arab, and guilty of dealing everything from drugs to weapons out of Sheidalin since we opened our doors seven years ago.'

JD raised his brows. 'Those are trash sites. Nobody believes that shit.'

'You'd be surprised,' Thorne answered glumly, wanting to tell JD that he didn't understand. Thorne had heard the slurs for years, some behind his back, others to his face. And people did believe 'that shit', or it wouldn't continue to be written.

'Then talk to them. Give them what they want. Give them an interview and set the record straight.'

Thorne shook his head. 'It could backfire. You know how they say that journalists should tell the story without becoming part of the story? I'll talk to the press on behalf of a client, but I don't want to *be* the client.'

'You *are* the client, Thorne,' JD said gently.

Thorne blew out a breath. 'I know. And if it comes to it, I will talk to them, but the very thought makes me want to throw up.' He rubbed his temples. 'I'm more concerned about the impact this is going to have on the club. If Sheidalin goes belly-up, thirty people will be out of work and on the street. I have savings, but not enough to pay their salaries for all that long.'

JD shot him a surprised glance. 'You're not really thinking of doing that, are you? Paying them out of your own pocket?'

'Of course I am. Most of our employees live paycheck to paycheck. They can't afford not to get paid.'

JD just blinked at him. 'You have that much money?'

Thorne shrugged uneasily. 'Jamie and Phil gave me some cash when I graduated from college. Told me to go backpacking in Europe. I invested it instead. I'm comfortable.'

'Wow. Well, I doubt Lucy and Gwyn are going to allow you to use your own money.'

'Then our employees will quit, because they'll have no other choice. And when we finally do start up again, we'll be doing so with a green crew.'

'I think you can worry about that later,' JD said quietly. 'But for the record, it's really decent that you'd be willing.'

Thorne's chuckle was one hundred percent mirthless. 'You don't have to sound so surprised.'

'Shut up, Thorne,' JD replied, but the words held no real heat. 'You assume everyone's thinking the worst of you.'

'Because they usually are.'

'Well, that might be true,' JD allowed. The light changed and he turned left. 'Where do I go from here?'

'I'll direct you. Is it too much to ask that you stay in the car and let me talk to Ramirez alone?'

'Yes. Mostly because I need to be able to alibi you.'

'Hope they'll still believe you,' Thorne muttered.

'What's that supposed to mean?'

'Just that hanging with me could be hazardous to your reputation. I'm now a "suspected drug dealer". Oh, and murderer. Let's not forget that.'

'Joseph doesn't believe it. Neither does Hyatt.'

Thorne found the energy to roll his eyes. 'It won't matter soon.

I'll be tried and convicted in the court of opinion. And I'll be damned if I drag you all down with me.'

'Jesus, Thorne, you're making me depressed. Stop it. We're going to figure this out. You forget Lucy is an equal owner in your little den of iniquity. If you think I'm letting her go down on a sinking ship, you're insane. I'll patch the fucking ship myself if I have to. I'll toss you one of those circle things.'

'You mean a life preserver? Turn right at the next light.'

JD made the turn. 'Try not to have all three of you doing hard time on a chain gang just yet, okay?'

'I'll try.'

He said no more, giving terse directions until JD had pulled up in front of Ramirez's place. It was a nice house on about five acres of land, so the nearest home was around the bend. The house was dark, but the lawn appeared to have been freshly mowed. Thorne started to get out of the car, but JD stopped him, handing him a pair of latex gloves.

'I don't have a good feeling about this,' he said quietly.

'Me either.' They'd chosen to arrive at quarter till eleven, so that if Ramirez really was going to meet Thorne, he wouldn't be home right now. But the house didn't just seem empty. It had a still, abandoned feel to it that was foreboding.

The two of them went up the front walk, JD looking around with a fierce intensity. 'No cameras,' he said, then unsnapped his holster and drew his weapon, holding it along his thigh, keeping it pointed at the ground.

The gun Thorne carried was heavy in his pocket holster. He followed JD's lead and drew it. It was Clay's, but Thorne owned a similar model. He didn't like guns, but was practical enough to have become proficient with their operation.

JD opened the mailbox and pulled out several fliers. 'Announcement for a party at the rec center,' he murmured. 'From a week ago.'

They approached the front door and JD sighed. 'Fuck.'

'What?'

JD looked at him. 'You can't smell that?'

Thorne drew a breath and grimaced. 'Yeah. Now I can.'

It was the odor of decomposing flesh. Somebody in that house was dead.

'I gotta call this in,' JD told him.

'I know. At least we didn't go in. I have that much of an alibi.'

JD gave him a distracted nod. 'Put your gun and the holster in my trunk. I don't want anyone seeing you with it. It'll make things harder for you in the long run.'

Thorne did as he was told, then sat in the passenger seat while JD called for backup.

Annapolis, Maryland,
Monday 13 June, 11.15 P.M.

He'd been awake, waiting for Kathryn to get home, so he answered on the first ring. 'Hello?'

'Thorne's not here,' Patton said grimly. 'But about a dozen cops are.'

He was not surprised. He'd figured Thorne would put him at the top of his suspect list, but he'd hoped to keep him guessing for a little longer.

He was surprised to hear the cops were there. Their cooperation with Thorne was something he hadn't anticipated, but he should have. That they hadn't arrested him right away was a major disappointment.

'Are you visible?'

'No. And I've altered my face, which was a good idea because the cops have cameras rolling. They're looking for whoever might have met Thorne tonight.'

'I'd have done the same,' he murmured. 'But things should start to change for Mr Thorne after tonight. The police will be less willing to cooperate with him' – or protect him for that matter – 'now that they know he's been dealing from his nightclub.'

'Maybe,' Patton said. 'Maybe not.'

He frowned. 'And that is supposed to mean exactly what?'

'You've got a police radio, sir. Turn it on.'

He disconnected the call without another word and flipped on the scanner. And frowned. Then cursed.

Units had been dispatched to Ramirez's house.

Thorne. But how had he known where Ramirez lived? Surely the man hadn't been foolish enough to share his address. He'd found no record of it in his files, at least. Maybe Ramirez hadn't known that Thorne knew. *The fool.*

Thorne had suspected him before. Now he knew for sure.

Nothing had really changed, of course. He'd laid out the plan with care and would see it through. But he'd have to rattle Thorne a little more. Put more pressure on his inner circle, rendering them afraid to stand too close to him. Or at a minimum, render them useless by forcing them into hiding.

He picked up the phone and redialed Patton. 'I think you might be right. The discovery of Ramirez changes things.'

'I made it look like a robbery, just like you said, but they won't buy it now.'

'You're probably right about that too. I have one more assignment for you tonight.'

Dead silence. 'I dropped those two at the warehouse, just as you asked.'

'I know you did.' He wondered if Patton had managed to keep his supper down as he'd done so. 'This can be accomplished more conventionally. I'll send you an address. There may be an officer guarding outside. You may dispatch the officer as you see fit. Any occupants of the house itself can be hurt, but not killed.'

'Got it.'

'I'll be waiting to hear your summary, Mr Patton.'

'Of course. Later. Sir.'

He ended the call and slid his phone into the pocket of his dressing gown. Unsettled, and annoyed to be, he headed downstairs to make a pot of coffee. In his younger days, he'd been able to stay up all night with no issues, but he was beginning to feel his age.

Plus, he'd had an active day. Carving up those Circus Freaks boys had been labor-intensive. Satisfying, though.

He paused outside the nursery, listening, opening the door when he heard Benny's fractious wail. The boy stood in his crib, tears streaking his beautiful face. Not hesitating for a second, he picked the child up and cuddled him close, settling into the rocking chair.

He'd convinced Margo to stay with him in case Benny needed care during the night. His physician was on call should the child's fever worsen. He knew she'd complied primarily to assuage his fears, rather than because she was actually worried about Benny. She was convinced it was only teething and he was sure she was right, because his personal physician had confirmed it.

Margo had not been happy when she'd called earlier in the evening, after the physician had examined Benny and left. She'd accused him of thinking she was not a good mother, which couldn't have been farther from the truth. He'd begged her indulgence and with a sigh she'd agreed.

However he'd achieved it, he was happy the boy was here. He felt a little closer to Colin every time he held Benny in his arms. The child had already quieted, a combination of the rocking chair and the finger he'd offered for Benny to gnaw.

A rustle of silk had him looking toward the door. Margo stood in the doorway, her face in shadow. 'Papa,' she whispered.

'He's fine,' he murmured, continuing to rock. 'Just fussy.'

She crossed the room and knelt beside the chair, touching her son's forehead. 'His fever has broken,' she said gratefully. She stroked Benny's cheek. 'Does that taste good, little man?' She glanced up, met his eyes. 'You're going to spoil him.'

'That's what grandfathers are supposed to do,' he said with a smile for the child in his arms. 'You should sleep. I have to stay awake for a while anyway.'

'Why?' she asked. 'Is Kathryn okay?'

'She's fine.' He sighed. 'But Thorne found Ramirez.'

Margo frowned. 'How?'

'He must have followed him.'

'That makes sense.' She frowned. 'What are you doing now?'

'Nothing you have to worry about.'

Her eyes narrowed. 'Papa?'

'Fine. I'm hitting him a little closer to home. *His* papas,' he said mockingly, because he did not believe such things were natural or proper.

'Will you finally give a kill order?'

She hadn't agreed with his decision to have Patton intentionally miss Gwyn and Stevie earlier today.

'Not yet,' he said soothingly, unwilling to disturb Benny, who'd started to fall asleep. 'Patience.'

Even in the semi-darkness, he could see her rolling her eyes. 'Yes, Papa.'

Her sarcasm made his chest tighten, because in that moment she sounded very much like his Madeline. How he missed her. He pressed a kiss to Benny's forehead. 'You are very sweet,' he whispered. 'Your grandmother would have loved you so very much.'

Margo's smirk drooped. 'I'm sorry. I know you miss her.'

'We were married for nearly thirty years. Every day that I wake without her seems like a thousand years. Which is why I have not given a kill order. I want to draw this out. I want him to feel pain.'

'Striking his papas is a good first start. He loves them.'

'I know. I only wish I could be there to see his torment.'

Baltimore, Maryland,
Tuesday 14 June, 12.55 A.M.

Thorne said nothing as JD got back in the car and started the engine, sending the A/C blasting. JD had been inside the Ramirez house for an hour with Hyatt and Joseph Carter. During that time, one of Hyatt's detectives – not Brickman, thankfully – watched Thorne like a fucking hawk, daring him to move a muscle.

Thorne hadn't had the energy to even flip the asshole off. Not that he could really blame the guy anyway. *This is starting to look bad even to me, and I know I'm innocent.*

He'd texted Gwyn a few times, cursory one-word answers to her questions.

Are you okay? she'd asked.

No.

Is your contact alive?

No.

Are you still with JD?

Yes. That hadn't been exactly true, but it met the spirit of her question.

Come back to me soon.

Yes. He'd swallowed hard as he'd typed the three letters, then added, *Sorry.*

For what? And don't be an idiot.

He'd almost smiled at that. *Thank you.*

You're welcome.

He rested his head against the window, patiently waiting for JD to speak.

'They've been dead for at least a week,' JD said finally.

'They?'

'Ramirez and his wife.'

'Fuck,' Thorne breathed.

'Indeed. At least the A/C was on. It was pretty miserable in there.'

Thorne absorbed the words. At least a week. 'I hadn't heard from him in about a week. Not until I texted him Sunday after I woke up. The phone he used was a burner that he kept secret from Tavilla. Someone's either gotten his phone or knows his number to spoof it on his replies to me.' He blinked hard and forced himself to focus. Why? What had happened a week ago? Nothing that he could think of. 'So even if I'd given Joseph and Hyatt his name during the meeting this afternoon, it wouldn't have made a difference.'

'No.' JD sighed. 'I'm not telling you any of this, by the way.'

'Any of what?' Thorne asked.

JD's mouth quirked dryly. 'Yeah.' He blew out a breath. 'He was shot in the gut. It wouldn't have been a slow death. She was shot in the head.' He rubbed his temples. 'But she'd been tortured first. Lots of little punctures in her torso and groin. Not by a knife. Maybe a screwdriver.'

'Fuck.' Thorne swore again.

'They suffered. Both of them.'

Thorne scrubbed his face with his palms. 'Am I a suspect?'

259

'No. But they will ask you why Ramirez agreed to sell you secrets. He was one of Tavilla's top men.'

'I know. I was surprised too. He wouldn't tell me, but I figured it out. His nephew was gunned down by one of Tavilla's thugs in a drive-by shooting. He wasn't a target, but Tavilla's boys sprayed the house with bullets and the nephew got caught in the crossfire. Died.'

'Did Ramirez ever confirm that?'

'Yes, once I presented my theory. He hated Tavilla, but he was not "in a position" to take him out. Which meant he feared retaliation on his family. He has children. Given that his wife is dead too, we should check on them.'

'We found their addresses on some mail on the hall table. We'll contact them, don't worry.'

Because if JD and the cops had seen the addresses, the killers had too. 'Were Ramirez and his wife eviscerated?'

'No. That seems to have been reserved for Patricia and the two Circus Freaks guys. So far,' JD added grimly. Thorne knew the cop was thinking about Lucy, Gwyn and Stevie.

'Were they killed here?'

'It doesn't appear so,' JD said. 'Why?'

'Just thinking about what Frederick told us. About there being seagulls in the background on the call from the fake detective to Sally Brewster.'

'Right. Bernice Brown's friend. Did Frederick check on Mrs Brown, by the way?'

. 'Yes. She and her cousin have relocated. She didn't tell him where. She said she'd be in touch.'

'We're going to need to talk to her at some point.'

'I know, but she's pretty spooked. I don't think she'll be coming out of hiding any time soon.'

They were quiet for a while, when both their phones started ringing at the same time.

'Shit,' JD barked.

'Fuck,' Thorne said at the same time, because this could not be good. 'Mine's from Jamie.'

'Mine's from Lucy,' JD said.

They answered the phones simultaneously. 'What's happened?' Thorne demanded.

'Thomas.' Jamie sounded terrified, and Thorne had to fight back nausea.

'I'm here. Tell me what's happened.'

'It's Phil. They got him.' Jamie's voice rose, hysteria breaking through. 'They got him, Thomas.'

No. No, no, no. He found himself chanting the words in his mind for the second time that night, and fought for calm. 'Where are you?'

'On my way to the hospital. Frederick's driving me.'

'Which hospital?' Thorne asked.

'County.' It was JD who replied, having obviously heard it from Lucy. He put on his emergency flashers. 'I'll get Thorne over there,' he snapped into his phone. 'You and Gwyn stay the fuck put.' He hung up and pulled away from the curb, radioing Hyatt. 'Something's happened to Phil Woods. I'm taking Thorne to the hospital. Will keep you informed.'

Thorne returned his attention to Jamie. 'We're on our way. Tell me what happened. Where is Sam? And Agent Ingram.'

'Sam's unconscious,' Jamie said hoarsely. 'He was hit in the head. Ruby's on her way to the hospital. Ingram . . . God, Thorne. He might not make it.'

Fuck, fuck, fuck. Thorne drew a breath and let it out. 'One at a time. What happened to Phil?'

'He had a heart attack. He lost consciousness for a while, but came out of it long enough to call 911. Ingram also called before he passed out.' Jamie's voice broke. 'Blood loss.'

'Who found them?'

'I did. Frederick and I got there about a minute ahead of the first responders. Frederick took care of Ingram and I rushed into the house. Sam was on the floor near the front door. And Phil . . .' He choked on a sob. 'Phil was lying on the floor in the kitchen. I checked his pulse. It was really irregular. Ingram managed to call 911 for an ambulance. I called for two more, for Phil and Sam.'

'All right,' Thorne murmured, more for his own benefit. 'Is Phil conscious now?'

'I don't know. I couldn't ride with him in the ambulance. My chair . . .'

His chair wouldn't fit in the back of the ambulance. *God. Poor Jamie.* 'Phil will understand when he wakes up,' Thorne said, amazed to be maintaining his calm.

'I know. Frederick wouldn't let me drive.'

'Good. Frederick's got a head on his shoulders. Let him take care of things at the moment. How did they get in the house?'

'I don't know. It's not like Phil not to set the alarm.'

'I know. We'll figure that out. For now, know that he will be okay.'

'What if he's not?'

'He will be,' Thorne said forcefully. 'I'll be there in . . .' He looked to JD.

'Fifteen minutes,' JD said.

'I heard,' Jamie said, his voice breaking again. 'Hurry, Thorne. Please.'

'I am.' He swallowed hard. 'Phil loves you. He will fight for you.'

'But he was so tired. What if he's *too* tired?'

Jamie sounded like a frightened child and it was breaking Thorne's heart. 'I'm on my way,' was all he could think to say. 'I love you.'

Jamie sobbed once. 'Me too. We just got here. Frederick is stopping at the ER door. Hurry.' And he hung up.

Thorne pressed his fist to his mouth. 'Gwyn's okay?'

'Yes. Clay and Stevie are sticking close. Ford and Taylor are backing them up. Paige is taking Ruby to the hospital. She's apparently a mess. Ruby, not Paige.'

God. Ruby and Sam were so damn happy. And they would continue to be, he told himself sternly. Sam was a tough bastard. But Ruby . . . 'This can't be good for Ruby or the baby.'

'Let's not borrow trouble,' JD said sternly. 'We have enough of our own already.' He turned on his siren and punched the accelerator. 'Hold on.'

Hunt Valley, Maryland,
Tuesday 14 June, 4.30 A.M.

'Good Lord, Gwyn.' Lucy tiptoed into Clay's kitchen, Wynnie in her arms. 'You scared me. I didn't expect anyone to be in here.'

Gwyn looked up from the article she'd been reading on her laptop. 'I was banished.'

Lucy chuckled. 'Why?'

'I was pacing and everyone was trying to sleep, but there's no way I can. Not with Thorne so wound up over Phil. And Sam. And Agent Ingram.' His texts over the last few hours had all been the same. *Still waiting. No news.* 'I kept asking if anyone else had news, but I was doing it kind of often.' She was actually annoying herself with her anxiety, so she didn't blame the group for becoming impatient.

Yawning, Lucy settled herself in one of the chairs and cradled her baby to her breast. 'I know there hasn't been any news, because JD just called me.'

'Then why did he call you?'

'He says it's because he found a big bag of your dog's food in the back of Jamie's minivan and figured you'd be needing it. I think he really just wants to see me and the kids. He does that sometimes when the stress starts to build, but don't tell him I said so. He thinks he's being all stealthy about it. Anyway, he wanted to be sure someone was awake to take the dog food, because he can't stay long.'

'Thank you. Thank him, I mean. I was going to have to go out and get some.'

'Like anyone's going to let you do that.' Lucy rolled her eyes. 'What are you doing?'

'Well, I went through the club's books, making sure that there wasn't any trail that would lead from Mowry to the Circus Freaks, because the cops will subpoena our files. It's just a matter of time. I mean, I could see the pattern now that I know it's there, but I don't think even a seasoned forensic accountant will find any irregularities. But my audit didn't take as long as I thought it would, so I started looking into the Lindens, specifically Patricia. She gets mentioned a lot in the society pages, but I went back to the articles around the time of Richard's murder.'

'Anything interesting?' Lucy crooned, not wanting to disturb Wynnie, who was suckling with concentrated determination.

'Linden Senior and Mrs Linden had both been married before. Richard and Patricia weren't blood relatives. But they took very pretty family portraits. I found an archive in the Lindens' company website with the Christmas portraits they took every year. Patricia was devastated by Richard's murder and apparently the media attention was pushing her toward a breakdown. Her parents sent her away to relatives in Europe, where she finished high school. Everybody paid a price for Richard's death. Thorne and Sherri most of all. I found a photo of the two of them together in one of the articles covering her death. Sherri was very pretty. You could tell she was a dynamo, just from her picture and what her friends said about her when she died.'

'Looks like Thorne has a soft spot for tiny dynamos,' Lucy said fondly. She cocked her head. 'That was the front door. JD's here.'

'I'll tell him you're back here,' Gwyn said, shutting down her laptop and hurrying to the front door where JD was setting the bag of dog food against the foyer wall.

'Thank you,' Gwyn said, and he smiled down at her wearily.

'You're welcome. Where's Lucy?'

'She's in the kitchen with Wynnie. How . . . how long are you gonna be here?'

He gave her a knowing look. 'Not long. I'm going back to the hospital.'

'Take me with you?' Gwyn begged. 'Please? Thorne keeps texting and I know he's losing his mind. I just want to be there with him.'

'Security is good there,' JD said after considering it. 'Give me a few minutes with Lucy and I'll be back out.'

She threw her arms around his neck. 'Thank you.' He patted her back, but his face looked stunned when she stepped back. 'What?'

'That's the first hug you've given me. Like that, I mean.'

264

Because she'd met JD right when everything with Evan hit the fan. *But now I'm back. I'm really back.* 'It won't be the last.'

Baltimore, Maryland,
Tuesday 14 June, 5.40 A.M.

Hospitals were noisy places, even at night. Gwyn remembered that from the two days she'd spent in the hospital after Evan. But she mostly remembered the relief at being able to leave. The arm Thorne had placed around her as he'd helped her into his car. The gentleness with which he'd laid her in his bed and kissed her on the forehead and told her that everything would be all right.

It's always been him, she thought, slowing her step as she and JD approached Phil's room in the cardiac ICU. His room was easy to spot – it was the only one with an armed police officer standing guard outside.

There had been a lot of armed officers elsewhere in and around the hospital. They stood outside the rooms belonging to Sam and Agent Ingram, and by the doors to the waiting rooms where their families and friends had gathered.

The waiting room was where she and JD had gone first. Joseph was there, sitting with Mrs Ingram, who'd been weeping. That did not bode well. They found that Sam had been moved to a regular room and Ruby was with him. She'd had a sonogram, at Sam's insistence. Word was that the baby was okay, so the news wasn't all bad.

Gwyn got to meet Sally Brewster, the pediatric nurse, who'd come to sit with Frederick during her break. Frederick looked worn and so damn tired. But clean, because JD had driven him home for a shower and a change of clothes.

JD had been simply amazing, which really came as no surprise. She'd observed him being amazing to Lucy for the last four and a half years.

Now he was being amazing to Gwyn herself, walking her to Phil's room, where Thorne and Jamie kept vigil. Because now that she was here, she was a little apprehensive. Thorne had told her

265

explicitly to stay at Clay's. She was nervous about what he'd say when he saw her.

Then she raised her chin. This relationship didn't have a chance of success if Thorne thought he could command her. She'd nip that in the bud right away.

Still, she was glad JD was with her.

'You sure you want to do this?' he whispered.

'If this were Lucy's dad, would you?'

'If this were Lucy's dad, I'd have set off firecrackers to send him over the heart attack edge,' JD said dryly. Because Lucy's dad had been an abusive bastard. 'But I get your point. I'd want Lucy with me if I were in Thorne's position.'

'Thank you.'

She approached the room on tiptoes. As she peeked around the doorway, her knees went weak. Phil's eyes were open and he was looking up at Jamie, who held his hand. Thorne stood off to the side, tears on his face. But she could see that they were good tears.

Thorne inhaled then, and his shoulders stiffened as his body turned toward the door. His dark brows furrowed, his jaw going tight. 'What. The. Fuck?' he whispered loudly.

'Shh,' Jamie scolded, then followed his line of sight. 'Come in, Gwyn.'

Gwyn obeyed, her feet carrying her to the bed, her eyes not looking at Thorne. She leaned in and stroked Phil's pale cheek with one finger. 'Hey there.'

'Hey, Amber Kelly,' Phil whispered, one corner of his mouth hooking up. 'Thorne is not pleased with you.'

'I know,' she whispered back. 'But I think he's going to have to get used to that.'

Phil's eyes were tired, but they managed a small sparkle. 'I knew you had it in you.'

Jamie's chuckle was watery. 'Mount St Thorne is about to explode. Take him home. Or somewhere.'

She kissed Phil's cheek, then went around the bed to kiss Jamie's. 'Taking him home now. I'll make sure he sleeps.' She reached for Thorne's hand. 'Come on.'

He let her take his hand, but he didn't say a word. Not until they were outside in JD's SUV. Then he let it roar.

'What the actual fuck?' he shouted, so loudly that her ears rang. 'JD, what were you thinking?'

'That we had excellent security at the hospital and that she was likely to be duct-taped to a chair by everyone at Clay's who was trying to sleep but couldn't because she kept pacing and asking everyone if they had news.' JD sighed. 'And that you might need her.'

Thorne huffed out a breath. 'It was stupid.'

No, it wasn't stupid. And Gwyn was aware that he hadn't denied needing her. So she'd see where this went. An angry Thorne could be interesting.

Which was interesting in and of itself. Because there wasn't one bone in that man's body that frightened her, even when he was about to explode with what he considered to be justified rage. He'd never hurt her.

'Can we go to my place, JD? Or even a hotel? Clay's house is completely full and I think Thorne's going to need to yell at me a little.'

'A lot,' Thorne muttered.

'You're still under surveillance, Thorne. Joseph has someone waiting outside Gwyn's place already. That's where we figured you'd go.'

And for that, Gwyn gave JD another big hug when he walked them up to her condo and made sure they were locked safely inside for the night. Then she turned to Thorne, who was staring out the window, his expression thunderous and brooding.

'Go ahead,' she said. 'Let me have it.'

Sixteen

Baltimore, Maryland,
Tuesday 14 June, 7.15 A.M.

G*o ahead. Let me have it.*

Thorne knew what she meant by the words. Which was *not* the way he wanted to take them. He stood at her window, his hands fisted at his sides because he wanted her so goddamn much. He wanted to turn around and grab her, kiss her, throw her over his shoulder and toss her on the bed. He wanted to strip her, touch her. Worship her.

He was vibrating with it. His skin felt too thin, too tight. Like he'd split out of it any minute. *Let me have it.* His brain replayed the words over and over, taunting him, because he couldn't do what he wanted to do. Not tonight. Not ever.

I wasn't drugged the whole time. Evan had hurt her. Broken something inside her. *But she's healing. Not broken anymore. She said so herself. So let her have it.*

It would be so simple to listen to the devil on his shoulder. But he wouldn't. He couldn't. It was why he'd told her to stay put tonight.

Yes, he wanted her safe, but logically he'd already come to the same conclusion that JD had. There'd been plenty of security at the hospital. She would have been safe there.

From shooters. But not from me.

The realization had shaken him soundly. *She's not safe from me.* He'd kissed her tonight. He wanted to do it again. So much.

'Hey.' She was behind him all of a sudden. Poking him in the back. '*Hey.* I'm *talking* to you. Don't ignore me.'

'Like I ever could.' He flinched. He hadn't meant to say the words aloud.

She grabbed a handful of his shirtsleeve and pulled. 'Talk to me, dammit.'

He whirled then, gripping her shoulders and holding her at arm's length. 'You don't want to hear what I have to say right now,' he warned in a low growl that he didn't even recognize as his own voice.

Her eyes widened. Then narrowed. Twin streaks of ruby red rode high on her cheekbones, and she was breathing very deliberately. 'What do you have to say?' she asked, and then her tongue stole out to wet her lower lip and he couldn't stifle his groan.

He closed his eyes. He was trembling now. He'd been trembling in the hospital when he'd looked up and seen her. He'd wanted her in that moment. Had wanted to lose himself in her body. Had needed some kind of valve for the pressure that had spiked in his head.

Pressure that was now ten times higher and spiking everywhere.

'Thorne,' she whispered. 'Look at me.'

He didn't want to. He wasn't going to. But then she begged, 'Please.'

He looked down into that beautiful face, and his breath caught. She wasn't afraid. She was aroused, her eyes hot and snapping with desire. 'Tell me,' she demanded hoarsely.

'God, I want you. I want to lay you down and . . .' He shuddered, his body so hard that it ached.

'And?' She rolled her shoulders, easily escaping his hold because he'd kept it gentle. Even when he wanted her so much he thought he'd explode, he could keep his hands gentle. She stepped closer and he stepped back. Her mouth quirked up in amusement and she took another step closer. His giant step back put him up against the wall.

She took one more step and was plastered against him, her hands flat on his chest, rubbing up the fabric of his shirt. Her eyes were still hot and aroused. Her hands did not tremble.

She wanted this. Wanted him. 'What, Thorne?' she pressed. 'Lay me down and what?'

His head dropped back, hitting the wall with an audible crack that he barely even felt. 'I want to see you. I want to touch you. Every inch of you. I want to come inside you and then I want to *come* inside you.' He whispered the last words and felt her shudder before becoming aware of small hands on the buttons of his shirt. Undressing him.

And then she had his shirt open and her lips were brushing his skin and he couldn't breathe. 'Please,' he said, his eyes still closed, the words like gravel in his throat. 'If you aren't serious, stop now. You're killing me.'

The click-clack of her shoes hitting her floor as she took them off was the only warning he got before she launched herself onto him, wrapping her arms around his neck. His hands automatically found her butt, his arms trapping her legs against his sides. She leaned in to kiss him, hard. Then she licked his lip. 'Kiss me, Thorne.'

And then he was. He was kissing her and she was opening for him and it was everything he'd ever wished for. His tongue swept inside her mouth, tasting her, and she made a hungry noise deep in her throat.

Then she ripped away, breathing hard, her legs wrapped around his hips, her hands on his face. 'This is what I want to happen,' she murmured. 'I want you to take me into the bedroom and do all the things you just said. But I don't have any condoms.'

Frustrated disappointment hit him like a rogue wave. 'Fuck.'

Her eyes managed to be aroused and serious at the same time. 'I'm clean. I got tested obsessively after . . .' She shook her head hard, as if flinging the thought away, then met his eyes squarely. 'Are you? Clean, I mean?'

'Yes. I've been tested twice in the last two years. Once for an insurance policy and then in the hospital on Sunday.' He swallowed hard. 'It's been a long time for me, Gwyn.'

Her thumbs stroked his cheeks. 'How long?'

He hesitated. 'Four and a half years.'

Her eyes widened. 'You . . . waited? For me?'

'I didn't want to. I wanted to get on with my life. But I couldn't. I couldn't walk away from you.' A shiver rippled over his skin at the thought of burying himself inside her. 'I might not last long.'

Her lips curved sweetly. 'We've got time.' Then she leaned in and kissed him again. They were halfway to her bedroom before he realized his feet had started moving. He finished the trip in a few big strides and set her down, so that she stood on the bed. From this angle, he was looking up at her.

And he loved what he saw. He touched her blouse. 'Tell me I can take this off.'

'You can take it all off.'

Hands shaking, he did. He slipped the blouse over her head, pressing kisses down her throat, between her breasts, so enticing in the lacy bra. He unhooked it with one hand and she laughed breathlessly.

'I don't want to know how you got so good at that,' she murmured, then she was gasping and moaning as he pulled the bra away and sucked one of her nipples into his mouth.

He released her, pressing kisses between breasts that were more than a handful even for his big paws. 'You're so pretty,' he said.

She blushed. 'I want to see you.'

He held his arms out and she pushed the shirt from his shoulders, humming her appreciation. 'You have the most beautiful skin.' She dropped kisses across his pecs. 'I saw you once,' she confessed. 'In the shower. At the club.'

'I know.' He unbuttoned her skirt, groaning when she stepped out of it, leaving her wearing only a tiny pair of black lace panties. He cupped her breasts, loving the feel, the weight. 'I saw you watching me.'

Her eyes flew wide. 'You're lying.'

'I would never lie to you.' He grinned at her. 'I was preening for you that day.'

She kissed her way from his cheek to his neck, her tongue stealing a lick. 'It worked. I dreamed about what you looked like for months and months. I got a lot of mileage out of that one accidental

271

peek.' She pulled his belt loose. 'Take off your pants. I don't want to have to remember what you looked like. I want to see.'

His pants hit the floor a second later and she let out a long breath as she stared at the bulge in his briefs, which were at that moment cutting off his circulation. 'Wow.'

Her fingers traced his length and he wanted to . . . *Not yet. Let her lead this dance.* There would be other times for him to take the reins. *But not today.*

He was jerked from the conversation with himself by her hands grabbing his waistband and yanking his briefs to his thighs. She followed them down, dropping to her knees on the bed. And then . . .

'God,' he barked. Because her mouth was on him, hot and wet and . . . perfect. 'Please. Yes. Please.' His hands went to her hair, but he wouldn't let himself thread his fingers through it, wouldn't let himself hold her head, wouldn't urge her to go faster or deeper.

She pulled off his cock, licking her lips. 'I'm not breakable, Thorne.' She winked up at him. 'I promise.'

He didn't have a chance to ask her what that meant, because she was on him again and there was no way he could tell her to stop. There weren't the words. But he wanted more than this. Wanted to feel what it was like inside her. So he picked her up and laid her on the mattress, then ripped the pretty black lace down her legs, revealing the trimmed patch of dark hair he'd only dreamed about.

He stood there for a moment, staring. And then she bent one knee, opening herself to him. His eyes flew to hers and she winked again. His brain short-circuited, and then he was on his knees on the floor, pulling at her legs until her ass was hanging off the mattress and his mouth was on her.

She made another hungry noise and undulated against his mouth in a rhythm that drove him crazy. He pulled away, shaking his head.

'I want you to come when I'm inside you.'

'Then hurry up,' she said with a strangled laugh.

He dove onto the mattress, rolling to his back and pulling her upward and over, so that she straddled him. 'I've thought about this a million times,' he whispered. 'I want you to ride me the first time. I want to see your face when I fill you up.'

Another one of those breathy moans escaped her throat. 'Yes.' Bracing her palms on his chest, she set her hips so that his cock was right there. At the entrance. But . . .

She was crying. Tears welled in her eyes and slipped down her face.

'What?' he whispered, panicked, because he'd rather die than hurt her. 'We can stop.' It might literally kill him, but he'd do it.

'No. Don't you dare stop. It's just . . . I thought I'd lost this forever. This connection. I'm so glad it was you who brought me back, Thorne. Thank you.' She leaned in to kiss him, and slid down so that the head of his cock slipped in.

Tight. And bare. 'Never,' he gasped. 'Never done it like this.'

She didn't pretend to misunderstand. 'Me either. You're so hot.'

That made him grin. 'I know.'

She laughed. 'Shut up. I meant temperature.'

'Hot-blooded, that's me.' But the light moment passed by and they were serious again, eyes locked as she slid all the way down.

Then he couldn't hold her gaze anymore, because his eyes were rolling back in his head and he was biting his tongue not to come right away. She lifted and fell, harder and harder, and he forced himself to look up at her face, not wanting to miss a second of her taking her pleasure.

She sped up, rocking on him, gorgeous little whimpers coming from her throat. And then her back arched, her head falling back like a flower too heavy for its stem, and she was coming, clamping down on his cock so hard he couldn't hold back another second.

Grabbing her waist, he planted his feet on the mattress for purchase and thrust upward once, twice, and then it was like he was flying. He came, shouting her name, just like he'd dreamed so many times.

I love you. He wanted to say it, to scream it, but stopped himself. It wasn't time yet. He knew that. But it would be time eventually. He'd waited seven years. He could wait a little while longer.

Baltimore, Maryland,
Tuesday 14 June, 2.45 P.M.

Gwyn woke to find the sun high in the sky outside her bedroom window, the ceiling fan spinning lazily, and more than half of her bed taken over by a huge, sprawling man who slept on his stomach, snoring softly. The sheet was pooled at his waist, showing off acres of muscle and the tattoo that she'd always wanted to trace with her tongue. They'd been in too big a hurry for her to do so the night before. Both times. They'd just had too much lost time to make up for. Too much stored-up need.

Next time, she promised herself. In the light of day, while the world did its own thing outside her window. Next time she'd take her time and lick him all over.

She might have snuggled closer, but her cell phone was buzzing with an incoming call, the number an unfamiliar one. 'Hello?' she answered, and Thorne immediately woke, his eyes doing a quick tour of the ceiling before landing on her. His slow smile was enough to make her want to end the call and jump him. Again. And again.

Shifting to his back, he reached for his own phone, checking his texts. Then, rolling onto his side, he propped his head on his forearm, smiling a little smugly when he saw her gaze glued to his bare chest. God, the man was built.

'May I speak to Amber Kelly?' The voice in Gwyn's ear was smooth, cultured and female.

It took Gwyn a minute to remember that Amber Kelly was the name she'd given to the hair salon owned by Angie Ospina, the woman Thorne had rescued from Richard Linden's clutches nineteen years ago.

It seemed nearly nineteen years ago that she'd made the appointment, rather than only a little more than twenty-four hours.

'This is she,' she said cheerfully, because she was supposed to be eloping tonight. She blinked rapidly, bringing back all the details she'd used in her phone call yesterday.

'I'm calling from the Heavenly Salon, confirming your appointment for five thirty.'

274

Gwyn glanced at the clock. *Just enough time to get there.* 'I've been looking forward to it all day,' she gushed. 'See you in a little while.'

She ended the call, then snuggled back down on her pillow so that she and Thorne were face to face. 'How is Phil?' she asked, pointing to his phone.

'Resting comfortably. He sent Jamie home with Frederick to get some sleep. They stopped by Clay's to pick up Julie, and now they're headed to Frederick's. Jamie's house is still a crime scene.'

'Sam?'

'Ruby texted. He's fine, and she is too.'

'And Agent Ingram?'

He frowned. 'Still critical. He hasn't woken up yet.'

She reached out to rub at the deep groove that bisected his forehead. 'Not your fault, baby.'

'I know. At least we know how the shooter got in. Phil was finally lucid enough to tell Jamie what happened. He got a text on his cell phone – from my number.'

'Shit.'

'Exactly. The text said that I'd lost my key. Phil was making hot chocolate in the frother for Sam and asked him to open the door.'

'Spoofing site again.'

'Yeah. Sam opened the door, and *pow*, he went down, but Phil didn't hear.'

'Because he was running the frother. It's so loud.'

'Right again. Phil saw the intruder and yelled, but Ingram was bleeding, and Sam was unconscious.'

'But he saw him?'

'Not really. The intruder was wearing a mask.'

'Of course he was,' Gwyn murmured.

'Phil might not have been able to see his face, but he got a good hit in.' Thorne's lips curved a little. 'He picked up the frother, tossed the hot milk in the intruder's face, then hit him with the metal pot. It didn't stop the guy, so Phil picked up a ceramic cookie jar and hit him with that too. The jar shattered.'

'So the shooter may have left some blood behind on the broken pieces?'

275

'If he left anything behind, it was too small for Jamie to see. He saw the cookies all over the floor when he rushed to Phil's side, but the jar was gone. The intruder picked up all the pieces. So there was probably blood on them, or he was afraid there would be. The guy never actually touched Phil, although Phil said he was holding a club – probably the one he hit Sam with. The doctor says it was likely a combination of the exertion of Phil fighting back and general fear that triggered the heart attack.'

'But he's going to be okay,' Gwyn said positively. 'The doctor said so.'

A small smile. 'Yes, he did. Who was on the phone?'

'The salon, the one that your old classmate owns.'

He frowned again. 'You can't keep that appointment.'

'Why not?' She narrowed her eyes at him. 'And don't even bother to say it's not safe. I know it's not safe. Which is why we have to make this thing stop as quickly as possible. It's not like you can go in my place.' She raked an appreciative gaze over his body. 'No offense, but there's no way you'd fit in at a salon like that.'

'I could get a haircut,' he muttered.

She laughed. 'Baby, they'd take one look at you and a fight would break out over who got to put you in their chair. All the stylists would be stabbing each other with their shears and blood would flow.'

He rolled his eyes. 'Stop it.'

'Why?' She smirked at him. 'It's true. There is no fucking way I'm letting you anywhere near a bunch of women in a beauty salon. They're worse than a pool full of piranhas.'

'You're not going in alone,' he snapped.

'Okay,' she said quickly, chuckling when he realized he'd all but agreed she could go. 'You can wait in the lobby.'

His scowl returned. 'You can't do this. What if Angie is connected with Tavilla in some way?'

She blinked at him. 'That's a leap.'

'He got details from someone. The only people who knew about that damn key ring are either dead or too scared to talk to anyone.

276

Now we're down to the original cast of characters – Richard's three friends and Angie.'

She thought about that and he was right. 'There is a connection between Tavilla and somebody in your past,' she agreed. 'Detective Prew knew.'

Thorne frowned. 'I've thought of that too. He was so helpful. Made me suspicious.'

'Plus we gave him a road map of where we'd be yesterday. How else would someone know we were going to be at the EMT's apartment?'

'I know,' he said, still growly. 'I need to check him out. But don't think you've distracted me. You're still not keeping that appointment. We'll get someone else.'

'Who?' she challenged. 'Lucy? Stevie? Paige? They're all new moms with babies. Maybe Ruby? She's only seven months pregnant. No? That leaves me, unless you want to tell Hyatt and have him give the job to one of his female officers. And of course Hyatt will be *so* forthcoming with whatever they find out,' she finished sarcastically.

'Now you're just playing dirty,' he grumbled.

She smiled, knowing she'd won. 'Poor baby. Little me, such a threat to big strong you. Should I make it up to you?'

He actually pouted. 'We don't have time. We have to get to Bethesda by five thirty.'

Pushing him onto his back, she rolled on top of him and slid down his body until she straddled his hips, her palms flat on his hard abs. She shivered as she rocked back and felt his very hard cock nudging her flesh. His hands gripped her waist, his eyes meeting hers, and her heart actually hurt with all she saw there. Desire, of course, but so much more. How could she have missed it for so many years?

'Thank you,' she whispered.

His brows crunched a little. 'For what?'

'For waiting for me.'

'You're worth it,' he whispered fiercely, the second time he'd said the words. She had no doubt that he believed it with every fiber of his existence. Someday she might believe it too.

Until then, she'd show him what *he* was worth. Everything. *He's everything. And he always has been.* She leaned in and kissed him slowly, luxuriously. 'You are so beautiful,' she murmured against his mouth. She licked his lip and his hands slid down her back to her butt. 'I can't believe you're here. In my bed.' And suddenly she found herself hoping that she really had been worth the wait.

He pressed his head back into the pillow so that he could see her face. 'What?'

She scraped her teeth over her bottom lip, already a little swollen from their kisses. 'Nothing,' she said when the question in her heart wouldn't form into actual words.

'No.' He brought his hands to cup her face so tenderly her eyes began to sting. 'It's not nothing. Tell me.'

'I guess . . .' She looked away, hoping the tears in her eyes would drain back to wherever they had come from. 'I guess I just hope it was worth it. That I was worth it.'

He tugged her chin until she was looking at him again. 'I just said you were worth it.' His lips curved. 'Weren't you listening?'

'Yes.' She tried to pull away, to slide down his body and make him forget the question entirely, but he held her in place easily, one hand on her ass, the other gripping her chin.

'Gwyn.' Just her name, but said so sweetly that she blinked, sending the tears down her face. He wiped them away with gentle fingers. 'Talk to me, love.'

Love. God. 'I just . . . You waited a long time. For me. And I know you've . . .' her cheeks burned and he swept his thumb across her heated skin, 'experienced a lot of . . .' She closed her eyes, too embarrassed to speak. 'I need to get ready for my appointment.'

'No. Talk to me. And look at me. Please.'

She forced her eyes to open and the words to leave her mouth. 'I don't want to disappoint you.'

He frowned. 'You couldn't.' Then his eyes widened. 'You mean in bed? You're asking if I enjoyed it? *Seriously?*'

She wished she'd never brought it up. 'I know you enjoyed it,' she muttered.

'Twice,' he said smugly, and she laughed, which made him smile. 'What's this about?' He squeezed the ass cheek he still held firmly. 'If you can't talk to me, who can you talk to? Come on.'

'You waited for me for a long time. I just want it to be worth it.'

His smile became rueful. 'If it had been any more worth it, I'd be sharing a room with Phil in the cardiac unit.' He threaded his fingers through her hair, gently working through the tangles. Always gently. Even when he'd been angry with her, he'd been gentle. 'Gwyneth Bronwynne Weaver, it was worth it. If I had to wait ten years more, it would have been worth it.' He gave her hair a tiny tug. 'Having said that, I'm glad I *didn't* have to wait ten years more. I might have exploded.'

Her chuckle was watery. 'You say the sweetest things.'

He pulled her down for another kiss that left her wanting more. She ran her lips over his jaw, down his throat, until his voice rumbled deep in his chest. 'I hate to say this, but we really do need to be going soon if we're going to make it to Bethesda.'

Her hand wandered down his chest to his groin, closing around him. He was still so hard. She squeezed and he groaned.

'Dammit, Gwyn. Don't be a tease. That's not fair.'

She glanced at the bedside clock and did the math in her head. 'I don't have to do my hair. That'll save at least fifteen minutes. If I put my makeup on in the car, that'll save another fifteen.' She grinned down at him. 'I can do a lot with half an hour.'

Her only answer was another groan as she disappeared under the sheet and took him into her mouth.

Bethesda, Maryland,
Tuesday 14 June, 5.15 P.M.

The traffic gods had smiled on them, Thorne thought as he pulled into the salon's parking lot fifteen minutes early for Gwyn's appointment with Angie Ospina. The lot was filled with Mercedes, BMWs, a few Bentleys, and even a Maserati. Fire-engine red, of course.

'Swanky,' Gwyn murmured. 'No wonder she took out loans. The rent in this neighborhood is astronomical, and she actually owns her place. I bet her mortgage alone is more than she's been bringing in on average.'

News of Angie's loans had come via Alec Vaughn just minutes before. Gwyn had been on the phone with him almost the entire time that Thorne had been driving them from Baltimore to Bethesda. Alec really was an IT whizz-kid. Clay was lucky to have him as part of his company and Thorne was grateful that he was sharing the young man's remarkable hacking skills.

'What exactly did Alec say?' he asked.

'That Angie took the first loan from Linden Senior ten years ago. Although a payoff seems far more likely than a loan. She took out a second mortgage with a local bank four years ago, then someone made her a private loan in the amount of . . .' Her voice trailed off. 'Holy shit, Thorne. Four hundred thousand dollars. That's on top of the second mortgage.'

Thorne's eyes popped wide. 'That's a lot of money to privately loan someone. She must be hemorrhaging money to need that kind of cash infusion.'

She frowned. 'But that's the weird thing. She's not losing money. She's making payroll and still putting away what looks like a small profit.'

'Then why would she need a loan? Who made the loan?' he added because the 'why' wasn't a question either of them could answer at this point.

'Alec can't trace it yet. But the timing is interesting.' She lifted her brows at Thorne. 'The four hundred grand was deposited into her bank account a month ago.'

'Tavilla could have been poking around a month ago, although it probably wouldn't have been him personally. He generally doesn't get his hands dirty. Always uses his right-hand men to do the blatantly illegal stuff. Definitely worth checking into.'

'I don't know if it was Tavilla or not.' She was frowning at her phone. 'But the loans – including the second mortgage – were all deposited at the same time of year. Actually in the same month, within a three-day window.'

That was interesting. 'The anniversary of something?'

280

'Makes sense to me.' Gwyn checked the time on her phone. 'I should be going in soon. You can come in with me, but it's risky. Your photo is all over the news.'

He released his seat belt. 'I don't like you going in there alone.'

She didn't really either. It was just a beauty salon, but if Angie was guilty of something and felt cornered, it could get dicey. Gwyn had a .38 in her girdle holster beneath her blouse and a knife in the thigh holster that was covered by her knee-length skirt. Watching her dress had been a conflicting experience for Thorne – both arousing and terrifying. He hadn't come this far to lose her.

Her phone buzzed with an incoming text. 'It's Alec again,' she said. 'He's asking me if I've gone in yet. I'm telling him no, and why. Hmm,' she said a few seconds later. 'He says he's brought reinforcements and to tell you to drive to the McDonald's one block north of here.' She responded, voicing as she typed. 'My appointment is in ten minutes.' She chuckled. 'He says, "This will be worth it. Thorne will be happy. We are in a white van."'

Thorne immediately pulled away from the salon and began to drive. 'I like to be happy, but call him. I want to make sure it's him and that we're not getting spoofed again.'

Gwyn did as he asked. 'What's up, kid?' she said, putting Alec on speaker when he answered.

'I'm busy,' he snapped.

'We needed to know it was you.'

'Oh.' His voice softened. 'Didn't think about that. Sorry. It's me. Gotta go.'

'There it is,' Thorne said. 'The white van. And there's Ford.' Taylor's fiancé sat behind the wheel. The panel behind him slid open, revealing Alec, who waved Gwyn inside.

Thorne lowered the window so that he and Ford could talk. 'He's going to wire her,' Ford explained. 'We didn't want you to tell her not to go in, in case we couldn't get here in time, but traffic wasn't too bad. Park your SUV and get in the van. We'll park close enough to the salon that you can storm the place if you need to.'

Thorne breathed easily for the first time since leaving the safety of Gwyn's bed. 'Thank you.'

Ford grinned. 'Thank Clay. This was his idea.'

'Excuse me,' Alec protested. 'It was my idea. I just made Clay think it was his.'

Gwyn smiled at both young men. 'Whoever had the idea, I thank you two for coming all the way out here.'

Alec was checking the connections as Thorne climbed into the van. 'You have a tail, you know. Black SUV. Escalade.'

Thorne pulled the van's door shut. 'I know. Detective Hector Rivera. He's a member of Joseph's joint task force. JD introduced him to us when he dropped us off at Gwyn's condo this morning.'

Ford glanced in his rear-view mirror. 'You know you could have come back to Clay's house,' he said seriously. 'They have lots of room.'

'I know,' Thorne said. 'But I can't help thinking that if I'm not there, they're safer.'

'I don't think that's true,' Alec said. 'I think this Tavilla asshole is going after the people who are important to you. Whether you're there to see it or not seems immaterial.'

'You're probably right,' Thorne admitted. 'But I still don't want to paint targets on their backs any more than I have to. We need to go now. It's almost five thirty.' He sat next to Gwyn on the middle seat and Alec moved up front with Ford.

Alec waved his hand. 'Make it so, Number One.'

Ford snorted. 'You are such a geek.'

'And proud to be.'

Gwyn grabbed Thorne's hand. 'I'm glad he's proud to be a geek, because he knew how to wire me up.'

'Me too.'

They pulled back in front of the salon with a minute to spare. Gwyn grabbed Thorne by the tie and pulled him down for a hard kiss. 'It's going to be fine.'

Love you, he wanted to say, but he held it back. 'Be careful,' he said instead.

She winked as she got out of the van. 'Count on it. We have unfinished business.'

He watched her saunter away, then glanced at the two younger men in the front seats. Both stared at him open-mouthed.

'Wow,' Ford murmured.

'That was . . . wow,' Alec echoed, then he grinned. 'You've been holding out on everyone, Thorne. Just think of how excited the ladies are going to be over *this* news. I can't wait to tell them.'

'Too late,' Ford said smugly. 'Just texted Taylor. Everyone will know in about three seconds flat.'

Thorne wanted to be annoyed. He really did. But he was too damn happy. Giddy. Like a damned teenager.

Then Alec waved his hand. 'Gwyn's in the salon. I'm recording this, but if we're quiet, we can hear.' He connected his phone to the processor he wore behind his ear, then put the phone on speaker so that Ford and Thorne could hear too.

And that fast, Thorne's giddiness turned to dread. She'd better be careful. They both had too much to lose.

Seventeen

Gwyn glanced around the reception area of Angie's very upscale salon, taking in the displays of expensive cosmetics and hair products, all high-quality stuff. It was good she'd given a fake name, she thought wryly. She had enough cash for the salon service itself, but she would have been tempted to splurge on the makeup, and her credit card clearly said *Gwyn Weaver.*

Interspersed among the product displays were several framed magazine and newspaper articles, many with Angie's photo, so at least Gwyn would recognize her on sight. Angie had received 'Best Of' awards for the salon and 'Businesswoman of the Year' awards from the local chamber of commerce as well as several women's professional organizations. She'd achieved success and the respect of her community.

Gwyn really hoped that she wasn't in league with Tavilla. *But if she is, I'll help take her down.* No way was this woman going to hurt Thorne. Not again.

'Amber Kelly,' she chirped to the woman behind the desk. 'I have an appointment with Angie.'

The woman smiled wanly. She was young, pale, tall, pencil thin, and dressed all in black. 'You're our bride-to-be. Congratulations. Would you like some champagne?'

'Please,' Gwyn gushed, bouncing on her toes, which in four-inch heels was harder than it looked. 'This has just been the perfect day.'

And it had been. She still wore the glow of sex with Thorne,

284

although that last time had seemed like so much more. She'd been more than content to give him pleasure, but he'd wrested control only a few minutes into her efforts, rolling her to her back, sliding into her . . . reverently. She'd held his gaze the entire time, and even though she'd had to crane her head back to do that, it had been worth it.

Worth it, worth it, worth it. Those had been the two words he'd uttered over and over as he'd taken her, each roll of his hips as gentle as a slow wave. Bracing himself on his hands, he'd held his body high over hers, careful with her, like she was fragile and precious.

She'd felt precious. And even though they'd tried positions where she was able to feel his skin with every slide of his flesh into hers, this one seemed far more intimate.

When she'd come, it had been so hard she'd seen white lights twinkling all around her. And when he'd come, it was with a silent intensity that made her shiver all over again.

'Wow,' the receptionist murmured. 'I am so very jealous of you right now.'

Gwyn blinked to find the woman holding out a flute of champagne. She accepted it with a polite but puzzled frown. 'Why?'

The receptionist's smile turned sly. 'You know that scene in *When Harry Met Sally* where Meg Ryan fakes an orgasm? I have a feeling I just watched the real thing.'

Gwyn laughed, slightly embarrassed, then even more so when she remembered that Thorne, Alec and Ford were listening to every word of her conversation. 'Guilty as charged,' she managed, taking a sip of the champagne to cover her discomfiture. 'Oh my. This is really good.'

'Only the best for our clients. Come with me. Angie is ready for you.'

Gwyn was directed to a stylist's chair behind the wall that provided the clients with privacy from those waiting in reception or anyone walking past the big windows looking out onto the street.

Despite the salon's elegance, the stylists' stations looked much like those in more financially accessible places. There was a chair in front of a mirror surrounded by lights. Tucked into one edge of the mirror was Angie's cosmetologist license, and below that, several photographs. Some of them were of Angie – the woman hadn't really changed that much from the photo she'd found – but all of them featuring the same young man. Angie was a slender Hispanic woman, her high cheekbones and flawless complexion making her pretty enough to have been a model in her youth. Not that she was old. She'd been in Thorne's graduating class, so she couldn't be much older than he was.

The young man, though . . . Gwyn found herself leaning forward to study his face. He was a teenager, a recent high school graduate if the little number dangling from the tassel on his cap was anything to go by. He was startlingly . . . familiar. Blond hair, bright blue eyes and a dimpled smile that managed to be warm and slightly self-deprecating all at once, as if he was uneasy being the center of the photographer's attention.

'Hello.'

Gwyn jerked her eyes up to the mirror, where Angie herself stood behind the chair, smiling at her. Gwyn smiled back. 'Hi. Thank you for fitting me in.'

Angie's smile grew, and a dimple popped in her cheek. Exactly in the same position as that of the boy in the picture. 'It was my pleasure, Miss Kelly. I like to have a little hand in happily-ever-afters. Weddings are my specialty.'

'I'm just Amber.' Gwyn settled into the chair and fingered the ends of her hair. 'I want to look princessy, but my guy likes it long, so he made me promise that you wouldn't cut it.'

'Then we shall do both,' Angie said, and draped a cape over her, drawing it around her shoulders to snap it at the back of her neck. 'Where are you going for your big night?'

My bed was just fine for our big night, Gwyn thought, but she smiled brightly into the mirror. 'Paris. I've never been and I'm so excited!'

Angie was studying her hair, testing the springiness of her curls and the weight of it. 'When do you leave?'

'We have an eleven p.m. flight out of Reagan National.' Gwyn had made sure that the flight existed, just to be on the safe side. 'We'll get there in time for a late lunch or an early supper and we've made arrangements with a little chapel for an evening service.'

'So I need to style it so that it lasts at least until then,' Angie said seriously. 'Flights are hard on hair. I'll have to use some pretty strong hairspray. Is that okay?'

Gwyn nodded dreamily. 'That'll be fine.'

After a trip to the shampoo bowl, Gwyn was back in Angie's chair, staring again at the photos of the young man. 'I can't help but think that I've seen that boy somewhere,' she said conversationally.

Angie spared a glance at the photos, her expression softening. 'No,' she said almost sadly. 'My nephew lives in Iowa. I don't get to see him all that often.'

Iowa. Gwyn had to take a breath so that she didn't reflexively stiffen in the chair. Detective Prew had said Angie had gone out west to 'some state with corn' during Thorne's trial. If her nephew lived out there, she'd probably stayed with family.

'You look very proud of him,' she remarked. 'I can see that you're related. You have a dimple in the same place.'

Angie smiled again, revealing said dimple. 'We do.' She cast another longing glance at the photograph, a glance that was decidedly . . . maternal. 'Liam is a good boy. I'm proud of him.'

Gwyn knew that look. She'd seen it in her own mirror every time she thought of *her* 'nephew', usually on his birthday, but it was also the look she'd learned to bury whenever anyone said the word 'son'. Because Aidan wasn't Gwyn's nephew any more than Liam was Angie's.

'I can see that,' she said quietly. *You should tell Thorne.*

About what? Angie's son or mine?

Both. You know it's the right thing to do.

And she did know that. She also knew it would be a hard thing to say. *My son.* She'd never spoken the words aloud to anyone, not even to Lucy, not since that awful day she'd signed the papers so that her beautiful boy could have the life he deserved with parents who could provide for him.

Because she wouldn't have been able to. Not then. She remembered the scared, unemployed, uneducated young woman who'd foolishly believed the man she'd thought she'd spend the rest of her life with when he'd told her he loved her. *Water under the bridge, Gwyn.* After all these years, the only thing she had left was self-recriminations, and they never helped.

She wondered what Angie's circumstances had been and mentally did the math. If Liam had recently graduated high school, he'd be about seventeen or eighteen.

About the same age as Aidan, who'd turned eighteen ten months before. That had been the kicker for Gwyn. The nudge she'd needed to get on with her life. To get counseling so that she could dig her way out of the darkness in which she'd been floundering since Evan. Because Aidan's parents had promised they'd tell him he was adopted when he turned eighteen, or if he asked, whichever came first.

Hopefully he'd want to meet Gwyn someday, and she wanted to have her life together when and if that day ever came.

Her eyes were drawn to a photo of Angie and Liam together, smiling. 'How old is he? Your nephew?'

Another wistful smile. 'Eighteen just last month.' But she brightened then. 'He's coming to Baltimore for college.' Her whole demeanor changed. 'He was accepted to Johns Hopkins, into their biomedical engineering department.'

'Whoa,' Gwyn said, suitably impressed. 'He's a genius.'

'He certainly is,' she said proudly.

'And now you'll be able to visit with him more often than before.'

'I will.' Angie did something magical with her hands, and Gwyn's hair was suddenly up, delicate curls framing her face and making her look years younger.

'Oh!' she exclaimed softly, and Angie beamed.

'I thought you'd like it this way.' She tugged and poked pins into the do, murmuring apologies when Gwyn winced. 'Gotta make sure it stays.' She winked in the mirror. 'For Paris.' She took a step back, surveying her work. 'I'm going to find the heavy-duty hairspray,' she said. 'Just relax for a minute or two.'

When she was gone, Gwyn resumed her study of the photos. Young Liam had turned eighteen a month ago. Right about the time that four hundred thousand dollars had been deposited in Angie's account. The same month that years earlier the Lindens had given her money for her business.

And then Gwyn knew why the boy's face was so damn familiar. Glancing around for Angie, she pulled out her phone and studied the photo she'd snapped late Sunday evening while sitting at Phil and Jamie's kitchen table. It was the photo of the Linden family that Jamie had included in his case file. She enlarged it until Richard Linden's face filled her screen, then glanced up at the mirror, where an almost identical face stared back. The only difference was Liam's smile, which he'd clearly inherited from his mother.

'Angie is Liam's mother,' she whispered, hoping Thorne could hear her. 'And Liam is Richard's son,' she added, swiping the photo closed just as Angie came back shaking a can of hairspray.

'Let's get you fixed for Paris,' she said.

Gwyn forced herself to smile back. '*Merci*.'

Bethesda, Maryland,
Tuesday 14 June, 6.10 P.M.

Thorne sat back in his seat, stunned. 'Did she just say what I thought she said?' he asked Alec and Ford. The three of them had been gathered around Alec's phone, which he'd had on speaker while recording everything that was said inside the salon.

Thorne had needed to pull himself from his own thoughts when Gwyn had spoken the words so quietly. *Liam is Richard's son.*

He'd been stuck back on *Guilty as charged*, unable to hide his reaction. Not the burning of his cheeks and certainly not the hardening of his cock. But he'd borne it, because he was *not* adjusting himself in front of the other two.

Luckily, the conversation had shifted to Gwyn's plans for Paris and what she wanted done with her hair. Still, his pants had remained uncomfortably tight.

'She said Liam is Richard's son,' Ford said slowly. 'And Angie is Liam's mother? So . . . Richard Linden and Angie?'

'If so, then Richard raped her,' Thorne said harshly, remembering the look of sheer terror on Angie Ospina's face all those years ago.

'He treated her like she was his plaything. The timing is right, if the kid just turned eighteen. So the Lindens must have been paying her for more than her silence in refusing to testify on my behalf. They've been paying for their grandchild.'

'How does Gwyn know this?' Alec asked skeptically. 'It seems like a huge leap.'

It did, Thorne had to admit, even though the notion made so much sense. He shook his head. 'I don't know. We'll ask her.'

Ford gave a low whistle. 'Here she comes. Gotta say, Angie is good at her job.'

Thorne could only stare as Gwyn left the salon, a cheerful smile on her face that he knew was completely forced. But Ford was absolutely right. She was gorgeous. She had been before she'd gone into the salon, though.

He opened the side door and helped her climb in. As soon as the door slid closed, the smile evaporated from her face. 'Did you hear what I said?'

'That Richard is Liam's father?' Ford asked. 'We heard it.'

'But we're not sure where it came from,' Alec added honestly.

'What happened that we couldn't see?' Thorne asked her gently, because she was trembling. 'How did you know?'

She straightened her spine. 'It was how she looked when she talked about the boy. She said he was her nephew. But there is no way that's the truth.'

'You sound certain,' Alec said cautiously, and she shot him a look so . . . *hard* that Thorne blinked. It was not a look he'd ever seen on her face before. Ever.

'I am,' she snapped, then closed her eyes on a sigh. 'Call it intuition, but I just knew.'

'Okay,' Alec said slowly, but his doubt was still clear.

Opening her eyes, Gwyn pulled her phone from her purse. 'Look at this.' She showed them the selfie she'd taken in front of Angie's mirror, the chair spun so that both her face and the back of her hair were visible. She enlarged the selfie, readjusting the placement so that a vertical row of photos stuck in the mirror's edge was visible. 'Look at the young man in these photos.'

'Oh my God.' Thorne immediately saw the resemblance and was taken back nineteen years. 'Richard,' he murmured. 'Liam could be his twin.' He shot Gwyn a look of pure admiration. 'You are very good.'

Her cheeks pinked up at his praise, but the hard look in her eyes remained. 'I kept thinking I'd seen him before, and then she said he lived in Iowa.'

Ford frowned. 'Why is that important?'

Thorne understood. 'Because that's where they grow corn.' He told Ford and Alec what Detective Prew had said about Angie going out to visit relatives in Iowa around the time of his trial, and how she'd stayed away for two years. 'There was about six months between my arrest and my trial. If Angie was raped around the time of my hallway brawl with Richard and his friends, she'd have been showing by then. If she'd already been assaulted – and made pregnant – I can see her being afraid of the Lindens' threats.'

'Huh. Wow.' Alec had pulled up his own photo of Richard from the Internet. 'There is an incredible resemblance.'

Ford leaned over to see the photo. 'It makes a lot of sense. Really good catch, Gwyn, but what does all this mean with respect to what's happening now?'

'I don't know.' She frowned slightly. 'Maybe nothing. Except that the Lindens knew that Angie had had Richard's baby. Maybe they didn't know right away, but they did as of the time of the first loan, when she started the salon.'

'They paid her for her silence,' Ford said with a frown. 'I suppose it could have been some under-the-table child support, but I'm wondering if it's more likely that they bribed her or she extorted them.'

Gwyn shrugged. 'Regardless of why they paid her, they did, and without publicly acknowledging that the boy is their grandson. That's the important part, because if word got out that Angie was pregnant and Richard was the father and that he'd raped her, it would have given the police another possible suspect – Angie's father, perhaps, or someone else in her family.'

'But the Lindens were determined that I be found guilty,' Thorne said slowly, mentally rearranging the puzzle pieces that had been in such disarray in his mind. 'Enough that Richard's father lied in court about altercations I'd had with Richard. Why?'

'Good question,' Gwyn murmured. 'Maybe Linden Senior was trying to divert attention away from someone else. Rich people hate scandals.'

'True,' Ford agreed. 'That would make sense if they already knew about Angie's pregnancy.'

'Definitely something to consider,' Gwyn said. 'I also wonder how many other people had a reason to kill Richard. Could Angie herself have done it, Thorne?'

Thorne shook his head. 'Whoever did it had to have been able to physically overwhelm him, then cut him open and bash his face in. Angie isn't tiny, but I can't see her being physically able to do all that. Besides, the Lindens had as much contempt for her as they did for me. She was a scholarship kid too, and the Lindens never let us forget that they paid our way.'

'Sound like real assholes,' Ford muttered.

Thorne nodded. 'They were. If they suspected Angie was involved, they might have turned on her then too.'

Gwyn bit at her lip. 'Linden Senior was willing to perjure himself on the stand. That's desperation. He really wanted you to take the fall. So I think you're right. If he'd had anything credible on Angie at the time, he would have used it rather than risk the legal consequences of making up stuff about you. But why did he want you blamed for this crime so badly? It's almost as if he was protecting someone.'

'So they not only knew Thorne didn't do it,' Alec said, 'but they had an idea of who did?'

'Or *why* they did.' Thorne rubbed his temples, feeling a headache coming on. 'I keep coming back to the key ring. That is a weird thing to shove into a carved-up body. Weirder to shove into Patricia's body all these years later. It means something. I guess the question remains: who knew about the key ring?'

'You mean, who knew about the key ring who's also still alive,' Gwyn clarified. 'The person who put it there knew, either because he was Richard's killer,' she said, ticking off on her fingers, 'or because he – or she – was *with* Richard's killer if he didn't act alone. The EMTs knew, but one of them is too scared to talk and the other is MIA. The ER doctor knew, but he's dead. The ME claimed not to have seen it, and Lucy has vouched for his integrity. The ME tech knew and he's dead, his wife living a good life in Chevy Chase.'

Alec scowled. 'I'd forgotten about her. I meant to run some background and financial checks but I lost the thread. I'll get on that ASAP.'

Thorne was studying Gwyn. 'What do you mean, "with Richard's killer"?'

She shrugged. 'You said his injuries were extensive. In the trial transcripts, the prosecutor used your size to insinuate you could have done it.'

'You read the transcripts?'

She nodded. 'That night at Jamie and Phil's. I couldn't sleep, and Jamie left them out on the table. Anyway, the prosecutor put forth that someone huge had to have committed the crime. Jamie countered that it didn't have to be a single someone. It could have been two people or even more, that Richard was a punk and he treated enough people badly that there could have been others with motive. He even mentioned Angie as one of those people, because Richard had groped her in the hallway, but the prosecutor objected on the grounds that Angie had said that the groping had never happened. It could even have been one or more of Richard's friends. Even if they weren't there with him, they might have known why someone shoved a key ring in his gut.'

Thorne nodded again, because he'd been thinking the same thing. 'Let's start at the top. Darian Hinman was Richard's best friend and he doesn't live too far away.'

'We've been instructed by Clay to remain with you, rendering assistance where necessary,' Alec told them. 'Clay wants this whole mess settled so he doesn't have to worry about Stevie getting shot at again. We'll take you wherever you want to go. That way the Fed tailing you only has to chase one vehicle.'

'I'm sure he'd be grateful,' Thorne said dryly. 'But we'll take Gwyn's car.' Because there was no way he was making these kids a target. 'Thanks, guys. I do appreciate your help. I just hate that I'm putting you in harm's way.'

Ford shrugged and started the van. 'Sooner we clear this up, the better for all of us.'

'And don't worry about trying to lose us,' Alec added with a smirk. 'I have the address from Clay. He got it from Frederick, who got it from Jamie.'

'Of course he did.' But even as he sighed the words, his throat closed up. He was so damn grateful that he had these people, people who cared.

Please don't let them get hurt, he prayed. *Please don't let anyone else die.*

Chevy Chase, Maryland,
Tuesday 14 June, 7.05 P.M.

'Wow,' Gwyn breathed as Thorne drove them around a perfectly landscaped bend at the end of the long driveway leading to the home of Darian Hinman. 'We're never going to get to him for even a hello. These are the kind of people who have butlers and maids and valets who say "sir" and put your socks on for you.'

Thorne chuckled, just as she'd hoped he would. His hands loosened their death grip on the steering wheel, at least a little. 'I hope I'd think of something better for them to do than put my socks on for me.'

He pulled the car up to the front of the mansion, which was lined with actual pillars, like it was some antebellum antique. *It might actually be*, Gwyn thought, taking the place in. It had a rolling front lawn where honest-to-god peacocks strolled without a care.

'I wonder if Hinman's butler cleans up after those damn peacocks,' Thorne said dryly. 'Talk about fucking pretentious.'

She nodded. 'Pretentious. That's the word I was looking for. I keep expecting women in hoop skirts with parasols to come round the house any minute. Is this joint as old as it looks?'

'Yep. Property records say the main house was built in 1851. It's been in Hinman's family from day one.' He glanced up to his rear-view mirror, frowning slightly at the sight of Ford and Alec approaching in their van. The black SUV with Joseph's hand-picked agent brought up the rear.

'Alec and Ford are not going to leave you,' Gwyn murmured. 'You're going to have to be okay with it.'

'No, I don't have to be okay with it,' he snapped. 'I might not be able to make them leave, but I don't have to be okay with it.'

'Fair enough.' She cast her gaze up at the three-story mansion. 'I find myself admiring this place kind of against my will.' She glanced at Thorne. 'Does that make me a bad person?'

'No.' He reached over to cup her jaw. 'It's a beautiful structure. Does that mean you want a place like this, maybe even a little?'

Gwyn laughed, but leaned into his touch. 'No way. That's way too many toilets to clean.'

He leaned over the center console to brush a kiss against her cheek. 'That's what I'd get the butlers and maids to do. I have to say, you'd look awfully pretty in one of those fancy dresses with your hair done up like that. Princessy.'

She blushed. 'Stop making fun of me,' she mumbled.

'You think that?' He tugged her chin until she faced him. 'I was being serious. When you came out of that salon today, you took my breath away.'

She smiled at him, pleasure lighting up her dark blue eyes. 'Thank you.'

He kissed her forehead, then let her go. 'I don't suppose you'd stay in the car or go wait in the SUV with Joseph's guy?'

'No and no. His name is Detective Rivera, by the way.'

'Don't want to know,' he grunted as he extracted himself from Gwyn's small car. 'Don't want to get attached to them in case they get hurt.'

'I suppose that's fair too,' Gwyn allowed. 'But remember his name, just in case you need to speak to him.'

'I'll answer to just about anything,' the detective in question said as he approached. 'Agent Carter said I should accompany you on this visit.'

'So I don't punch Darian Hinman in the nose?' Thorne challenged.

'No,' Gwyn said. 'So *I* don't punch him in the nose.' Because she wanted to. This was one of the Neanderthals who'd beaten Thorne all those years ago. Beaten him and kicked him until he could barely walk. 'Asshole.'

Rivera grinned. 'If you do punch him, I'll have to take you in and Joseph will have you confined. He told me to tell you that.'

Thorne rolled his eyes. 'And your obedience was such a hardship.'

'Nope,' Rivera said cheerfully. 'I wanted to say that.' He looked over his shoulder at Alec and Ford, who wore amused looks. 'You can stay in the van if you want, guys.'

'Nope,' Alec mimicked, just as cheerfully. 'Our boss told us to stick close, just like yours did. Shall we?'

Gwyn led the way, watching the sidewalk for gaps in the mortar that would destroy the heels on her newest shoes. Thorne was at her side seconds later, though.

'Do not get separated from me,' he commanded.

'Fine. But I still say we're never gonna get past the butler.'

'That's why I'm here,' Rivera said, more seriously. 'I've got a badge.'

Well, at least he'll be good for something. Then she abandoned the thought to enjoy the front garden before they knocked on that grand front door. The hedges lining the walkway had that wonderful old-garden smell that tickled her nose, making her smile.

'What?' Thorne asked, looking down at her with a fond smile of his own.

'The hedges. My aunt had them in her garden in Baltimore.'

'The aunt you named your part of Sheidalin for?' he asked, and it took her a second to remember that she'd said as much on Sunday evening when the group had met in her apartment to strategize.

'Yes,' she said, stiffly now, and he frowned. He hadn't believed her Sunday night either. She'd seen it in his face as she'd studied him in the mirror on her living room wall. She saw it now and was grateful to be coming up to the front door.

With any luck, he'd be sidetracked enough that he'd forget about the question. *But you do have to tell him about Aidan sooner versus later.*

Yes, but later. Much later. When she'd gotten used to this new thing they had going and had more stable ground beneath her feet. Then she'd confess her deepest regret.

She drew one more deep breath, wanting the calming scent of the hedges. But what she drew in was the antithesis of calming. What she drew in was the antithesis of life. *Oh God*, she thought as queasiness rolled through her stomach.

'Fuck,' Thorne muttered. 'Not again.' He turned to Rivera. 'Do you smell it? Something or someone is very dead in there.'

One look at Rivera's face answered that question. He was already reaching for his radio. 'I'm your alibi. You're welcome. Go wait in your vehicles, please.'

Gwyn was only too happy to comply. Backing away, she covered her mouth with her hand, desperately needing fresh air and trying not to gag. She found herself being supported by Alec and Ford, each young man taking one of her arms.

'Dammit, I hate that smell,' Ford muttered.

'I, on the other hand, love it,' Alec said sarcastically. 'Fuck, Ford. Everyone hates that smell.'

Back at the car, Gwyn drew in huge lungfuls of fresh air. Thorne was still standing next to Rivera as the detective called in the obviously dead something on the other side of the door. Whoever or whatever it was, it had been dead for some time.

Gwyn could only hope Thorne had an alibi for that time too.

Eighteen

Hunt Valley, Maryland,
Tuesday 14 June, 7.30 P.M.

'Hey, baby.' Frederick kissed the top of Taylor's head when she let him in through Clay's front door. 'How's your sister?'

'Happy as a clam,' Taylor reported. 'Ford and I took her riding in the cart this morning and she loved it.' She grinned. 'She even held the reins for a little while.' She smacked his arm lightly when he frowned at her. 'Relax. It was with Gracie. She's the best-trained horse here on the farm. I control her with verbal commands and Ford had a secondary set of training reins. Do you really think we'd do anything dangerous with Julie? With anyone here on the farm?'

Chastised, he shook his head. 'Sorry. You're right. Thank you for taking such good care of her.' He looked around. 'Where is she?'

'In the kitchen with Cordelia and her aunt. Izzy's making cookies with them.' She gestured with her head toward the study. 'Pops is waiting for you.'

She entered with him, taking one of the two leather chairs in front of Clay's desk where her 'bio-dad' – her words, not his – sat studying his monitor, one hand absently patting the infant resting in the sling he wore strapped to his body. Something about the sight of the big man cradling the tiny baby made Frederick's chest tight. He missed those days. Missed the times he'd cuddled his girls.

Someday he'd have grandchildren, but not any time soon. Both Taylor and Daisy had had their adolescence stolen from them by his naïvety and stupidity. They deserved the chance to live their lives before taking on the responsibility of families of their own.

Taylor cleared her throat meaningfully, making Clay look up. He motioned to the other chair. 'Sit,' he said distractedly to Frederick.

'Please,' Taylor inserted, as if rebuking a child.

Clay rolled his eyes. 'Please,' he repeated.

'Am I in trouble?' Frederick asked lightly.

Clay scrubbed his free hand down his face. 'No. I'm just watching Stevie. She and Paige are calling on the elite.' He pitched his voice to sound snooty.

'Stevie's wired for audio and video,' Taylor explained. 'She and Paige have gone to talk to the women from Patricia's fund-raising group, trying to find out more about her husband and possibly the boy she was . . .' Her forehead crinkled. '"Affair" sounds wrong. If he's that young, it's assault. But I'm not sure what to call it until we figure out who the kid is.'

'Have they found anything so far?'

Clay rolled his eyes. 'Only that most of these women have way too much time on their hands.'

'Not fair,' Taylor chided. 'Several of them do amazing work for the community. But a few play a lot of tennis and get a lot of mani-pedis,' she allowed.

'What's a mani-pedi?' Frederick asked.

Clay cut Taylor off with a look when she started to explain. 'That's not what I wanted to talk to you about,' he said.

Because Clay had asked him to come over as soon as he'd dropped Jamie off to see Phil.

'Sorry if I made you wait,' Frederick said. 'Jamie finally got to sleep, so I wanted to let him rest before I had to wake him up to go back to the hospital.'

And then he'd stopped to check on Sally Brewster, who was just fine. He'd been extra worried about her after all the violence the night before.

Clay waved his hand. 'That's okay. That's more important, actually. What I want to discuss will take a few days anyway.' He nodded at Taylor. 'Tell him. I can't talk and watch Stevie at the same time.'

It was Taylor's turn to roll her eyes. 'Not like she's a former cop,

299

or that Paige is a world martial arts champion, or that both of them shoot as well as you do,' she said sarcastically, earning her a faux glare from Clay.

'Don't be disrespectful,' he said, and Taylor laughed.

'Okay, Pops,' she said cheerily, laughing again when Clay's eyes narrowed. Every time Frederick heard her laugh, he knew he'd made the right call in selling his ranch in Northern California and moving his household to Maryland. 'So,' Taylor said, her expression growing serious. 'Clay and Stevie are going to postpone the baby's christening.'

He wanted to say *no, don't do that*, but he didn't, because he knew that Clay and Stevie were being prudent. So many of their friends were also friends of Thorne. Having the christening meant they'd all be in the same place at the same time, and Tavilla's man had already proven he could get onto Clay's property – in broad daylight.

'It'd be like shooting fish in a barrel,' he murmured.

'Exactly,' Clay said grimly.

'But they don't want Tavilla or any of his cohorts to know the christening is cancelled. Stevie's taking the baby to Chicago. Clay's old partner Ethan lives there with his wife. They can protect them there. They want the bad guys to come here. They want them to think that we are happy and helpless.'

Frederick nodded, liking the plan. 'And the rest of the women and children?'

'Are all being evacuated for the weekend, including Julie,' Taylor said.

Clay looked up from the monitor, his expression fierce. 'Tavilla is playing with Thorne and we're caught in the crossfire. Chad Ingram is still fighting for his life. Sam is out of commission for several weeks, as is Phil, meaning both Ruby and Jamie are distracted, which is completely understandable. Hell, *I'm* distracted, which is completely understandable. I don't want to worry about my wife and children getting shot at every time they leave the house. I don't want you to have to worry that someone is going to get to Julie, or for JD to be constantly worried about Lucy and his kids. We can't sustain this level of vigilance for that long.'

'I think Thorne plans to offer himself up if it continues,' Frederick said grimly. 'Jamie's terrified that he will.'

'I thought the same thing,' Clay said. 'We can't let him do that. It won't matter anyway. Tavilla doesn't seem to want Thorne. He wants to *hurt* Thorne.'

'So all the women and children are shipping out. I like that.' Frederick glanced at Taylor. 'What are you going to do?'

'I'm going with them. I have to protect Julie, at least until they get there. Once they arrive, I can fly back. Apparently Ethan's wife knows some nurses, volunteers at a local women's shelter that she runs. They've offered to help out. I can be back by Saturday morning.'

'I told her to stay up there,' Clay said, and Frederick wondered if the man knew he'd wrapped one big hand around the baby he cradled against his chest. 'She doesn't listen to me. So I thought you could tell her.'

Frederick laughed at that. 'You think she'll listen to me? You must have a much higher opinion of me than you should.'

'Told you,' Taylor said smugly.

Clay shot her a real glare. 'Brat.'

'That's fair,' she allowed. 'I'm still coming back. I'm one of your best shots. JD might be better than me, but only if he's having a really good day.'

'Brash brat,' Clay amended.

'Brash genes,' she said with a smile, then reached over to grab Frederick's hand. 'And super-brash training.'

Because Frederick *had* trained her well. He'd had her practice both her shooting and martial arts every single day. She'd have earned a black belt had she trained in a traditional dojo. She was a fierce fighter, one he'd have been proud to have on his own team back in his army days. Except that she was Clay's daughter too.

'You should listen to your father,' he said quietly, and meant it.

Clay gave him a grateful look, but Taylor just shook her head. 'You know I love you both, and it gives me warm fuzzies that you get along so well, but just let it go. Both of you. What's next?' she asked, turning to Clay. 'You said you don't want to send out a blanket email canceling the christening because it could fall into the wrong hands, and Tavilla could get tipped off and then not come here at all. But assuming he does come here thinking we're having a christening, how do we make sure other innocent people don't show up and get hurt?'

'We're going to have to do this the old-fashioned way and call people, one at a time. Most of the folks attending know Stevie was shot at. Most of them I trust implicitly. What we're going to say is that she strained her old injury when I pushed her out of the way, and she doesn't think she's up to coping with all the guests at once. So we're just going to have family and godparents attend this Saturday and we'll throw a big bash later in the summer.'

'Who are the godparents?' Frederick asked.

'Stevie's sister is Mason's godmother,' Clay said. 'And my friend Ethan is his godfather. Ethan and his wife had already planned to fly in tomorrow night. Ethan will still do that, then drive back with Stevie and the others. I trust him with my life. And, more importantly, with Stevie, Cordelia and Mason's lives.'

Frederick frowned. 'That seems dangerous too, though. They'll be sitting ducks on the open road.'

Clay acknowledged his concern with a nod. 'We've planned to do a vehicle switch. Leave in our own personal vehicles, drive to a covered garage, then transfer to other vans. JD and I will drive our personal vehicles away, playing decoy. Paige and I have added a few bodyguards to our staff in the last year. I've pulled them out of rotation and they'll accompany the group. They're fully vetted, all former cops or military. I trust them all. I've coordinated operations like this before.'

Clay might trust his staff, but Frederick didn't know them. 'I'll go too.'

Clay shook his head. 'I want to go as much as you do, but that's kind of the point of the operation. We stay and take care of the investigation and drawing Tavilla's men.'

Frederick drew a breath. 'That has to be good enough for me then.' He glanced at Taylor. 'Where does Ford fit into all this?'

'He's helping us drive up there.' She glanced at the wall clock, a small frown furrowing her brows. 'Right now, he and Alec are with

Thorne and Gwyn. He hasn't checked back in almost an hour. I'm getting a little worried.'

Just then, all three of their phones buzzed at the same time. *Not good*, Frederick thought, his intuition confirmed when he looked at the screen. *Well, shit*. 'Mine's from Gwyn,' he murmured.

'Mine's from Alec,' Clay said.

Taylor sighed. 'Ford. They've got another nasty-smelling corpse.'

Darian Hinman was dead. 'One more link to Thorne's past eliminated,' Frederick said quietly. This was insane. 'We're definitely moving the kids out.'

'Yeah.' Clay's body had tensed, but his hand on his son remained gentle. He took sheets of paper out of his printer. 'I divvied the names up and wrote the script below. These are all the guests we need to cancel on, and what I want you to say. If anyone asks why I didn't call myself, tell them that I will contact them as soon as I can.'

Frederick hesitated, then decided he'd be remiss not to take care of one detail before beginning. 'Look, I want to warn Bernice Brown's friend, Sally Brewster. She knows what happened to Phil, Sam and Agent Ingram last night. She knows to be careful, but I think she needs to know about this latest death.'

Taylor's eyes widened. 'Sally Brewster? The lady who tried to talk to Julie?'

'Yes. I've spent some time with her.' She'd come by the waiting room the night before and sat with him during her break, just holding his hand while they waited for word on Phil and the others. 'She actually spoke with one of Tavilla's men who was posing as a detective. What if Tavilla thinks she's a loose thread too?'

Clay considered it, then nodded. 'It'll be on the news soon enough. Darian Hinman is a big fucking deal in the financial world, and it's related to Thorne, so it's going to be major headlines.'

Frederick started to text Sally, then recalled the spoofed number through which she'd been threatened to begin with. He dialed her number, hoping he wasn't waking her. Her hours were all over the clock.

She answered on the second ring. 'Frederick?'

'Yes. I wanted to let you know that there's been another death related to Thorne, this time to his past.'

'Oh no. I'm so sorry.'

'I am too.' *But only because this guy had information we needed.* Knowing what he knew about Darian Hinman, he wasn't going to mourn him. 'I just wanted to make sure you were okay.'

'I'm fine. My son is here with me. He's a police officer, so I'm well guarded.'

Frederick heard voices in the background, then a man came on the line. 'Mr Dawson, this is Ed Brewster, Sally's son. I wanted to thank you for making sure that she got home safely after her shift. My sister and I appreciate it.'

'It was the least I could do.'

'Did you just tell her that someone else is dead?'

'I did. Darian Hinman. He's a corporate bigwig. But nineteen years ago, he was friends with the brother of the woman murdered on Sunday morning. Both are connected to my colleague Thomas Thorne.'

'Thorne's club was closed down for drugs.' Ed Brewster sounded doubtful.

'He's being set up. We're going to fight the charges. Look, don't condemn him just yet. He's a good man. And even if you don't believe that, keep an eye on your mother. The people behind this don't leave loose ends.'

There was a beat of hesitation on the other end, followed by a sigh. 'I know.'

Frederick frowned. 'What do you mean?'

'Mom told me about her conversation with the guy who tried to pump her for information. She said she gave him a fake address, but turns out it wasn't fake.'

Dread pooled in Frederick's gut. 'Explain, please.'

'The address she gave was a space at the trailer park. When she visited Bernice, that space was unoccupied. I checked.'

Frederick swallowed hard and looked up to see both Clay and Taylor staring at him. 'What happened?'

'Someone moved their trailer into the space. The vehicle was set on fire. The doors were blocked so the occupants couldn't escape. It happened in a national park, so it was under park police jurisdiction. I wouldn't have known if I hadn't specifically checked. Two people died of smoke inhalation, a professor on sabbatical and her husband.'

Bile burned Frederick's throat. 'Dear God.'

'I know. Give me your email address. I'll send you a copy of the police report.'

'Thank you,' Frederick managed, and rattled off the address. 'Can you take some time off to stay with your mother?'

'I already did, as soon as I read that report. I made her take a leave of absence from the hospital too. They won't get to her.'

'Good.' Frederick swallowed again. 'If you leave town, I don't expect you to contact me with your location, but I'd appreciate it if you could somehow let me know that she's okay.'

'Will do.' Another hesitation. 'Thank you again.'

'You're welcome.' His phone pinged with the incoming email. 'Thank you for this information. Your email just came through.'

'Don't open it,' Clay barked.

'Who's there?' Ed Brewster snapped.

'My daughter and . . . my friend.' He wasn't in the mood to go through their oddball relationship at the moment.

'Oh, you mean her other father. I helped my mom run her search. I know everything about you that she does.'

'Wonderful,' Frederick muttered.

Brewster chuckled. 'I can tell you that she hasn't blushed like this in twenty years. So when this is all over, you should come by and meet her children.'

'Ed!' Sally shouted.

Frederick felt his own cheeks heating and cleared his throat. 'What she said.'

Brewster chuckled again. 'I don't beat around the bush. I also told her that contacting your daughter like that was really stupid and she's lucky you were nice about it.'

'I'm not ever telling you anything again!' Sally said loudly, and that made Frederick smile.

'Yeah, yeah, promises, promises,' Brewster said good-naturedly.

'Tell your daughter's other father to run my attachment through whatever scrubber he uses. It'll be safe. No viruses. I'd appreciate a heads-up on this case whenever you can.'

'Same goes.' They disconnected, and Frederick found Clay and Taylor staring at him open-mouthed. Wordlessly he handed Clay his phone.

'I'm forwarding the message to my own email,' Clay said. 'I'll run it through a scrubber.'

Frederick kept his eyes on the baby swaddled to Clay's chest. Safe territory. Babies couldn't judge. 'That's what her son said you should do.' But he could feel Taylor's gaze on him and risked a glance.

Her mouth had curved into a sly smile. 'You *like* her!' she crowed. 'Sally Brewster. You really like her! You old charmer, you.'

He frowned at her. 'I'm not old.'

She clapped her hands, much as Julie did when she was happy. 'Awesome. It's about fucking time.'

Frederick shifted his eyes back to the baby. 'Stop.'

She snorted. 'No way. This is too good. I've got to tell Daisy. But first I'll tell Ford. He'll tell his mom. Then everyone will know.'

He grabbed her arm, but gently. 'No. Don't. It's . . . Just please don't.'

She sobered abruptly. 'Dad, you deserve to be happy. You at least deserve a date with a nice woman. If this woman is nice, we are all going be just fine.'

It wasn't 'everyone' he was concerned with. It was himself. 'Just . . . back off, baby. Please.'

Her mouth tightened into a flat line. 'For now, okay. But I'm not letting this go. Sounds like her son isn't against her seeing you, from what little I could eavesdrop. You get a little reprieve until all this shit quiets down, but I *will* bring it up again.'

She got up and kissed his cheek, went around the desk to kiss Clay's, then leaned in to nuzzle the baby. 'He's going to need feeding soon. I've got some of Stevie's expressed milk in the fridge downstairs. I'll warm a bottle and bring it to you.'

'Thanks, honey.' When she was gone, Clay met Frederick's eyes.

'You brought her up,' he said with a shrug. 'Who she is is totally on you.'

Frederick laughed in spite of his agitation. 'Who she is is awesome.'

Clay smiled. 'That is a true statement.' He sobered then, turning to his screen. 'Brewster's son was telling the truth too. No viruses.' He scanned the police report with a sigh. 'Goddammit.' He cast a furtive glance at the baby. 'I hope he can't understand what I say yet. I've got to stop cursing. Just maybe not this week.' He handed Frederick's phone back to him. 'The attachment is safe to open.'

Frederick read it, then echoed Clay's sigh. 'We need to pass this on to JD so that he can tell Hyatt.'

Clay lifted a brow. 'Or *we* could tell Hyatt. Or Joseph.'

Frederick eyed him over the desk. 'You can do it. I guess Joseph is okay, but I do *not* trust Hyatt.'

'I don't either,' Clay admitted. 'But Stevie does. I'll call him. I've got to tell him not to come to the christening anyway. He's on the guest list.'

Shaking his head, Frederick took his share of the guest names and headed off to another room to begin making calls.

Chevy Chase, Maryland,
Tuesday 14 June, 8.15 P.M.

'What the actual fuck, Thorne?'

Thorne lifted his head from the table in the interrogation room where he'd been separated from Gwyn, Ford and Alec. JD Fitzpatrick had entered the small room – thankfully alone – and he was furious.

'I don't even know where to start with that question,' Thorne said. 'Give me a hint.'

JD dropped into one of the chairs with a heavy sigh. 'Why didn't you call me? I would have come with you.'

'Because you ran yourself ragged all night and you needed to sleep. And when you woke up, you needed to stand watch over Lucy and my godson and Gwyn's goddaughter.' He pressed his fingers to his temples. 'And because I didn't expect to find any more dead bodies.'

JD's expression relaxed at that. 'I thought you didn't trust me.'

Thorne laughed mirthlessly. 'You're just about the only cop I *do* trust. I don't want you to get into trouble because we're friends.'

JD smiled at that. 'Aw, Thorne, I think you almost care.'

Thorne met his eyes. 'I do care. And I care about Lucy. I love her like a sister and I don't want to see her widowed. Or worse.'

Sobering, JD nodded. 'I agree. Okay, so here's what needs to happen now. Joseph spoke to me after Detective Rivera called him for reinforcements at Darian Hinman's house.'

'It was Hinman? The dead body?'

'The ME will have to make the determination, but it appears so. Same height, weight and hair color. They'll compare dental records, probably.'

Because the victim's face was beaten past recognition. Just like Patricia's. Just like the two Circus Freaks drug dealers found with their bodies stuffed with Sheidalin matchbooks.

Thorne hadn't even had an opportunity to address that set-up. Tavilla was keeping him hopping. And scared. 'Was it just Hinman?' He thought of that huge mansion. 'Was anyone else found?'

'No, just Hinman. He was single and had only a few household staff with key access. We're working on figuring out where they are now and why no one noticed he was missing.'

That was a good question. A VP of a company couldn't just not show up for work without raising flags. 'What was stuffed in his body? Am I allowed to know?'

JD's expression instantly smoothed out. Became unreadable. And Thorne knew the answer was not going to be good. 'Actually, it was another medal,' he said.

Thorne closed his eyes. 'Darian was on that championship soccer team with us during our senior year. Please tell me it was his.' But he knew it wasn't going to be.

'No.'

Thorne opened his eyes, met JD's. 'It was mine?'

JD nodded. 'Afraid so. Or one that someone had engraved to look like yours.'

'Which is why they've kept me separated from Gwyn and the others.'

Another nod. 'And she is loaded for bear. I don't think I've ever seen her this upset.'

'Am I finally under arrest?' Thorne sucked in a breath. 'Wait. Don't tell me they sent you in to arrest me.'

'No. I'm not here to arrest you. I'm here to take you and Gwyn home. Or wherever you'd like to go, as long as it's not out of town. Joseph is collecting Ford and Alec as we speak.' He stood up and held out a hand. 'Come on, before Gwyn wears a trench in the floor of her interview room.'

Thorne didn't move, just sat there staring up at JD. 'Why am I not under arrest?' he asked.

JD sat back down. 'Because you, Thomas Thorne, are a lucky fucker. Rigor's passed, so the ME put TOD somewhere before thirty-six hours ago.'

Thorne did the math. 'Sometime before Monday morning. When I was either with everyone at Gwyn's house or at Jamie and Phil's with Gwyn. So I might have an alibi?'

'Yes, but maybe something even better than that. Hinman's security system has cameras inside and outside, all feeding to two DVRs. Only one DVR had been stolen. The other was hidden in a storage shed. Apparently, Mr Hinman had suspected his lovely young ex-wife of cheating on him, which would have triggered the prenup he'd made her sign. He'd known that she knew about the first DVR, so he'd had a second installed in the gardener's shed. Rivera found it when he did his first search of the property.'

'And he's still alive, right? Rivera?'

JD looked startled. 'Yeah, why?'

'Because I want to thank him, and for that I have to allow myself to remember his name.'

JD chuckled. 'Yeah, you can let yourself get attached. Anyway, Hinman was captured by the security camera leaving his house at eight forty Saturday night. At nine fifteen, all his household staff got a text from his phone telling them to clear out and not come back until next week.'

'Spoofed?'

'Not sure yet. Hinman's phone hasn't been found. They're pulling his call log now, but it'll take a little while.'

'Didn't the staff find that unusual?'

'Not really. Rivera found Hinman's butler's name and number taped to the phone in the home office, so he knew who to call. The butler said that Hinman sometimes brought home "women who wore another man's ring", and when he did that, he wanted no witnesses. Saturday night, the camera caught his car pulling into his garage at eleven. A masked man, the same size as the guy Sam caught on your security camera, dumped the body where it was found tonight, then left on foot immediately afterward. No movement was seen after that, inside or outside the house.'

Comprehension dawned and relief shuddered through him. 'He was killed during our poker game at my house on Saturday night.'

'I think so. So your alibi is better than decent, which is why you're not under arrest right now.' JD stood up again. 'Come on. Gwyn's probably paced that trench so deep that she's in the basement.'

Thorne found himself being tugged to his feet, his friend's hands squeezing his shoulders hard. And his eyes stung. Irritated with himself, he looked away.

JD squeezed his shoulders once more before dropping his hands to his sides. 'Ready?'

'Yeah.' He looked around, feeling like he was seeing the walls surrounding him for the first time. 'This is the second time I've been in an interrogation room as a suspect. Can't say I liked it any more the first time.'

JD grimaced sympathetically, then checked his phone and groaned, aggrieved. 'Gwyn's giving me hell. Can we please just spring you now?'

Thorne found himself smiling. 'Yes.'

Gwyn was waiting for them in the lobby, pacing anxiously. Her face lit up when she saw them and she launched herself into his arms. He caught her easily, lifting her until her shoes dangled from the ends of her toes, shuddering out another relieved breath when she lowered her forehead to his.

'Are you all right?' she demanded in a hoarse whisper.

'I'm fine. Let's go home.' To whose home, he didn't care. As long as she was with him, it would be home enough for him.

'Clay's,' she said in his ear. 'They've called a meeting.'

He reared back, suddenly afraid. 'What else has happened?'

She patted his cheeks lightly. Comfortingly. 'No one is hurt. It's just strategy. You should probably put me down now. People are beginning to stare.'

He glanced around, annoyed to see the occupants of the Montgomery County police department's lobby gawking. He held her a few moments longer, just to be contrary, then carefully lowered her until her feet touched the floor. He took her hand, happy when she curled her fingers around his.

They were halfway to JD's car when Thorne stopped in his tracks. 'Wait. If the guy dumped Hinman's body and immediately left, that means he didn't get my medal from Hinman. His killer already had it.'

JD's brows lifted. 'I wondered how long it would take you to figure that out.'

Gwyn frowned, looking between them. 'What did I miss?'

'We'll tell you in the car,' JD said. 'Come on. I want to get out of here before something else happens that I have to bail you two out of.'

Nineteen

They'd decided to stop by the hospital first, because visiting hours were almost over and Thorne needed to see Phil. After everything that had happened – both good and bad – he needed to touch base with the men who'd stood with him through the old nightmare. And who'd become targets because of this new one.

On the plus side, Gwyn hadn't let go of his hand since they'd left the police station. She still clutched him, her heels clicking against the shiny tile as she walked at his side through the long hallway of the hospital's cardiac care unit. She'd pretended to be okay, but he could see the stress lines at the corners of her mouth and wished he could exchange them for one of those grins that had once been so effortless.

Before this nightmare. Before Evan. *I wasn't drugged the whole time.* The words ate at him. He needed to understand them. He needed to find a fucking minute when he wasn't dodging Tavilla's bullets – both real and metaphorical. His friends were targets, his father had been assaulted, a fucking drug-dealing gang leader thought that he'd challenged them, his nightclub had been closed down, his employees were out on bail for drug charges, for God's sake, and people he visited kept being dead.

And in the middle of it all was Gwyn. She was his oasis, except she had her own nightmares. *I wasn't drugged the whole time.*

He needed to know what she saw when she closed her eyes. He needed to find a way to make it go away for her. He desperately

312

needed to keep her safe. To make her happy again. And he was doing a piss-poor job of any and all of those things.

He'd find time to figure that out. After he visited Phil. After he made sure Jamie really was okay. And after he met with the friends who were risking their lives to help him keep his ass out of jail.

'I need to tell Clay that we're going to be a little late,' he murmured.

'I already did,' JD told him, following closely behind them.

Thorne threw an appreciative glance over his shoulder. 'Thanks, man.'

JD pointed ahead, at the doorway to Phil's room. 'Look, there's a line.' It was true. On one side of the doorway, a nurse stood typing at a rolling workstation, glancing furtively into the room, a frown bending her lips.

On the other side of the doorway, Frederick leaned against the wall, weary but alert as he constantly scanned the area for threats. 'Once a soldier,' JD murmured, and Thorne remembered that JD had been one too, a sniper actually.

'What kind?' Gwyn asked. 'I've wanted to ask, but he doesn't like to talk about it.'

JD made an impatient noise. 'Then don't ask him to talk about it.'

'I'm not,' Gwyn said pointedly. 'I'm asking you.'

JD repeated the noise. 'I don't exactly know, but I know that look. I wore that look.'

'Still do,' Gwyn muttered. 'It's a little freaky, JD.'

'That's probably why Frederick doesn't want to talk about it,' JD snapped.

'He was Special Forces,' Thorne told her quietly. 'That's all I know. All I needed to know. The man can take care of himself, which was what I'd been asking about when he agreed to work for the firm.'

She nodded. 'That's all I needed to know too.'

'Didn't know he'd be needing all those skills, though,' Thorne grumbled guiltily, and Gwyn squeezed his hand. So hard that he winced. 'Ow. That hurt.'

'Poor baby,' she said, sounding zero percent sympathetic. 'Stop blaming yourself. It's getting damned old.'

313

'What she said,' JD added.

'How is he?' Thorne asked, because they'd reached the nurse, who looked up from whatever she'd been typing. Her smile eased his heart.

'Doing great. They'll probably release him tomorrow or the next day.'

'To rehab?' Thorne asked, hating that he was wishing Phil could stay here a little longer, until it was safe. There was still a cop stationed between the elevator and his room. Just having seen the officer there had lowered Thorne's blood pressure.

'For a while. And after that, his insurance should pay for home visits from a nurse.'

Thorne's brain was already wondering how he'd care for Phil when he was released, because he sure as hell wasn't leaving it all up to Jamie. 'Can we go in?'

The nurse craned her neck to see into the room. 'He's got two in there with him now. You'll need to wait until one of them leaves.'

Thorne stretched to see around her, blinking. 'Detective Prew?' His eyes flew to Frederick's, his brows raised in question.

Frederick shrugged. 'He showed up ten minutes ago. Brought Phil a book. Some biography, I think. Plus some crayon pictures from his grandson.'

'Oh, right.' He'd nearly forgotten what had gotten them talking to Prew to begin with. 'They've known each other for years. Prew's son was one of Phil's students.'

'That makes me feel better,' Frederick admitted. 'I was a little taken aback when he just showed up.'

'Why are *you* here?' Gwyn asked. 'I thought we were meeting at Clay's.'

'We are. I'm here to transport Jamie. Nobody goes anywhere alone for a while. One of the new rules we'll talk about tonight.'

JD gave a grunt of agreement. 'And you two don't go anywhere without me.'

Thorne frowned. 'What about Detective Rivera?'

'Joseph needs to pull him into the investigation, so you're stuck with me.'

Thorne nodded once. 'I feel better about that,' he said, because he still felt bad that JD had believed he didn't trust him.

JD's lips quirked. 'Good to know.'

Prew picked that moment to lift his eyes to the door. When he spied Thorne, he immediately came toward him. 'Give me a second to tell him goodbye and I'll be out of your hair. Visiting hours are almost over anyway.'

When Prew was gone, Thorne reluctantly let Gwyn's hand go so that he could take the man's place. He breathed more easily once he saw that Phil did look better. 'I feel bad,' he said when he saw the hardcover on Phil's lap and the stack of childish crayon drawings on the bed at his side. There were stuffed animals and several Sudoku books sitting atop a stack of three file boxes. 'Presents galore and I didn't bring you anything. What is all this?'

Phil smiled and more of the pressure on Thorne's heart lessened. 'The drawings are from Prew's grandchildren and the stuffed animals are from some of my students. The boxes are Jamie's. Files from your office. Anne brought them, along with the Sudoku puzzles for me.'

Behind him, Gwyn made a growling sound at the mention of Anne, who she'd never liked but who she had no reason to worry about. 'Ask Thorne to bring you some pictures from his coloring book,' she said, slipping her hand in his again.

Thorne blushed, thinking about the Kama Sutra coloring book she'd given him – and the positions they'd personally tried that afternoon. 'The nurse said only two at a time. She's going to kick you out.'

'She said I was small and looked quiet,' Gwyn said, snickering.

'Boy, is she wrong,' Jamie drawled. 'But may I say that you look stunning.'

She lifted a hesitant hand to her pretty hairdo. 'Thank you. Today was my appointment with Angie.'

Phil's eyes widened. 'I'd forgotten all about that. What did you learn?' He patted the side of his bed and Gwyn sat down. He tugged on one of the curly strands Angie had left free. 'And you do look lovely.'

315

'Thank you.' She smiled at Phil, and Thorne felt his heart lighten just a little more. This, he realized, was respite. A little pocket of lovely in a storm of shit.

I'll take it. I'll take it and keep it and remember it when it gets bad again.

He glanced over at Jamie to find him smiling too, paternal joy in his eyes. That made his cheeks heat and he ducked his head, dragging the extra chair closer to the bed.

Gwyn's smile faded as she began to tell them what she'd deduced about Angie, Liam and Richard.

Phil's mouth flattened. 'Sonofabitch. I *knew* that boy had hurt her. But it didn't occur to me that he'd *raped* her. Goddammit.'

Jamie cast a quick look up at his monitors. 'Easy there. We don't want the nurse chucking us all out of here. What are you going to do next?' he asked Thorne.

'I need to talk to the other two members of Richard's posse, so I—'

Gwyn interrupted him with a loud harrumph and arched brows. 'I?'

Thorne sighed. 'We – which includes JD, because I know he's standing in the damn doorway glaring at me – will pay a visit to Officer Chandler Nystrom and Colton Brandenberg's sister. If for no other reason than to warn them.'

Both Phil and Jamie frowned, and Thorne realized they hadn't heard the latest. He gave Phil a cautious glance. 'Because Darian Hinman is dead. Murdered.'

Phil nodded once, his expression lethal. 'Not gonna cry over him. I can still see your face after he kicked you in the head.'

'You're not suspected, are you?' Jamie asked, frowning.

'No,' Thorne said simply, because he'd already given Phil too many surprises for the day. The two of them didn't need to know that his own medal had been found in Hinman's body. 'And after I see them, I'm going to check on Ming, Mowry and Laura. I called them all this morning. They were okay. Not happy about having arrest records, but hopefully we can get those expunged once we clear everything up.'

'But first, we're due at Clay's for a meeting,' Gwyn said, kissing

Phil's scruffy cheek. 'So we need to say goodnight.'

'Visiting hours are over anyway,' Jamie said. He wheeled his chair closer to the bed. 'My ride is waiting outside in the hall. You kids skedaddle. I'll meet you there.'

'So is ours.' Thorne leaned in to whisper in Phil's ear. 'Love you. Take care of yourself.'

Phil's eyes softened. 'Love you too, and I will.'

Thorne rose and offered Gwyn his hand. 'See you at Clay's, Jamie.' They left the two alone to say their goodnights and went into the hall. 'I don't think they've spent a night apart in years,' he murmured to Gwyn.

She patted his arm sweetly and tilted her head so that she could meet his eyes. 'He'll be out soon and they'll be together again, and then this experience will just be a bad memory.'

And once again he found himself thinking about *her* bad memories and wondering what exactly had happened to push her into checking out of life for four years. *Stop wondering for now*, he told himself. *For now, enjoy the smile on her face, because it's real and it's all for you.*

That was sound advice, he decided. 'You're right. Let's go.' Because the sooner they got this meeting done, the sooner he'd be back in her bed, holding her in his arms.

Hunt Valley, Maryland,
Tuesday 14 June, 9.40 P.M.

Dinner at Clay's was pizza, and Gwyn's stomach started growling as soon as the scent of cheese and pepperoni hit her nose. 'Oh my God,' she groaned. 'We forgot to eat today.'

Lucy met them at the door, giving JD a kiss hello before slinging her arm around Gwyn's shoulders. 'You didn't feed them, JD?'

'They never said they were hungry,' JD protested, then bent down to scoop up the toddler racing toward him. 'Hello, you,' he said, then blew raspberries on his son's stomach. 'I'm starving too. Bailing out your friends is hard work.'

He started to walk to the pizza boxes stacked on the living room coffee table, but Jeremiah had other ideas. Lurching out of JD's arms, he leapt into Thorne's, smacking a kiss on his stubbled cheek.

The little boy giggled, rubbing his chubby fingers over Thorne's jaws. 'Tickles. Up. Wanna fly.'

Gwyn stopped walking at the look on Thorne's face. He was smiling at Jeremiah with a love so pure it almost hurt to see. How had she missed this? Did he want this? A family with babies?

Do I? Can I? She'd been content to hold Lucy's babies, believing it was likely as close as she'd ever get to having another child of her own – something she'd long ago promised herself she'd never, ever do again.

But it would be different this time. She wouldn't be young, broke, uneducated and terrified. *I'd be pushing forty, juggling a business that I hope I still own after all this is over . . . and terrified.*

'What?' Lucy demanded. She gripped Gwyn's chin and tilted her face up. 'You look like you just got diagnosed with a terminal illness.'

Gwyn blinked, quickly bringing her expression back to neutral, but it was too late. Lucy had already seen. 'It's nothing.' She shot her best friend a pleading look when Lucy opened her mouth to argue. 'Please. It's nothing.'

'But . . .' Lucy frowned, clearly upset. 'I heard you were all sexy together this afternoon. Wasn't that true?'

Gwyn wanted to roll her eyes. 'Ford and Alec are little gossips.'

'Well, yeah. But were they wrong?'

'No,' she admitted. 'I'm really hungry. Can I eat before you grill me?'

Lucy stepped back, blinking away hurt. 'Of course. Sure.' She'd started to turn toward Thorne, who had lifted Jeremiah over his head and was jogging toward the pizza, both of them making plane noises. Gwyn grabbed her arm.

'Wait.' It was just the two of them in Clay's entryway now. 'They weren't wrong. I just . . . It's hard to take it all in, okay? Give me some time.'

'Enough time for you to tell yourself all the reasons it won't work?'

318

Gwyn looked away. 'Probably.'

Lucy's arm came around her shoulders again. 'It was Jeremiah, wasn't it? Seeing Thorne with him?'

'A little, yes. I guess I missed how he looks at him. I've been out of it for so long, I just . . .' None of what she'd said was untrue. It just wasn't all of the truth.

Lucy smiled. 'You mean how Thorne looks at Jeremiah like he loves him? You didn't miss it before. Not really. Thorne doesn't usually let that show unless he thinks no one's looking. He's all gruff when there are witnesses, but when it's just him and Jeremiah? I've seen that look before. That he wasn't guarding it just now says a lot, I think. He's opening up. This experience, this horrible, terrifying experience, has gotten him to accept affection from the group. So it's not all bad.'

'No, not all bad,' Gwyn murmured.

Lucy squeezed her shoulders. 'And it's gotten you to open up and maybe see things you hadn't seen before too.'

'Maybe,' she allowed. She swallowed hard. 'He's a good man.'

'He is. And if you're about to say he deserves someone better, I will personally kick your ass.'

'Let's avoid that,' Gwyn said dryly, because that had been exactly what she'd been thinking. 'I really am hungry. Can we have this conversation later?'

'One second,' Lucy begged. 'Just one detail, please. Was it what you'd hoped?'

Gwyn's lips twitched, her smile breaking through despite her best efforts. 'Okay, fine. It was stellar. Far better than I'd ever dreamed. Are you happy now?'

'Yup.' She smiled and steered Gwyn toward the food. 'Sit and eat. We'll pull everyone together. By the way, that was an amazing piece of deduction today. You did good, girl.'

'Thanks.' Piling her plate high, she found Thorne taking up most of a loveseat, leaving just enough space for her to snuggle in beside him. They ate steadily, pausing to greet Jamie and Frederick when they arrived and to nod as the chairs around them filled with their friends.

Gwyn could feel Thorne tensing as everyone came together. She leaned away from him so that she could see his face. It was at times like this, when she was tucked up against him, without the benefit of four-inch heels, that she felt overwhelmed by the sheer presence of him. And in a totally good way.

The man was lickable. Which she now knew for herself.

At the moment, her lickable man had schooled his expression, but she wasn't fooled. 'Stop it,' she muttered. When he looked down at her, she just smiled at him. 'Friends, Thorne. They are here because they want to be. They help you because they want to. Just like you did for them.'

He nodded stiffly. 'I know,' he said quietly. 'I just can't stand the thought of any of them getting hurt because of me.'

Lucy settled on the arm of the loveseat next to Thorne. 'It wouldn't be because of you. It'd be because of a sick, sadistic bastard who has his nuts in a twist because you once told him fucking no.'

Thorne pursed his lips, but this time it was to hide a smile. 'Did you just say "nuts in a twist"?'

Lucy smacked a kiss on his cheek. 'I did. And I'll say it again, more loudly, once all the kiddies are downstairs.'

'Who's watching them?' Gwyn asked, even though she knew the answer. She missed caring for her goddaughter. Providing childcare to Lucy's kids had been of the things she'd looked forward to, but Taylor had stepped forward to take the job and Gwyn had let her, because she knew the young woman was still finding her place in her new family's world and helping out was an easy niche to carve. This Gwyn understood. Helping Lucy with the kids had been healing as well as allowing her to support Lucy. *Because I was a pretty shitty friend when it came to almost everything else.* Babies didn't judge, didn't ask questions. They just loved you.

'Taylor and Ford,' Lucy said, just as she'd thought. 'Taylor's got an earbud, though, because she wants to know what's going on up here. Sam's here, by the way. In the house, I mean. Ruby's with him, resting in one of the bedrooms upstairs.'

'And Agent Ingram?' Gwyn asked.

Lucy smiled. 'He woke up. He's not out of the woods yet, but his chances are much better now.'

'Thank God,' Thorne said quietly. 'I've been afraid to ask.'

Jamie rolled his chair next to Gwyn. 'Frederick and I stopped in to see him on our way out of the hospital tonight. His wife said he's been squeezing her hand, which is very encouraging. He's still on a ventilator, but it's good to have some hope.'

On that note they simply sat, Gwyn and Thorne and Lucy, linked together just as they'd been from the beginning. It was sweet. And powerful. They were her family. And now Jamie and all the rest of the people here had become her family too.

And the members of her family were very good at their jobs, she thought as Clay and Frederick rolled a free-standing bulletin board into the room. The board was covered with photographs, clustered around two central pictures – one of Cesar Tavilla and the other of Thorne.

'What the hell?' Thorne whispered, staring.

'It's our crime board,' Lucy said conspiratorially. 'Please notice that you're on the Good Guy side.' It was hard to miss. Two big signs had been tacked to the top of the board: *Bad Guy* and *Good Guy*.

Thorne's photo was one Gwyn had taken years ago as he'd played his bass on stage. He'd looked at peace in that moment, she remembered. And she'd wanted him then too.

It had been a long time since she'd heard him play, and she'd wondered why. But now she knew. It had been four and a half years. He'd been grieving too, because she'd gotten so lost in her own mind.

'I'm glad to see I'm a good guy.' Thorne put his plate aside to lean forward, forearms on his knees, scanning the display. There were dozens of photos and notes, with string connecting them.

'So,' Clay said. 'We got tired of being targets. We're taking charge. All of us, Thorne, and that includes you.'

'I can live with that,' Thorne said.

'We thought so.' Clay pointed to four Post-it notes, which someone had numbered one through four. Two simply had 'male' written on them, the third 'male/killer', and the fourth said 'female'.

321

All four were attached to Tavilla. 'We know he has at least four people helping him. The two men who drugged you and carried you into your house, the woman who called you posing as your client, Bernice Brown, and the mask-wearing guy who took the two guys away from your house, then returned, sticking around for a few more hours. We figure he was the one who probably killed Patricia.'

A photo of Patricia was positioned in the middle of the board, with string connecting her to both the 'male/killer' and a photo of Richard Linden, which connected to Thorne.

Thorne frowned. 'Probably?'

Alec nodded. 'I took a closer look at the video Sam retrieved from your house. The masked man was there, but there was another person there too.'

Beside Gwyn, Thorne shifted uncomfortably. 'Who?'

'I don't know. There's just a shadow in the hallway as the person goes from your bedroom to the garage. He – or she – never comes into camera view, but there are clearly two different shadows at one point. One from the masked man and the other from the second person.'

Thorne rubbed the back of his neck. 'That is . . . I don't know. It was bad enough knowing I had *one* creepy guy in my house while I was unconscious, but two? I'm wondering if it was Tavilla himself. *That* freaks me out.'

Me too, Gwyn thought. That Thorne had been that vulnerable . . . *They could have done anything to him.* She found herself being grateful that they'd 'only' drugged him. She swallowed hard. *It could have been so much worse.*

Alec shot him a sympathetic look. 'Sorry, man. I tried to get more definition, but I couldn't. I can send the file to the cops and see if they can.'

Thorne nodded slowly. 'Yes, please.'

'Send it to Joseph,' JD said. 'The FBI has better equipment than Hyatt's team at BPD.'

Alec nodded. 'You want to send it, JD?'

'That would be best. Let's email it to my Gmail account. Open me

322

a browser window.' Alec did as he was asked, then handed his laptop to JD, who tapped a few keys and handed the laptop back. 'This way nobody can subpoena you later.'

Gwyn leaned back, able to better see Lucy with Thorne leaning forward as he was. 'JD's becoming one of us.'

Lucy grinned and blew JD a kiss. 'And it's sexy as hell, isn't it?'

Gwyn shuddered. 'Ew. No.' JD was like a brother to her, just as Thorne was to Lucy.

Thorne shook his head at them. 'Ladies, focus.' He squinted at the photos. 'I see Patricia, the two Circus Freaks guys who tried to deal out of Sheidalin, Ramirez and his wife, and Darian Hinman. All victims. But who are the two people beneath Hinman?'

A woman and a man. Both were connected to a woman in nurse's scrubs who connected to Bernice Brown, the woman who'd been impersonated by whoever had lured Thorne out on Saturday night. Bernice Brown was also connected to Thorne and back to the mysterious female working for Tavilla.

Gwyn had a bad feeling about those two people, underscored when Frederick started to speak, then hesitated. 'Not your fault, Thorne,' he said. 'Remember that.'

Thorne slumped back into the loveseat. 'They're dead too,' he said flatly. 'Who were they?'

'A professor on sabbatical with her husband. Their trailer was parked in the space that Sally Brewster' – he pointed to the nurse – 'described to the man who called her asking her for Bernice Brown's location. Sally thought the space was unoccupied.'

'Oh no,' Gwyn breathed.

Frederick nodded. 'Sally's son is a cop. He had a bad feeling about the man pumping his mother for information, then someone using that same number to get information from Julie.'

'Ramirez's throwaway cell number,' Thorne said grimly.

'Well, yes, but I didn't tell him that,' Frederick said. 'He was convinced enough of the danger to take a leave of absence to watch out for his mother.'

Thorne leaned back, closing his eyes. 'At least she's safe then. Has anyone told Joseph the connection between those poor people and my case?'

'I did,' Clay said.

Thorne sat up abruptly. 'Have we checked on Bernice Brown?'

'Yes,' Frederick said calmly. 'I talked to Bernice and her cousin this afternoon. I told them about the couple who died, though they'd already heard about it. Bernice is pretty rattled. So is Sally. She feels like she condemned them to be murdered.'

'No,' Thorne bit out. 'It was Tavilla, snipping ends. He's damn good at that.'

Gwyn and Lucy shared another glance. Thorne looked at them. 'What?'

'You're not blaming yourself,' Gwyn said. 'That's an improvement.'

'It totally is,' Lucy said. 'I'll go next. It's not much, but I got a copy of the preliminary autopsy report for Patricia Segal. Cause of death was the stab wounds. She had excessive levels of GHB in her blood and a blood alcohol of .35.' She sighed. 'And there was evidence that she had been sexually assaulted.'

'Oh no,' Gwyn murmured. Lucy shot her a stricken *I'm sorry* look but Gwyn waved it away, hoping no one had noticed Lucy's reaction, because it was far too telling. 'Did the rapist leave anything behind?' she asked, conscious of how still Thorne had become beside her.

'A hair,' Lucy said sadly, and Gwyn knew the sadness was for her, not for Patricia Segal. Although it should have been for both of them, because no woman deserved that. *Ever.* Lucy squared her shoulders. 'Her body was released today. The funeral will be Friday. There will be a closed-coffin visitation with the family on Thursday evening.'

There was a moment of silence and Gwyn felt like everyone was staring at her. She didn't like it. 'We need a plan for Patricia's visitation and funeral. One of us needs to be there in case her killer shows up. We need to capture the faces of attendees.'

'I'm keeping a list of action steps,' Alec said. 'I'll add that one.'

'Thanks, Alec.' Stevie stood up and walked to the bulletin board. 'I've got to feed Mason soon, so I'm going next. Paige and I interviewed half a dozen of the women on Patricia's fund-raising committee today. We were trying to get more info on her husband, and on the young man she was sleeping with.'

'Patricia liked doling out information in small parcels,' Paige said with a grimace. 'She told one woman his hair color, another his eye color, another the size of his . . . well, you know.'

Everyone grimaced at that. 'Did she tell any of them his *age*?' Gwyn asked sharply.

'Just that he was over the age of consent,' Stevie said. 'Which in Maryland is sixteen.'

'The friend she told that to was pretty appalled,' Paige added. 'She said she pressed her for assurances that he was over twenty-one, but Patricia just giggled and said he made her feel younger. That she'd enjoy it until he went away to college in the fall.'

'Did she tell any of them his name?' Thorne asked, his face stony.

Because he'd represented young men who'd committed crimes, only to find that the source of their behavioral issues was being sexually assaulted by someone they should have been able to trust. Both male and female, their abusers had been pastors, priests, rabbis, teachers, scoutmasters, and many times the parent of a friend.

'No,' Stevie said. 'But she did tell one friend that he had muscles from playing lacrosse, and another that he had a scholarship. On a hunch that he went to the same high school as her son, we got a copy of the lacrosse team's most recent photo and did some cross-checking for seniors who'd received scholarships. We used the hair and eye colors she'd revealed and narrowed it down to these two.' She held up a high school yearbook and pointed to two of the boys.

Paige picked up the story. 'Then we found their coach. He's teaching summer school at the high school. We told him we'd gotten a report of one of his players potentially being the victim of a predator who was an older woman. We thought he'd be all "isn't that cool, wish I'd been that kid". Like, you know, that song "Hot for Teacher".'

'That attitude pisses me off so much,' Lucy hissed.

Thorne's hands had clenched into fists.

'Well, you wouldn't have been pissed off,' Paige said, 'because the coach was as appalled as we were. And very helpful. He told us that one of the players had a steady girlfriend and he doubted it was him.'

'But this one,' Stevie said, pointing at the page, 'Tristan Armistead, had been acting strangely during the entire second half of the year. Secretive, not showing up to team events. His grades suffered, as did his performance on the lacrosse field. He nearly lost his scholarship.'

'And,' Paige added, 'he'd been friends with Patricia's son, but then it was like they'd had a falling-out. The coach said that Patricia's son had come to him for advice because he was bewildered. He had no idea what he'd done wrong.'

'And then,' Stevie finished dramatically, 'the coach went really still and asked if the older woman was Patricia Segal.'

'Did you tell him that it was?' JD demanded.

Stevie shook her head. 'No. But he'd already figured it out. He asked if the boy was in any danger, and we told him honestly that we didn't know.'

'But that if he were our son, we'd be worried,' Paige finished. 'We asked if he could help us find Tristan, and he did one better. He went with us to the kid's house, but Tristan wasn't home. A neighbor told the coach that the family had gone on vacation but Tristan had stayed behind to feed the cat and bring in the mail. They hadn't seen him for a few days and the mailbox was stuffed.'

'We gave the coach and the neighbor our cards and asked them to call if they saw him.' Stevie handed over the yearbook to Paige. 'I need to go. Bye.' Leaning heavily on her cane, she made her way to the elevator.

'I'll make a copy of that yearbook page,' Alec offered. 'I'll enlarge Tristan's photo so Clay can put it on the board.'

'Can I see the yearbook first?' Thorne asked, and Paige passed it over.

'Tristan is the blond on the far left,' she said. 'He's standing right next to Patricia's son, Blake Segal.'

Thorne took the yearbook and Gwyn leaned closer to see. Then she gasped. 'Oh my God.' She grabbed the book and pulled it closer.

'Oh. My. God.'

'What?' Lucy demanded.

Gwyn looked up at Thorne. 'Look at him, Thorne. Blake Segal. *Look* at him.'

'I see,' Thorne said, his voice strangled.

'See what?' Lucy all but shouted.

Gwyn looked up to meet the alarmed gazes of their friends. 'Blake Segal could be Liam's twin.'

Alec's mouth fell open. 'What?'

She turned the yearbook around so they could see, then brought up the photo she'd taken on her phone in Angie's shop, enlarging it until Liam's face was visible.

'Oh my God,' Jamie echoed quietly. 'You're right. Is that possible? That Richard is the father of Patricia's son? That he raped his own sister?'

Hunt Valley, Maryland,
Tuesday 14 June, 10.15 P.M.

Swallowing back bile at the notion that Richard had sexually assaulted his own sister, Thorne expelled his breath in a harsh whoosh. 'But it might not mean anything. He was her brother. I mean, they carried the same genes. It makes sense that his nephew might look like him.'

'No.' Gwyn shook her head hard. '*No*. Remember I told you I was looking into Patricia's background? I found out that she left school after Richard was killed and didn't come back until after the trial. She went to Europe, supposedly. She was gone for over a year.'

'It still may not mean anything,' Thorne insisted.

Gwyn was undeterred. 'Richard and Patricia weren't blood siblings. Wait. Let me find it . . .' She was rapidly punching keys on her phone. 'Richard Linden's obituary. Here it is. "Richard is survived by his father, Richard Linden Senior, his mother, Elizabeth Hale Linden, his *step*mother, Judith Linden, and his stepsister, Patricia." She looked up at him. 'Judith was the one who was married to Richard Senior at the time of the murder, and she remains

327

the current Mrs Linden.'

'I've got Patricia's obituary,' Alec said. 'It was printed in this morning's *Washington Post*. "Patricia is survived by her mother, Judith Linden, her father, Harold Martelli, and her stepfather, Richard Linden Senior." You're right, Gwyn. There was no shared blood between Richard and Patricia. Totally different genes.'

Thorne leaned forward again and buried his face in his hands. 'God.' It was almost a moan, but he didn't care.

Gwyn rubbed his back soothingly. 'What's wrong, Thorne?' she murmured.

'How could he do that?' *And how could none of us have seen it? First Angie, now Patricia. How could we have just gone on every day with a rapist in our midst and not known?* But those words wouldn't come, so he repeated the ones he'd already used. 'How could he *do* that?'

'You know the answer to that,' Jamie said softly. 'Richard was simply bad. And this could have been why Linden Senior was so keen to have you take the fall for Richard's murder. He knew that someone else had a motive to kill Richard. Hell, Richard could have raped more girls than just Angie and Patricia. If his crimes had become public, it would bring scandal on their precious family name.'

'And on Patricia too,' Gwyn murmured. 'My God. She raised a child of rape.'

Thorne shuddered out a sigh, wondering what Gwyn was seeing in her mind. Wondering what Evan had done to her. 'I keep wanting to believe it was consensual,' he said hoarsely, mostly because he wanted to believe that the physical relationship Gwyn had had with Evan had also been consensual. 'But I know that's not true.' He knew that *neither* was true. And he thought he was going to be sick.

Hold it together. For her. Her hand was rubbing slow circles on his back and Lucy was stroking his hair, both comforting, but both utterly different touches.

'The key ring,' he said finally, needing something else to latch onto. 'If Richard was murdered because of someone he'd raped – either Angie or Patricia or, God forbid, somebody else . . . The key ring means something. It always comes back to that damn key ring.'

'Or maybe just the key,' Gwyn said thoughtfully. 'It's possible that the soccer medal had nothing to do with it. I wonder what the key fit. I wonder what Linden Senior knew about it, because somebody made it disappear.'

'And that usually means a money trail,' Lucy said.

Alec nodded, typing. 'We need to get more information about the widow of that ME tech,' he said. 'We need to find out where her money is coming from. Adding it to the to-do list.'

Thorne focused on Alec so that he didn't have to keep thinking about what had happened to Gwyn. Or to Patricia. 'How did you get to Angie's finances so quickly?'

Alec glanced up at JD as if to ask if he was going to turn him in.

JD rolled his eyes. 'Tell him. I'm kind of curious too.'

Alec shrugged. 'I basically did a Hail Mary and sent a Trojan in an email to the salon's email account. One of those "invoice attached" emails that you're supposed to delete. Whoever was manning the computer clicked right on it, and bingo, I was in their system. They've kept meticulous records. Every bank statement had been downloaded in a PDF and stored, labeled just as meticulously. It was just a matter of sifting through documents until I found what I needed.'

'I'm glad you're on our side,' JD muttered.

Alec grinned at him. 'I use my skills for good, not evil.' He sobered then. 'If the ME tech's widow is as careless, I could get lucky. If I am, I'll set the Trojan to self-destruct so that when Joseph's guys finally get there, they won't know I've been there already. If I'm not lucky, it could take a little longer to get into her system.'

'Do what you need to,' Clay directed. 'Just, you know, the usual.'

Alec looked amused. 'Don't get caught. Got it. But poor JD looks like he's got a stomach ache.'

JD grimaced. 'Yeah, but not because of you. I'm wondering now just how they lured Patricia to wherever she was abducted from. I mean, she was carefully chosen for her link to Thorne, but how? And why? Why now? How does Tavilla connect to her? He either lured her out or had her followed and snatched. Was it through this kid? The lacrosse player? Or did her husband find out about her . . . God, I don't even want to call it an affair. Did Judge Segal find out? I mean, he might not have cared about an ordinary affair, but his wife pursuing a barely legal kid who was her son's friend? That won't look good for him.'

Paige was biting her lip thoughtfully. 'Most of the ladies Stevie and I spoke to today said the marriage had issues. That it had been rocky ever since they'd known Patricia. She'd had affairs in the past, so they were used to that. It was the age of this young man that had them alarmed – and Patricia too, when she was sober. When she was sober – or less drunk, anyway – she feared her husband would find out and kill her. Her words, they said. They also said she wasn't sober very often. She drank a lot, apparently. Maybe we can understand a little bit of the why behind that now.'

Beside him, Gwyn tensed, but Thorne wasn't going to embarrass her by calling attention to it and fixed his gaze on the bulletin board with its photos and string, making himself focus on the case.

'*If* Judge Segal knew about the boy, I suppose it's possible that he set his wife up to be killed. He'd be too smart to kill her himself. Unless it was a crime of passion, of course, which this wasn't. It was too planned. If the judge was involved, he somehow connects to Tavilla because Tavilla somehow got his hands on Patricia and that damn key ring. If the judge isn't involved, we still need to know how Tavilla got to Patricia.' He stared at the photo of Patricia, feeling a pained sympathy for the assaults she'd endured, both in her youth and prior to her death. 'Can we get access to her cell phone records?'

JD looked uncomfortable. 'Both Hyatt and Joseph have them. What would you be hoping to find?'

'How she was lured out on Saturday night,' Thorne said. 'Was she called to meet someone, like I was? Or did someone slip something in her drink at a bar she went to voluntarily? I want to know how she was abducted.'

'I'll see if I can find out,' JD promised. 'Joseph has let a few things "slip" in front of me, like the details from Hinman's house today. He's trying to help us as much as he can.'

'Which we appreciate,' Clay said. 'But we can't ignore a possible connection to the judge, if for no other reason than that Patricia was afraid of what would happen if he found out. We need to know more about Segal and any possible connection he has to Tavilla. Paige, would Grayson be willing to do some digging for us? Perhaps see if there are any rumors about him?'

Paige's husband, Grayson Smith, was the senior assistant state's attorney, one of the highest positions in the prosecutor's office. He and Joseph's wife Daphne, also a prosecutor, had recused themselves, unwilling to jeopardize any case law enforcement was able to build by interfering with the investigation, but Grayson could still be a valuable resource.

'I'll ask him,' Paige promised. 'He has told me a few things, like that Segal's post is an appointed one, so he doesn't have to worry about pleasing an electorate. That can make him more vulnerable to rumor, though. He also said that Segal had a solid record against crime in the past, but that he's made some odd rulings recently. I was planning to dig into that first thing in the morning.'

Because it was getting late, Thorne realized. 'I'm sorry. I've kept you all up way past your bedtimes. We should wrap this up.'

Clay's expression became one of rueful amusement. 'The perfect segue if I ever heard one, because now it's my turn. Thorne, we made up signs for you for this part. Everybody?' Everyone in the room except Gwyn and Thorne reached for a piece of poster board they'd stored at their sides. Even Lucy and Jamie held them. 'Turn 'em,' Clay instructed.

All of them read *IT'S NOT YOUR FAULT, THORNE!* in various colors, scripts and fonts, and all were decorated with glitter and stars. At the bottom of Lucy's sign, Thorne could see a small signature. *Cordelia Maynard.* Stevie's ten-year-old daughter.

He had to swallow the sudden lump in his throat. 'Glitter? Wow, you guys went all out.'

'It kept Cordelia busy for *hours*,' Clay said dryly. 'I'm not ashamed to say that I'll use glitter to my own advantage if necessary. So this is the deal, Thorne, and if you even look like you're thinking that it's your fault, we have other props.'

'Water guns,' Paige said with such unabashed delight that Thorne laughed.

Clay smiled at him. 'So the consequences will be severe, just a heads-up.' He rolled his shoulders, as if preparing for a fight. 'Okay. We are postponing both the christening and the barbecue afterward, but have spread the word that the service is still on and that only friends and family will be attending.'

Thorne's mouth fell open. *No. No way.* 'But—' he started, only to see half a dozen glitter-covered signs being waved at him. He looked at Gwyn helplessly. She looked back, her eyes bright with unshed tears, clearly appreciating this expression of support.

'We're sending moms and kids to Chicago,' Clay went on. 'My friends are there and they'll take care of Stevie, Lucy, Paige and all our babies. Julie and Cordelia are also going, so we will only have adults in the house, and only adults who can handle a firearm.'

Thorne looked up at Lucy in shock. 'You knew about this?'

She nodded, her eyes soft. 'Yep.'

He checked with JD to find him nodding as well. 'The signs were my idea,' JD said with complete seriousness.

'The water pistols were mine,' Paige added smugly.

Thorne shook his head, unable to hold back his smile. 'Of course they were.'

'Wait,' Gwyn said, her mouth bent in a sudden frown. 'You're sending a bunch of new mothers and babies to Chicago *alone*?'

Paige looked offended. 'Bite your tongue, girl. We're not just a bunch of "new mothers". We are super-moms. Stevie and I can take care of ourselves. And Lucy can . . . well, she can hit any bad guys with her violin.'

Lucy feigned a shudder at the notion. 'Bite your tongue, girl,' she said, then smiled at Gwyn. 'Don't worry, Grandma. We'll be fine.'

'And anyway, we're not going alone,' Paige added. 'Grayson's going with us. He's been chomping at the bit because he hasn't been able to do anything else to help. He's being watched like a hawk,' she said apologetically. 'Damn judicial politics.'

He'd done a lot to help, though, Thorne thought. The prosecutor had fully supported Paige's involvement, even if it caused him political hardship later.

'Plus, Taylor and Ford are going with them,' Frederick said. 'And

Clay's friend Ethan. It's all arranged. We'll go on with the appearance of a small event attended by family and friends, and we'll make sure we're a target that Cesar Tavilla cannot resist.' He narrowed his eyes. 'All of your people in one place. All armed and ready for the motherfucker.'

Thorne opened his mouth, then closed it, because he was truly overwhelmed. These people had disrupted their lives. Risked their lives. *For me.*

Lucy chuckled. 'We have achieved the impossible. Thorne is speechless.'

Gwyn gripped his collar and gently pulled him down to kiss his cheek. 'Say thank you, Thorne.'

Thorne shuddered out a breath. 'Thank you,' he whispered.

'That's all?' Paige asked, pushing her lip out in a pout. 'I was hoping you'd fight us.'

Alec nudged her with his foot. 'You just want to use the water guns.'

'Damn straight,' she grumbled, making Thorne laugh again.

'Thank you,' he repeated, his voice finally steady. 'Really. Thank you.'

Twenty

Annapolis, Maryland,
Tuesday 14 June, 11.00 P.M.

He lifted his gaze from his computer lazily, or at least it would appear so to his guest. He'd intentionally made the judge wait, stewing the arrogant man in his own juices.

'Can I help you, Judge Segal?' he inquired politely.

The judge took an angry step forward, but was halted by Patton's grip on his arm. He attempted to shake Patton off. The two were well matched in terms of size and muscle, but Patton was twenty years younger and armed.

The judge was not armed. Patton had searched him thoroughly.

'You may let him go,' he told Patton.

The judge adjusted his suit coat with the air of a man who'd been wronged. 'Who the fuck do you think you are?' he hissed.

He folded his hands atop his desk. 'Cesar Tavilla. President and CEO of Los Señores de la Tierra.'

Segal shook his head, like that didn't matter. But it would matter. By the time this was done, it would matter a great deal.

By the time this is done, I will own the man.

Segal leaned across his desk to loom over him. 'You killed my wife.'

He blinked up at Segal. 'I did, yes.' He gave his wrist a shake and the blade he'd hidden in his sleeve came sliding into his hand. With a flick of his thumb, he opened the switchblade and jabbed it within a centimeter of the jackass's snarling face. 'With this very knife. Are we done now?'

Segal paled and took a step back, hands fisted at his sides.

He had to admit to reluctant admiration. He'd expected the judge to go running. The man was not a coward.

'That was not our agreement,' Segal gritted out.

Conscious that Patton had crept close enough to rip Segal away if necessary, he regarded the judge soberly. 'You would have had me murder a young man instead? The best friend of your son? A young man whose only crime was to believe your wife when she promised him a fairy-tale ending?'

Segal's jaw clenched. 'That was our agreement.'

'No, that was *your* agreement. *Our* agreement was that if you provided me with information with which I could discredit Thomas Thorne, then I'd refrain from reporting your judicial indiscretions to the bar.'

'But you were never supposed to *kill* my wife!'

He lifted his brows. 'You want me to believe you loved her? Truly?'

Segal swallowed hard. 'She was drinking herself to death. She didn't need your help.'

For a split second, he had some sympathy for the man's loss. Then he remembered with whom he was speaking. 'So you would have been fine with your wife killing herself and possibly someone else's loved one when she drove drunk?'

The judge looked away, swallowing again. 'No.'

'Because you weren't going to be able to hide her DUIs forever, Judge Segal.'

'I know that.' Segal's gaze returned, his eyes blazing. 'But you didn't have to rape her too,' he whispered hoarsely. 'She didn't deserve that.'

His mouth fell open. 'What are you suggesting?'

Segal's mouth twisted. 'I'm not "suggesting" anything. I'm *telling* you what was on the autopsy report. She was sexually assaulted. And I know it wasn't by the kid, because I know where he was all evening. He was waiting for her in the fucking park, which was where you were supposed to collect him.'

He sat back in his chair, horrified by Segal's accusation. Horrified

335

by what – according to the ME – had happened. 'You think I did that?'

'Who else could have done it?' Segal pointed to the knife he still held. 'You carved her up just like . . .' He cut himself off, looking away again.

'Like what, Judge Segal?' he asked quietly. 'Like her brother was carved up by his killer?'

Segal jerked a nod. 'She didn't deserve that.'

'Probably not. But she was unconscious at the time. She didn't suffer. Unlike her brother.'

'*I don't care!*' Segal cried, his eyes filling with what appeared to be honest tears. 'She was a *horrible* wife. She was a *horrible* mother. But she did *not* deserve to be raped. *Again.* And she did *not* deserve to die that way. I had to tell my son what had happened to his mother, because I knew the media wouldn't keep quiet. I had to tell my son that his mother was *raped.*'

A glance from the corner of his eye showed Patton to be as confused by the news of the sexual assault as he was. 'Must have been Harrelson and Schwab,' he said quietly. 'They brought her to me already drugged up.'

He sighed. 'I'm sorry, Judge Segal. This was not done on my command. If it helps, the men who abducted your wife are dead.'

Segal closed his eyes, sending the tears streaking down his face. 'Of course it doesn't help. Patricia's still dead. My son is still grieving.'

He tilted his head, considering. He'd been following Segal's career for years. The man was canny, never doing anything without a damn good reason. 'Your wife has been dead since late on Saturday. It is now Wednesday. Why did you wait more than three full days to confront me?'

'Because I've been busy,' Segal snapped. 'My son has been a wreck. I've had to reschedule my court calendar and arrange a funeral, on top of dodging cops and reporters.' His throat worked as he swallowed yet again. 'It was the autopsy report. I was furious that you'd killed her, but when I was told that she'd been raped too, I just . . . I had to do something.'

336

'This time, you mean?'

'Yes,' he hissed. 'This time. But just like before, there isn't anything I *can* do.'

'I understand that helpless feeling,' he said coldly. 'I felt it when my wife died after my son was incarcerated. And when my son was murdered in prison.'

Segal shook his head. 'That was not my fault.'

'That is still debatable, sir.' He steepled his fingers, considering what he'd do with the man. Segal had contacted him through Margo, and Patton had blindfolded him when he'd brought him here. That Patton had done so without his approval was a separate topic, and his assistant would be dealt with severely. 'I could kill you right now, you know,' he said to the judge.

'I know.' Segal lifted his chin and met his gaze squarely. 'But I wasn't completely stupid. I left a document in my safe deposit box, detailing what I'd done and the deal I'd made with you. And that I planned to see you tonight.'

Well, if he was bluffing, he was good at it. And there was really no reason to believe he wasn't telling the truth. The man had very little to lose at this point.

If I kill him, I risk being linked to Patricia's murder. Of course, Thorne already suspected as much, but the man had no evidence. There was no tangible connection. The police hadn't even sniffed his way. And he would know. He had resources in BPD, at all levels of the organization.

If I kill him, I lose a valuable resource on the bench. And those were alliances that took much longer to build.

If I let him live, he is a loose thread. Unless he is discredited for something entirely different before he can begin pointing fingers. Which I can do. Easily.

Decision made. 'You came to avenge your wife's honor,' he said finally. 'I can respect that. I won't kill you.'

Segal's laugh was darkly sardonic. 'Thank you ever so much.'

He bit back the temptation to bury his blade in the man's throat and kept his expression coolly neutral. 'You're welcome. Now, if you ever try to contact me again, by any means, you will regret it.'

Segal's nod was disrespectful. 'Same song, second verse. You kill me, I release my documents. It's called leverage.'

He smiled, the chilling smile that usually made men quake in fear. He was happy to see Segal was not immune. 'You still have someone to lose, Mr Segal.'

Segal paled. 'No. You wouldn't dare.'

'Dare? That is the wrong word to use.'

'My son is not part of this.'

'Everything that is dear to you is part of this. You upped the stakes. You can't whine when the house wins. Because the house always wins. If you ever contact me again, or if I hear the slightest whisper of my name in connection to yours, the boy dies. But first I will tell him exactly who he is. Are we quite clear?'

Segal ground his molars. 'Crystal.'

'Good.' He gestured to Patton. 'Please see that Judge Segal is returned to his vehicle, and make sure he goes directly home. It's late and the streets are dangerous. I'd hate for something to happen to him.'

Patton looked stunned, like he'd expected to be told to kill him. 'Yes, sir.'

'And then come back here.'

Patton swallowed. 'Of course.'

He watched Patton blindfold Segal and lead him away, none too gently, then picked up the phone and dialed Margo.

'It's late,' she said sharply. 'Benny is asleep.'

'I apologize,' he said stiffly. And he *was* sorry. In his anger, he'd forgotten about his grandson. 'But this is urgent. Segal has papers in his safe deposit box implicating me. I'd like you to get them.'

'That's not so simple, Papa,' she said doubtfully.

'But it is crucial that you do it. Use whatever resources I have at my disposal.'

'I will try.'

He drew a breath, irritated. He'd been too lax with her. She took advantage of her relationship to his son. *And to me.* Her obedience was not situational. He inserted cold iron into his reply. 'You will succeed.'

A beat of hesitation. 'Yes, sir.'

That was better. 'Thank you.'

Baltimore, Maryland,
Wednesday 15 June, 12.15 A.M.

They'd finally left Clay's very crowded house, and Gwyn was grateful for the quiet of her condo. She loved all of their friends, but she'd felt ready to bolt from the moment Lucy had basically outed her as a victim of sexual assault in front of them.

No. Not a victim. At least that wasn't all she was. A survivor. Who was finally living again. No way would she go back into the dark. It was too lonely there.

She removed the weapons she'd been wearing all day, placing the knives and one of the guns in her nightstand drawer before stepping around Tweety to lay the remaining gun on the nightstand on the other side of the bed for Thorne's use.

'Just in case,' she murmured to the dog, talking to him as she did every night. Except this night wasn't like any other, because this night she wasn't alone.

Through every thought, every movement, she remained acutely conscious of the huge man watching her from the doorway. 'I was lucky today,' she said conversationally, because she really wanted to stutter and pull a blanket over her head. She knew what he wanted to know. She knew she'd have to tell him, sooner or later.

Thorne was watching her with a combination of want and a kind of desperate trepidation. The want made her feel desirable, but the fear welling up within her was beating it down pretty damn well.

There were shadows on his face and questions in his eyes. The questions had been there off and on for most of the day, but after Lucy's little gaffe in front of everyone tonight, neither the shadows nor questions had faded. He wanted to know what had happened to her. With Evan.

And she was trying to think of any conceivable way to tell him without either of them falling apart. And failing miserably.

339

'How so?' he asked, his voice a low rumble that did things to her. Such wicked, delicious things.

Shivering, she threw a look over her shoulder. He'd taken off his shirt, and his biceps were straining as he gripped the sides of her door frame as if it was the only thing holding him upright. Her mouth went dry at the sight of all that beautiful skin. 'What?' she asked, having totally lost the thread of the conversation.

One side of his mouth lifted, but sadly. 'You said you were lucky today.'

She blinked before remembering. 'Oh. Right.' She turned to the safe, keying in the combination, but her fingers faltered midway. Her combination was a set of numbers, a birthday whose importance no one knew about. *Nobody but me.*

Well, her and the boy himself, along with his adoptive parents and anyone else in his world who'd attended his birthday parties over the years. *Which does not include me.*

She needed to tell Thorne about him too. But one big disclosure at a time. *Tackle the Evan shit. Then figure the rest of it out.* Briskly she re-entered the combination, because the safe had already reset itself. Popping open the door, she removed her larger .45 with the extended magazine and laid it on the nightstand. It was far too large and heavy to conceal comfortably under her clothing, but it was the weapon she felt most comfortable firing. And if they were surprised in the night, she wanted every advantage.

Leaving her other three handguns in the safe, she closed the door. 'I was lucky that Rivera was there today,' she said. 'He took my guns and held onto them until Joseph got there. Joseph gave them back to me. I mean, I have more handguns, but those conceal the best.' She turned to face Thorne, her smile firmly back in place. 'Joseph checked me for a concealed carry permit first, though.' She rolled her eyes.

'I wondered about that,' Thorne said. He shrugged, then dropped his hands from the door frame to his sides. 'Gwyn. I need to . . . we need to talk. I need to understand.'

She closed her eyes, feeling suddenly naked even though she was still fully clothed. 'I know. But I think I need some wine for this conversation.' She opened her eyes and found he'd moved out of the doorway. Silently he followed her to the kitchen, opening the bottle she handed him as he'd done hundreds of times before over the twelve years they'd been friends.

She got the glasses from the cupboard, then turned to him. 'Would you mind putting on a shirt?'

He took a step back, guilty apprehension in his eyes, and too late she realized that he thought she was afraid of him. 'No, not that,' she said quickly. 'It's just that I'd be able to concentrate better.'

Visibly relieved, he nodded and disappeared back into the bedroom while she filled the glasses. When he returned, buttoning a clean shirt, she'd put the glasses on the coffee table and switched on the gas fire.

He frowned. 'Are you cold?'

Which was fair, because the evening was warm and humid. 'No. But the fire is calming. Don't worry,' she added, when he looked abruptly worried. 'I'm not a pyro or anything. Some people find watching waves soothing. But for me, it's flames. It's meditative.'

'All right.' He sat on the sofa and didn't complain about its size for what might have been the first time. 'Tell me what you can,' he said gruffly. 'And if you can't, just tell me what you think I absolutely must know so that I don't hurt you.'

He looked up then, and her breath caught in her throat. His eyes were filled with so much pain. So much fear. But there was more there. Something sweet and lovely. Tender. And loving.

Toeing off her shoes, she sat beside him, as close as she could without sitting on his lap, waiting until he put his arm around her to snuggle her cheek into his hard pec. This would be easier if she didn't have to actually look at him.

'You won't hurt me,' she said quietly. 'I know that. I always knew that.'

'Then . . .' he cleared his throat. 'Why didn't you tell me?'

The hurt in his voice was unmistakable, and suddenly she needed to see his expression. Twisting to her knees so that they were face to face, she cupped his jaws in her hands. 'It wasn't because I didn't trust you, so if you're thinking that, don't. Please.'

341

'Okay.' He turned his head so that his lips were on her palm and kissed her there. 'Then why?'

She sighed. 'You were my safe place, Thorne. I didn't want you to know because I didn't want you to look at me like you were afraid of *me*. Like you pitied me. Like you knew. Because then I'd have to think about it all over again. He was dead. Gone. It was over. Everyone told me it was over.'

He lifted careful hands to her face, swiping tears from her cheeks that she wasn't aware she'd shed. 'But it wasn't over for you,' he whispered.

'No,' she whispered back. 'It wasn't. I tried to forget it. I did. But the only thing that helped was blocking it out. I'm good at blocking things out.'

'Join the club. You, me and Lucy. All champion blockers.'

'Until we can't anymore,' she said sadly.

He kissed her palm again. 'It's not like we're sharers, not voluntarily anyway. Lucy didn't tell us her story until she was forced to because she was being chased by a killer. I never told you about my trial. Or Sherri. I might not have ever done so, but you found me with a dead woman in my bed and I was kind of forced to.'

'Did you love her?'

'Sherri? Yes, I did.' His lips tipped up, the picture of melancholy. 'We'd talked about getting married when we finished college. We had a plan, most of which involved me doing things for her father so he'd accept me.'

Gwyn rested her forehead against his. 'I'm so sorry she died.'

'Me too.' He closed his eyes and swallowed hard. 'I'm sorry that I never pursued any of this nightmare before. I just let her killer go because it was . . . easier.'

'No,' she whispered.

'*Yes*,' he whispered back. 'It was easier to change my name to Thorne and start out fresh and never look back. I should have kept searching until I found her killer. I should have gotten her justice.'

'Baby.' She kissed his brow, then his eyelids, then his cheeks. 'You survived. You went through hell and came out the other side. Do you think she'd want you to suffer?'

Another melancholy smile. 'No. But she would have wanted me to fight for justice. The last day we had together, she was trying to get me to sue the school, to force them to let me back in after I was expelled.' His chuckle was watery. 'She wanted to contact the ACLU.'

'Sounds like she was a spitfire. What did you say?'

'About suing?' He chuckled again, this time fondly. 'I told her nothing good ever came of going to court.'

Gwyn grinned. 'Oh, wow. And look at you now. She would have been so proud of you, Thorne.'

He swallowed hard. 'I hope so. I really hope so. But I didn't mean to make this about me. I just meant that I don't blame you for keeping things to yourself. I'd be a hypocrite if I did.'

She kissed him again, softly. 'I know. I get it. I might have never told you about . . . what I'm going to tell you. But I did tell someone, and it did help.'

'Who?'

'My therapist. I've been seeing her for over a year, and I don't think I could have ever been here, taken this step with you, without her. But I didn't even tell her what really happened right away. I didn't have the words for months.'

'What made you seek her out?'

'I woke up one morning and my life was a mess.' She remembered the morning specifically. February seventeenth. Seventeen years after she'd given birth to a beautiful boy. For the past sixteen years, February seventeenth had been the day she'd woken to cry over the one photo she had of her holding her son. Knowing that he'd be eighteen in a year and that he'd be told of her existence was the motivation she'd needed that particular day. 'I needed to fix my life, but by then I didn't have the first idea of where to start. I went online and started researching therapists who worked with PTSD. I figured that was what I was experiencing.'

'And was it?' he asked.

'Yes, and the underlying reason was . . .' She closed her eyes, unable to look at him when she whispered the words. 'Being raped. By Evan.'

343

Annapolis, Maryland,
Wednesday 15 June, 12.40 A.M.

Patton had actually returned. He hadn't expected him to, but the man now stood in front of his desk, feet spread, hands clasped behind him, expression one of grim determination.

'I have to say, you continue to surprise me, Mr Patton.'

'I know what you think. And it isn't true.'

He leaned back in his chair, giving Patton a serious study. 'What do I think?'

'That I was careless and brought the judge here on my own.'

'You didn't?'

'No. Your daughter-in-law told me to. Sir.'

He frowned. 'Margo wouldn't have done that.'

'She did. I know you don't believe me, but that's the truth. She said you'd told her to send him over.'

His frown deepened. 'What I said was that I would come to the office downtown.' Which was where the judge had shown up demanding to see him.

'She must have misunderstood. She looked . . . tired. I think the baby is teething. Maybe she hasn't gotten enough sleep.'

'That could be true. Thank you for telling me the truth, Mr Patton.'

The man narrowed his eyes. 'You believe me?'

'You're here. If you'd been lying, you would have run. Or maybe you are lying and trying to employ reverse psychology?'

Patton shook his head. 'I have enough trouble with straight psychology.'

His lips twitched, certain that Patton was much smarter than he wanted anyone to believe. 'Well, I'll talk to Margo about getting more sleep. In the meantime, I have another assignment for you.' He handed him a list of names and phone numbers, each with a single sentence that would bring that person the most fear. 'Starting in the morning, call each of these people and read the sentence next to his or her name, then hang up. Use a throwaway phone with a voice-altering app so that each person hears a slightly different voice, just

344

in case they get brave and go to the cops. I don't think they will, though.'

'Who are they?'

He smiled. 'The less you know, the less you can mistakenly tell them.'

Patton folded the paper and put it in his pocket with a shrug. 'Yes, sir.'

The man was learning.

Baltimore, Maryland,
Wednesday 15 June, 12.40 A.M.

Being raped. By Evan.

Thorne had thought he was strong enough to hear the words. *I was wrong.*

Bile rose in his throat and he began to tremble where he sat, white-hot fury rendering him helpless as she knelt beside him, pressed against his side, her hands still holding his face like he was precious to her.

But her eyes were closed and she'd whispered the words as if they still shamed her. *Being raped. By Evan.*

'You don't have to tell me any more,' he choked out.

She opened her eyes and they held mild challenge. Milder reproach. 'You asked, Thorne. Which is it? Do you want to know or not?'

This was important. His answer was important. But he felt paralyzed, unsure of what to say. 'Do you want me to know?'

'No. But now that you've opened the box, you need to look inside or you'll always wonder. I'll know you're wondering and it'll make me crazy. So let's look in the goddamn box, then close it again.'

Her voice was calm. So calm. It unnerved him. 'All right.' If she could tell it, he could listen.

She nodded once, then slid back down to sit beside him, her head tucked against his chest. The two glasses of wine sat on the coffee table untouched, but he didn't think he could choke down a single sip.

'If you want both of those, you're welcome to them,' he said, pointing to the glasses.

'No. I . . . um . . . I pour it and usually end up dumping it down the drain.'

He hadn't known that. 'I think I'll buy you cheaper wine, then.'

She chuckled. 'Fair enough. Once the fire is going and I get into meditating, I don't want it any more. And tonight I'm thinking about Patricia, drinking too much. I don't want to fall into the same trap.' She sighed, her breath warm on his chest. 'My dad was a mean drunk. When I'm centered, I remember that. I don't want to go there.'

She'd not spoken of her father, not in a long time. All Thorne knew was that her parents were very strict and she'd run away to join the circus. He wondered now how much of that story was true.

But first things first. 'So. Evan. You said you weren't drugged.'

'Not the whole time, no. I don't think he meant to kill me. Not at first. At least that's what he said when he . . .' She trailed off and he felt her body shift. 'I figured out who he was, you know. That he was the killer. He'd put a tracker in Lucy's purse.'

'I remember that.' He'd been so fucking angry. He was so much angrier now.

'Well, he put one in mine too. When Lucy told me about hers, I got curious and checked, and sure enough, he'd been tracking me too. But he came in and found me looking for more.'

'In your purse?'

'No. In his gym bag. I'd seen something like the one in my purse before, but I didn't know it was a tracker. I found five more in his things. I think I just stared at them for the longest time. I wish I'd acted more quickly, looking back. I'd just started to dial Lucy when he came in. He was . . . not pleased.'

Thorne's stomach heaved, because he remembered visiting both Gwyn and Lucy in the hospital after their rescue. Lucy had a broken nose and a broken leg. Gwyn had two broken ribs, a broken finger and bruises. All over.

He clearly remembered the bruises in the shape of fingerprints around her throat. At the time, he hadn't wanted to think about how she'd received them.

He didn't want to think about it now. But she was right. He'd always wonder, and that wasn't fair to either of them. *So man up and deal with this shit now.*

'What did he do?'

'Well, he grabbed me and shook me, so hard I saw stars. I tried to run, but he caught hold of my hair and pulled me back. That was at three a.m.'

Thorne forced himself to breathe. Evan hadn't kidnapped Lucy until around eight the next morning. 'So he had you alone for hours.'

'Yes. I think it was at about seven thirty that he finally drugged me. I fought him, Thorne. I promise you I did.'

He tightened his arm around her shoulders, pressing her closer to him, his other hand stroking her hair, still in Angie's updo. 'I know you did,' he said hoarsely. 'I remember the bruises.'

'By the time we got to the hospital, it was more than twelve hours later. They . . . did a rape kit as a matter of procedure, but I told them I hadn't been raped. That it was . . .' She trailed off, her swallow audible. 'Consensual.'

'Why?' he murmured.

'Because by then he was dead and JD had saved Lucy and I was just a footnote to the whole nightmare. I was the "girlfriend of the serial killer", the woman who'd believed his lies. Who'd invited him into her bed. I felt stupid enough, Thorne. I didn't want to rehash what had really happened.'

'I understand.' He really did. 'It was like me changing my name to Thorne and moving on with my life.'

'Exactly,' she said, sounding relieved. 'For the record, he was pretty vanilla in his physical technique, but he made sure he humiliated me. Made sure it hurt. He was big, so it kind of hurt a lot.'

He was big. Evan had been six-four at least. *Big like me.*

Thorne thought he was going to throw up.

His hand tightened reflexively in her hair and she flinched. 'I'm sorry,' he said, immediately loosening his grip. 'Can I take these pins out? I like your hair down.'

347

'If you want,' she said, but not unkindly. 'They were giving me a headache anyway.'

'Why didn't you take them out earlier?' he asked, deliberately chasing this new topic, just to give them both a moment's respite.

'Because my hair was pretty and princessy.'

He huffed a chuckle and kissed the top of her head. 'I never quite get over what you women do to look pretty. Just looking at your shoes is enough to put me in traction.'

'Hey,' she protested, but there was no heat behind it. 'Don't diss the heels. Without them, I'd be staring at your belly button.'

He pulled out a hairpin. 'No, you wouldn't.' Although she likely would. 'But I can appreciate your legs in heels, so whatever floats your boat, babe.'

She worked a few of his shirt buttons free and pressed a kiss to the middle of his chest. 'I like looking here. You are a beautiful man, Thomas Thorne.'

He'd been called beautiful before, in dozens of ways by dozens of other women, but never had it given him the pleasure that Gwyn's simple words did. 'Thank you.'

She kissed his chest again. 'You're welcome.' She drew a breath and let it out. 'You ready for round two of the painful info dump?'

He hadn't thought she'd been fooled by his timeout. He concentrated on finding the pins in her hair, forcing himself to answer. 'Yes.'

'All right. Most of his abuse was focused on making me record a message he could play to lure Lucy. I refused.' She paused for a moment that seemed to drag on for hours, but it was less than a minute. 'I refused several times.'

His chest constricted painfully. 'Baby,' he whispered, and she patted his chest comfortingly.

'It was kind of empowering, telling him no,' she mused. 'I couldn't get away, couldn't even scream because he'd taped my mouth shut while he did his worst, but I *could* tell him no when he took the tape off and demanded I record the message. I wasn't going to help him kill Lucy, that was for damn sure. No reason she should have to pay for my stupidity.'

No. No fucking way. 'You weren't stupid,' he growled. 'He fooled all of us.'

She patted his chest again. 'I know that now. I even believe it sometimes. But that's certainly not what I was believing then. I was kicking myself for letting him use me. Which was what he reminded me of over and over during those hours. How he'd used me. How he'd manipulated me. How stupid I was to have believed his lies. How he'd laughed to himself every time he fucked me.'

Thorne leaned his head back against the sofa cushion, counting his breaths. *Breathing in, six, five, four, three, two, one. Hold for four. Breathing out, six, five, four, three, two, one. Repeat. Repeat. Repeat.*

Until you no longer want to dig him up and rip his corpse to shreds. Breathe. Breathe. Breathe.

He heard a choked sound and knew it had come from his own throat. But he couldn't make it stop. Couldn't swallow it back. *Breathe. Breathe.*

Hold it together. But he couldn't. He was flying apart, molecule by molecule.

'Thorne? Oh, honey.' Gwyn straddled one of his thighs and wrapped her arms around his head, cradling him to her breast.

Because he was crying, weeping like he hadn't done in years, not since Jamie had told him that Sherri was dead.

She rocked him, murmuring comfort into his ear that he couldn't hear because the dam had broken and he was sobbing loudly, holding her so tightly that he was sure she couldn't breathe. But she never asked him to let her go, so he held on.

She was dropping kisses on top of his head, pressing them to his temples, all while she rocked him, whispering to him. Comforting him when he was supposed to be comforting her.

He clenched his jaw, ground his teeth, fought to control himself. 'God,' he whispered. 'I'm sorry. So sorry.'

'For what?' she asked reasonably. 'For not stopping him? For not reading my mind afterward? For not killing him yourself?'

'Yes.' The word came out on a rush of air. 'All of the above.'

She released him only enough to kiss his forehead, his swollen eyes. 'You know what? If you'd known, you would have. I have not a single doubt.'

And somehow, that helped. 'What do I do now? For you?'

'Be here. And do what you did yesterday morning and again in the afternoon. Show me that you think I'm worth it.'

Worth it, worth it, worth it. He'd chanted the words as he'd claimed her as his own, as he'd made love to her, though inside his mind he was chanting *love you, love you, love you.* 'You *are* worth it,' he whispered. *I love you. So goddamn much.* But he didn't say that, because he didn't want to be feeling gutted and sad when he finally spoke those words. He wanted it to be perfect. Like she deserved.

'You make me believe that.' She kissed him again, this time sweet and sexy all at once. 'You make me believe that I can have forever, Thorne. And last week I would have said that wasn't possible. But now, I . . . I want that. Forever. With you.'

He opened his eyes to find her staring down at him, her hair half up, half down, smiling at him like he'd hung the moon. 'I love you,' he said, because the words simply wouldn't be silenced.

Her mouth dropped open, her eyes filling with tears.

He touched her lips, his fingers trembling. 'You don't have to say it back.'

She took his fingers, kissing them before wrapping her hand around them. 'I love you too. I think I always have. I was just too scared to admit it.'

He thought he might actually cry again. 'You're not scared now?'

'Of you? No. Of this? No. That I might mess it up? Hell, yeah.'

'You can't mess it up. Just be here. With me.'

'Okay,' she whispered. 'There's one more thing you can do for me.'

'What? Name it.'

'Don't let what I've told you stop you from touching me. You would never hurt me, Thorne. It's not in your nature. You're a protector.' She leaned in, pronouncing each word with emphasis. *'You would never hurt me.'* She nuzzled her cheek against his, whispering in his ear. 'I liked sex before Evan. A lot. I like it with you. A lot. He tried to steal that from me, and for four years I let him. Don't let him steal it from me any longer. From us.'

Exhausted, Thorne could only nod, but she seemed satisfied, because she smiled at him again. 'We've had a long-ass day. I'm ready to sleep. You up for that?'

'With you? Always.' He stood, hauling her up with him, pushing up her skirt so that she could wrap her legs around him.

'Just so you know?' she said as he carried her to the bedroom. 'I could totally get used to this.'

'Then that's my new goal.'

'What was your old goal?'

He nuzzled his face into her neck. 'Hearing you say that you love me.'

She went silent, then expelled a shaky breath. 'That was a good goal, Thorne,' she whispered, her voice thick with tears. 'A damn good goal.'

He sat on the bed, lowering her to her feet so that she stood between his knees. 'I thought so. Say it again. Please.'

Her eyes were shiny. 'I love you, Thomas Thorne.'

Hands on her hips, he pulled her closer so that his cheek rested against her breasts. The world might be going to shit around them, but for this moment he was content. Happy in a way he couldn't ever remember. 'Love you too.'

Twenty-one

Silver Spring, Maryland,
Wednesday 15 June, 10.00 A.M.

Thorne stared at the small drapery shop that doubled as home to the older sister of Colton Brandenberg, one of Richard Linden's posse. The one who'd most surprised him when they'd beaten him up nineteen years ago. The one who'd all but disappeared after high school graduation.

'What's wrong?' Gwyn asked quietly from the passenger seat.

'I'm . . . nervous,' Thorne admitted. He glanced into the rear-view mirror of the SUV that had been waiting outside Gwyn's condo when they'd come downstairs to meet JD. The SUV was one of Joseph's personal vehicles, and the Fed had asked Thorne and Gwyn to use it until this whole nightmare was over. With bullet-resistant windows and door panels, it was a gift worth its weight in gold.

JD, appointed their personal guardian for the duration, pulled up behind them in another of Joseph's SUVs. He didn't get out, waiting instead for Thorne.

Reaching over the center console, Gwyn tapped Thorne's arm. 'Why are you nervous?'

'Well, for starters, I'm worried she'll be dead.'

'That's actually fair. Why else?'

He sighed. 'Colton Brandenberg and I were friends once. I'd just started at Ridgewell and so had he. We were both new kids. We both played soccer and we both liked science class.'

'I thought you liked history and music.'

He shrugged. 'I liked everything. And I knew I had to nail all the

352

science classes if I wanted a scholarship. Colton was better at it than I was and my old school hadn't been as good as Ridgewell. I was behind. He tutored me until I caught up. Then in our sophomore year, he joined Richard's posse. I don't know why or how. Richard was pretty selective in who he let into his circle.'

'Like *Mean Girls*, but with boys?'

'Exactly. Even after he joined Richard, though, he wasn't an asshole to me. Not until that day at school.'

'When you dragged Richard off Angie.'

'Right. I don't know if Richard threw any actual punches, but he did kick me a few times. Colton threw some punches. Darian threw the first punch. Caught me in the jaw. Chandler, the one who's a cop now, he got in the second, an uppercut that had me biting into my tongue and spitting blood everywhere. And it was probably Chandler who did the most damage to my knee. But it was Colton who broke my nose that day. I remember lying on the floor of the hallway, just staring up at him as he lit into me. I was . . . I don't know. Stunned.'

'Betrayed,' Gwyn murmured.

'Yes. That too. That more, in fact. I don't know what to make of the fact that he disappeared.'

'Or that he seemed to be a zombie when he testified at your trial?'

'I don't remember that,' he confessed. 'I just remember wondering what I'd done to make him hate me as much as he'd seemed to that day. Because it wasn't just aggression, not like it was with Darian and Chandler. They were bullies. They'd have beaten up anyone that Richard told them to beat up. Colton seemed to hate *me*.'

She gave his arm a squeeze. 'Let's go talk to the sister. Maybe she can shed some light on it. Plus, we're kind of sitting ducks here.'

He jerked his head up, unable to believe that he'd forgotten to be careful. 'JD must be wondering if I'm insane.'

'I think he's known the answer to that for a long time.' She unbuckled her seat belt. 'He loves you anyway.' She leaned in to kiss his cheek. 'And before you ask, I love you too. Now move it, big guy.'

Smiling now, he got out of the SUV and helped her down. She

was significantly shorter today, having substituted her customary heels with running shoes at his request. Just in case.

'Everything okay?' JD asked cautiously as he approached them.

'Yeah. Just hoping everybody in there is breathing,' Thorne said.

JD grimaced in commiseration. 'Let's go make sure.'

The three of them marched to the shop's front door, which sported a colorful sign proclaiming: *Creations by Christina*. In the window was a mannequin wearing a beautiful lace wedding gown. A smaller sign at the mannequin's feet read: *Custom Designs Available On Request*.

Gwyn whistled softly. 'If she designed that gown, she's as talented as Prew's wife said.' She looked up at Thorne and JD, frowning when she had to crane her head back farther than usual. 'Who's on point?'

'Not me,' JD said. 'I'm here as your friend only. No official capacity.'

'I can pretend to be a customer,' Gwyn said. 'Like I did with Angie.'

'No, I'll be on point,' Thorne said. 'Worst that can happen is that she tells me to go to hell.'

He knocked on the door, but nobody answered. Tugging on the handle, he found it unlocked. *Because it's a business, idiot.* He opened the door and entered first, pausing in the doorway to make sure it was clear before gesturing Gwyn and JD inside, where a country music radio station warred with the whir of a sewing machine. The front of the shop was all fabric and big books of patterns and dressmaker's dummies in various stages of dress. An open doorway led to another room, presumably the sewing area.

'Hello?' Thorne called, and the sewing machine whir immediately ceased. A few seconds later, the radio was switched off and a woman came to the doorway. She was tall and thin, her dark brown hair streaked with silver.

Christina Brandenberg, Colton's sister. She'd graduated four years ahead of them, so Thorne hadn't known her in school. But he remembered her from the times he'd hung out at Colton's house, before Colton had been absorbed into Richard's circle of friends.

354

'Can I help you?' she asked warily.

'I hope so,' Thorne said. 'Do you remember me?'

She lifted her gaze to his face for a few moments without registering any shock, then closed her eyes. 'Of course. Tommy White. Although you don't go by that name anymore.'

'No. I don't. Look, I don't mean to bother you, but I'm looking for some information and it might involve your brother.'

She lifted her hand like a traffic cop. 'He's not here and I do not know where he is. I can't help you, so if you'd see yourselves out, I have work to do.' She started to turn, but Gwyn took a step forward and briefly touched her arm.

'Wait, please. Your brother could be in danger.'

Christina froze. 'I told you, I don't know where he is. I have no contact information for him.'

Gwyn nodded. 'I hear you. But have you seen the news?'

'Who are you?' Christina asked, narrowing her eyes.

'My name is Gwyn Weaver, and this is our friend JD Fitzpatrick. I'm . . . Well, Thorne is our friend. My priority right now is to clear his name.'

'Then you have quite a task ahead of you. Murder isn't an easy charge to skirt.'

'I know,' Thorne said carefully. 'I've already done it once.'

Christina looked away. 'I know. But I can't help you this time.'

This time? Thorne wanted to ask what she meant by that, but Gwyn took another step forward because Christina had turned to go a second time.

'I'm sorry,' Gwyn said, 'but I can't just walk away without at least asking a few questions and properly warning you. We went to see Darian Hinman yesterday. He was one of your brother's friends, and they were all friends of Richard Linden nineteen years ago. Darian was dead when we got there. He'd been dead for days and Thorne has an unshakable alibi for the time of the murder. He was with a group that includes a Baltimore homicide detective and the senior assistant state's attorney.'

'That has nothing to do with my brother,' Christina said, but her eyes flickered nervously.

355

'You could be right,' Gwyn said, 'but we don't think you are. Richard Linden's sister was killed shortly after Darian Hinman, just hours apart. There are indications that the same man did it. Someone is killing people *now* who were connected to Richard Linden *then*. Your brother was connected to him *then*.'

Christina swayed as all the color drained from her face. She put a hand against the frame of the open doorway to steady herself. 'Oh. Well.' She huffed out a breath that sounded far more afraid than dismissive. 'I still don't know what any of this has to do with Colton. He left the state after his graduation. He hasn't come back. I'd appreciate it if you'd leave now.'

Gwyn started to say more, but Thorne lightly gripped her elbow and tugged her back against him. 'Okay,' he said. 'We'll go.' He pulled a business card from his wallet and left it on her counter. 'My cell number is on there. If you think of anything, or if anyone bothers you, please call me.' He took a step toward the door, Gwyn in tow. 'And you should lock your door. I know you're a place of business, but the people behind this aren't playing around. They're snipping off loose ends, and eight people are already dead, two of them just for being in the wrong place at the wrong time. Please be careful.'

The three of them left, closing the door. Thorne heard a distinct click as Christina locked it behind them.

'At least she listened to you,' JD said as he walked Thorne and Gwyn to their borrowed SUV. He looked over his shoulder. 'She's watching us. What'll you bet she's on the phone with her little brother right now?'

'I hope so,' Thorne murmured. 'And I hope she's careful.'

JD clapped him on the shoulder. 'You warned her. That's all you can do. Where to?'

Thorne made a face. 'Chandler Nystrom, former cop turned personal security officer.'

'Mall cop?' JD asked.

Gwyn shook her head. 'No. Anne, our receptionist, was able to find his work information. He was most recently employed by Hinman Enterprises, after being relieved of duty by Howard County

PD, where he went after being relieved of duty by Montgomery County PD.'

'He works for Darian Hinman's father,' Thorne clarified. 'He's a security guard in their building downtown.'

'They're open for business?' JD asked, surprised. 'Darian's body was found not even twenty-four hours ago.'

Thorne shrugged. 'Jamie called the front desk to ask if they were receiving deliveries. They said they had business hours as usual.'

'Then I guess I'll follow you there,' JD said.

Chevy Chase, Maryland,
Wednesday 15 June, 11.00 A.M.

'I don't think this is going to end well,' JD muttered from behind Gwyn as Thorne pushed through the door into the building bearing Hinman Enterprises' name.

'I'm thinking you're right.' Positioned between them, she felt slightly claustrophobic, but she had a view of Thorne's back muscles flexing as he opened the door, and that was a silver lining.

The doors were draped with black, the mood of the lobby somber. The place was nearly all marble – the floors, the columns, even the walls. The building alone had to have cost a fucking fortune. But it was nearly silent, only whispers bouncing off the walls. It was like an opulent library.

Thorne tucked her against his side as soon as they were through the door. 'Old money,' he leaned down to whisper in her ear. 'Lots of it.'

'I figured that out,' she whispered back. 'Which one is Chandler Nystrom?'

Thorne paused to look around, and almost immediately saw the former cop. 'That's him, heading our way.'

Dressed in an ill-fitting uniform, Nystrom looked out of place in the lavish lobby. His face was as dark as a storm cloud.

Squaring his shoulders, Thorne pulled Gwyn closer. JD just sighed.

Chandler Nystrom had the build of an athlete who'd allowed his body to go to seed. His face was florid, broken capillaries criss-crossing his nose.

He's a heavy drinker, was Gwyn's first thought. She wondered why that was. He stopped in front of them and she was gratified to see that Thorne was easily eight inches taller. Maybe ten.

She was more gratified to see the flicker of apprehension in Nystrom's eyes as he had to look up to see Thorne's face. He was nervous. *Good. He should be.*

'What the fuck are *you* doing here?' Nystrom hissed.

Thorne didn't blink, didn't back down. But the hand he had on her back tensed. 'I've come to talk to you.'

Nystrom's face grew redder with fury. 'Well, you can just get out. *Now.* You have one *hell* of a lot of nerve. First you kill Richard, then Patricia, and then you just "happen" to find Darian's body. You should be locked up.'

To look at Thorne's face, one would never know he was affected by the words, but his hand on Gwyn's back twitched, tightening on the fabric of her blouse. Still, he met the man's angry gaze steadily.

'I haven't killed anyone. You know that now. And you knew it then too.'

Bleary eyes narrowed. 'You are full of shit, White. You always were.'

Again Thorne let the insult fly by. 'You're so upset by Patricia's death,' he said calmly. 'I wonder why you weren't more upset that she'd been raped by her brother when she was still in high school.'

The color drained from Nystrom's face and his mouth fell open. It took him ten full seconds to regain his composure enough to stammer, 'I have no idea what you're talking about.'

Thorne's hand relaxed on Gwyn's back. 'I don't know how you lasted as long on the police force as you did. Suspects must have had your number in a heartbeat. Your poker face is non-existent.'

Nystrom's nostrils flared, his rage returning. 'Fuck you, White.'

'Why did Richard's killer put his key ring in his body?' Thorne asked quietly, and once again Nystrom was struck silent for long seconds.

'There was no key ring,' he finally said stiffly. 'But you should know, since you killed him.' Thorne simply looked at him, and Nystrom grew fidgety. 'I said, get out. I *will* call the cops on you.' He stomped past them to open the door, glaring daggers at them. 'Out. This is private property and *you* are trespassing.'

'All right,' Thorne answered, never losing his cool. Gwyn felt a swell of pride at his self-control, because she knew this had not been an easy confrontation. The last time he'd seen this man was in court as Nystrom testified against him on a murder charge. The time before that, he'd seen Nystrom's boot as he'd kicked his head.

The three of them turned to leave, JD and Gwyn having said not a single word to the man. Thorne paused at the door and gave Nystrom his card. 'Be careful,' he said. 'Somebody is snipping off loose ends. Don't think they don't know who you are, even if they haven't revealed themselves to you.'

Sneering, Nystrom ripped the card into tiny pieces, tossing them out the door with great drama. They caught on the light breeze and scattered, falling to the grass outside. 'Fuck off, *White*.'

Thorne gave him a single nod and walked out, tucking Gwyn's arm through his, keeping his steps slow so that she didn't have to run to keep up. But they paused to listen when JD stopped in the doorway and handed Nystrom another card.

'I'm not here in an official capacity,' JD said quietly, 'but my boss said to give you his card. If you need help or think of anything that could be helpful, please call him. It's Lieutenant Hyatt. Two Ts.'

Nystrom's eyes narrowed to slits. 'Tell your boss that I don't need his fucking help.'

'He figured you'd say that,' JD said companionably. 'He asked me to tell you that he's got eyes on you, and for you not to wait until it's too late to call him. Your buddy was rotting by the time we found him.' He smiled. 'Have a nice day.'

He left the building and walked to where they'd parked the SUVs, leaving Gwyn and Thorne to follow in stunned silence.

'What was that?' Thorne exploded once they were at the vehicles.

'Did Hyatt really say all that?' Gwyn demanded.

'He did. He'd checked into Nystrom for me. Couldn't give me details, as the IA investigations are sealed, but he got enough dirt on the down-low to know Nystrom was going to be a problem. After Hinman was found last night, he told me to give Nystrom his personal message.'

'Huh.' It was all Gwyn could think to say. Maybe Hyatt wasn't quite so bad. At least he was aiming his grandstanding at someone who deserved it this time.

'Where to next?' JD asked cheerfully.

'You enjoyed that way too much,' Thorne grumbled. 'But I did too. We need to meet with Ming and Mowry to discuss the club. We've got employees who need to work.'

'Maybe we can call for food delivery,' JD suggested. 'If we've hit a lull, we should eat. I don't want a repeat of yesterday. I was hungry enough to eat the pizza and the boxes.' He left them and got into his SUV.

Gwyn swung herself up into her own seat, then threw Thorne a sultry look when he slid behind the wheel. 'I can think of a lot of other ways to spend the time,' she said.

Thorne choked out a laugh. 'You're a tease.'

She sniffed, pretending to be offended. 'I'm only a tease if I don't deliver.'

Thorne put the SUV in gear. 'We'll make it a fast meeting.'

Baltimore, Maryland,
Wednesday 15 June, 12.00 P.M.

Mowry was packed. Like, packed to move. Thorne frowned when he, Gwyn and JD entered his manager's small apartment and saw boxes stacked against the wall. Some were labeled with rooms – kitchen, bedroom, bath – but some had names. He saw his name, Gwyn's and Ming's written in Mowry's distinct handwriting.

'Where do you want this?' Thorne asked, lifting the takeout bags he'd picked up at the Ethiopian place they all liked. 'And what's with the boxes?'

Mowry closed the door behind them and gave JD a slightly irritated glare. 'I'll tell you later, Thorne. Put the food on the table. Ming's getting plates.'

JD put his hands up in a gesture of surrender. 'I can wait outside if you've got confidential business.'

Mowry shook his head. 'No, it's okay. Come in and eat. You'll hear what I have to say soon enough anyway. I'll tell these two, they'll tell Lucy, then she'll tell you. I might as well cut out the middleman.'

Thorne exchanged a glance with Gwyn, who looked as worried as he felt.

'Hey, boss,' Ming said when they got to the table. 'And hey to you too, Thorne.'

'No respect,' Thorne complained without heat, bumping Ming's fist when he held it out. The guy was every bit as big as Thorne. Maybe bigger. Ming was Samoan, his skin a shade more bronze than Thorne's. Their size, similar ethnicity, and love of rugby had drawn them together years ago.

Gwyn drew Ming down to kiss his cheek, her smile strained. 'So, you guys were okay yesterday. Pissed off, but okay. What's happened since?'

'Sit.' Mowry took the chair at the head of the table. 'Let's take care of the easy stuff first. Ming and I went over the books.'

Ming snorted. 'That wasn't the easy part.'

Mowry handed him a styrofoam box. 'Eat. I meant the easy part of the books. You know, the *good* news.' He said the word sarcastically as he opened his own meal. 'The part where we get to tell them we can only stay closed for another week before we run through our cash reserves. And that doesn't count paychecks. The liquor distributor is already demanding his money. It's not due until next week, but he's afraid the cops will seize our assets.' He shoved a bite of flatbread-wrapped beef into his mouth.

Gwyn's eyes flittered closed for a few seconds. 'That's the good news?'

Mowry swallowed, nodding. 'Yep.'

Thorne frowned. 'We should have more cash than that.' He'd been ready to front the paychecks, but he'd thought they'd be okay for longer than a week.

'Part of the bad news,' Ming said quietly. 'About half the reserves

361

have been siphoned off, all within the last two weeks.' He glanced at Mowry. 'The money had been funneled to petty cash and withdrawn.'

Gwyn closed her eyes again, shaking her head. 'Fuck.'

'Why fuck?' JD asked.

'Because Mowry handles petty cash,' Thorne said grimly.

'And because,' Mowry added, his stress clear in his tone, 'Mowry has been paying a member of the Circus Freaks gang for information about his band of brothers.'

'Which is how we knew who to kick out Sunday night,' Ming finished. 'But it makes it look like Mowry has been stealing from the club.'

'We know you haven't,' Thorne murmured. 'Is that why you're packed to run?'

Mowry cast another furtive look at JD, then sighed. 'Shit. Look, as soon as I got arrested, I knew I was going to have to leave.'

'Because of who you were before you came to Sheidalin,' JD said levelly, rolling his eyes when Mowry's own eyes popped wide with shock. 'Did you think I didn't check on you, Sheldon? On any of you who came in contact with Lucy, who got close enough to hurt her? After what we went through with Ev—' He cut himself off. 'Sorry, Gwyn.'

'It's okay,' she said, but her cheeks bore the dark flush of embarrassment. 'Did you know about me? About what Evan did?'

Ming tensed, and on a man that large it was a terrifying sight. 'What did he do?'

Thorne gave him a slight shake of his head. 'Later, man.'

Ming nodded, looking unhappy.

JD's nod was even less happy. 'I knew what you'd told them at the hospital and I knew that they did a kit anyway. I almost asked you about it, but it was your business. Your story to tell. I didn't even tell Lucy.' He winced. 'She told me last night and she knew I wasn't surprised. I can't ever get anything past her. She gave me shit for not telling her, I'll have you know.'

Thorne was torn between respect for the cop and the desire to tear JD's arms off and beat him with them. He'd known. For four fucking years. He'd watched Gwyn stumble through her life like a zombie and he'd said nothing. *I could have done something. I could have helped her.*

He looked up when he felt Gwyn squeezing the hand he hadn't realized he'd clenched into a fist. 'It wouldn't have mattered,' she whispered, once again seeming to read his thoughts. 'I wasn't ready to deal with it yet. I had to do it on my own. So it turned out okay. Let it go, Thorne.'

Gritting his teeth, he nodded. 'Okay. So you checked up on all of us, JD? Even me?'

JD met his eyes directly. Unapologetically. 'Yes.'

And Thorne had to admit he would have done the same. But this wasn't about him or Gwyn or even Evan. It was about Mowry, who looked ready to flee at any moment. 'What did you find on Mowry?'

'That he was a dumb-assed punk who played lookout for some dangerous men but turned them in when they robbed a store and killed the owner. He ran away with his guitar, his insides intact, and his head attached. And not a lot more. You met him when he came in to audition for the band shortly before you opened the club.' JD's smile was kind. 'And you got him a new ID so that the thugs he'd turned on couldn't find him, and gave him a new start.'

Mowry was staring at JD open-mouthed. Gwyn was staring at Thorne, her eyes soft. He'd never told her and he'd assumed she'd be angry to learn the truth so many years later, but he saw no anger. Only approval.

And because he wanted to drown in that approval but didn't have the time, Thorne forced himself to turn back to JD, studying him skeptically. 'How did you dig all that up?'

'I'm a detective,' JD said very slowly. 'My job is detecting. I find stuff out about people. It's what I do.'

Ming coughed to cover a laugh. 'Sorry,' he said when Thorne glared.

'Yeah, yeah, I get that you're all super-cop, but how?'

JD shrugged. 'I got suspicious when Mowry just showed up in the system. Next time you build a new ID, give the person a backstory, for God's sake. I started digging, asking questions here and there. It took me a while,' he admitted. 'It's a good ID. If you're worried that the cops are going to start investigating you, that's unlikely. And if I get wind that they are, I'll discourage it.'

'Why?' Mowry asked, clearly not buying JD's helpfulness.

'Because Lucy loves you like a brother. You've been good to her. And if that's not a good enough reason, I'll rent you a U-Haul truck and you can run.'

'They will investigate, though,' Ming insisted. 'The money is gone.'

Gwyn was feverishly tapping on her phone, accessing the bank account. 'Fuck,' she hissed. 'It really is gone, but as of today, not over the last couple of weeks.'

Ming looked over her shoulder at her phone. 'Huh. The ledgers give the same balance, but show the money being withdrawn over time.'

Gwyn shook her head. 'I looked at the ledgers on Tuesday morning – last time was three a.m. I spent hours combing through the books to see if there was anything that would catch the cops' attention. There wasn't. And the petty cash account was intact. So was the bank account.'

'You're saying somebody changed the ledgers between Tuesday morning and now?' Mowry asked. 'Who would do that? And how? And why?'

'That's exactly what I'm saying,' Gwyn said grimly. 'And I can prove it. I printed out the last year's worth of ledgers. As for who . . . Tavilla is trying to bring Thorne down. I don't know who could actually have made the changes, though. Somebody who had access to our server and who understands the accounting software. I don't know exactly how they'd have done it. But that's what happened.'

JD was nodding. 'Do you still have the printouts?'

'I do.'

'Good. Because the state's attorney may try to get a warrant for your books. We can't stop that, but we can show them that the existing books are doctored. That puts the rest of the evidence in question.'

Mowry shuddered in relief. 'I might not have to move.'

Ming clapped him on the back, causing him to nearly faceplant into his food. 'I still want what's in the box you were filling for me.'

Mowry straightened his back, wincing slightly. 'Fuck off, *Clive.*'

Ming took the jibe good-naturedly. 'I'll give you that one as a freebie because you're damn giddy right now. But call me that again and we shall have words, *Sheldon.*'

'Boys,' Gwyn warned. She closed her bank app. 'The ledgers can be verified, but the money is still gone. We have to be able to show it was stolen for the bank to replace it. If it looks like we withdrew it, we can't file a claim.'

'We'll worry about that later,' Thorne said. 'We can still make payroll.'

Gwyn looked close to tears. 'How? We've got so many people depending on us.'

'I can cover payroll,' Thorne said softly. 'Don't worry.'

She shook her head. 'I'm not going to let you clean out your savings for our company's payroll.'

He brought her hand to his lips. 'We'll discuss it later,' he said firmly, then looked at Ming and Mowry, who were watching them avidly. 'What?'

Mowry's grin was quick and sharp. 'About time. Way to go, Thorne.'

Ming's grin was slower to spread, but nearly split his face. 'Ditto, boss.'

Thorne had to bite back his own grin, because Gwyn was sputtering. 'What else?' he asked before she could get a word in.

Mowry put his phone on the table and spun it around so that Thorne and Gwyn could see it. 'This came in right before you got here,' he said. 'It's from my contact in the Circus Freaks.'

It was a text. '"Our bosses need to talk",' Thorne read. He'd been expecting some kind of summons ever since the Freaks' dealers had turned up dead, stuffed with Sheidalin matchbooks. 'Where and when?'

'*No!*' Gwyn exploded. 'Absolutely not.'

'You can't talk to the head of the Freaks, Thorne,' JD protested. 'Not right now.'

Thorne shrugged. 'I think it's better to talk to him than to start some kind of war over non-existent turf. I don't think he believes we were behind the death of his boys. If he did, he'd have done something already, like burning the club down, or my house, or Mowry's apartment building. He likes fire,' he added when JD stared at him.

'That's true,' Mowry said. 'They wouldn't have waited more than a day to retaliate.'

'How did they know we were on our way here?' Gwyn asked suspiciously. 'It seems too much of a coincidence that they messaged you right before we arrived.'

'They're probably watching us,' Thorne said. 'Another reason to believe that they don't think we're involved. They want us to know they're watching and that they haven't killed us yet. Tell your contact I'll be happy to meet with his boss.'

'I don't like it,' JD grumbled. 'It's not safe.'

'I think it would be less safe if he turned them down,' Mowry said.

'Agreed.' Thorne glanced at Gwyn.

She nodded grudgingly. 'I'm going with you.' She held up a finger to cut off his interruption. 'And if you say it's not safe for me, then it's not safe for you.'

He narrowed his eyes at her, considering the risk. She was right, unfortunately. 'Fine. What else?' he asked his employees.

'Just Laura,' Ming said. 'She quit.'

Thorne stilled. 'What do you mean?'

'She quit,' Ming repeated. 'I called her this morning and asked if she could come for this meeting, and she told me then. Said she was going home to her folks. I told her she should wait until everything died down, that if she still wanted to quit, we'd give her a reference. She was determined, though.'

'Where are her parents?' Gwyn asked.

'In Virginia.' He shrugged. 'I reminded her that she couldn't leave the state. She got pissy and said she wasn't going to skip bail. I couldn't blame her for wanting to go home. She was in holding longer than we were and she was not happy about it. At least her mom was able to watch the baby all night.'

366

'We'll go talk to her,' Gwyn said. 'If she really wants to quit, we won't stand in her way, of course, but she needs to know we'll see this drug charge through with her. Either Jamie or Frederick will continue to represent her.'

Ming looked uncomfortable. 'She said she'd be getting her own lawyer, that she didn't trust you all not to railroad her.'

Gwyn bit her lip. 'Guys, did Laura have access to the server?'

Mowry shook his head. 'No. Well, yes, but only to the inventory database.' His eyes narrowed. 'You're suggesting she took the money?'

'She's not here,' Thorne said. 'And she's putting distance between us. We have to at least consider it. We'll ask Alec to trace the changes to the accounting software and the bank withdrawal. In the meantime, we'll go see her.' He stood up, pulling Gwyn to her feet. 'Mowry, call your contact to see if he really texted that or if we're being spoofed. Once it's verified, call me. I want to hear voices from here on out.' He squeezed the manager's shoulder. 'And seriously, if something changes and you do need to run, do what you have to do. But call me afterward. I'll help you.'

Mowry nodded. 'Thanks, boss. Will do.'

Twenty-two

Baltimore, Maryland,
Wednesday 15 June, 1.45 P.M.

Gwyn's mood was dark as Thorne parked their borrowed SUV in front of the crab shack that acted as the Circus Freaks' front office. It was really old. Paint peeled, shutters were missing, and windows had been boarded up. Perched on the banks of the Patapsco River down by the docks, the place was definitely ramshackle. But not abandoned. Twenty motorcycles were parked outside. And amazing scents wafted through the SUV's air vents.

Steamed crabs with Old Bay seasoning, one of the few pleasant memories of Gwyn's childhood. It was almost enough to make her sigh happily. Except she wasn't happy. At all.

'I want to say again that this is a stupid idea, Thorne.'

He glanced over at her, his expression equally dark. 'So noted, but it's too late for you to change your mind. I don't have time to take you somewhere safe, and there is no fucking way that I'm leaving you in the SUV.'

'I didn't say I'd changed my mind,' she said tersely. She was going in with him, no matter what. Didn't mean she had to like it.

His reply was equally terse. 'Good.'

They sat in silence for a full minute before he blew out an angry breath and voiced what was worrying them even more than their meeting with the leader of the Circus Freaks. 'How did we miss this thing with Laura? I thought she was happy and honest.'

Gwyn pinched the bridge of her nose. Their missing bartender had proved to be an even bigger issue than they'd feared. Not only had she quit, but she'd cleaned out her apartment. And not only had she done that, but her neighbors hadn't seen her in a month, and none of them had seen her with a baby. Ever.

The woman they'd hired and nurtured and treated as one of their own had truly gotten one by them. A big one. How big was not yet known.

Gwyn did not have a good feeling about any of this. 'I don't know. We put her through the same hiring process we've used for years. The same background check. I mean, I didn't do it, but you did.'

'No, I didn't,' Thorne murmured. 'I was busy with a case. Anne did it.'

Anne Poulin, Thorne's beautiful, tall, willowy French receptionist who Gwyn had disliked on sight. Well, French Canadian anyway. Didn't matter. The woman still oozed sex.

Gwyn frowned. 'Why didn't you ask me to . . .' She let the question trail off, because she knew the answer. She'd always done Thorne's hiring at the firm. Until four years ago. But Laura had been hired six months ago. 'I was better when we hired Laura. Why didn't you ask me?'

'You might have known you were getting better,' he said wearily. 'I didn't know any such thing and I didn't want to push you.'

'Next time, push me,' she said.

'So noted,' he replied once again, and she sighed.

'I'm sorry, Thorne. I shouldn't have questioned you on that one. I'm upset.'

'I know.' Taking her hand, he pulled it to his mouth and kissed her knuckles. 'In hindsight I probably should have pushed you. I let you stew too long.'

'I told you that you were more patient with me than I am with you.'

'Well, that's true.' He checked his phone. 'I left a voicemail for Anne, asking her about Laura's background check, but she's never called me back. You?'

'She wouldn't call me. She doesn't like me.'

She thought he'd deny that, but he shrugged lightly. 'She's jealous. Everyone compared her to you and it annoyed her.' He squared his shoulders. 'We should go inside and talk to Alistair.'

'Who is that?'

Thorne's smile was wry. 'The boss of the Circus Freaks.'

'And his name is *Alistair*? Why didn't he change it to Rocco or something?'

'Rocco was taken. Plus . . .' He hesitated. 'Nobody ever makes fun of him. Let's just leave it at that.'

'Lovely.' She patted her stomach, comforted to feel the handgun holstered in the girdle she wore. 'Let's get this over with.'

Gripping his hand tightly, she entered the shack, blinking to get used to the darkness. It was a familiar sight, picnic tables covered with newspaper and piles of crab shells – the only way to truly enjoy blue crabs.

Thorne bent down to whisper in her ear. 'If we don't die, let's get a bushel to go.'

That made her laugh, so when they came face to face with the biggest, burliest man she'd ever seen, she was still smiling. The smile faded away as she craned her head back to see his face.

'Holy motherfuck,' she muttered under her breath. Alistair was *enormous*. He towered over Thorne, for God's sake, with a bald head and a handlebar mustache that would have made him look comical had it not been for the wicked scar that ran from his left eye to disappear beneath the facial hair. His eyes were blue. And cold. His leather vest was covered in gang patches, his skin in tattoos. It was only the steady pressure of Thorne's hand on the small of her back that kept her from turning to run for her life.

Keeping a firm hold on her, Thorne stuck his free hand out for the gang leader to shake. 'Alistair. It's good to see you again.'

The man shook Thorne's hand. 'Likewise,' he said in a voice that was more growly than any one of the motorcycles out there. He eyed Gwyn. 'I didn't know you were bringing your lady friend. I'm afraid these benches are the only seats we've got.'

'It's all right,' Gwyn said. 'I grew up on a crab boat. I've sat on much worse.'

He tilted his bald head, studying her. 'You're Gwyn Weaver. You manage Thorne's club.'

death is not enough

'I am.' She lifted her chin, meeting his eyes. 'It's my club too. You're Alistair. I'm afraid I don't know your last name.'

His mustache twitched. 'Nobody does. Let's sit down.' He waited until they were seated – Alistair on one side of the table, Thorne and Gwyn on the other – before leaning forward. 'Where was your crab boat?' he asked, his tone challenging.

'A little nothing town called Anderson Ferry on the Eastern Shore.'

'I've been there.'

'I'm sorry,' she replied without missing a beat. She'd run away at sixteen and had only been back once. And that had ended very poorly.

His mustache twitched again. 'Crabs were good,' was all he said, then sat back, his palms flat on the newspaper. 'So, Thorne. You've got yourself a situation.'

'That I know. Do you know anything else? Something that would be news to me perhaps?'

Cold blue eyes regarded them. 'I owe you a debt,' Alistair said. 'That is the only reason you're still breathing.'

Gwyn drew a breath and let it out slowly.

Thorne was as steady as he'd been with that douchebag Chandler Nystrom just hours before. 'I didn't have anything to do with your boys getting killed. I hope you know that.'

'I do. But it wouldn't have mattered. If I hadn't owed you anything, I would have been . . . remiss had I not avenged my brothers. But I do owe you. Because of you, my son has a life. Avery's doing well, by the way.'

Ah, Gwyn thought. Avery was the young man that Thorne had represented in court – and the one he'd encouraged to testify against Tavilla's son, Colin. Now a few things made more sense.

Thorne's lips curved. 'I know. I get a card every Christmas.'

'His mama raised him right.' Alistair drummed his fingers on the table briefly, then stilled them. 'Once we're done here, my debt is paid.'

'Understood. And thank you for not killing us,' Thorne added dryly.

Another mustache twitch. 'You're welcome. Your bartender was a plant.'

Gwyn blinked, stunned. A quick glance up showed Thorne doing the same.

'What do you know about our bartender?' she asked, because Thorne was still blinking. 'We're talking about Laura, right?'

A single nod. 'She didn't go by that name when she tried to infiltrate the Freaks. She introduced herself to us as Bianca. She attached herself to Bart and for a while she fooled us. Luckily for us, Bart was a jealous bastard and followed her one night because he suspected her of cheating.'

'Bart *was*?' Gwyn asked.

'He was one of the young men found stuffed with your matchbooks,' Alistair said, his eyes growing even colder, something Gwyn hadn't thought possible.

'I'm sorry,' she murmured. That meant Bart had been at Sheidalin on Sunday night. 'Did she recognize him?'

'He recognized her,' Alistair corrected. 'But she must have seen him too, because he's dead.'

'Where did she go the night Bart followed her? Back when she was trying to infiltrate the Freaks?' Thorne asked, but his tone said that he already knew the answer, and in that moment, so did Gwyn.

'F—' She broke off the curse, unsure about biker gang etiquette. 'No way. Are you saying that Bianca, Laura, whoever she was, was working for' – she lowered her voice – 'Tavilla?'

Alistair nodded once. 'She left Bart's bed and went to the restaurant Tavilla enjoys.'

'Bruno's,' Thorne said flatly.

'High cuisine,' Alistair sneered. 'He's an arrogant prick. Thinks because he wears two-thousand-dollar suits and sips champagne with his pinky out that he's some kind of *gentleman*.'

'When he's just a common thug,' Thorne murmured, even though he also wore an expensive suit. 'Like the two of us.'

Alistair grunted. 'Not as good as the two of us. Smarmy little punk.'

Thorne chuckled. 'I wish you were legit, Alistair. I'd invite you to my poker game.'

The mustache twitched again, this time revealing a glimpse of white teeth. 'I'd rob you blind.'

'I know.' Still gripping Gwyn's hand, Thorne raked his other hand through his hair. 'We missed something on the background check.'

Alistair nodded. 'I'd have to agree with that.'

Gwyn cleared her throat. 'How did your guys end up at Sheidalin on Sunday?'

One massive tattooed shoulder lifted. 'I sent them there. I've had my eye on your club for years. Too bad it's closed. Really. Even if we weren't able to strike a deal with you on the inside, we've made a mint selling to your clients as they leave.'

Thorne winced. 'I don't want to know that. Now I have to stop you when we open again. Because we will open again.'

'I wouldn't want you to get bored, Thorne,' Alistair drawled. He pulled a piece of paper from a pocket inside his vest and handed it across. 'Final payment on my debt.'

Thorne unfolded it and frowned. 'Who is . . .' He squinted. 'That's Laura. Bianca. Whoever.'

'Her real name is Kathryn. She's worked for Tavilla for years. What's wrong?'

Thorne had grown very, very still. At last he seemed to shake himself, then he refolded the paper and slid it into his own pocket. 'Thank you, Alistair. Truly.'

Alistair looked like he'd press the issue, and Gwyn sensed that this was a topic Thorne would not discuss. She leaned forward, catching the biker's eye. 'If I may . . .' she began, encouraged when he nodded. 'Why is your club named Circus Freaks?'

'Because I come from a circus family,' he answered, surprising her. 'My grandfather was a strongman. So was my father. He was even bigger than me.'

'I'm glad to hear that,' she said sincerely, and it was true. 'I know sideshow performers, and they're salt of the earth. I'm glad you're not just using their name.'

Alistair studied her. 'You were a contortionist.'

Again he'd surprised her. 'Everyone always remembers that,' she grumbled. 'I was also a tightrope performer.'

'Not such a good one, since you got hurt. Which is why you left the circus.'

It was a fair assessment. 'You really did your research.' That factoid wasn't in the bio posted on the club's website.

'Of course. I figured he'd bring you. You've been joined at the hip for days.'

'You've been watching us,' she said, injecting just a tiny bit of challenge.

'And I'm not the only one. Be careful, little contortionist,' he said very seriously. 'Some of the people watching you are not as nice as I am.'

'We will.' She offered her hand. 'Thank you again for not killing us.'

He took her hand in his meaty paw, shaking it gently. 'You're welcome. Now go. My hospitality only extends so far.'

Gwyn rose, tugging Thorne with her. He followed, his brows knit. Clearly troubled.

She waited until they were in the SUV before asking, 'What was that?' He gave her the paper and she scrutinized the photo of Laura, aka Bianca, aka Kathryn, apparently. 'She looks really different. Not just hair color, but she wore facial prosthetics or something when she worked for us. Her face is almost like a stranger's.'

'Not so much,' he said. He opened his phone, swiped and tapped the screen, then handed it to her. 'This is a photo Ramirez sent to me last August.'

A tanned man in a suit and tie sat next to Cesar Tavilla, who had a pretty young woman perched on his knee. 'Is that Gage Jarvis?'

The man who'd killed his wife and tried to kill his daughter because she'd witnessed the murder. Thorne had helped Joseph and JD catch him, and this act of decency had drawn Tavilla's attention once again.

'Yes. Look at the woman on his knee.'

Gwyn enlarged the photo and gasped. It was the woman they'd

known as Laura. The woman who'd set them up on drug charges and who'd likely cleaned out half of their cash reserves.

'She worked for us for six months,' Thorne said. 'And all the time he was waiting. Just waiting.'

Her blood ran cold. 'He's been planning to take you down for a long time then,' she murmured. 'He pulled the trigger when his son died in prison.'

Thorne started the SUV and pulled away from the crab shack. 'Laura slipped right through the background check. We need to talk to Anne and find out how this happened. Can you call Jamie? He's got all the employee files. He can give us her address.'

Gwyn started to do as he asked, then froze, her pulse leaping into the stratosphere. *Holy shit. Holy fucking shit.* She enlarged the photo to maximum scale, her heart threatening to break through her ribs. 'Thorne,' she whispered. 'Oh my God. Pull over. Now.'

With a screech of brakes, he complied, pulling onto the shoulder. Wordlessly, her hand trembling, she handed him back his phone.

She knew the moment he spotted the woman standing in the back of the room, behind the seated Tavilla. Dressed in a simple white sheath dress, her blond hair in an elegant twist, she exuded wealth and dignity.

Thorne's mouth opened, but no words came out. He swallowed, moistened his lips. 'Anne,' he said hoarsely. 'How?'

'I don't know.' But she did know that if she'd been halfway human for the last four years, Anne wouldn't have been hired in the first place. 'This is a problem.'

'Yeah. She's had access to all our client records at the law firm. She knows everything.'

They sat in silence, trying to absorb this new truth. The silence was broken by the buzzing of Thorne's phone. Caller ID was Jamie. He put him on speaker.

'I'm here with Gwyn,' Thorne said, his voice still hoarse. 'Is it Phil?'

'No,' Jamie said, his own voice tight. 'Phil is fine. I'm standing outside his room right now. But we have some new developments.'

Thorne's laugh was painful to hear. 'So do we. You go first.'

'I've gotten several phone calls from clients. Someone is blackmailing them with information that they swear was told only to you.'

Thorne closed his eyes. Again he tried to speak and couldn't.

'Are you there?' Jamie demanded.

'He's here,' Gwyn said. 'It's Anne, Jamie. And Laura from the club. They both work for Tavilla.'

There was a moment of shocked silence. 'What? Are you sure?'

'Yes. We have a photo showing them together. All three of them. Laura's real name is Kathryn. We don't know Anne's yet.'

'This is a nightmare,' Jamie murmured. 'I have to think. Is Thorne all right?'

Thorne was staring out the window, his normally dark skin gone gray.

'No, he's not all right, but I'll get him safely to you.' She checked the side mirror. JD had stopped behind them, but he hadn't approached yet, which she'd expected him to do. Instead he was sitting gazing straight ahead. 'What else has happened, Jamie?'

'Stevie was shot at again. She's okay, but the bullet grazed her arm. It was her cane arm and she lost her balance and went down. No more bullets were fired, even though she was a sitting duck at that point. She said the shooter was either incredibly skilled or incredibly clumsy.'

Thorne had grown deathly pale. Gwyn unsnapped her seat belt and twisted to her knees, reaching for his chin. 'Thorne. Thorne!'

He stared down at her, devastated anew. 'He's taking it all apart. Piece by piece. My family, my friends, the club, the firm. Phil. Stevie.' He seemed to age before her eyes. 'You.' He pushed her from her knees back to sitting, then kept pushing until she lay sideways, her head on the console. All the while his hands were gentle, but shaking. She allowed it, allowed him to get her out of view of the windows, not reminding him that Joseph's SUV was nearly bulletproof because she didn't think he would even hear her words.

'I'm okay, Thorne,' she said instead, keeping her voice calm. 'Stevie's okay. Phil is okay. We are all okay.'

'He could be out there. Anywhere. I should have shipped you off somewhere safe. Why didn't I send you somewhere safe? Why didn't I . . . I should have . . .' His voice broke. 'But it wouldn't have helped,' he whispered, sounding so damn vulnerable.

Fear skittered through her. This wasn't Thorne. This wasn't *her* Thorne. 'What wouldn't have helped?' she asked quietly.

'*Thorne.*' Jamie's voice cracked through the phone, filled with the same fear.

But Thorne didn't answer. Gwyn grabbed a handful of his tie and yanked with all her strength. She tipped her head up, fixing her gaze on him. 'What wouldn't have helped? Offering yourself?' she demanded when he continued to say nothing.

He nodded. 'He doesn't want me to die. He doesn't want me to physically suffer. He knows this is worse.' He swallowed. 'So much worse.'

She tugged his tie, bringing him closer until his face was inches from hers. 'We aren't going to let him win.' She glanced at the phone. 'Right, Jamie?'

'Right,' Jamie said grimly. 'Meet me at Clay and Stevie's. We'll figure out what to do.'

As soon as she ended the call, JD's face appeared at the window, looking even more haggard than Thorne. New fear grabbed her throat, because JD was pale and shaking. *Lucy.* 'No,' she whispered. 'No, no, no.'

JD tapped on the window and Thorne seemed to wilt, his whole body shaking now as he popped the lock and opened his door. JD gripped the frame, his shoulders sagging.

'She's alive,' JD rasped. 'Lucy. And the kids. But our house is on fire. She got them out in time. They're okay.'

Thorne turned in his seat, facing JD. 'I'm . . .' He didn't say the word 'sorry'. He just grabbed JD and pulled him into an embrace, taking the other man's weight and holding him as he shook. Gwyn slid over the console, draping her body over Thorne's back and holding them both. They clung that way until JD got hold of himself and pulled away, wiping at his wet cheeks.

'Oh God,' JD murmured. 'This sucks.'

Gwyn snorted a surprised laugh, wiping away her own tears. 'Yeah, it does. Where is Lucy now?'

'On her way to the airport with Joseph,' JD said.

'Airport?' she asked cautiously. 'That was fast.'

'Yeah.' JD's lips twisted. 'She kept her head. Called Joseph first because she knew that once she called me, she'd have to stay on the phone to keep me from losing my shit. Joseph picked her and the kids up and took them straight to Martin State.'

The small airport served private jets, Gwyn knew. A few of the higher-priced bands that had played Sheidalin had flown into Martin State. 'Does Joseph have his own plane?' Joseph was rich, but she didn't know he was *that* rich.

'His father does. Joseph's sent cars for Paige and Stevie too, to take them to the airport.'

'And Julie?' Gwyn asked, thinking of Frederick.

JD nodded, still shaky. 'Yes. She's still at Stevie's. Joseph was pissed off at me for not telling him about the plan to drive them all to Chicago. He's taking them there himself. He insists flying is safer.' He ran his hands through his hair. 'I need to get to the airport. I need to see them before they go.'

Gwyn took a long look at Thorne. Giving JD comfort had seemed to bring him back from his own abyss. The haunted look was gone, replaced with the grim determination she'd come to rely on. 'JD isn't safe to drive,' she murmured.

'But I am. You take JD. I'll follow.' He kissed her, hard and fast. 'I've got your back.'

'I know you do.'

Annapolis, Maryland,
Wednesday 15 June, 4.40 P.M.

He rewound the video and played it again, smiling as he thought of the way the former homicide detective had gone down with just one small bullet graze. His body camera had caught it all, so beautifully it was as if he'd hired a movie director. Stevie Mazzetti-Maynard had hit the ground without so much as a yelp, though, and for that he reluctantly admired her.

When she'd realized what had happened, she'd been more pissed off than hurt or even afraid. By the time she'd crawled across the pavement to get her cell phone, then crawled closer to the big black SUV she'd been driving, he'd had his rifle disassembled and in its case. By the time she'd called the police, he was in his own vehicle.

And by the time sirens could be heard, he was driving the other way.

He wished he could see Thorne's face when he learned of the latest shooting. The last time, he'd trusted Patton with the job, because he was to have intentionally missed, which Patton had done. This time, though, it had required a little more finesse. He didn't want to kill Stevie Mazzetti-Maynard. He just wanted Thorne to know that he could. He'd hit her just enough to cause pain, but not enough to cause serious injury.

And he could do it at any time to any of them. And he would. Tomorrow they were planning to leave. At least some of them. The most vulnerable. They were sending their women and children away in vans. Driving them to 'safety'.

He didn't plan to kill them. Not yet. But he would show them that they couldn't escape him. Though if after he shot at their tires they crashed into a tree and suffered all kinds of injuries . . . that would be just fine.

He hoped they planned to properly secure the children in car seats.

He paused the video at the sound of a light knock on his office door. 'Come in.'

Margo stuck her head in. She did not look happy. In fact, she appeared nervous. 'Hi, Papa.'

He waved her in and pointed to the chair. 'Is it Benny?'

'No, he's fine. Just teething and drooling.' She glanced down at her blouse. 'I changed twice before I left the house this morning.' Squaring her shoulders, she folded her hands in her lap. 'I have bad news for you. They've already gone.'

He froze. 'Who?'

'The women and children. They were flown out by private plane. About an hour ago.'

His eyes narrowed. 'You knew nothing of this?'

She moistened her lips. 'No. I didn't make any of the reservations. It was handled by the FBI. The shot you fired on the ex-cop this morning, followed by Patton's arson at the Fitzpatrick home, prompted them to fast action.'

Rage flared within him, but he put it aside. They were protecting their most vulnerable. 'Where will they go?'

'I'm trying to get my hands on the flight plans. I can tell you that the plane is owned by Agent Joseph Carter's father. The Carter family owns several pieces of property all over the country as well as abroad. I assume they'd go to one of those places.'

He drummed his fingers on the desktop, attempting not to feel like a child who'd had his favorite toy stolen. 'I see. What about the fire? Patton left the box?'

'Yes. When the fire cools, they'll find it filled with matchbooks from the Crabshack and Circus Freaks patches. But I don't think they'll buy it.'

'Why not?' he snapped. 'Alistair's love of fire is well known.'

'Because Alistair doesn't believe Thorne is responsible for the deaths of his two gang members. He and Thorne met today at the Crabshack, right about the same time that Patton was setting fire to the Fitzpatrick home.'

Margo delivered the words with no emotion whatsoever. Still they felt like a rebuke. A reprimand. 'How do you know this?'

'Same way I know that they'd planned to ship everyone to Chicago by van. I can still hear every word they say in the Maynard home. The men, along with Gwyn, arrived moments ago. Thorne and Gwyn were arguing because Gwyn refused to get on the plane.'

'So she's still here? She'll have to be good enough for now.'

Margo hesitated. 'They also know about me.'

His hand closed into a fist. 'How?'

She shrugged delicately. 'I don't know. But there was a lot of "Fuck Anne" and "If I get my hands on her . . ." You know. The usual. They don't know who I am, but they know I work for you.'

'You heard all this?'

'Clear as a bell. The microphone I stuck in the box of client files broadcasts beautifully. And so far there's been no attempt to block our signal.'

He blew out a breath. He hadn't thought this would be easy. Thorne's friends were a formidable group. He *had*, however, expected them to turn on the defense attorney, or at least abandon him. He had to admire their loyalty. 'They don't know that we can hear them?'

'No. They think they're arranging a temptation that you won't be able to resist.'

'The christening on Saturday.'

'Yes, sir.'

'Good. Let's let them keep thinking that. Let me know as soon as you find out where the women and children have gone. I haven't finished playing with them yet.'

'Of course.'

'Have you found a way into the judge's safe deposit box for that incriminating letter?'

'No, sir. Not yet, but I'm still working on it.'

'Work faster.'

She rose. 'I will. If you need anything, I'll be in my office.'

Twenty-three

Hunt Valley, Maryland,
Wednesday 15 June, 4.45 P.M.

The mood in Clay's living room was more than dark, Frederick thought, wishing he knew what to do but too deep in his own funk to help the others. The normally noisy house was strangely quiet.

The kids were gone. The moms were gone. In the end Joseph had taken Stevie, Paige, Lucy and all their kids, including Cordelia and Julie, plus Ruby *and* Sam, because if the shit hit the fan, the man might not be able to get out of the way. If Clay's house was set on fire like JD's had been, Sam would be a liability, his concussion still causing any fast movements to result in debilitating vertigo. It had been a bitter pill, but he had swallowed it stoically.

Joseph had even arranged for Phil to be transported to a private hospital with security equivalent to that of the Secret Service. But that meant that Jamie had needed to decide whether to stay with Phil or Thorne. Both Phil and Jamie had decided that Thorne needed him more, so Jamie sat in his chair next to his son. Because Thorne *was* his son, in every way that mattered.

Frederick had taken a seat next to Jamie, because he was certain that even though Jamie felt no regrets about his choice, he still worried about Phil. Giving Jamie his support seemed like the only thing Frederick could do, at least as long as they were all in this waiting pattern.

Because Taylor had gone with Julie, Gwyn was the only woman left in the room, and *that* had been a truly epic battle. Thorne had tried to bodily force her to get on the plane, but Gwyn had

382

more grit than anyone had expected.

And more moves. The woman could slither and slide and contort her body in ways that still confounded Frederick, and he'd witnessed the whole thing. It was like Thorne had been handling a slippery fish.

Now Gwyn perched on the arm of the loveseat that Thorne had commandeered. Both sat with their arms crossed, still angry with each other. Clay stood at his back window, brooding at the sunset, and JD alternately paced and brooded with him.

JD's house had burned to the ground. Lucy had grabbed her children, then had gone back in for her violins. Everything else had been destroyed, and they now had only the clothes on their backs. And the violins. JD had been too relieved to see her alive to scold her about risking herself to save the instruments. Frederick suspected that might become an issue later, however. The rest of them had wisely maintained silence on the matter.

Everyone, including Frederick, glanced at their phones with irritating frequency. The plane was still in the air, but would be landing very soon.

'Anything?' Jamie murmured, leaning to glance at Frederick's screen.

'That depends,' Frederick answered quietly, feeling as if he were in an oppressive library. 'The plane has Wi-Fi, so Julie's sent me lots of pictures. She's having a ball. It's only the second time she's been on a plane. Taylor has Julie, Cordelia and Paige singing "Ninety-nine bottles of chocolate milk on the wall", and Stevie's about to go nuclear.'

Jamie chuckled. 'Chocolate milk?'

'They're not old enough to sing about beer.' He touched the photo of his smiling daughters, feeling wistful. 'I guess Julie is, but . . . not really. I haven't done a good job with her.'

'What?' Jamie shook his head. 'You've done a fine job. Stop that.'

But Jamie was his friend, so he had to say that. 'A stranger found out more about my daughter in an hour than I ever knew.'

'Sally Brewster?' Jamie asked. 'Look, she's a nurse. A pediatric nurse. She's trained to talk to young people. And it sounds like Julie

383

connected with her. Maybe she just misses having a mom.'

'Maybe. Sally's offered to spend time with her after all this is over.'

Jamie's brows rose. 'Sally? Huh. You gonna let her?'

'I think so. I've checked her out. She's legit. A really nice person.' Frederick hesitated. 'And we've been texting.'

Jamie's grin spread across his face. 'You sly dog, you. You *like* her.'

'God. You sound like Taylor.'

'Taylor's smart. I don't mind sounding like her.' Jamie leaned over, bumping shoulders. 'So what do you text about?'

Frederick shot him a withering look. 'I'm going to hurt you.'

Jamie snickered. 'Fine, fine. Just go with it, man. You're too tight.'

'You two sound like teenaged girls,' Thorne grunted from where he sat sprawled on the loveseat, arms crossed over his chest, the picture of manspreading.

Gwyn smacked his chest with a backhand that made her wince. 'That is a patronizing and condescending thing to say. And shit, why didn't you take off that damn vest? It hurts.' Joseph had insisted they all don Kevlar vests for their trip from the airport back to Clay's house, handing them out like candy on Halloween.

'Still wearing mine,' Frederick said.

'Me too,' Jamie added. 'Why aren't you? They're not that uncomfortable.'

And would come in handy should Clay's house be torched by a gunman, forcing them to flee like rats off a sinking ship. The knowledge that that could happen, coupled with the memory of the smell of smoke on Lucy and her children's clothing when Frederick had hugged them goodbye . . .

Yeah. It was sobering, all right. He was relieved he'd gotten his girls far away. He'd be even more settled when he heard from Daisy. She was not answering any of his calls. He'd had radio silence for the past week, and that wasn't like her. She'd texted him twice. Once to give him her travel itinerary, and then to tell him that she was alive and receiving his texts, but that was before he'd told her not to come to Baltimore yet, to delay her departure. Since then, he'd heard nothing.

So he was worried.

'I took the vest off because it was huge,' Gwyn said, ripping him from his thoughts. 'It came down past my butt. I can't sit down properly in it.'

'You won't sit down at all if you're dead,' Thorne muttered. 'You should be in Chicago.'

'I should be *here*,' she replied. 'This mess with the club affects me too. As does the mess with the firm. I'm still listed as an officer and an employee.'

Thorne scowled. 'You're fired. All of you, from all of it.'

'Doesn't matter.' She kissed the top of his head, affection showing through her irritation. 'Even if you fire us, it's because you love us. So you're stuck with us.'

'Until you're all dead.' Abruptly he stood up. 'I can't just sit here. I need to do something.' He strode to the bulletin board and made a savage noise at the photo of his office manager, now placed next to the photo of Tavilla.

Anne Poulin, Frederick thought. She'd fooled them all. *Even me.* Not that he'd ever had a great read on women, but . . . Only Gwyn had had reservations, though Frederick had chalked that up to jealousy.

Again he'd been wrong. Gwyn had an intuition about the woman that they'd all ignored. Even Gwyn herself.

'Who is the real Anne Poulin?' Frederick asked. 'She passed the background check. I began reviewing the employee files the day all this started. Mowry's inconsistencies stuck out like a sore thumb, but Anne's record raised no flags. She has a past, a work history, social media, even elementary school photos on her parents' social media. I found a copy of her work visa and cross-checked it against the government record. It's legit. She moved here from Montreal five years ago for college. She's continued to take classes. For a fake identity, this is exceptionally well done. And I know how to fake identities.'

Clay turned from the window. 'I know,' he said dryly.

Because Frederick had created the fake identity that had allowed him to hide Taylor from Clay for years, believing him to be a violent, vengeful man. He'd been wrong about Clay, but he was not wrong about this.

'You're right, though,' Clay continued, confirming his thoughts. 'It's a good fake. I'll ask Alec to do some digging.'

At that moment all their phones began ringing, calls from every-one. 'They're there,' Frederick murmured after talking to Taylor. 'Safe at Ethan's.'

'Thank God,' Gwyn breathed.

At the window, JD sagged forward, resting his forehead against the glass. Clay gave his shoulder a supportive squeeze. 'Come on, JD. They're safe now, and we can get to work sending Tavilla to hell so that we can bring them home.'

JD nodded. 'Except we don't have a home.'

'You can use ours,' Frederick offered. 'Julie and I can stay here until you rebuild.'

JD smiled wearily. 'We'll talk. But thank you.' He slumped on one of the sofas. 'Let's bring this fucker down, Thorne.'

Thorne nodded. He hadn't moved from the bulletin board, his body still rigid. 'Right. I need to find him. Tavilla.'

'And do what?' JD asked.

'Stop him.'

Gwyn sighed. 'I would like nothing more than to put a bullet in Tavilla's head, but as soon as we do that, we go to prison. I think he'd like that.'

'From the grave,' Thorne muttered.

'But we'd still be in prison,' Gwyn said carefully.

'Not "we",' Thorne corrected. '"I". And it would be worth it.'

Jamie pinched the bridge of his nose. 'So what say we come up with an *actual* plan that doesn't make me defend your ass on a murder charge a *second* time?'

Thorne turned, his mouth quirked up on one side. 'Yes, Dad,' he said, his tone slightly mocking, but there was affection under it. 'We tried Chandler Nystrom and he's a no-go. He might talk under torture, but I don't know. I'd like to try, except that would just make

Jamie scold me again. Tavilla had Patricia killed. We know that, right? I'm really asking. Because there are so many bits of string connecting so many pieces of this puzzle that I could weave a rug.'

'He's involved,' Clay said. 'Whether he killed Patricia himself or not, he is involved. His trigger was the death of his son.'

Thorne nodded slowly. 'But Anne's been with us for a whole year. Whatever Tavilla's got planned, he put this in motion a long time ago.'

'So just snuffing him out at this point wouldn't necessarily stop him,' Gwyn said. 'Please promise me that you're not really considering it.'

Thorne shrugged. 'If I have to, I will. If I seek him out and he tries to kill me, I will. But I won't take a potshot at him while he's walking his dog. If he has one. At least the club will be okay now that we can show that our bartender was in his employ. The bartender – Laura or Bianca or Kathryn or whoever – was the only one with drugs. And the notoriety will just draw crowds when we finally reopen. It's the firm that concerns me. What do we know about the clients getting blackmail calls?'

'Six clients called me,' Jamie said. 'I assume there were more who haven't come forward yet, or who won't. Each got a call from a different number. Each described a different voice. High, low, raspy, male, female, distorted. Whoever made the calls used a voice-alteration app of some kind. Each person was threatened with exposure of their worst secret, things they'd disclosed to you. None were given blackmail terms yet.'

'So just enough to stir them up,' Thorne murmured. 'If this gets out, I could be up on charges with the bar.'

'Given that Anne-fucking-Poulin works for *Satan*,' Gwyn ground out, 'I think the bar will understand. However, your reputation may not survive. Nor will the firm.'

Thorne sighed. 'I know. That's really not my biggest concern at the moment. I'm more worried that the firm is discredited and that any of our employees who has to get another job afterward will be sullied. At least we have fewer employees affected by the firm than the club.' He tapped Tavilla's photo. 'Our goal is to stop him. We do

387

that by exposing his plan and the fact that he's pulling the strings. We destroy his financial base so that none of his employees get paid. That way, any contracts he has out on any of us won't be carried out.'

'Tall order,' JD said, 'considering neither Baltimore PD nor the FBI has been able to stop him.'

'True.' Thorne chewed on his lip. 'But he had that damn key ring. And my medal, the one Darian Hinman's killer left in him. Tavilla had to have gotten them from somewhere. Brent Kiley, the EMT we talked to on Monday, said he'd seen the key ring in Richard's body, but denied taking it. The only person left in the chain is the ME tech, who's dead.'

'But whose widow is still raking in enough fourteen years later to live in a ritzy part of town,' Jamie said. 'If the ME tech took it, then who did he give it to?'

'Somebody with enough money to pay off the widow.' Thorne pointed to the photo of Linden Senior.

'Not just him,' Gwyn murmured. 'The Hinmans had money too. I mean, that lobby we walked into this morning was something straight out of a museum. Also, by the time the ME tech died, Patricia and Judge Segal were married. He wasn't a judge then, of course. He was barely out of college. But his family had money too. The Lindens, Hinmans and Segals all had the means. We assume the Lindens had a motive, but what if they weren't the only ones?'

Thorne huffed an impatient sigh. 'We need to get that fucker Nystrom to talk to us. Or find Colton Brandenberg. If Richard was molesting his sister or Angie or anyone else, they would have known something about it. Richard was not subtle. Somebody on this board knows something that ties Tavilla to Patricia. When we find that person, we have to get them to roll on him.'

'You mean Joseph and I do, right?' JD looked concerned. 'BPD and the FBI. Not you, Thorne.'

'I don't care who takes the credit,' Thorne said. 'I just want him stopped. Where is Alec on the ME tech's widow's bank records?'

Clay took out his phone. 'Texting him to come give us a report.'

'Where is he?' Frederick asked.

'In his room downstairs. I sense you judging me for texting.'

Frederick heard the humor in his voice. 'Maybe a little. I'm supposed to be the old man.'

Clay grinned. 'Not touching that one. One, I'm too tired to get up and call down there. Two, if he's got his processors off, he won't hear me yelling anyway.'

The door to the basement opened and Alec joined them, but he looked frustrated. 'I was just about to take a break.' His hair stood up on end, like he'd been shoving his hands through it. 'I've been searching for a way into the widow's home system, but she's wily and my Internet's been wonky. You guys may have to take the low-tech road and simply ask her.'

Thorne sighed. 'She's the only loose thread we have – that ties to my past anyway. We still have the judge, his son, and Tristan Armistead, the boy Patricia was . . . involved with? Molesting? Shit.'

'Stevie was on her way to Tristan's house when she got hit,' Clay said. 'She and Paige had stopped at the school to check in with the coach. They never got to talk to him. He was out today. They were leaving the school office when the shot came.' He rubbed his face with his palms, shuddering. 'God. Stevie had stopped dead in her tracks for at least ten seconds when she got shot. The gunman had time to set the shot up, but it was the lightest of grazes. She barely needed stitches. Which, you know, I'm happy about, but . . .' He shrugged, looking gray. 'Ten seconds is a long time. If the gunman had any skill at all, he could have hit her right in the heart.'

'But he didn't,' Gwyn said, reaching over to pat his arm. 'What made her stop?'

'Oh.' Clay shook his head as if to clear it. 'She got a text from my number. Said that the house was under attack, that Cordelia had been shot and was being airlifted to the ER.'

'Oh,' Gwyn breathed. 'Poor Stevie.'

'Yeah.' Clay swallowed. 'We'd set up a code between us, a word we'd use so that she'd know it was me. By the time she figured out that the text was a spoof, she was hit.'

'That's a good idea,' Jamie said. 'We need to have a word. What—'

'Stop,' Alec interrupted. He looked around, a tense frown creasing his brow, then put his finger over his lips and ran downstairs. No one said a word, no one even moved a muscle until he returned holding a scanner.

Shit. Frederick recognized that scanner. It was used to search for listening devices. *No. No, no, no.* He exchanged horrified glances with everyone else in the room as Alec did a thorough search before dropping to his knees in front of a stack of boxes.

'No.' Jamie covered his mouth, cheeks gone pale.

Holy fuck. Frederick met his eyes. 'Anne,' he mouthed, and Jamie nodded miserably. They were the boxes of client files that Anne had brought to Phil's hospital room the day before, and that Frederick had piled in the corner of Clay's living room because leaving them in Jamie's van had been too insecure.

Motherfucking shit.

Alec emptied one of the boxes, carefully scanning the contents as he stacked papers and file folders on the floor. Finally, he got to the bottom of the box and pulled out a padded envelope. He gave a yank, and the cardboard box split down the side, revealing a wire.

And the microphone. Alec held it up for them to see, eyebrows lifted in question.

Clay pointed at the door. 'Get rid of it,' he mouthed, and Alec nodded.

'I'm sorry,' Jamie said as soon as the door was closed. 'They're my boxes.'

'Stop,' Clay said. 'You didn't know that you couldn't trust your office manager. Let's just try to figure this out. When did you put them there?'

'Yesterday evening,' Frederick said. 'So they heard all the plans we made last night.'

JD ran a trembling hand through his hair. 'They knew about the evacuation plans then. That we did it differently may have saved their lives.'

Frederick's gut dropped. 'I said they were safe at Ethan's. I said it softly, but I said it. Depending on how sensitive the microphone is . . . Anyone who does a background check on you, Clay, knows who Ethan is.' Clay and his former partner had co-owned the personal security business that had grown into Clay's existing private investigation firm.

'I'll call Ethan now,' Clay said, already dialing. He shared the information with his friend, then ended the call. 'He's putting additional security measures in place. He'll be watching. That's all we can do for now.'

Alec came in from outside, dusting off his hands. 'I felt like throwing it in the manure pile,' he said, 'but I want a chance to pull it apart. I disconnected it and put it in the gun safe in the trunk of my car. It's lead-lined.'

'That's good,' Clay said. 'How did you know to look for it?'

'My Internet connection was being disrupted. Sometimes that happens downstairs because I'm so far from the router in Clay's office. I figured it'd be better up here, but it was even worse. I'd done a routine sweep before everyone started gathering here a few days ago, so I knew this was new.'

Clay's pride was evident in his expression. 'Good work. I want to go over this house again with a fine-toothed comb. Until then, we discuss nothing here.'

Thorne took out his phone and typed out a text, but didn't send it. *We'll check out the ME tech's widow.* He passed the phone around. 'Okay?' he asked aloud.

'Fine,' Clay said. 'JD and Frederick, you go with them.' He indicated Gwyn. 'But you need a vest if you're going. Stevie has a few extra ones upstairs in her closet. Next to the sparkly evening gown she wore when we went on a cruise.' His lips curved a little, as if remembering. 'You can't miss them.'

'Thanks.' She kissed his cheek and took the stairs two at a time.

Thorne glared at Clay. 'You could have asked her to stay here.'

Clay snorted. 'Yeah? No. I got enough problems with Stevie. You want Gwyn to stay here, you deal with her. Jamie, I need your help. Alec, get him a scanner and a long-handled extender. If you would, Jamie, scan every wall on this floor. Alec, you take downstairs. I'll take upstairs. Scan the perimeter, up to the ceilings, then back and forth along the carpet.'

'Got it.' Jamie grabbed Thorne's arm. 'Do not do anything stupid. Do not make me ground you.'

Thorne smiled. 'Okay, Dad.'

And that time it hadn't been mocking at all.

Chevy Chase, Maryland,
Wednesday 15 June, 6.20 P.M.

Eileen Gilson, the ME tech's widow, lived on a beautiful tree-lined street where a sporty Mercedes and a tidy Kia sedan vied for the only available space in front of her townhouse. Luckily her neighbors didn't seem to be home, so Thorne was able to find a place to park. The four of them had said little on the drive from Clay's house, despite Alec declaring the SUV free of listening devices.

Thorne felt edgy and paranoid and he had to draw a breath before getting out of the car. 'We're going to overwhelm her,' he said as the four of them gathered on the sidewalk.

'I'll take the lead,' Gwyn said. 'You three can be my entourage.'

Without waiting for argument, she hurried up the walk and knocked on the door. A woman in her mid forties answered. She was small and fit-looking, with straight black hair cut in a sharp angle that followed her equally severe jawline. Her gaze scanned their faces, coming to rest on Thorne's.

'Hi,' Gwyn said. 'We're sorry to bother you, but we'd like to talk to you. I'm Gwyn Weaver, and this is—'

The woman lifted her hand. 'I know who you are. You and Mr Thorne, anyway. Come in,' she said. 'We've been expecting you.'

Casting a perplexed look at Thorne over her shoulder, Gwyn followed, but came to an abrupt halt when she entered the small sitting room. Thorne nearly knocked her over, and stumbled when JD ran into him. But he immediately saw why she'd stopped short. Three suitcases stood at the base of the staircase.

And Detective Prew sat on the sofa, a small blond woman at his side.

'Okay,' Gwyn said slowly. 'But *we* didn't expect *you*.'

'No,' Thorne agreed, wondering what the hell was going on. 'We did not. Frederick and JD, this is Detective Christopher Prew, recently retired. Detective, my associates, Frederick Dawson and JD Fitzpatrick.'

'My wife, Delia,' Prew said.

Eileen Gilson motioned to the four chairs she'd pulled from the dining room table into the sitting room. 'Now that we've made all the introductions, please have a seat. I apologize in advance that I don't have more comfortable seating for you.'

'You knew we were coming,' Gwyn said.

'Yes,' Eileen confirmed.

'Why are you here, Detective?' Thorne asked when it became clear that she planned to say no more than that.

'I'll explain,' Prew promised. 'I did call Phil, hours ago, but he'd been moved to another hospital. I wasn't at home and didn't have the business cards you gave me. Is Phil okay?'

'He's fine,' Thorne answered. 'Just . . . security.'

Prew's gaze flicked over to JD. 'I understand. I was sorry to see your house in the news, Detective Fitzpatrick.'

JD nodded once. 'It's just stuff. Everything precious is safe.'

Prew smiled. 'I'm very glad to hear that.'

Gwyn's eyes narrowed. 'How did you know we were coming?'

Prew cleared his throat. 'Well, I may have been a trifle harsh with the hospital, trying to reach Phil. They wouldn't give me Jamie's number either, but after they hung up on me, they called him to tell him that I was pestering them. Jamie called me and I told him that I was here. He said to sit tight, that he'd let you know, but that was only a few minutes ago. I'm sensing that he didn't tell you.'

Thorne's phone picked that moment to buzz. He checked it to find a text from Jamie, complete with their code word. 'He just did. So back to my question. Why are you here, Detective?'

'My wife was at the beauty parlor today. She called me on my cell and told me to haul ass over there.'

'Not in those words,' Mrs Prew protested mildly. 'Chris had asked me to keep an ear open for any rumors or gossip about Patricia Segal. I was stunned to see Ms Gilson in one of the chairs, though. We hadn't seen each other in quite a while.'

Eileen nodded, meeting no one's eyes. 'She overheard me talking to my son on the phone. I was telling him that we had a last-minute trip planned and that he should meet me here.' Her smile was strained. 'He's in college. He had plans already. I was rather . . . insistent. I didn't realize that my voice had carried.'

Mrs Prew looked a little uncomfortable. 'It really didn't. I was actively listening because I knew that Ms Gilson was a person of interest for you. After she hung up with her son, she called a neighbor to ask her to collect her mail until she could have it forwarded. I got the impression she was leaving town for a while. So I called my husband.'

Thorne wasn't sure how he felt about the retired detective sharing facts about the case with his wife, then realized he'd have done the same with Gwyn.

'We followed her here,' Prew said, 'saw she was loading up her car, and asked her to stay. You need to tell them,' he said gently to Eileen.

She drew a shaky breath. 'I know. It's just hard after all these years.' She rose and walked to the front window, wringing her hands. 'I wish my son were here. I'd feel a lot better about telling you this if I knew he was safe.'

'Your son was threatened?' Gwyn asked, her voice much softer.

'Yes. He's the only reason I kept this secret for so long. Him and the fact that I didn't want to go to prison.' She rubbed her arms briskly. 'Okay. My husband, Kirby, worked for the ME's office when Richard Linden was murdered. He prepped the body. You already know about the key ring. And according to Detective Prew, you've already figured out that Kirby took it.'

'Why did he?' Thorne asked.

'Because . . .' Eileen closed her eyes. 'He was honest. Until that moment, he was so honest. And that moment, that bad decision, it ruined our lives. The victim's father asked him for it. Came right into the morgue and asked him. Kirby said he was shocked and said no. So the man offered to pay him.' She shook her head. 'We were pretty desperate at the time. I was pregnant with our son and on bed rest. I'd lost my job and we had loans and . . . He did the wrong thing.'

'Come and sit down with us, Eileen,' Gwyn said kindly. 'The window may not be the wisest place to stand right now.'

Eileen jerked away and walked back to her seat, nervously looking out of the window from across the room. 'God. This is a nightmare.'

Gwyn patted her hand. 'I know. We've been living it this week, but you've lived with it a lot longer, haven't you?'

She nodded, swallowing thickly. 'Yes.'

'When did you know what your husband had done?'

'Not for five years.' She covered her mouth, her eyes filling with tears. 'I always knew something had happened, because one day Kirby was happy, and then he wasn't. He wasn't the same after that. For a while I thought he'd cheated. I was flat on my back and not able to do anything. But he insisted that he hadn't, that the body of the Linden boy had just hit him hard. And I'd read about the case in the paper, so I believed that.'

Mrs Prew pulled a tissue packet from her purse and gave it to Eileen. The woman nodded her thanks and dabbed at her eyes.

'It was when our son was four and a half that it all came out. He was diagnosed with leukemia and we . . . we were devastated. We were also poor. Kirby was going to school at night, and I was work- ing part-time and we had insurance, but it didn't cover everything. And what it didn't cover bankrupted us in the first month. We were desperate. And then, all of a sudden, we had money. Lots of it. Enough to pay for our son's treatment. I demanded to know where Kirby had gotten it, and that's when he told me about the key ring. That he'd gone back to the boy's father and told him that he'd tell the police about it if he didn't pay him more money. Linden did and our son lived.'

'But your husband didn't,' Thorne said quietly.

'No. He never got over any of it, though. If he'd had a bad time when he took money for the first time, he was overcome by guilt the second time around. He'd stand at our son's bedside and cry. He swore me to secrecy. Said we'd go to prison if anyone found out.

395

And then one day, I got a visit from the police saying that my husband was in the morgue. That he'd responded to the scene of a shooting and a "stray bullet" hit him. But I knew the truth. I knew he'd been silenced.'

'Why didn't you say anything then?' Prew asked.

She laughed bitterly. 'And end up like my husband? My son was in remission, but that could have changed at any moment. I knew that. I was the only person left to take care of him. And then, about two weeks after I buried Kirby, there was a knock at my door. It was Mr Linden. He said that he knew I'd said nothing and that I was smart. He said that if I continued to be smart, everything would be fine. I was too scared to say a word. The next day, money was deposited into my account. That's continued, every month, ever since.'

Frederick leaned forward. 'Where does the money come from? Is it an account in Linden's name?'

'No. It comes from a corporation. I tried once to dig through the layers to get to who actually owned the company, thinking that if I could show it was Linden, I could get free. But I couldn't untangle it.'

'What do you mean, get free?' Gwyn asked.

'I tried to keep working, deposited all my paychecks in a separate account, figuring that if I had to, I could just walk away. Then one day one of Mr Linden's attorneys showed up with the keys to this place. Said that Mr Linden was afraid I'd leave town. That if I tried, he'd claim that I'd extorted money from him and that I could go to prison. Which is ironic as hell. So I've stayed here where he can watch me.'

'Did you have contact with Mr Linden again?' JD asked.

'No. It kind of became . . . my life. And then I read about what happened to Linden's daughter, Patricia. I nearly came forward, but . . . I didn't. I started packing instead.' She dropped her eyes, appearing ashamed. 'And then Darian Hinman was found dead. I knew he'd testified at your trial, Mr Thorne. Kirby had followed every detail. He'd told me everything. I knew Hinman and Richard Linden had been friends. And now Brent Kiley, the EMT, has been killed, and—'

Thorne jerked forward in his seat. 'Wait, *what*?'

Her eyes widened in surprise. 'I read it on the news. When I was in the salon. His body was found this afternoon. That's why I wanted my son to come home, so we could get away.'

Thorne twisted in his chair to stare at JD, whose mouth was slightly open.

'I didn't know,' he murmured.

Thorne nodded. 'We need to talk to your boss.'

JD nodded grimly. 'You're right. We do.'

Prew frowned. 'I'm sorry. I thought you would have heard. I thought that's why you came here.'

'No,' JD said. 'We've been a little busy with another shooting and a house fire.'

Frederick held out his phone. 'Here it is. Brent Kiley was found this afternoon by someone from his firehouse when he didn't show up for his shift. There are no details yet.'

'I'll get them,' JD vowed. Joseph had been busy carting the moms and kids to Chicago, but Hyatt could have called. Should have called.

Eileen searched their faces. 'What are you going to do with me?'

'Nothing,' Thorne said. 'I'm not a cop and JD is here as my friend, not in an official capacity. But it would make a difference if you gave a statement. The key ring is important. Richard Linden's killer thought so. His sister's killer agreed. So did Darian Hinman's. That Linden Senior has paid you for years for your silence means that he knows it's important too.'

She looked away. 'I'm sorry, but I can't. I'll be on record and I'll have to testify. There won't be anywhere on earth safe enough for my son.'

You fucking bitch. Thorne's temper broke free. 'Look at me, Eileen,' he bit out, using the voice that made hardened criminals sit up straight and tell him everything. He waited until she'd dragged her gaze to his. 'You have been silent for fourteen years because you were afraid. We all get that. We are afraid. I am afraid. My friends have been shot at. My employees have been injured and set up for crimes they did not commit. My father was attacked in his home.

397

And this afternoon, someone set Detective Fitzpatrick's house on fire. His wife and children were inside. His children, Eileen. Babies.'

Her gaze skittered away again and he had to resist the urge to grab her face and force her to look at him. She had information that could get them a warrant to search Linden's home and office, if the corporation could be traced to him. He'd hoped she'd do the right thing, but her jaw had taken on a stubborn line.

This was a woman who'd taken money for her silence. She'd embraced the lifestyle the money afforded. She was not going to testify willingly.

'Look at Detective Fitzpatrick,' he spat. 'Look at him and tell him that your kid is more important than his babies. No? You asked what we'll do with you. I don't know about them, but I know exactly what I'll do. Do you have any idea how many requests I've had from reporters asking me to tell my story? Hundreds. Many from national, international networks. What I will do is give them what they want. And I will be sure to tell everyone what you have done. I will be sure to tell them about the Mercedes you drive, the lifestyle you enjoy, the job you do not have.'

She looked at him then, eyes filled with hate. And fear. Whether that fear was because of him, or Linden, or even Tavilla, he didn't know and did not care. 'You wouldn't dare,' she challenged, but her voice shook.

He laughed as bitterly as she had. 'Watch me. Someone is taking my life apart, bit by bit, hurting the people I love. I have nothing to lose.'

He held her gaze as the seconds ticked by. Then she jerked a single nod. 'Fine. But I want protection for my son.'

No fucking way, he wanted to snarl, but bit it back. This wasn't the kid's fault any more than it had been Thorne's fault when Richard had been murdered.

Gwyn placed a hand on his and Thorne realized he was trembling. 'We can ask,' she said quietly. Calmly. Thorne shuddered and felt his anger draining away. He was too exhausted to hold onto it any longer, but Gwyn had taken the baton and he was grateful.

Eileen folded her arms over her chest. 'All right. It would seem I don't have much choice.'

She really didn't. He felt a prick of conscience that he was forcing her hand, then remembered how JD had sobbed in his arms that afternoon. His friends – his family – were hurting. And he could make it stop. Somehow he would make it stop.

He dug deep and found his courtroom presence, and with it, his calm. 'Just so that we are perfectly clear,' he said coldly. 'You're agreeing to testify that your husband tampered with evidence, turned over the key ring to Richard's father for money, then later blackmailed the Lindens in exchange for his silence. Then, after his death, you continued to accept money for your silence. Is this correct?'

Her jaw flexed as she ground her teeth. 'Yes. That is correct.'

It was enough to get a warrant for Linden's records. Hopefully that would lead to a connection to Tavilla, because that was the one piece of the puzzle that continued to elude them.

'Thank you,' he said stiffly. 'We appreciate your cooperation.'

Twenty-four

Annapolis, Maryland,
Wednesday 15 June, 6.45 P.M.

The thud caught his attention and he turned from the view outside his porthole. He'd always loved this view, but now . . . it didn't seem to matter. It hadn't mattered since he'd lost Madeline. It had been two years. Two long years.

At least she hadn't lived long enough to bury their son. She wouldn't have survived that. *I barely have.*

'Patton's back.'

He turned to the chair in front of his desk where Kathryn sat, her legs crossed. She wore a pretty black cocktail dress that made her legs look long and elegant.

'I know,' he said. 'I think he's delivered something I requested.' Or, more accurately, some*one*. 'You look lovely tonight. You should always wear dresses. I hated the uniform they made you wear at that club of Thorne's.'

She smiled at him, a dimple creasing her cheek. 'I don't know. It made me feel badass, wearing all that leather. Although I gotta say the bra chafed and I couldn't sit down in the pants. Still, I looked hot.'

In hindsight, he could have used a little more time to put his plan together. He'd had to do some things too quickly. He would have preferred to have Kathryn in place longer. The movement of money, the hiding of drugs behind the bar . . .

It had been sloppy. The charges against Thorne's people would never stick, but that was okay. They'd get off lightly this time, but

400

next time the police would be less inclined to believe the best of him.

And I'll keep attacking. Slowly. Insistently. He had time, after all.

Nothing but time now.

Kathryn rose fluidly and came to put her arms around his neck. 'I hate to see you like this,' she whispered. 'So damn sad.'

He shrugged. 'It'll pass.'

She rested her cheek against his shoulder. 'Madeline wouldn't have wanted this for you.'

'No. Probably not.'

'She warned me, you know. To watch for this.'

He leaned back to look down at her. Kathryn was lovely. Young, of course, with smooth alabaster skin and wide brown eyes that sparkled with intelligence. She was a good reader of people too. She was the one who'd told him to jettison Gage Jarvis the summer before. That he couldn't be trusted.

She'd been right. She'd also warned him about Ramirez. The man had been weak, falling for Kathryn's charms. Cheating on his wife. His pillow talk had ultimately doomed him, because he'd told her how devastated he'd been over the death of his nephew, the last male of their family. *She picked up on the hate that I did not.*

'What did Madeline tell you to watch for?'

He'd never cheated on Madeline. At least not conventionally. His wife had been bedridden for much of the later years of her life. She'd known she would die and had hand-picked Kathryn, giving him her full blessing.

Kathryn had certainly made getting over her death easier. But on nights like this, he still missed his Madeline so much he ached with it.

'Your melancholy.' Kathryn caressed his face. 'She said she'd have to drag you out of your own darkness sometimes. That I shouldn't let you get too sad. I know you miss her. I know you miss Colin. But I've got something to cheer you up.'

She was kissing her way to his ear when they were interrupted by a knock. He sent her back to the chair with a reluctant wave and opened the door. 'Yes, Mr Patton?'

'He's here.' Patton indicated the punishment room with a jerk of his head. 'Be careful. He's waking up earlier than I expected.' He rubbed his jaw. 'Got me with his hard skull.'

'Thank you. Where is Margo?'

'She said she was working from home. The baby has a cold and she didn't want to take him out. She's got enough of Weaver's shit to go through to keep her busy most of the night, she said.'

When he raised his brows, Patton rolled his eyes. 'Yes, sir. Your grandson's mother says "shit". I'm sorry to break it to you.'

He found himself smiling. 'I've heard her say it over the years. More times than she should have. Come back in a few hours. I'll be done with Mr Nystrom by then.'

Patton gave him a salute, then jogged up the stairs, closing the door behind him. He turned back to Kathryn, his smile widening. 'I think I've found a solution to my melancholy.'

She smiled back. 'May I watch?'

He leaned in to give her an indulgent kiss. 'Sure.'

'Why are you killing Nystrom?'

'Because he's weak. He was questioned by Thorne this morning. He said all the right things, but he'll crack if Thorne leans on him again. Especially after hearing about Hinman's death. He was very scared, and scared men do stupid things.'

'They expected you to trust them,' she said with a shake of her head. 'But they sold you information on their friend. They really should have expected the knife in their own backs.'

'Exactly.' He tugged off his tie. 'Should I use the knives or clubs?'

She toed off her shoes and unzipped her dress. 'Why not both?'

He chuckled. 'You are the best.'

She shimmied out of her dress, grinning at him. 'I know.' She paused, then sobered. 'I'm worried about Margo.'

He laid his suit coat over his desk, turning to her with a frown. 'How so?'

'She's been . . . off. I mean, yes, she should be sad because she misses Colin something awful, but it's more than that. She's working herself so hard. Being a mom is tough enough. I've tried to help her out, I've babysat Benny as often as I could. But she never rests, even when I'm there to watch him.'

Kathryn and Margo had always been close. Together they'd come up with the plans to infiltrate Thorne's businesses when he'd refused to represent Colin, acting for the Freaks' son instead and ultimately sending Colin to prison. Margo's skill set had been perfect for an office manager, and she'd applied to Thorne's firm as soon as it was certain that her alias would survive the background check.

Margo had been in her role as Thorne's office manager much longer than Kathryn had worked at the club, and had been able to gain access to many more parts of Thorne's business. Trust took time.

But he'd hated sharing Kathryn with Sheidalin, which was why it had taken him so long to allow her to work there. Once she had started, however, the girls had incorporated photos of Kathryn with Benny to flesh out 'Laura the bartender's' social media presence. That way, she had a reason to keep strict hours and to reject social overtures. That way, she came home to him.

'Do you think Margo needs a vacation?' he asked.

'Yes. Somewhere there is no Internet and she can't work. Maybe we can pull up anchor and sail somewhere warm, sunny and exotic.' Kathryn's smile was impish. 'She and I are both currently un-employed.'

He chuckled. 'Plan something and run it by me. We'll celebrate when this is over.'

She clapped her hands. 'In the meantime, we party with Chandler Nystrom.'

Baltimore, Maryland,
Wednesday 15 June, 7.00 P.M.

'I'll just be a minute,' Gwyn said, unlocking her front door while Thorne, JD and Frederick hovered over her. She'd gotten used to the mild claustrophobia induced by their protection. 'Poor Tweety. He'll be crossing his legs for sure.'

'I'll walk him,' Thorne said tersely. 'You get his things together.'

She didn't take any offense at his tone. She knew he was barely holding it together, wired so tightly he was about to snap. The news of the EMT's death had hit him hard.

403

If I'd only told Hyatt and Joseph that Kiley saw the key ring, he'd whispered to her once Joseph had arrived to deal with Eileen Gilson and the four of them had returned to Gwyn's. *The police would have known that Kiley had critical information and they might have protected him.*

Not your fault, she'd whispered back.

Brent Kiley had kept his secret for too many years and he'd paid for it. His fear for his family had been legitimate, but his refusal to do the right thing had led to the collapse of his marriage, leaving him alone with piles of empty pizza boxes and beer cans.

Thorne hadn't let it go. *I could have forced him. Like I just did with Eileen Gilson.*

Maybe. But the EMT hadn't cared about anything enough to be used for leverage. Eileen, on the other hand, did. Both her lifestyle and her son. Gwyn had disliked the woman on sight, and that Thorne had thought she'd been compassionate showed just how off-kilter he'd been thrown by this whole mess. Unable to convince him, she'd just held his hand, hoping that Eileen's testimony would enable them to get a warrant.

He'd immediately called Christina Brandenberg, the sister of the still-missing Colton. She hadn't answered his call and he'd left her a message that someone else related to their shared past had been murdered. He urged her to come forward, for protection if nothing else. And once again he begged for her help in finding her brother.

He even called the number he had for Chandler Nystrom, leaving him a warning message, despite the despicable way the former cop had treated him that morning.

Then he'd closed his eyes in silent misery, as Frederick brought them to Gwyn's condo to collect her dog. They'd decided to stay with Clay because there was strength in numbers.

It felt desperate, because it *was* desperate. That Thorne was offering to walk her dog made a grim kind of sense. Because Tavilla wasn't going to kill Thorne. *He'd kill me and enjoy watching Thorne suffer.*

'I hope you left that animal some food,' JD grumbled. 'He always looks at me like I'm a pork chop.'

'He does not.' Chuckling, Gwyn pushed the door open and . . . froze. 'Oh my God.'

Because her apartment was trashed. Completely trashed. Her sofa was ripped up, the leather knifed to ribbons, stuffing on the floor. The mirrors on the walls had been smashed, glass littering the carpet, which was also strewn with pictures ripped from the walls.

'Tweety.' She bolted into her apartment, only to have three sets of arms grab her back.

'Stay here,' JD ordered. 'Frederick?'

'I'll hold onto her,' Frederick promised, because Thorne had already gone running into the apartment.

Gwyn sagged into the older man, her breath coming in pants. Her home. Her safe place. Not anymore.

'Did you set the alarm?' Frederick asked her gently.

'Yes, of course.' Her voice broke. 'I know I did.'

Frederick stroked her hair. 'Try to breathe, honey.'

'Found him!' Thorne called. 'He's okay.'

Gwyn choked back a sob. 'Thank God.'

Thorne and JD came back together. 'It's clear,' JD said. 'Come in, shut the door.'

'I left Tweety in the bathroom,' Thorne said, 'until we clean up the glass.'

'He'll need to go out,' Gwyn said, her mind refusing to comprehend the catastrophe she was seeing. 'He needs to pee.'

'He already did,' Thorne said, taking her from Frederick's arms into his own. 'We can clean the bathroom. The rest of the place may be harder. It's a mess. I'm so sorry.'

She reached around his neck, wishing for her heels just to get closer to him. He solved that by picking her up and holding her to his chest. She buried her face in his neck and breathed him in.

'Not your fault,' she whispered. 'None of this is your fault.'

'Did you have your laptop on your desk?' JD asked.

'No. I left it at Clay's. I was using it to review the books Monday night.' There was that then. Her documents were safe. Except . . .

Her gut clenched and she abruptly pushed away from Thorne.

405

'Let me down.' He immediately complied and she ran to her bedroom, throwing open her closet.

It was empty. Completely empty. Hangers were scattered on the floor and every shelf was bare. *Oh God. Oh no.* Her knees wobbled and she held on to Thorne, who'd been right on her heels.

It was gone. Her fire safe, holding her important papers. Her life. Her secrets. Could they open it? Probably. It had a keyed lock. Not terribly hard to jimmy.

And what would they find? Her birth certificate. Her passport. And all the newspaper clippings she'd collected over the years. Some of Thorne, a few of Lucy. One of herself, on the tightrope. But most were of Aidan. A few from his childhood, usually a grainy photo in a school newspaper about an award. The better clippings came when he'd entered high school. Number 54. Offensive line.

That whoever stole the safe could identify him was a given. His last name was on the back of his jersey. And if they figured out who he was to her? Less likely, but exact relationships weren't necessary. The existence of the clippings screamed his importance. Her stomach twisted painfully. She needed to warn him. *That could be complicated. I need to figure out how.*

'They took your clothes?' Frederick asked, coming up behind them.

'No,' JD said. 'They're mixed in with bedclothes on the floor over there by the bed. But they're trashed too. Ripped up. Sorry, Gwyn.'

She didn't care about the clothes. Turning in a slow circle, she took in the smashed cosmetics and perfume bottles, the broken mirror, the mattress on which she and Thorne had first made love. It had received the same treatment as the sofa, slashed with a knife, stuffing everywhere.

And then she got the real message. Her gun safe stood open, but the guns were still there. 'They knew my combination. That's how they got past the alarm.'

'You used the same combo for your security alarm as your gun safe?' JD asked.

She nodded numbly.

'The alarm was 0-2-1-7,' Thorne said, because he'd always known it. He just didn't know what it stood for. His voice became thoughtful. Questioning. 'I never knew your safe was the same combo.'

'Yes,' was all she could say.

'Who else knew?' JD asked, his phone out, ready to call this in to BPD.

'Lucy. That's it. Except . . .' She turned away from the open safe to the less upsetting mess on her dresser. 'Anne. She came home with me once. I had car trouble and Thorne and Lucy were busy. She said she had to use the bathroom, so I asked her to come up. She could have seen me put in my alarm code.'

'When did this happen?' JD asked. 'At the club? Because you haven't worked at the firm in a couple of years.'

'I still worked there from time to time as a paralegal. When Thorne or Jamie had really sensitive cases they didn't trust to anyone else.'

'Right,' JD murmured. 'You told Hyatt that on Sunday when Thorne was in the hospital. I thought you were lying, actually.'

She glanced up at him sharply. 'You would have let me lie?'

JD nodded soberly. 'To protect Thorne? Hell, yeah.'

She was able to smile about that. 'Thank you.'

'But how did Anne get past your dog?' Frederick asked.

Gwyn shrugged. 'He knows her. She always had a treat for him, every time we came into the office or every time she brought papers to the club for Thorne to sign. I thought her giving him treats was sweet at the time, but now . . .'

Thorne threaded his fingers through her hair. 'We can replace everything.'

'Not everything. I had a fire safe. On the closet shelf. It had all my important papers in it.' Her stomach gave another heave. *God.*

'Did it have the same combination?' Frederick asked.

'No. I had a key.' Her voice was calm now, surprising her. 'But if she was able to copy a key to my apartment – which I assume she did, since she managed to disable the alarm – she probably has a key to the fire safe too.'

Thorne had his hand around the back of her neck, providing just enough pressure to reassure without any pain. 'Do we need to stay here?' he asked JD. 'I'd like to get her back to Clay's.'

JD nodded. 'Yeah. Let's lock up. I'll request a uniform to stand watch until we can get CSU here to process the scene.' He smiled sadly at Gwyn. 'Looks like we're both going clothes shopping soon.'

'Looks like.' A whimper caught her attention, followed by scratching. 'Poor Tweety. We're lucky he hasn't dug through the door.'

'He tried.' Thorne took her hand. 'I think your bathroom will need a severe overhaul when this is over.'

Please God, let that be soon. They were fraying at the ends. All of them.

They could only maintain vigilance for so long before one of them made a mistake. Got hurt. Or worse. And then Thorne would wish he was dead.

Which was exactly what Tavilla wanted.

Hunt Valley, Maryland,
Wednesday 15 June, 9.30 P.M.

Thorne threw his phone on the dresser in the guest room he and Gwyn were sharing in Clay's basement. He had to take a moment to breathe. To calm himself. She didn't need his frustration now. She'd had a shock of her own. Her home had been invaded, her sanctuary destroyed.

Still fully clothed, she lay on the bed, propped up by pillows. Tweety sat on the floor, his chin on the edge of the bed, watching her. As if he too knew she needed extra care tonight.

She looked up from her laptop. 'Anything?' she asked cautiously. She was still too pale, her brow furrowed in worry.

He knew the feeling.

'No.' He sat down on the bed, forearms on his knees, and hung his head, huffing a tired chuckle when Tweety shifted his chin from the edge of the bed to his knee. He scratched the dog behind his ears. 'I tried to call them both again. Both Nystrom and Christina

Brandenberg. Both went to voicemail. Hers rang like ten times, but his just went straight to voicemail.'

'She's ignoring you then. He's either blocked you or turned off his phone.'

'I know. I just . . . God, Gwyn. I don't want anyone else to die.'

'I know, baby.' She put the laptop aside and crawled so that she could drape her body over his back, resting her cheek between his shoulder blades. 'I know.'

'I asked Alec to search for Colton Brandenberg. I don't know what else to do at this point.'

'Hopefully Alec can work his magic for us,' she murmured, sounding so totally not like herself that he twisted abruptly to catch her face in his hands.

'We will stop this,' he promised. 'We have to.'

She nodded, leaning into his palm, then jerked away at the knock on their door. 'Yes?' she called.

'It's me,' Alec said through the door. 'You guys decent?'

Thorne felt his cheeks actually heat. 'Yes,' he said, embarrassed. 'Come in.'

Alec stuck his head in tentatively, then opened the door wider so that he could enter. 'I found Brandenberg.'

Thorne blinked. 'So quickly? How?'

Alec gave him a look that was slightly annoyed. 'Because I'm damn good at my job? I figured that if he'd gotten so upset that he had to be medicated during your trial—'

'Wait,' Gwyn interrupted. 'What?'

'I read the transcripts and I read Jamie's notes. The behavior Jamie described sounded like a friend of mine who was on serious sedatives for anxiety and depression. Maybe even bipolar. I never asked him about his diagnosis. But he was a zombie, just like Jamie described Brandenberg. I figured if he was that upset, maybe we couldn't find him because he'd changed his name. Just like you did.'

God, the kid is good. 'Had he?'

'Yep. I played with a few variations, looked at name-change records in Maryland around that time, and bada-bing. I sent the information to your phones.' Alec paused a second, his gaze resting on Gwyn a few seconds longer than seemed necessary. 'Okay?'

She nodded. 'Sounds great, thanks. What's his new name, and where is he?'

'He is now Brandon Colt. He's an old-fashioned country doctor, lives in Appalachia. Has a traveling practice. He works with communities in need. I sent you a link to an article that someone wrote about him last year. He owns a twenty-year-old truck and that's it. No address, no property records. The reporter was doing a series on lung ailments in the old mining towns and mentioned him. Said he was "unfailingly humble" and didn't want any credit.'

'Penance,' Thorne said quietly. This he understood.

'That's what I took away,' Alec agreed. 'Kind of like all the pro bono work you do. You were just lucky enough to have Jamie's financial support coming out of your trial. Looks like Dr Colt has no one.'

'Very few people have no one,' Gwyn said. 'His sister knows where he is. She just didn't want to tell us.'

'Fair enough. I found a phone number for him, but it went to voicemail when I called. I used a burner number, so he might not take calls from numbers he doesn't know, but I kind of doubt that, him being a doctor and all.'

'Thank you, Alec,' Thorne said sincerely. 'We have one more place to start in the morning.'

'You're welcome. One other thing.' He took a few steps into the room, handing them each a Post-it note. 'I've set all the house alarms. If you need to leave, use this code or the screeching will really hurt your ears.'

Gwyn took her note and folded it in half. 'Not your ears?'

He grinned. 'Nope. My room is rigged with a bed shaker and strobe lights that are activated with the alarm. When I take off my processors, I hear *nothing*. And I'm about to take them off for the night.' He waggled his brows. 'Just . . . give me two minutes to get settled before you two start anything, okay?'

He pulled the door shut, leaving both of them staring after him.

'Well,' Gwyn said with a half-laugh. 'That was subtle.'

Thorne blew out a breath. Because he really wanted to start

something with her. To lose himself in her body and get out of his own head. For just a little while. He'd wanted it all day, but now . . . She'd had a shock. She wasn't herself.

But she'd also challenged him not to assume.

Cautiously he reached for her, sighing his relief when she crawled into his lap and put her arms around his neck. 'We've got about a minute and a half that we have to be quiet,' she said. 'We can neck till then.'

He smiled at her. 'I'm glad you're here.'

She arched one brow. 'You mean I was right not to get on Joseph's plane this afternoon?'

He kissed her lightly. 'No. I still wish you were safe. But if you had to be stubborn, I'm glad you're here with me.' He rested his forehead against hers. 'I really need to escape my own head right now,' he confessed.

'Me too. But . . .' She drew a breath. 'I need to tell you something. And it's not going to be simple.'

He stilled, because he'd sensed something like this was coming. Ever since she'd looked into her closet and seen that her fire safe was gone. 'What was in the safe, Gwyn?'

'You noticed.'

'Yeah. You didn't care about anything else. Just the fire safe. Why? Birth certificates are replaceable.'

'I know. Just about everything in the safe was technically replaceable. But if Anne, or whoever the hell she really is, opens that box, it . . . well, it gives them ammunition to use against me. To make me suffer. Which makes you suffer.'

He sat back, waiting. The dog, also sensing her distress, leaned against Thorne's leg, his head on Gwyn's thigh. Absently she stroked his ears. 'I ran away from home when I was sixteen.'

'That I knew. To join the circus.'

'Well, actually it was to follow a boy. A man. He'd just graduated from the University of Maryland. He'd gone there on a music scholarship.'

'So he was older. Like, twenty-one?'

'Twenty-three. My father forbade me from seeing him, more

411

because he had long hair and played the guitar than because he was older than me. So of course seeing him was what I wanted to do most in the world. I was rebellious.'

'That I also knew,' he said dryly.

Her lips tipped up. 'Yeah, yeah. I fell for this guy. He had a job on the boardwalk at Ocean City, playing in a band at one of the clubs. That's where I met him. I liked to hitch a ride into Ocean City because it was a lot more exciting than Anderson Ferry, where I grew up.'

Thorne knew about Anderson Ferry, because it was also where Lucy had grown up. 'It doesn't sound like a welcoming place.'

'Not if you didn't fit in. Which Lucy and I certainly didn't. Anyway, I met Terrence that summer and we . . . got it on.'

'You were sixteen,' he said flatly, not wanting to picture her with anyone else, especially a long-haired musician.

'I told him I was eighteen. He bought me beer. We had sex. It was supposed to be a fling, but then my dad found out I was seeing him and had a cow. I kept seeing him and my dad was exceedingly unhappy. My father was a believer in strict discipline. A church-going man. When he was unhappy, he hit with a belt or made us cut our own switch, which was . . . abuse. When he got drunk, his hits became serious abuse.'

Thorne gritted his teeth, hating that they had parental abuse in common. 'How often did he get drunk?'

'A lot. I pushed him. But that's no excuse. He hit me hard when he found out I was seeing Terrence. I mean, really hard. I ended up dragging myself over to see Lucy's mother. She was our town doctor then.'

Thorne swallowed hard, fighting to keep a lid on his fury, because he wanted to drive to Anderson Ferry and tear Gwyn's father's head right off his neck. 'I know. I met her at Lucy and JD's wedding. Did she report your father?'

'No. She asked me if I wanted to report him, but I said no, so she just cleaned and stitched my cuts and bandaged me up. I told her that I wanted to get away, and she loaned me some money. I hitched a ride into Ocean City and went to Terrence's room at the boarding house. He took one look at me and wanted to kill my father.' She stroked Thorne's tight jaw. 'Kind of like you do right now.'

He swallowed again. 'The thought has entered my mind.'

'I know.' She sighed. 'Turned out Terrence was getting ready to go home. To Sarasota. His parents had supported him getting his degree, but agreed that he'd come home after graduation to be part of the family act again. He belonged to a circus family. Tightrope walkers. Terrence was also an archer. Did a William Tell type act where he shot an apple off his assistant's head.'

Thorne's brows shot up. He'd never heard this part of her circus story. 'Were *you* his assistant?'

'I was. And I was *fabulous*.'

'I'll just bet,' he grumbled.

'No need for jealousy. He's been out of the picture for almost twenty years. But *that* year, he took me home with him to Sarasota. It's a circus town, you know. The winter home of Ringling when it was operating. Huge circus museum. Used to even have a clown college. Lots of circus people still live there. Anyway, his mom took me in. Fussed over me. His dad wanted to kill mine when Terrence told them what happened. They were nice people.'

'Were?'

'Yeah, they died in a hit-and-run. They were tightrope performers, but they died crossing the damn street a few months after Terrence and I had left the circus. I traveled with them for a couple of years, until I was eighteen. Worked for my keep. Started out sweeping and shoveling shit, but I had some skills. I'd done gymnastics in high school. Dreamed of the Olympics, but we never had the money for that kind of coaching. But I wasn't bad, and I was . . . flexible.'

'Of this I am well aware,' Thorne said, hoping to pull a small smile to her mouth.

She did smile, just a little. 'Yeah, well. There was this woman there who did a contortionist act. She trained me and I was good. I could get out of all kinds of locked boxes and tied ropes. Learned to pick locks, get free of chains.'

'That's how you knew how to pick locks when we'd go under-cover, investigating for the firm?'

413

'Yep. Picking locks is a bankable skill. I was cute back then. Made good tips.'

'You're cute now.'

'Thank you,' she said, rolling her eyes. 'I wanted to try the tightrope, though. Which did not end well.'

'You got hurt.'

'Yeah. There was a net, but one of the other performers fell on top of me. My back still aches when it gets cold. But the hospital needed my medical records and it came out that I was just eighteen. Which meant I'd lied about my age. I agreed to quit so that the circus – and Terrence's family – wouldn't get into any trouble for hiring me without proper ID. Terrence wasn't happy, though, and he'd lost his archery target. He wanted to leave. His parents were chill, and they kissed us both and gave us a little cash, and off we went. Terrence had put together a band and I played piano and sang. At the beginning, I only knew church hymns, but I learned a few things from Terrence.'

He growled. 'I don't want to hear any more about him.'

She sighed. 'You have to, because none of that was in the fire safe.'

'What was?'

'I got pregnant. I was eighteen. And a half. He and I had been traveling with the band for about six months. I went to tell him the news and found out that I wasn't his only port in a storm.'

Thorne was still stuck on 'pregnant'. She'd never mentioned a baby, so either she'd never had it or she'd put it up for adoption. He gathered his wits, though, because she'd stopped talking. He latched onto the topic that felt less like a minefield. 'Terrence was cheating.'

'Yeah. With one of the other singers. I hated her. I threw a hysterical fit and she left. I told him about the baby and he wanted me to get rid of it. I couldn't. I know some women do and I support their choice, but it wasn't right for me. He gave me an ultimatum. So I left and went home to Anderson Ferry. My mother and father were not happy to see me. And when I told them I was pregnant, they threw me out.'

414

Thorne clenched his teeth so hard that a sharp pain speared his jaw. 'I really hate your parents, Gwyn.'

'Me too. I didn't have anywhere to go. Terrence's parents were gone. I had one great-aunt in Baltimore. My mother's aunt, who they rarely spoke of except to pray for her immortal soul. I found her and she took me in, no questions asked.'

'Your Aunt Aida. Your letters for Sheidalin.'

'Kind of. I loved my aunt, but she was much older and in bad health. I got my GED while I was pregnant, but I had no real business skills. She helped me see that I couldn't provide a good home for a baby and that I needed to be able to fend for myself, because she wasn't going to be around for much longer. She might have been the family bad girl, but she had the kindest heart. She knew some people who knew some people, you know? And through them we met the couple who adopted him.'

Him. 'You had a boy?' he asked, unprepared for how much the question hurt.

'Yeah. I named him Aidan, after my aunt. The couple liked the name and kept it.'

'That's your I-D-A, then,' he said, and she nodded. 'What happened to the family?'

'They're in Virginia, near Richmond. Aidan just graduated from high school. He's going to Virginia Tech next year to play football.'

'So what was in the fire safe? Pictures of him?'

'I only have one photo and it was in there, but it was just a copy. The original is in my safe deposit box at the bank. That's the only picture I have of me holding him. The rest are newspaper clippings. Most of them are from his high school football games.'

'You ever see him play?'

She closed her eyes, but not before he saw the pain there. 'Once. Just once. I couldn't stay. It hurt too much. It was a big game. Homecoming. Lots of people there and it was cold, so I could wrap a scarf around my face. No chance of his parents seeing me. I didn't want to intrude. I just wanted to see him. But I had to leave.'

He could imagine her sitting all alone in the stands, her heart

415

breaking. His was breaking just listening to her. 'Did you see him any other times?'

'Occasionally, yes. Sometimes – and I'm not proud of this – I'd go to his neighborhood and watch for a glimpse of him. Just playing. I wanted to be sure he was okay. That he was happy. That they really were good people. He was always smiling.'

He sighed, picturing that too. 'You think Anne will be able to open the fire safe?'

'I'd be shocked if she hasn't already. Other than you and Lucy, that boy means more to me than anyone else in this world. If I were them and I were trying to figure out how best to hurt you, I'd pick me. And with Lucy now out of reach, Aidan is the only one they can use to hurt me.'

'We should contact his parents then.'

'I was hoping you'd say that. I . . .' Her eyes filled with tears. 'I can't, though.'

'Why not?'

'Because he was eighteen in February.'

Oh. Oh God. 'The seventeenth is his birthday?' *0-2-1-7.* How many times had he entered that alarm code without knowing what it stood for?

She nodded. 'His parents said they'd tell him about me when he turned eighteen and leave it up to him whether to contact me. He's been eighteen for four months now and I've heard nothing.'

'Maybe they didn't tell him.'

She shrugged. 'All the more reason I shouldn't call them. I don't want them to think I'm pressuring them. That wouldn't be fair. Plus, what if he picks up? That could be awkward, and even more unfair to him. I was going to ask Jamie to contact them, as my lawyer. But . . . you could, if you wanted.'

If he wanted . . . Yeah, he wanted to do this for her. He hoped he was strong enough. 'I'll ask Alec to get me the number.'

'He already did. He sent it to my phone.'

'Oh. That's what that look was for.'

'Yeah. He was trying to preserve my privacy. He didn't ask who they were.'

'Alec's a good kid.' He tilted her chin up, kissed her gently. 'You know this doesn't change how I feel about you, right?'

She swallowed hard. 'I'd hoped it wouldn't,' she whispered.

'You did what was best for Aidan.' He remembered the early years, right after he'd met her. She'd struggled to make ends meet. Struggled to get her degree, to make a life for herself. She'd been too proud to accept his help, had eaten a steady diet of ramen for the first year or two. 'He's had a good life, right?'

Her nod was shaky. 'I believe so, and I've watched. Carefully. Later, after I had my degree, I wanted to change my mind. I wanted him back, but I couldn't have done it, even if I'd had a legal leg to stand on, which I didn't. He was happy. Every time I've seen him, he's been happy.'

She reached for the dog, palming the side of his head as he leaned against them, once again sensing her mood. 'I've been hoping to hear from him for months. But if I don't, I'll be okay. Just the hope . . .' She faltered. 'I woke up the morning he turned seventeen and grieved, like I always have. Then . . . I looked around and knew I'd fallen so far into depression, retreated so far from life that even if he did seek me out, I'd be no good for him. I had a year to get good enough. I figured that it had taken me three years to get as bad as I was, that digging my way out wasn't going to happen overnight, but that I could do it in a year.'

'You had a goal,' he murmured. *Would she have worked so hard to dig her way out for me if I'd had the courage to tell her how I really felt four years ago? Probably not.* She hadn't been ready then to embrace that part of her that Evan had stolen. But motherly love . . . He thought of Stevie and Lucy and Paige with their babies. That was powerful. Powerful enough to yank Gwyn toward the light.

'I did. I found the therapist and then I found Tweety.' She smiled. 'And then I found you. Right where you'd been all along.'

He opened his mouth to say something wise. Something comforting. But all that came out was a hoarse 'I'm so glad you did.' Because he hadn't been sure how much longer he could have lasted.

'Me too.' She drew a breath, checked the time. 'We should call them now, even though it's late. If something happens during the night, I wouldn't be able to forgive myself.' She handed him her phone, Alec's email opened, before sliding off his lap.

'You want to be here while I call?'

'No. I think I'll go upstairs and get some water. Come on, Tweety.'

Annapolis, Maryland,
Wednesday 15 June, 10.05 P.M.

He zipped his trousers, feeling languid and well rested after fucking Kathryn in his shower. Kathryn lounged on the sofa behind him, looking long-leggedly sexy in his shirt. She'd been especially passionate tonight, because for her, watching him dismember a man was an aphrodisiac. It was just one of the things he'd come to love about her.

Nystrom was dead, his body cooling in the punishment room. Patton would deal with him in the morning.

'What are you going to do about Thorne?' Kathryn asked.

'I don't know,' he said honestly. 'He's whisked all his people away. I know where they are, but getting to them will be tricky. They're getting wise about texts too, so we'll have to come up with something else.'

She shrugged. 'They can't keep their families separated forever. They'll come home, they'll return to normal, and when they least suspect it, you'll get them again. In the meantime, you've got his clients angry with him and his club is closed.'

'You're right,' he said, smiling. 'Are we staying here tonight or going home?'

'Let's go home. I mean, Nystrom was fun while he was screaming, but now, knowing he's dead and getting nasty is kind of a turnoff.'

He didn't care much. The sight of a cooling corpse had never bothered him. 'Give me my shirt then,' he said. He grabbed his cell phone from his desk to slide it into his pocket, but noticed a new text from Margo, accompanied by two photos: one a grainy picture of a young man in an American football uniform, the second of a woman holding a baby. He flicked the screen to expand the photo, then realized the woman was a very young Gwyn Weaver.

Found you something, the text read. *His name is Aidan. What do you want me to do with him?*

He smiled and held out the phone to Kathryn, who'd tugged on her black dress and was now handing him his shirt.

'Oh, Margo,' she cooed. 'She hit gold.' She gave the phone back. 'What are you going to do?'

'What do you think I should do?'

'Have Patton pick him up,' Kathryn decided after a moment of thought. 'Drug him and leave him somewhere to be found.' She smiled. 'Just to show her that you can. Send her a photo. That'll hurt her enough for now. You don't want to break her yet. She's Thorne's favorite. You want to torment her until she has no choice but to leave him. Because she'll have to blame him sooner or later.'

'I like it.' He texted Margo the instructions, then added: *Good work. Get some sleep, my dear. I'll see you tomorrow.*

Hunt Valley, Maryland,
Wednesday 15 June, 10.05 P.M.

Thorne waited until he'd heard Gwyn climb the stairs, then dialed the number for Aidan's adopted family.

'Hello?' a man answered.

'Hello. I'd like to speak to Randy York.'

'If you're selling something, I'm not interested.'

'I'm not,' Thorne said quickly. 'Please give me just a moment. My name is Thomas Thorne. I'm sorry to be calling so late. Gwyn Weaver asked me to contact you.'

The man sucked in an audible breath. 'I know who you are. You're Gwyn's partner. The one who's wanted for murder.'

Thorne had to take a second to regroup. He should have anticipated that people outside the city had read about their situation. 'That is not entirely correct. I *am* Gwyn's partner.' In every way. 'But I am *not* wanted for murder.'

'That's not what I hear on the news.'

Thorne pinched the bridge of his nose. 'Well, I can give you references in Baltimore PD and the FBI and you can check for

419

yourself. For now, I'm calling on Gwyn's behalf. If you've been following this story in the news, you'll know that my family, my friends and my businesses have been targeted.'

A beat of silence. 'You're saying someone's trying to set you up?' The man's doubt was clear.

'Call Special Agent Joseph Carter. He'll give you the truth. For now, I am calling on behalf of Gwyn,' he repeated. 'Please, Mr York. This is important.'

'What? What does Gwyn want?' Now there was fear in the man's voice.

'To warn you. Her apartment was broken into tonight. Ransacked. Her safe with her important papers were stolen. Among them were some newspaper clippings of your son she'd collected over the years. It may be nothing, but she's worried that they'll go after Aidan to hurt her. Which will hurt me.'

'That's . . . preposterous.'

'My other business partner, Lucy Fitzpatrick, barely escaped a burning house with her two children this afternoon. Her son isn't quite three. He is my godson. Her daughter is almost one. She is Gwyn's goddaughter.'

'Oh my God.'

'My adopted father is in a cardiac care unit because someone broke into his home and attacked him. One of my investigators has a concussion and the officer who was guarding them is still in critical condition after being shot.'

'Oh. Oh no.' He dropped his voice to a hushed whisper. 'And you think these people will hurt Aidan?'

'Like I said, it could be nothing, but she wanted you to be aware so that Aidan could be on his guard. She figured he'd still be living at home, that he wouldn't have left for college yet.'

'Yes, he's still here.'

'That's good. That will ease her mind. You can tell him what you wish. But she trusts that your first priority will be to keep him safe.'

An extended exhale. 'All right. My wife and I will discuss what we'll tell him. For now, he's safe in his room. Do the police have any suspects?'

'I . . . I don't know. I'd suggest you call Agent Carter for that information.' He gave the man Carter's phone number.

'I'll call him first thing in the morning. Why . . . why didn't Gwyn call us herself?'

'Because she didn't want to put you on the spot. And she didn't want to risk Aidan answering. She especially doesn't want to pressure him.'

'That's kind of her.' He hesitated a few beats. 'We told him. When he was eighteen. We told him that we'd adopted him. We told him what we knew about his birth mother. His reaction was . . . typically Aidan. He's a stoic kid. Keeps his emotions close to the vest.'

'Like his mother,' Thorne said softly. 'Look. Gwyn suffered a terrible trauma four years ago. It was the knowledge that Aidan was turning eighteen soon that helped her find her way back to who she'd been before.'

'I know about that. I keep up with her too. In the news, I mean. My wife and I were so glad to read that she was all right after that attack.'

She wasn't all right, Thorne thought. *She's not totally all right even now. But she will be.* He'd make sure of it.

'I'm not telling you this so that you feel pressured either. I just want you to know that Aidan continues to be important to her. If he ever chooses to meet her, she'll be ready. For now, it's important that he's kept safe.'

'Thank you. Can I reach you at this number? The one you called me from?'

'For now, yes. It's a temporary line. You can also reach me through Agent Carter.'

'Thank you for calling. I hope you work through all this soon.'

'So do I.'

Twenty-five

Hunt Valley, Maryland,
Wednesday 15 June, 10.35 P.M.

Thorne checked his phone for the thirtieth time in fifteen minutes. Gwyn hadn't come back from her water-getting expedition and she should have. He'd gotten up to go find her several times, but forced himself to sit. She'd needed space. He'd give her space.

But he was worried. They were in a locked house with better security than Fort Knox, and she hadn't been out of his sight long enough to take a really long shower. But he was losing his mind. Was that what they were going to be reduced to? Traveling in groups? Sleeping in the same house? Sequestering the moms and children hundreds of miles away?

Yeah. Apparently they were. *Nobody can sustain this. Tavilla knows this. His son went to prison and he's put us in prison.*

Had the tables been turned, it would have been poetic justice. But this was hell.

So stop whining and make him stop. But first, find her. Ease your mind.

Clay's downstairs was eerily quiet, the toys in the playroom stacked and abandoned. 'Gwyn?' he called, but there was no answer. He jogged up the stairs and stopped short. She was sitting at the kitchen table with Clay and Jamie, the latter stroking her hair as she hugged her enormous dog and cried into his neck. Tweety actually looked sad. Both Clay and Jamie wore expressions of pity.

Thorne's heart threatened to break all over again.

Clay pointed to a stack of T-shirts and jeans. 'I found some of Stevie's pre-baby clothes. They're more likely to fit Gwyn now.' He winced. 'Don't tell her I said "pre-baby". She'll hurt me.'

Gwyn choked on a laugh that sounded more like a sob. 'Yeah, she will,' she said, but didn't lift her head.

Jamie shot Thorne a helpless look. 'I think it just hit her that she's lost about everything in her apartment.'

No, that wasn't it. She wasn't crying over the loss of her things. But Thorne wasn't going to tell them the truth. Aidan – having him, losing him, being afraid for his safety, mourning that he'd turned eighteen and hadn't contacted her . . . All that was Gwyn's story to tell, if and when she decided to do so.

'Hey,' he murmured, crouching down beside her and pushing the dog away when a wet tongue came out to lick his face. 'You're exhausted. Let's get some sleep. All of us. We have work to do tomorrow. Tavilla has had us on the run. Now it's time to make *him* run.'

'Straight to fucking hell,' Clay muttered.

'I'd drink to that,' Jamie said grimly.

'How?' Gwyn asked, her face still hidden in Tweety's fur.

'By attacking the people he cares about. We know of two women – our office manager and our bartender. They were in that photo from last summer, taken at that Italian restaurant, Bruno's.'

'Where he still hangs out,' Jamie said.

Thorne nodded. 'I imagine the police have the place under surveillance. We know he has offices. Anne was a really good office manager.'

Gwyn snorted her derision. 'Bullshit.'

Jamie smiled. 'She's an evil bitch from hell, but I'm going to agree with Thorne on this one. That woman had an amazing filing system, and she never missed a birthday. Maybe she does office management for Tavilla too.'

Gwyn lifted her head. Her face was tear-streaked, but she was still the most beautiful woman Thorne had ever seen. 'You could have something there.'

'There was a child in Laura's social media,' Thorne went on. 'Or Bianca or Kathryn or whoever she is. It may not have been hers, but it belonged to someone. Babies get colds, get shots, need pediatricians.

We start there and see where it takes us. The point is, we have options. Let's get some sleep, and we'll plan tomorrow.'

'Okay.' She wiped her eyes on her sleeve, then grabbed the stack of clothing. 'Thanks for the clothes, Clay. And I won't tell Stevie what you said, because your son would be in kindergarten before you got laid again.'

Clay made a face. 'Thank you.'

She smiled at him. 'You're welcome. Come on, Tweety.' She waited until they were back in the guest room before turning to Thorne. 'Did you reach them?'

'I did. His father thanked me for the warning, and said he would keep him safe.'

She hesitated. 'They've told him, haven't they? They told him and he doesn't want to meet me.'

'Give the kid some time,' Thorne said, dodging the actual answer. 'Come here.' He led her to the bed and began unbuttoning her blouse. 'I'm going to put you to bed and give you a massage, and you're going to sleep.'

Hunt Valley, Maryland,
Thursday 16 June, 1.10 A.M.

Gwyn woke in a strange bed, but she wasn't afraid because she knew before she'd opened her eyes that she was with Thorne. He held her half sprawled over his body like he was an oversized pillow. Her head rested on his chest, his arm was around her shoulders, his hand firmly gripping her butt. One of her legs was lodged between his powerful thighs, and when she tried to move, he rumbled out a warning.

'Watch the knee, babe.'

Because she was only inches away from his groin. And his very erect cock. She slid one hand down until she could grab it. His rumble became a moan.

Tipping back her head, she kissed the underside of his jaw and wondered how long she'd been asleep. 'Did you sleep?'

'No,' he murmured. 'Just holding you.'

She rolled her shoulders experimentally, feeling no pain. 'That was some massage.'

'That was the plan,' he said. 'To make you feel better.'

She'd fallen asleep minutes into it, so there had been no mutual pleasuring. No satisfaction.

That was going to change. 'You know what I really liked?'

'The part where you melted into the mattress when I rubbed your shoulders?'

'Of course that. But I was thinking about Tuesday. In my bed.'

'Mmm.' He played with her hair. 'Which time?'

'All of them. But mostly when I was on my back and I could see your face the whole time.' She could hear his heart starting to beat a little faster. 'I was hoping we could do that again. Maybe soon? Like now?'

The next thing she knew, she was on her back and he was sliding down her body, lifting her legs over his shoulders, licking into her. She moaned quietly, not because she worried about anyone hearing her, but because the moment seemed too important, too sacred, for loud shouts and grunts and pleas for more.

'Thorne,' she whispered.

He lifted his head. 'What do you need?' he whispered back. 'Name it.'

She brushed his hair with her fingertips. 'Just you. Only you.'

He kissed the inside of her thigh, a soft brush of his lips. Then he was licking again, so gently, a luxurious lapping that stirred her, but not to a frenzy. Not yet.

She stretched like a cat, gripping the brass bars of the headboard, crying out when he worked two big fingers into her.

'All right?' he murmured.

She undulated her hips, grinding down on his fingers. 'Yes. Feels good. Don't stop. Please don't stop.'

'I won't,' he promised, a smile in his voice, then went back down on her, sucking her clit as he worked in a third finger.

She wasn't feeling calm and quiet any more. The need to come was spiraling upward, and she arched, needing to move. 'Thorne, now. Please. I'm ready.'

He paused to look at her, and she could see his amusement in the dim light. 'I'm not,' he said. 'You're impatient.'

'Damn right.' She swiveled her hips, trying to entice him, and he groaned.

'Impatient and mean,' he said.

'Impatient and *impatient*,' she corrected, wriggling against his fingers. 'I'm five seconds from doing this myself.'

Chuckling, he took a final lick, then pulled his fingers free and crawled up her body, his huge muscles rolling, his body sleek and graceful. She widened her legs to give him room. He planted his fists on either side of her head and rubbed up against her sensitized flesh.

'Thorne,' she moaned. 'Come on.'

'Shh,' he murmured. 'Let me.'

She opened her eyes and met his, and her heart stuttered. *There* was the look, the one she'd wanted to fall into and never leave. 'Yes.'

He hummed deep in his throat. 'Yes what?'

She smiled at him, letting go of the bars to brush her fingers over his cheeks. 'Whatever you want.'

He shuddered, hard. 'I want it all. All of you.' Canting his hips, he positioned himself and slid inside, and she cried out, filled again.

She'd never felt this full, not with anyone else. Not just her body, but her heart. Her soul, connected to his. And it was glorious. Her eyes abruptly stung and she blinked hard, feeling the tears slide down her face and into her hair.

Immediately he froze. 'Did I hurt you?'

'No.' She cupped his face. 'No. It's . . . perfect. You're perfect.'

He shuddered again. 'So tight. God. Not gonna last long.' He surged into her harder, picking up the pace, his eyes never leaving hers.

She wrapped her legs around his hips, lifting into him, meeting each thrust. Her orgasm built and built until suddenly it was *there*, crashing over her like a wave on the shore, stealing her breath, leaving her shaking and gasping his name.

He held himself perfectly still as she spasmed around him, then groaned, deep and guttural, as his own body whiplashed, his thrusts growing frantic and uncontrolled.

She could only watch, exhausted. Mesmerized. *He's beautiful.*

He threw his head back, arching until his body stretched taut above hers, like a powerful god rising from the sea. And she could feel him lose himself, feel him throbbing inside her, feel the heat of his come as it filled her as surely as he had.

He collapsed then, his trembling arms giving out. He caught himself, bracing his forearms on the mattress as violent shudders shook his body.

'Oh God,' he panted. He dropped his head, his hair tickling her cheek. 'Gwyn.'

She lifted a tired hand to stroke his hair. 'Thank you.'

He huffed a laugh. 'I think I'm supposed to thank *you*.'

She trailed her fingers down his face to the back of his neck, now hot and sweaty. And still perfect. 'Not just for the sex.' Her lips curved. 'Although that was amazing. Thank you for giving me back myself. I was so afraid for so long that I'd never be able to be like this again. And I couldn't have been with anyone but you.'

He kissed her then, so sweetly and full of joy. 'I love you.'

Her sigh was simple contentment. 'I love you too.'

With a little groan, he slid out and rolled onto his back, taking her with him. She let herself be arranged how he wanted her, which was exactly how she'd woken up, sprawled across his chest, one of his big hands on her butt. Her ear to his heart.

This was peace. And she'd take it for as long as she could. Which would be until morning, if they were lucky.

Hunt Valley, Maryland,
Thursday 16 June, 8.30 A.M.

Peace lasted until midway through breakfast. Seated at Clay's kitchen table and practically swimming in Stevie's too-big 'pre-baby' clothes, Gwyn was starting her second cup of coffee and tabbing through the news coverage online.

'Well?' Jamie asked, pointing to her laptop.

She shrugged. 'It's a mixed bag, although it looks like public opinion is starting to swing our way. Tavilla himself hasn't been

427

named as a suspect, probably because Joseph and Hyatt want all their ducks in a row first.'

'They need to fucking hurry up,' Frederick grumbled.

Thorne came in from the study, a frustrated frown on his face, and Gwyn patted the empty chair next to her. 'Colton Brandenberg still isn't answering?'

'No.' He slumped into the chair. 'Neither is Nystrom or Christina Brandenberg. Thanks,' he added when Frederick filled his coffee cup. 'JD's on the phone with Hyatt. They're going to be circulating the photo of the baby in Laura's Facebook photos to area pediatricians. They're positioning it as a possible child endangerment case because she's implicated in the murder of two Circus Freaks members. They recognized her as one of Tavilla's operatives who'd tried to infiltrate their gang, and then they were dead. It's a circumstantial link at best, but enough for BPD to try to find her through the baby.'

Gwyn blinked in surprise. 'Alistair will verify that she tried to infiltrate the Freaks?'

Thorne snorted. 'Hell, no. But Prew did, at least that the murdered men knew her. Remember, he followed them after Ming and Mowry tossed them out of the club Sunday night. Prew remembered them talking about the bartender, and when they called their boss, they asked if they should bring her in. Hyatt's not thrilled with approaching this as a child endangerment, but it sounds like he's cooperating at least.'

'Too little, too late,' Gwyn muttered. 'Would have helped if he'd told us about the EMT's murder himself. Makes me wonder what other secrets he's keeping.'

'A few,' a new voice said, and they all looked up to see Joseph Carter coming through the kitchen doorway, Clay right behind him. Joseph looked disgruntled, but Clay seemed a little smug.

'Joseph,' Thorne said with a nod. 'Why are you here?'

'I came to get you,' he said, then gave Clay a sour look. 'You didn't have to search my briefcase.'

'I had Alec scan Joseph and his briefcase for listening devices,' Clay said, a twinkle in his eyes. He and Joseph were close, but they seemed to take great delight in needling one another. 'Anything that comes in or out gets scanned. No exceptions.'

Joseph rolled his eyes. 'Jesus,' he muttered. 'Can I at least have some coffee?'

Thorne gave it to him, stone-faced. 'What other secrets?'

Joseph sat down and took a big gulp, wincing because it was hot. 'Nystrom is dead. You can stop calling him.'

Thorne flinched, then closed his eyes. 'Fuck. How?'

'Quite painfully, I'd imagine.' Joseph shook his head. 'One of those things that I wish I could unsee.' He tilted his head. 'How many medals did you have in high school, anyway?'

Thorne gave him a look of bewildered irritation. 'What?' Then his shoulders sagged. 'He had one of my medals in him?'

'Yep. And not much else.' Joseph took another gulp of coffee, grimacing. 'Let's just say that I have not had a pleasant morning, and leave it at that.'

'Where was he found?' Clay asked.

'In his house. He wasn't killed there, though. His cell phone records show that he called Hyatt last night. It was his last outgoing call.'

'JD gave him Hyatt's card,' Thorne said. 'Told him to call if he needed help. I gave him my card, but he ripped it up.'

'He waited too long to call Hyatt,' Joseph said. 'But you were good to try to help him, Thorne.'

'Not entirely altruistic on my part,' Thorne admitted. 'I was sure he knew about that fucking key ring.' He squeezed Gwyn's hand when she took his. 'I've been trying to reach Christina Brandenberg too. God, I hope she's not dead. She's the sister of Colton, who was the third of Richard's posse back then. He's a doctor now, apparently. At least he tried to do some good. She's protecting him.'

'I know,' Joseph said calmly, sipping from his cup. 'That's why I'm here. I got a message through the switchboard this morning from a Dr Colt. He and his sister are on their way to see me.'

Gwyn's mouth fell open. 'You could have led with that.'

Joseph narrowed his eyes. 'I got another call this morning. From a Mr York.'

Gwyn felt the blood drain from her head. 'What?'

Thorne winced. 'I told him to call Joseph for verification. I'm sorry. I forgot to tell you.'

Because he'd given her an amazing massage, then more amazing sex. She patted his hand. 'It's okay. What did he say?'

'He wanted to know if Thorne's story was true,' Joseph answered. 'I verified it. Next time, a heads-up would be nice.' Then his narrowed eyes softened. 'You should have told me, Gwyn. I would have given them protection.'

Gwyn's face heated as Clay, Jamie and Frederick stared at her. She dropped her gaze to her cup. 'I had a baby. Gave him up for adoption. Records of him were in my fire safe.'

'Oh,' Jamie said softly. 'That's why you were crying last night. Oh, honey.' He wheeled his chair over and pulled her close, pressing a kiss to the top of her head. 'I'm sorry. I didn't know. I would have said different things.'

'I know you would have, but thanks.' She leaned into him for a moment, wishing he'd been her dad too. She returned her attention to Joseph. 'Is Aidan okay?'

Joseph frowned, and Gwyn's breath started to come in pants. Beside her, Thorne stiffened. 'No,' she said, hearing her own hysteria.

Joseph sighed. 'We don't know that anything's wrong. He's just not at home. His father was frantic when he called. The young man's friends say they had a party last night and that Aidan left with a girl. The girl says he left her house just before dawn and was going home.'

'Oh God, oh God, oh God.' Gwyn clamped her hand over her mouth and turned into Thorne's arms, which tightened around her.

'His father said he was at home when I called last night,' Thorne said.

Joseph sighed again. 'Yeah, well, he thought he was at the time. Mr York decided he wanted to talk to me first thing this morning before frightening his son. His friends admitted that Aidan had snuck out the window. That he'd been doing it for years.'

Like me. He's like me. Crawling out of windows to parties. Tavilla's got him, and now he's going to die. Like Nystrom.

'Gwyn.' Thorne gripped her shoulders. 'You need to breathe. You don't know that he's going to die. He could be with another friend.'

Gwyn hadn't even realized she'd said the words aloud. 'You don't believe that, though.'

Thorne squared his shoulders. 'No, I don't. But I also know we're not going to find him by losing our shit. I'm going to tell you what you told me on Sunday. I'm not going to give you time to process this. I need you here with me now.'

No, no, no, no. The chant filled her head. She wanted to curl up into a fetal position. She wanted to rock herself, like she had done right after leaving the hospital. After Evan.

No. Not going back there. Get it together, Gwyn. She dragged in a breath. 'What are you doing to locate him, Joseph?'

'The local field office is treating this as an abduction. They're forming the task force as we speak. I didn't want you to hear this on the news or from someone else.'

She jerked a nod. 'Thank you. Will you raid Tavilla's home and offices?'

'Not right now. We don't have anything connecting him to this that would allow us to get a warrant.'

She leaned into Thorne, breathing him in. Picturing all the yarn on the bulletin board connecting the victims to the perpetrators. The connections they couldn't yet explain were those to Tavilla. Why he had chosen to kill Patricia, and how he was tied to Linden Senior. And, of course, that motherfucking key ring.

'What about Linden Senior?' she asked. 'Can you bring him in?'

'For extorting Eileen Gilson into silence, yes. Maybe for interfering with the investigation into his son's murder nineteen years ago. But that's not enough to connect him to any of the rest of it.'

'Brandenberg will do that,' Thorne said. 'He has to. He's the only one left.'

Joseph put his empty coffee cup aside. 'Then let's go talk to him. He's meeting me and Hyatt in half an hour.'

Baltimore, Maryland,
Thursday 16 June, 9.30 A.M.

'What did Clay say?' Gwyn asked as they exited the elevator on the homicide floor of BPD. She, Thorne and JD had driven here with Joseph, while Frederick and Jamie had followed in Jamie's van.

Clay had stayed behind with Alec, who had now thrown himself into the search for the real Anne Poulin, not the woman who worked for Tavilla, but the one who'd left Montreal on a student visa. The real Anne Poulin was another link to Tavilla because she had once existed, but had been apparently erased and replaced by the woman who'd worked for Thorne for a whole year.

Tweety had also stayed behind, but Thorne was rethinking that decision, because Gwyn was still pale and dangerously on edge as she waited for an answer to her question.

He slid his phone into his pocket. 'He was staticky at the end because of the elevator, but I got the main gist. Stevie got a call this morning from the coach of Patricia's son's lacrosse team. He'd found Tristan Armistead, who confirmed he'd been "seeing" Patricia. He was seventeen when she first approached him. He'd been both elated and terrified by her attentions. He was being seduced by an older, experienced woman, but he also knew Patricia's son would not understand. When Patricia was murdered, he was afraid but didn't know who he could go to for help.' He narrowed his eyes at Joseph. 'He also said that one of Hyatt's men had already spoken to him. Told him to lay low.'

Joseph's eyes widened, showing rare shock. 'I didn't know that.'

Thorne believed him. 'Tristan said the cop who interviewed him accused him of calling Patricia to lure her away from home the night she was killed. He denies it. Says he'll give access to his cell records to disprove it. He heard from his teammates that his coach was looking for him, and contacted him. He's been sweating bullets for days, thinking the cops were going to arrest him or that Judge Segal was coming for him.'

'Who was the cop?' Joseph asked, dark color staining his cheekbones. He was pissed. Good. So was Thorne.

'Gave his name as Detective Hooper.'

Frederick gasped softly. 'That's the same name the guy gave to Sally Brewster, the one who was looking for Bernice Brown.'

'Because Bernice Brown supposedly lured *me* out on Saturday night,' Thorne said, 'after which two innocent people were killed in their trailer because someone thought Bernice was there.'

'But Detective Hooper doesn't exist,' Frederick said. 'I checked.'

'True,' Thorne said, 'but the man Tristan described reminds me a lot of that prick Brickman.'

'Like it's a shock that he's dirty,' Gwyn said bitterly. 'I hated that man on sight.'

JD was staring at an unoccupied desk in the bullpen. 'You know, when I finally met Cesar Tavilla last year, he was sitting right there. At that desk.'

'Tavilla was . . . here?' Thorne asked. He hadn't known that part.

JD nodded. 'Yeah. I'd been looking for him everywhere but hadn't found him. He has offices but never seemed to be there. I left loads of messages with his receptionist. We were looking for Gage Jarvis for murdering his wife. It was urgent because we were afraid he'd go after his daughter, who'd witnessed it. We knew Tavilla had seen Gage Jarvis because you gave us that photo, Thorne.'

'That I got from my contact Ramirez,' Thorne said grimly. 'Who is now dead. You're saying that Tavilla just showed up? How'd he get past security?'

'Good question. He wasn't on the security camera in the lobby, which meant someone found an alternative way to get him in here. We opened an investigation, but didn't get anywhere. As far as I know, it's still an open case in IA.'

'We figured that Tavilla had inside contacts,' Joseph said, his jaw grim. 'He's been able to stay a few steps ahead of us for years. Fuck. I didn't like that prick Brickman either.'

'What do we do with this information?' JD asked him quietly. 'Is Hyatt compromised?'

Joseph grimaced, agitated. 'Shit.' He straightened his spine and smoothed his expression. 'We'll keep the news about Tristan quiet for now. I'll tell Hyatt myself after this meeting with Dr Colt. If

Brickman is in the room, I'll find a reason to get him to leave.'

'This should be interesting,' Thorne muttered. He put his arm around Gwyn and drew her close. She leaned into him, her step momentarily faltering.

She was terrified for the boy she'd had to watch growing up from afar, and she had every right to be. She'd seen what had been done to Patricia first-hand and she knew about the others. He had no words of comfort, so he tightened his grip, holding her up.

'Just a little longer, baby,' he whispered, hoping like hell that was true. Her nod was jerky, but she was still with him, so he'd have to be satisfied with that.

He braced himself as he stepped into the conference room, the same room he'd been brought to after Gwyn and Stevie had been shot at. Right after they'd talked with Brent Kiley, the EMT. Who was now dead.

Colton Brandenberg came to his feet when they entered, his expression exhausted. And haunted. His sister remained seated beside his chair, giving Thorne a look of apology. He nodded to her, because he understood protecting one's family. He'd do anything for his.

'Tommy,' Colton said quietly. 'Or is it Thomas now?'

'It's just Thorne. Thank you for coming in.'

The man shook his head. 'Don't thank me,' he said darkly. 'Please.'

Shit, Thorne thought wearily. *What now?*

He helped Gwyn into a chair on the other side of the table and sat beside her, conscious of Frederick and Jamie behind him. Joseph took the chair on Thorne's left and Hyatt made the introductions.

'Dr Brandenberg wouldn't tell us anything until you got here, Thorne,' he said, his irritation clear. 'Now that you are, let's get this show on the road.'

Colton cleared his throat. 'It's Brandon Colt now, but people just call me Colt.' He spoke with an accent that he hadn't had when they were teens back in school, and Thorne wondered how long he'd been in Appalachia.

'Why shouldn't I thank you?' Thorne asked. If Colt wasn't going to help them, he'd rather know now than continue to hope for a revelation.

'Because I should have said something nineteen years ago,' Colt answered bitterly.

'But I'm telling it now and I hope it will help.' He drew a breath, gripping his sister's hand hard. 'My sister didn't know any of these details until earlier this morning, when I arrived in town.' He lifted a brow at Thorne. 'I got your message. How did you track me down?'

'I have enterprising friends.'

'You must. No one's found me in nineteen years. Because I changed my name and ran away.' He blew out a breath. 'Because I was a coward. I was terrified of Richard Linden's father. And Gil Segal.'

Thorne stared at him. 'Segal? Judge Segal? Why?'

'Not now, not because he's a judge. I was afraid of him back then. He was dating Patricia when she was in high school. Her parents had forbidden her to see him because he was so much older. He was in college and she was only fifteen. She didn't listen.'

Beside him, Gwyn sighed softly, but said nothing. Thorne took her hand under the table and squeezed it.

'Patricia was always unhappy,' Colt continued. 'At first we thought she was just moody. What the hell did we know? We were kids and we knew nothing about girls. By "we", I mean me, Chandler and Darian. Richard was the expert. He'd had sex a lot more than we had. Trouble was, he had to force the girls to give it to him.'

'You knew he was raping girls?' Thorne asked.

'No. Not at first. Not really until after we beat you up.' He dropped his gaze. 'For which I have been ashamed ever since.' He looked up, met Thorne's eyes. 'I'm sorry, Tommy. I mean Thorne. I was one hundred percent wrong that day.'

Thorne wasn't ready to accept his apology, so he just nodded. 'Tell us about Patricia.'

'Richard believed that Angie Ospina liked him. He wanted to believe it, at least. The day we beat you up, he'd boasted that she'd been all over him the night before. He suggested she might be up to

435

taking a few of us on at once.' He grimaced, as if still finding the notion contemptible. 'Chandler and Darian were all for it. I . . . wasn't. There was the typical macho bullshit. You know, asking if I was a pussy, or if I wasn't into girls at all. What they didn't know then is that I wasn't.'

It took Thorne a second. Then . . . 'Oh.'

Colt nodded grimly. 'Yeah. Oh. I obviously wasn't out then and it was critical to me to keep my secret. To seem as straight as I could be.' He glanced at his sister. 'Our parents were conservative. If they'd known, I'd have been thrown out.'

His sister's smile was tight and sad and loving all at once. 'I'd have taken you in.'

'Like you could afford another mouth to feed back then,' Colt said with a shake of his head. 'But I know you would have tried.'

'I always wondered why you hung with Richard and his friends,' Thorne said. 'You'd always been so nice before.'

'I know. I hated them. I hated myself. I was a mess. Not all of my rage that day was aimed at you. I was having trouble at home too. When you did the right thing that day, saving Angie, something in me just snapped. All that self-loathing just . . . It took over and I just remember being so mad. Like I couldn't see clearly. You were the most accessible target, and again, I'm sorry. I tried to find you after your trial, after I got my shit together, but you'd changed your name too.'

Thorne was more inclined now to give him absolution, but he'd wait to do so until they were alone. And after Colt actually gave them some useful information. 'I understand your mental state at the time,' was all he said. 'Can you tell us about the day Richard was killed?'

Colt's eyes registered the fact that Thorne had not accepted his apology, but he nodded. 'Richard was at the school that night because he was going to take your bass and destroy it. Darian, Chandler and I went with him, but I had a last-minute panic attack and refused to go inside. They laughed at me and left me outside. They had a key to the school – Richard had stolen it from his father, who had it because he was on the board or some bullshit. But they left the door cracked open with a brick so that I could join them if I changed my mind. I ducked behind a bush when Gil Segal got there, and he was . . . well, like a charging bull. He didn't see me, because I was hiding. Like a coward.' He drew a steadying breath. 'He grabbed the brick and ran inside. The door closed and locked behind him.' Colt looked away, his eyes focusing on the past. 'A few minutes later, the door busted open and Chandler and Darian came running out, white as ghosts and babbling that Gil was killing Richard, gutting him with a knife, screaming that he'd never put his filthy hands on Patricia again.'

He blinked, and his eyes refocused on Thorne. 'They ran, Chandler and Darian. I tried to run too, but I was frozen. It couldn't have been more than a minute later that you and Sherri arrived. I could see you on the curb, talking.' He swallowed. 'I always liked Sherri. She was kind to me, even though I was a mean, hateful mess.'

Thorne's throat closed. 'Yeah,' he whispered hoarsely, vividly remembering the girl he'd loved. 'She was kind.'

Gwyn squeezed his hand, resting her head against his arm. Understanding his grief. Not begrudging him a single memory of his first love. Gwyn was kind too, he thought. Under her sarcastic, prickly cactus exterior, she was a marshmallow. He had the sudden certainty that Sherri would have totally approved.

'You and Sherri went inside with your key,' Colt went on, 'and a few seconds later Gil Segal came out, all wild-eyed and covered in blood. He looked around and I thought he'd see me, but he didn't. He tossed a knife into a bush about five feet from the one I was hiding behind, then threw the brick . . . far. I don't know how far away exactly, but it landed in the parking lot. Split into pieces.'

Thorne frowned. 'That would have been close to a hundred feet.'

Colt shrugged. 'I heard it hit. I was surprised too, when I was getting my thoughts together for this morning, but I also remembered that Gil was on the track team in college. He did shot-put. A brick weighs only about a third of what a shot weighs in college. He was big. And really strong. He fucking terrified me that day. Literally was huffing like a bull.'

'The police never found the brick,' Jamie said from behind them. 'They did find the knife, though. What happened next?'

'Gil stood there huffing, like I said. And then he just went still. Again, I thought he'd seen me, but he pulled a cell phone from his pocket. It was the same kind Richard had. It might have been Richard's. He called 911 and reported intruders in the school. Said he could hear screams. Said for the cops to hurry. Then he hung up and ran away. Not like Chandler and Darian had done. He didn't tear out of there like a bat out of hell. He just jogged to his pickup truck and drove off.'

Thorne sucked in a breath. 'Pickup truck? Fucking hell. *He* killed Sherri and her father? Gil Segal, who's now a fucking *judge*?'

Colt looked tired. 'I don't know for sure. Probably.'

Gwyn was pressing her forehead against Thorne's arm and Jamie clutched his other shoulder. Supporting him.

'Okay,' Thorne breathed. 'Okay.' He closed his eyes because they were stinging with tears. *I walked away.* Allowed a killer to go free. *I'm sorry, Sherri. I'm so damn sorry.* He drew a breath, let it out. 'What about the key ring?'

Colt looked ill. He opened his mouth, then sighed. 'God.'

'Just tell them,' his sister urged. 'It'll all be over with.'

Colt's nod was shaky. 'It was the evening after we beat you up. We'd gone to Richard's house because he had the best video game system and his parents had an unlocked bar. They weren't home that night, the parents. Patricia came down to get some vodka and I remember thinking, "What the hell?" She was only fifteen.' His lips twisted bitterly. 'Richard poured her a drink and Patricia took it upstairs. Later, when we were all pretty drunk, Richard took out the key ring and dangled it in front of us. We were like, you drilled a hole in your medal, are you insane? He said it was his special good luck charm, not that he needed luck. He showed us a little baggie filled with powder. Called it his "yes dust". Said it made them all say yes. Or at least not say no. Then he went upstairs. Came back down a little while later looking relaxed. Like he'd just gotten laid. Chandler and Darian were cheering him on. He gave them the key. Told them to go for it.'

Thorne swallowed back the bile that burned his throat. 'He had a key to Patricia's room?'

438

Colt nodded. 'I . . . I left. Ran home. Threw up in the bushes on my way. I didn't know what to do with the information. I started to tell my father when I got home, but he was going off about how you, Tommy, were a troublemaker. How I should stay away from thugs like you and stick with "guys with class", like Richard. That making those friends in high school would pave the way when I got older. All I could think of was Richard dangling that key in front of us.' He shook his head, his self-loathing written all over his face. 'The next day at school, Richard and the others gave me hell for running away the night before. Questioned my masculinity again. When they decided to break into the school on Sunday night, I went with them. I actually had the thought that I could get that key away from Richard and throw it in the river. But Gil Segal must have found it first, because it ended up in Richard's body.'

Thorne's eyebrows shot up. 'How did you know about that?'

'I caught up with Darian and Chandler after they ran from the school. We met up at Darian's house. The Hinmans didn't have an unlocked bar, but they did have a fridge full of expensive beer. We got drunk again, and Darian and Chandler told me. They'd seen Gil shove the key in Richard's gut after he sliced him open. Which was after he'd beaten his face in with the brick. We made a pact never to tell. Then I got home and heard that Sherri had been killed in a car accident. A hit-and-run. With a truck. I knew Gil had done it. I knew he'd kill me too if I said a word. So I didn't. I let a killer walk free.'

His sister cleared her throat. 'To be fair, Colt had a breakdown after that. He was catatonic. My mother called me. I was out of college and living on my own by then. I came straight home and Colt was in his room, rocking back and forth, mute.'

Like Gwyn, Thorne thought. *After Evan.*

'You were hospitalized?' Jamie asked Colt.

'Yes. I was put on a seventy-two-hour suicide hold. When I got out, my father sent me to a private clinic. I was allowed out to testify in Thorne's trial. I never told anyone at the clinic what had happened. Maybe I would have healed faster if I had. I did heal, though, enough to be on my own. I was scared to go home. Scared to run into Darian or Chandler or, worse, Gil. One thing that did come out of therapy was me.' He made a face. 'My parents were less than enthusiastic. Cut me off financially. I decided to make a break of it and change my name. I got into a decent school and took on loans for med school, payable with service in disadvantaged communities. I paid off my financial obligations years ago, but I stayed.'

'Penance,' Thorne murmured.

'Yes,' Colt confirmed. He spread his hands on the table. 'That's all. I hope it helps.'

Joseph and Hyatt shared a glance. 'We can get warrants now,' Joseph said.

Hyatt nodded. 'This together with Eileen Gilson's testimony can get us a warrant for Linden Senior's financial records.'

'And for his house?' Gwyn asked, startling them. She hadn't spoken a word since they'd entered the room. 'Because if Richard had a key back then, someone put a lock on Patricia's door. And if someone put the lock there, they knew she had reason to need to protect herself.'

'Her parents,' Colt said grimly. 'One or both of them knew she was being molested by Richard.'

'Or at a minimum that he'd assaulted others, or had a predilection,' Gwyn said. 'They knew the significance of that key. They paid Kirby Gilson for it before Richard's body was autopsied. If the key became public, they'd have to acknowledge that they were harboring a sexual predator.'

'You're right,' Thorne murmured. He hadn't thought of that. 'Thank you.'

A kiss to his biceps was her answer.

'What about Segal?' JD asked. 'He knew too. He murdered Richard and then covered it up. We need to get a warrant for his arrest too.'

'We can bring him in for a chat,' Joseph said. 'I'd like to hear about his tie to Tavilla.'

'I'll ask him to come in,' Hyatt said. 'They have the viewing today, but it doesn't start for a few hours.'

Everyone started to move, but Frederick and Jamie both lifted their hands. 'Excuse us,' Frederick said. 'But as Thorne's attorneys, we want to clearly state that we expect a statement from the BPD and the FBI formally clearing him of any and all suspicion. Dr Colt wouldn't be here today were it not for Thorne's request. His businesses and his integrity have been hit hard by these blatant attempts to frame him.'

Thorne had to swallow again, this time out of gratitude. His guys had his back.

'We also expect this statement to be made in a press conference dedicated to this purpose,' Jamie continued. 'It will not be buried in the verbiage of statements on other topics, nor will it be attached at the end of another press conference like an afterthought.'

Jamie wasn't asking. He was telling. And both Hyatt and Joseph were nodding. 'We can do that,' Joseph said.

'Excuse *me*,' Colt's sister cut in. 'But what about Colt? The other two in Richard's circle of friends are dead. Will you protect my brother?'

Joseph stood. 'We can do that too. Come with me, Dr Colt. We'll get you situated in a temporary safe house.' He turned to Thorne. 'I want the rest of you to go home. Lay low. Let Hyatt and me do our jobs.'

Thorne nodded. 'Of course.' But he had no intention of hiding in Clay's house. He had to find leads on locations for Anne Poulin and Laura, because they would lead him to Tavilla. The wheels of justice moved too slowly and he wanted his friends – his family – out of danger.

Twenty-Six

Baltimore, Maryland,
Thursday 16 June, 12.15 P.M.

He looked away from his risotto when Patton leaned down to murmur in his ear. 'Sir? A word, please?'

'Of course.' He offered his lunch companions a quick apology before following Patton to Bruno's kitchen. Kathryn would tend to them for a few minutes. She was good with his clients and customers. Most of the men simply liked stealing glances at her cleavage. As long as they never touched, he could live with that. 'What's wrong?'

Because anyone who worked for him knew not to disturb him in business meetings. He was five minutes from landing a lucrative shipping contract that would enable him to expand his control of the docks. Whoever controlled the docks controlled the flow of . . . well, everything. And he wanted to control everything.

'The police are searching Linden's home.'

His jaw tightened. He'd expected that to take a good while longer. 'How did they get a warrant?'

'A man came into the police station to meet with Lieutenant Hyatt and Agent Carter this morning. Thorne and his group were also there.' Patton hesitated. 'His name is Brandon Colt now. It was—'

'Colton Brandenberg.' He slid his hand into the pocket of his trousers to hide the fact that he'd clenched it into an angry fist. 'That's impossible. He's dead.'

Again Patton hesitated. 'No, sir, he's not.'

442

He was already dialing Margo's number. 'Why is Colton Brandenberg alive?' he asked acidly when she answered, bypassing any greeting. It had been her responsibility to ensure that the man and his conscience wouldn't become a problem.

'He's not,' Margo said. In the background he could hear the baby crying. A door closed and the sound became muffled.

'What's wrong with Benny?'

'More teething. He's got one cutting through.' She sighed wearily. 'What is this about, Papa? I've had very little sleep.'

He pushed away any feelings of compassion. In this, she was not his daughter-in-law, the mother of his grandson. She was his employee and she had royally erred. 'Colton Brandenberg met with law enforcement this morning.'

She gasped. 'That's not possible. Ramirez killed him. I saw the body.'

'Did you do a positive identification?'

A beat of silence, then two. 'No,' she admitted. 'Ramirez forced Brandenberg's truck off a mountain road. It rolled into a ravine and there was a fire. His face was ruined.' More silence. 'What did Brandenberg tell them?' she asked timidly.

'Enough for them to get a warrant to search Linden's house.'

'Well, we knew that was a possibility when we chose Patricia as Thorne's "victim". All of this was done to discredit Thorne, remember? Not to actually have him imprisoned. A prison sentence would have been like hitting the Powerball.'

Her logical tone grated on him. He was spared what would have been an angry retort when Patton lifted a reluctant finger. 'There's more,' he whispered.

'Wait,' he barked at Margo before muting the call. 'Why didn't you say something?'

Patton looked away. 'You were already dialing her.'

He'd sought to teach Patton manners, not to beat him down. It appeared he'd be searching for a new right-hand man very soon. Margo was clearly not up to the task either. At least not now. Her attention was too fragmented.

'Well? What is it?'

443

Patton looked green. 'They've brought Judge Segal in for questioning.'

He literally felt the blood drain from his head and swayed on his feet for a second before gathering his composure. 'When?'

'I got the notification just as I was coming into the restaurant. He's been at BPD for about ten minutes by now.'

He gritted his teeth. The judge would talk. He'd break. *Because he's weak.* 'Go to his home. Do what you have to in order to make his son come to the door. Then take him. Do not kill him. Do you understand me?'

'Yes. Sir,' Patton added quickly.

'Take Kathryn with you. She can lure him out. Send me a photograph of him once you've taken him.'

'Yes, sir.' He started to turn, then paused. 'Is that all?'

'Where is the other boy? The son of Gwyn Weaver?'

'I dropped him off, just like Margo told me to. She has the photos you asked for.'

'Good. Go.' He unmuted his call. 'Are you still there?'

'Yes,' Margo said, sounding worried. 'What's going on?'

'They've brought the judge in for questioning.'

'*What?* No. That's not possible.'

'You didn't hear any of this with your hidden microphone?'

'No.' A long pause. 'It's gone quiet.'

'In other words, they found it.'

'I . . . I think so, yes. Perhaps.'

He drew in a breath. 'Send me the photos of the boy.'

'Gwyn Weaver's son?'

'Yes. Do it now. Then call your mother to take Benny. Your *distraction* could have ruined all my plans.'

'I'm sorry, Papa.'

'Sir,' he corrected. 'In this, I am "sir".'

Another beat of silence. 'I'm sorry, *sir*.' There was anger in her voice and he didn't care. She'd fucked this up. Badly. 'What can I do to help?' she added, and it sounded like she was speaking through clenched teeth.

'Come to the boat. Immediately. Wait in my office.'

'Yes, sir.'

Less than a minute later, Margo's email with the photos of Gwyn Weaver's son appeared in his inbox. He flicked through them until he found one that would work. It was a photo of the Weaver kid in the back of Patton's SUV. It had been taken in the darkness of a windowless garage, the only illumination the dome light in the hatch. Just bright enough to see the lump of a figure covered in an old blanket.

Not enough light to see a face. The blanket covered his clothing, and a cap, slightly askew, covered his hair. It was a generic enough photo. It could have been nearly anyone's son.

He froze for a moment as a sudden harsh pain of longing swept through him, compressing his chest and making it hard to breathe. *Colin.* He missed his son. But he forced his lungs to function and pushed the grief to the side. He'd grieve later, when he was alone. Right now, silencing Judge Gil Segal was his key priority.

He attached the photo to a text and added: *Be smart. Be silent.* Then he hit SEND. That was the best he could do until Patton and Kathryn retrieved Segal's son. Then he'd send more texts showing the boy's face. The judge was weak, but he wasn't stupid. And even if the boy was Richard's spawn, the judge loved him like he was his own flesh and blood. He'd make the right choice.

And if the judge didn't make the right choice?

He could make life difficult. But ultimately there would be nothing he could say to the police that wouldn't incriminate him even more.

Yes, I approached Segal. Because his obsessive research into Thomas Thorne had yielded a better result than he'd ever imagined possible. That the man had been acquitted of murder was a matter of public record. But someone had murdered Richard Linden nineteen years ago, and he'd continued asking questions until he'd dug the truth out of Darian Hinman and Chandler Nystrom. It hadn't been cheap, but he'd considered it one of the best deals he'd ever made.

He'd considered killing them at the time, but feared it would warn Thorne as to what was coming. And he'd wanted Thorne caught completely unaware.

Yes, I threatened Segal with exposure. But not for money. He didn't need money for one, nor did the judge have any to spare. He and his wife had spent their fortunes. Segal was a financially desperate man.

He was also very afraid of Thomas Thorne, having lived in fear for all these years that Thorne would discover his secret. Segal had never expected the boy he'd known as Thomas White to simply walk away. He had expected Thorne to avenge his Sherri.

It's what I would have done. I never would have walked away. He'd known that Thorne was weak, but the discovery of his cowardice had cemented his opinion.

As a young man Thorne had been broken by the trial, by the loss of his Sherri, and by the betrayal of his family. That fracture in his character still existed, but he had covered it by changing his name, reshaping his life so that it wasn't visible. Nevertheless, underneath it all was a broken man, afraid that all he'd built could be taken away.

So on that knowledge he'd made his plans. On that knowledge he'd offered Segal the opportunity to make his fear of Thorne go away forever.

The judge had accepted his offer. Had provided him with everything he'd needed to set up the crime. Except, of course, the victim who'd been found in Thorne's bed.

Killing Patricia's young lover would have been the most stupid thing he could have done. And unfair. Patricia hadn't deserved to be spared. And the discovery of her body in Thorne's bed had kicked off his plan so much more effectively.

But the judge wasn't supposed to have been suspected of murder. That was never part of the plan. He wouldn't have been either, not if Colton Brandenberg had been killed the way he was meant to have been. Now that the truth had come out, Segal might try to sacrifice him to make a deal.

In the end, whatever Segal told the police would be the judge's word against his own. Anything he said would be viewed through the lens of a man accused of Richard's murder. Even the boy with whom Patricia had been having her affair would come forward to say that Segal had threatened him.

The trouble was Thomas Thorne. Thorne would keep pushing the investigation. That was a certainty. Any charges brought against the judge would remove the spotlight from Thorne. He might even be cleared. And he had the feeling that Thorne would push to uncover how the judge connected to everything that had happened to his businesses and his friends. *How the judge connects to me.*

For the first time, he had doubts about his ability to achieve his plans. Killing Thorne was now an option he had to consider.

The return of Colton Brandenberg was a game-changer. Margo's misstep had tipped the balance precariously. Perhaps he'd assumed too quickly that she'd be an adequate successor. She'd always seemed so together. Always so intelligent and cool-headed. But when the pressure got too high, she'd screwed up.

He had expected too much of her, he knew that now. She was grieving Colin and caring for the baby, all at the same time. She'd be punished for her mistakes, but he had to admit he'd made mistakes too.

Grief would do that to a person. But now he had some difficult decisions to make. He dialed Kathryn.

'I'm with Patton,' she said after answering. 'We're on our way to pick up the judge's kid. We had to lose our tail. Looked like Feds this time.' She hesitated. 'I can't lie, Cesar. This situation is bad. Brandenberg showing up like that . . . alive? He was the block that could bring down the whole tower. Margo promised us that he'd been taken care of.'

'I know,' he said grimly. 'The judge will take the fall for Richard's murder and will not attempt to implicate me. Especially once we have his son.'

'What about Thorne? He's not gonna back down. You have to know that.'

'I know,' he said again, even more grimly.

She sighed. 'Hate to be the one to tell you this, but all that time we thought you had? It just got shortened dramatically. Thorne will not give up investigating you until he finds something that sticks. And in the meantime, he and his people will be a pain in the ass. They've already located the Poulins.'

He shrugged. 'I covered that eventuality a year ago, when I sent Margo to work for him.' They'd eliminated the Poulins. But he frowned, because they were supposed to have eliminated Colton Brandenberg too.

'I know, but I'm saying that they are digging and will continue to do so. Eventually they will uncover something we haven't planned for.'

She was saying what he was thinking, even though he did not want to be thinking it. 'You're saying I should just end him, rather than watching him suffer.'

'I'm saying you might not have the luxury of choice.'

'Kathryn,' he growled.

'*You* think you should end him, don't you?'

He found himself pouting like Benny. 'Yes. He is no longer worth the trouble. I agree.'

'Then that's what you should do. But be aware that bringing him in will not be easy. You can't just send Patton after him. He and his friends will be on their guard. Whatever you do, it will have to be quick, surgical and overpowering.'

'Such as?' He already knew how he'd play it, but he wanted her take. And as he listened to her plan, he realized once again how much he trusted her judgment. 'Can you make it happen?'

'Of course,' she said confidently. 'I'll have to pull some of your men away from their normal responsibilities. I won't touch your bodyguards, but I need your highest-ranked men on the street.'

He could forgo the income his men normally generated in a single day. Their customers might go to their competition for the day's drugs, but they'd be back. If not, his people would eliminate the competition. 'Do it. I have to get back to my lunch guests. They will be wondering where I've gone. What did you tell my lunch guests when you left?' The men who were about to award him a lucrative shipping contract.

'That you'd just received contracts from one of your Russian clients and needed me to translate them.'

'Perfect as usual. Message me when you have the Segal boy and when you've planned the hit on Thorne.' He ended the call and made his way back to his table, where his clients were finishing their meal. 'I am so sorry, gentlemen. I hope the food has been delicious?'

One of them, a big barrel-chested man, pointed to his empty plate with a chuckle. 'Hated it,' he said with a smile. 'Had to be forced to eat every bite.'

The other man looked appropriately wary. 'I hope everything is all right.'

Because no sane businessman made such a lucrative deal with a man who catered to drama.

'Everything is just fine. A minor issue, easily resolved.' He waved to a server, who refilled their wine glasses. 'Where were we?'

Hunt Valley, Maryland,
Thursday 16 June, 2.50 P.M.

'We need to do something,' Frederick murmured to Clay and Jamie. The three of them sat watching Thorne, who was miserably watching Gwyn, who stared out of the window on to Clay's backyard with a vacant expression. They hadn't heard anything from the Feds in Virginia who were searching for her son.

'I can't even imagine what she's going through,' Jamie murmured.

'I can,' Clay said flatly.

Frederick winced, because he'd been the cause of Clay's pain. He was the one who'd hidden Taylor from Clay for most of her life. Gwyn had wondered if her son was alive or dead for a few hours. Clay had wondered for *years*.

'Stop it,' Clay grunted impatiently.

'Stop what?' Jamie asked.

'I'm talking to Frederick. He gets this guilty look on his face. I wasn't blaming you.' Clay elbowed Frederick lightly. 'It was our wife's fault.'

'Oh, right.' Jamie shook his head. 'I forget you two shared a wife as well as a daughter.'

'Not my finest memory,' Frederick said.

'Nor mine,' Clay added. 'Besides, you understand what Gwyn's going through. You spent sleepless nights wondering where Carrie was when she ran away.'

Pain, both remembered and new, speared Frederick's heart. 'I did.' He glanced at Jamie, who looked curious but was too polite to ask. 'My oldest daughter didn't acclimate well to life on a ranch in the middle of nowhere.'

'When you went into hiding,' Jamie said. 'To protect Taylor.'

'Yeah,' Frederick said bitterly. 'For nothing. There was no threat, but I didn't know that at the time.' *Because I didn't ask the right questions. I simply reacted.* A father, protecting his child. 'Carrie ran away, back to Oakland, then to LA. She . . . OD'd. She didn't make it.'

Jamie gasped softly. 'I'm sorry, Frederick. I didn't know.'

'I don't talk about her often.' Because it still hurt so damn much. 'But yeah, I know about that kind of worrying. I did it. Every night. Wondered if she was all right. If she was in the gutter somewhere. If she was homeless, addicted. All of which were true. I don't have a happy ending to her story to cheer Gwyn up.'

'Yes, you do,' Clay said. 'Because you recognized the signs in Daisy and got her help.'

'No, Taylor recognized the signs in Daisy. I was too focused on turning my daughters into killing machines so that they could defend themselves against a threat that wasn't even real. Taylor begged me to get Daisy help and that's the only reason I let my daughter out of my sight long enough to go to rehab.'

'But you did,' Clay insisted. 'And she's well. Right?'

'Right.' At least according to the last reports he had of her. She'd stayed away from liquor stores. Her meal charges on her credit card had all been small – enough for food, but not booze. At least not inordinate amounts of booze. 'But I haven't heard from her in too long. Not in a few weeks. She's not returning my calls or my texts.'

Clay's brows rose. 'Did you ask Taylor? They're so close, maybe Daisy has been communicating with her instead.'

'I have asked Taylor. She's danced around the question. She has talked to Daisy, but won't tell me why Daisy isn't talking to me. She answers everything else or tells me how well Julie is doing in Chicago.'

Jamie frowned. 'Call her and demand an answer. We can't have you distracted with your own worries right now. You need to know your daughters are okay. All of them.'

It was a good point. Stepping away from the group, Frederick dialed Taylor.

She answered on the first ring. 'Dad, what's wrong? Have you heard anything about Gwyn's son?'

He could hear road noise in the background. 'Not yet. Where are you?'

'In the car with Joseph. He picked me up at the airport.'

He frowned. 'You're coming home?' It had been her plan when she'd left, but he'd really hoped she'd stay safe in Chicago. He should have known better.

'Yes. Traffic's snarled up, but I'll be there soon. Bye, Dad.'

'Wait. I called to ask you about Daisy. I need to know she's okay.'

A beat of silence. 'She's okay, Dad. I promise.'

But there was something awkward in his daughter's reply. Something she wasn't telling him. 'Taylor, I've just been advised that I cannot afford distractions right now. Please tell me what's going on. Why is she coming home early? Why isn't she talking to me?'

Taylor sighed. 'You've been monitoring her, haven't you?'

His defensive hackles raised reflexively. 'What are you talking about?'

'Oh, come on, Dad. You ask me for the truth and then you play dumb? You had someone following her around Europe, spying on her.'

His cheeks heated. 'Not spying. Exactly.'

'Then what *are* you calling it? Exactly? I'd be pissed too. You'd better not be spying on me,' she added darkly.

'I'm not. Look, I just . . . I wanted to be sure she was okay.'

'She is. Physically anyway. But she's awful mad, Dad. You've got some charred bridges to rebuild.'

'Is she still coming home?'

'Yeah. So be thinking about how to make this right. I need to go. Love you.'

451

'Love you too,' he murmured. Pocketing his cell, he rejoined the others. 'Daisy is okay. Just angry with me.'

Clay's brows went up. 'What did you do?'

He slumped into a chair. 'Had her followed around Europe.'

Jamie winced. 'Even I knew not to do that, no matter how much I worried about Thorne back then.'

But Clay looked sympathetic. 'I can understand the impulse. I can also understand why she's angry with you. She's twenty-five years old. Hardly a child.'

'I was worried about her, out there with all that temptation. I wanted her to try her wings, but I didn't want her to get them singed. France has such a drinking culture. There are bars every-where.'

'There are bars everywhere in the US,' Clay said logically. 'You're going to have to learn to trust her, Frederick.'

'I know.' He rubbed his temples. 'But at least I know she's alive. So I eliminated the distraction. Replaced it with another, but I can at least push that aside enough to focus on them and this.' He pointed to Thorne and Gwyn, then to the bulletin board, still covered with photos and string. 'What can we do?'

Clay shrugged. 'Find Tavilla and beat the shit out of him, then leave him for rival gangs to dissect and dismember?'

Jamie nodded. 'I like that idea. I kept wondering when we were talking to Joseph Carter and Lieutenant Hyatt if they know where Tavilla is. We know he hangs out at that restaurant sometimes. The one where the photo of Anne and Laura was taken.'

'I'm sure they have that place under surveillance,' Clay said. 'While you were at the police station with Joseph, Alec and I spent the morning looking for records of Anne Poulin in Montreal. Alec found a report on a sixteen-year-old runaway with that name. He found a phone number for the family and I left a message, but their voicemail greeting was in French and my French is worse than nil. I left my phone number, plus Thorne's and Joseph's. We haven't heard back. We haven't found any birth or death records for her. It's more difficult when you cross borders, which I'm sure Tavilla knew and took full advantage of.'

'And tracing the kid in the bartender's social media?' Frederick asked.

Clay shook his head. 'Nothing yet.'

A phone buzzed on the coffee table, startling them. 'It's yours, Thorne,' Jamie called, and Thorne rushed over to answer it. The expression of mixed hope and dread on Gwyn's face as she turned from the window broke Frederick's heart.

'I don't recognize the number,' Thorne said.

'It's a Montreal area code,' Clay told him as Thorne hit ACCEPT and SPEAKER with a trembling finger.

'Yes?' Thorne's voice betrayed none of his tension.

Clay was on his own phone, texting, presumably to Alec, because the young IT whizz slipped into the living room from Clay's office, his laptop open.

'Hello.' The voice was wobbly and . . . French? 'I'd like to speak to Thomas Thorne?'

Yes, French, Frederick thought, his heart sinking along with Gwyn's expression as realization hit that this was not about her boy.

'This is Thorne,' Thorne said. 'How can I help you?'

'My name is Fannie Poulin,' the woman said, her speech stilted. 'I heard your voicemail. I apologize for my English. It is not my first language.'

'It's fine,' Thorne assured her. 'How can I help you?' he asked again.

'Your voicemail . . . you said you were looking for my daughter Anne.'

'We are. When did you last see her?'

'Face to face, maybe ten years ago. But we speak on the telephone.'

Thorne frowned, clearly thinking the same thing that Frederick was – that this felt too convenient. 'She hasn't visited you? Not in all this time?'

'No. She has let me know she is still alive. That is all. She ran away, you see.'

'Why?' Thorne asked. He looked at Alec, who waved at him to keep talking. He was recording the conversation, hoping to get some clues to the identity or location of the speaker.

'Because her stepfather was . . . They did not get along.'

'I see. Do you have an address where we might reach her?'

'I do.' She recited it and Thorne noted it down. 'Why are you looking for her?'

Thorne hesitated, visibly weighing his words. 'We have reason to believe she might be in danger.'

'Oh no.' The woman's voice wobbled again, this time with fear. 'If you would, please let me know when you find her.'

'We will. Thank you.' Thorne hung up and sighed. 'Who believes that was legit?'

Frederick shook his head. 'She didn't even ask why her daughter was in danger or where you were located or how you knew her. I'd want to know all of that if my daughter ran away.'

Surprisingly, Alec disagreed. 'It was legit in that her voice is consistent with the one on the voicemail greeting. That number is the one in Montreal's phone listing. It was also the one listed in the police report on Anne's disappearance. The i's are all dotted. If you want to double-check, call the number back and see who picks up. If it's spoofed, it won't be the same woman.'

'Call from one of the burner phones,' Clay said. 'See if the same person picks up for a stranger.'

Thorne did so, and they were all a little surprised when the same woman answered. 'Hello?'

'Hello, Madame Poulin,' Thorne said quickly. 'I'm sorry to bother you, but I was hoping you had some photographs of Anne.'

'Only old snapshots from when she was small. They are packed away.'

'I see. You don't have anything recent?'

'No,' the woman said sadly. 'Nothing. I wish I did.'

'Well then, thank you for your time.' Thorne ended the call and turned to the group. 'This could be a legit lead,' he allowed. 'Maybe it feels wrong because everything else we've had to find out the hard way. This just dropped in our lap.'

'It hardly dropped in your lap,' Alec protested. 'Finding that missing person report was damn difficult. You act like I just pulled it out of my ass.'

Thorne raised his hands, palms out. 'Sorry. I didn't mean to insult you. I'm just . . . skeptical.'

'Then be skeptical,' Alec grumbled. 'But don't call this easy.'

'Sorry,' Thorne apologized again. 'Don't worry, Alec. I know how lucky I am to have you.'

Alec nodded, still disgruntled. 'Anne's address is an apartment building. Appears to be a walkup.'

'Then I'm out,' Jamie said, disgusted. 'Give the address to Joseph. Let him investigate it.'

Thorne looked doubtful. 'I'll have him meet me there. But I'm not giving this away. If it's a real lead, I want to find Anne. I want to find out who she is to Tavilla.'

Alec's mouth flattened. 'That's smart, especially since it seems your Fed has been holding back on you. A bunch of black suits are searching the judge's house as we speak. Got themselves a warrant and everything.'

Thorne's mouth opened. 'How do you know that?'

'It's on the police scanner and now the news. Reporters are gathered in front of Segal's house. Nobody was home, so they broke the door in. They're carting out computers and boxes of files. One of the reporters says the judge has a recent history of odd rulings, which Paige told us a few days ago. I was looking into it when Clay told me Ms Poulin was calling.'

'Fucking hell,' Thorne muttered. 'I trusted Joseph.'

'You still can,' Clay insisted. 'He has a Fed agenda, but he'll do the right thing. I trusted him with my family, Thorne.'

'You're right. I know it.' Thorne rubbed the back of his neck. 'I'm edgy.'

'You have a right to be,' Clay said kindly. 'We all do. Take a breath and think this through.'

'Maybe Joseph just hasn't had a chance to tell you yet,' Frederick said.

'He was driving the car with Taylor when you talked to her,' Thorne said, unconvinced. 'He could have told us then.'

Clay's sigh was exasperated. 'Maybe he's busy. Let's call him with Anne Poulin's address and have him meet us there.'

455

Thorne made the call then huffed a frustrated breath and hung up. 'Went straight to voicemail. He must be on his phone. I'll text him to call me. I don't want to leave this information on voicemail. I want to be sure he's heard me. Who's with me?'

Frederick and Clay said, 'Me,' at the same time.

'And me.' Gwyn followed them to the door.

Thorne stood in her way, blocking her path. 'No.'

She looked up at him stubbornly. 'Yes. The closer I stick to you, the safer I am. If I'm with you, it's less likely I'll be shot or carved into pieces or blown to bits, because he doesn't want to kill *you*.' She looked up at Thorne, her eyes stark. 'And if I hear bad news about Aidan, I'm going to need you.'

Thorne looked like he'd say no again, but those last few words had his posture softening. 'All right. But stay close.'

Hunt Valley, Maryland,
Thursday 16 June, 3.10 P.M.

Shot or carved into pieces . . . Huddled in the back of their borrowed SUV, Gwyn choked back the bile that burned her throat. Either of those things could be happening to Aidan right now.

Because I care about him and because Thorne cares about me. She'd seen the devastation on Thorne's face, because he knew this was true. His family, his friends, they were all being tormented because he cared about them.

He knew that sooner or later they would break, the strain too much to endure. So far no one had been seriously hurt, except for Agent Ingram and it appeared he'd survive. He was still in ICU, but had been upgraded from critical to serious.

But if one of them died? Then what? Thorne would walk away to protect them, she knew that already. He'd give himself up to Tavilla, and if that didn't work? She didn't want to think about it.

She glanced over at him, needing to see his face. Needing him to tell her that this was going to be all right, that Aidan would be found alive, that Tavilla would be arrested, and that all of this would *stop*. But his gaze was darting in every direction, trying to spot a threat in time to neutralize it. In the front passenger seat, Clay did the same. Frederick drove grimly, as if anticipating an obstacle course.

I shouldn't have come. They'll try to protect me first. She'd opened her mouth to ask Frederick to turn around, to take her back to Clay's, when Thorne's phone buzzed.

'Joseph,' he answered. 'I've been trying to reach you.' He told him about the call from Montreal. 'I wanted to be sure you got the message. We're just leaving Clay's house. I want you to meet me at Anne's address.' Joseph must have told him to go back to Clay's, because Thorne's brow crunched in a frown. 'No. I'll see you there. Why didn't you tell us that you were serving a warrant on Judge Segal's home?'

Gwyn was distracted from Thorne's conversation when her own phone buzzed with an incoming text. A photo. The preview screen showed a blanket-covered figure, and new dread settled over her. She opened the text and couldn't stop the cry that escaped her throat.

It was Aidan, lying on a concrete floor in a heap. Blood pooled around his head. 'No,' she cried hoarsely.

Thorne leaned over to look and swore. Slowing to turn onto the road at the end of Clay's long driveway, Frederick looked up into the rear-view mirror and—

The sudden impact stole Gwyn's breath and had her crying out again, this time in pain. From the corner of her eye she'd seen the approaching Hummer roar out of the trees, a split second before it rammed them broadside. Frederick struggled to maintain control as their SUV was pushed off the road, careening down a slight hill to smash into a tree.

Then everything was suddenly still, too still. Pulse skyrocketing, Gwyn pushed her hair out of her eyes to look up. The airbags in the front and sides had deployed. Frederick was on the phone, calling 911. Thorne was searching for his own phone, having dropped it during the collision. Clay was blinking rapidly, his side of the SUV having taken the brunt of the collision with the tree.

The first bullets hit the tires in sync – one, two, three, four – like a well-oiled machine. The next ones smashed into the bullet-resistant windows from all sides, rocking the SUV in little jiggles but not penetrating the interior of the car.

'There are at least six gunmen,' Frederick said grimly to the 911 operator. 'You still with us, Clay?'

'Yeah,' Clay said unsteadily. He pushed the now-deflated airbag aside and reached to his feet, bringing up the rifle he'd placed there.

This is it, Gwyn thought, and drew her weapon from the girdle holster. She handed it to Thorne as the next barrage of bullets hit. The glass was compromised now, little protrusions pushing into the car interior. She could no longer see through it.

She pulled a smaller handgun from the holster at her thigh and racked it, making sure there was a bullet in the chamber.

'I'll get out,' Thorne said, his voice tight and thin. 'Let them have me.'

'No!' the three of them shouted in unison.

Thorne racked the slide of the gun she'd given him. 'You are going to die. This glass can't hold much longer. I will not be the cause of this.'

Slipping his phone into his pocket, Frederick shared a glance with Clay, who nodded. 'Here's what we're going to do,' Frederick said calmly, with authority. 'Thorne, take your hand off the door handle.'

More bullets pelted the windows, these in a steady stream, all aimed at one target – a one-inch-square area of glass on Frederick's window.

Thorne complied. 'And then?' he asked acidly.

'Clay and I will open our doors, roll out and start shooting. You and Gwyn wait five seconds, then do the same. We'll take out as many as we can for you. It's six on four. Not bad odds.'

And they were all wearing Kevlar, Gwyn thought, releasing her seat belt. *We can do this. We have to do this.*

'On my count,' Clay said. 'One, two, three.'

Frederick and Clay threw their doors open and started firing, but Thorne grabbed Gwyn and pulled her to the floor, throwing himself over her before reaching up and opening her door. For a moment, all she could hear was shooting. She struggled against Thorne, then felt him jolt. Then shudder.

'Fuck,' he snarled. 'Dart gun.' He fell on top of her, nearly

458

suffocating her. 'Don't fight,' he ordered thickly. 'Let them try to move me. Then shoot.'

The shooting abruptly stopped and Gwyn's heart stopped with it. *Frederick and Clay.* They had to be all right. Then she heard a barked command: 'On your knees.'

That hadn't come from either of their guys. Dammit.

But at least the two men were still alive enough to be forced to kneel.

Atop her, Thorne was still breathing. 'Love you,' he whispered in her ear.

'Love you,' she tried to whisper back, but it was becoming increasingly hard to breathe.

Suddenly Thorne was sliding off her, a grunted curse coming from somewhere near his feet. 'Fucker's heavy. I didn't give him that much, I swear to fucking God!'

'Better not have,' another voice said. 'Boss gutted the two who OD'd him the last time. Nasty.'

'Great, thanks.'

Pulling an extra clip from her girdle holster, Gwyn lifted her eyes in time to see her door opening. As instructed, she propped herself on her elbows, took aim and unloaded her clip.

'Holy fuck!' The man moaned as he staggered back, and Gwyn reloaded, on autopilot. A second man slammed her door closed. Twisting, she sat up, her back against her car door, the pockmarks in the armored metal poking into her skin. Thorne had been pulled out of the vehicle onto the ground. He lay on his back, his face and all his muscles gone slack.

'Sonofabitch,' she yelled. If they'd killed him, she'd—

Her door flew open and a pair of arms grabbed her from behind. 'No!' she cried, desperately trying to twist free, but the arms held on.

'Get her fucking gun,' the man holding her ordered. 'She's like . . . like I'm holding a fucking snake.'

Aiming down, Gwyn shot at the booted feet. The man cursed in shock, grabbing her wrist so hard she felt something pop. She dropped the gun and wrenched free, falling to the ground. Rolling to her feet, she began to run away from the SUV, toward Clay's house.

'Freeze!' a voice called. 'Take another step and loverboy dies.'

She faltered, turning to see a masked man on one knee next to Thorne, his gun pointed at Thorne's temple. *Run!* She could hear Thorne's voice in her mind, but her feet wouldn't move.

'Smart girl,' the man said.

From where she stood behind the SUV, she could see the entire battlefield. The truck that had rammed them was an older-model Hummer and had sustained no damage at all, but their SUV was completely trashed.

Two of the masked men lay on the ground, unmoving. Their black clothing was dark and shiny, and blood was pooled around them. A third man lay in a fetal position on her side of the SUV. He was rocking and moaning.

She felt grim satisfaction for only a split second. Yes, she'd taken one out, but there were three left. Two stood over Clay and Frederick, who were both stony-faced. The third, who knelt beside Thorne, came to his feet.

'I'm probably older than you are,' Gwyn said flatly.

'What?' the man asked, and even with his face covered, she could tell he was giving her a puzzled look.

'Don't call me "girl". I'm older than you are.'

'Pack a damn fine wallop too,' the man grumbled. 'We deserve double pay for this job. Get your ass over here. I'm not chasing you.'

Probably because she'd shot his foot, at least once. *Good for me*, she thought as she moved to Thorne's side, dropping to her knees and taking his hand, her heart beating so hard she could barely breathe.

She found his pulse easily, slow but strong. They hadn't killed him. Relief hit her like the truck had hit their SUV, leaving her lightheaded and grateful that she was kneeling, because she wasn't sure she could have remained standing.

The man whose foot she'd shot wasn't injured so badly that he couldn't function. He motioned to the two men guarding Clay and Frederick. 'Cuff 'em, hands and feet. Then one of you stand guard over them. The other, come and help me with Thorne.'

A van appeared from a nearby clump of trees that had been

concealing it from view. It rolled to a stop next to Thorne. The men opened the side door. Then one grabbed Thorne's feet, the other gripping under his arms, and together they swung him into the empty cargo area and cuffed him with zip ties.

The man in charge swept into a bow, gesturing to the open van door. 'Get in, or I throw you in,' he snarled.

With a helpless look back at Frederick and Clay, who were watching grimly, Gwyn climbed into the van, freezing at the sight of the woman behind the wheel.

Laura. Their bartender. Aka . . . 'Kathryn,' Gwyn snarled her name.

Kathryn laughed, surprised. 'Well, hello to you too. I'd like to know how you found out my real name, but we'll handle that later. Please restrain her. And make sure she's not carrying anything else.'

The man did so, then climbed in after her. He pointed to the second man. 'Go help him get the bodies in the Hummer, and stow the two old guys. We'll meet you there.'

Then the door was closed and Kathryn eased the van up the hill and back onto the road. Stepping on the accelerator, she sped toward town.

'I'd welcome you,' she said cheerily as she drove, 'but you won't be around that much longer. And the time you have left will not be enjoyable.'

Twenty-seven

Hunt Valley, Maryland,
Thursday 16 June, 3.30 P.M.

Frederick watched the van drive away, disgusted with himself. 'Fuck this,' he muttered. 'The white van that took Thorne and Gwyn is driving away.' He'd phrased it as carefully as he could, hoping he was still connected to the 911 operator and that he wasn't tipping off the gunmen that he'd just reported Gwyn and Thorne's disappearance.

'I know,' Clay muttered back. 'He called us old.'

Frederick snorted a shocked laugh. 'Shut up. This is serious. What are we going to do?'

'You're going to shut the fuck up,' the guard snarled. 'Or not.' He delivered a kick to Clay's ribs. 'I'd enjoy fucking you up. The guy you killed was my cousin.'

Clay breathed out slowly, and Frederick had known him – and trained with him – long enough to know that that long breath masked a moan of pain. Arching his back and neck, Frederick looked around and saw the man who'd helped drag Thorne into the van. He was walking toward the Hummer, favoring one leg. The man who Gwyn had shot in the foot had left with the white van, so either he or Clay must have injured this guy. They'd have to use that fact in their favor.

Frederick glanced at Clay and saw him noting the same thing.

The man who'd kicked Clay squatted beside them. 'The boss is going to slice you up while you're still alive. I've seen him do it before. The guy gettin' sliced always screams and screams until he

462

passes out. The boss lets him come to, then starts all over again. I'm hoping he lets me help this time. I hope he lets me cut you.' Holding his handgun by the barrel, he swung it up like he was about to bring it down on Clay's head. Clay closed his eyes and gritted his teeth against the blow.

Rocking up to his knees, Frederick was about to throw his body into the gunman's when another shot rang out. The gunman jerked, then crumpled into a moaning heap. Frederick sat back on his heels, stunned.

'What the actual fuck?' Clay muttered. He rolled onto his back and sat up, the movement ungainly. His wince indicated that he probably had a cracked rib or two.

The other guard began to run for the Hummer, but five more shots rang out, four of them hitting the tires, just like their attackers had done to the SUV. The would-be driver changed direction and headed for the trees, but soon came out with his hands raised, dragging one leg, two young women with rifles behind him. One was tall, with long black hair, the other a petite blonde.

Frederick let out a harsh breath. 'Oh my God.'

'What?' Clay's back was to the direction of the trees and he twisted his body, doing a one-eighty rotation on his ass. 'Taylor?'

'And Daisy.' Frederick's eldest daughter did not look happy to see him.

Taylor came running when she saw them. 'Dad! Pops!' She kicked the handgun away from the now-bleeding man, then dropped to her knees, pulling a switchblade from her boot. She cut the zip ties and inspected their faces, then mouthed *Wow* at the ruined SUV.

'What happened here?' she asked.

'I could ask you the same question,' Clay said, rubbing his wrists. He looked at the Hummer, all four of its tires now flat. 'Nice shooting, baby.'

'I only did one side. Daisy did the other.' Taylor popped to her feet, searching the pockets of one of the dead gunmen.

'What are you doing?' Daisy asked impatiently.

'Finding zip ties. Here they are.' Taylor dug them out and cuffed

463

both survivors, because the one who had been about to brain Clay was still breathing. And moaning. Loudly.

'You can relax now,' Taylor told Daisy, who lowered her rifle but did not appear convinced.

'You said it was calm and quiet out in the country,' she said to Taylor, and Frederick was very aware that she was ignoring him completely.

'It is, except for this week.' Taylor extended a hand to both him and Clay, pulling them to their feet. Clay groaned softly and Taylor looked concerned. 'What happened?'

'Probably a bruised rib,' Clay said, and Frederick didn't correct him. Clay had reached for his phone and was dialing. 'We need to call this in. Did you pass a white van? They took Gwyn and Thorne.'

'Yes,' Taylor nodded grimly. 'Joseph is chasing them.'

'Voicemail,' Clay said, then texted the information to Joseph.

'How did you two get here?' Frederick asked as Clay dialed 911, stepping away to report their status. Hopefully the cops would be on their way after Frederick's first call, when they'd still been in the SUV.

'Joseph had picked up Daisy from the arrivals terminal at BWI and we were most of the way here when you called,' Taylor said. 'He was planning to drop us off at Clay's and head back to Judge Segal's home when he got Thorne's call. He heard the crash and knew you needed help. Luckily Thorne had just told him that you were leaving Clay's house. The 911 dispatch was feeding him information as you gave it to them, Dad. Joseph got your message that Thorne and Gwyn had been taken away in a white van. We were almost to Clay's driveway, so he stopped his SUV and told us to get out, because he was going to follow and he didn't want us in the line of fire. Joseph had extra rifles in the SUV, just in case we ran into trouble on the way from the airport. Daisy and I knew that you two were in danger, so we grabbed the rifles and got out. The white van passed by a few seconds later. We could see your wrecked SUV and this asshole –' she jabbed the toe of her boot into the gunman still writhing on the ground '– about to hit Clay with his gun. So I shot him. Then we saw the other asshole running away and we brought him back. Now you know it all.'

'Good timing,' Frederick offered, but Daisy deliberately looked away.

Taylor sighed at her sister's wordless rebuke. 'Not good enough, because they got Thorne and Gwyn.' She visibly tried to relax her bunched shoulders. 'Joseph was on the phone with one of his people when Thorne first called him, by the way. His team is searching the judge's house.'

Frederick nodded. 'We knew that. Alec caught it on the scanner.'

Taylor frowned. 'He'll catch this on the scanner too, and will be worried.'

'Hold on.' Frederick called Alec and assured him that he and Clay were okay, but that Thorne and Gwyn had been snatched. Before he could hang up, Jamie took the phone. 'What's happened?'

Frederick sighed. 'They drugged Thorne and dragged him away. Threatened to shoot him if Gwyn didn't cooperate, so she did. The last time I saw him, he was alive and breathing.'

'Oh my God,' Jamie whispered. 'No. Please.'

'I'm so sorry,' Frederick murmured. 'There were seven of them in two vehicles, including the driver of the van. We got three of the gunmen, between Clay, me and Gwyn. One of the survivors went in the van with Thorne and Gwyn. The bartender was driving.'

Jamie moaned. 'No. I told him to let Joseph handle this.'

Frederick wanted to reassure him, but all he could do was give him the facts. 'Joseph is in pursuit right now.'

'Okay,' Jamie whispered. 'I have to tell Phil. This could kill him.'

'We're going to get them back,' Frederick said firmly. 'I swear we're going to get them back.'

'How . . . Why are you there? Did they leave you?'

'No. Like I said, they had two vehicles. We were going in the second one, but that's when Joseph arrived. We have a survivor, who knows where they were going. We'll get him to tell us.'

'How?' Jamie asked, sounding so lost.

Frederick glared at the man who'd tried to run away. 'Don't worry about that. He will talk to me. I have to go. I'll call you back.'

Clay finished his call to 911 at the same time and walked over. 'What are you going to do?' he said under his breath.

'Don't ask,' Frederick said gruffly. 'Plausible deniability.'

Clay looked torn. 'Don't do anything you can't live with.'

'I can't live with Tavilla gutting Gwyn while Thorne watches,' he spat bitterly.

Clay nodded. 'What can I do to help?'

'Make sure my daughters don't see this,' Frederick whispered.

'Okay.' Clay squeezed his shoulder. 'Thorne would want you to keep your soul intact.'

Frederick was pretty sure Thorne would be more concerned that Gwyn not be murdered. He walked to the man who lay on the ground on his stomach, his hands and feet secured by zip ties. *So let's see if we can't make Junior here tell us what he knows.*

Looking over his shoulder, he saw that Clay had taken the girls a short distance away and was talking to them intently. Probably filling them in on everything that had been happening.

He bent over the survivor, keeping his voice quiet but deadly. 'Tell me where you were taking us.'

'Go to hell,' the man spat, his spittle landing on Frederick's shoe.

'I probably already am,' Frederick muttered, yanking him to his knees. Twisting his fingers in the man's hair, he jerked his head back. 'Tell me.'

The asshole tried in vain to twist out of Frederick's grip. 'Go. To. Hell.'

Goddammit. He did not want to do this. Crossing his fingers, Frederick jabbed them down into the hollow of the bastard's throat, ignoring the hacking cough and the writhing. Abruptly he pulled away. 'Tell me.'

Lungs heaving, the man turned toward him and threw up. Luckily Frederick had been anticipating that and jumped out of the way.

'Tell me,' he growled, and put his fingers back on the same spot. He tapped. The man puked again.

'No,' he begged. 'No, no, no.'

Palming the front and back of his captive's head, Frederick

466

pressed . . . hard. A sharp scream of agony burst free and Frederick released him. The man collapsed on the ground, shaking, the front of his trousers growing dark as he lost control of his bladder.

Frederick grabbed him by the hair again, jerking him upright. *'Tell me.'* He put a little pressure on the hollow of his throat. 'Tell me and I'll stop.' He added more pressure, aware of the time passing. The cops would be here in a minute, and as soon as this guy heard sirens, Frederick's leverage was gone. 'He won't know it was you.' A little more pressure. A little more puking. 'Tell me.'

'A boat,' the man rasped. 'He's on a boat.'

'That's good.' Frederick eased off, then pressed again. 'What's the name?'

'Señ . . . Señor del Mar.' He bit the words out and moaned. 'He's going to kill me.'

'Not if I catch him first,' Frederick whispered. 'That's your best hope right now. Where is it docked?'

The scream of sirens started up in the distance, and the man spat at Frederick again, tears streaming down his face. 'Go to hell.'

Frederick released him, letting him tumble to the ground. 'Tell me where it's docked. If we get to him, he can't kill you. I'm your best chance at surviving this.'

The man moaned. 'Chevalier. Now leave me alone.'

Suddenly drained, and feeling the full impact of his actions, Frederick stepped away and made a beeline for the trees where the van had been hiding. Dropping to his knees, he retched, losing everything he'd eaten that day. Which, luckily, was not a lot. His head fell forward, vile memories swirling in his mind, memories he truly thought he'd buried forever.

But there was no such thing as forever.

And they'd seen. His daughters had to have seen him, or at least heard the bastard's screams. Everyone in a five-mile radius had heard the bastard's screams.

God. I am a horrible person. At least now they could find Thorne and Gwyn. *Need to get up.* But his body would not cooperate, his knees buckling every time he tried to stand. He was shaking all over.

'Shh. It's all right.' Taylor's voice was warm in his ear, her hand rubbing his back in slow sweeps. 'You're okay. We're okay. We'll get Thorne and Gwyn back.' She pressed a water bottle into his hand. 'Drink.'

He struggled with the cap. 'Fuck,' he muttered.

She knelt beside him and pressed her lips to his temple. 'Let me help you, Dad.' She took the bottle from his hands and managed the cap in a single capable twist, then eased him back so that he sat on his heels. Lifting the bottle to his lips, she whispered, 'Drink.'

He obeyed, more than aware that their roles had switched, his child caring for him. He rinsed his mouth and spat, then drained the bottle in a few greedy gulps. He was still shaking, but not as violently.

She stretched her arm across his back. 'You're okay.'

'I know,' he murmured. 'But I wish you hadn't seen that.'

'Well,' she said practically, 'I can't disagree with you there.' She pulled at him until his head rested on her shoulder. 'What did you find out?'

'He's got a boat. The *Señor del Mar*.'

'*Lord of the Sea*,' she said softly. 'Makes sense. Tavilla's gang is Los Señores de la Tierra, or Lords of the Planet.'

Yes, it did make sense. 'It's docked at a marina called Chevalier. We need to get word to Joseph. Maybe he'll know where it is.'

'Clay will tell Joseph. He's behind us, texting him now.'

'Listening,' he murmured unhappily. He hadn't wanted anyone to see him torture the man into confessing. Clay was supposed to have kept his daughters from witnessing that. And if Clay and Taylor had been listening, Daisy probably had been too.

Taylor sighed. 'Yes, we were listening. He was worried about you, Dad. So was I.'

'I'm okay,' he said. 'Because you told me so.'

'Then it's true, because I'm rarely wrong.' She laughed when he scoffed at that. 'The marina being named Chevalier makes sense too,' she added. 'It means knight. If he's the Lord of the Planet, his gang would be his knights.'

That Tavilla had likely named his marina was troubling. That meant it might not be an actual marina at all, or not a public one, at least. 'The man's a fucking poet.'

'Hopefully a dead poet, soon enough.' She blew out a careful breath. 'How did you learn how to do . . . what you did?'

The word is 'torture', baby. But he didn't say that. No need to make this uglier than it was. But the answer came spilling out of him before he could call it back. 'Experience.'

Her flinch was tiny. 'You were trained when you were in the army?'

'No.' He clamped his lips together, unwilling to say more.

But Taylor was a smart cookie. She went very still and exhaled another careful breath. 'Daddy?' she whispered, her voice suddenly small. 'Did that happen to you?'

It was his turn to sigh. 'We are not going to speak of this.'

'Please. I need to know.'

No, you don't, baby. You really don't. But again he answered. 'Central America in the eighties. I was captured for a few weeks. It's over.'

'No, it's not. Not if it does this to you. But . . . I'll respect your wishes.'

'Thank you.' He looked down at his clothes. 'I need to change.'

'Yeah, you do. Come on, Dad. Let's go to Clay's house and get you cleaned up.' She rose, then pulled him to his feet with her.

His knees still wobbled, but he could lock them in place. 'Thanks, honey.'

She blinked a few times. 'I love you, Dad.'

He turned and . . . sighed. Because Daisy and Clay still stood there. Hoping so hard, he opened his arms, and then breathed again when Daisy walked into them and hugged him.

'You smell really bad, Dad,' Daisy whispered.

He bent to kiss the top of her head. Her mother had been so tiny. 'I know. I'm sorry.'

'I'm still really mad at you. But we'll talk later.'

'That's fair.' He nudged Taylor. 'That asshole kicked Clay in the ribs, really hard. Make sure he takes care of himself.'

'Sure thing.' Taylor left him to put her arm around her other dad.

'Clay seems nice,' Daisy murmured.

'He is.' He turned to look at her. 'And you did some great

469

shooting today. You saved us. Thank you,' he said.

She tipped her head back, lifting one side of her mouth. 'You're welcome.'

She walked with him out of the trees to where the police were now gathered. He was surprised to see Joseph with them.

'You're gray, Frederick,' he said.

'Thank you. Did you lose the van with Thorne and Gwyn?'

Joseph pointed to his SUV, looking frustrated, which for him was a big deal. The man didn't show a lot of emotion. 'Yeah.' His windows were shot up nearly as badly as those in the SUV he'd loaned them. 'The good news is the glass holds against a hell of a lot of bullets. My wife will be pleased.'

Frederick wished their glass had held against a few more bullets, because then Thorne and Gwyn would be safe, but he bit the words back. If they hadn't had the loaner SUV, they'd all have been dead in the first barrage. 'Does what Tavilla's man told me make sense?'

'Not yet. Chevalier isn't showing up in the marina listings. He could have been lying to you.'

'Maybe about the marina.' Because he'd heard sirens by then. 'I think the name of the boat is real.'

Joseph gave him a long, long look, as if he knew exactly what Frederick had done. 'All right,' was all he said.

'Can my dads go home now, Joseph?' Taylor asked him. 'They're kind of banged up.'

'Yes, of course. I'll send someone by to get their statements shortly. I've got to get to the police station. The evidence found in the search of the judge's house is starting to trickle in. I'm hoping there's something there that can tie him to Tavilla.'

Frederick wanted to explode. 'That he just attacked us and took Thorne and Gwyn isn't enough?'

Joseph shook his head. 'Unless I can get the guy you've tied up to admit that Tavilla is his boss, no, the attack is not enough. We can't prove he ordered it. We can search for him, but he's been in hiding since last summer.'

'Can you at least put a uniform on that restaurant he likes?' Frederick asked, frustrated with the slow progress. Because Tavilla had Thorne and Gwyn in his hands. And they all knew what he did to his enemies.

His stomach threatened to revolt again and he battled it back.

'I have,' Joseph said grimly. 'He was there today for lunch, but he manages to lose every tail I put on him. Bastard's slippery.'

'It wasn't Detective Brickman on watch, was it?' Clay asked acidly.

Joseph gave him a don't-be-an-asshole look. 'No. Detective Brickman has been put on administrative leave. The problem is, the detective's gone AWOL.'

'For God's sake,' Clay muttered. 'Really, Joseph?'

'Hey,' Joseph said sharply. 'He'd gone AWOL before you told me about his visit to Patricia's . . . victim. I can't bring myself to call a newly-turned-eighteen-year-old her lover. Anyway, we're trying. You have to know that. Thorne and Gwyn are friends of mine too.'

Clay looked away. 'I know.'

Frederick managed a jerky nod. 'I need to update Jamie. I'm sure he's losing his mind.'

'Wait,' Clay called when Joseph turned to go. 'What about the address Thorne gave you? For Anne Poulin?'

'It was an empty apartment,' Joseph said. 'I think you were tricked into leaving your house. They were waiting for you.'

Frederick had figured as much, but it was a bitter pill to swallow. 'You'll call us when you hear something?'

'Of course,' Joseph said kindly.

Annapolis, Maryland,
Thursday 16 June, 5.05 P.M.

She was on a goddamn boat. This was bad. It would make rescue problematic, especially if Kathryn and company decided to set sail.

Gwyn stumbled into the small room below deck, pushed by an irritated Kathryn. Apparently, something had occurred back at the crash site and Frederick and Clay were not en route. Gwyn wanted to cheer at this, because it meant they were safe. At the same time, it meant she had to save Thorne all alone.

471

Thorne, who'd been brought aboard in an old refrigerator box. Kathryn and the two men under her command had pushed and shoved the box into a small launch and sailed it out to a yacht that had to have been a hundred-fifty-footer. Gwyn might have been impressed had she not been so fucking terrified.

That they hadn't blindfolded her didn't bode well at all. They'd been brought to a mansion on the water outside of Annapolis, then she'd been escorted to the small launch while Thorne had been boxed up and hauled on a handcart. She'd hoped he could breathe in there. She needed him to hold on until she could figure a way out. She was handcuffed, but that was all. And handcuffs might be escapable. She'd done it before, after all.

The box was shoved into the room after her and she heard a quiet moan from inside. So he was still alive, at least. That had her shuddering in relief.

'Fucker,' one of the men muttered as he kicked at the box. Not one of the six gunmen who'd attacked their SUV, he'd been riding shotgun with Kathryn in the white van.

Kathryn had called the man Patton as she had driven them from the crash site to this private yacht club. Very private. Gwyn hadn't seen a frickin' soul the entire time they'd been in the launch. Which again did not bode well. Even if she managed to escape, who was she going to ask for help?

The remaining gunman had removed his mask once they were a few miles from Clay's house. Of course it was Detective Brickman. He'd sneered at her and she'd wanted to kick him, but she'd restrained herself. She might need that kick later.

Kathryn and the two men closed the cabin door and she heard a click. They'd locked it from the outside. Which was to be expected. The room was dim, the only light coming in through a porthole close to the ceiling, and the sun was on the other side of the boat. There were overhead lights, but she saw no switches.

Two chairs sat in the middle of the room, bolted to the floor. Manacles on chains hung from the back of them and were attached to the two front legs. The red stains on the legs of the chairs were probably not paint.

A steel table was mounted to one wall, hinged so that it lay flush against the wall at the moment. It too had manacles dangling from chains. And more red stains that were also probably not paint.

She jerked her eyes away, because her mind was already conjuring images of what had happened on that table. Those chairs. *And what might happen to me.*

Her terrified gaze fell on a person in the corner. A boy. Her heart sped up. *Aidan?* But as her eyes adjusted to the light, she saw that this young man was slender and blond, where Aidan was big, broad-shouldered and dark-haired.

She swallowed back her disappointment and her fear. *Not Aidan.* Was her boy dead? That pool of blood he'd been lying in, was it his? *Oh God, oh God, oh God.*

'Stop it,' she muttered aloud. Dissolving into a panic wasn't going to help anyone right now. Not Aidan, not Thorne, and not the live kid in the corner.

Who didn't seem to be moving toward her, so, judging him not to be an immediate threat, she dropped to her knees beside the box that contained Thorne. 'You okay?' she murmured. A low moan reached her ears. He wasn't awake yet, but he wasn't fully unconscious either.

That wasn't bad, actually. They were waiting for him to wake up before getting under way with her torture. *And I'm not going to think about that, because it'll scare me to fucking death.*

'Who are you?' she called softly to the person in the corner. He didn't answer, so she crawled toward him. She was a few feet away when she realized she'd seen his photo before, in the yearbook, the night they were all together at Clay's house. 'Oh. I know you. You're Patricia's son. Blake.'

He lifted his head, his eyes sunken, skin sallow in this light. He was grieving. He'd lost his mother less than a week before. 'Yes. Who are you?'

'Gwyn Weaver. You haven't seen any other boys your age, have you?'

He shook his head. 'Did you lose one?' he asked, trying to sound snarky, but the tremble in his voice gave him away.

473

'Yes, I did. My . . . son.'

Blake's expression changed. 'I'm sorry,' he said quietly.

'Do you know why you're here?'

He shook his head. 'Do you?'

'I know why I'm here, yes. There's an unconscious man in that box and he loves me. They intend to kill me and make him watch.'

His eyes closed, his throat working. 'God,' he whispered.

'I can guess why you're here,' she went on. She needed this kid on her side. If she could get her hands free, she might be able to climb out of the porthole, but she'd need a boost. 'What do you know about your dad?'

He frowned. 'He's a judge.'

'Okay. That's true. The police are searching your house right now. He's suspected of . . . a lot of things.'

His jaw tightened. 'You think he killed my mother.'

Her eyes widened. 'Do you think that?'

'No, but I heard my mother's friends talking about it.'

Oh, honey. That had to have been hard to hear. 'Actually, no, I don't think your father killed her. But I think he knows who did. That person is the one who plans to kill me. I'd really like to avoid that.'

'What do you think *I* can do?' he asked, shrewdly guessing her intent.

'Help me get to that porthole.'

His eyes bugged. 'You are shitting me. You can't fit through there.'

'Watch me. But I have to get out of these cuffs first. Are you tied up?'

'My hands are cuffed behind my back too.'

'Well, shit.' She was going to have to do this the hard way. At least Kathryn had made her remove her Kevlar vest when she'd been forced into the van. Had she still been wearing it, she wouldn't have had the freedom of movement to do what she needed to do. 'You might not want to watch this.' Drawing a breath, she forced her body to relax and slipped her shoulder out of joint.

She sucked in a breath. She'd forgotten how much that hurt. 'Sonofa*bitch*,' she hissed. The young man was watching avidly.

Tucking her knees to her chest, she swung her joined hands under her butt and popped the shoulder back in.

'Sonofa-*fucking*-bitch,' she swore. She rolled her shoulders, blinking away tears. 'God*damn*, that hurts.'

'But it was frickin' cool,' he said, sounding genuinely impressed.

'Sure. It is cool when it's not *you*, y'know?'

With her hands in front of her, she had a prayer of unlocking the cuffs. They were on too tightly for her to slip her hands through. She had just the tool to do the job, but she had to get to it. She hiked up her skirt and fumbled with the now-empty thigh holster. In the seam she'd hidden two of the hard plastic lock picks that she'd used most when doing performance art. After several tries, she managed to work one of them to the small hole she'd left in the seam. She pulled it out, feeling very pleased with herself.

However, picking the handcuff lock would be the hard part. Lock-picking was a delicate task and she hadn't had much practice recently. She dropped the pick the first two times and had to force herself to relax, to not think about the fact that Thorne was helpless in that box and Aidan might be dead somewhere. Instead she hummed one of Thorne's favorite songs and felt her muscles begin to unwind.

If Thorne could hear her and know she was near, that was a bonus.

It took two more tries, but eventually she managed to pick the lock, freeing one of her hands. It would do for now. She crawled over to the box and ripped at a seam, tearing away the back.

She couldn't stop the whimper that escaped her throat when she saw Thorne lying there unmoving. His beautiful face battered and bruised.

The sound propelled her back into motion and she pushed at his massive shoulder as gently as she could, maneuvering him so that she could get to the cuffs at his back. He moved with her, although he said not a word. She made quick work of the locks, then tucked the cuffs into the back pocket of his pants and rolled him onto his back. Massaging his arms to help his circulation, she gave him a quick visual once-over. No blood, no obvious gunshot wounds.

She leaned in to brush a kiss over his lips. 'I'm going to get out of here,' she murmured. 'I'll be back for you. I love you.'

His eyelids fluttered open. 'Run,' he rasped. 'Get away.'

'I'll have to swim. We're on a boat.'

'Fuck,' he whispered, and she had to fight the urge to laugh.

'Indeed.' She took another second to touch his face, then pushed to her feet. 'Your ankles are bound with zip ties. I need a knife.'

Thorne lifted to rest on his elbows, giving his head a hard shake, looking around the room for the first time. 'Shit. What is this place?'

'A boat with a torture room,' she told him. 'Welcome to Chez Tavilla.'

'Check the cabinet on the wall,' the kid said from the corner. 'They were talking when they dumped me here. Thought I was still out of it. The woman said she wished she had the key, that . . .' He drew a shuddering breath. 'That she'd left her knife in the . . . butler.'

Gwyn looked over from the walnut chest bolted to the wall. Blake's eyes were closed, his jaw taut. But tears ran down his face.

She returned her focus to the lock, inserting the pick. 'What do you mean, in the butler?'

'My . . . tutor. Officially, anyway. Unofficially he was . . . He took care of me. Ever since I can remember.' He shuddered another sob. 'He called himself "the manny".'

'I'm really sorry,' Gwyn said softly, keeping the glee out of her voice, because at just that moment the chest's lock turned and . . . 'Holy fucking shit.'

Thorne twisted his body to see the cabinet. 'Wow.'

There were knives of every size and type, all neatly displayed. Gwyn chose a pocket switchblade for herself and a large hunting knife for Thorne. Kneeling at his feet, she sawed at the zip ties with the hunting knife, then handed it to him once she'd freed him.

She dropped the switchblade in her skirt pocket, glad the pocket had a button. Hopefully she wouldn't lose the knife in the water. She glanced back up at the weapons, re-evaluating her plan. If they were armed with knives, they could fight back when the cabin door opened, which it inevitably would. Tavilla was coming for them. She'd overheard Kathryn and her minions discussing it.

476

While they reloaded their semi-automatic weapons.

Gwyn discarded the notion of relying on fighting back. Only a fool brought a knife to a gunfight.

'Can you stand? I need a boost to the porthole. I was going to ask the kid for help, but you're taller. It'll be easier for me to reach it if you're lifting me.'

Thorne forced himself to his feet, swaying dangerously before staggering to the wall below the porthole. He was tall enough to see out of it easily. He huffed an irritated breath. 'We're a long way from shore, babe.'

'I know. I was conscious when they brought us here.' She glanced at the porthole again. She needed less constriction for such a long swim, so she lifted her blouse enough to rip at the Velcro holding her girdle holster in place, then did the same for the thigh holster.

While she took off the holsters, Thorne turned his attention to the porthole. 'Hasn't been opened in a while,' he grunted. 'It's stuck.'

Both of them winced when the clamp holding the small window in place finally gave, because the porthole's hinge creaked. Loudly.

Gwyn lifted her arms and, bracing his weight against the wall, Thorne spanned her waist with both hands. Her hands cupped his face and she kissed him hard. 'I'll get help.'

'You get *safe*,' he rumbled gruffly. 'I love you.'

Then he lifted her to the porthole and she wedged her shoulders through, stifling a cry when the skin on her upper arms scraped away. The salt water was going to hurt like hell.

Thorne lifted her higher, and she shimmied until her hips slid through. Gripping the edge of the porthole, she bowed her body until her feet were free and she was dangling over the water. Belatedly, she wondered about sharks. Especially since her arm was now bleeding.

Don't be ridiculous. She was in far more danger from Cesar Tavilla than she was from sharks. She pulled herself up so that she could see through the porthole to where Thorne was watching her, his expression a mix of relief, fear and hope. And desperate love.

'Love you too,' she whispered, and then let herself fall into the bay.

Annapolis, Maryland,
Thursday 16 June, 5.25 P.M.

Thorne heard the soft splash and closed the porthole. *Yes.* Gwyn had escaped. She should never have given herself up back at the crash scene. She should have kept running. In his mind he'd been screaming for her to do exactly that, but his body and his voice had betrayed him.

'I know who you are,' the kid in the corner said quietly.

'Oh?' Thorne reached him in a few unsteady strides and dropped to his knees. 'Turn around. I'll try to get your cuffs off.' The kid – Blake Segal, the judge's son – complied, and Thorne fumbled with Gwyn's lockpick. 'Gwyn's better at this than I am.' His fingers burned like fire, his circulation still coming back after lying on his cuffed hands for so long.

'You're Thomas Thorne. The man who my father said killed my mother.'

Thorne paused, then went back to picking the lock. 'What do you think?'

'I think you're being set up, just like my dad.'

Well . . . The 'just like my dad' part was a hundred percent wrong, but Thorne could pacify the kid for a little while if he needed to. He might need him should the opportunity to escape arise.

He hadn't expected to be put on a fucking boat. His mind replayed the sight of Gwyn disappearing from the porthole, and the splash, and he hoped like hell that she was a strong swimmer. She'd been raised on a crab boat, for heaven's sake. She *should* be a good swimmer.

The lock on Blake's cuffs gave and he turned around, rubbing his wrist and giving Thorne the first look at his face.

Holy shit, the kid looked just like Richard Linden. It was like going back nineteen years.

'What?' the kid asked. 'You just went . . . I don't know. Like you saw a ghost.'

'I kind of did,' Thorne murmured, then forced his body to cooperate as he lunged to his feet, because he needed to put some

478

space between himself and this kid who looked so damn much like the asshole who'd almost ruined his life. His head went dizzy and he remembered being in the hospital on Sunday, feeling the same way. 'Deja-fucking-vu all over again.'

Blake was studying him like he was some kind of microbe under a microscope.

'What?' Thorne demanded.

The kid shook his head. 'I'm trying to decide what I believe about you.'

Thorne sighed. 'I'm innocent. I hope that's what you choose to believe.'

'Did you kill my uncle Richard?'

Thorne was shocked. 'No. I tried to save him.' *And he wasn't your uncle, kid. He was your father.*

'I read about that a few years ago. All about the trial, I mean. My mother didn't want me to and my father forbade it.'

Thorne's mouth quirked up. 'So you *had* to do it. I can understand that.' He blew out a breath. 'Look. I'm sorry about your mother. I hadn't seen her in almost twenty years. I didn't even see her Sunday morning. I was unconscious.'

'I read that too. Online.' He fidgeted with the other cuff.

'Stand up. I'll try to unlock that one too.'

Blake complied once again, lifting his hand while continuing to study Thorne's face. 'Did you know my mother well?'

'No.' He set to work on the second cuff. 'She was a few years younger than me. And shy.'

'I can't picture her as shy,' he murmured. 'Did you know my . . . uncle?'

The deliberate pause had Thorne glancing at Blake's face, and he realized the kid knew. Or at least suspected.

'Yes.'

Blake made a frustrated noise. 'And? What was he like?'

Thorne sighed. 'You aren't going to like my answer, so can we pretend like you didn't ask?'

'No.' Blake grabbed his shirtsleeve. 'I need to know. Nobody would ever tell me anything, and I *need* to know.'

Thorne heard the lock click open. He removed and pocketed the cuffs. Gwyn had already put the other pair in his back pocket. He scanned the floor, scooping up her discarded cuffs. Her gun holsters were like flags proclaiming she'd escaped. He picked them up too, rolled them up, and . . .

His chest hurt. *Lavender*. He could smell her perfume. He shoved her holsters under his shirt and turned to Blake Segal, who watched him with something akin to desperation.

'What exactly are you asking, Blake?' Thorne asked carefully.

'I look like him.'

Thorne didn't pretend to misunderstand. 'You do. A lot.' He went to the knife chest and began arming himself from the dozens of blades, sliding a stiletto into one pocket and a sheathed short-hilt military-grade utility knife into another. These were Tavilla's tools, he knew, and he wondered how many people had been murdered with them.

'Have you ever killed anyone?' Blake asked.

'No. Beat up a few, but only if they threw the first punch.' He glanced sideways at the kid. 'Should I trust you with a knife?'

'Yes,' Blake said soberly. 'But if you threaten me, I'll do my best to kill you.'

Fair enough. 'I won't threaten you,' Thorne promised, and hoped the kid wasn't a sociopathic liar like his father had been. He handed him a medium-sized blade with an easy-to-handle hilt.

'Was Richard my father?'

Thorne drew in a deep breath and carefully closed the doors to the knife chest. 'Yes. I believe so, anyway.' He turned to face Blake, whose eyes were now closed, his breathing fast and shallow. He couldn't imagine what the kid was feeling, so he offered no platitudes. 'You suspected?'

'Yeah. They told me I was adopted. Then later, when I saw pictures of my uncle, they told me that they'd picked me because I reminded them of his baby pictures.'

'That's . . . so wrong.'

Blake nodded. 'He raped her? My mother, I mean?'

'I think so. That's the testimony we heard from a man who was once one of' – *your uncle's? your father's?* – 'Richard's friends. Well, not a friend, necessarily. More like one of his followers. He was popular back then.'

'Until he was dead.' Blake sucked in a sudden breath, as if something had just occurred to him. 'Who killed him, if it wasn't you?'

Thorne found himself hesitant to answer. 'Look, kid. Blake. Let's get out of here, okay? Then I swear I'll answer any question you've got to the best of my knowledge and ability.'

'You just did,' Blake said dully. He took a deep breath. 'What do you need me to do?'

The question came none too soon, because there was a scratching at the door. Someone was unlocking it.

Thorne gestured for Blake to return to the corner where he'd been, then hid himself behind the door, his heart pounding so hard it was all he could hear. He scanned the room, looking for any other evidence that Gwyn had escaped through the porthole.

He found nothing. *Good. Let them look for her on board.* Even buying her a few extra seconds could make the difference. Unfortunately he hadn't thought to arrange the box to make it look like he was still in there.

The door opened and a slender man walked in. Thorne had no idea how many people were currently on this boat, but there would soon be one fewer. When the slender man had entered far enough, Thorne shut the door behind him and grabbed him, clapping one hand over his mouth and one arm around his throat.

This guy would be an easy win. He was puny. He was . . .

Shit. He was Detective Brickman. *Fuck this.* He couldn't kill a cop. Even a dirty one. He put the knife blade carefully against Brickman's throat. 'Do not move,' he breathed. 'Do not make a sound or I will slice you from ear to fucking ear.'

He could feel Brickman's shiver. *Good.* Quickly he grabbed the smaller of Gwyn's holsters from inside his shirt and rammed it in Brickman's mouth, then he shoved the cop to the floor, knelt across his legs, and yanked his hands behind his back, restraining him with the same cuffs that Brickman had used on him.

'Karma's a bitch, isn't it?' he murmured, then used the second set of cuffs on Brickman's ankles. He dragged the cop to the corner behind the door and covered him with the remnants of the refrigerator box. He turned to find Blake Segal staring at him with wide eyes.

'Holy shit,' the kid breathed. 'Why didn't you kill him?'

'Because he's a cop,' Thorne said, and the kid's eyes grew even wider. 'Sorry to be the one to bust your bubble, kid, but not all cops are good.'

'Oh, I know,' Blake said grimly. 'Not all judges are, either. I don't believe my father killed my mother, but he's taken bribes recently. I heard my parents fighting about it, right before Mom . . .' Voice breaking, he looked away. 'Fuck.'

Thorne wished he had words to give the kid. But he didn't, so he focused on priorities. He disarmed Brickman and tucked the gun into the back of his own waistband, then patted the cop down, finding Brickman's phone.

Yes. He dialed Joseph, relieved when the man answered on the first ring. 'Carter,' Joseph said briskly.

Thorne's throat grew abruptly thick, surprising him. 'It's Thorne.'

'Thorne? Where are you?' Joseph demanded.

'I don't know. On a boat somewhere.' Thorne looked at the kid. 'Do you know where we are?'

Blake shook his head. 'No. I was pretty groggy when we got here. But it wasn't far from my house, I don't think.'

'Who's with you?' Joseph asked.

'The Segal kid. Blake. He's okay. So am I.'

'That makes sense. His father hasn't said a word, even though we've pulled compelling evidence from his home and office.'

Thorne hesitated, then spoke his mind, because Blake was eighteen and not really a kid. 'They didn't blindfold Blake. See if that makes a difference to the judge.'

'I will. Um, what about Gwyn?'

'She got away. She's swimming for shore.' *I hope. God, please let her be okay.* 'Brickman's here. I've cuffed and gagged him. This is his phone.'

'Good. I'll stay with you. Don't hang up. We're going to trace the call.'

'I won't.' He wished Gwyn were here. She was the only one who'd been conscious enough to pay attention to their surroundings. 'We're going to try to get the hell out of here,' he said, to both Joseph and Blake. 'We're in some kind of torture room and I don't want to wait for Tavilla to arrive.'

'Especially since he didn't have Blake Segal blindfolded,' Joseph agreed. 'Just be careful, Thorne.'

'I will.' He met Blake's eyes, saw him square his shoulders. 'Can you swim?'

'Yes. But there's no way we're fitting through that porthole.'

Thorne almost laughed. 'We're going to make a break for the deck. Run like hell, jump off the boat and swim for shore. I'll be right behind you, but I'm a bigger target.' *And I'm not wearing Kevlar anymore*, he realized. It must have been removed in the van, when he was still unconscious. 'If they get me, you keep going. Got it?'

'Got it.' Blake hesitated. 'Thanks.'

'You're a victim of all this, same as me. I want both of us out of here alive.'

A loud banging on the door had them both jumping.

'Fuck, *Dick*man,' a man's voice thundered from the other side. 'Open the damn door. You've got the motherfucking key.'

Trusting Joseph not to speak, Thorne put Brickman's phone on speaker and shoved it in the pocket of his trousers, then pointed Blake to his corner. If Brickman didn't say anything, the guy outside the door would get suspicious and call for reinforcements.

Not even wanting to try imitating Brickman's whiny voice, Thorne gripped the hunting knife, opened the door, and yanked the man inside. He got a chance to yell once before Thorne plunged the knife into his throat. He was gurgling blood before he hit the ground.

Thorne stared at him for a long minute, frozen, horrified at what he'd done. He'd taken martial arts, he knew how to fight, he'd seen enough street fights, both on video and reconstructed, as part of defending his clients . . . But this was real. *I did this.*

Then he was crying out as pain seared into his back, through his

483

gut. His hand reached back and felt the slim hilt of a knife. Felt the blood already soaking his shirt. Felt the barrel of Brickman's gun slipping from his waistband.

Motherfucking sonofabitch.

He turned to find a smiling Cesar Tavilla, Brickman's gun in his hand. 'Welcome aboard, Mr Thorne. I've been expecting you.'

Twenty-eight

Annapolis, Maryland,
Thursday 16 June, 5.30 P.M.

Gwyn treaded water, wanting to scream at the pain when the salt hit the scraped skin on her arms. But the sting became bearable after a minute or so, and then she could be a little exultant. She'd done it! She'd escaped!

And now she had to swim a long way. They were moored a half-mile from shore.

It had been four years since she'd been in a pool. Swimming laps had once been part of her daily workout. Until Evan. Afterward, it had been all strength training and kickboxing. Activities she could use for self-defense.

Her swimming skills were rusty and her shoulder still throbbed from pulling it from its joint so that she could escape the handcuffs. But at least the water wasn't too cold. She eyed the shore, where Tavilla's enormous beach home rose from the sand, two stories tall above its stilts. She wouldn't chance going near the house, and she hadn't seen any other houses nearby when they'd driven in. But there was a boat tied to the dock.

It appeared to be the same launch that had brought her to the ship. Ignoring the pain in her shoulder, she swam along the yacht, stopping to tread water when she got to the stern. Yeah, that was the same launch, because there was currently no boat tied to the ladder.

Someone had left the yacht, for now, at least. She hoped that bought Thorne some time. And once she got to the dock, she could steal the launch and go for help. *If* the keys were in the ignition, as they had been when Kathryn had driven it earlier.

If not, she'd make her way to the road and walk until she flagged down a passing car. Either way, the dock was where she needed to end up.

She let herself drift for a moment to test the current, then reset her sights on the dock. *I can do this. I have to.* Thorne needed her. So did the Segal kid. *I will do this.*

Breaststroke would be the easiest on her shoulder and would allow her to keep an eye on the dock when she came up for air. Drawing a deep breath, she started out.

Annapolis, Maryland,
Thursday 16 June, 5.30 P.M.

Thorne staggered out of the cabin, getting a few yards up the narrow hallway before sinking to his knees. He wasn't trying to get away at this point. But if he could distract Tavilla, maybe the kid could escape and follow Gwyn to safety.

Gwyn. Part of him needed her there with him, but mostly he was so damn relieved that she'd gotten off the boat. *Run. Don't come back.*

She'd send help. If it was at all possible, she'd send help. He just hoped he could hold on until then. *Because goddammit, it hurts.*

Tavilla grabbed him by the collar and leaned down, his breath hot against Thorne's ear. 'Up!' he snarled. *'Stand up.'*

Thorne felt the cold barrel of a gun against his temple. 'You won't kill me,' he said hoarsely. 'You want to hurt me. Not kill me.'

Tavilla's laugh was bitter. 'This morning that was true. It no longer is.' He jabbed the gun harder. 'Move. Now.'

'No.' He needed to stay away from that room. He forced his body to go limp.

'That is fine,' Tavilla said, his voice becoming mild seconds before the toe of his boot slammed into Thorne's ribs.

Thorne couldn't stifle his moan and thought of the phone in his pocket. He might not survive this, but if Joseph was still listening – and hopefully recording – he could go out doing some good. Plus, the longer he gave Gwyn to get away, the better her chances of survival. And that was the most important thing.

'Why?' he croaked. 'Why do all of this?'

'Because my son is dead, *Mr* Thorne.' Another vicious kick, this one to his hip. 'And you are responsible.'

'Your son is responsible, *Mr* Tavilla,' Thorne shot back, grinding his teeth to keep from whimpering in pain. 'He committed the crime.'

Tavilla dragged him a few feet toward the room from which he'd come, then paused to lean against the wall, panting. 'This is ridiculous. I know how to make you move.' He left Thorne on the hallway floor, his footsteps receding back to the torture room.

At once there was a shout of fury. 'Where is she?'

Thorne held his breath, waiting for him to find Blake Segal, but all he heard was more shouting and the sound of the big box tearing.

Tavilla came back, kicking Thorne once again. 'Where is she? Your lover?'

'I don't know.' It was true. He didn't know. He hoped she had made it to shore. *Please be safe. I love you.*

'And the boy? The judge's son?'

He's hiding. Thank God. 'I don't know,' Thorne said again.

Tavilla kicked him once more, this time in the head.

'Yes, you do, Mr Thorne.' His voice quieted. Became so cold that Thorne shivered. 'And I know just how to make you tell me.'

Annapolis, Maryland,
Thursday 16 June, 5.40 P.M.

'I want to kill that fucker,' Jamie whispered, his voice choked.

Frederick glanced away from Judge Segal, who was seated alone at a table in one of BPD's interrogation rooms, and studied Jamie's reflection in the one-way glass of the observation room. His friend's face was contorted with the pain that came from knowing that his child was in danger and there was no way to help.

Frederick was familiar with that expression. He'd seen it in the mirror daily after Carrie had run away. Later, after she'd been found dead, his reflection had shown the consuming grief of losing her. He sent up a prayer that Jamie would never know that agony.

Frederick didn't want to kill Segal so much as he wanted to do the same thing he'd done to the gunman in the wood – make him talk, no matter what he had to do. Because whatever he'd pried out of the gunman hadn't been enough. They knew they were looking for a boat, but they didn't know where.

Joseph had helicopters conducting aerial searches, but so far, they'd found nothing.

'I get wanting to kill him,' JD murmured from where he stood on the other side of Jamie's chair. 'But we're going to have to trust Joseph and Hyatt to do their job.'

'Which is *what*?' Jamie hissed. 'Where the fuck are they?'

Because Joseph had abruptly left the room to take a call on his cell phone, Hyatt following behind him. The two had been gone for several minutes, serving to heighten the tension in the observation room.

Frederick remained silent, squeezing Jamie's shoulder before returning his gaze to Judge Segal, who sat alone at the interrogation table, his expression neutral. But the grip he had on his thigh was white-knuckled. He was nervous. He should be. The FBI/BPD task force had found evidence that Segal had taken bribes. Big ones.

Still the man had not cracked. Hadn't even asked to see his attorney. Which did not make sense at all.

The door to the interrogation room opened and Joseph and Hyatt re-entered, looking grim.

Jamie gasped, and Frederick squeezed his shoulder again, even though his own pulse had begun to race, wondering what had happened. 'Keep it together, Jamie,' he whispered. 'They'd tell you first if it was something bad.' Like if Thorne was dead.

No. I'm not going to even think it.

Joseph sat across from Segal. Hyatt sat beside the judge, encroaching on his personal space without actually touching him. Segal looked uncomfortable, but he didn't move an inch.

'You should have told us that Tavilla had kidnapped your son,' Joseph said bluntly.

Segal flinched, the remaining color draining from his face. 'You found him? Blake?'

'No, but we know that Tavilla has him on a boat, in some kind of torture room.'

Segal's eyes closed, but not quickly enough to hide the abject terror in his eyes. 'You're lying.'

Both Joseph and Hyatt narrowed their eyes. 'You know we're not,' Hyatt said quietly. 'What do you know about this torture room?'

'Nothing,' Segal insisted stiffly. He opened his eyes, having regained some of his composure. 'Absolutely nothing.'

Joseph studied him. 'I heard his voice. He didn't think he'd been taken too far from your house, but he was groggy because he'd been drugged by his captors.' He paused. 'Blake wasn't blindfolded, Judge Segal. He's seen their faces.'

Segal sucked in a breath, the full import of that statement clearly registering. 'Dear God,' he whispered.

'We know they're on a boat,' Joseph repeated. 'We know it's called the *Señor del Mar*. We know it's docked somewhere called Chevalier.' He gave Segal a sharp look. 'We were hoping you could help us.'

Segal licked his lips nervously. 'How? How could I know?'

'Because you conspired with Tavilla to eliminate Thomas Thorne.'

'Oh,' Jamie breathed. 'They found something.'

On the other side of the glass, Segal attempted to sneer, but the beads of sweat on his upper lip gave him away. 'You're fishing, Agent Carter.'

In answer, Joseph slid a piece of paper across the table. Hyatt leaned in to look over Segal's shoulder, shaking his head. 'That looks bad to me, Judge,' the lieutenant said with mock sympathy. 'An account in your own words. Signed by you.'

Segal had immediately stiffened when he saw what was written on the paper. His hands trembled as he snatched it off the table, not, it seemed, in fear, but in rage. 'Where did you get this?'

'From your safe deposit box,' Joseph said. 'We had a warrant. Signed by a judge.'

'Always risky to pen a confession to be shared in the event of your suspicious death,' Hyatt added, still mocking. 'Especially if you don't die.' He reached over Segal to tap the bottom of the page.

'It says here that you visited Tavilla on his ship, where you confronted him about the murder of your wife Patricia. He admitted to the crime "freely" and threatened your son if you told anyone.'

Joseph lifted his brows. 'It looks like he jumped the gun on you. He's got your son now.'

Segal lowered the page to the table, folding his hands atop it. 'Who told you that Blake was on the boat?' he asked, shoulders sagging in defeat.

'Thomas Thorne,' Joseph answered tersely. 'He's on the boat too and they're trying to find a way off it.'

Segal closed his eyes again. 'Thorne?' he moaned. 'Thorne is with my son? Oh my God. He'll kill Blake. He'll kill him.'

Hyatt's jaw tightened. 'You know, *Judge*, you should be relieved that it's Thorne with your kid. A lot of men would use this as an opportunity to exact revenge for allowing them to be accused of a murder that you fucking committed. But that is not Thorne's style.' He shook his head. 'He's more likely to take a bullet so that your kid can escape.'

Jamie made a sound that was too close to a whimper.

Heart hurting for him, Frederick squeezed his shoulder again. 'You don't know that anyone's taking a bullet,' he said quietly. 'Hopefully this asshole will tell them where the fucking boat is.'

'But Hyatt,' Jamie whispered. 'He . . . That was a really nice thing he said there.'

JD cleared his throat. 'Nice and true.'

'He's right,' Joseph said to Segal. 'Now help us save them before it's too late.' He leaned across the table, getting in Segal's face. '*Where is the boat?*'

Segal withdrew a handkerchief from his pocket and mopped his brow. 'I'm not exactly sure. It's somewhere off Muddy Creek Road. Near the mouth of the river.'

Joseph sat up sharply. 'Rhode River?'

A nod. 'I think so. Or one of the creeks. I was blindfolded, so I'm not sure.'

Hyatt frowned. 'How do you know that much if you were blindfolded?'

Segal flushed, the twin streaks of red dark against his pale face. 'I had a tracking device on me, but it . . . malfunctioned at the end.'

Joseph's face also bent in a frown. 'Tavilla allowed you on his boat without checking for a tracking device?'

If anything, the man's flush deepened. 'He checked. His gorilla – Patton – strip-searched me, the fucker. I had it . . .' He lifted his chin. 'I had it hidden. I was hoping to get his exact location for further leverage.'

Joseph's eyes flared wide in surprise, but the reaction was so brief that Frederick might have missed it had he not been watching closely. 'Oh. Hidden. Got it.'

Frederick exchanged glances with both JD and Jamie. 'Oh my God,' he murmured. 'He hid it up his . . .'

JD winced. 'So it would seem.'

Jamie closed his eyes, his relief palpable. 'Muddy Creek Road. That's a relatively small search area. They'll be able to find Thorne. They can get to him in time.'

Joseph lowered his chin to speak into the microphone clipped to his lapel. 'Detective Rivera, did you get that?'

The door to the interrogation room opened and Rivera stuck his head in, an earpiece clearly visible. 'Yes, Agent Carter. I've relayed it to the search team. They're changing course to intercept Tavilla's boat.'

'Any other news from Mr Thorne?' Hyatt asked.

Rivera shook his head, chancing a quick glance out of the corner of his eye at the mirror. 'No, but we're still connected.'

'To Thorne,' Jamie whispered. 'They still have Thorne on the phone. He's still alive.'

Annapolis, Maryland,
Thursday 16 June, 5.50 P.M.

Gwyn felt like throwing up. Swimming in the bay was completely different to swimming in the pool. It wasn't a windy day, but the waves still tossed her around, and she'd swallowed too much water. But she'd made it. *Thank you. Thank you.*

Swimming under the dock, she dragged herself onto the sand, giving herself a moment to rest before inspecting the boat's ignition. *Please let the keys be in it. Please.*

It was quiet here. Quiet enough that she heard the slamming of a car door.

Dammit. Somebody's here. Hurry. Forcing herself to move, she waded over to the boat. It had a small ladder on the side so that anyone in the water could easily climb aboard. She pulled herself high enough on the ladder to see the ignition.

No keys. Fuck. She could pick a lock, but she'd never been good at hot-wiring. That had been Thorne's expertise.

Voices suddenly split the quiet. Two women, calling to one another.

Fuckety fuck, fuck, fuck. Gwyn knew one of those two voices. Laura or Kathryn or whatever the fuck her name was.

Stop. Calm down. Drawing a breath, she focused, because in that split second she'd become over-the-top angry and frustrated. The voices were coming closer, and she needed to think.

As smoothly as possible, she slipped back into the water and under the dock just as footsteps thudded above her head.

'You okay?' That was Kathryn. *Fucking bitch.*

Stay calm.

'Not really.'

Gwyn blinked, because that sounded like Anne, her voice small and tentative, much as it had been when she was working for Thorne. *Not French, though. Faker.* But maybe the tentativeness wasn't faked.

'Is he very angry?' Anne asked.

A long pause. 'Yeah, hon. He is.' Kathryn sighed, her words full of gentle reproach. 'You really fucked up, not making sure that Colton Brandenberg was dead.'

'But that was Patton's fault, not mine.'

'I wouldn't take that tone with him. Just . . . say a lot of "yes, sir" and "no, sir". I've noticed how tired you are doing double duty. Triple duty, really. You were working for Thorne during the day and Cesar in the evenings, as well as taking care of Benny. Of course

492

you're going to be tired. I even commented to him last night that you needed a vacation. Just play that up. He'll be angry and he'll yell and scream, but we have this contained.'

'You have the judge?' Anne asked hopefully.

'No. The cops have him. But we do have his kid. Had to kill the butler to get him out of the house, but the kid's on the boat. The judge will stay quiet.'

'What about Thorne?'

'We have him too. Him and his bitch girlfriend.'

Gwyn scowled. *Calling* me *a bitch?* Cocking her head, she listened harder, because those last words had been muttered.

'What did she do?' Anne asked.

'She and her flunky bodyguards took out three of my men.'

Another long pause. 'Your men?'

'Well, Cesar's men.' Kathryn laughed. 'Don't get upset, little sis. I'm not horning in on your territory. But he will need some help while he regroups and you tend to Benny.'

Sisters. *Kathryn and Anne, or whatever her real name is. They're sisters.*

'Tend to Benny?'

'Well, yeah.' Kathryn had stopped laughing. 'He's not going to trust you again anytime soon. You realize that, don't you? Margo?'

Margo. *Anne Poulin is really Margo.* Things were starting to fall into place now.

'It wasn't my fault,' Margo insisted. 'I'll convince him. Will you stand up for me?'

'You know I—' The sultry tones of a tango interrupted. 'Cesar, we're on our—' She stopped short. 'Nowhere? She's tiny and bendy. Did you check under the beds and in the closets?'

Shit. They know I'm gone. I should have been quicker. But she'd swum as fast as she'd been able. She knew that. Holding her breath, she waited.

'The kid too? Fuck, Cesar! I had them tied up. I patted them down myself.' Kathryn sounded annoyed. 'I'll check the security tapes. Give me two seconds.'

'Do we need to go inside to check?' Margo asked.

'No. I can access the cameras from my phone.'

Of course she can. Gwyn's pulse began to race and she felt for the knife she'd buttoned into the pocket of her skirt. Closing her hand over the hilt, she flicked the catch, releasing the blade. She wasn't going down without a fight.

'Gwyn?' Kathryn called. 'We know you're under the dock. I can see you right now.'

Gwyn looked up at the piling. Sure enough, there was a camera. *Dammit.*

'You might as well come out,' Margo added. 'There's nowhere to run.'

Gwyn said nothing. *Come down here and get me.* She might not make it out alive, but she'd do her damnedest to take one of the bitches with her.

There was quiet above, and then footsteps along the dock above her head. Gwyn backed up until she was wedged between the top of the dock and the beach. *Tavilla wants to use me to hurt Thorne. So they probably won't shoot me.* At least not much.

Still her heart hammered. Tightening her grip on the knife, she waited.

There was a loud thump in the boat. One of them had climbed in. Gwyn glimpsed a long blond ponytail. Anne. *No, Margo.*

And then a hand grabbed her hair, twisting and yanking. And even though she knew it was Kathryn . . . it wasn't. Even though she knew Evan was dead . . . it didn't matter.

She froze, her heart pounding out of her chest, leaving her lightheaded and dizzy. He'd grabbed her by her hair and . . .

Bile rose in her throat as she remembered the things he'd done. Again and again. An agonized cry burst from her throat and she struck out, twisting in his grip, the knife in her hand hitting something hard.

A screech cut through the air, followed by a torrent of curses.

It was the screech that snapped her back into her mind. It was high. Falsetto. Not deep. Nor were the curses. *Not Evan.*

The hand in her hair fell away and she backed up, crablike.

Kathryn. Not Evan.

Though it didn't really matter, because both of them had pointed a gun at her face.

Gwyn blinked at the barrel as it came closer.

'Get in the fucking boat,' Kathryn gritted out. 'Now.'

Gwyn heard a splash behind her, followed by Margo's not-French voice. 'I've got her, Kat. Are you okay?'

'Yeah.' But Kathryn sounded breathless, and there was pain in her voice. The water around her arm was red. She was bleeding profusely.

I've got her. Ha! But Gwyn's joy was short-lived, because Margo had a gun of her own, this one with a silencer.

'Get in the boat, Kat. I won't let her get away. Once we have her locked down, I'll stitch up your wound.'

Kathryn waded by Gwyn on her way to the boat. 'Fucking cunt,' she muttered, and Gwyn felt a blinding pain as the butt of Kathryn's gun connected with her cheekbone.

Margo focused on Gwyn. 'Thorne lives as long as you're alive. I'm already in trouble with my father-in-law.'

Wait. What? Margo was Tavilla's daughter-in-law? *We had his daughter-in-law working for us for a whole year? Shit.*

'At this point,' Margo continued coolly, 'I'll kill you where you stand rather than risk his anger if you get away again. So do us all a favor. Extend Thorne's life and your own by getting in the fucking boat.'

Gwyn's eyes were watering, both from the pain radiating across her face and the gutting disappointment of losing her chance to help Thorne. But despite her blurred vision she could see that Margo's gun was a .45 with a shiny silencer. The woman meant business. Gwyn drew a breath, then nodded, ignoring the stars still twinkling in front of her eyes.

'Good choice,' Margo mocked. She waited until Gwyn had climbed the small ladder into the boat, then followed her in. 'Can you drive, Kat? I need to watch this bitch.'

Kathryn nodded. 'I think so.' She swallowed hard. 'This . . . is pretty bad, Margo.' Weakly she pointed at the yacht. 'I hope I can get up the ladder.'

'I'll help you,' Margo promised. 'Tide's just starting to go out, so there aren't as many rungs to climb.'

Kathryn gripped the steering wheel, her jaw set in determination, and the launch started out toward the yacht. With its powerful motor, Gwyn could see the trip wouldn't take long.

She watched the dock grow smaller and steeled her spine. She'd figure out another way. She'd get help for Thorne and Blake Segal. *I will. I have to.*

Once they reached the yacht, she didn't fight Margo when it was time to climb on board. She'd bide her time, waiting for another opportunity to run. She'd expected it to happen before the launch left the dock, as soon as Margo put down her gun to apply a tourniquet to her sister's arm, because Kathryn was still gushing blood. But Margo didn't do that. Nor did she tend to her sister when they got to the yacht. After forcing Gwyn up the ladder, she climbed up herself, then extended her arm over the side, hauling Kathryn up.

Kathryn collapsed on the deck, her face whiter than snow. 'What the fuck, Margo? That hurt like hell. You were supposed to help me, not drag me.'

Margo rose to her feet gracefully. Then casually shot her sister between the eyes.

Gwyn froze, gaping. 'What the . . . Oh my God,' she whispered. She lifted her eyes to Margo, shocked. 'Why?'

'Not your business,' Margo snapped. 'Now get down the stairs or I'll do the same to you.'

Twenty-nine

Annapolis, Maryland,
Thursday 16 June, 6.05 P.M.

'Go,' Margo commanded, nudging Gwyn down the stairs into the hold and along a hall to an open door. Gwyn gasped. *Thorne.*

He was on his knees, his hands covered in blood. His face was pale, his blood-soaked shirt hanging open, displaying a half-dozen knife wounds. The wounds were deep enough to bleed but not deep enough to gush.

Deep enough to torture. *Tavilla tortured Thorne.* The bastard himself stood behind him, his gun to Thorne's head.

Gwyn started to run to him, but Margo grabbed a handful of her hair to stop her. 'Stay,' she commanded, like Gwyn was a dog.

Thorne looked up and met her eyes, and Gwyn wanted to weep. He was in pain, so much pain. But fear mixed with the pain when he saw her, and he suddenly seemed defeated.

No. No, Thorne. It's not over yet. She thought the words as hard as she could, hoping he'd somehow understand.

'Ah, Margo,' Tavilla said smoothly. 'What do you have for me?'

'I found her trying to escape. Kathryn didn't do a very good job watching her.'

Tavilla frowned. 'Where is Kathryn? She said she was bringing you back.'

'She's dead,' Margo informed him conversationally, as if she were telling him that it was raining outside.

Tavilla's mouth fell open. 'What?' he asked quietly.

497

She shrugged. 'Bullet right between the eyes. She's up on deck if you want to check.'

Tavilla continued to stare, a muscle in his cheek beginning to twitch. 'Who did this?'

'I did,' Margo replied.

Gwyn's gaze jerked away from Thorne's in time to see Tavilla grow pale with shock. 'You . . . I . . . I don't understand, Margo.'

'I know you don't. But you need to.' She shifted the gun away from Gwyn just long enough to shoot Tavilla in his right arm, before calmly returning the barrel to Gwyn's temple. Tavilla looked down, both shocked and perplexed to see his weapon now on the floor. He fluttered his fingers helplessly, staring at his bleeding arm, then looked up at Margo.

'Why?' he asked, sounding sadly childlike.

Her laugh was bitter. 'Because of Colin. All this time you've blamed Thorne for Colin going to prison, for Madeline dying when he was incarcerated, for Colin getting murdered in the prison yard. But it wasn't Thorne's fault. It was yours. You couldn't let him have a normal life. You were going to have a son to carry on your name, your fucking legacy, no matter what Colin wanted. You pushed him to kill his best friend. You pushed him to do the thing that landed him in jail. And for what? To stir up trouble with another gang. Well, guess what. You're going away. Forever. And *I'll* carry on your damn legacy.'

'I would have let you have it all,' he said mournfully.

'No, you wouldn't. You'd have given it to Kathryn. You know, at the beginning, I didn't want it. I just wanted Colin.' Her voice broke. 'I just wanted the two of us to have a normal life with our son. But you wouldn't let Colin go. So now I'm taking it all.'

Gwyn locked eyes with Thorne. Then she looked at the gun Tavilla had dropped on the floor, about eight inches behind Thorne's left foot. Thorne was fading fast, but he managed a slight nod.

Margo must have noticed it, because a sudden vicious pull on Gwyn's hair made her cry out, her eyes watering once again. This time, however, she didn't flash back to Evan. Keeping her gaze on

Thorne's, she blinked the moisture away as the barrel of the gun ground into her temple.

'Kick the gun away,' Margo commanded, maneuvering Gwyn by her hair until she was inches from Tavilla's dropped gun. 'Over there against the wall.'

No, no, no, Gwyn thought, mentally scrambling for a Plan B but coming up with nothing. She could only obey, kicking the gun where Margo had commanded.

'Good girl,' Margo said sarcastically. 'Now, on the floor. On your face.'

'Let go of my hair, and I will,' Gwyn snapped, sucking in a gasp when Margo yanked it once more before shoving her away. She fell hard, landing on her stomach, able only to see Margo's face and Tavilla's back.

Thorne was all but hidden from her.

'You,' Tavilla breathed quietly to Margo. 'You lied to me. You said that Brandenberg was dead, but you knew he wasn't, didn't you? You *knew* he'd come back. And the Brown woman. Bernice. You knew she wasn't dead before using her name to lure Thorne out of his house.'

'Brandenberg, yes. I knew about that. Ramirez never went after him and nobody died a fiery death. But the Brown woman really was a mistake. We knew that if she lived, she could be part of Thorne's alibi – that he was rushing to save her when he was abducted. She really was supposed to be dead, because I knew her denying making the call would get all Thorne's friends whipped up and searching for clues.' She shook her head. 'Patton simply fucked up and torched the wrong trailer.'

Margo leaned to one side, glancing into the room where Gwyn and Thorne had been held. 'But it looks like Patton isn't a problem any longer. I'd planned to kill him, but Mr Thorne saved me the trouble. In fact, *all* of your upper ranks are gone, Papa. You could thank Kathryn for that, pulling six of your top men off duty to go after these two. But you can't, because she's dead.' Tavilla's back went rigid, his right hand clenching into a fist at his side. 'Now four of your top moneymakers are dead, one's in custody, and the only one left is . . .' She looked around, frowning. 'Where is Brickman?'

Gwyn ground her teeth. Thorne was bleeding out and Tavilla and Margo were bickering like an old married couple. *Do something.* She readied her body to spring, but Tavilla seemed to relax, his rigidity simply melting away.

'He'll be happy to know you planned to get rid of everyone in my upper ranks when you took over,' he said, a smile in his voice. 'Won't you, Detective?'

From where she lay, Gwyn could see Margo tense, even though there was no one behind her. It was a child's ruse, but it looked like the woman just might fall for it.

'I never said that,' Margo replied, looking from the corner of each eye uncomfortably.

Tavilla's stance grew more confident as Margo seemed to shrink, finally giving in to quickly check over her shoulder.

Which was when he leaped at her, going for the gun in her hand. The pair of them fought for it, giving Gwyn the opportunity she'd been waiting for. Crawling across the floor on her belly, she reached the weapon she'd kicked to the wall a moment after a cry of pain was followed by the loud thump of a body hitting the floor.

Thorne lay on the floor on his side, one arm stretched toward Tavilla, who was sinking to his knees, a short hilt sticking from his back. Margo still held the gun with the silencer, her arm outstretched. She seemed to be uninjured, but Tavilla had a hole in his head.

Good.

Margo's gaze fell to the gun in her hand, and for a second Gwyn thought she'd drop it, but she simply aimed at Thorne and—

Gwyn gripped the gun she'd retrieved from the floor and fired at Margo's chest. Margo staggered back, falling on her ass. But there was no bloodstain blooming on Margo's blouse, no cry of pain. *Kevlar. The bitch.*

Struggling to her knees, Margo aimed again, but this time at Gwyn.

On autopilot, Gwyn raised the gun once more, this time aiming higher. Squeezing the trigger, she controlled her breathing, keeping her hands steady.

Just as she'd practiced over the last four years. So many times. This time the bullet found its target, and Margo's head snapped back as the bullet hit her squarely between the eyes. She toppled sideways, the gun in her hand falling to the hardwood.

Gwyn let out a sobbing breath. 'Thorne. Thorne!' She crawled to him, dropping the gun on the floor and pressing her fingers to his throat. Feeling for his pulse. Then shrieking when someone grabbed her shoulder.

She looked up to see a very pale Blake Segal looking down, a phone in one hand, towels in the other. 'Is he alive?' the kid was asking, but Gwyn could only see his mouth moving. The gun's report had fucked with her hearing.

She grabbed at the towels and began pressing them to the knife wound in Thorne's back. 'Yes. But barely. Whose phone is that?'

Blake crouched beside her and pointed behind them to the room where they'd been held. 'It belonged to the guy with the knife in his throat – the big one who brought you and Thorne in. I've been on the phone with 911. They're almost here.'

Gwyn's muscles threatened to turn to jelly with relief. 'Tell them to send a helicopter. He's lost so much blood. Tell them!' she insisted when he said nothing into the phone.

'They can hear you,' he shouted. 'You're yelling.'

She winced. 'Sorry.'

Thorne stirred, reaching behind him to grab at her arm. 'Hey.'

Lightheaded with relief, she leaned over him, putting her mouth against his ear. 'You better not die, Thomas Thorne. Do you understand me?'

His mouth quirked in a small but smug smile. 'Yes. Love you.'

Her eyes began to burn and she blinked the tears away. 'I love you too.' She looked over to see Blake bringing more towels. The kid dropped to his knees and pulled the blood-soaked ones away, replacing them with new ones. 'Thank you.'

'You're welcome.' He glanced up and she realized how young he was. Just a year younger than Aidan. 'I have a message for you from someone named Carter,' he said.

She stiffened. 'Yes?'

'He said to tell you "he's okay".'

A new wave of relief had the tears coming in earnest. *Aidan*. 'Oh God,' she whispered, and Thorne squeezed her hand. But so damn weakly. She focused on keeping him calm and comfortable while Blake put steady pressure on the wound.

Saving him. Just like Thorne did for Richard. Blake's father. It was a circle that Thorne would find ironic when he woke up. Because he would wake up. Roughly she cleared her throat. 'Look, Blake, if you need anything when we get out of here . . . just ask, okay?'

He swallowed hard. 'I will. Thank you.'

Thorne gestured weakly at the phone Blake had set aside, still connected to 911. 'How did you know our location?'

Blake shrugged. 'Used Patton's fingerprint to unlock it and checked our GPS coordinates on Google Maps.'

Thorne rolled his eyes. 'Smart. Should have thought of that. Where were you hiding?'

'I hid in the closet, under a blanket. He was in too big a hurry to check.' Blake's throat worked as he tried to swallow. 'I was lucky,' he tried to say lightly, but the effect was ruined when his voice broke.

'Smart,' Thorne said again.

Gwyn pressed her fingers to his mouth and her mouth to his ear. 'Be quiet now.'

He kissed her fingers, opening his eyes enough to meet hers. 'Don't leave me.'

'Never.'

Baltimore, Maryland,
Monday 20 June, 11.45 A.M.

Thorne woke from his umpteenth nap that day and smelled lavender. 'We've got to stop meeting like this,' he murmured, and was rewarded by Gwyn's watery chuckle. She'd kept her promise, not leaving his side for more than a few minutes at a time since he'd been airlifted to the trauma center.

She reached out to stroke his arm, which she'd been doing

502

approximately fifteen times an hour, but he wasn't complaining. Apparently he'd nearly died, and her constant touches were her way of assuring herself that he was still alive.

And she wasn't the only one. Jamie squeezed his ankle briefly. 'You okay?'

'Fit as a fiddle,' Thorne told him.

Jamie snorted. 'A beat-up fiddle.' Between Thorne and Phil, who'd been moved from the high-security hospital to the cardiac rehab unit in the same hospital as Thorne's, Jamie was constantly on the go. At the moment, he looked worn out, but the lines of worry were finally easing from his face, and that gave Thorne peace of mind.

They'd moved Thorne from ICU to a regular room that morning, so he was preparing himself for visitors. Gwyn had shaved him after his trembling hand had nearly slit his own throat. The doctors assured him the shakiness would fade.

Which would be good, but there'd been an intimacy to being shaved by the woman he'd loved for so long. When he'd whispered that to her, she'd blushed and promised to do it whenever he wanted.

Something to look forward to.

He adjusted the bed so that he could sit up, and patted the space next to him, wordlessly asking Gwyn to cuddle up against him. He was worried about her. She was pale and looked like she'd lost weight in the few days that he'd been out of it. But she'd be okay because he was okay. And vice versa.

She sat on the edge of the bed, linking their hands. 'You've got a whole contingent of visitors in the waiting room. Jamie and I have made it clear that we reserve the right to tell them to come back later if you start to get tired.'

'Bring 'em on,' he said, even though he could already feel a yawn starting. Stupid surgery. Stupid injury. Fucking stupid Tavilla. Thorne hated feeling so weak. But it could have been so much worse.

Joseph and Hyatt were first. 'You look better,' Joseph said.

'Which isn't exactly hard to do,' Hyatt added.

'I'd flip you both the bird, but it would take too much energy,' Thorne said. 'Is this my debriefing?'

503

'Kind of,' Hyatt said. 'We got most of what happened on Tavilla's yacht from the phone calls you and the Segal kid had ongoing.'

Thorne recalled sliding Brickman's cell phone into his pocket, still connected to Joseph.

Joseph pulled up a chair and sat down. 'The audio from your phone was muffled, but we got the general gist. Gwyn and Blake Segal filled in the blanks.'

'And Brickman,' Hyatt said gruffly. 'He's singing like a damn bird. I'm . . . I apologize on behalf of the department. Brickman's been arrested and relieved of duty, of course.'

'Of course,' Gwyn murmured. 'Was he able to fill you in on Tavilla's operations?'

Hyatt nodded. 'Yes. He'd been working for Tavilla for a few years. He's already rolled on a half-dozen others in BPD who had ties to the organization or who were selling Tavilla information. He also gave us the woman who was Tavilla's admin assistant for twenty years. Her name is Jeanne Bruno. Her husband owns the restaurant where Tavilla would hang out. Jeanne was a close friend of Madeline, Tavilla's wife, who is now deceased.'

'Her death came at the end of a long battle with heart disease,' Joseph said, 'but it also came days after Colin Tavilla was found guilty and sent to prison.'

Thorne sighed. 'For which Tavilla blamed me.'

'Passionately,' Joseph said dryly. 'Jeanne has – had – two daughters.'

'Let me guess,' Gwyn cut in. 'Drizella and Anastasia.'

Joseph's lips twitched. 'Not too far off. Margo and Kathryn.'

'Aka Anne and Laura,' Thorne said. 'The firm's admin and the club's bartender. What about the baby? The one Kathryn posted on her Facebook page as her own?'

'It's Margo and Colin's baby,' Joseph said. 'Born after Colin went to prison. Kathryn was the baby's aunt. We found the child when we arrested Jeanne Bruno. Jeanne has been charged with all kinds of criminal enterprise. She's being held without bond and the baby is in foster care.'

'Margo seemed to really love Colin,' Gwyn said quietly.

'Although I'm not sure how much of what she said can be believed, considering she'd double-crossed Tavilla and was planning to take over. She *said* she only decided to take over after Colin's death, but . . .' She shrugged her disbelief. 'She worked for us for a year.'

'Tavilla set up her false ID years ago.' Hyatt looked incredibly weary, and Thorne found he had a little compassion for the brash lieutenant. 'He'd been watching your businesses for some time and knew the kind of person you'd want to hire. Plus, he discouraged anyone else from working for you.'

'What?' Thorne looked at Jamie. 'How?'

'By offering them jobs with higher salaries at competing firms and threatening them when they wouldn't take those jobs.' Jamie shook his head. 'I tracked down some of our applicants and they admitted that they'd been too afraid to come forward.'

Thorne felt some of the blood drain from his face. 'Our admin assistant before Anne . . . She was in a car accident and had to quit. Was Tavilla responsible?'

Jamie nodded, briefly closing his eyes. 'We didn't know, Thorne. She didn't know either. She doesn't blame you.'

Gwyn's hand tightened on his. 'How did you find this out?'

'We got Margo's laptop,' Hyatt said. 'She had notes galore, including incriminating files on your clients' – he held up a hand to stem Thorne's impending explosion – 'which we've sealed, pending the review of a third-party mediation panel who will determine what we can and cannot access for our investigation.'

Thorne bit the inside of his cheek, the sudden pain in the top of his head indicating that his BP had skyrocketed. This was unacceptable. This was wrong. He hadn't come this far only to have his clients fucked over.

Jamie glanced up at the bank of monitors. 'Thorne, you need to calm down, or the nurse will come in here and throw everyone out.'

Thorne jerked a nod. 'Who's on the panel?'

'Grayson,' Joseph said. 'And Daphne.'

Thorne relaxed. Grayson Smith, Paige's husband, was one of only two prosecutors he trusted. The second was Joseph's wife Daphne.

'And Frederick and me,' Jamie added. 'Don't worry, Thomas. We won't let your clients be screwed over.'

Thorne let his head fall back against the pillows, the pain in his head receding. 'Okay. What else did you find in Margo's laptop?'

'A list of your clients she intended to blackmail once she'd taken over Tavilla's operations,' Joseph said. 'According to everything we could find, those initial calls were as far as it went. That list was sent to the third-party panel as well. One of the things that won't make you angry is the tie between Tavilla and Judge Segal. Segal crossed Tavilla's radar about eight months ago. Tavilla had been digging into your past, figuring out the best way to hurt you. He had a multi-pronged attack – your friends, your businesses and your integrity. Ultimately he wanted you in prison, but he hadn't planned to kill you.'

'Then why did he have us brought to his boat?' Gwyn asked.

Joseph grimaced. 'According to Brickman, Tavilla had decided you weren't worth the trouble. He'd planned to tie your deaths back to the judge, specifically revenge for his wife's death and the kidnapping of his son. That way, if Segal claimed Tavilla had killed his wife, no one would believe him.'

'But Margo had other plans,' Thorne said. 'She killed her own sister.'

'She might have been a little . . .' Hyatt tapped his temple. 'But she kept amazing records.'

'Best office admin we ever had,' Jamie said morosely.

Gwyn frowned. 'Hey.'

Jamie's smile was indulgent. 'You know we all love you, Gwyn, but your filing system was a huge pile of papers.'

She sighed. 'That's fair.'

Hyatt didn't smile. 'As best we can figure, she planned to make it look like her father-in-law and Thorne had killed each other. That way, Tavilla's clients would continue to do business with her.'

'What about Tavilla's connection to Patricia?' Thorne asked. 'Did her husband give her up?'

'We don't think so,' Joseph said. 'Once we started searching

Segal's home, we had enough for a warrant for his safe deposit box. He'd written a detailed account of his dealings with Tavilla, who approached him about his connection to Thorne. Tavilla knew months ago that Segal had killed Richard Linden. He had paid Darian Hinman and Chandler Nystrom for the information. He also somehow knew that the judge had always been looking over his shoulder, expecting Thorne to figure it out. Or maybe it was just guilt. Whichever it was, Tavilla exploited it, convincing Segal that helping him get rid of Thorne would be in his best interest. The judge didn't fight him too hard.'

'Did Segal know that Tavilla planned to kill Patricia?'

Joseph shook his head. 'Not according to the papers he left in his safe deposit box. He and Tavilla had agreed on a "different target". The judge's words, not mine. My personal opinion is that Segal believed Tavilla was going to kill Tristan Armistead for having an affair with Patricia. Tristan had been lured to a bench in the park. He thought the invitation had come from Patricia, but her phone records don't show her having sent the text that he received. I think Segal texted Tristan himself.'

'But Tavilla killed Patricia instead,' Gwyn said.

'Yes.' Joseph lifted a shoulder. 'Once that happened, everything was set into motion and Tavilla snipped off all his loose ends.'

'But why did he need the judge?' Thorne asked, squinting in confusion. 'He had the story from Darian Hinman and Chandler Nystrom.'

'Segal believes that Tavilla planned for him to be the fall guy,' Hyatt answered. 'That if everything fell through, he would be suspected, especially since he'd threatened Tristan Armistead for sleeping with his wife. Once Patricia was killed, Tavilla knew that the judge couldn't come forward without incriminating himself over Richard's murder and making himself a suspect in the murder of his wife.'

'He didn't draft the papers we found in his safe deposit box until after Patricia was killed,' Joseph added. 'He realized then that he needed leverage.'

'What about Linden Senior?' Thorne asked.

'Keeping the "why" quiet – Patricia's being sexually assaulted by Richard – was what Linden Senior was all about,' Hyatt said. 'He admitted to it when we pressed him.'

Thorne was stunned. 'He admitted it?'

'He had to,' Jamie said, 'what with Eileen Gilson's testimony that her husband was paid for the key ring and then later killed over it. Plus fourteen years of bank deposits that paid for her silence.'

'Linden didn't have to admit it,' Joseph corrected. 'He could have fought us in court. But we were able to convince him that if he didn't admit it, we'd order a DNA test on his grandson. Blake would be revealed in court records to be the son of Richard and Patricia. Which we already got Judge Segal to admit to separately, so it was kind of moot.'

'Blake knows,' Thorne said softly. 'He told me so, right before Brickman and Patton came into that room where we were being held. How is the kid? Gwyn and I have been worried about him.'

Joseph frowned. 'How did he find out?'

'Same way we did,' Thorne said. 'He saw a photo of Richard. He guessed that Richard had raped his mother. I suppose we need to decide if we want to tell him that he's got a half-brother. Angie Ospina's son Liam is a product of Richard's rape too. If I were him, I'd want to know.'

'You should probably leave that decision to Angie,' Gwyn recommended quietly. 'Liam is living in Iowa now, but Angie told me that he's been accepted to Johns Hopkins. He'll be in Baltimore in the fall, attending classes. At this point, I don't know if Liam even knows that his aunt Angie is really his mother. That's a much bigger bombshell to drop than him having a half-brother.'

'I agree,' Jamie said. 'You might want to know, Thomas, but like you said, those young men are products of rape. And part of that information, as a victim, is Angie's to share.'

Hyatt's mouth fell open. 'What?'

Joseph's eyes widened. 'Explain. Please.'

'Oh, right.' Thorne told them how they'd known that Angie had also been raped by Richard. 'We got a little distracted after we found that out. I would say she has a right to a civil judgment against the

Lindens, but they've been paying her for years. It's not quite child support, but she's been compensated.'

'Jamie's right,' Hyatt said unexpectedly. 'It should be her call. She's the victim. I don't name rape victims without their consent.' He looked at Joseph. 'Is that all you have?'

Joseph nodded. 'We do have some good news for you, Thorne.'

Hyatt hefted the shopping bag he'd brought in with him. 'We found several of your sports medals in Judge Segal's safe deposit box.'

Thorne blinked. 'So he had them? All this time?'

Hyatt nodded. 'Yes, but that's not the only thing he had. We found four large boxes in his basement filled with your possessions.' He drew two thick photo albums from the bag, along with some framed photos. 'We're clearing them out of evidence as quickly as we can, but I had these expedited.'

Thorne was . . . speechless. And almost too afraid to hope that the albums contained what he thought they did. Gwyn reached for them with care, bringing them to her lap.

Her smile was sweet. 'Can I?'

He nodded, saying nothing. Hoping. Hoping.

'Oh, Thorne,' she laughed breathlessly. 'Look at you. You're so cute.'

Jamie rolled closer. 'Oh, wow.' He sounded delighted. 'You really are. Phil is going to *love* seeing these.'

Thorne forced himself to look at the album she held, and a lump rose in his throat. 'Oh my God.' He traced a finger over a photo of him with his real father, Thomas Thorne. He remembered the day. He'd been four and his dad had taken him to the aquarium. The album was filled with pictures of his father. 'I . . . I thought these pictures were gone forever.' He huffed out a breath and chanced a look up at Hyatt. 'Thank you,' he whispered.

'Least we could do,' Hyatt said gruffly. 'There were other things in the boxes. Trophies and comic books. Stuff like that. We'll be getting it to you as quickly as we can.'

'Was there a ball?' Thorne asked, again fearing to hope. 'A rugby ball?'

Hyatt nodded. 'Yes. Signed by a lot of players.'

'It was my dad's.' His voice broke and he cleared his throat. 'I thought it was all gone.'

Gwyn brought his hand to her lips and kissed it. 'I'm so glad it's not.'

Joseph's smile was gentle. 'Segal admitted that he'd gone by your house the day after you were arrested. He'd come down from the adrenaline high of killing Richard and told Patricia what he'd done. Linden Senior had already gone ballistic because of the key that Segal had shoved in Richard's body. One of the cops on the scene – not Prew, but one of his colleagues – had given him the heads-up, and Linden Senior had already bought the key ring back from Kirby Gilson, the ME tech. Segal was feeling antsy by then, and paranoid. He wasn't sure what you'd told your mother and stepfather, Thorne. So he went by your house, and that was when he saw your belongings at the curb. He loaded them all into that truck of his.'

The mention of Segal's truck had Thorne's mind snapping to Sherri. 'Did he admit to killing Sherri too?'

'Not yet,' Hyatt said. 'But the prosecutors are working on him. They'll be offering him all kinds of deals for information,' he added with disgust.

Joseph chuckled. 'I won't tell Daphne that you said that. She's lead on Segal's case. It's the only perk she's had out of all this. She's wanted to be in the thick of it with you, but she knew that once we caught someone, she'd need to be conflict-less.'

'I'm glad she's on the case,' Thorne said sincerely. 'And I'm glad that Grayson's home so that he can help.' He knew that Grayson and the rest had returned from Chicago the day after Tavilla was killed. Lucy had been to see him every day, and the others had spaced their visits, timing them for when Jamie had been with Phil, because Thorne had only been allowed two visitors at a time in ICU.

'We're all going to be busy for a while. The paperwork on Tavilla's victims alone is . . .' Joseph shuddered. 'And those are the victims we know of.'

'How many?' Thorne asked, afraid to hear the answer.

Joseph sighed. 'Altogether we have nineteen present-day victims. Some of those were Tavilla's kills. Some were Patton's. We're sorting through that now. We have Patricia, of course. The two members of the Circus Freaks that he stuffed full of Sheidalin matchbooks. Ramirez and his wife. Darian Hinman and Chandler Nystrom. The professor and her husband who were killed by mistake in their trailer. Brent Kiley, the EMT. According to Segal, Tavilla also killed the two men who drugged you and Patricia, Thorne. Margo killed her sister, Kathryn.'

'And Tavilla,' Gwyn added.

Joseph shrugged. 'That depends on who you talk to. The ME lists COD as exsanguination. But he wasn't sure which of the wounds killed him – Margo's two bullets or Thorne's knife. So, Thorne, you can have that honor if you want.'

Thorne shook his head. 'No. No, thank you.' He still remembered the horror at having killed Patton. He would have killed again, because it was self-defense, but . . . 'No.'

Again Joseph's smile was gentle, as if he understood. 'Then we'll list Tavilla in Margo's column.'

Thorne swallowed back bile. 'Thank you.'

'You get credit for Patton, though,' Hyatt said, oblivious to Thorne's emotional distress. 'And Gwyn gets credit for Margo and one of the thugs who attacked your SUV. Frederick and Clay each got one too. Your friends did well.'

Gwyn squeezed Thorne's hand, comforting him wordlessly. They'd each killed their first and, hopefully, only people. They'd done what they'd had to do to survive, as had Frederick and Clay. None of them were happy about what they'd done, but they'd live with it.

Jamie cleared his throat. 'Of course, we also have the people who made it – Phil, Sam, Chad Ingram.'

'And Blake Segal and Aidan York. We can't forget them.'

Thorne felt Gwyn stiffen beside him and asked the question he knew she wanted to ask but couldn't bring herself to do so. 'Joseph, what happened with Aidan York? All we heard was that he was okay.'

'He was found shortly after you two were taken. He'd been on his way home from his girlfriend's house just before dawn. Kathryn and Patton were waiting for him to come out, but caught him sneaking in. They drove around with him for a while and dumped him. He appears to have no injuries. That's all I know. I'm sorry, Gwyn.'

She jerked a silent nod.

'Thanks,' Thorne said, caressing Gwyn's hand with his thumb, wishing he could comfort her. But she'd heard nothing from the Yorks, parents or son. And she wouldn't push them. It made Thorne angry on her behalf, but he'd respect her wishes and wouldn't push either.

Joseph stood up. 'We're done for now, Thorne. Get some rest. You too, Gwyn.'

'And . . . thanks,' Hyatt added with a grimace, as if the word tasted bad.

Thorne waited until they were gone to laugh hollowly. 'I thought he'd choke on the thanks.'

Jamie chuckled. 'This is a big day, young grasshopper. You got an apology *and* a thank-you from BPD. We should celebrate.'

Thorne relaxed against the pillow, Gwyn on one side and Jamie on the other, memories of his father in the album on Gwyn's lap. Phil was resting comfortably in the cardiac rehab wing. His family, his friends, all safe and accounted for, and that was what really mattered. 'I am celebrating. Right here. Right now.'

Epilogue

Baltimore, Maryland,
Saturday 29 July, 2.30 P.M.

'Everything is amazing, Thorne,' Clay said. 'Thank you.'

Thorne smiled at Clay and Stevie, who'd taken a few moments away from their guests to seek him out where he sat on a stool behind the bar at Sheidalin. Everyone was having a good time, dancing to the family-friend band and socializing, but he wanted everything to be perfect for the christening after-party, as it had been dubbed. 'You're welcome. But Gwyn did most of it.'

'That's what she said about you,' Stevie said. Her eyes were equally watchful, because someone else was holding her baby.

'Sally's a nurse, Stevie,' Clay said. 'And I checked her out thoroughly before we even invited her.'

Gwyn joined Thorne behind the bar, sliding her arm around his waist. 'Because Frederick really likes her. Say's she's his "companion", because it's silly for him to have a girlfriend at his age.'

'They've been dating for almost six weeks,' Thorne said. 'He says his girls like her better than they like him.'

Clay winced. 'Taylor and Julie are teasing when they say that. Daisy . . . I'm not so sure. She's still really pissed off at Frederick.'

'She should be.' Gwyn frowned. 'I love that man, but he truly messed up when he hired spies to follow her around Europe. She's twenty-five, for God's sake.'

'His heart was in the right place,' Clay said sadly. 'But you're right, Gwyn. I hope he and Daisy patch it up. Life's too short for arguments like that.'

513

'Definitely true,' Stevie said. 'Hopefully they'll have time to hash things out. Daisy's been talking like she misses California. She might be going back.'

Clay shrugged. 'She knows she'll always be welcome for visits. Oh, crap. I see Cordelia eating another cupcake. That's her seventh. We're going to be praying to the porcelain god tonight if she doesn't slow down on the sugar.'

Stevie followed him back into the sea of people, leaving Thorne and Gwyn alone.

'I admire Stevie,' Gwyn murmured. 'But I don't think I'd want to do that. You know, have a baby at our age.'

'I told you I was okay with that,' Thorne said, and he really was. He enjoyed babysitting for their friends' children, but he was always relieved to give them back. Especially if they had dirty diapers. He was no fool. *And speaking of no fool . . .* He tugged Gwyn until she sat on his knee. 'Besides, we have our hands full with Blake.'

Because he and Gwyn had taken the young man in after Thorne had been released from the hospital. Blake was a good kid, who had nobody. His mother was dead, the man he'd called his father for his whole life was going to prison, and they'd had to bury the man who'd been his 'manny' since he was three years old.

Thorne looked at it as paying it forward, doing the same for Blake as Phil and Jamie had done for him. The kid was very little trouble so far. He'd been accepted to the engineering program at Georgetown University and was slowly adjusting to his new life.

Blake knew he had a half-brother in Liam Ospina. Gwyn had told Angie about him, and Angie had decided that it was best to expose all the secrets. Liam had been angry at first, at Angie, and at Gwyn and Thorne for interfering in his life. But he'd been polite to Blake. With Liam coming to Baltimore for university, there was a chance these two brothers could have a relationship.

'Where *is* Blake?' Gwyn asked, looking around.

'He stepped out. Said something about an errand.' Thorne knew exactly where he'd gone, but was unwilling to say anything to Gwyn in case Blake's attempts didn't pan out. It was looking bleak. The kid should have been back almost an hour ago.

But at that moment Thorne got a signal from Ming, who was welcoming guests at the door. A thumbs-up. *God.* He'd come. *He's here.* His heart started pounding, because he really wanted this for Gwyn.

Blake cut through the crowd, a tall, dark, broad-shouldered young man behind him. His hair was wavy, but clipped short. Thorne wondered if he'd have ringlets if it got too long.

Gwyn was talking about the new bartender they'd hired – who'd come with stellar references and a background check that could have satisfied the CIA's vetting process – when she went suddenly still.

'Oh my God. Thorne.' She looked up at him, questions in her eyes. 'Is that . . . Am I . . . ?'

'Yes, it is,' Thorne said, 'and no, you're not dreaming or crazy.'

Mouth slightly open in stunned surprise, she gazed at the tall young man behind Blake, then slid off Thorne's knee and came out from behind the bar. Her face had paled, but there was hope in her eyes. Thorne prayed it would go all right.

'Aidan,' she said quietly. 'It's a pleasure to meet you.' She extended her hand formally. 'I'm Gwyn Weaver.'

'I know.' Aidan looked down at her, because the kid had to be six-three. 'I . . . I hope it's okay that I came. Blake suggested it would be a good place to meet.'

Gwyn turned to Blake, tears in her eyes. 'Thank you.'

Blake blushed. 'It was nothing.'

She turned back to Aidan. 'I . . . I'm so glad you came. I'm so happy to meet you.' She seemed overwhelmed, then took a deep breath to calm herself. 'Do you want to chat? I'd like to do that. To find out about your life.' She pointed to an empty table far from the band. 'Can you stay a little while?'

Aidan nodded, and the two of them sat down at the table. They were quiet for a moment, just looking at each other. Then, as Thorne watched, they seemed to hesitantly begin to talk.

'You're wrong,' Thorne said to Blake. 'This wasn't nothing. This is huge to her.'

'I know,' Blake said softly. 'She's been good to me. I wanted to do something nice for her.'

'Well, you succeeded. And now I'll have to top it. Thanks, kid.'

Blake grinned. 'I'm going to get some food. I'm starving.'

'Of course you are,' Thorne murmured. 'Kid'll eat me out of house and home.'

'You ate six times more,' Jamie said as he wheeled over.

'Maybe seven times,' Phil added, looking fit and healthy. 'Is that . . . ?'

'Yes,' Thorne said. 'Blake kept inviting him until Aidan agreed just to shut him up. Cross your fingers that it goes well.'

'Fingers and toes,' Phil said. 'This is a nice party, Thorne. It's good to see the club open again.'

'And we hung our shingle out for business at the firm two weeks ago,' Jamie said. 'We've gotten a lot of good press clearing us, so we're getting clients. So far, so good.'

It *was* good. It was all good. Because everyone who mattered to Thorne was here, under this roof. For this moment in time, everyone was safe and happy. He'd take this moment and hold on to it, because it wouldn't always be like this.

But whatever came his way, he wasn't alone anymore. He was connected to every person in this room. Some more so than others, he thought as Gwyn shot him a look nearly giddy with joy. This was his family, and for today, everything was good.

About Karen Rose

Author photo: © Deborah Feingold

Karen Rose was introduced to suspense and horror at the tender age of eight when she accidentally read Poe's *The Pit and the Pendulum* and was afraid to go to sleep for years. She now enjoys writing books that make other people afraid to go to sleep.

Karen lives in Florida with her family, their cat, Bella, and two dogs, Loki and Freya. When she's not writing, she enjoys reading, and her new hobby – knitting.